THE SEVENTH WAVE

Emma Sinclair (a pseudonym) was raised in Kent and joined the BBC to work on television programmes in the fifties and sixties. Through her marriage to an RAF officer, she has travelled widely and now lives with her family close to the New Forest in Hampshire.

The Seventh Wave is Emma Sinclair's first novel for adults, although she has written children's novels under her own name.

EMMA SINCLAIR

The Seventh Wave

This edition published by Diamond Books, 1999

Diamond Books is an Imprint of HarperCollins*Publishers*
77-85 Fulham Palace Road,
Hammersmith, London W6 8JB

First published in Great Britain by
Piatkus Books 1992

Copyright © Emma Sinclair 1992

The Author asserts the moral right to
be identified as the author of this work

ISBN 0-261-67079-4

Set in Times

Printed in Great Britain by
Caledonian International Book Manufacturing Ltd, Glasgow

For all sad words of tongue or pen,
The saddest are these: 'It might have been' ...

Maud Muller by John Greenleaf Whittier (1856)

CHAPTER ONE

1941. The bright February afternoon had faded into grey twilight and Abby Nichols was cold. In spite of this, she walked slowly along the street of Victorian terraced houses as the keen east wind coursing along the Thames cut through her short, threadbare woollen coat. She was nine years of age, small and pale with long titian hair partly covered by a knitted hood and a tiny ungloved hand folded frozen and rigid about the letter it held.

Abby was turning into Victoria Place when a familiar wail was heard in the distance. The sound was instantly taken up by the Bermondsey siren. Mournful and penetrating, it sent an undulating howl across London which, nightly bombarded by the Luftwaffe, was now the most dangerous city in the world. The droning sound of approaching aircraft caused the girl to pause. Her green eyes turned skywards. High above the barrage balloons, two squadrons of German bombers were following the silver line of the Thames. A sudden crack of anti-aircraft guns sent shells to pepper the sky even as Spitfires appeared out of nowhere to harry the squadrons. Abby's fascinated gaze followed the falling bombs. Flame and smoke flashed across the river as the weapons found their target and the docks blazed. A close whistling sound, followed by a deafening explosion, sent the little girl sprawling to the ground. Her shock was brief, and finding her feet, Abby ran to the doorway of number nine. Turning the handle, she ran down the narrow hallway until she came face to face with a woman who stared down at her incredulously.

'Abby! What on earth are you doing 'ere?' Evelyn Carr was switching off her gas cooker before joining her son in the Anderson shelter. 'Is your Mum with you? No?' She grabbed the child by the arm and pulled her through the scullery door to a small back yard dominated by the shelter.

As Abby climbed down the steps into the musty gloom, she saw Eddy, one year her senior, sprawled on the lower bunk reading a comic.

'The blighters are early tonight,' murmured Evelyn as she shut the door and lit a paraffin lamp. A small woman with a tendency towards plumpness, anxiety and lack of sleep now kept her gaunt. In her thirty-eighth year, Evelyn looked older. Her brown hair, set in a neat roll around her head, was greying at the temples, and lines fanned out from her eyes, kind eyes which made people turn to her whenever things looked bad. They were fixed on her son just now. 'Eddy, put that away. You'll ruin your sight in this bad light. Now then, Abby, perhaps you'll tell me just what you're doing out at this time of the evening. Your Mum'll be worried sick.'

'It was Mum what sent me,' said Abby, holding out the letter. 'With this.'

'At this hour?' Puzzled, Evelyn took the letter and peered at her best friend's handwriting in the glow of the lamp. Eileen Nichols was asking her to keep Abby for the whole of Sunday since she was expecting a visitor she did not wish her daughter to meet. She would explain later. Meanwhile would she please make sure that Abby was home before dark in case of a raid. Thoughtfully, Evelyn folded the letter and looked at the pretty girl.

'Did your Mum tell you what she'd written in this?'

Abby was taking off her hood and shaking her hair into place. It fell in soft curls about her shoulders so that even Eddy was caught in admiration. 'No. Why? Is it somefink about me then?'

Evelyn bit her bottom lip and shook her head. 'No, luv. Not really. She just thinks it would be nice if you spent Sunday with us. She's got someone coming and reckons you'd be bored.' She folded the letter and placed it in the pocket of her overall. 'Tell 'er it's just fine. And tell your Mum that next time she's to come round 'ere when the siren goes.' She sighed, knowing her friend would sooner take her chance under the stairs than in an Anderson shelter.

Abby's thoughts were racing. Memories of her mother's strange behaviour that day came flooding back.

Everything had been fine until a letter arrived in the afternoon post. After that her mother had smacked three-year-old Helen, shouted at Abby and read the letter so many times it was obvious something was wrong. Finally, Eileen Nichols had written this hasty note, charging her daughter to deliver it and return before dark. But Abby had dawdled, not wishing to return to that frenetic atmosphere. Now she was caught in a raid and her mother would be even more angry. Abby's mind turned to her father. She remembered him standing by the fireplace in his khaki uniform, and realized now that she couldn't visualize his face. He had been killed at a place called Dunkirk. A tall man with dark hair and a loud voice, but no face: that had been her father. Supposing he was not dead after all but returning home on Sunday! Supposing all this was to be a surprise for her. As hope bubbled up inside the child, one look at Mrs Carr's worried face sent it crashing.

The raid was a bad one and each bomb seemed closer than the last. Then came an explosion which shook the shelter and extinguished the lamp.

'Blimey, that was close,' murmured Eddy. He re-lit the lamp and turned to Abby. 'Did you see the planes?'

Abby nodded and felt important. 'There was 'undreds. Saw the Spitfires too.'

'Dogfights! Wow!' Eddy's eyes opened wide. 'Lucky you.'

'And all the bombs falling and ...'

A deafening explosion cut short her graphic description and sent the door flying off its hinges. Earth fell onto them, causing Abby to scream as again they were plunged into

3

darkness. The shelter's corrugated iron roof had been split asunder and the packed soil around it had fallen through the gap.

'God 'elp the poor devils who copped that lot,' Evelyn said.

Unnerved, the three sat in silence as the noise of the raid continued and the bells of an ambulance grew closer.

Evelyn's heart sank with dread as she estimated the direction the ambulance had taken. Which of her neighbours would not see daybreak? Please God, she prayed silently, let Eileen and her baby be safe. She wiped more dirt from Abby's hair, settled the child under a blanket and urged her to sleep. At the same time she resolved to spend no more nights close to the docks. She would have to start the nightly trek west to the Underground, and lie on a dirty platform all night long while trains pulled in and out spilling their passengers onto the sleeping Londoners. Like it or not, Eileen would be made to join her.

Facing her bomb-blasted house in the grey light of dawn, Evelyn despaired at the gaping hole in the roof and the paneless windows, then reminded herself how lucky she and the children had been. Many had died in that raid, while they lived and still had a house.

Victoria Place had been lucky that night. Blast-damaged houses were still dwellings for all that. People stood around chatting about the raid, while others set about clearing the debris and glass which lay in the road.

Leaving Eddy sleeping in the Anderson, Evelyn walked along the road, holding Abby's hand more tightly than she realized. From Pelham Street she turned into Albert Road, then stopped dead in her tracks.

Abby blinked in confusion at the huge pile of smoking rubble and the men crawling over the ruins, trying to help trapped victims. She tugged at Evelyn Carr's hand. 'Come on. Mum'll be waiting for me.'

A policeman approached and told them to go no further. 'Five 'ouses gone down in that lot. Land mine.'

'Is anyone ... I mean,' stammered Evelyn, ''ave they got anyone out yet?'

'Not yet. They're doing their best, but it's going to be a long job.' He shook his head and the gesture spoke volumes. There was little hope for those buried under the great smoking pile.

Slowly the full horror of that land mine came into focus for Abby. This was where her home should be. 'Where's Mum.' Her voice was a strangled whisper. 'Where's my Mum?'

'Come on, luv,' murmured Evelyn, trying desperately to keep calm for the child's sake. 'We'll go back to my 'ouse. Let the men get on.'

With a sudden scream, Abby twisted away from Evelyn's firm hand and raced onto the ruins crying for her mother. Before she was lifted kicking and shouting from the ruins, she managed to grab an old battered rag doll, now charred by the bomb. The doll had been hers from birth, made with loving patience by her mother, and Abby called it Pixie.

Frantic with grief, Evelyn held Abby close. 'There, there. Don't cry, luv. Don't cry ...' Her voice broke. The policeman touched her arm.

'Take her home. I'll be in touch with you as soon as there's news. Any next of kin?'

'Not that I know of.' Evelyn patted Abby's head to comfort her. 'But I'm an old friend, and this little girl's known me all her life. So she's all right with me.'

One look at Evelyn Carr's shattered face told the groups still chatting in Victoria Place what had happened. They gathered around to offer their sympathies. When they learned that Evelyn intended to take the children to the Underground that evening, they shook their heads in warning.

'You wouldn't get me down there, not after what 'appened in Balham. The river poured in after a bomb 'it the station and people were killed in the panic.'

An elderly man added his story to the list of disasters

5

the Underground could bring. 'In the City a bomb sent people 'urtling onto the line, and they was electrocuted. Me and the missus is going to try the caves at Chislehurst. They say it's the best place to be.'

Later that afternoon Evelyn found herself pushing a borrowed pram containing two rolled-up mattresses, three blankets and a flask of tea and sandwiches. As she walked along with Eddy on one side, and Abby on the other, she wondered what her husband Harry would think if he could see her now. He would be angry at her for allowing Eddy back from Wales where he, like Abby, had been evacuated at the start of the war. But the children had been desperately homesick, and Eileen had missed Abby, so in the end both women had allowed their offspring home. Evelyn was worried about Abby. Since her screams the child had become very quiet. She was touched by Eddy's attempts to comfort the little girl. Shy and retiring, he was a gentle boy, and just old enough too to feel compassion for a friend. All day he had been talking to Abby, trying to reach the girl, as though waking her from sleep.

At Chislehurst, the crowds on the train spilled onto the platform and started down the slope towards a wooded dell, forming an orderly queue.

The smell of damp earth and woodland filled Abby's nostrils but she hardly took in where she was. Eddy had talked of caves and caves meant darkness. She was afraid of the dark. So was Helen, who now lay under the ruins of their home. She would be crying, as she always did when their mother put out the light. Sharing the same bed, Abby would comfort her sister, though in truth she shared the same terrible fear. Eddy urged Abby forward, saying: 'It won't be dark. People 'ave got candles. It'll be all right.'

As they approached the narrow entrance under the hill, Eddy took Abby's hand. A dark-haired boy with deep brown eyes, he was good-looking in a gaunt fashion. A

6

lock of hair fell over his forehead so that he was always sweeping it back or shaking his head to shift it, giving him an air of restlessness he did not possess.

At the entrance, Evelyn paid the penny and was given a pass. 'Guard it with your life,' the Cave Captain told her. 'Without it, you'll lose your pitch. You have to be out by nine o'clock each morning and back no later than ten o'clock at night. You're in the Druid Section.'

Then they were entering the long corridor of chalk, relieved that someone had installed electric lights along the vast network of caves. People were everywhere, sitting on their mattresses or on chairs, some standing in groups talking to those in neighbouring pitches, some eating, some knitting, others queuing for the toilets. Some families sought privacy and festooned their pitches with curtains, while others openly undressed their children to settle them for the night.

The Druid section was further from the entrance than the Saxon caves and both Abby and Eddy began to fear they might get lost for ever. At last, Evelyn was able to put the mattresses on the floor and cover them with the blankets. The Cave Captain informed them that there was a canteen where cups of tea and a bun or sandwiches were available. 'We've even got a church,' he said, smiling at Evelyn's astonishment.

'Gawd, what a journey. I must be barmy doing it.'

The voice came from an old lady who had suddenly appeared beside them. 'Carted this lot from Lambeth. Where you from then?'

'Bermondsey,' said Evelyn. 'My name's Carr. This is my son Eddy and this is Abby.'

Abby looked at the old lady. With white hair piled in a tangled mess on top of her head, a high-necked white blouse and long black skirt over buttoned boots, she seemed to have stepped out of another age. A cameo brooch was pinned at her throat. This, and the woman's florid cheeks, gave the only touch of colour to a figure that was all black and white.

'I'm Mrs O'Connor,' she said, dropping her large shabby bag. Shrewd eyes watched the man who had helped her and was now setting her mattress on the floor. 'You are a luv. Thanks.' She grinned widely, displaying several missing teeth. 'Everyone's bin kind. Couldn't 'ave managed otherwise.' She looked about her wearily. 'This is a rum do, ain't it? Always swore old 'Itler wouldn't chase me out of me 'ome, but I'm desperate for a good night's sleep.'

As the old lady settled into the pitch beside theirs, Abby stared about her and dreaded the lights going out. The blackness of a cave was the blackness of a grave. Soon her mother and sister would be in a grave, she knew, yet she could not accept it. God would not let such a terrible thing happen, not when Jesus loved little children. If she prayed all night, then surely he would reunite her with her family tomorrow. Resolved on this line of action, Abby's spirits began to lift.

Evelyn produced cheese sandwiches. The cheese was stale and the margarine bitter, but everyone was hungry. Until this moment she had been too worried about her immediate plans to come to terms with the tragedy. Now, however, the anguish stabbed at her. What of the child who was now an orphan? No busybody of an official was going to drag poor little Abby into an orphanage. Hell would freeze over before she allowed that to happen.

Later, as Evelyn held up a blanket in her outstretched arms, Abby lay fascinated at the strange spectacle of Mrs O'Connor shedding her garments. Rheumatic fingers struggled to untie the tapes holding up two white petticoats. Once out of these, Mrs O'Connor stood in a cotton camisole top over a whalebone corset which was laced through and through at the back. The camisole discarded, the fingers fumbled at more tapes until the hideous restriction of the corset lay on the chalk floor. Mrs O'Connor gave a deep sigh of relief, scratched ecstatically at her midriff, and climbed under a blanket still wearing her long winceyette bloomers and vest.

As everyone settled down for the night Abby, lost and frightened, lay looking up at the lights, her nostrils filled with the distinctive smell of musty chalk. She prayed, until the exhaustion of the day finally overwhelmed her.

Back home to more bomb damage in Bermondsey, Evelyn marvelled that they had heard nothing of the raid from the caves. Looking around her own house, she knew she would have to get an army of people in to repair it. She gave the children breakfast, then told Eddy to keep an eye on Abby while she visited the local police station.

Realizing why she was going, Abby pleaded with her to be allowed to go also, but Evelyn was firm. 'No, luv. You stay with Eddy. Be good and brave for me, won't you? I'll be back before you know it.'

But Evelyn was gone a long time, her route to the police diverted because of two unexploded bombs. When she finally reached her destination, it was to hear there had been no survivors from Albert Road. A temporary mortuary had been set up in the church hall, and it was there that Evelyn formally identified the bodies of Eileen and her infant. Helen could have been sleeping but for the grey pallor, while Eileen bore the scars of her sudden death on her face. When Evelyn asked about the funerals, she was told that all would be done according to the edicts of Christian burial.

'A mass grave!' Evelyn could not stifle the sob. 'Don't seem right − all those poor people.'

'But it has become necessary during these past months, Mrs Carr,' had come the kindly answer.

But there were other problems to deal with that morning. Abby needed a new ration book, since everything she owned had been destroyed. This meant a long queue at

9

the Council Offices to get the child reinstated as a member of the living since the clerk had Abby listed as dead.

'And she has no living relatives, you say?' the clerk asked.

Evelyn was on her guard instantly. 'No. But she's known me all 'er life, thinks of me as an aunt. It'd be cruel to take 'er away from me now.'

'I'm sorry, but the policy is that orphans be taken into care.'

'No. You can't do that. Not after all the child's been through. She's safe with me. Each night we're travelling to the Chislehurst Caves, and in the day I've got my 'ouse in Victoria Place. Please leave 'er with me.'

The clerk glanced at his watch and sighed.

'The child would be far better off in the country in a Barnardo's home.'

'No she wouldn't. Who would love her there? We love her very much.' Evelyn was becoming alarmed, and her voice was shrill.

'But what happens if your home is bombed? Should anything happen to that child now, I'd be held responsible.'

Evelyn leaned forward and lowered her voice. 'I'm sorry, I know it's 'ard for you too. Look, suppose I promise to give you all the details of where Abby's living, and 'er progress, will that do?'

There was a long pause, and the clerk smiled. 'All right. We'll give it a try. But you must report to me each month on the child's progress, and see to it that she gets an education. Otherwise ...'

'Yes, I know,' said Evelyn quickly. 'Thank you very much. It means a great deal.'

It was bitterly cold and flurries of snow settled on Evelyn's face as she returned to Victoria Place. Abby was sitting on the doorstep and jumped to her feet when she saw her. Evelyn hugged the little girl to her, murmuring softly: 'I'm sorry, luv. But Mummy and 'Elen are safe with Jesus now. They didn't suffer. They just went to sleep.'

Abby tensed and twisted away, shaking her head from side to side in disbelief. 'No. No!'

Evelyn drew her close once more, trying to fight back her own tears. 'There, there. Jesus is with them and 'e loves little children, so your sister ...'

'If 'e loves 'em, then why does 'e let 'em die like that?' cried Abby.

Evelyn found herself saying the things she had heard all her life and yet never believed. 'It's all part of a greater plan which we just don't understand. But one day you'll see them yourself up in 'eaven, and it won't be a mystery any more.' What rot, she told herself. 'Suffer the little children,' Jesus had said. Well, they were suffering all right under that sod Hitler.

Abby heard her words but they brought little comfort. She had fallen asleep when she had promised God that she would pray. It was all her fault that her sister and mother were dead. Mrs Carr was telling her that she could stay with them. The words brought home to Abby, for the first time, that she was an orphan now and had no one else in the world. Tears sprung to her eyes and she began to cry.

'Always? You mean I'll always be able to live with you, Mrs Carr?'

Evelyn nodded, her face set grim. 'Always, luv. I promise you that.'

When they returned to the caves that evening, Mrs O'Connor was already in her pitch, seated on a wooden chair and searching her large shabby bag until she brought out a bottle of beer, two handleless cups and a pack of playing cards.

'I can tell from yer face, luv, that the news is bad,' she whispered to Evelyn. 'Poor little mite. Is she to live with you?' When Evelyn nodded, the old lady went on. 'Thought we'd play a game of gin rummy. You do play,

I 'ope. Meanwhile, get some of this milk stout down you, girl. Got iron in it, that 'as. Do you the world of good.'

Abby watched as the two women drank and then asked, 'Are you *very* old, Mrs O'Connor?'

The deep lines about the eyes etched into even deeper grooves as the old lady grinned. 'Yes, little sparrer. I'll never see seventy again.'

Grateful for the beer, Evelyn began to feel a little more human again and asked, 'But what about your family? Where are they?'

The pale eyes turned sad and the white head shook a little, causing the two whiskers, which grew from a chin mole, to quiver. 'Me 'usband's bin dead these past fifteen year. I do 'ave a son but don't know where 'e is now. Arthur didn't get on with 'is Dad, 'e didn't. Left us both twenty year back. Last I 'eard, 'e was livin in the North somewhere.'

Abby frowned in disapproval. 'Don't your son never write to you then?'

'Sssh, luv,' said Evelyn. 'It's rude to ask questions.'

Too young to know how to express her grief, Abby knew only fear, confusion and a sense of deep loss. She clung to Evelyn by day, and screamed out in her sleep at night. Each morning they returned to Bermondsey, where Evelyn would queue at the local shops for food to supplement the meagre rations. When the convoys could not get through to the besieged British Isles, the rations had to be cut even more, and Evelyn went without in order to feed the children.

There was no school for Abby and Eddy after the building was razed to the ground by bombs. This worried Evelyn, who stopped visiting the clerk with her monthly reports, but delighted the children, who soon became uncontrollable ruffians, chasing each other through bomb sites and the ruins of riverside warehouses. After listening to Children's Hour and having a tea of scrambled powdered egg, they would head for the Chislehurst train. The nights were lighter and the days warmer.

The wooded dell by the caves was a mass of green now and birdsong greeted the Londoners each evening. Abby noticed how many more people were taking shelter in the caves, most of them from Silvertown which was more or less a burned-out shell. For these people, their pitch number was their only address. She wondered where they went to during the daytime, and shared Evelyn's fear that one day they too might have no house to return to.

One evening, as the train pulled into Chislehurst, Abby saw a lone figure on the platform bench. White head bowed on her breast, the old lady's arm rested on the familiar brown shopping bag beside her.

'Look!' cried Abby. 'It's Mrs O'Connor. Why isn't she in the cave?' She ran across the platform and shook the arm gently.

The white head trembled slightly, then shot up. 'Gawd, girl! You did give me a fright.'

'Why are you sitting here, Mrs O'Connor?' asked Evelyn with growing concern.

'I've nowhere else to sit,' came the sharp reply. 'Been bombed out, I 'ave. Got 'ome this morning to find the 'ole block of flats gone. Fifteen dead. I told 'em they should come to the caves, but they wouldn't listen. Fifteen! I've known them donkey's years.'

Evelyn drew in a sharp breath. 'That's dreadful. Oh, I am sorry, dear.' She placed a comforting arm about the old lady.

'There ain't nothing left. Nothing.' The fleshy chin trembled and the tired old eyes began to fill with tears. 'Not even a rotten photo. Seventy years and all I 'ave to show for it is this tatty old bag. What use is it, Mrs Carr?' She forced a smile. 'Bin 'ere all day, I 'ave. Didn't know where else to go. The porter's bin kind. Let me sit in 'is

13

room by the fire, and gave me some of 'is sandwiches.'

'But you must 'ave friends, or relatives to 'elp you now.'

Mrs O'Connor shook her head slowly from side to side. 'Did 'ave. But those who ain't passed on 'ave all moved away.'

'Come on, you must be ready for something to eat.' Evelyn urged the old lady to her feet.

'Not 'ungry,' said Mrs O'Connor, picking up the large shabby bag. 'Couldn't 'arf murder a milk stout, though.'

Evelyn smiled. 'I'll nip out and get you one later.' As the small group wandered down the slope and into the dell, she knew what she must do. 'Now you're not to worry, dear. You come back to my 'ouse each day. It's no bother. I'm cooking anyway, so one extra makes no difference at all.'

In May Eddy discovered the Druid's Altar. He came running back to the pitch in high excitement, speaking of blood sacrifices and ghosts. When he saw Abby's eyes grow wide, he embellished with sheer imagination where he deemed the facts unexciting.

Evelyn was knitting and smiled at Mrs O'Connor who seemed engrossed in the evening paper. 'Oh, rubbish, Eddy. Where do you get such nonsense from?'

Before Eddy could answer, the old lady spoke. 'Today's the tenth. It's my Arthur's birthday. Now let me see, he'll be forty-eight. Glad I saw the date. Even if I can't send the boy a card, I like to remember 'im on 'is birthdays.' She dropped the paper and looked into the distance. 'The last birthday present I ever gave 'im was a woollen muffler and gloves.'

Later, when the two women joined the queue at the washing area, Abby lay on her bunk thinking about the old lady's sad life.

'I think that Arthur's a rotter to leave 'is Mum like that,' she whispered to Eddy. 'Especially now that she needs 'im. Why don't 'e write?'

'Cos 'e don't want 'er to find out where 'e is and then get caught up with looking after an aged parent.'

Abby frowned, hugging Pixie tightly. 'I'd never 'ave left my Mum. And I 'ope you don't never leave yours neither, Eddy Carr.'

Eddy, who had been trying to read a comic, stared at his friend crossly. 'Leave it out. As if I would ignore Mum when she's old! And don't you be such a bossy boots.' He was just about to settle back once more when he caught sight of the owner of the caves making his evening rounds, and checking on the giant fan which stood at the end of their section.

'There goes Mr Gardner. Must be exciting discovering caves.' He watched as the owner walked on out of sight, then leaned back on his bunk. 'Do you realize that if one of them fans breaks down, we might never wake up again!'

Abby opened her eyes wide. 'What? Is there any chance of them stopping, then?' she whispered in fear.

'Shouldn't think so,' Eddy now dismissed the subject lightly.

Abby slept fitfully that night. Each time she opened her eyes her thoughts drifted to the night sky high above the caves and she wondered vaguely if there was an air raid taking place. She could not hear the roar of engines, nor see the bright moonlight gleaming on silver wings as wave after wave of German bomber squadrons headed for London and one of the biggest mass air attacks of the war. Before the night was over, the city was ablaze from east to west, twice the area of the Great Fire, and nearly fifteen hundred people were dead and eighteen hundred more seriously injured.

The following day, rumours were rife as people waited for the few trains running. Most of the main line stations had been bombed. 'So has St Paul's,' people murmured in despair, 'and Westminster Abbey, the Houses of Parliament and even Buckingham Palace.' Listening to all this, Evelyn's heart sank to its lowest ebb yet.

A pall of smoke hung over the city and everywhere was ruin. Most of the bridges across the river were unpassable. Streets were blocked off; buildings still burned, untended by the overstretched fire services. A tram lay on its side in the middle of the road and an ambulance had smashed into a building. Everywhere there were bomb craters, rubble and unexploded bombs, and the Carrs' long, circuitous route home took them through roads no longer recognizable. If anything could break the spirit of London it should have been this, the worst raid of all. People stared grimly at the ruins of their city, but their spirit was one of anger and defiance, summed up by Mrs O'Connor's remark:

'Blimey, it'll take ages to get this sodding lot cleared up. We'll 'ave to use the shops in India Street now. I 'ope their butcher's as good as our old one.'

'St Paul's is still there,' said Abby. 'I saw it clearly.'

Heart in her mouth, Evelyn turned into Victoria Place, and breathed a sigh of relief as she saw her home was still there, along with all the other terraced houses. They lacked windows once more, and people were out brushing away the debris, but truly it seemed that Victoria Place lay under the protection of some magic spell. 'Maybe,' she murmured quietly, 'maybe there is a God after all.'

There was no disguising the seriousness of this raid – even the BBC news bulletins could not do that – but whereas Westminster Hall had blazed and the House of Commons had been bombed, the main body of the Houses of Parliament still stood. St Paul's had been damaged but, like Buckingham Palace, it had survived the night.

While she and Mrs O'Connor kept the house going and shared the chores, Abby and Eddy continued to grow wilder, playing with other children among the bomb sites. There were houses to explore, charred beams to climb and cellars to hide in. There were wild flowers too, forcing their way through the ruined wasteland, and Abby's heart lifted to see them. Her favourite was the red poppy. Hard as it had been for this flower to reach out for life in a dead land, it had finally succeeded.

'Hitler's invaded Russia.' The voice came from an elderly man in the neighbouring pitch. 'Invaded Russia, would you believe!'

'The silly sod.' Mrs O'Connor was pouring milk stout into a beer glass. 'Still, if 'e leaves London alone, then I don't care.'

'That's just it. He is.' The man tapped the *London Evening News* excitedly, then handed it over to Evelyn. 'The blitz is over. Look at the headline!'

Evelyn scanned the page. 'Moscow's turn now,' she read aloud. 'Poor devils. Still, that's what comes of supping with the devil. A short while ago, Stalin and 'Itler were chums.'

It was late September when the blow fell. Abby had been helping Evelyn and Mrs O'Connor to bottle apples when there was a loud rap on the door. Evelyn's heart dropped when she saw it was a woman dressed in the uniform of the Women's Voluntary Services.

'Good afternoon,' said the woman. 'Are you Mrs Carr?' When Evelyn nodded, the woman went on. 'And you have in your care a child by the name of Abigail Nichols?'

Evelyn felt quite sick, and cursed herself for not keeping her promise to the clerk. 'Yes. But she's all right. I know I should have gone to see the clerk as I ...'

'I'm afraid we're at cross purposes.' The woman smiled. 'May I come in?'

Evelyn showed the woman into her living room, where Mrs O'Connor and Abby were waiting wide-eyed with curiosity.

'I'm Mrs Channon,' said the woman, opening her large

17

leather briefcase. 'It's about Abigail that I've come to see you.' Quickly she informed them that a relative of Abby's had come forward and offered the child a home. 'He's a cousin of Mr Nichols – the late Mr Nichols, I should say. His name is William Glenister, and he lives near Canterbury.'

Evelyn wiped her damp hands on her overall and frowned. 'I've never 'eard of 'im. And I'm quite sure that Eileen didn't 'ave no relations, or Tom either.'

Abby listened in alarm, and crept closer to Evelyn for comfort. She felt the motherly arm about her and knew that this strange woman would never be allowed to take her away. Mrs Carr had promised and this was her home now.

Mrs Channon looked anxious. 'Perhaps it would be better if the little girl didn't listen to our conversation. She is Abigail, I take it?'

Evelyn's arm tightened on the child. 'Yes. This is Abby. We love 'er very much. She's family now.'

'Nevertheless,' Mrs Channon insisted with raised eyebrows.

'Abby,' murmured Evelyn, 'would you mind writing the date on the bottle labels for me? It'll save time afterwards.'

For a moment Abby clung. She knew these women were going to argue about her future. She felt she had a right to be there, but at length, she walked slowly back to the small kitchen, leaving the door open.

Evelyn watched her go, closed the door quietly, then turned to face this woman who had the power to ruin all their lives. 'Whoever this man is, he can never give Abby the love she's found with us.'

Mrs Channon smiled sympathetically. 'I can see how much you care for the child, and I wouldn't dream of breaking up this family, but a relative has the first right, and we are bound by that edict. Now even though you have never heard of him, I assure you he exists and is genuine. He is well off — he owns a large department store in Canterbury — and has two lovely children and a caring wife. Furthermore, he lives in the country. Now what could be better for Abby than that?' Mrs Channon fumbled in her briefcase and took out a folder with pages of notes inside it. 'It seems that Mr Glenister got in touch with the local authority about five weeks ago. Apparently he paid a visit to the child's mother last February, after learning of the death of his cousin through a friend. When he arrived at the house, however, he found nothing but a pile of ruins. Only later, on making enquiries about the grave, did he learn that Abigail had survived.' She looked up from her notes and saw the stunned looks on the faces of the two women. 'He can give her a good home, and an education, Mrs Carr. After all, when did the child last go to school here!'

The question was rhetorical, but Evelyn knew she was beaten. She remembered Eileen's last note. Was this the very man that her friend had wanted to keep Abby from meeting? 'I know it all sounds very fine and that,' she stuttered, 'but I'm not sure that Abby would be 'appy with this Mr Glenister. In fact, I've good reason to think that 'er mother would not like this.'

Mrs Channon was growing impatient and the voice took on a firmer tone. 'What you think is immaterial. The child's welfare must come first. Abigail is to go to her uncle's house tomorrow. I'll be here to collect her at noon.'

'We stay at the Chislehurst caves each night,' snapped Evelyn. 'So I doubt if I can get things organized by then.'

'Why don't I come down to collect Abby from there? It will save a lot of time.'

'She's to come 'ome and 'ave a good breakfast first,' said Evelyn sharply. 'I'm not pushing the poor little mite off like she was ...' her voice cracked, and tears filled her eyes. Choking with emotion, she turned away, and buried her head in her hands. 'Please go. Go!'

19

Mrs Channon stood up. 'I'm so very sorry. But we are doing our best for the child. One day, you will all come to see that.'

Abby wept for most of the day and would heed no words of comfort. Instead she rounded on Evelyn, shouting, 'But you promised. You promised I could stay with you always.'

Her accusing eyes filled Evelyn's heart with anguish, and all efforts to make the child understand were in vain. Mrs O'Connor's grief was matched by her fury.

'All those interfering la-de-dah ladies coming down 'ere and bossing us around! Who the 'ell do they think they are?'

Each night Abby had brought her rag doll to the caves and slept with it close beside her, drawing comfort from the last remnant of her old life. Tonight she needed Pixie more than ever, as once again her world was collapsing about her.

Eddy, who had been very quiet all day, gestured for Abby to follow him through the caves. She did so, and found herself standing before the huge chalk ledge, known as the Druid's Altar.

'Why are we 'ere, Eddy?'

Eddy looked embarrassed. 'You'll write to me. Promise?'

Abby nodded. 'And you must promise to write to me.'

He nodded but there was something else on his mind. 'You'll forget me soon enough and then you'll forget your promise.'

'Never!' Abby grabbed his hand and squeezed it hard, tears smarting her eyes once more. 'Never, Eddy. I won't never forget you.'

This was all the encouragement Eddy needed. 'Then let's make a pact now, 'ere, in front of this altar.'

'A pact?'

'A promise to marry, when we're grown up.' There — he had said it. Now she would laugh at him.

But Abby just smiled through her tears and nodded. 'All right. But if it's a pagan altar, won't God be cross with us for making a pact 'ere?'

Eddy shrugged. It had seemed romantic somehow. What had God got to do with it? ''Course not. It ain't used by Druids these days, so it can be whatever we want it to be.' With that, he took from his pocket the remains of a candle and a box of Swan Vestas. Lighting the candle, he fixed it on to the ledge of chalk, and taking Abby's hand placed it on the altar beside the candle. Then, placing his hand over hers, he intoned solemnly:

'I, Edward George Carr, promise to marry you, Abigail Nichols, when we're grown up.' He turned to her. 'Go on − now it's your turn to promise.'

'I, Abigail Nichols, promise to marry you, Edward ... I didn't know your second name was George ...' She pulled a face.

'Get on with it!'

'Promise to marry Edward George Carr when I grow up.' She watched as Eddy blew out the candle. 'Are we engaged now?' When Eddy nodded, she went on, 'Then you must never go back on your promise or God will punish you.'

'That goes for you too,' said Eddy. 'Come on, let's get tea and a bun.'

Dressed in the old green coat, and carrying the few clothes she possessed in a large brown paper parcel, Abby boarded the train for Canterbury the next day, rag doll under one arm and gas-mask case hanging from her shoulder.

Mrs Channon took her things, leaving Abby to say her farewells in private.

Evelyn looked up into Abby's tear-stained face, and tried to choke back her own tears. 'You'll be all right, my luv. You'll like it with your aunt and uncle, I know you will. Be a good girl now and don't forget to write to us.' She kissed the child lovingly then turned away before breaking down completely.

Mrs O'Connor stepped forward. Taking Abby's face into her old wrinkled hands, she gazed into the sad, lost, green eyes and forced a smile. 'Now then, sparrer, no tears. It's gonna be a great adventure and you'll 'ave two cousins to play with an' all. Think of all those lovely green fields to run about in! Better than old bomb sites any day.' She pulled the little face nearer and planted a large kiss on the smooth forehead. 'Gawd bless you and make you 'appy. Don't forget to write to us, now!'

Eddy stepped up just as the whistle blew. ''Bye, Abby. Don't forget your promise.' The train started to pull away from the platform, and he ran along beside it. 'Don't ever forget your promise . . .'

'I won't,' cried Abby, leaning from the carriage and waving. Slowly the train moved out of the station until the three figures she loved best in the world could be seen no more.

CHAPTER TWO

Milicent Glenister lit a cigarette and stared out of the window of Ferndene Lodge. Angry and agitated, she inhaled deeply to ease her nerves, then exhaled a cloud of smoke which drifted about the green velvet curtains.

A tall, attractive woman, Milicent was slender with a proud carriage and a cold manner. Her brown hair swept upwards to form small curls on the crown of her head; her chic blue woollen dress, with its padded shoulders and straight skirt, was brightened by a small diamond and enamel brooch, a present from her first husband. Though in her late thirties, no tell-tale lines fanned out from the cool blue eyes that scanned the country lane.

Turning away from the window, she wandered across the large drawing room to the boudoir piano and began to play. As the strains of Schubert filled the house, her eyes took on a distant look and her anger began to melt away. Once a teacher of music, it was only in music that Milicent could find her true self. All else was a sham. Her life was a sham: an unhappy struggle for acceptance in a world where she met only rejection. Her second marriage was no happier than the first, but what future could a divorced woman expect? Her hands paused on the keys. She should count her blessings with William Glenister, dubious though they might be.

Suddenly her hands slammed out a chord. *Damn the man.* How could he do this? Without the courtesy of discussing his plans with her, he had announced that his cousin's child would be coming to live with them. Not once had he thought to ask if she minded, or whether she would be able to manage. His bald statement brooked no argument. When he spoke of the child's background Milicent had been appalled. *A cockney from the slums*! Everything she'd done to achieve acceptance into Canterbury's society would now be jeopardized.

She finished her cigarette and immediately craved another, but there were only three left in her golden cigarette case and there was no knowing when she would be able to buy more. Food was difficult enough, but cigarettes were a rare commodity, to be used sparingly. Her thoughts returned angrily to William once more. How stupid he could be at times, stupid and thoughtless and selfish. It was true he had given her security when she needed it most, had proved himself to be a good provider and father to the children. In all this she could not fault him. But he was wrong for her in every other way.

There was a quiet knock on the door and a plump woman walked in. Since the full-time maid had joined the Land Army, Mrs Blackstock came in from the village two mornings and one afternoon each week.

'Excuse me, Mrs Glenister, but what time will they be arriving? I was wondering about tea, you see.'

Milicent shrugged. 'Goodness knows. I expected them long before this. Let's give it another fifteen minutes.'

'Yes, Mrs Glenister. But I'll have to leave at four today. My daughter's coming over with her baby, and I haven't seen them for some time.' Mrs Blackstock hovered by the door. 'Is the little girl to have tea in here, as well?' Her eyes swept anxiously across the Wilton carpet, the polished mahogany tables and chintz covered suite. 'I mean, I could give the child tea in the kitchen, if you prefer.'

'Would you?' Milicent breathed a sigh of relief. 'That's a good idea. I should tell you now, Mrs Blackstock, that this child comes from the dock area of London, so goodness knows what her upbringing's been like. She's an evacuee. We know nothing of her.'

24

The grey eyebrows shot up in surprise. 'Evacuee? Oh. I understood from your son that she was a relative.'

Milicent forced a light laugh. 'Good heavens, no. Richard has misunderstood. I told him we were going to encourage her to call us Aunt and Uncle, just to make the poor child feel at home.'

Mrs Blackstock was not so easily fooled. Her employer was hardly the kind of woman to take in an evacuee and no WVS officer would send a child to the threatened South East. Still she smiled and said quietly, 'Well, I think that's a right nice thing for you to do, Mrs Glenister. I hope the poor little mite will soon settle in.' With that she left the room, closing the door quietly behind her.

Still holding the cigarette case, Milicent stared at the engraving on it wistfully. It was of a large house, built in the neo-classical style, imposing and rather ugly. Nevertheless, she had expected to enter it as a welcome member of her first husband's family. They were wealthy and had walked with princes. But she was from the wrong background and, since her husband was the youngest son and wanted to be a doctor, rather than enter the family firm, they were treated with indifference. This alienation set the young marriage ripping at the seams. It ended after only three years, when Milicent walked out without any settlement, and returned to her widowed mother's Victorian villa in Folkestone. There she gave piano lessons to supplement their meagre income and pay for her mother's doctor's bills. After her mother died, she was desperate, and it was then, during a concert at the Leas Cliff Hall, that she met a young man with a South London accent. At first, she'd thought him beneath her, but his good looks and gentle persistence had finally won her over. On learning that William Glenister had inherited two shops from his uncle, she swallowed her pride and married him.

Milicent gave William Glenister no peace until he had

built up his business, selling both shops and borrowing from the bank in order to purchase a large department store in Canterbury. Already popular, it had become, with Milicent's guidance and eye for quality, the most prestigious store in town, boasting a restaurant where a ladies' trio played light music in the afternoons. She spent years cultivating the 'right' friends and playing bridge with those who formed Canterbury's social fabric. She served on various committees and was well known in the city. Within the confines of her middle-class existence, Milicent felt secure and comfortable. Now all of this was to be put in jeopardy by William's cockney niece!

Without even realizing it, she took out another cigarette and lit it with a trembling hand. Arguing with William once he had set his heart on a thing had always been a fruitless exercise. He had called her a snob when she tried to stop the child from coming here. And with the balance of the argument in his favour, she knew there was no chance of winning. After all, they were talking about an orphaned niece, a girl of ten who had been living in caves. How could she fight that? God, how she hated this war. It had turned the world on its head and swept away all the old rules.

Milicent returned to the piano. As ever, when she played this Schubert *Impromptu*, her thoughts went to her first husband, since this had been his favourite piece also. There had been no communication between them for years and she wondered where he was now. In the army or working in a hospital? Was he alive or dead?

The sound of the Canterbury bus pulling in at the stop along the lane brought Milicent out of her reverie. She glanced at the clock. It was ten minutes past four, and Mrs Blackstock had left five minutes earlier. She got up from the piano stool: her hands tightened on the cigarette case. *This is it,* she thought, walking out into the large hallway. She would have to face the girl alone.

*

Abby was tired, and unimpressed with Mrs Channon, who had slept throughout the entire train journey. At the station they had waited three quarters of an hour for the double decker bus in a cold, biting wind. It had taken another half an hour to wind its way through narrow country lanes to Ashton Green.

Still carrying her rag doll and gas-mask, Abby alighted, taking in the High Street bordered by timbered houses set among trees. A herdsman was driving his cows along the narrow lane; except for him there was no other movement. She had never seen a place so quiet or so pretty, yet already she was longing for the bustle and noise of London, and the security she felt with Mrs Carr, Eddy and Mrs O'Connor. She stood there, lost and frightened, desperately afraid that her aunt, uncle and cousins might not like her, or she them.

The area known as the Green was a triangular patch of grass set between the church, three shops, the forge and a public house. Mrs Channon paused and consulted a piece of paper upon which was a hastily drawn map of the area. 'The oast house should be on our right,' she murmured, looking about her anxiously. 'Oh, yes. There it is further along the lane. Come along, Abigail. Best foot forward!'

At length they came to Ferndene Lodge, a rambling two storey house of dark brick with bay windows and lattice-paned glass, spoilt only by the wartime criss-cross tape which scarred all buildings. Built at the turn of the century, the house stood well back from the road behind a wooden fence, and was dominated by a huge chestnut tree, the leaves of which were already changing to russet and gold. Overawed at the size of the place, Abby just stood staring. Beside the building was a brick garage with dark blue wooden doors. One door stood partly open and Abby could just make out the outline of a car hidden beneath black tarpaulin.

Walking along the gravel path, they came to the front

27

door which opened immediately. Abby stared up at the tall woman who stood there, but Milicent's eyes were on Mrs Channon, whom she greeted cordially enough. When she did look down at Abby, her eyes held unconcealed hostility and the child's heart sank.

'So,' murmured Milicent with a sigh, 'you are Abigail.'

'I'm always called Abby.' Her voice was a frightened whisper.

'Not here. I do not approve of diminutives.' Milicent's voice was sharp, as she bade them both enter the house. 'You will be called Abigail, and will call me Aunt Milicent. Do you understand?'

Abby nodded, her sense of loss and fear growing rapidly. This aunt did not like her. Yet she would have complete control over her life until she was grown up and able to look after herself.

Ushered into the drawing room, Mrs Channon sank thankfully on to the settee. 'I've brought the only clothes the child possesses in this parcel. And here's her ration book ...' The voice trailed off as she searched in her handbag. Milicent meanwhile urged Abby to take off the threadbare coat which she carried straight to the outhouse to be burned at the soonest possible moment. Wondering if the child had lice in her hair, she slammed the kettle down onto the gas stove, wishing with all her heart that Mrs Blackstock could have stayed longer to deal with the girl.

As they waited for tea to be brought, Abby's eyes swept the room. It was dominated by the piano which had several silver-framed photographs standing on it. The fireplace was made of brick with a mahogany mantel and in the hearth comforting flames licked the lumps of coal which Mrs Blackstock had put on just before leaving. On a coffee table in front of the settee was a copy of *Vogue*. Abby shifted and fidgeted on the edge of her seat, wondering what the word meant.

'Sit quietly,' said Mrs Channon. 'And be very careful not to spill your tea on this lovely carpet. This is a very nice home, Abigail. I hope you're grateful to your aunt for taking you in like this.' Then the door opened and Milicent wheeled in a trolley upon which was a silver tea service with bone china cups and saucers. On the lower tier was a large Victoria sponge and Abby eyed it hungrily. But when her aunt handed out small napkins and cake forks, Abby became confused and dropped both onto the floor.

Milicent eyed the girl in despair. 'Place your napkin on your lap, and eat your sponge with the fork, Abigail.'

After Mrs Channon left, Abby stood alone with her aunt at last. She felt herself swung around by the shoulders as anxious fingers searched her scalp. The fingers were hard and uncaring, as they parted the titian tresses, causing the child to wince with pain.

After satisfying herself that Abby had no lice, Milicent led her up the stairs to her room.

'We store apples in here during the winter months, that's why it smells. Of course, we'll have to find somewhere else to store them now.'

The small spare room stood at the rear of the house and faced north. Cold and sparse as it was, Abby could hardly believe that she would have such a room all to herself. The single bed was covered with a blue folkweave counterpane which matched the curtains. A thin rug covered bare boards and over the small iron fireplace hung a picture of mountains. Abby's eyes lingered over the oak dressing table and single wardrobe, then moved on to the window. Through it she could see a long garden which ended in a row of poplar trees.

Milicent untied the paper parcel. 'Now then, let's see what you have in here, child.' She unpacked a pink winceyette nightgown, some underwear and two woollen jumpers, then turned to the girl and sighed. 'Is this all? No spare skirt, or dress?'

29

Abby shook her head solemnly.

'Marvellous. That's just marvellous. How am I supposed to clothe you, I'd like to know?' Her eyes narrowed as she caught sight of the charred rag doll which Abby was clutching to her. 'My dear child, what on earth is that?'

Abby backed away, holding the doll more tightly than ever. Her aunt moved towards her swiftly, forcing her back into a corner.

'Good heavens, it must be alive with fleas,' said Milicent. 'Give it to me at once.'

'No!' said Abby.

'At once, I said.'

'Leave Pixie alone,' said Abby, almost in tears. 'She's mine. You can't 'ave 'er.'

No child had ever spoken to Milicent in such a manner before. Angered, she advanced on Abby, trying to pull the doll from her. 'Give it to me, I say! I won't have that lice-infested thing in my house.'

Abby stared up at her, gripping the doll tightly, her expression one of fear and hatred. 'She ain't got fleas. And you're 'orrible. I want to go 'ome. I want to go back to Mrs Carr.'

Milicent gave a sharp tug and wrenched the doll from Abby's grasp. As she did so the child let out a scream of rage and despair.

'I 'ate you ... I 'ate you!'

For a brief moment Milicent stared down at the child's blazing eyes, shocked beyond belief. Even the sight of the little girl sinking to the floor and sobbing, as she rocked back and forth on her heels crying for her mother, did nothing to soothe her anger. 'You'll stay in your room, until I call you.'

Shaken more than she cared to admit, Milicent paused in the hallway. Well. That was it. William would certainly have to do something about this situation. Picking up the telephone, she rang his office.

'Hello. Is everything all right? Has Abby arrived yet?' he asked in his calm, cheerful voice.

'Yes, Abigail has arrived – and no, everything is not all right. We have some serious talking to do, and this time you're going to listen to what I have to say.' With that she slammed down the receiver.

Taking the doll to the bonfire site at the far end of the garden, Milicent poured a little paraffin over the pathetic bundle and lit a match. As she watched the doll burn, she felt a twinge of pity for the child, knowing how much her own children valued their toys. Yet she had no choice; it could be diseased.

Watching from her bedroom, Abby saw the flames and wished her aunt would burn also. Screaming with rage she banged on the window, then threw herself onto the bed, where all the suppressed grief of the past now mingled with fear for the present. Burning Pixie was like burning her mother and Helen, for the old toy was all that remained of her family. Now it, too, was gone. Burying her face in the bedspread Abby cried, huge convulsive sobs shaking her small body, as her mind filled once more with the horror of the rubble under which her mother and sister had lain. At last, worn out with weeping, she fell asleep.

A slamming door awakened Abby. Cold and shivering, she sat up and remembered the warmth of Victoria Place. She wondered how long she had slept as she heard a girl's voice drifting up from the hallway. Any minute now, she thought, her door would open and she would come face to face with one of her cousins. But thirty minutes passed, and she was still alone in her room.

She walked over to the window and looking out, saw a thin wisp of smoke curling upwards from the burned rag doll. It pained her to look, so she let her eyes wander to the poplar trees beyond. The garden was large, and dominated by the inevitable Anderson. Surrounding the shelter were rows of lettuce and vegetables, and several old apple trees, heavy now with fruit, bordered the garden. Abby recalled how she had been helping to bottle apples on the very day she learned she was to be dragged away from her second family.

At that moment, she heard another door slam. There were voices in the hall, then thundering footsteps on the stairs and her bedroom door was flung open. A boy stood on the threshold, smart in his grey school uniform, blond hair shining like corn in August, his shy smile broadening into a friendly grin. Abby judged him to be older than she by a good two years.

'Hello. I'm Richard.' Before Abby could respond, he entered the room, grabbed her by the hand, and pulled her towards the door saying: 'Crumbs, it's freezing in here! Why didn't you stay in the kitchen? Come on.'

Richard did not let go his charge until she was safely seated at the kitchen table, feeling the glowing warmth of the Aga stove. On the table were slices of bread, a jam dish and the Victoria sponge. Richard walked over to the Aga, and poured boiling water from a kettle into the earthenware teapot. 'Mother's gone to a meeting. She'll be back later. We have dinner around seven, after my homework.' He looked around him in exasperation. 'Where is she? Stella!' His cry was answered by footsteps coming along the wide hallway.

Stella entered and barely glanced at her cousin as she fumbled in her satchel for a ruler. She was almost as tall as Abby and strongly resembled her mother. Her hair was drawn into two rigid plaits with purple bows at each end to match the braiding on the blazer of her school uniform and her full lips were set in a pout which told the world she was sulking.

Richard sensed the bad atmosphere and took charge. 'Here's Abby. Abby, this is Stella.'

Stella stared at her cousin with cold curiosity. Her mother had told her that Abby was a common, rude little slum brat and would be gone by the morning. Stella had heard this with great relief. What would her friends think of a cousin who came from the slums and who had lived in a cave, for goodness' sake? Now here she was sitting at their kitchen table. How stupid Richard was at times, and how like him not to be practical. She found her ruler at last, and said haughtily, 'I've got to finish some homework, so I'll take my cake and tea upstairs.'

'No you won't,' said Richard sharply. 'You'll sit at the table and eat properly.'

'Who do you think you're bossing about?' shouted Stella. She turned to Abby with narrowing eyes. 'Mummy says you've been living in caves. Is it true that you eat from newspapers instead of plates?'

Abby could have hurled her cup at the rude girl but thought it might upset Richard who was being kind to her. 'Course it ain't.'

Stella's eyes fixed on her cousin and she slowly sat down at the table, driven by hunger and curiosity. 'Mummy says all cockneys eat nothing but fish and chips which they buy wrapped in old newspapers.'

'Oh,' said Abby, munching a mouthful of sponge. 'That. Fish and chips is different.'

Stella wrinkled her nose. 'Sounds disgusting.'

'That's enough,' snapped Richard, darting a black look at his sister. He knew they should be trying to make Abby feel welcome instead of cold-shouldering her. 'My father won't be home until much later, because he's a warden on fire-duty most nights. He couldn't go into the army because he's forty and has a heart condition.' Richard immediately wondered why he had said that. Was he apologising for the fact that his father had been spared while Abby's had been killed? He wished she would say something. He could tell she had been crying. She was unhappy with them, and that perturbed him.

'How old are you?' he asked.

33

'Ten last June,' came the whispered response.

'Ten!' Stella gave a curt laugh. 'I'm nine, but I'm as tall as you already. You're going to be a titch.'

Abby ignored her and drank her tea, feeling the warm liquid flow through her body, blanketing the awful chill, and lifting the despair a little. She had met the Stellas of this world before, even if they hadn't such posh accents. She could deal with the silly girl. It was Aunt Milicent who frightened her. And what would Uncle William be like?

'I go to St Monica's school,' said Stella. 'Last night Mummy said you'd be going to the village school. That was before . . .' she stopped suddenly.

'I'm going to the King's School in a year,' said Richard. 'Only the school's not in Canterbury now. It's been evacuated to Cornwall, so if the war isn't over by then, I'll be going to Cornwall, too.' He frowned. 'We get lots of air-raids here, you know. That's why we were sent to Yorkshire.'

'To a great-aunt who was beastly,' said Stella. '"Beastly Bertha", we called her. I hated her.'

'She didn't like us either,' said Richard. 'We lived near an army camp, and I got into a lot of trouble for climbing into an army tank on the moors.'

Abby stared at him in growing admiration. 'What happened?'

'It started moving down the hill, and ended up in the river. Good thing the water was shallow! The soldiers were furious and Auntie nearly had a fit. So we came back home. That was last March. I don't want to be evacuated again. I want to stay here.'

Abby wanted him to stay, too. Richard was her only friend in this house. In a way, he reminded her of Eddy, though they were poles apart in looks and speech. 'If the war ends, you won't 'ave to go away,' she said hopefully.

Richard shook his head. 'Oh, I'll be boarding anyway, even if the school returns to Canterbury.'

'Boarding?' Abby frowned. 'What's boarding?'

'Living at the school, silly,' sneered Stella. 'Don't you know anything?'

Abby was shocked. The idea of anyone living at school was unheard of in her world. Evacuation was bad enough but to be sent away from home without reason was the cruellest thing she had ever heard. Aunt Milicent truly must be wicked if she wanted this for her son.

'Don't your Mum love you then?' she asked quietly.

Richard looked surprised and laughed. 'Of course she does.' He stood up and started washing the dishes. 'You'll like Canterbury. And we live by the river. If it's fine on Sunday, I'll show you around after church.' He turned awkwardly, noticed that Stella had left and said, 'Look, I have to finish an essay. Will you be all right sitting here? I'll give you a book to read if you like.'

Abby's eyes brightened. 'I like comics best.'

'Sorry. We're not allowed to read them,' said Richard.

Abby sighed. Memories of swapping comics with her friends in Bermondsey glimmered like a light through the darkness she was feeling. Eddy had loved *The Eagle* while *The Beano* was her favourite. A house without comics was a cold, hard place to endure.

That evening, Milicent gave Abby a bath and washed her hair with carbolic soap before rubbing vinegar into the dark red locks. She then made Abby sit on the bathroom stool for fifteen minutes before rinsing it off.

'Now then, I want no more cheek from you, my girl. Go down to the kitchen and sit by the stove until your hair is dry.'

Clad in a pair of Stella's old pyjamas, Abby sat alone by the Aga while her cousins did their homework in their own rooms. She felt mortified. Never in her life had she had lice in her hair. Her mother had always kept her scrupulously clean, bathing her twice a week in the zinc bath before the blazing fire. Bath nights had been warm and fun. The bathroom in this house was big, and had hot and cold taps fixed to both sink and bath. Yet, even as she marvelled, Abby hated the white tiled room. Like the house, it was large and lonely.

Dinner was a nightmare for Abby. Glancing at the array of cutlery in confused silence, she then used the wrong spoon for her soup. Milicent quickly corrected her. Abby then reached for the sugar sprinkler, assuming it was salt, and shook it over her fish and boiled potatoes, causing howls of laughter from Stella. Richard came to her rescue, switching plates and saying, 'I don't mind sugar on fish at all. Might improve it.'

In bed that night, Abby lay wide awake, unable to sleep in the deep silence. Never having slept alone before, she now found it an unnerving experience. As she tossed and turned, Abby heard the front door open and shut again quietly: a man's voice, low and indistinct, then the louder tones of her aunt. Climbing out of bed, she opened her door a little and stood there listening.

William Glenister was surprised to find his wife still up, waiting for him. He was tired and hungry and just wanted some peace and quiet before retiring. 'Drizzling again,' he murmured, slipping out of his mackintosh and placing the warden's helmet on the porch to drip onto red tiles. 'Still, at least we've plenty of cloud cover. Jerry might not bother tonight.' He turned at once, walked past his wife and made straight for the drawing room where he warmed his hands by the dying fire.

A thick-set man with greying hair, William Glenister seemed older than his forty years, with a distinguished manner which belied the thin trace of a cockney accent. The many years spent in Canterbury had changed his speech, but there was still a quality in it which surprised some and beguiled others. It was warm, soft and comforting. He might not be top drawer, they thought, but Mr Glenister was as solid and trustworthy as the Cathedral itself.

36

'Thought you'd be in bed by now,' he murmured, as his wife followed him into the room.

'Did you.' The tone of Milicent's voice put him on his guard. She wasted no time in coming to the point. 'That child cannot stay in this house, William. You must make other arrangements.'

'Oh, not again.' William sighed and sank into the armchair. 'Christ Almighty, we've been over this ground time and time again. I've told you, my mind is made up.'

'Is it!' snapped Milicent. 'Well, you'll just have to think again. You wait until you hear her speak, and watch her table manners. Wait until she's been as rude to you as she's been to me. Then I daresay you'll change your mind quickly enough. That child belongs in an orphanage. She's nothing to do with us.'

'She's blood kin,' said William wearily. He gave a deep sigh. 'Come on, Mil. She's only a mite. You must give her time to adapt.'

Through the crack in the bedroom door, Abby could hear her aunt's raised voice, but her uncle spoke too quietly. An orphanage! Her aunt wanted to put her in an orphanage! Horrified, she moved out onto the landing, and looked down at the light flooding into the hallway from the drawing room.

'Time won't change her class,' Milicent was saying.

'Have you forgotten that her class is my class?'

'Well, it damned well isn't mine or the children's,' cried Milicent. 'I won't have our lives ruined like this. As for class, you were never from her background.'

'I'm working-class, Mil, whether you like it or not. Working-class made good, but they're my origins.'

'Oh, don't be stupid.' Milicent had heard him on this soapbox before and it irritated her beyond measure. How could he accuse her of snobbery when he gloried in the class war himself?

'She stays,' said William flatly. 'And that's that.'

Milicent turned on him in fury. 'What on earth is so special about this girl? Two weeks ago you didn't even know of her existence. Now our lives are to be turned upside down because of her.'

'Don't exaggerate,' said William tersely. Switching on the wireless set, he lit his pipe and settled back in his armchair.

But Milicent did not like losing. 'If she does stay, then it's on my terms, William. Those terms mean telling people that she's an evacuee, not a relation. I've already said as much to Mrs Blackstock, so there can be no going back on it now.'

'You've done what?' William looked at his wife incredulously. 'Are you mad?'

'On the contrary.' Milicent stood in the doorway, a sly smile playing on her lips. 'It's the only way I'll accept the child.'

'But the children ...'

'They've already been briefed,' Milicent cut in sharply.

William got to his feet slowly, his face white with anger. 'You've told the children to *lie*? Told them to deny their blood kin simply because she's from the wrong class according to Milicent Glenister?'

'You left me no option,' Milicent replied, then retired to her room.

Abby rushed back to her bed at her aunt's approach, and lay there with her heart pounding. So she was to stay here, because Uncle William had put his foot down, but no one was to know who she was. Later, she heard a tread on the stair and saw her door open slowly. A man stood there, looking down at her, and she shut her eyes, pretending to be asleep. When she opened them again, he had gone.

Abby awoke late the following morning. The house seemed silent and she wondered what the time was. Dressing quickly, she walked down the stairs and entered a cold and empty kitchen. Where on earth was everyone?

'Your uncle's at the store, and Richard and Stella are at school,' said her aunt, returning from the garden with a large cabbage which she now prepared to clean.

Abby stared up at her aunt in disbelief. 'School! But it's Saturday.'

Milicent explained tersely that public schools had lessons on Saturdays, likewise Stella's convent. Lessons would be followed by Games, so neither of the cousins would be home until four thirty at the very least. And then Stella had a riding lesson.

'Can I go and watch?' asked Abby.

The thought sent a shudder through Milicent. 'No. I'm afraid not. You'll just have to amuse yourself, my dear, and not get in my way.'

Abby spent most of the day outdoors, exploring the garden, the outhouse and the small orchard. It was here she discovered the green wooden gate that opened onto the river bank. Looking down into the flowing waters of the Stour, and long tendrils of weeds waving gently beneath the surface, she wondered if the river coursed its way seaward from London and for one brief moment imagined stealing a boat and rowing upstream until she found her way home. A keen wind soughed through the willows on the far bank, the rustle of their leaves breaking the stillness of the sunless afternoon. Abby watched them for some time, missing the noise and bustle of London. Mrs Carr always used to have the wireless on, but Aunt Milicent never listened at all, it seemed. These woods and surrounding fields would never be the same as the old bomb sites that she and Eddy used as playgrounds. Was he missing her as much as she was missing him? she wondered.

When Stella returned, Abby watched her pull on her riding boots.

'Can I come and watch you ride?'

Stella shook her head. 'No.'

'Why not?'

'Because Mummy said that my friends wouldn't like you. You're too common.' Stella spoke with all the innocent insensitivity of a child who was merely stating a fact. With that, she rushed to the porch, found her riding crop, and vanished without so much as a goodbye.

Abby sat down on the bottom stair, crushed. Common! Mrs Carr had said that about a neighbour. 'Common as muck she is, with her dyed hair.'

But I'm not common, she thought angrily. *I don't have dyed hair*. Aunt Milicent had spoken of class. She, it seemed, was the wrong class and that was why no one, except Richard, liked her. Abby supposed class meant rich. You had to be rich to live in a big house like this. Yet it was more, she thought. It had something to do with using the right spoon and placing napkins on the lap at mealtimes. Stella had laughed at her for not knowing these things.

That evening Abby met her uncle for the first time, and liked him instantly. He was warm and kindly, and had brought some gym-slips and blouses for her to try on. 'You'll need these for school on Monday.' Turning to his wife, he said, 'It would have been easier had you brought the girl into the store. How could I know what size she is?'

Abby saw the reproachful glare her aunt hurled at Uncle William, as she snapped, 'I think you know the answer to that one. I've made my position quite clear.'

After church the following morning, Richard, true to his promise, led Abby out through the garden gate and along the muddy river path. The wind was keen, but the day was crisp and golden, perfect for country walking. Half a mile north of the village they came to a wooden footbridge which spanned the deepest part of the Stour. On the far side, the path led upwards through a thickly wooded copse, then wound its way onto downland where sheep grazed.

'We call this Stapledown,' said Richard as he strode

towards the summit. 'You get a super view of the city from here. Look.'

Breathless, Abby gazed down on Canterbury. Barrage balloons hovered high above, yet the Cathedral still dominated the skyline. Richard pointed out the ancient Roman wall, then Ashton Green. 'You can just see the church between the trees.'

Abby followed his pointing finger. The square tower of St Michael's seemed almost lost among giant yew trees. Beside it she could make out a few of the older cottages where smoke curled up from tall chimneys. Following the trail of smoke, Abby's eyes came to rest on a large stone mansion set in acres of parkland. A lake shimmered in the sunlight and three horses grazed in a paddock close by.

'What's that house, then?' she asked.

'Wickham Place,' answered Richard.

'Blimey! Whoever lives there must be blooming rich.'

Richard smiled, then sat on the ground, heedless of the cold and damp. Abby did likewise, plucking at a blade of grass and gazing about her with interest. Today she liked the country and the oasthouses set among hop gardens. There were orchards in plenty and she realized now why Kent was known as the Garden of England.

'Why does Aunt Milicent want people to think I'm an evacuee instead of your cousin?' she asked suddenly.

Startled at the suddenness of this question, Richard looked away in embarrassment. 'Does she? I mean, I don't think that can be right.'

'No. I 'eard them talking about it. What will *you* tell *your* friends?' She stared at him curiously, worried that he, too, might think her common.

'That you're my cousin, of course,' lied Richard, feeling his face burn. He had been opposed to his mother's suggestion from the start, but she'd insisted. Abby's speech was a disgrace and her manners impossible. When he'd

41

replied that his friends wouldn't give a fig about Abby's speech, she had turned on him angrily.

'If you let me down in this, Richard, then I shall have no alternative but to send her to an orphanage. That may sound harsh, but I know the world we live in. Now I want your solemn promise to obey me in this matter.'

When he'd pointed out that they had been brought up not to tell lies, she merely said there were times when a small lie did the greater good all round. And so he had promised. Now he found himself telling more lies to avoid hurting Abby's feelings.

At that moment, a pony and rider appeared on the crest of the hill. The girl on the chestnut mare was about Richard's age. Her long hair fell like spun gold from beneath her riding hat and she sat in the saddle as though born to it. When she caught sight of Richard, and the small, thin girl beside him, she reined in her mount and rode towards them.

'I'm not so sure I should speak to you, Richard Glenister, since you chose to ignore me after church this morning.' The voice was clipped and authoritative, and the deep brown eyes stared out of a round, flushed face.

It was then Abby remembered where she had seen the girl before. Only that morning she had walked in stately procession with her parents along the aisle of the church to the front pew. No sooner had the three closed the small door to the pew than the choir started along the nave towards the altar, carrying the golden crucifix before them. This family had arrived last, and when the service was ended, no one moved before they had made their way out of the church. Clearly, they were very important.

Richard was blushing to his eartips and looking nervous. He gestured towards Abby, introducing her in a clumsy manner. 'This is Abby Nichols. She's ... she's staying with us for a while.' He turned to Abby. 'This is Samantha Fellowes.'

Abby smiled up at the girl, wondering at Richard's refusal to say the word 'cousin'. She turned towards him expectantly, almost willing him to go on. 'Abby's been bombed out, and she's an orphan now, so ... so she's come to live with us.' Richard looked down at his shoes, but could feel Samantha's eyes burning into him. 'How simply awful for you,' said Samantha. 'Where did you live?'

'London,' said Abby, her heart like lead. She'd thought Richard stronger and more true. Now she knew better. He had failed her, denied her true identity when face to face with his own friends.

Samantha was eyeing Abby, curiosity mixed with jealousy. She had known Richard for two years now, and, although they met rarely, harboured a secret crush on him. 'I've an aunt who lives in Knightsbridge. Did you live near there?'

Abby frowned and shook her head. 'I dunno. Is it near Bermondsey?'

The puzzled look on Samantha's face changed to one of dismissive practicality. 'I'll be late for luncheon,' she said wheeling her pony about. ''Bye, Richard.' With that she urged her mount back down the hill and disappeared into the spinney.

'Sammy's all right, really,' said Richard as he started down the hill towards the river. 'Her father is the local squire. He's Sir Gerald Fellowes. You saw the whole family in church this morning.' Guilt-ridden, knowing how much he must have hurt Abby, he walked on, not daring to look into her face. But what else could he have done? He had never wilfully disobeyed his mother.

Abby followed him slowly, her pride refusing to discuss the matter. He was what he was – his mother's son. Still,

43

she should be grateful to the one person who had shown her kindness when no one else had.

Abby's days at Ashton Green began to fall into place once she had breached the frightening barrier of returning to school after such a long absence. So far behind was she in her lessons that the staff despaired, and sent her to the Remove, where most of Abby's colleagues were dull-minded children who would rather be anywhere than in a classroom. In this Abby was different. She wanted knowledge desperately. But when the time came for her first exam, she was mortified to be faced with a maths paper which meant nothing to her. Too far behind in her studies to catch up with the maths curriculum, Abby had been left chewing the end of her pen while others unravelled the mysteries of decimals and fractions. To Abby, it was a moment of humiliation she would never forget.

The routine at Ferndene Lodge was rigid and left Abby hovering on the brink of family life. Each evening, Richard and Stella would arrive home from school, spend one hour on homework, then an hour each at the piano, have dinner, give a further hour towards studies then get ready for bed. On the rare occasions when they had friends in, Milicent made certain that Abby was banished to her bedroom, or sent on an errand. Samantha Fellowes was the only visitor Milicent actively encouraged. She'd often arrive on a Sunday afternoon, tether her pony to the fence and seek out Richard. Her confidence was inbred, and fed on her ability to get her own way in all things. Milicent was mere putty in her hands. Not so Richard. His curt and bored manner would have deflated any other ego, but only made Samantha more determined.

'Why do you encourage the girl?' asked William one day. 'Anyone can see that Richard doesn't want her around. And when she's here, poor little Abby is made to stay in her room. It's ludicrous.'

44

'I see nothing ludicrous in their relationship,' Milicent said.

'What relationship?' William's eyebrows shot up. 'If you're thinking what I think you're thinking, then forget it. Girls from Samantha's background don't marry into trade. She'll wed into her class, just as Richard will wed into his.'

Milicent smiled and said, 'Of course.' Her innermost thoughts she kept to herself. She loved her son more than anyone else in this world, and her ambitions for him were boundless. One day he would grow to see Samantha in a very different light. Time would take care of that. And she was a very patient woman.

CHAPTER THREE

Glenisters Store occupied a prime position in Canterbury. Formed from three sixteenth-century merchant houses, its timber frontage and small-paned windows gave it an air of quality that matched the merchandise within. Since the war, however, the mahogany shelves which had contained silk lingerie and cashmere twinsets were almost empty, and uniforms took priority over civilian wear.

In his office, William Glenister checked his accounts and wondered how long he could stay in business. The limited stock he was able to get relied entirely on the availability of coupons rather than money. At this time, he was just keeping his head above water. He had dreamed of opening another store in Folkestone, then another in Maidstone, but if the war continued much longer he would have to sell up and start again.

He walked across to the window. The High Street was bathed in May sunshine. He marvelled that a market-stall holder from Woolwich should find himself doing so well in this city of ancient houses set within Roman walls. Born and bred in South London, he'd expected to die there, selling cheap clothing in the market place beside the Arsenal factory. Now Woolwich seemed a world away and there were times when William missed his old life. Today was such a day. He missed his friends, especially the cousin he had become close to before he died at Dunkirk.

You were Jack the Lad then, Glenister. Now look at you! Sober as a judge and old before your time.

William turned from the window, heavy of heart. For all his success, he felt a failure. How ironic that the uncle who'd left him his small shops in order to help had, in the end, only destroyed. *I'd have been better left shouting my head off in the market square*, he thought bitterly. At least then he would have married someone from his own background, instead of Milicent. What on earth had attracted him to her in the first place? Was it her looks or his vanity?

Vanity, you stupid beggar. The vanity of an ill-educated working-class man, wanting a middle-class woman of culture. She was a challenge. Could Jack the Lad succeed out of his class, as well as he'd succeeded within it? Milicent's first response to his overtures had been unenthusiastic, but he'd persisted until she was standing beside him at the Registry Office. After the first year, he'd spent every waking moment regretting his foolishness. Yet it was true that without her, he could never have come this far. What would a man from his background know about crystal or porcelain and the world of classic fashion? And if, at first, he'd been uncomfortable at her social gatherings, he soon became used to the well-bred elite Milicent cultivated. Even so, he dreaded going home to the cold atmosphere she always managed to produce, and was thankful for his war duties. Fire watching and patrolling the streets as an air-raid warden kept him sane.

A soft knock on the door broke William's reverie. 'Come in.'

The door opened slowly and Richard's head appeared. 'Am I disturbing you, Father?'

William smiled. Everything had its good side, and the children were the good side of his disastrous marriage. 'Of course not, son. Who's that behind you?'

Richard and Abby entered the office, each carrying a package wrapped in recycled paper.

'Mother sent me in for another jacket, since I ripped my old one, and it was too short in the arms anyway. Abby needed shoes, since Stella's don't fit her. Mrs Wellings

47

served us, and Mother said I was to leave the coupons for you to sort out.'

'Did she now.' William knew this dodge of old. Being the owner of a store would, in Milicent's eyes, exempt his family from rationing. 'Tell your mother I'll take them off the books tonight, but she's not to do that again. Why should my family have special privileges not accorded to others? It's unfair. And it's illegal.'

Richard nodded in high embarrassment. His mother was always doing things like this. He hated it, just as his father did.

William turned to Abby. Seeing the worried look in those large green eyes caused him to regret his stern remarks. This child never had anything new. Milicent kept her coupons for Stella, handing cast-offs down to Abby instead. He smiled down at her.

'Well, are you going to show me the shoes?'

Abby opened the paper and took out a pair of black lace-ups. 'Mrs Wellings measured me foot and all. I'm a size three now.' She gazed lovingly on the shining new leather, then wrapped the shoes once more.

'Abby's only been into town three times since she came to live with us,' Richard was saying, 'so I've promised to show her the Cathedral and the spot where Thomas à Becket was murdered.'

'How nice,' said William drily. 'Don't be late for the bus home.'

'We won't. Thought I'd show her the King's School as well.'

'Well, off you go then, you bloodthirsty little pilgrims. If there's an air-raid ...'

'I know, Father. Take shelter. Don't worry, we'll be fine.'

Too restless to work, William turned back to the window and watched the children walk along the narrow street of ancient houses towards the Cathedral. His wife's attitude to Abby had changed very little in the eight months she'd lived with them, and this had sent the child into a quiet shell which only Richard could penetrate. William had hoped normal family life would help Abby forget the horror she'd lived through, but when he saw the distant expression on that small face, he knew his hopes were in vain.

In the Cathedral, Richard showed Abby the scene of Becket's martyrdom, giving a graphic account of his murder at the hands of the barons. He even made her believe the darker shading in the stone floor was a bloodstain. Abby listened to him in horror, unsure about this huge and cavernous building. She had never been in a cathedral before and found it daunting, preferring to gaze at the river from the ancient Weaver's house, or look up at the thick Norman walls of the West Gate.

Richard then showed her the King's School, in the Precincts of the Cathedral, and she was amazed that any school could be so ancient.

'But you'll be going to Cornwall, you said.'

Richard nodded. 'To Carlyon Bay. The school's taken over a hotel. It'll be great! Right by the beach.'

A shadow crossed Abby's brief day of happiness. She hated to be reminded of Richard's departure and pushed the thought from her. Three months was a long time. The war might be over by then, and Richard would not have to go away at all.

Each week Abby wrote to Mrs Carr and received a reply which usually included a hastily scrawled note from Eddy giving all the news of life in London and the Chislehurst Caves. She lived for these letters and wrote long chronicles back, but had only once revealed the truth about how she felt. That had been in her first letter, and Milicent had confiscated it and made Abby write a very different letter. She then subjected her to a lecture on how fortunate she was to live in such a house, when she might easily be in an orphanage. Never again did Abby dare to write the truth.

After a long quiet Sunday tending his garden, William Glenister left home to take up his watch as air-raid warden. It was a clear night and mild. He gazed up at the moonlit sky and felt a gentle breeze on his face.

The sods will be over tonight, as sure as God made little apples. Poor bloody London. His thoughts were grim as he walked on through the village, checking as he went that no chinks of light were showing through the blackout curtains. Entering the church, he climbed to the tower and took up his fire watching position. His view across the countryside was unobstructed and he could see the outline of the Cathedral against the moonlit sky.

As the first wave of bombers approached, Abby opened her eyes and listened to the throb of their engines, knowing they would pass on overhead to their main target. The warning had blared out over Canterbury some minutes earlier, but Aunt Milicent had decided not to bother going to the Anderson. The chances of anything falling on Ashton Green were remote. At the sound of the first explosion Abby shot up in bed. By the time she had reached her window, two more had followed. Looking out she saw a strange bright glow in the sky. Parachute flares were being dropped on the city, lighting up the night sky so that every house could be seen. The flares were followed by more bombs. Racing for her door, Abby collided with her aunt.

'Into the shelter, Abby,' said Milicent, banging on Richard's door then rushing along to Stella's room. 'Come on, you two!'

In the garden they paused for a brief moment and gazed up at the sky. Stella bounced up and down in excitement. 'Look, oh, look! It's fantastic. I can see the planes!' She was practically thrown into the shelter by her mother who then turned to the others, urging them to hurry.

Richard's face was clearly visible in the strange light.

'It's a deliberate raid,' he said. 'But why? Why Canterbury?'

The first wave of bombers had moved on and already another was approaching, their wings shining in the light of the flares. Soon a different glow hung over Canterbury and the smell of burning drifted across the Kent countryside. 'Poor, lovely, old city,' murmured Milicent, her heart as heavy as lead. 'Dear God, why?' But she knew why. Recently the Allies had bombed Cologne. Clearly this was a revenge attack.

As Milicent lit the paraffin lamp, her eyes fell on Abby, hunched in the corner of the lower bunk. The child was rigid with fear and for the first time she felt pity for the little girl. Leaning over, she touched the child gently on the arm saying, 'It's all right. We're safe out here in the country.'

'What about Father?' asked Richard. 'Where's Father?'

They fell silent knowing that every warden would be heading for the city to help. William was probably there already digging people from the rubble, risking his own life without a thought.

When the All Clear finally sounded, they stood in the garden looking up at the flaming sky. A long pall of smoke drifted towards Ashton Green, bringing with it the terrible smell of charred wood and acrid fumes.

Aware that the war was not a distant thing after all, Richard was fearful for his father, a fear that was expressed in anger. 'Bastards,' he cried out. 'Filthy German bastards.'

'Richard!' Milicent looked at her son in dismay. 'Don't ever let me hear you use such language again.'

Richard ignored her, saying, 'I don't care. They're evil and I hate them.'

Milicent wheeled on her son. 'Be quiet. You don't know what you're saying.'

Later, as she put the kettle on to make a pot of tea, her fingers shook as she struck the match. Anxious as she was for William, it was her son's words of hatred that made her tremble so. She had been wrong to keep the children here.

William did not return home for forty-eight hours. When he did he was weary to the bone and sick at heart. 'Everything to the east of the Cathedral has gone. One third of the entire city. The blighters didn't get the Cathedral, thank God.'

'Have there been many casualties?' Milicent asked.

'Couldn't say how many for certain. About fifty dead, but many injured.' William sank into his chair and placed his head in his hands. His hair was white with dust and his face covered in soot and dirt. He thought of the dead and dying he had dragged from the rubble. Such pictures could never be erased.

'How badly damaged is the store?' asked Milicent, lighting a cigarette.

William sighed and looked up. 'The interior's a shambles and the ceiling's down in Children's Wear. But I expect we can soon put things right.'

Milicent stared ahead, remembering her son's words. 'Frankly, I don't think anything can ever be put right again.'

The rubble was cleared away. The Cathedral stood proud and strong beside the wasteland. The people of Canterbury had seen a miracle and counted their blessings.

Abby discovered that she, too, had a blessing. Her talent for art was first noticed by a teacher at the village school, who promptly took it upon herself to nurture the gift. In Abby she found a willing pupil and a fast learner, and they talked of art scholarships.

Abby spent most of the summer holidays with a sketch pad on her knee, trying to capture the willows hanging over the river, the horses waiting at the forge, and the women in the Land Army as they toiled in the fields. She and Richard would cycle along the narrow country lanes, dodging army lorries and soldiers until they reached an old barn or oast house which had to be captured on paper. Their favourite place was Stapledown, where Richard had taken her on that first Sunday. Abby only climbed to its summit when Richard was with her, thinking of it as their special place. High on the downland, with only a lark's song to break the silence, the two would gaze down on Canterbury and say nothing, content in each other's company.

That autumn, Richard left home for Cornwall, and Abby was desolate without him. She found solace in her art, becoming so prolific that Mrs Blackstock complained.

'You know, dear, I really can't clean your room properly unless you do something about all those pictures. Can't you find somewhere to store them? The attic, for instance?'

Abby had been in the attic only once before, with Richard, and found it a little frightening. Climbing the narrow wooden staircase, on her own, Abby opened the creaking door and felt the old fear return. The light from the small gabled window showed only the outline of discarded things covered in dust. Making her way slowly past two Victorian dining chairs with horsehair protruding from the velvet covering, a pile of suitcases and a trunk, she came to the oak chest which had belonged to her aunt's mother. The top two drawers were already full, and Abby stared at the dark blue velvet curtains enviously, seeing herself in a ballgown of such richness. The two bottom drawers were empty and into these Abby placed her sketches. This done, she stood up and looked around with growing curiosity. So many old and fascinating things, she thought.

The trunk in the far corner caught her eye. Raising the lid, Abby found herself gazing on a pile of clothes. She drew out a twenties-style dress of crêpe de Chine, a white fur stole, several sequined evening bags and a woollen dress of dark green which flared at the bottom. Everything was out of date and smelling of mothballs. Under the clothing, Abby discovered a leather-bound photograph album. Of all the people in the photographs, she recognized only her aunt, much prettier and younger than the woman she knew now. Her hair was short and wavy, her dresses long with softer lines than those of today. In many of the pictures a tall, fair-haired man stood beside Milicent. Both looked happy and relaxed. Other pictures showed her with three young children. The photograph Abby liked the best was of the three of them on their bicycles waving towards the camera.

Abby stared at the children, wondering if these were cousins she knew nothing about. She would never be able to ask, since there would be hell to pay if it were known that she'd been rummaging through the trunk. The last photograph was the blond man again, this time kneeling beside a huge Alsatian dog. In the background stood a mansion. As Abby studied the picture she realized it was the house etched onto her aunt's golden cigarette case.

The warm spring of 1944 gave way to the wettest June people could remember. Then came news of the Allied landings in Normandy. Safe in his store, William Glenister hardly knew whether to be relieved or dismayed. If his own neat village had been turned into a quagmire, then what must conditions be like on the battlefields of France? Please God, not another Somme, he prayed. But as he listened to the bombers thundering overhead on their nightly missions to Germany his spirits lifted. *They're giving Jerry a pounding. It'll all be over by Christmas.*

The first time Abby saw a plane with its tail on fire, she marvelled at its ability to go on flying in such a straight line. Then the flame went out, the plane glided down onto Canterbury, and she heard a distant explosion. Another plane followed, its tail of flame reminding her of a comet.

'How can they fly when they're on fire?' asked Abby, staring up from the garden.

'I don't know,' said Stella.

As they stood watching, more planes with tails of fire came flying across Canterbury, dodging the flak.

'They're not planes,' Milicent explained. 'They're bombs. Flying bombs.'

Abby looked up at her aunt in disbelief. 'But what about the pilots?'

'There are no pilots,' murmured Milicent, her spirit at its lowest ebb yet. 'The Germans have produced a new weapon. Somehow, I don't think the war will be over for some time.' As she urged the girls into the shelter, she thanked God that her son was safe in Cornwall.

By day and by night the drone of flying bombs could be heard as guns pounded the skies. So many were brought down on the villages of Kent that the run became known as 'Bomb Alley'. However, many got through to London, which had not known such an onslaught since the worst days of the Blitz.

Eddy wrote to Abby giving her the latest news in his barely readable scrawl.

Everyone's pouring into the caves these days. More than 15,000 people and there's a notice at Charing Cross saying that the Chislehurst Caves are full. It's the doodlebugs what's doing it. Our house was damaged again when one fell on Mrs Roberts. She's dead. We was standing in the yard when it happened. I saw the flame go out when the thing was right above us. Mum pushed me into the shelter. The ack ack caught the wing, and the thing tipped away from us onto Mrs Roberts instead. The shock was bad for Mrs O'Connor, but she's all right now. The house is such a mess we're staying with Mum's friend in Lewisham. Mrs O'Connor's roomatism is better these days, and she swears it's spending our nights in the caves what's done it. She likes it there and knows everyone. We had a film show the other night and a week earlier a band and dancing. I'm glad you like your school. I

*loathe mine. Teachers don't know nothing anyhow.
It's in Lewisham and we spend most of our time in
the air-raid shelters instead of the classrooms, singing
daft songs and testing our gas-masks. Found more
shrapnel the other day. Your aunt sounds posh, so
do your cousins. I expect you're posh too now. You
won't want to know us no more. Maybe you won't
never come back to London. Maybe you've forgotten
the promise you made at the Druid's Altar.*

    *Mum and Mrs O'Connor send their love and remind
you it's your turn to write.*

Love and kisses,
Eddy

Abby placed the letter in an old shoe box with all the
other letters she had received from the Carrs. How silly
Eddy was, thinking she could forget them. She smiled as
she remembered that last evening when they had taken
those childish vows before the altar. She wondered if
he had changed and longed to see them all again. One
day, when the war was over, she would take the train
to London and visit the woman she still thought of as
a second mother.

The flying bombs were followed by another deadly
weapon, known as the V2 Rocket. It arrived without
warning, soundless and with an even greater explosive
power, to devastate London. No one knew when the
world would suddenly explode about them.

The rockets kept Richard away all summer and when
they ceased Uncle William insisted he remain in Cornwall
until the war was over. Milicent missed her son dreadfully
and frayed nerves made her particularly short with the
girls. It was unfortunate that Abby chose this moment
to bring up the subject of an art scholarship.

'Mrs Holford has asked me to give you this letter,'
said Abby.

Milicent had been trying to calm herself by playing some

Chopin, and was not pleased by this interruption. 'Who on earth is Mrs Holford?'

'One of my teachers. She thinks I'm good enough to go on to the College of Art after I've left school.' Abby's eyes shone with pride and high expectations.

Milicent read the letter and smiled wryly. 'So this Mrs Holford thinks you scholarship material, does she?' The voice was dangerously thin. 'And what exactly does she think you're going to do at this College of Art?'

'Well, I'll be taught properly to paint and sketch and ...'

'Paint and sketch!' Milicent gave a harsh laugh. 'My dear child, I've been an art lover all my life and there's one thing I do know. No one makes a living out of art. You'd be enjoying yourself at our expense for another three years, and then you'd have to be re-trained for something else. No, my dear, I won't even consider the matter.'

Abby stared at her aunt in dismay. Everything she had hoped for was dashed to pieces. 'But Mrs Holford thinks ...'

'I don't care what Mrs Holford thinks,' cried Milicent. 'I'm sure the woman means well, but she must be mad if she thinks we're going to carry you once you're old enough to earn your own keep. Really, child, don't you think you owe it to us to leave school as soon as you can, and find work to pay your way in this world?'

Abby was close to tears. 'But you see, Aunt, I thought fashion design would be a career. I've been making my own things now for some time, and if only I could learn properly, then I *would* be able to earn a living.'

'My dear child, you might have a talent for art but you'll never amount to anything more than a gifted amateur. Anyway, Mrs Holford's jumped the gun, don't you think? You've a few more years' schooling yet.'

The subject was closed. But Abby told herself Mrs Holford would be able to convince her aunt when the time came.

*

57

Another bleak Christmas came and went, and still the war did not end. It was a cold St Valentine's Day, and the family gathered around the fireside, Stella with her knitting, Abby with her book, Milicent with the latest copy of *Vogue* and William with his newspaper.

Milicent looked across at Abby and frowned. 'Why aren't you getting on with that blouse?'

'I've finished it,' said Abby, wrenching her thoughts away from the adventures of Sir Percy Blakeney. 'It's pressed and hanging in the wardrobe.'

'Why didn't you show it to me?' Milicent asked, wishing Stella had Abby's skill.

'I didn't think you'd be interested.'

The thin eyebrows lifted. 'Don't be impertinent, child. Of course I'm interested.'

At that moment William switched on the wireless. He glanced across at Abby, thinking how pretty the child was now. Her hair glowed in the firelight, falling in soft curls around the small oval face dominated by large green eyes. She'll break men's hearts one day, he thought.

Big Ben's chimes heralded the nightly chronicle of cities bombed, planes lost and missing, and the latest offensive as the Allies and Russians closed in on Germany. Abby was concentrating on *The Scarlet Pimpernel* when a strange sound from her aunt made her look up. Milicent had her hand to her throat, and was staring ahead in horror.

'God in heaven, how could they!' Milicent was on her feet pacing the room like a caged tiger. The newsreader was announcing the Allies' devastating bombing raid on Dresden.

'Why?' cried Milicent, in growing hysteria. 'That lovely city!'

'There must be a reason or they wouldn't have done it,' said William. 'It's a great industrial city comparable to Sheffield.'

'Rubbish!' snapped Milicent. 'It's a beautiful city, with no strategic importance at all. So why bomb it?'

'Why bomb Canterbury?' said William. 'It had no strategic importance, but that didn't stop them from trying to wipe it off the map.'

'It's a barbaric act,' said Milicent. 'And the war's almost over anyhow.'

'But will Hitler give in, and save thousands of lives?' snapped William. 'The Germans brought this on themselves. Save your sympathy for those who have suffered because of them.'

Abby looked at the porcelain shepherdess on the mantel, and remembered Richard's warning. '*Careful. It's Dresden china, and Mother will go mad if you break it.*'

'Daddy's right,' said Stella. 'The Germans deserve all they jolly well get ...' The words ended in a gasp, as Milicent struck her cheek.

'Don't you ever let me hear you speak like that again.'

Stella staggered backwards, her eyes filling with tears of rage and hurt. 'You wouldn't have struck Richard!' With that Stella ran from the room, screaming hysterically. Milicent ran after her. There were footsteps on the stairs, then a bedroom door slammed and all was quiet once more.

'Does Aunt like the Germans then?' Abby asked, shocked by the scene. 'She's so upset about Dresden!'

William sighed. 'Many years ago, she lived there. Long before Germany thought about war. She taught a family English, and gave them piano lessons. I daresay she's worried about them.'

Abby gasped. Aunt Milicent had lived in Germany? Among the very people who bombed and killed English people? It was the most shocking thing she had ever heard. Germany was a place of storm troopers, the Gestapo, torture chambers and concentration camps. That anyone should willingly go to such a place seemed inconceivable.

William frowned. 'Look, Abby. What I said about the

Germans asking for it was wicked and wrong. Your aunt is right to be worried. The children she taught were just like you and Richard and Stella. Now that Dresden is burning, it will be ordinary people like them who are suffering the most. How can that be right?'

Abby frowned and looked at her shoes. 'But the Germans *aren't* ordinary. They like Hitler, so they must be wicked. Richard thinks so too. He says that if the Germans weren't the most wicked people in the world, they would have killed Hitler long ago.'

William tensed at these words. 'No, Abby. It's more complicated than that.' He fell silent for a few moments, then stood up, and murmured, 'I'd better go and talk to your aunt.'

Left alone, Abby picked up the delicate porcelain shepherdess, wondering how it was that the people who made a thing of such beauty could wreak such havoc on the world. The idea that there were ordinary people in Germany had never occurred to her. Her thoughts turned to the children in the photograph album. Were they caught up in all that horror? She wanted them to go on living, whoever they were, and not be lying dead under a heap of rubble like her mother and sister. For the first time in her life, Abby was aware of compassion, and in that moment, she said goodbye to her childhood.

CHAPTER FOUR

Four years later, on St Valentine's Day, Abby remembered that terrible scene at Ferndene Lodge as she sat in the Cathedral sketching one of the apostles. The figurine of St Peter conjured up the shepherdess that had stood on the mantel and all the horrors that had come to light when the war ended.

Abby paused and studied her work critically. The sketch was good but her aunt had been right to call her a gifted amateur. Milicent had not changed her mind about art college and had tried to force her niece into a nursing career. It had been a transparent ruse to get Abby out of the house and into residence at a teaching hospital. But her obdurate refusals matched Milicent's stubbornness. Furious, Milicent sent her niece to work at a small back street haberdashery in Canterbury.

'Why can't I work for Uncle, if I'm to work in a shop,' Abby had asked. 'Glenisters has a large fashion department.'

'We operate a policy of not employing members of the same family,' Milicent replied. 'You can hardly expect us to change the rules to suit you.'

Plausible as this might sound, Abby knew the real reason. Her aunt wouldn't want her friends to see Abby working at Glenisters as a shop assistant. But those friends were not likely to come into Mrs Ryder's shabby old Button Shop. The past bleak months had been made tolerable only by the thought of seeing Richard. Abby's feelings for her cousin had grown stronger and she lived for term endings when he came home.

Since the King's School had returned to its rightful home

in the Precincts of Canterbury Cathedral, Abby wandered into the city whenever she had the chance in the hope of catching a glimpse of Richard. She spent her lunch time within the Precincts, ostensibly to sketch, but always studied the groups of youths walking from the school in case he should be among them.

That was her reason for being here today, on her afternoon off. The choir was at practice, and as the strains of 'In Paradisum' filled the echoing nave Abby felt a great sense of peace wash over her. She had grown to love the Cathedral, not just because it brought her closer to Richard, but because it made her feel safe and strong.

As the last strains of the music died away, Abby headed across the Precincts towards the King's School once more. A group of youths passed her in the Mint Yard, but Richard was not among them. He rarely was, and she told herself this silly nonsense must stop before people began to notice her and tongues started wagging. Yet it had become exciting never quite knowing whether he would show up or not. On the occasions when Abby did see Richard, he would sometimes leave his friends to have a few words, marvelling that anyone could be as keen on art as she was. Other times he merely waved and walked on, unaware that his actions had the power to enrapture or devastate.

Abby slowed her pace. That morning she'd received a Valentine's card and, with trembling hands, tore open the envelope. When she saw it was from Eddy, her excitement turned to disappointment. How like him to remember, and how typical of Richard not to have even realized it was St Valentine's Day!

Leaving the Precincts, Abby headed for her bus stop. The wind cut through her thin coat, but it had been all she could afford from her light wages. Now that she was taller, Stella's cast-offs no longer fitted. Forced by necessity to make her own clothes, Abby's talent had increased, and she turned out stylish skirts and blouses from all materials, often using designs of her own making.

Jealous of her cousin's talent, Stella made light of it. The two girls had never become real friends and, as far as Stella was concerned, her cousin was still the common girl from the slums who could not be introduced to her friends. In truth, Stella found herself pig-in-the-middle between the highly favoured Richard and the unfavoured Abby, and was struggling to find her own identity. But Stella had a vain streak which irritated her cousin and brother. 'Do you think I look like Jean Simmons?' she asked Abby one day. 'Everyone else thinks I do.'

'Do they really!' Abby was in no mood to placate, having just heard that Stella was applying to the Royal Academy of Dramatic Art, while she had been denied her chance of trying for an art scholarship. 'I don't think you look anything like her!' In this Abby was truthful. Stella's colouring was all she had in common with the beautiful young film star.

'You're only jealous,' she said, turning on Abby with blazing eyes. 'Jealous because no one even notices you.'

Abby blamed herself for her present predicament. Ages ago Richard had told her to speak to her uncle about the art scholarship. But she knew her aunt and uncle were not happy and worried if she set them quarrelling over her Aunt Milicent would win, and she'd be packed off to a Barnardo's Home quicker than she could say 'sorry'. One day she'd take charge of her own life, and move to London. But not before Richard went to university. At the age of eighteen it would be possible, with her uncle's consent, to leave home. Then she would try to get a position in one of the larger stores, working with materials and fashions. Her heart was set on fashion design and she had the ability to sketch and sew. Given time and money, she might even be able to start up on her own. Was this a pipe dream? Probably, Abby smiled to herself. But she had ambition, and talent, and maybe fate would handle the rest.

*

Summer came and with it long sunny days which were used to the full. As soon as Mrs Ryder locked The Button Shop, Abby hastened into the Precincts and sat on the grass sketching studiously. On such golden evenings, only hunger drove Abby home, more often than not without a glimpse of Richard. With final exams looming large, he had little time for relaxation, and was hoping for a place at Oxford to read Law.

Exams over at last, Richard returned to Ferndene Lodge exhausted but relieved. However, he soon became worried as he noticed his father coming home late each night, smelling of whisky. His mother was also out nearly every evening, playing bridge or serving on some committee or other. When the two were together they hardly said a word to each other.

Sensing Richard's troubled spirit, Abby tried to comfort him. 'They're just caught up in their own lives, that's all. Two very busy people.'

Turning to Abby for companionship and warmth, Richard found she'd blossomed into a lovely young woman. Slight though she was, her figure was fully developed. And what colouring the girl had, with her long red hair and dark green eyes. She had developed poise and was so well-spoken it was hard to remember her background. Amazed at her talent for art, Richard insisted on framing his favourite sketches and watercolours. He'd even tried arguing with his mother about Abby's future, but to no avail. 'That issue is dead and buried, Richard. Abby well knows it.' Richard said no more on the subject and made no mention of it to Abby. To do so would serve no purpose, save to hurt, and in any case Abby seemed happy enough.

Abby *was* happy, imbued with a new self-confidence from Richard's attentions. He insisted on taking her to the tennis club, where he introduced her to all his friends as his cousin. They went boating along the Stour at Canterbury, and cycled through the country lanes of their childhood.

They climbed Stapledown once more, and remembered the barrage balloons that used to float high over the city. Abby also remembered the day she first saw Samantha Fellowes, when Richard had been embarrassed by the presence of his cockney cousin. Samantha had long since been banished to a country boarding school, and was now in Switzerland being 'finished'. Abby thanked God for it.

One day Richard dragged Abby to the top of the Cathedral's famous Bell Harry Tower to view the new buildings being raised in the eastern part of the city. The modern architecture sat uneasily beside the medieval past, a permanent scar to remind people of the war. As Richard pointed out places of interest, Abby watched him with growing love and wanted desperately to put her arms around him. She reminded herself that they were cousins. Second cousins but cousins all the same, and she felt unsure about such a relationship turning into anything more intimate. But how long could she go on like this, she wondered, before Richard realized the strength of her feelings for him? She would never have the courage to voice her feelings, though she'd seen a certain look in his eyes at times that held more than cousinly affection.

Richard left for Oxford in the first week of October. On the morning he left the family were up early. The autumn day promised to be warm. Ashton Green was bathed in soft golden sunshine, muted by a slight mist; cobwebs veiled the rose bushes like jewels and the chestnut tree had turned to brilliant russet-brown and gold.

William placed his son's luggage into the boot of the car. 'What a day! Indian summer.' Rubbing his hands vigorously, he continued in a false, hearty tone. 'You should have a good journey. Now you know what to do when you reach Charing Cross.'

'I know, Father. And I'll be just fine.'

As they drove into Canterbury Abby did not trust herself

even to look at Richard. Her eyes were red and puffed from weeping and her throat felt constricted.

At last Richard was safe in his compartment, surrounded by luggage. As the train pulled out of Canterbury West, leaving smoke billowing along the platform, Richard leaned out of the window and waved. He was staring at Abby but could not see the tears streaming down her face. Milicent had seen them however, just as she'd seen how close the two had become during the summer months. At first she had been alarmed, but once Merton College had accepted Richard she knew the budding romance was over.

'Goodbye, my darling Richard,' Milicent sighed. 'By the end of the week you'll hardly give any of us a thought. By Christmas you'll be a changed person.' The words cut through Abby like a knife, but she kept her eyes on the small figure, still waving from the distant train, until he was out of sight.

'Keep still or I'll never get this hem straight,' Abby told Stella as she pinned the long yellow taffeta skirt of the gown she'd made for her. 'Yes. That's about it. Now then, turn around slowly.'

Stella turned slowly before the long mirror. 'Yes,' she said at last, 'I like it. Anyway it's heaps better than that childish thing Mummy wanted me to wear.'

Abby studied the tightly fitted bodice, the flowing skirt and the straight collar-line with a critical eye. She had worked hard so that her cousin could wear the gown to the New Year's Eve party at Wickham Place. The invitation had arrived a week earlier and was for Richard and Stella only. Abby had pretended that she had no feelings about the matter, but it hurt.

Stella piled her long dark hair onto the top of her head and pouted into the mirror. 'I think I look even more like Jean Simmons with my hair up. I'll wear it up at the party — and I don't care what Mummy says.'

'She'll never let you,' murmured Abby, her thoughts inside Wickham Place, visualizing a ravishing Samantha dancing with a mesmerized Richard.

As if reading her mind, Stella murmured, 'I think it's rotten that you haven't been invited, but then Sammy's my friend and Richard's too. She's always had a thing for him. Even Mummy and Daddy aren't going. It's mostly Samantha's friends — a kind of "welcome home" before her coming-out party. I wish I could be a debutante! It's embarrassing not to be. It *makes* you socially, and I'll never be made.' Stella took off the dress carefully. 'I hope I get an invitation to her "coming-out"!'

Don't bank on it, thought Abby. *It's Richard she's after and I don't think the Fellowes are spending all that money in order for her to marry into trade.*

Hanging the gown on the wardrobe door, Stella went on. 'If I pass my audition to RADA then I might stay with Samantha's aunt in Knightsbridge. Mummy doesn't want me mixing with the wrong people.'

Abby laughed at this. 'I always thought I counted as one of the "wrong people" and you've lived with me nearly all your life.' She yawned and glanced at the small bedside clock. 'It's nine thirty and I'm nearly dead.' Closing the door softly, Abby saw her aunt in the hallway. Milicent was wearing the fur coat and matching hat she saved for special occasions.

'Going out, Aunt Milicent?' Abby asked.

Milicent looked up, startled. 'Oh ... yes. I'm off to play bridge and I'm very late.' She went out, slamming the front door behind her.

Bridge! At this hour? Abby didn't think so. Her aunt never went out this late, although it was often after midnight when she returned.

On Abby's bedside table was a letter, from Evelyn Carr, opened hastily that morning. She took it from the envelope and tried to imagine the family she'd left so long ago.

The news was not good. Mr Carr had been unwell

since coming home from the war. His condition had been diagnosed as emphysema and, at forty-six years of age, he was living the life of a semi-invalid. Eddy was an apprentice engineer, working in a factory and going to evening classes. It would be years before he earned enough money to make up for his father's lack of a pay packet. And Mrs O'Connor suffered from acute rheumatism since leaving the caves.

She says it was the chalk and the temperature which kept her well in the caves. I used to laugh, but now I believe it. Our poor old house was shaken to bits after the bombing and the council won't do nothing because it's condemned. They're going to pull the whole street down and build flats one day. Until then, we're to go into a prefab. I told them it would be over my dead body. I've stuck to my house through everything Hitler could throw at it, and I'm damned if I'll live in a hut because the council say I must. We've fixed up the place as much as we can, and, with a bit of luck, we might hang on here.

Abby put the letter back into the envelope, and thought the Carrs had no more control over their lives than she had over hers. It seemed that in order to gain control you had to have independence − and that meant money. Money could have taken them out of that small and damp terraced house with its outdoor lavatory, and into a house like Ferndene Lodge. Yet what little they had, they wanted to keep. Abby's years in Ashton Green had shown her higher living standards, and she would hate to live in Bermondsey now, but those months when she and Eddy had played among the ruins seemed sunnier than any others since. That tiny house filled with smells of cooking and boiling clothes had been home. She remembered the huge mangle in the yard which needed two people to manage it, one to feed the sheets through and the other to turn the handle.

Abby tried to remember the house where she'd been

born, but that image – and her mother's face – had become faded. When she thought of her sister, she was left with the sweet smell of a toddler fresh from her bath and the light shining on golden curls. That was all.

At the Falstaff Hotel, William Glenister looked at his watch. It was just after nine thirty. He drained his second glass of Scotch, and thought about the new store he wanted to open in Folkestone. Since the war had ended, his profit margin had inched up slowly, but Britain was now an almost bankrupt country paying off its American debt and business loans were hard to get.

Each evening he came to the hotel for a meal and a quiet hour, delaying his return to the cold, unfriendly house his wife was pleased to call 'home'. He wondered if she thought he was having an affair. If so she had never accused him of it. Strange that! Most women would have done. But Milicent wasn't most women. She lived in her dreams, and those dreams had never included him. He felt locked out, just as the pilgrims had been locked out of Canterbury when the city gates had closed on them for the night. They too had sought shelter at this inn, where he sought it now.

Driving home in a lashing downpour, William stopped at a traffic light. When the lights changed, he passed another car as a woman in the passenger seat lit up a cigarette. In that brief moment, William saw it was Milicent, and froze. Shaken, he tried to take a firmer control on the wheel. *Who the devil is she with?* He had never seen the man before, but now he understood why she had never quizzed him about his own behaviour.

In his drawing room William poured another Scotch, and walked about in a state of high agitation. *Fool!* he thought over and over again, *damned stupid fool. You've been cuckolded, Glenister.* It was the last thing he expected of his wife. That Milicent did not love him was no revelation but that she'd risk destroying their precious reputation was. If he had seen her, then half of Canterbury must have seen her too. Like most cuckolds he was the last to know about it.

'Is that you, Uncle?'

William swung around to see Abby standing on the threshold. 'Abby! I thought you were in bed!'

'I was.' She looked at him and frowned. He'd been drinking and seemed upset. 'I . . . well, I just thought I'd check. In case you were a burglar.'

'I'm sorry, chick.' The sight of her took the anger out of his heart and in its place came a sense of concern. 'Do you often get frightened when you and Stella are left alone?'

Abby smiled and shrugged. 'Why should we?'

'And are you left alone a great deal late at night?'

The question put Abby on her guard. Surely Uncle William knew that his wife played bridge nearly every other night.

'Not a great deal. Aunt's usually here anyway.'

And I should be too, thought William with a sudden surge of guilt.

Alone in her room, Abby felt alarmed. What on earth was going on? There was Aunt Milicent creeping out dressed to the nines, and now here was her uncle looking like thunder and drinking heavily. If only Richard were home. Just three more days, then he'd be back, she told herself, and then everything would be just fine.

When Richard put off his homecoming to join a party at a large country house, Abby thought her worst fears had been realized. She went to the station to meet him and stood awkwardly while he kissed his mother and sister dutifully. When it was her turn to be greeted, he looked embarrassed and merely nodded.

During dinner, Richard spoke happily about his law studies, the societies he had joined and the new friends he had made, but Abby noticed his eyes went everywhere to avoid meeting hers. Her dismay increased in the days that followed when Richard spent more time with his old school colleagues than he did at home.

'He's getting just like Daddy,' snapped Stella. 'Well, who cares if he doesn't get home for meals? All the more for us.'

'You can't blame him,' Abby had replied. 'It's only natural that he should want to see his old friends again.'

'I suppose we're not good enough for him now that he's at Oxford and has friends with large country houses,' Stella remarked. 'Perhaps we should wear bags over our heads or something.'

Only when he saw the invitation to the Fellowes' party did Abby sense something of the old Richard. At first he thought Abby's name had been left off by mistake, but his mother soon put him right.

'But that's disgraceful,' he said, glancing towards Abby who was writing out her Christmas cards. 'It's an insult and I'm jolly well not going if she isn't invited.'

Milicent stopped decorating the tree, alarmed. 'Don't be foolish, Richard. Abby's never been a friend of Samantha's. It's no insult. Anyway, she doesn't mind one bit, do you, dear?'

The question was rhetorical so Abby just went on writing. But her eyes mirrored the warmth that flowed through her at that moment. Richard still was her champion! She looked up and smiled at him.

'What *are* you doing on New Year's Eve, Abby?' Richard asked.

She shrugged. 'Haven't really given it much thought.'

'Well, I've had three offers from friends, so we'll go to one of their parties and I bet we have a much better time.'

Abby looked at him in surprise. Did he really mean to forego such an invitation just to be with her? The look in his eyes told her that he did. She had been wrong this past week. He *did* care for her. Maybe he was afraid to show his true feelings in front of his family, afraid perhaps of his mother's reaction?

'You can't mean it,' Stella was wailing. 'After all the work Abby's put into my gown. You're to be my escort.' She burst into tears. 'You *know* how much I've looked forward to it!'

Abby's moment of joy was over. Stella's plight filled her with guilt and alarm. 'Richard, please don't do this. Stella's been looking forward to it so much. And I did work hard on her gown. She looks lovely in it.'

Milicent stood poised by the tree with tinsel trailing from her fingers. Common sense told her that this was a time for her to be silent. Abby's kind heart would do more than a mother's chiding tongue to bring Richard to his senses. But she was not pleased with her son's sudden outburst.

Abby was still looking up at Richard. 'Please. She can't go unescorted now, can she?'

'All right.' Richard succumbed. 'But just who the hell does Samantha think she is?' With that he stormed out of the room and went up to his own. Soon the strains of *Tintagel* came floating towards them, and Abby knew he was reliving his schooldays in Cornwall once more.

She remembered how he enthused about the coastline, the rugged cliffs and wild Atlantic rollers. 'Did you know,' he once said, 'that every seventh wave is the largest? Sailors know it. Especially after storms. We used to stand on the cliffs counting them and the seventh seemed to have built up, so that when it hit the rocks it was almost devastating.' When he had discovered Bax's tone poem, he spent hours playing the record, saying how he could see the waves in the music and feel the great ocean swell. 'There's something about Cornwall,' he would say. 'It has ... well, it has a *calling*.'

Listening to the music now, Abby sensed that all was not well with Richard. And whatever was wrong, he was taking solace in his childhood. What was she to make of that?

Her aunt's voice interrupted her flow of thoughts.

'Really, I don't know what's got into the boy these days.

72

Such a fuss over nothing.' Milicent tied a blue bauble onto the tree and sighed. 'Maybe it's the strain of studying Law. I do hope he isn't having second thoughts.'

'Maybe he's in love,' said Stella innocently. 'He's up in the clouds one minute and hell on earth the next.'

'Oh God, I hope not.' Milicent half turned towards her pale-faced niece and said, 'I don't want him to get romantically involved just now. It would be a catastrophe, especially if the girl in question is from the wrong background.' She looked straight at Abby and smiled sweetly. 'But I know Richard. When he does marry, it'll be to someone with the right credentials who'll help further his career, not hinder it.'

Abby's heart had frozen at her words. Had they been aimed at her, or did her aunt seriously think that Richard might have met someone else? Either way, the message was plain enough. She tried to carry on writing cards but her eyes were filling with tears, and she could see nothing. This was going to be the worst Christmas of her life.

On Christmas Day the entire family attended the morning service at St Michael's Church. After the choir followed the Crucifix along the nave singing 'O Come All Ye Faithful', Sir Gerald and Lady Fellowes left their pew, with Samantha following closely behind. Dressed in deep blue with matching hat over her blonde hair, she looked expensively stunning, and her large brown eyes fixed on Richard as she walked past.

Abby saw the look, and burned with anger. She followed the family out into the aisle. The progress out of the church was slow as the congregation stood talking to the vicar and his wife before moving away. At last, it was her turn to shake hands with the Reverend Morrant and wish him a Happy Christmas. No sooner had she done so than Richard started pulling on her arm and Abby found herself being taken towards the Fellowes'.

Lady Fellowes stood in her fur coat and matching hat,

listening politely as Milicent did her best to sparkle. She was no fool and knew Mrs Glenister for what she was: a shallow social climber. As Richard and Abby joined the group, she asked him how he was enjoying life at Oxford. Richard answered politely, his eyes on Samantha as he then said:

'And this is Abby. You remember her, surely, Samantha. She's lived with us for years.'

Samantha said nothing, but nodded. It was her mother who looked taken aback. 'Abby? Goodness me, not the little girl who came from London during the war?'

Abby smiled, wondering what Richard thought he was doing. This was so embarrassing. 'Yes.'

Lydia Fellowes stared at her. 'I'd no idea you still lived in Ashton. What are you doing with yourself these days?'

'I work in Canterbury,' said Abby, seeing the look of horror on her aunt's face.

'I see.' Lydia Fellowes was far too well bred to ask why Abby was not training for some profession, or at least doing a Cordon Bleu course. Her look of puzzlement changed to one of concern. 'My dear, I had no *idea*! You really must forgive us. Your name was not put on the invitation. It's all my fault, I'm afraid. Please do come to Samantha's party on New Year's Eve.'

Abby's first inclination was to stand on her pride and refuse politely, but one look at Lady Fellowes' expression caused her to changed her mind. Here was true breeding, she thought, and to refuse would be churlish.

'Thank you, Lady Fellowes. I should love to come.'

'God, how embarrassing,' murmured Milicent, as the family walked along the church path towards the lychgate. 'I've never felt so humiliated in my entire life.'

'Neither have I,' said Stella tersely. 'How could you, Richard! And on Christmas Day too.'

'How could I what?' Imbued with confidence, Richard was enjoying his moment of triumph.

'You *know* what you did,' snapped Stella. 'You were so

74

obvious too, wangling an invitation for Abby like that. I could have died on the spot.'

'Why?' laughed Richard. 'You heard Lady Fellowes. It was all a mistake. What's the big deal?'

'How else could she have answered?' said Milicent. 'You put her in a most embarrassing position. As for you, Abby, I'm surprised you accepted. It was up to you to decline.'

'Why?' asked Richard. 'Why was it expected that she should decline?'

His mother turned to him with blazing eyes. 'Stop all this, Richard. I've had quite enough.'

'We've all had enough,' murmured William. Angry with his wife, and desperate for a drink, he admired Richard for the stance he had taken. 'Abby did the right thing. I think she handled things very well.' He smiled at Abby and added, 'You go, chick, and have a good time.'

As the Fellowes' Rolls Royce eased its way along Church Lane, Samantha could hardly contain her fury. 'Mother, what on earth made you ask that Abby to the party?'

Lydia looked at her daughter and frowned. 'Did *you* know the girl was still living with the Glenister family?'

'Of course. But she isn't a Glenister. She's just a girl from the London slums that they were kind enough to take in. Just because she grew up in their home doesn't mean she's the sort we invite into ours.'

'But my dear, that's a dreadful thing to say.' Lydia stared at her daughter long and hard. 'How cruel you can be. It's not the way you were raised. I blame that school. It's the height of bad manners to invite two children from one family and leave out the third.'

'Oh, you don't understand, mother,' said Samantha, turning to her father for support.

'Seems a nice sort of girl to me,' said Sir Gerald. 'Speaks well, seems to know her way about. I'll send Roberts over with the invitation tomorrow.'

Samantha stared out the window, wondering if she was foolish to be jealous of Abby. Surely Richard's feelings for her would be as brother to sister by now. Yet she was perturbed. Perhaps it was catching a glimpse of Abby in the village a few days earlier. At first, she had not recognized this girl with the outstanding colouring and beauty. When it dawned on her that this was the same skinny child who used to speak with a cockney accent, she had allowed fear to take hold. Ever since childhood Samantha had thought of Richard as hers. She bit her lip. Well, let her come. How could a girl like Abby outshine one who was already being tipped as a future debutante of the year?

William was very quiet during Christmas, angry that he had been cuckolded and unsure that he could do anything about it. Abby was also quiet, her thoughts centring on what to wear to this party. What a fool she had been. She shouldn't have accepted. Like Cinderella she had nothing to wear to the Ball. And, unlike Cinderella, she had no Fairy Godmother with a magic wand. On Boxing Day, she remembered the velvet curtains hidden away in the attic, and asked her aunt if she might use the material.

Milicent turned to her niece in surprise. 'The attic! Have you been poking your little nose into things that don't concern you?'

'No, Aunt.' In her anxiety about the dress, Abby had completely forgotten that her trip to the attic was a secret. 'Ages ago I took some of my sketches up there. I put them in the chest, and remember seeing the curtains. Please, Aunt. If you don't want them any more, couldn't I . . .'

'Make a gown out of them?' Milicent was shocked. 'My niece wants to go to Wickham Place in old curtains?'

She stared at Abby for some time. Then, with exasperation, she gave in.

'Oh, very well. But you must be careful. Velvet is a far cry from taffeta, and murder to work on, and the edges are faded with the sun. How you'll cut out the best pieces and still have enough for a decent dress is beyond me. If it looks a sight, you're going to have to plead illness. I won't have you shaming us.'

Hardly able to believe her luck, Abby went up into the attic and returned with three long blue velvet curtains. In the few days left to her, she worked each evening in her room until finally falling asleep in the early hours from sheer exhaustion. Using a *Vogue* pattern of a Dior design, Abby boned and lined the bodice to push up the bosom, then laced the neckline with a double edging of broderie anglaise. Shoulderless, the gown nipped in tightly at the waist then fell full and long. At last, in the small hours of New Year's Eve, the dress was finished.

'It's made well enough, I suppose,' said Milicent, casting a critical eye over the dress, 'but it's far too sophisticated for a girl of your years.' She was standing at the door of Abby's room staring at her niece in amazement. It was eight o'clock and Richard was already outside in the snow trying to crank-start the second-hand car his father had bought him for a Christmas present. 'Now Stella's gown is very nice. But for you to wear *that* is ... well ... I think you should cover up.'

Abby tossed her hair back defiantly and adjusted the *décolletage* so that her lovely sloping shoulders could be the more readily admired.

'Come on, Abby,' called Richard from the hallway. 'I've got the car started.' He stared open-mouthed as she appeared at the top of the stairs. She looked ravishing with her long hair cascading over her shoulders and her body encased in rich blue velvet.

Abby had never seen Richard in black tie and dinner jacket before. How handsome he was, she thought, and how aristocratic with his blond hair crowning those Adonis-like features. He put her in mind of someone, but try as she might, she could not recollect who.

Richard adjusted his tie in the hall mirror. 'God, I hate being trussed up like this.' He slipped his old duffle over the dinner suit and looked up at Abby.

Shabby coat about her shoulders, Abby walked slowly down the stairs and took Richard's arm. Afraid that her high heels might slip in the soft snow, she clung to him as they walked along the drive towards the car.

Milicent watched them go with envy. She would have given anything to be included in the invitation, and secretly had hoped that her long and unstinting work during the war years with Lady Fellowes might have provided a passport into that society. *Everything now depends on you, Richard*, she thought. *Play your cards right and that world can be yours.*

By the time Richard had turned the car into the drive of Wickham Place, the snow had settled. At the end of a long strip of white, the manor house spread before them. Abby leaned forward in her seat, her eyes wide and her lips parted with growing apprehension. She'd never been inside the house, although the grounds were familiar enough from all those summer fetes and the huge VE Day children's party. Would her dress be all right? Would anyone notice that the material had once adorned the windows of Ferndene Lodge? Would Samantha resent her presence and embarrass her before the world?

'I'm hopping mad that Mummy wouldn't let me wear my hair up,' said Stella. 'Anyone would think I was still a child. Do I look passable?'

Abby nodded, thinking how pretty Stella looked. Her dark hair, long and thick, was parted in the middle and held off her face by two bows. For one brief moment, she did, indeed, look a little like Jean Simmons.

'You look marvellous, Stella,' she said, wishing she could feel as confident about herself. Oh God, she wanted to go home. It was all going to be a disaster.

Richard escorted the girls into the large entrance hall, suddenly wishing he were at the local pub with Abby. What on earth were they all doing here anyhow? Unlike his mother, Richard had no illusions about his place in life. He was the son of a store owner who just happened to have caught the eye of the daughter of the manor. He ought to have stayed away, but with Stella's shattering disappointment, Abby's persuasions and his own ridiculous behaviour on Christmas Day, here he was, trapped.

A huge Christmas tree dominated the oak-panelled hall. After the bleakness of the war years, the shimmering beauty of the tinsel and fairy lights took everyone's breath away. Garlands of holly, ivy and mistletoe wreathed the staircase and banisters and Abby noticed the portraits hanging on the stairway, ancestral portraits of an old and well-connected family.

A maid came forward to take their coats.

'Don't leave me, whatever you do,' whispered Abby, grabbing Richard's arm. His reply was drowned in music and voices as they joined the line of guests waiting to be greeted by their hosts.

Lady Fellowes took Abby by the hand and smiled warmly. 'My dear, I'm so glad you could come. You look lovely.'

Abby moved on and found herself standing before Samantha. Tall and slender in a gown of white chiffon, blonde hair piled on top of her head, she resembled a Greek goddess.

'Good evening,' said Samantha, smiling with her mouth only. 'What a sweet dress.' She then turned to Richard and the brown eyes softened into a true smile as she whispered: 'And I'll see *you* in a few moments.'

They walked on into a large room, dominated by an Adam fireplace above which hung an ornate, gilded mirror. A group of young men stood beside the fireplace, and Richard's heart sank as he recognized the tallest of them, a dark-haired Lothario by the name of Jeremy St John-Tennant. He'd always been one of Samantha's admirers and was a pain in the neck to everyone else. Richard had met him several times at the tennis club and they'd taken an instant dislike to each other: Jeremy, because of Richard's closeness to Samantha, Richard because of Jeremy's arrogance and determination to prove himself the better of the two, not only at tennis but at life.

'Do you know anyone here?' whispered Abby.

Richard gazed around vaguely, aware that Jeremy had seen them. 'Hmm ... one or two. Well, no one really.'

'Well, we can't just stand here like lemons,' said Abby.

'Of course you can't.' Samantha's words were followed by a light laugh as she took hold of Richard's hand and pulled him towards the fireplace. 'Come on, you remember Jeremy, don't you, Richard? And these are Piers and Robert Langrish, my cousins.' She introduced Stella and Abby, then clung to Richard more closely, saying, 'Now you've got to dance with me. These young men will look after your ladies.' She turned to Jeremy wagging a finger. 'I'm relying on you now. See that they have a good time!'

Abby flushed with anger. *How dare she!* She looked at Jeremy, and saw that she was not the only one who was angry. 'Please don't put yourself out on my account,' she snapped. She felt a light touch on her shoulder, and swung around with blazing eyes.

Robert Langrish looked startled. 'I just wondered if I could get you some punch.'

The evening did not go well for Abby. Though she was surrounded by eager young men, and danced until her feet were sore, her spirit was low. Richard had not danced with her once. In fact, she'd hardly seen him since Samantha dragged him from her side. She felt betrayed and hardly noticed the appraising male eyes, young and old, following her around the room. Even Jeremy found her irresistible, his anger having evaporated the moment she snapped at him. But Abby was unimpressed with him, her mind on Richard and Samantha. Had he no idea how she felt?

At the supper table, she saw Richard helping Samantha to the cold buffet spread before them. He looked up and, for a brief moment, their eyes met. She saw his guilt and he read her anger, then both looked away quickly. Abby started flirting with Jeremy, knowing Richard could see them. She laughed at his appalling jokes, and allowed him to fill her plate with salad and cold chicken. When Piers and Robert beckoned Abby over to their seat in the far corner, she walked across the room, knowing Jeremy was following with the two plates. There was safety in numbers, and the Langrish brothers were decent, likeable youths. Jeremy whatever-his-name was far too free with his hands and kept gazing into her eyes until she wanted to scream. It was her own fault, she knew; her efforts to make Richard jealous had given him encouragement.

Robert escorted Abby towards a sofa, where Jeremy immediately sat down beside her, while the Langrish boys settled themselves on the floor.

She smiled at them both. 'This is a beautiful house,' she said. 'Did Samantha say you were her cousins?'

Piers nodded, his auburn head bent over his plate. 'We are, for our sins.'

Robert laughed. 'We grew up with Sammy, practically. She spent a lot of time at our place during the war.'

'And where exactly is your place?' asked Abby.

'In the Cotswolds,' answered Piers.

Abby smiled. 'Why did you say "for our sins"?'

Robert laughed. As the elder brother he felt it his duty to prevent Piers from embarrassing them both. 'Oh, nothing. You know how it is with cousins.'

'Come on, she's a pain and always has been,' said Piers. 'Always wants her own way — and usually gets it too. Now people are saying she'll be the deb of the year when she comes out. She'll be bloody impossible then.'

Won't she just, thought Abby. 'They're an old family. I mean they've got a . . .'

'A lineage that goes back to Charles the Second! Well, who hasn't.' Jeremy sounded bored with the conversation. 'Ours goes back to Elizabeth. She gave us our lands. We had to sell the estate in Norfolk when my grandfather died, but we still have Kelthorpe.'

Abby had never heard such a conversation. 'Kelthorpe?'

Jeremy looked at her in surprise. Was she being deliberately obtuse? 'It's one of the largest estates in Nottinghamshire, and the oldest. Bess of Hardwicke used to visit.' His eyes hovered over her shoulders and rested on her cleavage. 'Did I hear Samantha say you were that fellow's sister?'

'I'm Richard Glenister's cousin,' said Abby firmly. As she spoke she remembered that distant Sunday on Stapledown when such a thing could not have been said.

'Visiting for Christmas?' asked Jeremy.

'No. I live with the Glenisters.'

'Oh?' Jeremy's fork was poised in the air as he waited for her reply. 'Why?'

Robert saw Abby's growing discomfiture and intervened. 'Don't be so bloody nosy, Jerry.'

At that moment, Abby caught sight of Richard across the room, searching for someone. *Has Samantha slipped away from him then? Grown bored, has she?*

Suddenly Richard was before her, asking for the next dance. For one moment, Abby thought of refusing, then she stood up slowly, accepting his invitation with cool grace.

On the dance floor they moved around at arm's length, saying nothing, while the band played 'Bewitched, Bothered and Bewildered'. Richard thought the choice very apt. He hardly knew what to make of Abby. She had certainly seemed happy in the company of that arrogant St John-Tennant. But then she was an innocent, and knew nothing of the world.

'Don't let that silly cove make a fool of you,' he said. 'He's a nasty piece of work.'

Abby looked up at him sharply. 'Are you saying that because someone has been attentive and charming to me, it follows that he's up to no good? My word, how highly you rate me.'

'I didn't mean it like that,' sighed Richard. 'I just meant ... well ... he has a bad reputation and I don't want to see you hurt.'

Too late for that, thought Abby, wanting to hit him. What had it to do with Richard whom she danced with, when he had shown no interest in her whatsoever? Her body tensed, and she moved even further from him.

'We must look like a couple of tailor's dummies,' Richard said, pulling her closer to him. 'I've been trying to dance with you all evening, but you seemed to be doing pretty well without me.'

Abby looked up, her defensive mantle falling away as she felt the closeness of Richard's body for the first time. 'All you had to do was ask.'

'Easier said than done. I've been a prisoner since we walked in.'

Abby gave a curt laugh. 'This is hardly the Bastille.'

Richard stiffened in anger. 'I'm supposed to be a gentleman, not a boor. And this is the home of my hostess. I can hardly walk out on her when she refuses to leave my side, now can I? You've no idea what it's been like.'

He looked so perplexed that Abby wanted to laugh. 'It must have been hell.'

Richard looked down at her tenderly. 'Anyway, we're together at last, so let's enjoy ourselves. The old year's about to pass and I want to see the new decade in with you.'

As he pulled her close to him, the last remnants of anger left Abby. She leaned her head on his shoulder: something she had previously only dreamt of and, enveloped in his embrace, felt her pulse racing as her body stirred in a way she had never known before. Yet it all seemed so right and so natural with Richard.

'Abby,' he murmured close into her ear, 'I'm not good with words, but there's something I've wanted to say to you for so long. Only I had to pick the right moment.' He held his breath as Abby lifted her face up to his. Her lips were tantalizingly close as they softened into a smile.

'And what is it you have to say to me?' she whispered, her heart pounding.

'You're determined to make me say it, aren't you?' grinned Richard. 'Well then — I love you, and I've loved you from the day I first left for Oxford.' He sighed with relief. 'There. I've said it. Have I shocked you?'

Abby's eyes filled with tears of happiness. 'Oh, Richard. You don't know how long I've waited to hear you say that.' She felt his breath on her neck. 'But why didn't you write to me, or ask for me when you phoned?'

'I tried writing, but when it came to it I couldn't put such personal feelings onto paper. And when Mother kept answering the phone, I lost my nerve. I was afraid, I suppose. Afraid I'd frighten you off, and shock Mother into a heart attack. But that's all behind us now. We'll tell my parents as soon as we go home.'

'No!' Abby felt a warning note buzz through her head. 'No, don't do that. Not yet. Your mother will try to break us up. And anyway, you have your degree to get first. I don't want to do anything to prevent you getting on, and if you tell her now ...'

'All right.' Richard tried to calm her. It might be better to play their cards close to their chests where Mother was concerned. 'You're not worried because we're cousins, are you?'

Abby shook her head, and heard him say:

'You do want to marry me?'

'Of course!' How could she tell Richard his mother was her enemy? He thought Aunt Milicent would be against their love simply because they were so young. He'd no idea of his mother's strength of feeling against her.

At that moment a long roll on the drums announced that midnight was approaching, and the dancers moved into the other room to recharge their glasses.

Richard held her close. 'All right. We'll play things your

way and keep it to ourselves. But let's seal our vows on the stroke of midnight.'

'Like a secret engagement?' Abby smiled.

Richard nodded. 'Funny to think that it will soon be 1950. A new decade.' He released his arm. 'I'll get us some champagne.'

As Abby stood inside the doorway, she heard Samantha's high-pitched laughter, and saw her sweep Richard into her own circle, as the chimes of Big Ben rang out the New Year. She started as a firm hand clutched her arm and pulled her across the room.

'Stop wriggling,' said Jeremy, ignoring her protestations. 'I've filled our glasses.'

'I'm seeing the New Year in with Richard,' said Abby, trying to pull away from him.

Jeremy laughed. 'I think he's otherwise engaged. Look.'

Following his eyes, Abby saw Richard kissing Samantha.

'Happy New Year,' Jeremy staggered toward Abby and planted his wet lips over her astonished mouth. Disgusted, she pulled away from him, but his grip on her arm was painful. 'Wassa madder? Not good enough for you, then?' Leering, he went on: 'Thass rich coming from a docker's brat.' He clutched her tightly, and brought his lips close once more.

Mustering all her strength, Abby slapped his face and Jeremy reeled back in astonishment, his hand on his reddening cheek.

'Why, you bloody little slut,' he said. 'D'you think we don't know about Abby Nichols from the slums? You're all the same. Lead a chap on then . . .' She dealt him another blow and was lost among the crowd by the time he had recovered.

Tears were pouring down her cheeks as Abby tried to find her way out of the room. She saw Richard and Samantha, hands linked, as they sang 'Auld Lang Syne', and rushed past the revellers out into the cold night, without waiting for her coat. Her high heels slipped and twisted in the deepening snow, as she ran along the drive, but she neither noticed nor cared, so great was the rage and humiliation inside her. She paused in the High Street, suddenly feeling exhausted. It was snowing again and the flakes settled on her bare shoulders.

Ferndene was in darkness as Abby let herself in, thankful that her aunt and uncle were at their own party. She stood in the kitchen beside the Aga and let the heat thaw her rigid body. *Oh Richard! This was to have been our very special night; our own secret pledging. I believed you. Now I know it was just the drink talking.*

She moved away from the stove, thinking that, by the time Richard fell into his bed, he would have forgotten all that he had said. Should he be unlucky enough to remember, then he would be too embarrassed to face her again.

God, how it hurt! Abby went into the drawing room and raked the dying coals of the fire until they sparkled into life once more. This done, she fell back onto her heels, a shivering, humiliated shadow of the girl who had left for a party only a few hours earlier. She had never felt so wretched in her life. Heartbreak was physically painful. Why had Richard not pushed Samantha away as she had Jeremy? His so-called love was too frail to withstand impediment whereas hers was steadfast. Love must transcend all things, and be constant. It was clear Richard simply did not love her.

Convulsive sobs shook Abby as she knelt before the hearth, a small figure in a sodden velvet ballgown. She'd lost both the man she loved and her identity in one night. The only thing to do, she told herself, was to leave this house at first light, and find her own life back in London. Abby took her hands away from her face. *The Carrs!* That was it. Of course. *I'll go back to London, to Mrs Carr, Eddy and old Mrs O'Connor. I'll go home!*

The back door slammed shut, then Richard was in the room, his duffle coat hanging from his shoulders, his hair an untidy mess, and his expression one of surprised anger.

'What the hell happened to you? I searched everywhere. Damn it all, Abby, you should have told me if you were getting a lift home.' His voice trailed off when he saw her tear-stained face. 'What is it? Has something happened?'

Abby could hardly believe she was hearing him correctly. 'Keep away from me,' she hissed, as he moved towards her. 'Don't touch me.'

Richard was dumbfounded. 'What on earth ... your dress is soaking wet. Who brought you home?'

'No one.'

'What? You don't mean you actually walked?'

'Why did you do it?' cried Abby, rising slowly. 'You promised, and then ... oh, go away and leave me alone.' She rushed past him trying to stifle her sobs and, in the doorway, collided with an astonished Stella.

'Hey! What's going on?' Stella watched as her cousin ran up the stairs closely followed by her brother.

Richard caught Abby's arm. 'I think I deserve an explanation.'

'*You* deserve an explanation?' Abby stared at him with blazing green eyes. 'I'll tell you something that might serve as an explanation. Tonight, thanks to you, I was mauled and humiliated by that oaf of a man, because you weren't around when you promised you would be.'

Richard frowned. 'Do you mean that St John-Tennant creep? Well, I warned you about him. Why didn't you come and join us?'

Abby's eyes narrowed and the words choked in her throat.

'Look,' Richard continued, 'I know what we agreed and I meant to come back, but Sammy got hold of me and ... well ... I don't know, it all got so –'

'Merry?' Abby interjected.

'I looked for you afterwards ...'

'*Afterwards!*' Abby turned swiftly on her heel and

stormed up the remaining stairs. Slamming the door behind her she heard Stella say:

'Well, of all the ingratitude! After all you did to get her an invitation.'

Those words hurt more than anything else, stripping Abby of her last shred of dignity. She wept most of the night, her world shattered along with her dreams. *Tomorrow,* she kept telling herself, *tomorrow morning I will say goodbye to this house and this family for ever. I'll stay with the Carrs until I get a job in London, and then I'll rent a place of my own.* No one in this world could be relied on. Therefore it made more sense to rely only on oneself. If you never loved, you never got hurt.

She would not make the mistake of loving again. Tomorrow would be the start of a new life and a new woman.

The following morning, however, the world was silent and blanketed in white. Abby could hardly move her head off the pillow, and felt like someone had taken a hammer to it during the night. Her body ached from head to foot; burned one minute and froze the next.

Stella came into her room at nine o'clock, bright and breezy. 'What a Sunday!' she said. 'Nothing's moving. No buses. No trains. Can't get the car out of the garage. I'm about to dig the front path. Aren't you ever going to get up?' Stella glanced at the sweating figure huddled under the blankets. 'I say! You look awful. Fancy coming home like that without a coat or anything. You worried Richard sick. What *did* happen, exactly?'

'Go away, please,' groaned Abby from her pillow. 'I feel awful.'

'Shall I bring you up some aspirins?'

'Would you?' murmured Abby. 'Stella, you haven't told your parents about last night, have you?'

'No. They're still in bed. Richard looked in on you earlier, but you were out for the count. I think he's gone back to Samantha. They were on the phone earlier. Then she phoned back asking if there was something wrong because he sounded strange, and she invited us to join her house party for snowballs. I think that's where Richard is now. But it's too cold for me.'

Abby contemplated Stella's words in misery, conjuring up a vision of Richard and Samantha laughing as they threw snowballs at each other. Jeremy was in that vision too, somewhere, and both men must have had a moment of amusement at the complexities of young women. Illness or no illness, as soon as the trains were running, she would leave this house for good.

As Abby lay ill in bed, Richard struggled through the deep, virgin snow that covered the narrow lanes. All night he'd lain awake, trying to make sense of Abby's strange behaviour until he'd come to the conclusion that the Honourable Jeremy St John-Tennant had gone too far. Perhaps attempted rape! Why else would Abby run home alone, without her coat and in such weather? At eight thirty, he'd telephoned Wickham Place, got Samantha out of her bed and demanded that Jeremy meet him by the gatehouse.

Samantha sounded bemused. 'Richard, you're still drunk. Go back to bed.' But he had stirred her into action with his angry insistence.

Jeremy was already at the gatehouse, nonchalantly leaning against one of the huge stone pillars which dominated the end of the driveway.

'Well, here I am, Glenister. Is it pistols at dawn then?'

His stupid grin sent a wave of anger through Richard. It was what Abby had refused to say which had sent his imagination racing, and that grin confirmed his worst thoughts. Walking straight up to Jeremy, Richard brought his fist into the surprised face.

'*Bastard!*'

Blood pouring from his nose, Jeremy staggered backwards, then, recovering from the shock, he hurled himself onto Richard. The two locked in combat, rolling in the snow, their fists pounding into each other until, spent with the fight, Richard finally hauled Jeremy to his feet. Pinning him against the stone pillar, he gasped: 'If you ever touch Abby again, I'll kill you.'

Jeremy's face was bloodied and bruised. He felt dizzy and could not catch his breath.

'God's teeth, what has the bitch been telling you? All I did was try to kiss her.'

'And what else?'

'Nothing. I swear it! Not unless she found the home truths too hard to take.'

'Home truths?' Richard frowned.

'Oh come on, Glenister. She's just like all the girls from her class. Lead a chap on and then ... well, she couldn't take it, could she?'

Richard stared at him for a moment. 'What's all this about her class?'

A grin of triumph spread slowly across Jeremy's face. 'She's the daughter of a docker, isn't she? A girl from the slums. Did you think we didn't know?' The grin widened. 'Social climbing upstarts, the whole damned lot of you.'

Richard released his grip on Jeremy. 'No wonder she found you so repulsive. What has her background got to do with you, or anyone else for that matter?'

'Nothing at all, dear boy, until she starts thinking herself equal to us.'

Whatever Richard did to him now, Jeremy thought, victory was his. Physically he'd lost the fight, but emotionally Glenister had been knocked for six. He wasted no time in consolidating his victory. 'Sammy told me. Until then I thought your little cousin carried things off rather well.'

There now! Samantha the shining goddess had fallen to earth with a resounding bump. Richard would never forgive the insult to his family. Now Jeremy was in with a chance once more. 'I shan't forget this, Glenister,' he called as Richard walked away. 'One day you'll pay for it. Believe me, you'll pay for it!'

Richard staggered home through the snow, every bone

in his body aching, his face swollen and bleeding. He should have beaten that idiot to a pulp, he told himself, but Jeremy wasn't worth it. He blamed himself. Samantha must have become jealous and let her tongue run away with her. *Bitch! Damn it!*

Stella met him in the kitchen, horrified at the state he was in and almost frightened by his anger.

'Don't you dare breathe a word of this to anyone,' Richard said, his voice as sharp as a honed blade. 'I'm not kidding. It's too bloody serious.'

'I won't, I promise.' When Stella realized he wanted to see Abby, she shook her head. 'You can't. She's ill. Well, is it any wonder! Whatever you have to say can wait until she's feeling better.'

'How ill is she?' Richard asked. 'Shouldn't we get a doctor?'

'She isn't that bad.'

But when Richard crept into Abby's room, and placed a gentle hand on the sleeping girl's forehead, he realized her temperature was high.

'Let her sleep,' whispered Stella from the doorway. 'She's had two aspirins. Sleep's the best medicine, and you look as though *you* could do with some after you've cleaned up.'

Later, when Abby awoke, Jeremy's words kept running through her mind. *'Do you think we don't know about you, Abby Nichols, from the slum?'* She didn't care what that idiot said. But Richard mattered, and if her background caused him embarrassment, they were doomed anyway. She thought about the young men she had met at the party. Some charming and likeable, some idiots, but all groomed to run far-flung posts of the Empire one day. Their backgrounds were established. Richard was on the edge of that world, and if Samantha had her way he'd one day be a part of it. Aunt Milicent was right. How could the wife of a barrister come from Bermondsey? Last night Richard must have realized this, and the love that was fuelled by alcohol had died in the sober light of day. Her aunt had tried to warn her but she had not listened. Abby closed her eyes and let sleep engulf her once more. When she woke again, it was dark.

The bedroom door opened and a light beamed in from the landing. Richard stood on the threshold. 'Abby,' he whispered, 'are you awake?'

Having no strength to talk, Abby closed her eyes and pretended to be sleeping. Only when she heard the door close quietly, did she open them again.

The following morning Richard slept late while the world crashed in on Milicent. News of the fight was all over the village and the telephone at Ferndene Lodge did not stop ringing until she took it off the hook. Those of her friends who thought her too 'uppity' took great delight in the whole affair.

'I do hope Richard wasn't hurt,' said Edith Buckingham from the Bridge Club. 'But, my dear, how absolutely priceless! Of course, I shan't say a word. You can rely on me. I'm glad Richard's unharmed. But fancy, your son hitting the son of a Viscount! His father is Lord Kelthorpe, you know. Samantha must be a little madam, to have men fighting over her like this. It's quite romantic.'

Mortified, Milicent ran upstairs to confront her son. Richard had never seen his mother so angry, and tried to placate her by saying he had been defending Abby's honour.

For a moment Milicent was too stunned to speak. Then she found her voice. 'Abby? *Honour?* You fought the son of a Viscount, because of *Abby*? Have you lost your senses?' As Richard tried to explain, she cut in. 'I don't want to hear any more about it. You abused your position as a guest in the Fellowes' home. I can't believe it − my son bringing shame on us in this way, and for what? Abby! What did she do then? Make a fool of herself?' Before Richard could answer, she continued: 'I knew she would. Class is class. Her background will always let her down, and anyone close to her. Remember that in future!'

Richard tried to defend his cousin but even as he was speaking, Milicent marched out, and made her way to Abby's room, ready to face her niece. But when she flung open the door, Milicent found only a neatly-made bed. Frowning, she glanced about the room until she saw the sheet of note paper on the small oak dressing table. Picking up the letter, she read the neat handwriting in disbelief.

Have gone to London. I'm sorry for everything. Please don't look for me, I'll be all right.
Love, Abby

Milicent tore the note into small pieces then crunched them into her clenched hand. 'No, young lady — I shan't come looking for you. Don't worry!'

CHAPTER FIVE

As the train pulled into Charing Cross Station, Abby remembered too late that she should have left it at London Bridge. Packed with people, the station had a curious smell of smoke, stale fish and fruit: a smell which conjured up memories of crowded platforms and over-full trains, of people trying to leave the bombing and soldiers heading back to camp.

Pulling her long woollen scarf about her head, Abby pushed her way through the crowded concourse and headed out into the Strand. For one moment she stood overwhelmed by the traffic, noise and bustle of London. The snow had brought havoc to the railways, and people who should have been at work hours earlier were still struggling to get there.

London was a degree or two warmer than Canterbury. The snow, melting into blackened slush, had been swept into the gutters where it now formed a watery barrier for people to stride over. A car backfired, and startled pigeons circled Trafalgar Square in noisy panic before re-settling once more. Turning into Whitehall, Abby walked quickly towards Westminster, noting how things had changed. Gone were the piles of sandbags that had stood outside every entrance and ground floor window. Gone too were the uniforms of Abby's childhood, when every man or woman wore khaki, navy, or air-force blue. Tin hats had been replaced by bowlers, and unflattering short skirts by Christian Dior's New Look, full, feminine skirts reaching to the calves.

Big Ben struck eleven as Abby stepped onto Westminster Bridge and crossed the river. Her wonder at being in

London was overshadowed by heartbreak and horror at what she had done. Her isolation was complete. Aunt Milicent would never take her back now, and supposing the Carrs were not pleased to see her? They had no idea she was coming and might not welcome the intrusion into their lives.

If only she could stop aching and shivering! At this very moment, she ought to be warm and cosy in her bed at Ferndene Lodge instead of walking in a cold wind. A sudden feeling of weakness swept over Abby and she staggered against the wall for support. The moment passed, and slowly strength returned to her painful limbs, but she paused before walking on to look over the parapet to the South Bank, where men were working on the new Festival of Britain site, fascinated by the strange shapes growing out of the rubble of the Blitz. After years of austerity, the Labour Government meant to show the world its hope for the future, and confidence in British design and engineering. The new concert hall was already being called the Festival Hall. Plain and stark in its concept, many decried it as a monstrosity, while others applauded its modern simplicity. Abby thought it rather bleak. Much of the exhibition was to be in the great Dome of Discovery which would have the largest unsupported roof in the world. She had seen pictures of what the exhibition would look like, but found it difficult to imagine the great finished dome, the pavilions, restaurants and many other buildings, some of which were to be made entirely of glass.

Abby took comfort in the familiar rattling of the old and noisy tram as it trundled on its track towards Bermondsey, but she was shocked to see how shabby and battered everything looked after Canterbury. Were these mean streets really her home? Everywhere there were gaps where houses once stood. Some of these had been reclaimed by nature, while others were filled with rows of prefabricated cream houses. After Ashton Green and Ferndene Lodge, Abby wondered if she could return to such a life. But she had burnt her boats, and made her choice. Her choice was Bermondsey.

At the corner of Albert Road Abby paused and gazed in astonishment at the wasteland of overgrown weeds where once her home had stood. How small and depressing the remaining terraced houses seemed, she thought. The smell of the polluted Thames and the noise of the riverside brought back the memory of a long-ago Sunday afternoon. She stood with her father on the Woolwich ferry, her nostrils filled with the smell of warm oil from the engines as she leaned over the guard rail to watch them shunting back and forth, propelling the old ferry across the river. Her father had bought her a bag of aniseed balls and told her that this was the only free ferry in Britain. She could remember his voice, but not his face; try as she might, she could not remember his face.

At last Abby left Albert Road and turned the corner into Victoria Place. Here, too, was a huge gap where a flying bomb had struck, but the Carrs' house was still standing with its narrow strip of garden and net curtains at the small bay window. The road seemed more narrow than in the days when she had run riot with Eddy and his friends. Opposite the Carrs' house stood a horse-drawn coal cart. Abby watched as the coalman, sack over his head and bending to his heavy burden, carried coal into one of the houses. She walked on towards number nine then hesitated to open the gate. Suppose she was not welcome? What if Mrs Carr sent her home with a sound 'ticking off'? Suddenly the front door opened and a woman emerged, her short greying hair neatly curled into the roll Abby remembered so well. She said something to the coalman, then returned briskly to the house once more. The coalman delivered two sacks to the Carrs, then the woman came back out with a yard broom and proceeded to sweep the step of coal dust. Suddenly aware of the girl, she paused, and turned towards her.

As Abby moved through the gate she saw the expression

on the woman's face turn to one of enquiry. 'Mrs Carr, don't you remember me?'

Evelyn frowned, then her eyes widened with recognition. 'Abby? It *is* you! It's our own Abby!'

At once the two were embracing, then Evelyn pulled back, her eyes filled with tears, and smiled. 'I didn't recognize you, luv. Oh, it's smashing 'aving you back like this. I never thought I'd see you again, but you've never been out of my thoughts, never. My gawd, it's freezing out 'ere! Come on in to the fire.' At the door she paused. 'But what brings you 'ere, luv? You're not in any trouble, are you?'

Abby shook her head a shade too vigorously. 'Of course not. I just wanted to see you again.' She forced a laugh. 'Look at us two, blubbering. Are you well? You look marvellous.'

This was not true. Evelyn looked tired, and much older than her forty-six years. The lines about her mouth and eyes were deeper, and her face was pale. Abby had remembered a tall, thin woman, but Evelyn was shorter than her by a good two inches, and had put on weight around her hips.

Evelyn urged her visitor into the main living room, where a coal fire blazed and crackled. 'We're all fine except Dad. I told you about 'im in my letter.' She examined Abby's flushed face, and frowned again. 'But you don't look too good, my dear.' She pressed a hand to her forehead. 'You're burning up. Sit yourself down. I'll make some tea, and get you an aspirin.'

Abby sank into the armchair gratefully, and looked about her at the oak dining table with a green velveteen cloth on it, the shabby oak sideboard and the little ornaments on the high mantel which Evelyn treasured so much. Nothing had changed. This was the room where everything happened – eating, ironing, playing cards, and, on Friday nights, bathing in a zinc tub before the fire. Wondering where Mrs O'Connor was,

Abby walked through to the kitchen-cum-scullery, and found the old lady peeling potatoes for the midday meal, completely unaware of the new visitor.

'Mrs O'Connor?'

The old lady turned her head slowly, then frowned in confusion. Slowly it dawned on her who this girl must be and her frown became a wide gap-toothed grin as she hugged Abby close. 'Well, sparrer, if you ain't turned out to be a princess!' The face was older, the wrinkles deeper and the whiskered chin quivered with emotion. 'When we waved you goodbye that day, I didn't think we'd see you again. But you was good and wrote regular, just as you promised. Now 'ere you are, luv, all grown up and a picture to look at.'

Later, as they sat drinking tea, Abby began to feel better and was eager to hear about their lives. Harry, always referred to as Dad by his wife, was still in bed after a very bad night.

'The poor old devil just walks about wheezing and gasping, clasping the bedposts for support. And there ain't a darned thing I can do to 'elp. It's 'is lungs, you see. They've packed up, almost.'

'Yes, you said in your letter,' said Abby. 'It's terrible! The war must have left so many ...'

'War?' Evelyn shook her head. 'It wasn't the war, luv, it was the fags. Been smoking like a chimney since I first met 'im. The doctor told 'im to stop, but would 'e listen? No, Dad would rather have 'is own personal peasouper to travel everywhere with 'im. Add to that the London peasoupers and one day 'is lungs just said, "enough is enough". Now it's only a matter of time.' Her voice cracked. 'The next fog, perhaps.'

'There must be something that can be done for him,' said Abby in alarm.

Evelyn sipped her tea and shook her head. 'The only thing would be to move out of London. Fresh air's what 'e needs.'

'Can't you move?' asked Abby.

Evelyn raised her eyebrows in surprise at Abby's naivety. 'Not a chance. This place was taken over by the Council and they 'ave a waiting list that would stretch from coast to coast. They'd put us on the bottom of any other list, since they give priority to people in their own areas seeking accommodation.' She put down her cup and looked at Abby intently. 'Now then, I want to know what brings you all the way up to the smoke in weather like this. What 'appened?'

'Nothing,' said Abby with false brightness. 'I've decided it's time I got a job. I'm going to search for a room and a job at the same time. I was ... I was wondering if you could put me up for the night. On the sofa, of course.'

'You're certainly not going anywhere with that temperature,' said Evelyn. 'Does your aunt and uncle know you're 'ere with us?'

Abby bristled. 'I'm old enough to do as I please now.'

'So they don't know.' Evelyn glanced knowingly at Mrs O'Connor. 'They must be worried sick.'

'Bin a row, 'as there?' asked Mrs O'Connor in a sympathetic tone. She leaned forward. 'Come on, gel, you can tell us.'

'It was stupid really,' Abby said. 'I fell out with my cousin, that's all. But I've been thinking about coming to London for some time. And my aunt won't care that I've left. Really she won't.'

There followed an awkward silence until Mrs O'Connor rose saying, 'I'd best get the dinner on.'

Evelyn waited until the old lady had left the room. 'You're wrong about your aunt, luv. She's probably climbing the wall wondering what's 'appened to you. When Eddy comes in I'll go with 'im to the phone box, and ring your aunt. I'd go now, but I never could get the 'ang of phones. I always push button B when I'm supposed to push button A.'

'There's no need to telephone.' Abby turned her gaze to the fire, her expression one of defiance. 'I don't want them to know where I am.'

Evelyn sighed. What on earth had got into young girls these days? They were all the same, wanting to leave home before they were old enough. 'I'm sure they love you very much,' she said. When Abby said nothing to this, a suspicion began to form in Evelyn's mind. Living in Victoria Place had made her aware of the terrible things some men did to the women around them. Surely such things didn't happen in the kind of society Abby had just left. But why then had she run away? Clearing her throat, and clasping her hands tightly before her, Evelyn tried to voice her fears.

'Now then, luv. You know you can say anything to me, and I'll take that secret to my grave.' She looked at the girl's bemused face, and remembered the small child handing her a letter during that fateful air-raid. This uncle of hers was the very man that Eileen had not wished her daughter to meet. She paused awkwardly. 'I mean ... has your uncle ever touched you? I mean, touched you in a way that an uncle shouldn't touch his niece?' There, she had said it – she could scarcely look at the girl, so embarrassed did she feel.

'No,' Abby said, her voice a shocked whisper. Such an appalling thought had never crossed her mind. How on earth had it crossed Mrs Carr's? 'Uncle William has always behaved in a proper manner.'

'Well, thank Gawd for that,' Evelyn said. 'Sorry if I shocked you, but it was a question that 'ad to be asked. I must know what made you run away when you're clearly unwell.'

Abby remained silent.

Evelyn sighed and stood up. 'Well, I'd best give Mrs O an 'and in the kitchen. Eddy'll be in soon. He's an apprentice electrician down at Cardington's factory. Went there from school at fifteen. They pay for 'im to go to evening classes so that 'e can catch up on the schooling 'e missed during the war.'

'How is he?' asked Abby. 'I can't imagine what he looks like now.'

'You'll see 'im soon enough,' said Evelyn, smiling. She patted Abby on the head gently. 'Now you rest quietly. You look all in.'

Abby sat quietly feeling weak and ill, the hushed voices from the kitchen made even more indistinct by the sound of pots and pans. She glanced around the room once more, so familiar yet so much smaller than she'd remembered. Still, one thing had not changed, and that was her love for Evelyn Carr and old Mrs O'Connor.

William's morning had been a hectic one. It was the first day of the January sales and Glenisters was full, in spite of the weather. He had heard nothing of the scandal caused by his son, nor of Abby's disappearance. Nor was he aware that Richard was already heading back to Oxfordshire. When the call from a public telephone in London was put through to him in his office, and a broad cockney voice assured him that Abby was safe in Bermondsey, and would be nursed until the 'flu had passed, his eyebrows shot up in surprise.

'Abby insisted I rang you and not your wife,' Evelyn was saying.

'Mrs Carr, I don't understand what you're talking about. Why is Abby with you? What's happened?' William asked, alarmed.

'That's what I'd like to know, Mr Glenister,' came the reply. 'Some tiff, I gather.'

'Look, I must have your address,' William said. 'I'll drive up and collect Abby. If she's ill, she should be at home.'

'You give 'er another couple of days. She shouldn't be moving around in this weather. Don't worry. Abby's all right with us.'

'But I must know . . .' At that moment there was a click and the dreaded dialling tone filled his ears. Puzzled and worried, William put down the receiver and tried to make sense of everything. Picking it up once more, he dialled his home number.

'Milicent? I've had a very strange telephone call from London.'

Hearing Milicent's account of the fight, and the shame that Abby had heaped on the name of Glenister, William thought his wife had finally gone out of her mind. 'She's driven Richard away. He's returned to Oxford . . .'

'If Richard punched some toffee-nosed cove in the face for insulting Abby, then all I can say is, good for him. But it doesn't explain why Abby ran away. For God's sake, Milicent, the girl is ill. How could you have let her go?'

Milicent suggested they resume this conversation when he returned home, and, determined to have the last word, said: 'I warned you that class was class. It was only a matter of time before Abby returned to hers. I'm only sorry she didn't go before driving Richard away.'

'Well he's a wessel-head and no mistake,' William said. 'What's the point of making a stand and then fleeing the field when victory is yours? If Richard had to leave, then why the hell didn't he go in search of Abby?' He paused as Milicent retorted with a stream of angry words, then took his stand. 'As for Abby, there's no way I'd let her return to that life. I'm bringing her back whether you like it or not.'

William slammed down the receiver, certain his wife had played a hand in all this.

Eddy crept into the darkened bedroom and gazed down at Abby sleeping soundly in his bed. She lay on her back, her right hand resting on the pillow, fingers lightly curled; her long hair falling in a tumble of curls; her expression soft and calm in sleep. As Eddy looked at her face – the long curling lashes and generous lips, still faintly coloured with lipstick – he found it difficult to believe she was the same skinny child he used to play with. He suddenly remembered a bank of chalk with a small candle flickering upon it as Abby pledged to marry him one day. Such things were best forgotten now, he thought. She was hardly the same person any more. His mother said she had a posh accent, too. Eddy stood for a moment longer just watching her, then left, shutting the door quietly behind him.

Later that evening, Abby joined the family in the living room, snug in Evelyn's old green candlewick dressing gown. She felt a little better, but had no appetite for food.

'You must keep your strength up, luv.' Evelyn tried to press her to eat.

'Feed a cold, that's what I always say. Feed a cold, starve a fever.' Mrs O'Connor hobbled across the room and bent her wrinkled face close to Abby's. 'I know what will do you good, gel.' She winked, then moved into the kitchen, returning with a bottle of beer. 'Milk stout!' she said triumphantly. 'This'll give yer all the strength and iron yer need. So come on, luv, get it down yer.'

Abby smiled and said, 'You haven't changed a bit, Mrs O'Connor. Do you still play cards?'

'Nearly every night,' said the old lady, grinning happily. 'If yer better tomorrer, we can 'ave a game of whist, the four of us.'

Abby forced herself to drink the dark bitter brew, aware of the old lady's hawk-like eyes.

Harry Carr, meanwhile, had put down his copy of the *Daily Mirror* and, gasping for breath, rose laboriously from the sofa to stand behind it, leaning on the back for support. His lungs needed all the room they could get, and sitting too long caused him great discomfort. He breathed heavily in uneven spurts, puffing air out of his mouth in short gasps.

Evelyn eyed her husband anxiously, then returned to her knitting. These days Harry lived in a world of his own, yet she could remember a time when he had been vigorous and full of fun, amusing children with his impressions of Popeye and chatting happily in the pub on a Sunday morning. That man had died some time during the war in a far-off land. Only a damaged shell had returned to her. Thank heavens there was her son.

'Pity Eddy's working late tonight. But 'e does need the overtime.' It was his money and her pittance from cleaning the local cinema which kept the family fed and clothed. 'I know 'e's just longing to see you again,' Evelyn added, wondering what Abby was making of them all. Mrs O'Connor had spoken truthfully when she said, 'She went away a rough little cockney and returned to us like a princess.' Abby had a refined air that matched her accent, and such things were very out of place in this street. Strange, too, how Eddy had to work tonight when Monday evenings were usually reserved for evening classes. He had always been a little shy, so it couldn't have helped him when she said how 'posh' Abby was now.

'You said you'd come to London to find a job,' she said to Abby. 'What sort of a job?'

Abby smiled wistfully. 'What I'd like is a job in the fashion industry. But since I'd need a diploma for that, I'll have to make do with something less ambitious.'

'Making clothes, you mean?' asked Mrs O'Connor.

'Well, I'd like to design them,' said Abby. 'But unless I can get training, I'll have to be content with selling clothes instead. Tomorrow I'll write to some of the big stores, like Harrods, and see if they'll interview me.'

Nodding her head in approval, Evelyn said, 'That sounds more like it. You want to keep out of the rag-trade, luv – those sweat shops with underpaid girls flogging their guts out for some sleazy man whose only interest is to sell badly-made things for as much money as possible. Harrods sounds better. I've never been there, but the King and Queen go, so it must be good.' Sensing the girl was troubled, Evelyn was determined to bring her out. 'Canterbury's near the coast, isn't it? I've always loved the sea. My aunt used to live in Southend, you know, and I used to visit her regularly when I was a kid. Now my cousin's got a place at Canvey Island, which isn't far from Southend. Me and 'Arry went down there for a weekend last summer while Eddy looked after Mrs O'Connor.'

'Looked after me!' scoffed the old lady. 'Blimey, gel, who do yer think woke 'im up every morning, cooked 'is breakfast and got 'im off to work on time? Who got 'is dinner and 'is tea? And who beat 'im at cards each night?' Mrs O'Connor grinned broadly. 'Eddy's a good lad. There aren't so many like 'im who'd be willing to keep old bones like mine company at night.' She turned to Abby. 'The only way I could get 'im to go to the pub, was to go with 'im.'

Evelyn laughed. 'My God, that must 'ave been 'ard for you, Mrs O!' It was well known that Mrs O'Connor liked her beer. Each morning she would take herself off to the Red Lion for half a pint and a chat with the neighbours. People in Victoria Place could set their clocks by the strange figure in black skirt and white blouse covered by a long black coat, who made her way along the street towards the pub on the corner.

Evelyn carried on speaking. 'We like Canvey. The people there are friendly. Most of them are Londoners anyway, so it's 'ome from 'ome, I always say. They commute each day. Then there are those who 'ave retired there. I wouldn't mind going if we 'ad the chance.'

Harry spoke for the first time that evening. 'It's all right, if you like marshes, sheep, the sea, howling wind and an oil refinery right on the doorstep.'

'It's lovely,' said Evelyn.

'It's bleeding flat and windy,' said Harry. 'Give me Bermondsey any time.'

You stupid man, Evelyn thought. *Can't you see that Bermondsey is killing you*? Then trying to subdue her anger, she changed the subject. 'Well I 'ope you find a job that you like, Abby. Still, a pretty girl like you won't 'ave no trouble getting an 'usband.' She fell silent at the look on Abby's face. Had she put her foot in it? Bending to her knitting, Evelyn allowed her mind to settle on a dream she'd been treasuring ever since Abby returned: to see this girl, whom she loved so much, married to her son. At first glance, it would seem that such a dream could never become a reality. Abby was a lady now. But Evelyn had taken a second glance, and felt that deep in her heart, Abby had not changed at all.

When Harry shuffled out to the lavatory, Evelyn leaned across to Abby. 'I tell you this – if we was given 'arf a chance, I'd move out of London tomorrer. Dad doesn't 'ave an 'ope unless we do. Of course 'e don't know I spend 'arf my life down at the Council offices begging them to move us out of the smoke.' She paused, remembering the expression on Abby's face when she had spoken of marriage. 'Is there anyone special in your life, Abby? A young man, I mean?'

Abby shook her head vigorously. 'No. I've no intention of marrying for years and years.'

Her thoughts were on Richard prancing in the snow with Samantha. She had no idea that her words had wounded. She loved Evelyn Carr and the old lady. They were like mother and grandmother to her. But coming back here after Ashton Green had made her realize that she could not thrive in their world: a world without music, literature or art. For all their affection, Abby knew she no longer belonged. It was class all over again. They were as firmly set within theirs as were the middle and upper classes. But what of the misfits like her who belonged to no particular class?

Mrs O'Connor's eyes had narrowed. 'Don't you want an 'ome and family, gel?'

Sensing she had shocked, Abby smiled. 'One day, yes. When I've made something of my life.'

Evelyn put down her knitting. 'Well, I wouldn't call working in a shop making something of your life.'

'When I was your age, I couldn't wait to get married,' said Mrs O'Connor. 'Still, Abby, you'll change your mind when Mr Right comes along and you want to raise a family.'

Abby thought of the old lady's son who had left home when still a youth and never contacted his parents since. So much for raising children.

'It's just ... well, it's just too early to speak of such things.' She glanced up at the clock which was striking nine thirty, and felt very tired suddenly. 'What time did you say Eddy would be in?'

'Don't wait up, luv,' said Evelyn quickly. 'It's 'igh time you was in bed.'

The next morning Abby was awakened by a soft knocking on the bedroom door. 'Come in,' she murmured. The door opened slowly and a dark-haired man appeared on the threshold. He was tall and swarthy, and that straight lock of hair was as much a nuisance to him today as it always had been. He pushed it back from his forehead and smiled.

'Eddy!' Abby exclaimed.

'Morning,' he murmured. 'Still feeling groggy?'

How handsome he was, thought Abby, rather like a dark-eyed gypsy.

'Sorry to wake you so early, but I 'ave to get fresh clothes.' He moved into the room, keeping his eyes averted from the disturbing sight of the tousle-haired beauty occupying his bed. 'I 'ave to be at work by eight. Anyway, don't let me disturb you.'

'I feel much better,' said Abby, genuinely pleased to see Eddy again. 'And I'm hungry.'

Eddy grinned, his white, even teeth gleaming. 'You always were, I remember.'

'Sorry I took your bed,' said Abby.

'I was fine on the sofa,' he lied, having spent most of

107

the night awake with the discomfort of a hard spring in his back. 'I often sleep on it so don't worry.' His voice was soft in the manner of certain Londoners and had a caring spark of humour in it which Abby found most comforting.

'Mum said you 'ad a bust-up with your relations.'

'Well, not all of them,' said Abby. 'But things had reached a point where it seemed best to leave.'

Just listening to her voice made Eddy's heart sink; that refined accent warned him that they were now worlds apart. She would go to a man from a better class, and the knowledge made him care all the more.

'So you've decided to settle in London.'

'Yes,' said Abby in a defiant tone. 'And I refuse to return.'

Eddy smiled. 'Good for you.' But he knew she would not have her way. She was under age and her uncle had been very concerned when his mother had spoken to him yesterday.

Hugging her knees Abby gazed around the room and said, 'You wouldn't let me into this room in the old days. It was your secret den, full of old junk – models, battered toy cars. Everything but the kitchen sink.'

Relaxing, Eddy added, 'And cardboard. I stored cardboard like a squirrel stores nuts. Came in useful though, that night all our windows were blown out and ...' He stopped suddenly, wishing the earth would open and swallow him. What a thoughtless fool he was. 'Sorry, Abby. Oh, God, I'm sorry.'

'It's all right,' said Abby. 'It was a long time ago.'

Eddy cleared his throat. 'But I'm a thoughtless dope just the same. I'll see you dinner time.'

'Don't you come home for lunch?' asked Abby in surprise. 'You did yesterday.'

Eddy frowned. 'Course not. I don't get off till noon.'

Now it was Abby's turn to feel embarrassed. She would have to remember the old ways or the Carrs might think her 'uppity'. From now on dinner was lunch and tea was dinner. As Eddy walked towards the door, a thought struck her. 'Eddy, do you have a girl friend? I mean — anyone special?'

A vision of Doreen Ford with her bleached hair, bad language and high-pitched giggle came into Eddy's mind. Most of the girls he knew were just like Doreen. Now he realized how low they were. 'No. There's no one. Must dash or I'll be late clocking on.' He closed the door, then opened it again, saying: 'Welcome back, Abby. It's good to see you again.'

Abby lay back on her pillow once more. He was the same dear, reliable Eddy she'd always remembered.

Mrs O'Connor had been dusting in the front room when she heard a car pull up outside the house. Puzzled, she drew back the curtain and saw a man in a loose tweed overcoat get out of a black Singer saloon and stride up the path towards the front door. All along the street other curtains parted while watchful eyes gazed out discreetly.

Thrown into confusion, Mrs O'Connor took off her apron, wishing Evelyn had returned from the shops. She shuffled down the hallway and slowly opened the door, suspicious eyes taking in the tall man standing there. Only when she was assured he was Abby's uncle and not some busybody from the Council did she allow William into the house.

'Mrs Carr's out shopping,' said the old woman, ushering him into the rarely used front room. 'But she'll be 'ome by and by.'

William gazed around the small, barely furnished room, and thought he could smell damp walls. 'How soon is "by and by"?' he asked gently.

'Soon,' said Mrs O'Connor. 'It's cold in 'ere, but we thought you was coming in another couple of days. The other room is, well ... not really suitable for guests. Abby's up now, I'll call 'er.' She paused, her flustered manner changing to one of protection. 'She ain't well enough yet to travel. And she ain't well enough to face a scolding. So don't be cross with 'er, will you, Mr Glenister. And don't keep 'er long in this room. It's too cold.'

As William waited, he was unable to understand why Abby had run to this awful place. No one ever went back. He would never think of going back. Glancing at his watch he saw that it was eleven fifteen. He had left Canterbury and his busy store hours ago. Kent was still snowbound and Wrotham Hill had been a nightmare. He was in no mood for women's pleadings. Abby would leave with him right now.

When he saw her standing in the doorway, a sage green jumper over her brown pleated skirt, he thought how tired and pale she looked. The silence between them lasted one full minute before Abby broke it.

'I ... wasn't expecting you just yet,' she murmured, staring at her uncle with wide green eyes.

'I see,' said William crisply. 'Planning an extended holiday?' He turned, and looked through the curtains at the houses opposite, then shook his head. 'Good God, Abby. What on earth possessed you to do this?'

Abby could scarcely answer. 'I had to,' she whispered. 'And this was the only place I could come to. They're very good to me here and ...'

William's eyes blazed. 'And what's that supposed to mean? Aren't we good to you? Do you think I don't care? What is it we've done? I know it has something to do with that damned party, but ever since the fight all hell's broken loose.'

Abby stared up at him in bewilderment. 'Fight? What fight?'

William sighed with exasperation. '*The* fight, of course.' He paused. 'You knew about it, surely?' When she shook her head, he went on. 'Richard sorted out the bloke who insulted you. Your aunt is furious. He's scarpered back to Oxford and you came running to this God-awful place.' He sighed once more. 'You're as white as death, chick. How are you feeling?'

'Much better, thank you, Uncle,' said Abby, her thoughts on Richard attacking Jeremy. It was incredible, marvellous and utterly fantastic. Unable to contain her excitement, she asked: 'Was Jeremy badly hurt?' Then an awful thought struck her.

'Richard! Was he hurt?'

'No, no,' said William. 'Both got bloody noses, but I gather Jeremy what's-his-name came off the worse for wear.' He smiled to himself at the thought of it. 'How come you didn't know? You were at home.'

Abby shrugged. 'No one told me. I was ill.'

'And still are,' said William. 'This place is damp. I'm taking you home, where you belong.'

Abby shook her head. 'I'm not going back. I can't spend my life in that awful Button Shop. I'm going to find work in London.'

'What kind of work?' asked William.

'Thought I'd try Harrods or Selfridges.'

'A shop?' He looked at her in amazement. 'What's the matter with Glenisters? Isn't it good enough for you?'

Abby frowned. 'But I thought I couldn't work there because we were related?'

William looked even more perplexed. 'Who told you that?'

'Aunt Milicent.'

There was a pause while William digested this piece of news. 'Whereas it's true that I have a policy of not employing people who are married, it hardly applies to you. I understood that you didn't want to work in the store.'

So Aunt Milicent had lied, thought Abby. It hardly surprised her.

'Anyway, I've decided to stay in London.'

'Like hell you will,' said William. 'I got you out of this slum and if you think I'd let you return now, you know very little about me.' He stood up. 'It's like an ice box in here. Let's be going.'

Abby knew she must comply. There was Richard, who had fought because of her. He did care, after all. On the other hand, there was her aunt.

'We'll go into the other room, by the fire,' she murmured. 'I'm sorry – I know what an awful journey you've had, when you should be at the store. But everything became impossible, and I don't see any future for me in Canterbury.'

William looked down at her gently. 'Is it true that you walked home from the party?' When Abby nodded, he went on. 'Without a coat?' He threw up his hands in a gesture of despair.

'How do you know all this?' asked Abby.

'Stella told me, of course.'

'Of course.'

Abby led the way into the warmth of the living room where Mrs O'Connor stood with Harry, both eyeing William with ill-concealed hostility. Abby introduced William to Mr Carr, and polite words were exchanged. But the old lady was in a fighting mood.

'You're not taking 'er back 'ome just yet, are you?' she said. ''Cos she ain't fit to travel.'

William smiled. 'Yes, I agree she isn't well. She belongs at home, in her own bed and with her own doctor in attendance. I'm very grateful for all you've done, but we've settled our differences and Abby's agreed to return. Isn't that so, Abby?'

Abby said nothing but nodded, her gesture conveying an unwillingness to leave which was not lost on Mrs O'Connor.

'It ain't right,' she said. 'The girl's unhappy with you, can't you see that?'

'Yes, I can,' said William. 'My niece is very talented, and she wants to go to an art school.' As Abby looked at him in surprise, he added, 'Richard told me, on Christmas Day. It's the first I knew of it.'

'I asked Aunt Milicent about it a long time ago,' said Abby.

'When you should have asked me.' William stood beside the fire and warmed his hands. 'Anyway, if you can get into an art college, then you shall. If you come home then you can work with me until September. I'll pay you well, and pay your fees at the art school.'

Abby stared at him in shocked disbelief. 'Really? I can go to an art school, after all?' When he nodded, she kissed him, then grinned at Mrs O'Connor. 'An art school! I can't believe it.'

Harry and Mrs O'Connor looked at each other in surprise. The situation had changed without warning, and they felt wrong-footed.

Harry leaned on the chair. 'You won't leave before Mum's returned, will you?' he gasped.

'They won't leave until they've 'ad their dinners,' said Mrs O'Connor firmly. 'Abby's not travelling without an 'ot meal inside 'er.'

Abby turned to her uncle. 'I can't leave without saying goodbye to Mrs Carr and Eddy.'

Evelyn arrived home at eleven thirty, put out by the sight of William Glenister in her living room. They all talked amicably enough, even though William wondered at the strange looks Evelyn kept giving him from time to time.

'She has to return home,' he said to her eventually. 'I'm her legal guardian and she's under age. She can't be alone in London.'

'She wouldn't be alone,' said Evelyn tersely. 'She'd be with us where we could look after 'er.'

When Eddy arrived home he was devastated to learn that Abby was leaving. He could hardly take his eyes off her as he answered William Glenister's seemingly endless questions. Yes, he liked his job and hoped to get into the Royal Electrical and Mechanical Engineers for his National Service. Yes, he did hope to see something of the Empire. There were enough trouble spots to go to, so with any luck he would see active service. As he answered these questions, he knew what William Glenister was thinking. Eddy Carr was a decent enough chap — but not good enough for his lovely niece. Did Abby think that too? Unable to stand any more, Eddy said his goodbyes with the excuse that he had to hurry back to the factory.

With a pang of guilt, Abby watched as he turned the corner of Victoria Place in his dark blue boiler suit. At last it was time to go. Evelyn hugged Abby closely.

'We'll miss you, luv. Don't leave it too long before visiting us again. And always think of this as your second 'ome.'

Mrs O'Connor kissed her. 'You come back now, sparrer!' she commanded. 'Don't wait until I'm pushing up daisies, neither.'

As William drove off, Abby turned, waved out of the window of the car and remembered a similar parting when she had been ten years old and Eddy had run along the smoke-filled platform shouting, 'Remember your promise, remember your promise!' This time he had left her abruptly, as though in anger.

Driving along the Old Kent Road, William and Abby talked about her future, and which art school would best serve her needs.

'I'd like to go to St Martin's in Charing Cross Road. They are the best when it comes to fashion courses,' Abby said.

William had been puzzling over something for a long time. 'Abby, when your aunt refused to let you go on to an art school, why did you leave it at that? It clearly means a great deal to you, so why didn't you come to me?'

Abby wondered if he could ever understand a child's fear of being sent to an orphanage. 'I didn't want to cause any trouble,' she said, then changed the subject. 'Will you write to St Martin's or shall I?'

'I will write, and I'm sure they'll take you. Your work is exceptionally good.'

'But what will Aunt say?' asked Abby at last. 'She'll be furious.'

'You're *my* niece; Ferndene is *my* home and Glenisters *my* store,' said William drily. 'I think I have the right to decide what to do with *my* money, don't you?'

Abby listened in growing amazement. Would he be so brave when face to face with the enemy? Or would he fall in the first hail of bullets?

The thaw had not come to Ashton Green, and Ferndene stood dark and shadowed beneath the snow-covered branches of the tall chestnut tree. Abby got out of the car, remembering how she'd felt arriving here for the first time. She felt the same way now, lost and afraid.

William opened the front door, and together they walked into the wide hallway. Ferndene was as cold inside as it was outside and she braced herself as her aunt opened the drawing room door.

Say what you like, Aunt Milicent, Abby thought defiantly. *I'll be leaving for an art school soon, so you can put that in your pipe and smoke it!*

Milicent ignored her, however, and turned to her husband, saying, 'How was the journey?'

'Awful,' said William, taking off his coat and hanging it on the hall stand. 'Warmer in London, though.'

The atmosphere here was like ice, he thought, deciding to stay home and give Abby support.

Looking straight through her niece, Milicent turned and walked back into the drawing room. Abby's greatest desire was to flee, but one quick glance at her uncle told her that she was expected to make her peace.

'I'm very sorry for all the trouble I've caused, Aunt Milicent.'

Milicent turned and stared at her. 'Yes. I daresay you are.' She drew on her cigarette with fingers that trembled slightly, then exhaled slowly. 'Tell me, Abby, have you been treated badly here?'

'No,' said Abby quickly. 'Of course not. What happened had nothing to do with ...'

'Then have you *always* held us all in such dire contempt?' cut in Milicent. 'Please do tell me, my dear, I'm sure everyone is longing to know.'

'Now then, Milicent, Abby's unwell,' said William, trying to defuse the situation. 'I think she should go straight to bed.'

Milicent's eyes flashed dangerously. 'Well, Abby, I'm waiting for an answer.'

'You don't understand,' said Abby miserably.

'No,' snapped Milicent. 'But it's high time you did, young lady. When you came to us all those years ago you had nothing; even the clothes you wore came from charity. We gave you a home, fed you, clothed you, and turned you from a rough-mannered cockney into a well-spoken lady. No easy achievement, I can assure you. Yet now you shame us, and drive our son away from his home.' Milicent's voice cracked at last, and her eyes filled with tears. 'I can't tell you how much that hurt.' She drew a handkerchief from the handbag resting on the coffee table. 'I think you'd better leave me now. What's done is done.'

But it was not over, thought Abby miserably. There was still the subject of her art studies to discuss. How would she and her uncle stand up before the tempest then? She climbed the stairs slowly to her bedroom, pausing as she heard the strains of Schubert's *Impromptu No 3*.

Thank God for Schubert, thought Abby. Thank God for music that calms. How would her aunt live without it?

In her room she switched on the electric fire, and unpacked the battered old case she'd borrowed from the attic. Excusing herself from dinner she went to bed. For the first time, Abby had seen Milicent vulnerable and hurt. Guilt and pain were something she and her aunt had in common, she realized suddenly. They both loved Richard and together had driven him away.

116

The bedroom door opened slightly and her uncle put his head round. 'How are you feeling, chick? Would you like a hot drink and some aspirin?'

'No, thank you,' said Abby. Then a thought struck her. 'Is Stella home yet?'

William nodded. 'I told her not to disturb you.' This was untrue. Stella had made it plain that she stood with her mother, and felt Abby had let them all down. 'You can see her tomorrow.'

Abby was just falling asleep when she heard the telephone ringing in the hallway below. Her aunt's voice came floating up the stairs.

'Yes, she's back, and perfectly all right.'

There was a long pause, during which Abby crept out of bed and onto the landing. Then gazed over the banister to where her aunt was standing.

'I told you she was fine. It was just an attention-seeking device. And I was very hurt that you should have gone like that. I know I was sharp, darling, and I'm sorry. Where are you, for goodness' sake?'

Realizing the caller was Richard, Abby was halfway down the stairs as William took the telephone from his wife. 'Look here, Richard, where the devil are you? Eynsham! That's near Oxford, isn't it?'

There was a long pause, then William spoke again. 'Well, if they're kind enough to put you up, you're better off staying where you are. You've only a few days before term starts, and you know what the trains are like in this weather. Take care, son.'

Turning, William saw Abby standing on the stairway, her long hair falling to her shoulders, her slender figure lost in the white nightgown which flowed about her. Her hands were clasped tightly and her eyes desperate with hope.

'Sorry, chick. Did you want to have a word with him? Damn, I never thought to get his number. Did you get it, Mil?'

Milicent glared at her husband. 'No. You snatched the

phone from me.' She looked up at her niece, and snapped: 'Get back to bed before you catch pneumonia. Don't you think you've caused enough trouble?'

Disappointed and angry, Abby returned to her bedroom. Damn her aunt for saying such things about her to Richard. Attention-seeking indeed! She would not see him again until Easter. How could she wait so long? There was so much she wanted to say to him, and so much she wanted to hear from him in return.

Four days later, a small package arrived addressed to Abby. Puzzled, she unwrapped a small pendant: a pearl in a silver mount. The note that came with it was brief and to the point.

I love you.
Richard

Abby kissed the pearl lovingly. Of course it wasn't real, but to her it was the most precious thing she had ever possessed, and she vowed to wear it every day of her life.

In the weeks that followed, Abby noticed that her aunt was keeping a low profile. Although as cool as ever in her attitude to her niece, she was treading carefully. The bridge evenings were cut to one a week, and she was always home by eleven thirty. Perhaps Uncle William's attitude had caused his wife to come to her senses at last.

Meanwhile, Abby liked her new job at Glenisters. Although she was only a junior sales assistant in Ladies' Fashion, her talents at dressmaking were often put to good use when the alterations lady was too busy to cope.

A few years earlier, Christian Dior had turned the fashion world on its head with his New Look. Women wanted to look feminine again, and Dior had provided the means. Yards and yards of material went into his outfits and ballgowns, causing the Government to call the New Look an extravagant folly and frivolous nonsense.

'What a colossal cheek,' Milicent had snapped. 'It's all right for Parisians to be in the height of fashion, but not the long-suffering English woman. And just who does this junior minister, Harold Wilson, think he is, intimating that we're unpatriotic for wearing fashionable clothes? He'll never amount to anything, you mark my words.'

British women ignored the government strictures and rushed to wear the Look, which became the accepted style of dress with its soft shoulders, nipped-in waists, full skirts and three-quarter-length sleeves. Abby loved it all, and each month eagerly awaited the arrival of *Vogue*. *One day,* she told herself, *I'll startle the world with a look of my own.* But at the thought a stab of anxiety swept over her. Her uncle had not yet broached the subject of her art studies with Aunt Milicent, though her interview with St Martin's was only two weeks away. Desperate that nothing should go wrong with her plans, she mentioned it to her uncle.

'Don't worry, Abby. I'll tell her when I get the chance,' he said, smiling.

'She'll try to stop it, I know she will. Uncle, you'll be ...'

'Firm?' William asked. 'Yes. You are going to whichever school takes you, and there's nothing your aunt can do to prevent it.'

Abby braced herself for the approaching storm, which came one evening at dinner. They had just finished the meal, when William told Milicent and Stella of the plans.

'How charming,' said Milicent, her eyes fixed on Abby. 'And just when did you and your uncle cook up this little plot?'

'Some time ago,' William replied. 'I decided that since Abby was so talented she ought to continue with her studies. Richard told me you refused to let her take up a scholarship years ago. It seemed pointless to say anything until we knew whether the school had accepted her. I'm pleased to say they have. Abby starts in September.'

Milicent stared at him, then gave a hollow laugh. 'And why this sudden interest? What good is art to the girl? She needs to be trained to earn a living. Art won't provide it. Are we expected to keep her for the rest of her life?'

'Will drama provide a living for Stella?' asked William. 'I don't think so. But when she got through that audition you couldn't wait to send her to RADA.'

Milicent threw her napkin down onto the table.

'Now you listen! Stella is *our* child, Abby is not. Abby should be grateful for all the years we have fed and clothed her. Is it too much to ask that she now starts supporting herself?'

'What's done is done. No sense in fighting over it.' With that, William left the dining room.

Speechless with rage, Milicent stood beside the table staring down at her niece. When at last she found her voice, she asked which school Abby was going to attend.

'St Martin's, in London,' came the weak reply.

'London!' Milicent took a deep breath, then nodded. 'Can't keep away, can you.' Slowly the expression of fury changed to one of thoughtfulness. 'Well, since you can't wait to return to your roots, we shan't prevent you.'

Abby remained at the table, too upset to move. She knew her aunt felt that the two men in her life had betrayed her for a worthless girl. It must seem that they had all turned against her, whispering in corners, plotting behind her back. Yes, thought Abby dismally, Aunt Milicent had good reason to feel shattered, while Abby Nichols had good reason to feel that she had just made a powerful enemy.

CHAPTER SIX

Milicent returned to her old ways, going out every evening and returning well after midnight. It seemed to Abby that she hardly cared what anyone thought of her any more and, indeed, seemed to be revelling in her husband's growing anger, willing him to bring matters to a head.

William, for some strange reason, said nothing.

Richard arrived home on Maundy Thursday, happy and full of news. William helped unload his luggage into the hallway, as Milicent threw loving arms about her son, declaring him to be much thinner.

'You're not eating enough, my dear.'

'I eat like a horse, mother,' laughed Richard, not adding that he drank rather more than was good for him as well. Seeing Abby, his blue eyes fixed on hers, and he murmured, 'Hello, there.' Covered in confusion, Abby turned her gaze from him. 'Hello, Richard. Did you have a good journey?' 'Not really,' he replied, wondering how long he and Abby must go on mouthing words that had nothing to do with their thoughts. It was a hopeless situation. Vaguely, he heard Stella's voice prattling on about her audition for RADA, and how they'd accepted her.

'I did the famous Lady Macbeth speech, you know ... "Out, damned spot, out I say ..."'

'Don't swear, dear,' said her mother disapprovingly. 'Come on, everyone, tea is all ready.'

Milicent wheeled the trolley into the drawing room and Richard fell back against the cushions of an armchair and sighed. 'Ah, this is the life. Nothing beats home.' Taking a cup of tea from his mother, he looked across the room at Abby and said, 'Dad tells me you're going to St Martin's.'

'Yes,' said Abby quietly, receiving the message in his eyes. *We'll be alone at last.* 'It's in the Charing Cross Road.'

Richard grinned. 'So is Foyles. You'd be surprised how much reading Law takes.'

Milicent froze, the cup halfway to her mouth. 'Foyles? Well, it's an excellent bookshop, of course, but Richard, you have the Bodleian, the most famous library in the whole world, at your feet. You're there to study. I don't want to hear of you junketing in London.'

Richard smiled and drank his tea. He noticed the pendant around Abby's neck, and continued to say with his eyes the words he dared not speak in this house.

Good Friday started off with grey skies but by eleven the sun was sending shafts of pale light onto the wind-blown daffodils and primroses. The clouds drifted away and the sun's warmth caused Abby to pause on the river bank. She smiled up at Richard beside her.

'Isn't this heaven?' Richard's eyes lingered on the full breasts outlined by her green jersey dress. Her eyes turned the same dark green as he moved towards her. Then they were in each other's arms and he buried his face in her soft, sweet-smelling hair. 'Oh, I love, I *love* you,' he murmured huskily. Gently he lifted her face to his and their mouths met, warm and passionate. As his ardour increased, Richard forced his tongue into her mouth. Abby pulled away, suddenly unsure of him and herself.

For a moment they just stood there, listening to the sound of the river flowing under the bridge. 'I'm sorry,' he said. 'It's real kissing. Sorry if I shocked you.'

'No, Richard, you didn't shock me,' Abby said; she was angry at her awkwardness, but his kiss had sent such a thrill through her that she'd acted without thought. Now she wanted him to embrace her again, but knew he would not. She took his arm and drew close. 'Do you remember the first time we walked here? The leaves were falling. Now they're just budding.' Walking among the willows,

Abby realized that she, too, was a mere bud, and Richard would be the one to bring her into full blossom. They must take things slowly, she told herself.

Richard picked up a small twig and, breaking it in half, gave one to Abby. 'Remember Pooh sticks?' They dropped the twigs into the river and raced across the bridge to see whose stick came through first. This child's play broke the tension, and suddenly they were laughing once more. Climbing up through the woodland path to Stapledown, they stood with their arms about each other, looking down at the Cathedral, their minds set on the future.

'Thank God you chose London,' said Richard. 'I'll take the car to Oxford in October so that I can pop down to visit you. Did Mother make much of a scene about the art school?'

Abby's mouth tightened. 'She thinks she's been betrayed by everyone.'

Richard stared out at the city, his face shadowing. 'Yesterday was horrendous. New Year seemed to hover over us like the sword of Damocles.'

'Did you really hit him?' Abby stared up at Richard, smiling with anticipation.

'Yes.'

'Because of me?'

'Of course. Do you think I'd risk a bloody nose for Samantha?'

Abby smiled. 'Have you heard from her?'

'Why do you ask?'

'That's a silly question.'

Richard paused. 'As a matter of fact, I've had three letters from her. It's embarrassing. I write back politely — what else can I do? It would put anyone else off, but she's so persistent.'

Abby's smiled faded. 'She's had everything she ever wanted, and she wants you, so beware. And this Jeremy St John-Tennant,' she murmured quietly, 'I hope your paths don't cross again.'

Richard grinned. 'I can deal with that chinless wonder. It's Samantha I'm trying to avoid.'

'You can't. There's church on Sunday.'

'I shan't go,' announced Richard. 'I know we've never missed a service on Easter Day, but, my love, this time I'm going to do just that.'

He drew Abby close, sending hot blood coursing through her veins, as he kissed her once more. Her legs felt weak and her body started to tremble.

This time Richard pulled away. 'I think we'd better get back.'

'Jesus Christ is Risen Today' sang the congregation at St Michael's Church on Easter Sunday. Abby turned the page of her hymn book, conscious of Richard close beside her. It had taken but one sentence from his mother to force him to church. *'My son does not run like a coward.'*

Face the music! Play the game! That was the life of an English gentleman, and the way Richard had been raised. Facing the music was one thing, thought Abby, but facing Samantha was something else again. There she was, looking more lovely than ever as she sat with her parents in their special pew. What would happen when the moment came for the Fellowes and their daughter to say good morning and 'Happy Easter' to Richard? Would they 'play the game' too, she wondered?

It was as Abby had expected: all smiles, and gentle conversation. 'Coming to the bun fight?' The breakfast was laid out in the Church Hall and although Milicent had said that she was looking forward to it, Richard made his excuses. Looking directly into Samantha's eyes, he shook his head.

'Sorry, I'll have to give it a miss. Masses of reading to do and today's the only chance I'll have.'

This was greeted by cries of 'Oh, how sad,' yet the Fellowes were glad to see their daughter away from the Glenister boy.

Samantha, however, was anything but pleased, and stared at him coldly. She looked like a duchess, in a dark blue velvet coat with matching hat. Mindful of the people watching, she pretended she was unconcerned that the moment for which she had longed was to end without a word passing between them. Abby smiled at her sweetly and, with a sense of mischief, said: 'And I'll have to cry off, as well. I might as well go back with Richard. Have a nice time, everyone.'

'That's put the fat in the fire,' laughed Richard as they hurried down the church path towards the lychgate.

Richard did no work that day or any other day, choosing instead to spend each precious hour of the holiday with Abby. They drove around the countryside, then walked along the lanes speaking of their future together.

'I'll have years of studying, I'm afraid,' he said, as they wandered along the old Pilgrims' Way. 'First I must get my degree, then work for the Bar exams. It'll be years before I become a fully-fledged, impoverished barrister looking for briefs.'

'We can't wait that long,' said Abby in dismay. 'I have four years of study too, but there must be some way for us to marry.'

'I'll give up Law and get a job in a bank or something,' said Richard firmly.

Abby gave him a look of disapproval. 'Give up your studies, after all you've worked for? I won't let you.'

'You can't stop me. No one can.'

'Then I'll give up my art studies, too,' she said resolutely.

Richard shook his head. 'Oh no. I won't let you do that. It means too much to you, darling.'

'As much as your studies mean to you. We'd both regret making such a move,' Abby said, and they walked on, leaving the problem unsolved.

The following day being a Bank Holiday, Richard and Abby drove off in the direction of Folkestone, through the Elham Valley where ancient timber houses nestled in woodland. Richard looked thoughtful as he drove. 'Mother didn't seem too pleased at our leaving,' he murmured. 'I'd assumed Father was staying home. Fancy going into the office today.'

Abby felt a sudden rush of anger. 'Oh, did you have a mind to bring your mother along too, then?'

'Of course not.' He glanced at her uneasily. 'I just think it's a pity that we've all deserted her. Stella's spending the day with friends, we're clearing off and Father's in his office.'

Abby felt like telling him that Milicent was probably only too happy to have her family out of the way. Unless, of course, the other man in her life was unable to meet her.

Folkestone was bustling with holidaymakers, most of whom had congregated around the old fishing harbour. Abby and Richard ate whelks from a stall, then wandered along the sandy beach towards the rocks beneath the cliffs. The sun brought the white chalk of the French coast closer to view.

'I'd no idea France was that near,' said Abby in astonishment. 'What a close call we had during the war. Imagine Nazis here! It makes me go hot and cold when I think of it.'

On their way home, they called into a pub which stood on the cliff tops above Folkestone. Inside, the saloon bar was snug and warm now that the sun had gone down.

'Mother told me once that she and Father used to come in here after walking along the cliffs,' said Richard.

Abby was incredulous. Aunt Milicent walking miles along a cliff top and coming into a public house? It seemed as likely as the King and Queen popping into Glenisters to do their Christmas shopping.

'It's true,' said Richard, wondering why she was laughing. 'This place is The Valiant Sailor, isn't it? This is their pub.'

It was dusk when they climbed back into the old Austin.

Their last day together was over. Tomorrow, Abby would be back at work, and Richard would be incarcerated in his room studying. They wouldn't have a minute alone: not one minute to be free, they thought simultaneously. Richard turned the car towards the main road and waited for the entrance to clear as another car pulled in. In that moment, both he and Abby saw the occupants clearly. The driver was a dark-haired man with a neat moustache. He was laughing as he talked to his passenger, and she laughed with him. The passenger was Milicent.

Richard froze at the wheel, but neither the driver nor Milicent noticed the little Austin. 'How long?' asked Richard at last. 'How long has this been going on?'

Abby saw his knuckles whiten as he gripped the wheel. 'I'm not sure. It's probably someone from the Bridge Club ...' Her voice trailed off when she realized how stupid that sounded. In the rear mirror she could see her aunt and the man walking into the pub. 'Don't read too much into it, Richard. They're probably just friends.'

'That wasn't my impression,' snapped Richard. 'How long, Abby?'

Sighing in defeat Abby answered. 'I think ... well, about the time you went to university, last October.'

Richard's voice was bitter. 'Does Father know?'

'Yes. I'm pretty sure he does. But he isn't saying anything, so you mustn't either. Leave it between them. It'll all blow over, you'll see.'

Richard was silent all the way home. It was the dark and menacing silence of contained anger and it frightened Abby. She longed to take away his pain with all the love she had for him. When he drove into the driveway of Ferndene and stopped the car, she turned to him, aching to put her arms about his tense body. 'Darling, don't be sad. I can't bear it.'

Richard half-turned towards her and whispered, 'I wouldn't have believed it of her. Not in a million years! My own mother playing around with other men!'

His anger had shut her out. Abby felt it consuming him and knew that nothing she said or did could change things. Their lovely day had been spoilt by Milicent.

Abby got out of the car, while Richard still sat there. She looked back at him, but he did not raise his head, or even seem to notice that she had gone. Dejected, she entered the house wondering how long they would have to live under the shadow of his mother.

Samantha sat in her bedroom and surveyed the gowns her mother had bought her for the 'season'. Her favourite was the Victor Steibel dress for her coming-out ball. Already she was imagining how she would look in *The Tatler*. For the presentation at Court, white of course, with long gloves; white too for the Queen Charlotte Ball, and heavenly outfits for the Derby, Ascot, Henley, Wimbledon and the many parties and balls that made up the season. She touched each outfit lovingly, remembering her father's shocked words.

'Good God, it's costing me a fortune! For what you've spent here, Lydia, we could have had the East Wing renovated and the roof re-done.'

'Exactly,' his wife had said. 'This house is falling apart at the seams. We have land, but these days that doesn't equal money. Spending it now will ensure that Samantha makes a brilliant marriage. And that should help us start work on this place.'

'Sounds pretty mercenary, doesn't it? Selling off our daughter like livestock.'

Lydia laughed. 'The aristocracy have been doing it for years. How else do you think they keep their lands and titles?'

Samantha thought of their constant arguments and remembered when the house had been full of servants. Now they were down to Roberts and his wife, and two jobbing gardeners. The East Wing had dry rot, the roof needed re-leading and the plumbing was a joke. To put this right, her parents were keen for her to marry Jeremy, the son of Viscount Kelthorpe and the grandson of the Earl of Penworth — what better match could they hope for?

'But why can't I have Richard Glenister to my coming-out?' Samantha had asked. 'Just because of that silly fight. It won't ever happen again.'

Sir Gerald had glowered at his daughter. 'If you think we're going to all this expense so that you can throw yourself away on the son of a shopkeeper then, my dear child, you can jolly well think again.'

'You're always telling me not to be a snob,' Samantha had replied. 'It seems I can treat him as an equal, as long as I don't sink so low as to marry him.'

'Now look here,' her father had said angrily. 'If that's what you have in mind, then send all these back to wherever they came from. There's no need to go through these silly shenanigans. Lydia, send back the clothes and cancel the invitations. There'll be no coming-out for Samantha.'

'Oh, Gerald, don't be so stupid.' Lydia treated his outburst as one treats the petulance of a small child. 'Samantha must have her coming-out. It's every girl's right and I won't have our daughter denied hers.'

And so the matter rested. But what use were all her beautiful clothes, Samantha wondered, if she could not have Richard? Each time she had tried on a gown she'd done so with him in mind. What would he think? Would he like the colour on her? It was all Abby's fault, she thought bitterly. How she hated that girl! The memory of Easter Sunday had not ended. Richard had rushed away instead of staying with her, and then Abby had smiled and gone off with him. She was just the type. Common to her finger-tips and jealous of those who had more than she could ever hope to possess. Well, she wouldn't have Richard, thought Samantha. To hell with the East Wing!

Milicent found Abby a run-down flat in Lamb's Conduit Street, close to Great Ormond Street Hospital for Children.

She was to share this accommodation with another St Martin's student, Susan Hillman, whose parents had arrived with her and were now staring at the flat in horror.

'It should be condemned,' whispered Mr Hillman to his wife. A solicitor, he silently determined that he would find somewhere else for his daughter. But London was still in the grip of a housing shortage and finding alternative accommodation would not be easy.

Milicent looked at the dirty cream walls, the two iron bedsteads and thin striped mattresses, then smiled with satisfaction. 'Well, student accommodation was never much. But I've spent the past month inspecting flats and this one is the best. And the rent is not to be sneezed at.'

Abby and Susan had met at the college interview, hit it off immediately, and decided to share together. Unfortunately they had left everything for Milicent to organize.

The sitting room was tiny, and had two wooden-based fireside chairs which should have been thrown on a bonfire years ago. In the fireplace stood an ancient electric fire with only one bar working. The kitchen sink was of well-chipped stone, and beside it stood a dirty gas cooker and one dingy cupboard. The bathroom boasted a 1920s bath, with a large brown stain where enamel should have been, and the geyser above it looked positively dangerous.

Mr Hillman surveyed it all in silence. Taking his daughter to one side, he whispered: 'No way, darling, are you going to stay here. I'll find somewhere better for both of you. Just give me time. Don't use that geyser — it'll probably blow up.'

Abby knew this was Milicent's way of getting back at her, but she hardly cared. She was going to study art and lead her own life at last.

Susan was a cheerful girl, slightly overweight and with curly fair hair which framed her round face, giving her the appearance of a rather tall child. Like Abby, she had been extremely nervous on the day of her interview and glad to have someone on her own wavelength to keep up her spirits. That they should have become friends was inevitable from their first encounter.

Abby's first year at St Martin's began with a foundation course that would lead to specialization for the National Diploma in Dress Design. She loved every minute of it. Her figure drawing improved dramatically. She now did costume and life portraits, as well as sketching gowns on models. Her circle of friends widened, and her old love of London returned, which was just as well since she walked across so much of it in order to save bus fares. Though Uncle William sent a cheque each month to cover food and rent, he forgot fares and heating bills, but Abby thought it would be wanting in gratitude to ask for more.

The first weekend that Richard drove into London from Oxford was mid-October. Since he had no idea where Lamb's Conduit Street was, Abby met him in Foyles bookshop in the Charing Cross Road, close to the school. They had then eaten at Lyons Corner House, before going on to the cinema. Overnight he slept on the hard floor, protesting that he was perfectly comfortable, and the following day they had walked in golden sunshine through Kew Gardens, and then along the tow path to Richmond. They climbed the hill, and looked down on the bend of the river Thames as it wound its way through fields and banks of willows.

'When I'm rich and famous, as an eminent Judge,' Richard had said, 'we'll have a house up here – along that Georgian terrace. Each morning when we wake up, we'll look out of our bedroom window and see this.'

Abby had looked down on the old stone bridge and the motor launches easing their way along the river. 'I think Richmond Hill will have to wait a long time for us.' Although she had spoken lightly, she wondered what had made her say it.

If Abby was careful with her allowance, Susan was pennywise to the point of parsimony, and never lost an opportunity to switch off a light or turn out the heater. 'Waste not, want not' had been the code by which her parents had raised her and although they never wanted for money they rarely spent it, either. It was the only thing about Susan which irritated Abby. But she put up with it until the day it all became too much.

'Oh Lord, I feel awful,' said Susan, sneezing again into her handkerchief. 'I'm sure it's 'flu. We bake in college and freeze in here.'

'Well, if you didn't keep turning off the heating, the place would have time to warm up,' Abby said, handing her friend two aspirins. 'I'll get you a warm drink, and put a hot water bottle in your bed.'

Bustling about in the kitchen, Abby heard the sound of Richard's car long before she saw it. Backfiring twice, it clattered along the street and pulled up outside the terraced block. She opened the window and leaned out. 'You're noisier than the Blitz!' she called. 'Where on earth have you been?'

Richard looked up and waved two theatre tickets in the air triumphantly. 'We've seats for *Carousel* tonight. That's why I'm late. I've spent hours queueing outside the box office. Get your glad rags on.'

Abby could hear Richard thundering up the uncarpeted stairs, and was waiting with the door open as he arrived, grinning from ear to ear. He folded her in his arms, kissing her hotly on the mouth before letting her go.

'Richard, it's marvellous. *Carousel!*' She hugged him in delight. 'But Susan isn't well. I'm not sure I should leave her.'

'Rubbish,' called Susan from the sitting room. 'I can hear you. How can your missing a show cure my 'flu?'

Abby made a pot of tea for Richard and Susan, then went into the cold bathroom for a quick bath. She switched on the geyser, but the flame did not light. Realizing the pilot had gone out, Abby held a match to the heater, and heard a muffled boom before she felt herself flung backwards across the bathroom. Heart pounding, she lay there dazed and shocked, and Richard's anxious face was the last thing she saw before passing out. When she came to, she was lying on her bed and she could hear a voice from the far end of a tunnel.

'Abby! Come on, Abby, snap out of it.'

Slowly Richard's face became clearer, and his voice louder. Abby felt strange, and her eyebrows were stinging. 'The geyser . . .' she tried to speak.

'It blew out,' said Richard, holding a glass of water to her lips. Behind him stood Susan, looking down at her, pale and concerned. 'I'll go down and phone for the gas people, and I think I'd better call a doctor,' Richard was saying.

'We don't have one,' Susan said. 'I could go down and get the landlady.'

'No!' Richard looked at Abby's pale face. Black soot was all over her forehead, and the front of her hair and eyebrows had been badly singed. 'I'll go. That bloody woman had better know that her geyser is dangerous. Abby could have been killed.'

'I'm all right and don't need a doctor,' Abby said. 'It's my fault, anyway. The pilot light blew out, and I forgot I had turned on the gas while I searched for the matches. I lit the match and . . .'

Richard dipped his clean handkerchief into the glass of water and started wiping her face and forehead gently. 'How on earth could the pilot light have blown out? The window doesn't open in there, for a start.'

'It didn't blow out,' Susan said feebly. 'I . . . I turned it out.'

Richard stared at her in disbelief. 'Why?'

'To save gas.' Her voice was barely audible. 'I forgot to tell Abby.' She stifled a sneeze then said: 'I'll telephone the gas board, you stay with her.'

Furious, Richard could only stare after Susan as she rushed away. 'I don't believe it,' he said at last.

133

Slowly Abby sat up, and touched her singed eyebrows. 'I do.'

'You should have a doctor to look at you,' said Richard.

Abby shook her head. 'No, I'm fine, and I want to see *Carousel*.'

'Well, I'm not taking a girl to the theatre looking as you do.'

Abby blinked at him. 'Why? What do I look like?' Pushing him away, she turned to the mirror, and the shock of her reflection nearly sent her flat again. 'No wonder my eyebrows hurt! I don't have any. And look at my hair,' she wailed, seeing the singed dark stubble above her brow. 'What am I going to do?' Sighing, she fell back into Richard's arms, and heard him chuckling.

'You're going to thank God you weren't blinded or worse. And I still love you even though you look the very devil. You could start a new fashion. You always said you wanted to.'

When Susan returned, she found them falling about with laughter and thought they must be mad. 'I'll put the kettle on,' she murmured.

'No.' Richard headed her off. 'Don't do anything until the place is given the all-clear. When is the gasman coming?'

'At once,' said Susan. 'I dialled 999 and told them there had been a gas explosion. They're sending the emergency services.'

'Oh, my God,' groaned Richard. 'This certainly is not the evening I'd envisaged. Any minute there'll be police cars, fire engines and ambulances.' With that, he rushed away to stop the invasion.

It turned out to be a perfect evening. Abby felt self-conscious about her hair and eyebrows on entering the theatre. Once the performance began she was past caring, all her thoughts on the young heroine who had lost the man she loved.

During the drive back home, a strange melancholy settled on her, and she felt threatened without knowing why.

'What is it? Didn't you like the show?' Richard asked.

Abby forced a smile. 'Loved it. Didn't you?'

Richard wrinkled his nose. 'I liked the music, but the story was too melodramatic for words.' He turned into Lamb's Conduit Street and saw, with a sinking heart, that the sitting room light was still on. Would they ever get a chance to be alone, he wondered?

The flat was filled with friends from the art school. Susan was sitting in one of the armchairs wrapped in a blanket, while all around her on the floor sat her fellow students. They were bright and breezy, considering the lateness of the hour.

'Hi, there. We found Pippa's party a bit of a bore, so came on here to find poor old Susan like this. Heard all about the explosion. Let's see your eyebrows, Abby? Gosh, look at your hair ...'

After another sleepless night, Richard took Abby to Hyde Park to spend Sunday alone with her. It was a cold, raw morning, sunless and damp. Seeing the fallen leaves, Abby realized that it would soon be Remembrance Sunday. She watched a small boy throwing bread to the ducks on the Serpentine.

'Richard, I can't go home for Christmas,' she said at last.

Richard looked down at her, and frowned. 'What? Why can't you come home?'

The silence between them deepened as Abby struggled with her thoughts. 'Something happened before I left, something turned your mother against me. I'm pretty sure it had nothing to do with my going to art school.'

Richard looked bemused. 'What?'

'Your parents had a terrible row. I heard them, Richard, but I couldn't understand what they were saying. It was awful. I've never heard your father raise his voice like

135

that.' She paused, her eyes still on the lake and the ducks gathering around the small boy. 'I told you I thought he knew about this other man. But there's something else, I don't know what, but I heard my name mentioned several times.'

They started walking on slowly and Richard placed his arm around Abby's shoulders. 'So?'

'I think your mother is under the impression that I told Uncle about her and this other man. Why else would my name come up? But I didn't, Richard. After that, Milicent hardly spoke to me. We travelled to London in silence. She was charming to Susan's parents, but when she said goodbye to me I felt she really meant it.'

'Rubbish,' said Richard angrily. 'It's Mother's fault there's a situation, not yours. We know what they were rowing about and it has nothing to do with you. And I'll tell you this, I'm not spending Christmas without you. If you're not at Ferndene, then I won't be either, and that'll only upset Father.'

Abby knew he was right, but still worried. 'If my being there is going to cause trouble, then surely he's better off without me?'

When Richard returned to Oxford later that afternoon, the problem was unresolved. Abby missed him deeply and, as she always did on these occasions, set to cleaning the flat from top to bottom, falling into bed exhausted at midnight.

Sleep, however, eluded her, as she thought again about Christmas. She could go to the Carrs and they would welcome her as they had on her many visits since starting at the art school. No doubt Eddy would be there, on leave from his REME camp at Aborfield. He'd been called up just one week after his eighteenth birthday last January. Then again, the idea of Christmas without Richard was so horrendous, she knew in the end she would go to him, wherever he was. Tossing and turning, she wished sleep would come to wipe the worries from her mind.

The issue soon resolved itself when news reached Abby that Uncle William had suffered a heart attack.

CHAPTER SEVEN

In a state of alarm, the family gathered together at Ferndene. From there, they went to visit William in the hospital. The attack had been sudden. 'A warning shot over the bow,' the doctor said. 'He's to take things more easily from now on.'

Richard went with Abby, since Milicent had decided her place was at home, beside the telephone, should she be needed at Glenisters. They sat beside the bed while William slept, both alarmed by the pallor of his complexion. When finally he opened his eyes, he saw Abby and smiled. She took his hand and squeezed it gently. The tired eyes closed once more and William slept on, comforted by her presence.

Richard looked across at her, his eyes brimming with tears. 'He doesn't even know I'm here.'

'He knows,' whispered Abby.

Allowed home for Christmas, William agreed willingly to all the doctor advised. 'Bed rest for another week, at least. No alcohol and no worries about work.' Leaving his patient comfortable in bed, the doctor had a final word with Richard. 'Whatever you do, make sure he's protected from stress. Your father's a sick man. This time, he was lucky.' These words struck a chill into Richard's heart.

In the drawing room, he found his mother sitting calmly by the blazing fire talking about decorating the house for Christmas. 'We're very late this year.'

'You heard, Mother, what the doctor said. No stress.'

She glanced up at her son. 'Yes, dear. Why are you looking at me like that?'

'Don't hurt him any more,' said Richard. 'That's all I'm asking.'

Milicent's brow creased, and her eyes darkened. 'Hurt him? What on earth are you talking about?'

'I know about your affair. Did you think you could keep it a secret?'

A shocked silence followed.

'I see,' Milicent said, at last. 'So it's Spy on Mother, is that it?'

'Of course not,' Richard said. 'We saw you that evening at The Valiant Sailor. Last Easter.' He paused, aware of an impending explosion. 'Though why you chose that pub I'll never know. You told me years ago that you and Father used to go there. Did you choose it deliberately? Or is it that you care so little for your husband, you didn't even make the connection?'

'How dare you?' Milicent's eyes flared. She rose, then, turning to confront her son, found she could not look into his eyes. 'His name is Brian Rivers. He ... well, we met when I was at a very low ebb. Your father was never here. It was inevitable that a Brian Rivers would come along one day. I found him attractive: someone I could talk to at last.' She lit a cigarette, inhaling deeply. 'I've often wondered how William found out. Now I know.'

Richard shook his head. 'You're wrong. If we could spot you both in Folkestone, don't you think you've been seen in Canterbury? This is a small place. Father probably saw you himself. He did not find out from either myself or Abby.'

'Abby!' Milicent said the name in a derisory manner. 'So you've been discussing your own mother with Abby, have you? Charming!'

'She thinks you blame her,' said Richard. 'But, believe me, she had no hand in it at all.'

Milicent stared at him for some time. 'Why does everything that happens in this house come down to Abby? There are five of us with cares of our own. Believe me,

Abby is the most insignificant of us all and I'm not the least concerned with what she thinks.'

'Why do you hate her so much, then?'

'Is that what she told you?' Milicent put the cigarette out. 'She's set us one against the other. Look what happened last New Year's Eve, for goodness' sake. Now please, Richard, no more.' Touching her brow, she frowned. 'My head aches. This has been a terrible week for me, yet instead of coming home to help, you pick a fight.'

'Sorry,' said Richard, feeling guilty. He walked towards the door, then paused. 'But what about this Rivers chap? How serious is it? Are you thinking of a divorce?'

'Of course not,' said Milicent. 'There's no question of such a thing.'

'Why not? Because you're worried about the effect it will have on Father, or ...'

'A scandal would ruin us,' Milicent broke in quickly.

Richard smiled thinly. 'I *was* going to say, "or because he's married too".' One look at his mother's face told him that he had guessed correctly.

'How did you know that?'

'I didn't. What about his wife? Has he any children? Just what are you getting into, Mother?'

'Enough of this inquisition.' Milicent turned on him angrily. 'What happens between Brian and myself is none of your business. Now, will you leave me in peace?'

Her son was not finished. 'Has it occurred to you that your behaviour has contributed to Father's heart attack?'

'That's a wicked thing to say!' said Milicent, going to the piano. 'If you must know, it's all over. I may be unhappy, but that shouldn't worry you.' Her fingers crashed down on the keyboard in loud discord, then moved in descending scales and arpeggios, venting all her anger onto the instrument she loved.

Richard left the room, doubting his mother had told

the truth when she insisted that her affair with Rivers was over.

'Trouble?'

Looking up, he saw Abby standing on the stairway staring over the banister at him. 'Yes,' he replied. 'But not the kind you had in mind.'

'What then?' She descended the stairs slowly.

Richard took her in his arms, and they stood listening to the angry music which filled the house. 'Don't worry about it,' he murmured, kissing her forehead, then burying his face in her sweet-smelling hair. 'It'll blow over. How's Father?'

'Comfortable, and asking for a cup of tea. He's upset to be missing the carols from King's College.'

'Christmas Eve!' The shock of it hit Richard. 'It's Christmas Eve and nothing's ready. We've no tree, no decorations, and I haven't wrapped a single present.'

'Well, there's food. Stella went to the butcher's to collect the turkey your mother ordered. Mrs Blackstock made a pudding and we've masses of sprouts, parsnips and potatoes.'

Richard sat beside the Aga watching as Abby prepared the tea things. There was a stillness about her which he found comforting. *Christmas Eve*, he thought. *Your father is very ill and you turn on your own mother. What kind of person are you, Richard Glenister?*

'Father doesn't have to miss the carols. Let's take the wireless up to him. Then we'll go and see if there's a Christmas tree left anywhere in Kent.'

Abby's eyes shone with emotion. 'Who would have thought we'd have been celebrating at all? Thank God, thank God!'

Richard rushed to her side and held her close. 'I know. It's been a bad time. Please God, it's over now. I only hope Mother realizes what a close call he's had.'

Later, as the lone choir-boy sang 'Once In Royal David's City', William Glenister lay back on his pillow, his eyes closed, a soft smile on his face. Now, at last, he knew it was Christmas.

Richard managed to find a small, scraggy tree and with Stella and Abby's help, decorated it in record time, but it was a subdued Christmas – not helped by Milicent's determination to produce copies of that year's *Tatler* for everyone to see.

'I knew you'd want to see the photographs of Samantha. She's in several issues. Look, this was her "coming-out" portrait. Isn't it lovely?'

Abby found herself unable to resist a peek – and rather wished she had not succumbed. Samantha looked like Royalty. Her hair had been cut and was combed flat to the head with soft curls framing the small, exquisitely chiselled features.

'The gown is a Steibel creation,' Milicent went on. 'And that diamond necklace she's wearing belonged to her mother's grandmother. An old family heirloom.' She went on, describing the Coming-Out Ball as the biggest event in the district for years.

'There were two huge marquees with lanterns crossing the drive, two dance bands, and the guest list ran into hundreds. I believe that half the aristocracy of Britain came to Ashton that evening.'

Richard grinned broadly. 'Oh, come now, the Fellowes may be landed gentry, but aristos they most certainly are not.'

'Don't you be so sure,' said Milicent, glaring at her son. 'Lady Fellowes is of noble birth.'

'How on earth do you know that?' asked Richard in amazement. His mother shot him a dark look. 'It's common knowledge to those who take an interest in these things.'

Stella sighed. 'Gosh, she's lucky. Fancy having a Coming-Out Ball! I must ask her what happened when she was presented at Court.'

'You'll do no such thing,' snapped Milicent. 'No

daughter of mine is going to show her ignorance in such matters. It simply isn't done.'

Stella turned to her brother mischievously. 'You're in the dog-house, you know. Samantha didn't say anything, but she was disappointed you didn't turn up for church this morning. Christmas morning, Richard!'

Milicent closed *The Tatler* and sighed. 'Yes, it was rather embarrassing. There was no need for you to stay behind with Abby. She's quite capable of ringing for a doctor should your father have needed one.'

'Everyone asked after him,' said Stella. 'And it wasn't politeness, they seemed really concerned.' She looked into the mid-distance, aware suddenly of just how much she cared for her father. 'Everyone seems to love him.'

Not everyone, thought Abby, and as her eyes met Richard's, she knew he shared the thought.

That evening when she went to say goodnight to her uncle he was anxious to talk.

'How's the art course going?' he asked.

'Hard work of course, but I love every minute of it,' said Abby. 'Soon I'll be studying pattern cutting, fitting, then colour and texture, and the history of costume. I can't wait, Uncle, and I mean to get my diploma. I won't let you down, I promise.' She went on talking to him quietly about her life in London. He seemed glad to hear she visited the Carrs regularly, yet clearly did not want her to get too involved with Eddy. But there was something in her uncle's eyes which told her he was ill at ease.

'I've talked far too long, so I'll say goodnight now.' As Abby moved away her uncle caught her hand and held her there. She sat down again.

William was clearly finding it hard to put his thoughts into words, and she waited patiently. 'Is your aunt treating you well?'

'Of course, Uncle. Why?'

'She hasn't been harsh on you,' he murmured. 'I mean . . . she hasn't said anything?'

'About the art school?' Abby smiled. 'No. She's accepted it at last. She's been too worried about you to bother with all that.'

William was visibly relieved. 'That's all right, then.' He closed his eyes, and murmured, 'Yes, I am tired now. I think I would like to sleep.'

Abby watched him for a few moments, feeling that there was something more, then she kissed him goodnight.

The day after Boxing Day, Milicent got Richard to drive her into Canterbury, and proceeded to 'take over' the management of Glenisters. Within twenty-four hours, she'd upset most of the staff. She ran checks on lines that had already been ordered then, deciding against several of these, insisted the orders be changed. She wanted to know the turn-over of each department, but would listen to no one, saying she needed their help, and not their hindrance.

William was constantly assured that all was well. Abby ran things at home, while Stella returned to London and her RADA friends, and Richard spent the rest of his holiday catching up on his Law. Before he left, he and Abby took William out for a drive to a village on the River Stour which had once been a Roman port, called Fordwich. The sun was bright and the day held the promise of spring, though January had not yet arrived. As they walked beside the river, William pointed out the medieval Town Hall and Crane House standing on the Stour.

'Haven't been here for years,' William said, walking slowly. 'There's always too much work. Then one day you find time has run out. It's a shock. I haven't done half the things I'd wanted to with my life. Good God, I've never been to Paris, or even York, come to that!' He shook his head. 'There's nothing like a heart attack to put things into perspective.' He turned to Richard and Abby. 'It's a short life, so make it a good one and take your happiness while you can.'

As they drove home, Abby was certain that they had her uncle's blessing.

When Richard left for Oxford, Abby decided to stay on and look after her uncle while Milicent managed the store. She worried about returning to London at all, but Mrs Blackstock put her mind at ease.

'Don't you worry, my dear. When your term starts, then off you go. I'll stay here until Mrs Glenister gets back in the evenings. And if I can't, I'll arrange for my daughter to pop in. I promise you, we won't leave him alone.'

Abby thanked her. 'He'll be back on his feet soon, the doctor says. I just hope he doesn't overdo things.'

'You're to stop worrying,' said Mrs Blackstock. 'He's in good hands.'

When the time came for Abby to say goodbye, William stood in the hallway with Milicent, as the taxi waited in the lane outside. 'Goodbye, chick,' he said fondly, kissing Abby on the cheek. 'You'll be back for Easter?'

'Don't be so silly, William,' said Milicent coldly. 'Abby has plenty of other places to spend Easter. She's young, with friends, and there are the Carrs.'

Both William and Abby stared at Milicent.

'Easter's a time for family,' said William.

'Nonsense. It's a time to travel. If you're well enough, I thought we might go to Paris. You said you'd never been there. Richard told me.' She turned to Abby. 'You'd best run along, dear, the meter's ticking over.'

As the taxi pulled away Abby looked back, and waved at her uncle. Didn't he realize that she'd just been turned out of the family home? Of course not. He hadn't seen the look in his wife's eyes, nor understood the meaning in her words. Paris, indeed! If Milicent went to Paris, it certainly wouldn't be with her ailing husband.

Leaning back on the leather seat, Abby watched the hedgerows rushing past and felt desolated. She had no home any more. She was leaving Ferndene for the last time.

Of course, she could ignore her aunt and bulldoze her way back into the family, but that wasn't her nature.

William did improve and by Easter was well enough to return to Glenisters, much to the relief of his staff. Knowing this, Abby told Richard she would not spend the holiday at Ashton Green.

'Well, then, neither shall I,' he said, his voice on the other end of the telephone loud and angry, much to Abby's distress. She was standing in the shabby hallway of the house in Lamb's Conduit Street, staring at the peeling wallpaper.

'You know I won't leave you, Abby.'

'But Uncle William will be very upset if you don't go home,' she said. 'Besides, where can we go? Susan's off to Bath for some huge family reunion, and you know how impossible things are here.' She was alluding to the strict rules laid down by the landlady who, although stipulating that the girls were to have no male visitors, had turned a blind eye to Richard on the understanding that both girls were to be in the flat when he came. 'I'll be all right. Go home to your father, Richard, or he'll be very hurt.'

But Richard could think of no-one except Abby. Since it was inconceivable that they could be alone in the flat under the eye of the nosy landlady, he swept her off to Cornwall as guests of Edward Markham and his parents.

The Markhams had a stone cottage on the Camel Estuary close to Padstow, and a ketch named *Moonraker*. For three days, they battled against Atlantic winds and waves to sail along the rugged coastline, mooring in fishing villages by night, then setting off on the morning tide to continue their journey.

At first, Abby had been afraid of the sea and the frail craft tossing and pitching on the Atlantic swell, wondering how people found such dubious pleasures enjoyable. She had never been so wet and cold, and longed for the night when she could look forward to sleeping in a dry bed.

146

When she slipped on deck, and thought she'd sprained her ankle, Richard was there at once to pick her up. She'd smiled up at him, expecting words of sympathy, but, after a cursory examination, he said: 'No broken bones. Watch where you put your feet next time. If you go overboard, we'll have the devil of a job finding you.' With that, he had walked away to check the rigging. What was it about boats, Abby wondered, that changed a quiet, considerate English gentleman into a domineering, short-tempered despot?

On a calm sunny evening they sailed back towards Padstow. Looking at the rugged shoreline, where breakers were crashing down on rocks, Abby had never seen anything so breathtaking. Then the cliffs gave way to sandy beaches and dunes, as they came into the estuary once more. Now she understood Richard's passion for Cornwall.

When the Markhams went off to visit friends in Plymouth, Abby and Richard explored Padstow's narrow and ancient streets. Later they drove north, and stopped to view the sea. The day was warm and the sun shone from a clear blue sky, turning the Atlantic to deep turquoise. A fishing boat rocked and swayed as it drew nearer to the coast; large herring gulls wheeled and circled above it, their cries filling the air. Arms about each other, Abby and Richard watched as the waves began to build, then rolled inland to explode against the cliff, sending spray so high they felt it on their faces.

'When you were at school in Cornwall,' said Abby, 'you discovered something about a wave which was larger than all others. The seventh wave.'

'Fancy you remembering that,' Richard said. 'I'd forgotten, myself.'

'You don't remember your letters to me?'

'I was a boy for heaven's sake,' Richard laughed. 'Now I come to think of it, we did count the waves. It seemed that the seventh was larger than the others.'

He looked at Abby, his heart full. She was so lovely,

and so vibrant, that the thought of spending his life with her made him dizzy with happiness. It was inconceivable that it could be any other way. He pulled her into his arms, and kissed her long and hard.

'I don't believe in your seventh wave,' said Abby at last. 'It's a myth.'

Rising to the challenge, Richard pointed seaward, saying, 'Let's put it to the test. A large wave has just come and gone, this is the first of the smaller ones. Watch how they build up.'

They watched in anticipation as the wave power built. The seventh began to break some way out, white foam tipping along the high wall of turquoise and moving towards them with menacing strength. Instinctively, they stepped backwards, heard the thunderous roar of its striking the breakwater, as a fountain of spray reached towards them.

Richard was grinning. 'Now then, Madam, have I made my point?'

'Coincidence, that's all,' murmured Abby, unconvincingly.

They spent the afternoon walking until ahead, in the distance, crowning the cliff-top, they saw the ruins of a castle.

'Tintagel,' said Richard, remembering the music he loved so much and the tales of knights, of round tables, of chivalry and love. 'King Arthur, King Mark, Tristan and Iseult ... there's a cauldron of legends right there.'

They climbed on. Then, taking out the sketch pad and pencils she always carried, Abby sat on a rock near a ruined archway, and set to work. 'Is it really King Arthur's castle?' she asked.

'He was supposed to have been born here. The castle belonged to the Duke of Tintagel, who was Arthur's father. And did you know we have our own Atlantis? Somewhere between Lands End and the Scilly Isles lies the lost land of Lyonesse. It was drowned by a tidal wave that wiped out a whole civilization. Even today sailors believe they can hear church bells from below the sea.'

Abby laughed and shook her head. 'Sailors, it seems, believe anything. What with seventh waves and ghostly churchbells, I'm surprised they have the nerve to leave shore. Come and sit for me in the archway.'

Richard settled back against the stone wall and gazed out to sea. The sun was still warm, but a dark bank of cloud was closing in from the horizon. 'Better hurry,' he said. 'There's a storm approaching.'

Abby sketched in the fair hair which curled slightly at the nape of Richard's neck. 'Wasn't Iseult King Mark's queen?'

'But she fell in love with Sir Tristan, and he with her. They drank a love potion, then ran off to live in the woods. One day King Mark came across their sleeping bodies, a naked sword between them. He banished Tristan from the land.'

'Don't move your head,' said Abby, frowning. 'Where did Tristan go?'

'Brittany,' Richard continued. 'He married, but because he still loved Iseult the marriage was never consummated. When he was wounded by a poisoned arrow, and lay dying, he sent a messenger for Queen Iseult, instructing him to hoist a white sail if she returned with him, but black if she did not.' He paused, thoughtful. 'She might have been standing here as the messenger arrived. Of course, she agreed to go. In Brittany, Tristan asked his wife to look at the approaching ship. Were the sails white or black? She told him the sails were black and Tristan turned his face to the wall and died. And Iseult, arriving too late to save him, died too, of grief.'

Abby paused and looked at Richard with loving eyes. 'Quite a romantic, aren't you?' she said, wondering what dramas had really been played out within those old walls. How much was truth and how much legend?

'Yes,' said Richard, reaching for her.

As ever with his touch, Abby felt a deep stirring, and longed for him with all her body. If only they could run off into woodlands to live out their lives in some mystic land! 'I wish this holiday would never end. I dread the thought of our parting again.' As she spoke dark clouds blocked out the sun, and an image of Milicent flashed through her mind. Shuddering, Abby clung to Richard for comfort.

The storm caught them long before they reached the village. A flash of fork lightning was followed by a loud crack of thunder and the sky exploded above them. They were soaked to the skin when they returned to the cottage. Abby was shivering, her hair in long wet strands about her shoulders.

'A hot bath for you,' Richard said, escorting her to the tiny bathroom. Then he stripped off in his bedroom, and put on a towelling dressing gown before returning to the warmth of the sitting room fire.

'Now I feel more human. Shall I run a bath for you?'

Richard turned to see Abby standing on the threshold wrapped in a blue towel, hair still damp and shoulders pink from the hot bath. Her face was radiant in the firelight, and her eyes shone like dark pools.

Richard could only stare at her, transfixed. She held his gaze. Then she was in his arms, clinging to him tightly as his mouth closed on hers, and both knew that this time they would not draw apart. Richard's ardour increased as his mouth moved down to her neck, then to her breasts, the towel falling from her body to reveal her smooth satin skin. Sweeping her up in his arms, Richard carried Abby upstairs to his bed.

Kissing her eyes, Richard stroked her breasts gently, feeling the nipples harden under his touch. His hands moved on to her firm belly, and she sighed and stirred to each caress. He pulled back for a moment in wonder. She was so beautiful, with her hair tumbling about the pillow, her eyes dark and wild, offering herself to him. He brought his mouth down on hers and they kissed.

Inflamed by desire, Abby thrilled to his every touch, as their passion heightened and engulfed them. She arched her body to his, gasping as he entered her. Then slowly they moved in unison, giving themselves up to each other, until her body quivered and exploded in one huge convulsive moment of ecstasy. In that moment, they were as one.

Afterwards, they lay in each other's arms, listening to the rain beating on the roof. It was a moment of bliss. Abby sighed and stretched with all the contentment of a cat as Richard gazed at her.

'God, I love you. Until now, I hadn't realized how much. I wish we could stay like this for ever.'

Abby stroked his broad, strong chest. '"Take your happiness while you can". Do you remember your father telling us that? Why did he say it, if not because he knew about us? And knowing, wasn't he saying that we should marry now, and not wait?'

Seeing the happiness fade from Richard's eyes as the old anxieties took command once more, Abby felt despair. She'd spoilt the most precious moment of her life by reaching for the moon. Of course, there could be no thought of marriage until Richard was safely called to the Bar. 'It's just ... I'm so afraid if we don't marry soon, then we never will,' she whispered.

'That's nonsense, darling.' Richard touched the tears falling down her cheeks. 'Of course we'll be married. Nothing can prevent that, save death itself. And we're too young to die.'

How could she make him understand this terrible foreboding? thought Abby. It had plagued her for years. She pulled him down to her, and passion engulfed their bodies once more.

On a wet day in May, the King opened the Festival of Britain and thousands gathered on the South Bank of the Thames to see Britain's contribution to future technology.

Home on leave, Eddy had managed to persuade Abby to go with him to the exhibition. He spent ages before the mirror, Brylcreeming his black hair, and combing back the offending lock. Glad to be out of khaki, he wore his light grey suit with a white shirt, and had polished his shoes until they shone. Although he had seen Abby twice since the cold January morning when she lay sick in his bed, the prospect of seeing her again set his stomach churning.

Eddy waited nervously on Westminster Bridge until he saw her alight from a bus. Wearing a cream cotton dress, with her hair in a pony-tail, Abby came towards him, laughing with delight. They toured flag-bedecked pavilions, and marvelled at the exhibits in the Dome of Discovery. The Skylon was attracting the most attention. Towering high in the sky like a long slim pencil, it seemed to be suspended in air.

'Isn't it marvellous,' said Eddy, with gleaming eyes. 'It's the future. A streamlined, efficient future with social equality, and a better standard of living for all.'

Abby was still gazing up at the Skylon. 'But what does it do?' she asked. She found it all too modern to take seriously.

There was even a new jet airliner, called The Comet. If this was the future, she mused, then H. G. Wells was welcome to it. Even the concert hall seemed sparse, though her friends had said the acoustics were perfect. Concerts were hardly Eddy's idea of a rollicking good night out, so she'd see when Richard took her.

An engineer, Eddy browsed through the machine displays which Abby did not understand, then looked bored when she lingered in a fashion booth. She wished Richard was with her instead of Eddy, and felt guilty at her selfishness. But Richard was preparing for exams, and their only communication had been by telephone. She missed him beyond all endurance and lived on the memory of that brief moment when they had become as one.

'How about a bite?' said Eddy, sensing her lack of

enthusiasm and putting it down to hunger. He led her into one of the pavilions where they ate eggs, sausage and chips. During the meal Eddy spoke endlessly of his time in the army.

'I'm glad I made it into the REMES,' he said. 'At least they train you to become skilled. Mickey Carter, my old mate at the factory, is a good engineer, but the stupid PSO sent 'im to the Catering Corps. Can you cop that? I mean, 'ow bloody stupid can you get?' He waved his fork at Abby. 'Anyway, I'm lucky, so I shouldn't complain. I'm learning to drive, as well. When I'm demobbed I'll buy an old jalopy. I'm trying to save, but on four shillings a day it's bloody nigh impossible, especially since I send Mum most of that.' Why was he talking on and on like this? Eddy wondered. Was it because of those large green eyes that were staring at him so intensely? God, she unnerved him.

'Tell me about yourself, Abby. You know, the art school and such. Do you like it there?'

Abby spoke happily about her hopes for the future, her friends, her lessons and Susan's near-lethal attempts to save money. 'Thank God, Richard was there, otherwise it would have been simply awful.' She was still talking about him twenty minutes later, failing to see the hurt in Eddy's eyes. 'It's going to be years before we can marry,' she went on.

Feeling crushed, Eddy managed a light smile. 'But then you'll be the wife of a barrister.'

'And a fashion designer,' said Abby. 'I don't intend to be just a wife.'

'Not the life I would 'ave expected for you when we used to play on those old bomb sites.'

Abby laughed at the memory. 'What a ruffian I was then! It was your fault, Eddy Carr. You and all those rough little kids you called your "gang".'

They walked around the exhibition until it was dark and the whole of the South Bank exploded into a blaze of

lights. Cries of 'Oooh!' and 'Aaah!' echoed around the
site as the Skylon shone like a beacon in the sky. This
was the first time Abby had seen London lit up. It was
beautiful and fantastic. They quick-stepped to the strains
of a dance band, then stood gazing over the parapet into
the dark waters of the Thames below.

Abby's thoughts drifted to the past once more. 'Do you
remember those nights in the Chislehurst Caves?'

Eddy smiled. 'The little church and the huge fans which
kept us all from suffocating.'

'And the Druid's Altar. We lit a candle there, the night
before I left for Canterbury. Do you remember?'

Eddy stared down into the water. 'When you promised
to marry me.'

'I know,' laughed Abby. 'The things children do!' She
turned, expecting him to share her amusement, but he
wasn't even smiling. Suddenly Abby wanted the earth to
swallow her up. What a stupid fool she was, prattling on
about Richard with no thought for Eddy's feelings!
Confused and dismayed, she shivered in the cool air and
ulled her cardigan more closely about her. 'I should have
brought a coat.'

'Come on,' said Eddy quietly, 'I'll take you 'ome.'

Because of the late hour, and knowing Susan had gone
to Bath for the weekend, Eddy thought it best to take
Abby back to Victoria Place for the night. He seemed
so relaxed and talkative on the tram that Abby decided
she must have misread his emotions earlier.

Evelyn was still up, and not at all surprised to see Abby
enter the house with her son. She kissed her warmly. Abby
told her about their day while Eddy went to make some
tea. At last, Evelyn yawned, and announced that she was
off to bed. 'I'll just change the sheets on Eddy's bed –'

'No.' Abby was firm. 'Eddy only has forty-eight hours.
He must sleep in his own bed.'

There was the usual gentle argument, but Abby had
her way. Evelyn went up the stairs to her bedroom,

leaving Eddy and Abby sitting before the dying embers of the fire.

'Does your mother know about Richard, and what he means to me?' Abby asked, at length. Sometimes she felt Evelyn expected her and Eddy to be more than friends.

'Didn't you tell her?' asked Eddy.

Abby shook her head. 'Well, no. It's just not a subject that's ever been raised. It's ... well ...'

'Difficult?' Eddy was looking at her strangely, almost accusingly.

'It is really,' said Abby. 'You see, I sometimes have the feeling that she thinks –' She paused awkwardly. 'Well, that she thinks that you and I are courting. I was hoping you could let something slip, in a casual way, to show her how things really stand.'

Eddy's dark eyes flickered and once again that unruly lock of hair fell over his brow. He pushed it back in an abrupt gesture that said more than his words. 'Yeah, I'll do that. Don't worry about it.'

She *was* hurting him, Abby knew for certain now. But what else could she do? She cared for him, but there was no comparison with her love for Richard. Yet caring made her feel responsible for him in some strange way. He went up to bed, leaving her staring sadly into the fading embers of the fire.

Richard did not share Eddy's enthusiasm for the Festival, likening it to the emperors of ancient Rome, providing a good spectacle to distract the people from the truth.

'Which is, that this country is still almost bankrupt and the Labour Government hasn't a clue how to get Britain back on its feet.'

Abby smiled. 'If you feel that strongly about things then you should stand for election one day.'

'That's exactly what I intend to do,' he replied. 'But even an MP needs a career. After all, you can be ousted at any time. If I have a law practice, then I've something else going for me.'

Earlier that evening Richard had taken Abby to the Festival Gardens in Battersea Park where, from the top of the Ferris wheel, they had looked out over the sprawling fairground, lit up like fairyland. They had wandered along treewalks, looked at the open-air sculptures, bought oranges from girls dressed as Nell Gwynne, and behaved like children.

Richard put his arm around her and kissed the top of her head. 'I do admit it's been a wonderful two days. Not like Cornwall, of course, but wonderful just the same. Next week we'll get tickets for the Festival Hall. I just hope to God we get a chance to be alone.'

Abby turned away, glad it was dark, so he could not read the worry in her eyes. She needed no doctor to tell her she was pregnant. She had missed two periods, felt nauseous in the mornings and kept having dizzy spells. Last night she had cried into her pillow, worried that she would have to give up St Martin's. And how could she tell Richard? He would be as shattered as she was, but with a baby on the way, they would have to marry – and marry soon. Unless her aunt and uncle came to her rescue, Richard would have to leave Oxford and find a job. How could she tell him? As it was, he was full of plans for the summer vacation.

'One of my friends has invited us to a villa in Nice. So how about it?' He stared down at her. 'Who knows, we might even get a chance to be alone again.'

Abby stuttered nervously. 'Oh, Richard, ... you ought to know ... we can't afford it. We can't afford to go away.'

'Nonsense,' said Richard. 'We'll be living in their villa, rent-free. We only need enough for spending, and I'll provide that.'

As they walked back to the car, Abby's courage deserted her. 'You go with them,' she said. 'It's not often you get

156

the chance, and your allowance won't run to both of us junketing in the South of France.'

Richard shook his head. 'You're coming, because I'm not going without you. Now get a passport. You'll need your birth certificate. And not another word, my love.'

Richard telephoned his mother as soon as he got back to Oxford, anxious to organize his summer holiday. 'Look, I need a passport. I'm off to France at the start of the holidays. Can you send me my birth certificate?'

Milicent's hand froze on the receiver, her mind spinning. 'Yes. Of course. France! But darling, this idiotic Government has cut the foreign travel allowance to twenty-five pounds. That won't get you far. Forget the whole thing and come home here after your exams.'

'I'll be staying with friends. Look, you'd better send it by registered post, just in case.'

'I'll bring it to you myself,' said Milicent, her voice sounding thin and shaky. 'I'd love to see Oxford. How about Tuesday?'

Richard's heart sank at the prospect of his mother arriving at the college. 'Well, that's a bit awkward. I've got a lecture and a couple of tutorials.'

'Saturday, then,' said Milicent.

'I'm revising, Mother.' There was a long silence. Richard sighed, defeated. 'All right, Saturday then. I was going to London, but ...'

'London? What were you going to do there?'

'I promised to meet Abby. We were going to the cinema.'

'Well then, you'll have to cancel, won't you,' came the icy reply. Milicent replaced the receiver, and stood there for a long time staring ahead into an emptiness that was like the emptiness of her life.

She lit a cigarette, and inhaled thoughtfully. All she lived for now was her son. If she lost him, then her life might as well be over. Damn that Abby! Why on earth was he going to London to be with her? She had hoped, with Richard at Oxford, and Abby enmeshed in her world of art, that their little romance was a thing of the past.

She wondered now about the sailing holiday at Easter. Richard had said they were with a party of friends. Was it possible they'd been alone together? Had her son been lying to her? If so, things were more serious than she'd realized. It was time to put a stop to it, and she would have to play a very careful hand indeed.

It was even possible that the very thing she feared the most, could be used to her advantage now.

'But Richard will marry you,' said Susan for the umpteenth time, in an effort to comfort Abby. 'I don't understand why you won't tell him.'

Abby shook her head tearfully. She had just learned from her doctor that she was in her ninth week of pregnancy, and felt nothing but horror now that it had been confirmed. 'But it's all too soon! We have our studies, our ambitions. I'm going to have to give up mine, and he'll feel that he must give his up too. Then, he'll blame me. I daren't tell my aunt or my uncle. They'd be horrified.'

'Why should Richard blame you? It takes two to make a baby.' Susan sighed and then said what she dared not say earlier. 'There is another way out. I don't know the first thing about it, but I could ask a friend at the college.'

Abby looked at her in horror. '*Abortion?* Kill our child?' She shook her head quickly. 'How can you even suggest such a thing?' Her mind fled to Cornwall. The child within her had been conceived in the goodness of their deep love and, whatever the cost, that child would be wanted and loved in return.

'I'm sorry,' said Susan quickly.

Abby smiled at her. 'No. You mustn't be. If I can't talk to you, then who can I talk to? I'm so mixed up and frightened. Everything's changing so fast. We'll have to get married. Aunt Milicent will go mad. She's determined Richard should marry Samantha and climb up the social ladder. Uncle William will be hurt that I brought Richard down, when he's spent so much on his education. How are we going to live? Oh, there's so much, Susan, so much more to having a baby than just ... well, having it.'

'What you and Richard think is all that matters. You're the ones who have to plan and from what you've told me about your uncle, I'm sure he'll help. Richard won't have to leave university. You'll live at Ferndene and then later ...'

'Ferndene!' Abby cut Susan off. 'No, it's out of the question. The very idea of Aunt Milicent glowering at me and making the kind of remarks she would constantly make, puts the whole thing out of court. So, you see, Richard would have to work.'

A long silence followed while Abby fell into dark confusion. Susan might be confident and reassuring, but she didn't know how strange Richard had been lately. Ever since his mother had visited him, he'd been a changed man, distant to the point of cool indifference, and Abby could not understand it. On Saturday, they had gone to Lyons Corner House as usual, but he said hardly a word, and seemed taken by surprise whenever she spoke to him. When she questioned his mood, the only answer had been the worried look in his eyes. She felt completely shut out. Was it something she had said? Or the age-old reason all women feared, that having once given themselves, they were no longer desirable? For them this could not be true. Richard loved her as deeply as she loved him and their lovemaking had strengthened this love, not weakened it. *He couldn't have turned against me,* she kept telling herself. *Not Richard. Not after all these years. Please God, don't let him stop loving me!*

Throughout June Abby slept little, and had a hard time keeping up with her work. Each day she returned to the flat hoping in vain for a letter from Richard, or a telephone message.

'It's his exams,' Susan assured her. 'He must be under

159

enormous pressure. After all, if he fails, then he's out.'

Abby looked at her. 'You mean he doesn't go back for the second year if he fails this year?'

Susan nodded. 'That's why he hasn't been in touch. He's burning the midnight oil. Give him a chance, and stop imagining things. Everything will sort itself out in good time.'

'No, it won't,' cried Abby. 'I'll never get my diploma now. I'll have to leave.'

'Now look,' said Susan firmly, 'when you and Richard are married you tell the school. Then, after the baby's born, you can continue your studies.'

Abby shook her head. 'As if they would let me. A married woman with a small baby? Anyway, Uncle would never pay my fees. He'll be too angry with me.'

'Stop crying,' said Susan. 'It's not the end of the world.'

'Yes it is. It is!' wailed Abby letting the tears flow. 'It's the end for both of us. I can't go to the college with a young baby to look after, and he can't go on studying with a wife and child to house and feed. We're finished, Susan. Finished. Perhaps he's guessed and that's why he doesn't want to see me any more.'

At that moment the telephone rang and Abby rushed from the armchair saying: 'It's him. It's him at last.' She was down the stairs in no time. 'Richard? Hello, Richard, is that you?'

There was a long pause, then Milicent's voice answered. 'Abby? I wish you wouldn't shout so. It's your aunt speaking.'

Abby's spirits plunged to new depths. 'Oh, it's you. I thought . . .'

'Yes, I know what you thought. Sorry to have disappointed you. How is Richard?'

'I don't know,' whispered Abby weakly. 'I haven't seen him for some time now.'

When Milicent spoke again, she sounded quite cheerful.

'Now listen, my dear, I must speak to you. I'll be in London on Saturday, so why don't we meet in Harrods for coffee? Say around ten thirty?'

Abby could hardly believe her ears. Her aunt wanted to meet her for coffee? Had the world gone completely mad? 'Yes, Aunt. Of course. Harrods on Saturday.' A terrible thought struck Abby. 'It's Uncle, isn't it. He's ill?'

'I'd hardly be coming to London if he was, now would I? I'm staying with Stella, but before I return to Canterbury I wish to discuss something with you.'

Abby put down the receiver, thinking Aunt Milicent was not good news and would bring none.

On the Saturday morning, as Abby was dressing carefully for this strange appointment, a letter came from the Carrs. Abby tore open the envelope and read Evelyn's familiar hand. Eddy was coming home that same weekend and, if Abby was at a loose end, they would all love her to come for dinner on Sunday. Abby could have wept. Dear old Victoria Place. Right now it seemed a haven from this nightmare. Nothing ever happened there. Nor were girls like her expected to get pregnant. That was the preserve of the cheap girls, the ones Eddy kept away from. Suddenly Abby felt like a leper. They would all look down on her. Much as she wanted to go on Sunday and be in the bosom of that loving family, she would feel dishonest, a cheat. They were decent people who held strong views. She placed the letter in her handbag as a reminder to turn up at the Carrs on time and pretend all was well.

Abby saw from her reflection she was looking her best. The blue cotton dress with cap sleeves and full ballerina-length skirt looked suitably demure with a matching blue skull cap and white gloves. Susan nodded in approval.

'Wish someone would take me for coffee and gateau in Harrods,' she said.

'You don't know Aunt Milicent,' said Abby, picking up her small handbag. 'There's something wrong. I'm the last person on earth she'd choose to have coffee with.'

Susan was holding a letter. 'Daddy's written to say we can let this place go. He's found a flat in Maida Vale. I know it's a long way from the college . . .' She paused as the sudden reality hit her. 'Sorry, I wasn't thinking. But it's only two weeks until the end of the term so I'll have to speak to our landlady today.'

Abby stared at her own reflection, and murmured, 'At the start of next term . . . where will I be then?'

Knightsbridge was bustling with Saturday morning shoppers, and Harrods thronged with well-dressed people as Abby pushed through the doors of the Food Hall. She wondered if she was too early, then saw Milicent standing by the coffee counter arguing with one of the assistants.

'Hello,' said Abby quietly, watching as the assistant ground a mixture of coffee beans into the blend which her aunt liked so much.

'Oh, there you are,' said Milicent, her mind taken up with the beans. 'That's right, a little more of the Kenya, I think. No, no, not that much, just . . . yes, that's right.' She took the coffee and paid for it, tutting to herself about the service. Taking Abby by the arm she led her towards the lifts, saying: 'The best store in London and I still have to fight to get things done!' She looked about her and smiled nevertheless. 'Still, it's good to come here. Have you seen the smoked salmon? It's no use taking that all the way home.' She paused and peered at her niece critically. 'You look very pale, Abby. Is there something wrong?'

'I'm fine, thank you,' said Abby quietly, getting into the lift. She studied her aunt, approving of the quiet green dress with the bolero top. But Milicent's taste in hats was too matronly by half.

The restaurant was already filling up when they arrived. After the waiter had escorted them to a table Milicent removed her gloves and asked if Abby would like some chocolate gateau. 'It's very good. Real cream, not that awful synthetic stuff you get everywhere else.'

Abby shook her head and settled for biscuits instead, wondering how long she would have to wait for Milicent's news. Her aunt spoke of this and that, remarking on a blouse she wanted to buy and discussing Stella's progress at the Academy. 'She's extremely talented, of course. I think she'll go far.' When coffee came, Milicent poured and then allowed a suitable amount of silence to fall between them before coming to the point. 'Now then, my dear. There's something I have to tell you. Oh, I promised I wouldn't, but that was some time ago, and I can see now that it just won't work. You have a right to know and I must put your considerations before mine.'

Abby had almost finished her coffee, and was now staring at her aunt with the cup poised at her lips. 'What is it? What's wrong?'

Milicent smiled and gave a little sigh. 'Have another cup first. You might need it.' She poured a second cup for both of them and lit up a cigarette. 'I would like to break it to you gently, but there really is no way.' She was using the sweet condescending tone she deemed to be diplomatic.

Abby was now visibly alarmed. 'Then tell me! Please — don't keep me in suspense like this.'

Milicent shrugged. 'William is not your uncle, my dear. He is your father.'

At first the words barely sank in, and Abby just shook her head. 'My father died at Dunkirk.' Why was her aunt saying such things?

'The man who married your mother died at Dunkirk, but she was two months pregnant when they married. I have it straight from William that you are his daughter. He told me last autumn, just before you came to London. It was a shock, I don't mind telling you, but I'm not one to bear a grudge. It isn't your fault that you're ... well, that you're illegitimate.' Seeing Abby's stunned expression she went on quickly. 'Your mother was going out with his cousin, but that didn't stop William from using her as a one night stand after she had drunk a little more than was good for her one riotous night. Of course, this was long before I met him. He was footloose and very fancy-free. Anyway, he left your mother and London, and only found out later that you were his daughter. How on earth she passed you off as premature beats me, but it seems that she did.'

Abby shook her head in sheer disbelief. 'I don't believe you. It's all lies! Filthy rotten lies. I don't know why you're saying such things. I'm leaving.' As she stood up her aunt gazed around nervously, and bade her sit down again.

'I'm not finished. Hear me out, please,' Milicent whispered. 'Do you think I'm getting pleasure out of this? Anyway, it seemed best that William should say nothing and let Eileen's husband think you were his own daughter.' She smiled wryly. 'Knowing William, I think he was only too glad to be rid of the problem. Men are like that. They don't want to know about fatherhood. All they want is a good time. They're all the same, my dear; don't let anyone tell you different.'

Abby was trembling, but her aunt went on. 'Anyway, when William heard that his cousin was dead, he wrote to your mother offering financial help with your upbringing. He said he would visit her, but when he got there it was too late. House and family had been blown to pieces. He assumed you were dead, too. Later, when he learned you had survived, it seemed to him that God was giving him a second chance. So he brought you into our home under the guise of niece. He had no choice. He knew there was no way I would allow his bastard offspring over the threshold. Things were bad enough as they were.' The sweetness had left the voice now, and these last words were uttered in bitterness.

Abby remembered a long forgotten scene. She was little, and caught in an air-raid. Her mother had given her a letter. She could see Evelyn Carr reading it by the light of the paraffin lamp even now. William had been the visitor her mother had not wanted her to meet. She began to feel sick again and murmured, 'Oh God ... dear God.'

'There's no need to look so shocked, girl,' snapped Milicent. 'Of course, your father and I had a blazing row when it all came out. I was shattered, I don't mind telling you. Wouldn't you be furious at such deception? Still you've had a good home with us, so you've no reason to feel hard done by. And you must understand this is extremely embarrassing. I found it very hard at Christmas, and there's always the chance that Richard or Stella might find out, which would be terrible, not only for you but for your . . . your father.'

Hearing Richard's name sent Abby into shock, and her body began to fail her. The noise in the room grew louder and she became hot as the room got darker. Something cold was pressed to her lips. Water found its way into her mouth, and she could hear her aunt's voice saying, 'Drink, Abby. Don't let's have a scene, please, dear.'

Obediently, Abby drank, and slowly the room returned to normal. The anxious waiter hovered and suggested that the young lady might like to rest in a quieter room.

'Thank you, but no,' said Milicent. 'I don't think that will be necessary. It was the heat, that's all. My niece is fine now.' Milicent looked long and hard at Abby, aware her careful words had done the trick, just as her words to Richard had done: two different truths for two different people. With any luck, she had parted them for ever. 'For goodness' sake, do pull yourself together, girl. I realize it's a bit of a shock, but it hasn't been easy for me either.' Milicent glanced at her watch and made a tutting sound. 'Is that the time? I must fly, if I'm to buy that blouse. You just sit for a bit longer,' she said, glancing at Abby's ashen face. Then she was moving across the restaurant and out through the doors.

Richard was her brother! The appalling thought echoed through Abby's head without mercy. She was carrying her brother's child. It was a nightmare, surely; just a nightmare and she would awaken soon. The waiter, hovering discreetly, brought Abby to reality. She was in Harrods, and her aunt really had told her this dreadful thing. Shakily she stood up and staggered towards the door.

She and Richard had lain together and made love. Incest! The worst of sins. And the child in her womb was the result of this sin. Like a sleep-walker she went out into the busy Brompton Road.

The traffic and crowds of people confused Abby. She had to get home. How? Which way was home? She dimly remembered arriving by the Underground. But now she needed air; she needed to be outside. If she walked long enough she might leave this awful nightmare behind her. As she stepped off the kerb, there was a screeching of tyres and a woman's scream as the taxi that had unsuccessfully tried to avoid Abby crashed into a lamp-post.

Abby lay on the ground, enveloped by darkness.

CHAPTER EIGHT

It was nearly one thirty when the black police car turned into Victoria Place and stopped in front of number nine.

Inside Eddy sat at the table with the rest of the family, eating his meal in silence, having just learned that Abby would spend the following day with them. He was caught on the horns of a dilemma. His best course lay in not seeing Abby again, yet he longed for her to walk through that door. If only his mother would leave well alone, but here she was, talking happily about Abby, and looking across the table at him with those sharp eyes that said, *'Why don't you get on with it?'*

It was Evelyn who answered the door. Confronted by the police, she stared in shocked silence, as they spoke of the unconscious girl in the Charing Cross Hospital, with no identification except a letter from this address.

Stifling a gasp of horror, Evelyn turned to see Eddy standing behind her. 'It's Abby. She's been in an accident!'

'How bad?' he asked, his heart pounding with fear.

'We can't tell you that, sir. If you would be so kind as to come with us?'

In a state of deep anxiety, Evelyn and Eddy sat in the police car, hardly speaking, save to answer questions. Eddy mentioned the aunt and uncle in Canterbury, suggesting that news of the accident would be better coming from him than the police.

'She's very close to us, you see,' sobbed Evelyn. 'I practically raised the girl. And one day, God willing, she'll ... well ... she'll be my daughter-in-law.'

Embarrassed, Eddy gave his mother his handkerchief,

knowing this was not the time to tell her how wrong she was.

Abby was lying in a long, dreary ward. Her face was bruised and swollen; her head and left arm were bandaged, and her ribs had been strapped. Both Evelyn and Eddy were taken aback when they saw her.

'She's been badly concussed,' the nurse explained.

As Abby opened her eyes, Evelyn kissed her gently, forcing a smile through her tears. 'Well, now, aren't you the daft one. Fancy stepping off the kerb without looking! Never mind, luv, you're gonna be just fine.'

Eddy took Abby's hand. Until this moment, he had not realized just how much she meant to him. His heart was too full for words. When at last, he found his voice, he tried to sound cheerful. 'I was 'oping we'd meet this weekend, but not like this. I told the police I'd ring your uncle.'

Abby's fingers tightened on his hand and her lips moved, though she made no sound. Only when Eddy leaned close did he hear her whisper: 'No. Please, no. They mustn't know.'

'Of course they must know,' he replied, then seeing her agitation increase Eddy thought it best to play along. 'All right. Whatever you say.'

Abby now was trying to say something else. He put his ear to her lips once more and heard her faint whisper.

'Susan. Tell Susan, she must come. Not Richard ... please ... please.'

'Susan! Right. I'll go to the flat and find her.' Eddy squeezed Abby's hand. 'We'll be back. You rest now and get well.'

Coming out of the ward, Eddy and Evelyn found the doctor waiting to see them. A grey-haired man in his late fifties, he had seen enough of human nature to make him despair. Young people today, he thought, had no morals. He looked at Eddy as he spoke. 'She's had a very lucky escape. The concussion is only superficial, but she has three cracked ribs and a broken arm. Did you know she was pregnant?' Seeing Eddy's shocked expression, he sighed. 'Nine weeks, at least. It's a miracle she didn't lose the child, but there's still a risk. She'll be in the hospital for a while. When she leaves, she'll need care.'

Evelyn was staring at her son with angry eyes. 'That's no problem, doctor, she can stay with us. We love 'er and will look after 'er. She's our responsibility now.'

Feeling poleaxed, Eddy walked from the hospital with his mother, not knowing what to say. It was Richard's baby, of course. But did he know? Abby had been so anxious that he should not be contacted.

'Abby doesn't want her family to know about the accident,' he said. 'Don't ask me why. But, considering her condition, I reckon we should do as she asks, don't you?'

Evelyn glared at him. 'Don't talk to me of her condition! I never thought I'd live to see the day when my own son couldn't be trusted ...'

'Stop, Mum,' said Eddy. 'We'll talk about this later. I'm off to find Susan − Abby wants her there. Can you find your way 'ome all right?'

'I think I know London well enough to find my way back to Bermondsey,' Evelyn replied. 'And I don't care what Abby says about not telling 'er uncle. She's in no position to know what she wants.'

'She knows exactly what she's saying. I don't want you telling anyone yet about the baby. Let's wait until Abby's better.'

Evelyn looked at him sharply. 'All I can say is I thought better of my son, really I did. But I see it's as much a shock to you as me. She should 'ave told you, the silly girl. Still, that's the least of our worries.' She bit her lip. 'We can't keep the accident from Mr Glenister. It's not right, no matter what Abby says.'

'At least wait until she can explain herself.'

Seeing his mother safely onto the bus, Eddy headed for the Underground, his anger growing. It was obvious that

Abby had told Richard about the baby and that he had turned his back on her and his responsibilities. It was always the way with privileged coves like him. Clearly there'd been a terrible scene and Abby, in a distraught state, had hurled herself before an oncoming taxi. Never in his life had Eddy felt the need for violence, but now he felt like killing Richard with his bare hands.

The Glenisters would disown Abby, as Richard had done, and she would have nowhere to turn, save to him. The thought warmed Eddy: a dream come true. She'd try to live through this alone, but he wouldn't let her. Not because he pitied her, but because he loved her.

She *must* turn to him, and his mother *must* go on believing Abby was carrying her grandchild. For himself, Eddy cared little. All that mattered to him was that Abby and her baby were loved and protected.

But would she let him be her husband and protector, when she loved someone else?

In his room at Merton College, Richard reread the letter he'd written to Abby, then threw it into the wastepaper basket. It was his fifth attempt. Her letters had called for reassurance. Reassurance of his love he could give, but nothing more. From the day of his mother's visit he had been like a dead man. He'd wanted his birth certificate, and she had brought him the Sword of Damocles. When he had worried about the effect of her news on Abby, his mother had been shaken to the point of fury. He had then explained their deep love and desire to marry.

'If that's truly the case, you must reveal nothing of what I've just told you,' Milicent had said. 'If you don't wish to lose her love, let things bide awhile. The longer you leave things, the better for both of you. Trust me, darling. I have only your happiness in mind.'

And so Richard said nothing, and had gone through agonies of doubt when they were together, and sleepless nights when they were apart. Did they have a future together now, or not? He pulled another sheet of writing paper towards him, then started again, ending with:

If you cannot find it in your heart to love me after this, then don't bother replying. I'd rather not read words of goodbye. But know this. Whatever you decide, I shall love you always.

Richard addressed the letter to the flat in Lamb's Conduit Street, then left it on the mantelpiece to post, certain he was doing the right thing.

Abby lay in the hospital bed, her heart broken and her mind in turmoil. *Richard is my brother.* It was all she could think about. Incest! How could she look Richard in the face again? What had once been so beautiful and right, was now ugly and wrong. And what of the child? A child made by her and Richard should be beautiful, but a child born of incest would be mentally and physically crippled.

She turned her face to the wall, wincing with pain at the movement. No one must ever know, she thought. Not Susan, not Eddy, and especially not Richard. *Richard!* She could never see him again, never. Far better to let him think she no longer loved him than to reveal the truth.

It was not until the following evening that Susan was allowed to see Abby. She sat at her friend's bedside, trying not to show her anxiety.

'I couldn't find any grapes but I brought some apples and oranges. It'll help with the hospital stodge.'

Abby smiled at her, feeling a little more human. 'Don't tell Richard where I am. I don't want him to find me ever again.'

'Oh, don't be so silly,' said Susan. 'When Richard hears you've been in an accident, it'll take a lot more than Susan Hillman to stop him from finding you.'

'We're finished,' said Abby sharply. 'I cannot see him

again, and I don't want him to find me. Please, Susan, I'm begging you. Do as I ask.'

'All this has something to do with your aunt, hasn't it? You went off to meet her and something happened. What?'

'I can't tell you.'

'Then how can I understand?' said Susan helplessly. 'I mean, Richard is bound to turn up at the flat, and I'm to say I don't know where you are? He'll never believe me.' She stared at her friend's face, pale beneath the bandaged brow, and decided that it was the concussion talking, not Abby. Perhaps it was best to play along and keep the patient calm. Patting Abby's hand gently, she said: 'All right. I'll do as you ask.'

'Thank you,' said Abby, breathing a deep sigh of relief.

'Eddy's taken a lot of your things back to his home,' Susan said. 'He told me that they were going to look after you, so I'll be moving into the flat at Maida Vale soon.'

An awkward silence followed this remark as both girls pondered Abby's uncertain future. The insecurity of it all appalled Susan. To be alone in the world with an illegitimate baby was the ultimate nightmare for any woman. 'You know, if you can't find anywhere ... later ...' she paused awkwardly, knowing such decisions were not hers to make, '...then you can always come to me.'

Abby smiled at her. 'Thank you. But that's a long way off. I can't think that far ahead just now. All I do know is that Richard mustn't find me.'

Susan looked at the hideous bruise on Abby's face. 'Does it hurt very much?'

'Yes.' Abby was not referring to her injuries.

'Still, you're lucky to be alive.'

Abby's eyes watered. '*Lucky to be alive!*' That was rich, when all she wanted was to die. She had cheated death once before. Had God spared her just for this? It would have been better to have perished in the rubble with her mother and sister.

As Susan left the hospital she felt sad, yet hopeful, for surely two people as deeply in love as Abby and Richard could not be parted for long.

Four days later, Richard plucked up enough courage to post his letter to Abby. It was picked up by the landlady in Lamb's Conduit Street and promptly ignored. She had no forwarding address for the girls and when neither of them came by for post, she grew tired of seeing the letter on the hall table, and threw it into the dustbin.

Though in torment mentally, Abby made good progress physically and was finally released after eight weary days in hospital. But it was a different girl who came back to the house in Victoria Place: a girl Evelyn scarcely knew. Abby said hardly a word, and spent hours staring into emptiness. Heedless of the world about her, she did not eat and rarely slept. Evelyn became so worried, she wrote to her son asking him to come home. Claiming Abby as his fiancée who was very ill after a road accident, Eddy managed to get compassionate leave.

Still in his uniform, he just stood in the sitting room, shocked. Abby was seated in the fireside chair, staring into an empty grate. Her hair was unkempt and in need of washing. Her hands were clasped tightly before her, twisting and turning in her lap, as though she were washing them. Eddy knelt before her and, taking her hands in his, spoke in a quiet but firm voice, hoping his words would break through the invisible barrier she had built around herself.

'I know you're worrying about the baby,' he said, 'but there's no need. I love you, Abby. I've loved you since that day you ran here from the Glenisters. Now you're running from them again, only, this time, I won't let you return.' He saw a flicker in those empty eyes and went on hopefully. 'I want to marry you. I want to look after

you and the baby.' At this Abby lifted her head slightly.
'Yes, I've known about the baby since the accident. So
does Mum. She thinks it's mine and I've let 'er go on
thinking it.'

Abby looked at the kneeling man before her. 'Eddy,'
she murmured once, then resumed staring into the empty
grate, as though searching for something hidden there.

Eddy was not beaten. He was prepared to kneel there
all night talking to Abby, if that was what it took to bring
her back.

Uncertain and desperately worried, Evelyn hovered
nearby until she could stand it no longer. 'It's no use,'
she whispered, her eyes moist with tears. 'You've done all
you can, son, but I think she's lost 'er mind. It must be
that blow to the 'ead. I'm gonna call the doctor, and see
what's what.'

Eddy nodded, thinking that Richard Glenister had a
great deal to answer for, and that he'd like to knock
him into next week. 'I thought, for one moment, that
I'd reached through to 'er.'

The doctor diagnosed trauma caused by the accident.
'We'll take some more X-rays,' he said. 'If they prove to
be clear, then you should consider psychiatric care.'

Evelyn stared at him in horror. 'What? Are you saying
our Abby's a nut case, doctor? No one from this 'ouse is
going into a loony bin. We love 'er, and I don't care what's
the matter, we'll take care of 'er. She don't need none of
that sic ... whatever you called it. She needs someone to
look at those X-rays again and mend 'er 'ead as well as
they've mended 'er arm.'

Two days before the X-rays were to be taken, Abby
seemed to awaken and take notice of the people about
her. Everyone crept around the house, speaking in hushed
tones. Then Eddy was there, saying kind things and being
cheerful. From time to time, Abby recalled his words
from a distant place. He had asked her to marry him,
and spoken of making a home for her and the child.

What had she replied? Try as she might, she could not remember.

After the X-rays were taken, Abby was given a clean bill of health. Life at Victoria Place slowly returned to normal, and Eddy started again to court Abby. She was touched that he should be willing to marry a woman who did not love him and who was bearing another man's child. Three times he asked, and three times she refused, saying it would be grossly unfair on him.

'But I love you, Abby,' said Eddy.

'And I don't love you,' she replied. 'At least, not in the way you would want me to love you. It's my fault that I'm pregnant, not yours, and I won't have your life ruined because I've ruined mine.'

'What will you do? Where will you go? Is the baby to be adopted, then? If not, who will take care of you both? Think, Abby, think,' Eddy persisted. 'You'd never forgive yourself for giving your child away. I love you more than anything else in this world, and you'd make me the 'appiest of men, if you'd become my wife.'

'But it would be wrong. I won't let you ruin your life in that way.'

'Ruin it!' Eddy grinned broadly and she thought how handsome he was. 'Marrying you would be the making of it.' He held her gaze. 'I know I'm not much of a catch, that you're used to men of a different class. But I'm no slouch, either. I'll make something of myself, Abby, and I'll provide a good 'ome for you and the nipper. Think of the child, then ask yourself — is my offer so terrible?'

'Don't say such things,' said Abby. 'I feel it would be quite wrong to marry someone I didn't truly love. I care for you deeply, Eddy, and always will. And, yes, there's a kind of love in that, but not the kind to make you happy.'

'Not the kind you have for Richard,' he said sharply. 'You said it was over. If it isn't, then you'd best get in touch with 'im, because time's running out.'

'It *is* over, it's *all* over.' Abby felt tired suddenly. If only Eddy would let her rest; but still he went on.

'Look, there's not much time left. I'm off to Germany next week, and goodness knows when my next leave will be. I'll go mad worrying about you and the baby. We could get a special licence, and be married in a few days.' He paused, and looked at her pale and tired face. 'Don't say no. Please, Abby, don't say no!'

For the first time since the accident Abby felt a shudder of emotion course through her body. Then she was in Eddy's arms, weeping convulsively. 'I can't ask you to take on another man's child,' she sobbed.

'You're not asking,' he said softly, kissing the top of her head. '*I'm* asking, and I'll go on asking until you say "yes". Now once again, will you marry me?'

Exhausted with emotion, Abby suddenly felt safe and warm in Eddy's arms, and knew she had no choice. Slowly she nodded her head.

'Thank God,' Eddy sighed with relief. 'You won't regret it, darling. I swear you'll never regret it.'

As Abby stood before the Registrar, however, she was already regretting it and wondered why she was there. This was not the wedding she had dreamed about. This was a sad, hurried ceremony touched with shame and a sense of unreality.

Susan stood behind Abby, wondering if her friend had gone completely mad. It made no sense that she should give up Richard for working-class, semi-literate Eddy, decent though he may be. As they'd searched the shops for something suitable for a pregnant bride, Susan had begged Abby to think again before taking such a step, but her words had fallen on deaf ears.

'Not white!' Abby had snapped at one point. 'White is for purity – and I'm anything but. I'd look better in scarlet, I think.'

Despairing of such utter nonsense, Susan had finally

picked out a pretty cream dress in nylon marquisette which flowed softly over the underskirt and bodice to fall in tiers from the waist.

Evelyn watched her son and Abby repeat their vows, her heart bursting with happiness. Finally her dream had come true. Abby was her daughter now and soon she, Evelyn Carr, would be a grandmother.

A few friends and neighbours came to the house in Victoria Place to drink the health of the bride and groom. Watching Abby cut the cake, Susan felt she was witnessing a tragedy. Eddy knew the child was Richard's, yet he was marrying Abby, all the same. Richard, on the other hand, had not been told; had not even been given the chance to make his peace with Abby.

She forced a smile as she kissed Abby goodbye. 'Well, Mrs Edward George Carr, I wish you all the best for a very happy marriage. You keep in touch, now.'

Abby grabbed her hand tightly, like one drowning. 'Yes. I will.' Her voice was tense and frightened. 'Don't forget me.'

As Abby watched Susan drive away, she saw her old life going with her. No more Richard; no more Ferndene; no more Uncle William; no more St Martin's School of Art; no more of anything.

In Oxford, Richard found himself unable to sleep or think. As each day passed without a word from Abby, he was tortured by doubts and fears. Unable to study, he paced the streets by day, and spent too much time in the pubs by night. Exams had been a disaster. His mind filled with thoughts of Abby, memory had deserted him. At last, on the 30th June, he drove to London to hear from her very lips the words he'd asked her not to write. When he found the flat empty, and the landlady unable to give him an address, Richard knew that Abby had fled from him in horror. Desolate, he found himself walking down the Charing Cross Road to the art school.

It was the last day of term and the foyer of St Martin's was filled with students. For an hour Richard stood back against the wall, watching frantically for Abby. At last, he saw Susan, heading towards the entrance with a group of chattering girls.

Richard stepped out in front of her. 'Where the devil is Abby?'

Surprised, Susan flushed to the roots of her hair and started to stutter incomprehensibly. Eventually she managed to say: 'She's left the college and the flat. I don't know where she's gone.'

'Left the college?' Richard repeated the words slowly. 'I don't believe it. She'd never do such a thing, so why say she has? I must speak to her. Tell her that, please.'

'I can't,' said Susan, wishing she were a million miles away from Richard's searching questions. 'It's no use. I can't say any more.'

'Why not?' Richard's eyes were blazing. 'What the hell is going on? Don't pretend to me, Susan. You know, and I mean to have your answer.'

Giving up the struggle, Susan sighed in despair and turned to him, her eyes filled with compassion.

Richard's blood turned to ice. 'What is it? What's happened?'

'She's married.' Susan could have choked on the words. 'Last week.' Richard's stricken face told her he found the news unbelievable. 'It's true. I'm sorry — I promised I wouldn't say anything to you, or tell you where she's living. I've broken one part of my promise now, but I mean to keep the other.' Richard was just gazing at her, too stunned to speak. 'Come along,' Susan said, 'this is no place to talk. There's a coffee shop around the corner.'

Sipping her coffee, Susan noticed that Richard still had not touched his. 'I'd no idea your quarrel went so deep.' After saying this and getting no response, Susan wondered whether to tell him about the baby and the accident. But Abby had been so adamant that he should not know, and she had promised. So Susan said nothing, though she could see, just looking at Richard's pale face, how much he really did love Abby. 'I'm sorry. I can't tell you how sorry I am.'

Richard shot to his feet suddenly. 'Don't be,' he snapped. 'It isn't your fault. If that's how she feels, then you're right. It is all over.'

With that he turned on his heel and walked out into the street, leaving Susan sitting there. It was unforgivably rude of him, he knew, but he had been suffocating inside that awful café.

It's all over, Richard told himself, *over and finished*. He left London and headed towards Oxford to collect his things and say goodbye. There would be no second year. He knew that without waiting for his exam results. Instead, National Service beckoned. He would welcome the chance to get away from England, and everything that made him think of Abby.

How could she have done it? he kept asking himself. To have turned from him was one thing, but to rush into marriage with someone else ... It must be her way of saying there could be no going back, and that surely revealed her reaction to his letter. It seemed that his mother had been right about her all along.

As the car sped on towards Oxford, his shock slowly turned to anger. And by the time he arrived at Merton College, his love had turned to bitterness.

CHAPTER NINE

In the last week of January, after a long and difficult labour, Abby gave birth to a healthy boy who weighed in at seven pounds and four ounces.

Though relieved her son was healthy and normal, Abby was soon overwhelmed by feelings of guilt. As she held her baby, and gazed down at his round pink face and deep blue eyes, she thought: *This is Richard's son. My own brother is the father of my baby!* Panic seized her. 'I won't feed him. I can't feed him.'

The midwife put her behaviour down to post-natal depression. 'You'll come round, Mrs Carr,' she said, taking the baby. 'You've had a bad time, that's all. He's a bonny lad, the bonniest in the ward. Enjoy him, get to know him. He won't break.'

What do you know about it? thought Abby bitterly. 'Take him away. Please.'

As the days passed, she did not 'come round', her fears and guilt blocking all maternal emotions. Only when Mrs O'Connor and Evelyn came to visit and made cooing noises over the baby, did she put on a pretence of motherly concern and held the child in her arms.

'Aaah, bless 'im,' murmured Evelyn, bursting with pride and happiness. 'Look at those little 'ands. He's a beautiful baby. Not like Eddy, who looked like a monkey for the first few days.'

'This one's almost ginger,' said Mrs O'Connor, touching the baby's crop of sandy-coloured hair. 'And 'e's gonna favour you, Abby. Thought of a name yet, sparrer?'

'Ross,' said Abby quickly.

Evelyn frowned. 'Ross? That's a queer name to choose. We don't know no one called Ross.'

'I like it, that's all.' She felt the need to keep something of Richard, even if it was only the first letter of his name.

'Ross Carr,' murmured Evelyn. 'Sounds like a Scottish fishing port, if you ask me. But I suppose we'll get used to it in good time.' She grinned at the baby. 'Eddy'll be over the moon. Pity he couldn't get leave.'

Thank God for it, thought Abby, grateful her husband was now in Hamburg. It was cruel of her and she knew it. Eddy had shown a rare sensitivity in never making sexual demands of her, not even on their wedding night. As yet, their marriage had not been consummated, for as much as he wanted her, he had been prepared to wait until after the baby was safely born, and Abby was well again. She dreaded the day.

Even after her return to Victoria Place, Abby found it hard to accept her infant son. When she looked at Ross she felt a guilt that seemed to weigh more heavily with each passing day. As the babe gazed up at her and made gurgling sounds which would fill any mother's heart with happiness, Abby found herself examining his eyes in fear, though she knew it was too early for any mental abnormality to manifest itself. Physically Ross was perfect. But who could say what the future would bring? Something terrible would happen, Abby was sure of it: God's punishment for incest. Then pity would sweep over her, pity for the child who would have to bear the brunt of that punishment. And when this pity came too close to love, Abby would turn her back on Ross, as though putting a barrier between them both. Love for such a child would only bring anguish later.

Evelyn watched Abby's coldness towards the baby with growing dismay, and did her best to make up for it, cuddling Ross when he needed love and attending to him when he cried. Each day she became more convinced that Abby's attitude was rooted in an unwanted pregnancy leading to an unwanted wedding. Deeply distressed, she

181

said nothing, unwilling to increase the resentment she was sure Abby was feeling. One day, however, her patience snapped when Abby walked out of the room, leaving her son screaming in his pram beside the window.

'Look at that. Ross needs changing, and she knows it,' Evelyn told her husband. 'I don't understand the girl, really I don't. Never in my wildest dreams did I think she could be like this. The doctor called it "post-natal depression". Never 'ad no fancy names like that when Eddy was born. In those days it was "stop moaning and get on with it".' Walking to the pram, she picked up the crying baby and gently rocked him to and fro. 'Girls these days are too pampered if you ask me.'

Harry nodded without hearing his wife. He had been up for most of the night, still suffering from the bad fogs earlier in the month. He switched on the wireless, and was beginning to doze when the music stopped abruptly and a solemn male voice announced:

'This is London.'

When Abby returned to the living room, she was surprised to see everyone so silent and grave. 'What is it? What's the matter?'

Evelyn was still holding Ross, but tears were streaming down her cheeks. 'The King,' she murmured. 'He's dead, poor man!'

'At Sandringham, this morning,' said Mrs O'Connor quietly. 'It seems 'e passed away in 'is sleep, God rest 'is soul.' The white head bent and the shoulders shook.

Shocked, Abby felt she'd lost a father. The King had always been there, and she'd assumed that he always would be.

Evelyn's voice broke, as she handed Ross to Abby. 'Such a good man too. So decent and kind. I blame 'er, I do really.'

Abby's eyebrows shot up. 'Who?'

'That Mrs Simpson.'

Harry shook his head. 'That's rubbish. The King was ill. It was obvious just by looking at 'im.'

'Wouldn't 'ave been if it 'adn't been for 'er,' snapped Evelyn. 'Think what it must 'ave been like for 'im taking over from 'is brother like that, and all through the war years too.' She blew her nose. 'No, I blame 'er.'

'So do I,' said Mrs O'Connor.

Abby stared at them in bemusement, knowing little about the events that shook the throne and kingdom in the thirties. 'Isn't it strange,' she murmured, 'Princess Elizabeth is now the Queen. I'll never get used to it.' Her face brightened. 'It's quite romantic, really. There'll be a Coronation.' The couturiers would be so busy, she thought, what with Coronation gowns, and dresses for the many balls and parties. Yet here she was, stuck in Victoria Place with a baby, unable to be a part of that excitement.

As if reading her mind, Evelyn turned to her daughter-in-law disapprovingly. 'First, we 'ave to bury our King.'

It was Susan's visits which helped to pull Abby through these dark days. Dandling Ross on her knee and cooing at him with all the maternal feeling Abby seemed to lack, Susan spoke of life at St Martin's, her latest disagreement with Bernard, her boyfriend, and her flat-mate's wastefulness. 'She leaves lights on, and is forever putting the three bars of the fire on full, instead of making do with one as we used to. Honestly, she thinks money grows on trees.' She passed on to Abby the things she had learned about design sketching and pattern cutting, and together they browsed over the latest fashions coming out of Paris.

One day, as Susan sat in Abby's room, repairing her make-up, she spoke bluntly. 'Surely you don't intend to remain here playing the good little housewife?'

'What choice have I?' Abby sat down on the bed, and sighed. 'I'm a mother. Oh, I make dresses for people, using Evelyn's old sewing machine, but most of the work consists of alterations. Still, the money helps.'

'It's hardly what you had planned for your life,' said Susan.

'No.' Abby hugged herself to keep warm. Dampness had never left this poor old house. 'But I have to do something. Eddy's army pay is a joke and doesn't go anywhere.' She put a hand to her brow and stared down at the floor despondently. 'Honest to God, Susan, I truly believe I shall go out of my mind.' As soon as she had spoken she regretted her words. 'No, that's ungrateful. Everyone's been so marvellous to me and I've been awful to them.'

Susan combed her blonde curls into place and smiled reassuringly. 'That will all change when you get out into the world again. I've been thinking – if you took a proper job with good wages, you could pay Mrs Carr to stay home so she wouldn't lose out by it. She could look after Ross while you became the breadwinner. Of course, you wouldn't have much left from your pay packet, but at least it would save your sanity.'

Abby looked at her. 'I think I lost that last summer.' A long silence followed this remark, which she broke with a strained whisper. 'Did ... did he come looking for me?' It was the first time she had dared to ask.

'Yes,' said Susan, after an awkward pause. 'He was desperate.' She turned from the mirror and looked her friend straight in the eye. 'You didn't tell him about the baby. Am I right?'

Abby nodded but said nothing, leaving Susan more confused than ever. 'Well, what on earth was he to think, Abby? You run out on him and make me promise not to reveal your whereabouts. In the end, to stop him questioning me further, I told him you were married.'

After another long and painful silence, Abby murmured, 'That must have come as quite a shock to him.'

'Oh, Abby, it was awful! He was devastated.'

'Don't,' cried Abby, tears in her eyes. 'Please don't tell me any more. I can't bear it!'

'I knew you still loved him,' Susan said. 'I don't understand, Abby. I'll never understand.' She stood up. 'I must be going. Come over soon and stay the night. We can have a long chat. Just like old times.'

It could never be like old times, thought Abby. Still, she took Susan's advice, and wrote off to several London department stores for interviews. *First*, she told herself, *be sure of your ground, so that you have a firm case to put to Evelyn.* Even so, she was quite sure that such a notion would cause the roof to cave in. And she was right. After an interview at Liberty, she was offered the position of Sales Assistant in the Materials Department. She told Evelyn and waited for the storm to break.

'What?' Evelyn looked at her daughter-in-law as though she'd proposed dancing naked at the local pub. 'Eddy's wife going out to work? Married women with babies 'ave their place, and it's in the 'ome.'

Patiently, and at great length, Abby explained her plan to Evelyn. 'You'll get back every penny of what you would earn at the cinema, and you won't have to clean the dirty floors and empty all those disgusting ashtrays. You'll be in your own home, with your husband who needs you, and with Ross.'

'Ross needs *you*,' said Evelyn. 'Of course, I love looking after 'im. He's a darling. One of the best babies I've ever seen, so good. But 'e needs 'is Mum, not 'is Grandma. Besides, Eddy'll go mad. You'll make 'im a laughing stock round this neighbourhood. They'll say that Eddy Carr isn't able to provide for 'is wife and child. That's what they'll say.'

'But they'll be wrong,' Abby persisted. 'It's just stupid prejudice. They were perfectly happy for women to go out to work in the war years. Many of them still do, and it's all right if it brings in the money ...'

'But these women 'ave got their kids off their 'ands. You 'aven't, and it's different,' said Evelyn firmly. But even as she spoke she knew in her heart that she must let Abby go. Maybe it was this resentment which caused Abby to be so uncaring with Ross. 'Very well,' she sighed at last. 'We'll give it a try.' Smiling, she added, 'Perhaps being out among people will put the bloom back in your cheeks again. So all right, luv. We'll give it a try.'

The minute she started working at Liberty, Abby felt her life was her own again. Surrounded by fabrics of all kinds, she was content for the next two months to measure, cut and stack the materials. She advised customers on choice and length of fabric, and quickly established her popularity among staff and customers alike.

She loved the ambience of the old building in Regent Street. The floors were built around a central well, which, looking down to the ground floor, gave a kaleidoscopic effect as people milled around among counters of colourful remnants. Often she would feel a nostalgic pang for the store in Canterbury. What was he thinking, that man who had been so kind and good to her? But had he? He was her father, a father who had denied her so that she had been allowed to fall in love with her own brother. Was that an act of kindness? Yet she supposed that he meant well. The world was full of the tragic consequences of those who meant well.

One evening she returned home to find Evelyn waiting for her in the hallway. 'This came for Mrs O'Connor,' she said, holding a buff-coloured envelope. 'It's from a solicitor, to say that her son has died. The poor old thing's been very upset, as you can imagine, but it seems that this son of 'ers was a partner in a firm up North. The letter's all legal jargon and that, and frankly, luv, I think you'd make more sense of it than I can.'

'Of course,' said Abby, taking the letter. 'Is Ross all right? Has he been good?'

'Out like a light,' whispered Evelyn. 'Which is just as well, since Mrs O's very down.'

'It's from Liverpool,' murmured Abby, as she read.

'Apparently he died more than four months ago and they've only just tracked Mrs O'Connor down. The last address her son had was Lambeth.' She looked at Evelyn sadly. 'How awful. Her son's been dead all this time and she's only just heard!' Abby read on. 'Well, she's lost a son and gained a legacy. Apparently his firm was a small engineering business. There's no wife or children, so his shares and estate go to his mother.' She frowned. 'Just think of it. All this time he's been living in comfort in Liverpool, and never gave a thought to his mother.' A worried look replaced the anger that had kindled in her eyes. 'How much have you told her?'

Evelyn shrugged. 'Hardly anything. I couldn't make 'ead nor tail of the letter. Why don't these solicitors learn to speak English?'

They walked on into the living room to find Mrs O'Connor pouring tea into four cups. The hands were shaking and the old lady kept her face turned from them.

'I'm so very sorry,' said Abby gently. 'I've just heard.' She sat down at the table, hardly knowing what to say about a son who wasn't a son. When the old lady turned to her, she read, not only grief in those eyes, but anger also. The son she thought dead had been living in the North all the time, and in comfort too. Abby wondered which would cause the most grief, a dead child or a child who was all but dead to the parent through his choice.

'I'm all right,' Mrs O'Connor's quivering voice whispered, as her wrinkled hand offered the cup and saucer to Abby. 'I'll be fine, luv. Now get this down yer before it gets cold.'

Abby drank her tea and read the letter through quietly once more before revealing its contents to Mrs O'Connor.

'There's the partnership, which means his shares in the firm go to you. If you wish to sell them, then his partner, a George Potterton, is willing to buy. Then there's the sale of his house, which realized fourteen hundred pounds. After solicitor's fees, this comes down to thirteen hundred and twenty pounds – which goes to you, Mrs O'Connor. The solicitor awaits your instructions in the matter.'

There was a long silence as Mrs O'Connor stared into the fire, her eyes thoughtful and sad. At last she spoke.

'All that money. All that money for me?' She shook her head in disbelief. 'Money instead of a son. It's horrible! For the sale of his house, you say?'

'Plus the shares,' said Abby.

Mrs O'Connor's eyes flickered and she stiffened. 'I don't want a single penny of it.' She turned to Evelyn and her face softened. 'No, but I want *you* to 'ave it. You deserve it more than anyone else I know. So I want you to 'ave the money and Eddy to 'ave the shares.'

Everyone stared at her in disbelief. Finally, Evelyn spoke. 'We couldn't possibly take it, dear. It's very kind of you but really ... no ... the money is yours. I wouldn't dream of taking such a sum off you.'

Mrs O'Connor crooked a gnarled forefinger and beckoned Evelyn to her side. 'What do I need?' she whispered. 'A roof over me 'ead, one good meal a day, a glass of milk stout on rare occasions and the love I get from all of you. So what use is my son's money to me now? On the other 'and, you've always said you wanted to move out of London. Well then, now's your chance. You can use this money to buy a small place in the country or by the sea like you've always said you wanted.'

Still Evelyn hesitated. 'I couldn't. It's your money and there are things you might want to buy ...'

'Things!' scoffed the old lady. 'I 'ad a flat full of things once. Took a lifetime collecting them and they all vanished in one second. At my age people want to get rid of their clutter, not collect more. Please, dearie, if you won't take it for yourself, then at least ...' she nodded in the direction of Harry, and mouthed silently, 'take it for 'im. Please.'

Evelyn took her hand and patted it gently, thanking the old lady for her generosity.

'Generosity?' Mrs O'Connor shook her head. 'Don't be

so daft. That's just money changing 'ands. Generosity is when you take in an old gel like me and make 'er one of your family. God knows your 'ouse is small enough without me taking up valuable room. Yet you wouldn't let me go into a council 'ome for old folk, thank God, and you've always made me feel welcome. So this is my way of saying thank you.'

To Evelyn it was a miracle. She was being given a sum of money which could mean the difference between life and death for her husband. Without delay, she wrote to her cousin on Canvey Island, asking her to look out for a small house.

Abby wrote to Eddy explaining the terms of the Will and Mrs O'Connor's gift to him. His reply sent a wave of alarm through her. Instead of selling the shares, he thought it would be better to take up the partnership. When he next came home on leave he would visit Liverpool and assess the situation himself. In the meantime, he would write to George Potterton, and ask for more details.

Liverpool! Abby was horrified. The idea of leaving London was unimaginable. She wrote again, saying that it would be better to sell the shares, so Eddy could start up his own small business when he was demobbed. His response increased Abby's panic.

You must be off your rocker to think I'd look such a gift horse in the mouth. Do you have any idea of what it takes to build up a business from scratch? I couldn't do it. Here's a going concern being offered to me on a plate. I'd be a dope to turn it down. If this partner of Arthur O'Connor's is willing to have me along, then so be it. I know we'll miss Mum and Dad and old Mrs O'Connor. I'll miss London too, but beggars can't be choosers.

He sounded very set on this venture. How could he understand her reluctance? In his world, wives had no careers of their own. Not that she had one now. Working in a shop was working in a shop, whether it be Liberty or Glenisters. Furthermore, if Evelyn did move to Canvey, who would look after Ross? She would be housebound once more, her taste of freedom over. Liverpool! Her life would be finished. Abby tried to calm herself. There were still nine months until Eddy was demobbed. What looked good from Germany might seem very different once he was back home. She must stop worrying, and take each day as it came.

Yet at night, as she lay alone, she told herself she'd been wrong to marry Eddy. Her mind and body still yearned for Richard. It seemed unreal that he was her brother. He was just – Richard, the man she loved and should have married. All other thoughts belonged in the world of nightmare.

Second Lieutenant Richard Glenister paused to adjust his sixty-pound back pack. The straps cut into the sores on his shoulder, sores caused by insect bites, which were turning septic in the steaming heat of the Malayan jungle. Sweat ran down beneath his bush hat, got into his eyes and soaked through his lightweight uniform. His boots squelched into rotting vegetation and marsh so that his feet were always wet.

Richard had been in Malaya for more than six months, yet still the heat and humidity sapped his strength. At the Jungle Warfare School in Johore, he'd endured an arduous training course that taught him to survive in hostile territory, command a patrol and engage the enemy in order to kill them. The enemy were communist terrorists who, after the war, had tried to seize control throughout the Far East. They hid in the vast jungle, attacking British patrols without warning, then melting away in thick forests as quickly as they'd surfaced. It was Richard's task to seek them out and destroy their camps.

He and his men were tired. Week after week they had

hacked their way through impenetrable bush then climbed steep hills before descending to the deep river valleys once more. It rained nearly every day, the deluge turning the jungle floor into a quagmire, so that men slipped and slid up and down the tortuous terrain, each weighted down with his pack, rifle and parang. At first each man had lived on his nerves, alert to the sounds of the jungle, fearing every cracking twig to be the enemy. Eventually the alertness gave way to a weary complacency, the senses lulled by the fierce, humid heat.

His pack readjusted, Richard reminded himself to treat the sores on his shoulder. It was a strict rule, and one which he hammered home to his men again and again: medicate each bite, sore or cut, for a sick man was a liability to his comrades in such a country. He walked on, aware of the patrol behind him. Though it was mid-afternoon only the merest glimmer of sunlight filtered through the jungle. Before him, three tribesmen scouts from Borneo, whose skills in tracking matched their deadly accuracy with knives and blow-pipes, led the way.

Suddenly one of the scouts turned and signalled. Richard quickly passed the signal on to his men. *Bandits!* His heart pounded against his ribs, as he slowly released the catch on his .303 rifle. A burst of gun-fire exploded from the jungle all about them. He and his men returned the fire. Though all his training had prepared him for this moment, Richard was shocked by its violence and ferocity. Then it was over. The bandits disappeared, leaving their dead for the patrol to find.

Richard bent over one corpse, a young and beautiful Chinese girl who, brainwashed by hatred, had become a hardened killer for her cause. Staring down at the still face, Richard closed her eyes, thinking she was no older than Abby. But Abby too was dead to him. *Don't look back*, he told himself.

Sergeant Edwards touched him on the shoulder. 'Come away, sir. She's quite dead.'

Richard stood up, thankful for Edwards, who was a regular and had served in this part of the world during the war. Unlike many regulars who thought little of the National Servicemen, Edwards looked upon them all as his own sons. In his early forties, he was a man of humour and experience who gave the nineteen and twenty-year-olds a feeling of security.

'Their camp must be close,' said Richard, knowing that his chances of finding it were slim.

The rain stopped that night but there was no moon, and the men on watch were jumpy. Richard knew the feeling only too well, when the hairs on the back of his neck rose at every sound from the jungle, and had him reaching for his gun. Yet he was the officer, God help him, the man who must show no fear, think clearly and encourage the others.

The next day, they hacked their way through the dense foliage until they came to a high ridge. Richard was thinking how strange it was that the men they now hunted had helped the British forces to fight the Japanese, when suddenly the scout signalled him to the summit. Richard lay on his belly, looked down into the clearing, and saw the terrorist camp. 'CTs,' he murmured to the sergeant who fell to the ground beside him and trained his glasses on the Malay manning the machine gun.

'We have the advantage of surprise, sir,' Edwards whispered. 'But the marshland down there will hinder our speed.'

Richard nodded. 'I realize that, but we've no choice. Form the men up, Sergeant.'

The Bren gun spat out fire, killing the terrorist manning the machine gun instantly, and Richard ordered his men forward. Leading the advance, he felt a searing pain in his right leg, and stumbled in the marsh.

'Go on!' he yelled. 'I'm all right. Watch your right flank.' Blood poured from his leg and the pain he felt was intense, but he was still yelling out orders as bullets flew around him. The fight for control of the camp went on for fifteen minutes, then just stopped. In the deadly silence that followed, Richard waved his men forward once more. He heard the shot before he felt the pain in his side, and Sergeant Edwards caught him as he fell. 'Did we get them?' Richard gasped, his vision blurred.

'Yes, sir. And the bastard who got you.' Edwards smiled to hide his fears. Blood was spreading over Richard's stomach. 'They left quite an arsenal too.'

'Good,' whispered Richard. The sergeant's face faded into dimness.

Slowly he became aware of movement and pain, and when he finally opened his eyes it took a while to make sense of his surroundings. He lay in bed at the far end of a long ward, with an open balcony running the length of it. There was a brilliant blue sky, and deep pink bougainvillaea trailing along the balcony. In the centre of the ward, four men sat at a table, while another hobbled along on crutches. Fans whirred from the ceiling, slowly cooling the humid air. Richard heard the rustle of starched linen, then a nursing sister appeared at the end of the bed, a stiff white veil covering dark hair. By her epaulettes he could see that she was a major in the Queen Alexandra's Nursing Service. When she saw he was awake, she smiled.

'Good afternoon, Lieutenant, nice to have you back with us.'

Richard had difficulty forming the words. 'How long?' His throat felt like sand-paper, and no sound came out. Gratefully, he drank the water the nurse held to his lips, and heard her answer his unasked question.

'You've been here for six days.'

Richard could hardly believe that was possible. Only a minute ago he was leading an attack! 'Where?' he managed to gasp.

'The Military Hospital, Singapore,' came the answer. 'First you were taken to KL but after emergency surgery you were transferred here for more surgery. You've had three operations, Lieutenant, two for stomach wounds, and one for your thigh.' She gently checked his pulse. 'You'll mend in good time. But it was a close call. A fraction of an inch higher, and the bullet in your stomach would have been fatal.'

Richard remembered the CT camp and bullets flying all around him. 'My men . . .' he gasped again. 'Did any of them . . .?'

She was ready for this. 'You were the only casualty. All your men returned safely. Everyone has spoken of your bravery, and how you stayed in command in spite of your wounds. You're quite the hero. Your sergeant told your Commanding Officer the whole story.'

Richard thought of Edwards, knowing that it was he who'd led the men back, and organized his removal to hospital. It must have been a feat of endurance second to none, carting a wounded man back through that terrain. He should be commended for what he had done, and Richard promised himself that would be his first task on leaving hospital. 'What happens now, Sister? How long will it be before I can rejoin my unit?'

The veil trembled as she shook her head. 'That's out of the question. It's up to the doctors, of course, but my bet is that you'll be sent to a convalescent hospital in England as soon as you're fit for the voyage.'

Richard heard her words with sinking heart. England was the last place he wanted to be. 'No, I want to return to duty.'

'The healing process is slow in this climate, Lieutenant.' Seeing his look of dismay, she tried to sound cheerful. 'Most men are only too glad to hear that news. You'll be able to see your family again.'

'Can't I be sent somewhere else . . .?' Richard's voice trailed off weakly. 'Australia, perhaps?'

'Sorry.'

'What about a desk job at HQ, in Singapore?'

The sister looked at him sympathetically. It was out of the question, of course. His wounds were serious, and would take months to heal. His days in the army were over.

Abby had spent twenty minutes with a customer, explaining to her the details of the pattern she'd just bought, and the material suitable for it, when she noticed a woman hovering nearby. Short and stocky, the woman was about sixty years of age, but was trying to look twenty. Her long peroxided hair was drawn back in a large velvet bow, while her make-up was so heavy, the bright red lipstick ran into the lines above her top lip. Abby had noticed her in the store before and wondered why she purchased so much material.

Returning to the business at hand, Abby took pity on the young customer, whose size and figure were all wrong for the pattern she had chosen, and sketched out a more appropriate design.

'You might be happier with a pattern on these lines. It would give you more length, and the seaming is less complicated,' she explained. 'Take this sketch to our pattern department and see if they can find something close to it for you to make.'

The young woman looked at her, in astonishment. 'You mean this isn't an established pattern?'

Aware that the peroxided woman had drawn alongside them, and was taking a keen interest in the proceedings, Abby explained quietly that it was an idea of her own, but that she was sure there would be something like it. 'Try *Vogue*. They're very good.'

'I will. Thank you for all your help. I'll make sure I come to you again,' said the young customer before departing with her sketch.

The peroxided woman stared at Abby with shrewd, hazel eyes and said: 'You seem to know your way around a design sketch. And you were quite right. She would have looked a pig in that other pattern.' Her voice was loud, and the accent foreign.

Appalled at her words, Abby glanced around nervously. 'Oh no, it was just that . . .'

'That you have an eye and she has none.' The woman smiled, though the thick-set face remained hard, and her eyes mirthless. 'Tell me where you learned about designing.'

Wishing the woman gone, Abby said, 'St Martin's.'

'You studied fashion design?'

'Only the foundation course. I left because of family commitments.'

The woman shrugged. 'And now you cut up yards of material for silly women who don't know what they're doing.' She gazed about her, saying, 'I'll take the black faille. Six yards please, and then four of the yellow taffeta. Put it on my account and have it sent with my other purchases to Maddox Street.'

'Of course, Madam,' said Abby. 'Could I have your name and address, please?' But the woman had already turned on her high heels and was walking away.

Seeing Abby's confusion, one of her colleagues came over to the table, and smiled. 'She comes and goes like lightning, expecting the whole store to leap to attention. We're used to her, of course.'

Abby sighed with relief. 'I'm glad to hear it. She left no name or address.'

'She's Justine Tate. Strange woman. French, I think.'

'Tate?'

'She married an Englishman long before the war. I think he's dead. Anyway, she buys most of her material from here.'

'In such quantities?' Abby asked.

'She's a couturier of sorts. Has her own salon in Maddox Street.'

A couturier! With her own salon! Abby thought of the woman until she finally decided that fate had sent Justine

Tate to her desk that morning, along with the inexperienced customer. Maddox Street was very close by, and it took no time to go there one lunch break, just to take a look at the place. The bay window of the salon was draped in pale green curtains, and held a display of freshly cut flowers. The brass plate said simply, 'Justine'. Abby longed to walk in and ask for a job. If only she had a diploma to wave at the woman!

In the event, it was Justine Tate who approached Abby on her next visit to Liberty. 'You seem to know your way around a pattern, but how good are you on a machine?'

Surprised at the question, Abby explained how she'd been making clothes for herself and others for years.

The pale eyes swept over her thoughtfully, then sharpened as doubt became decision. 'I need a young girl to train up. Are you interested?'

Abby's heart did a somersault, but she managed to sound calm. 'Yes. But I've no diploma and ...'

Justine cut her off with an impatient sound. 'I am Paris-trained. What use are your diplomas to me? I need someone who doesn't know it all and is willing to learn. Of course that someone would be a trainee, and paid accordingly. I would start you off on "making up", that is sewing on buttons, cuffs, and so on. Then we shall see if you are good enough to stay on with me for further training. Interested?'

Abby blinked and nodded vigorously. 'Very interested.'

'Good.' The bright red lips softened into what, for Justine, passed as a smile. 'Come and see me at Maddox Street tomorrow evening after this store closes.'

'I'll be there.' It was only as she watched Justine walk away that Abby came down to earth and thought about the trainee's salary. If there was one thing she could not afford, it was a cut in her weekly pay packet. All that night she thought about the job, knowing such an opportunity would never come her way again. To be taken on by a couturier was a dream come true. She'd make sacrifices. As long

197

as she could honour her agreement with Evelyn, and keep Ross fed and clothed, she could do without herself. By morning, Abby had made her decision. Chances had to be taken if she was to go forward in the career she had always wanted.

Justine's little empire consisted of an experienced cutter in her late fifties, and two senior machinists, who had trained at the Shoreditch College for the Garment Trades. All three had been trained by Justine to produce the couture clothes of the Paris fashion houses. As a Jewess, Justine had left France in the thirties, married in England, and never stopped reminding people that she'd once worked with the famous Coco Chanel, who was sadly no longer designing. No British couturiers could compare with the Paris names, she proclaimed to anyone willing to listen. The British simply had no idea how to dress, and never would.

As the new junior, Abby sewed on buttons, cuffs and collars under her employer's watchful eye. Justine need not have worried. Every task Abby undertook, she finished to perfection, her natural talent and keen eye manifesting itself at once.

For Abby's part, being trained by a Parisian who had once worked with Chanel filled her with enthusiasm for the work. Although paid a pittance by the parsimonious Justine, she was quick and eager to learn, constantly telling herself how lucky she was to have the chance.

Soon she was helping Justine drape muslin toiles over tailor's dummies. From the toile would come the final pattern and, when all was ready, this would be transferred onto the best materials. A perfect size twelve, Abby would sometimes stand in as a model, while Justine and her staff pinned and tucked the gown before final fittings on those clients who were lucky enough to have Abby's figure. Most, however, did not, and Abby was sad to see how little Justine did for them, just as she was disappointed to realize how few original designs came out of Maddox Street. Having

198

lost her flair for originality during the war years, in the skimpy utility clothing of the forties, Justine had never regained the heart or confidence to create something new. Instead she gave the clients what they wanted: copies of Hartnell, Amies, Dior or Balenciaga. To the society women who could not afford these top couturiers, Justine's prices were a gift from heaven.

Abby disapproved. For although Justine always gave her garments a slight twist on the originals, she knew the clients were passing off the gowns as such. Justine was aware of this too, but it brought her a steady income, so she had a strict rule that clients' names be kept secret. No appointments must clash or there would be hell to pay, since Justine had a fiery temper.

Fiery tempers were not confined to Maddox Street, as Abby found when Eddy returned home on leave in June. As Evelyn had predicted, he was profoundly shocked that his wife was working.

'It makes me look small among my mates,' he said. 'And what about the kid? Is it right that Mum should be looking after 'im?'

'But, Eddy, this job is what I've always dreamed about. I've been incredibly lucky. I know, at the moment, the money is poor, but I'm receiving training which would have taken years at college. You must surely understand how I feel about this. It's as important to me as your work is to you.'

'But you're my wife!' cried Eddy, unable to grasp her desire to go out to work. 'You prattle on about "special training," but all you're doing is working in the rag trade. You'd get better money on an assembly line. All right, so you're up West, but that don't make no difference. You're in a factory whether you like it or not − while your kid is without 'is Mum all day.'

Abby just stared at him. 'Ross is fine,' she said at last. 'Your mother copes very well. We came to an agreement which works for both of us.'

'She's right, son,' said Evelyn, desperate to save the day. 'The money Abby gives to me means I can stay at 'ome instead of going out cleaning. I'm getting too old to go out to work. Besides, I've got your father and Mrs O'Connor to see to.'

Abby glanced at her mother-in-law gratefully. Evelyn made it seem that a great sacrifice was being made so that she could stay at home. Seizing the moment, she added, 'You don't really want to send your poor mother out again, surely?'

Unable to fight them both Eddy gave up, reminding himself that he had pushed Abby into this marriage. He loved her and knew that if he was to keep her, then he must tread carefully – otherwise she might go running back to that Glenister fellow who had treated her so badly. Women were like that, his mates had told him. 'You've gotta show 'em who's boss,' they said. But Eddy wasn't the type to bully a wife. Abby was everything to him. He wanted to be everything to her – and that might take some time.

In bed at night Abby lay stiff with horror, hating Eddy's fumbling attempts to arouse her sexually. Unable to stir her, he could not hold back his own desire, and entered her clumsily. The act was over in a few brief moments, and he would lie gasping on top of her until she moved out from beneath him. Then they would lie silent, Eddy knowing he was failing her, and Abby unable even to act the part of the fulfilled woman. She was deeply unhappy, and knew she was making Eddy unhappy, but felt incapable of doing anything about it. Instead, she could only compare his feeble lovemaking with Richard's sensitivity and passion, and knew nothing and no one could ever take the place of those times.

Trying to make up for her lack of passion by being caring, Abby went out with Eddy to the cinema and the local pub, listened with his mates to tales of army life, and was constantly referred to as 'the Duchess'. She knew these young men talked about her and nudged each other knowingly, but refused to be fazed by them, telling herself that when Eddy came out of the army, they would buy a house away from such types.

Eddy went to Liverpool and returned full of enthusiam for the business and George Potterton. 'I can really make something of that firm,' he told his family. 'They make parts for machines which are on the way out, so I told George that a re-think would be necessary. Get up to date, I said, and the firm will go from strength to strength. Of course he's worried about letting down old customers, but that's the sort of attitude we can't afford to 'ave.'

'We?' Abby looked at him quickly. 'What do you mean, "we"?'

Eddy looked uncomfortable. The last thing he wanted was a row with Abby over the firm. 'Look, I'd be nuts to turn it down. The shares are worth two guineas each, and there are three hundred of them. That might sound a lot, but it's peanuts against the partnership.'

'I see,' Abby said stiffly. 'Well, it sounds like you've made up your mind.' With that, she went into the kitchen, feeling all the weight of the world on her shoulders. Eddy found her fighting to control the tears which were already streaming down her cheeks. 'I don't want to go,' she said, at last. 'Eddy, I'm telling you now, I just don't want to go to Liverpool. Things are beginning to happen for me in London. Can't you see that?'

Eddy shook his head, and looked at her in puzzlement. 'No, I can't see that at all. You work all hours, sewing dresses for a woman who pays you nothing. *I'm* offering you a sound future. I can make sure you and Ross want for nothing. Can she do that? What is there in London for us? Answer me that. When Mum and Dad move to Canvey who'll look after Ross?'

Ross! Always Ross! Abby felt like screaming, but Eddy was right and Ross was the chain that bound her to his will. 'I might put him in a nursery. There's a council-run place not far from here.'

201

'The poor little sod,' said Eddy. 'I didn't think you'd be so 'ard on 'im. After all, it ain't 'is fault that ...'

'Stop!' said Abby quickly. 'Don't say any more.' She ran an anxious hand through her hair, then wiped away her tears with the back of her hand. 'I'm not being hard on Ross. He's always been well cared for and always will be whatever happens. You want me to be what I just can't be. It isn't enough, I need to feel fulfilled ...'

'Fulfilled! You're a married woman with a child. Isn't that fulfilling? Isn't keeping a house and cooking and ...'

'Cleaning up after everyone?' she added. 'No, I don't think I'd find that fulfilling at all.'

'It don't matter what you think,' said Eddy angrily. 'You've got a duty, and it's in the 'ome.' Eddy sighed, then tried another tactic. 'All right, so you want to keep working. Well, there's no reason you can't make dresses in Liverpool. They don't walk around naked north of the Wash, do they?'

Abby gave him a withering look. 'Liverpool is hardly the home of haute couture.'

'What?' Eddy frowned. 'What's that when it's at 'ome?'

'Oh, never mind.' She tried to push past him, but he stopped her.

'Look, I'm sorry I spoke the way I did. I won't pretend I'm not disappointed, but ...' he paused, 'nothing's worth destroying our marriage over. If you don't want me to take up the partnership, then I won't.'

Abby looked at her husband's tormented face in dismay. She had hurt him again. 'Oh, Eddy! It meant everything to you.'

He came closer and put his arms around her. '*You* mean everything to me. I couldn't live without you, luv. If I 'ave to empty dustbins for a living, I'll do it just as long as we can stay together.'

That night Abby lay tense in the bed, having endured

another session of Eddy's love-making. The silence between them was noisy with accusations and counter-accusations, until she said, 'I know you think I'm frigid, but I'm so afraid of having another baby so soon after Ross.'

Eddy relaxed a little, though he did think Abby was frigid. According to his friends, a lot of women were. Sex was really for men anyway. Even so, he wished she would relax at his touch, instead of becoming stiff as a board. He lay on his back looking up at the ceiling. In the darkness, he could not see the crack which widened daily, or the peeling wallpaper, but he knew they were there. 'This is no place to bring up a baby anyway,' he murmured. 'As soon as I'm demobbed, we'll get our own little house. There'll be trees and a garden, just the place for children to play. Of course,' he added quietly, 'it won't be what we could 'ave 'ad.' Eddy became silent, picturing himself driving home from his business in Liverpool to a large detached house filled with happy children. There would be his three and Ross, although the latter would never be told that he was not a Carr. Closing his eyes he thought, London or Liverpool, the dream could still come true one day. He still had some months to go in the army, and in his letter to George Potterton had left his options open. Abby would come round in the end, he was sure of it. If she had another baby, she'd have no choice but to give up this silly career. Babies would do it, he told himself. Everything would come right in the end.

Lying close to Southend on Sea, Canvey Island was joined to Benfleet on the mainland by a road bridge. Its low-lying marshlands had been reclaimed from the sea over centuries, and were protected by walls and drainage dykes. A place of saltings, creeks and sheep, Canvey had become popular with Londoners because of its close proximity to the capital. Along its southern end were the esplanades, offering seaside attractions such as pools, cafés and bathing beaches. Eastwards lay the Thames Estuary, westwards the

Shell oil refinery at Coryton, and the north boasted views of Two Tree Island and, beyond that, Hadleigh Castle.

'Well, this is more like it. Beats blooming old Bermondsey every time.' Evelyn grinned at Abby and Eddy, who'd accompanied her to the island to see a bungalow for sale. It stood in a road filled with similar bungalows on the south side of the island. There was a good-sized garden in the rear, and a small one at the front. Inside were three small bedrooms, a dining-cum-sitting room, a small kitchen with a home-made 'lean-to', and a bathroom which filled Evelyn with delight. 'Imagine being able to run a bath from a tap! And we'll 'ave an inside toilet. About time, too. I loathe emptying chamber pots. It's your father what uses them, 'im and Mrs O'Connor. Can't expect them to go out in the middle of the night when it's cold.'

Eddy followed his mother, with the housing agent, around the bungalow, and gave advice wherever he could. The place was very shabby and needed a lot of work, but in time he could lick it into shape.

To Evelyn, however, the ordinary little bungalow was a palace, and she could scarcely contain her growing excitement. 'Our own place at last, and just what we can afford.' She frowned as she gazed out of the window towards the marshes and sea. 'Of course, I don't think it'll be so easy persuading your Dad that Canvey's better than London.'

'You'll 'ave to,' said Eddy sternly. 'If not, I don't reckon Dad'll survive next winter. Emphysema and London fogs don't mix. You've no idea what a shock I get each time I come 'ome.'

Abby, however, had misgivings. 'It's a nice bungalow, but don't you think this whole area is too low-lying? Think of the winter months. Suppose there's flooding?'

'Oh, there's little danger of that,' the estate agent stepped in smartly. 'The sea defences were strengthened years ago.'

Deciding to buy the bungalow, pending a surveyor's report, Evelyn walked with her son and daughter-in-law towards the sea. Abby was carrying Ross in her arms, and the child pointed to the sheep excitedly. It was a warm, hazy afternoon, and from somewhere out at sea, a ship's siren sent a mournful sound across the island.

Evelyn breathed in deeply. 'Hmmm, lovely! We'll be able to sit in our garden breathing clean air for once.' But in her heart she couldn't believe she was about to leave Bermondsey. Her roots were there, deep and strong, and suddenly she felt uncertain about the whole thing. Not for the world would she show it, though. Harry could not survive in London, therefore she would leave it.

On the journey homeward, Abby was quiet, staring out of the train window.

'Penny for them,' said Eddy. Ross lay curled against his shoulder, thumb in his mouth, eyes closing in rapid movements as sleep finally came.

Abby pulled herself back to the present and smiled. 'Oh, I was just thinking, wouldn't Southend itself be a better place to live?'

Evelyn shook her head. 'I've looked at the prices and they just don't compare. A bungalow like that in Southend would cost another couple of 'undred, and we just don't 'ave it. We can buy outright with Mrs O'Connor's money if we buy at Canvey. After all, no one's gonna give us a mortgage, are they?' She leaned back and smiled. 'And it's come at the right time. A letter came from the council saying we're all to be re-housed in the New Year. They're pulling down the properties in Victoria Place to build flats. Now who in their right mind wants to live in a flat? And isn't it just typical of them to move everyone around in the winter months? We're supposed to go to Borough Market, they said. Can you imagine? Still, we're independent of them now, so stuff the lot, that's what I say.'

As Abby watched her mother-in-law, she suddenly realized how old and tired Evelyn had become. The greying hair sat uneasily with her pallid complexion, and the dark shadows beneath her eyes told of wakeful nights and volumes of worries.

Eddy looked thoughtful. 'If they won't be putting anyone else into the 'ouse after you leave, then surely they'll let Abby and me stay on until the demolition squad move in.'

Evelyn frowned. 'Stay on! What are you talking about? Abby'll be moving to Canvey with us.'

There was an awkward pause, then Abby spoke. 'No, I thought you knew I'd be staying in London with Ross.'

Evelyn looked stricken. 'You can't mean to stay in Bermondsey alone all day, just you and the baby.'

'I'll be working,' said Abby, realizing she was now becoming the most unpopular member of the family that had always nourished her. 'And Ross will go into the Turner Street Nursery by day.'

'What!' Evelyn had come to love Ross deeply and the idea of parting with him, knowing he would be placed in the hands of complete strangers, caused her an anguish she had not known since the death of Abby's mother and baby sister.

She looked at Abby with pleading eyes. 'There's no need for you to work, luv, not now. Your place is with us. If you still want a little job, then you can get one in Southend. The buses go from Benfleet all the time.'

'I'm receiving training for a career of my own,' said Abby firmly. 'One day I hope to design clothes myself. Start up my own business.'

'Start up your *what*!' Evelyn exclaimed. 'You live in cloud-cuckoo-land, my girl. Women don't start up businesses.' She looked at her son angrily. 'Well, what 'ave you to say about all this?'

Eddy met her gaze, as if to say, *'I've tried, but it's useless. You know Abby. Say nothing more and give her time to come round.'*

Evelyn said nothing, but glared at Abby from time

to time with deep disapproval. What with this and the Liverpool fiasco, the girl was out of control. Eddy should put his foot down. She'd heard them both quarrelling about Liverpool. But then she'd decided that it was too far away and Abby was right to be wary. But this latest bombshell was different, and it made her angry.

When Eddy returned to Hamburg, Abby breathed a deep and guilty sigh of relief. Was it so wrong, she wondered, to want something more than Evelyn ever had? Was she wrong in continuing to live a lie? Evelyn thought Ross was Eddy's son, and Eddy had no idea that Ross was the result of incest. Was it not kinder to let them both go on thinking what they wanted to think?

As for Ross, God had smiled on the child, after all. Far from being handicapped, he was forward for his age. His eyes cornflower-blue, his hair the purest spun gold, he tended to chubbiness and laughed a lot. In short, he was the most contented baby a mother could hope to raise. But he had a long road to travel, and some day he might learn the truth about his parentage, no matter how much Abby tried to protect him from it.

What then? One thing only had become clear. Throughout the past months of guilt, shame and fear, Abby's natural love had won through. She had only realized it when Evelyn offered to take Ross with them to Canvey. It was then Abby knew she did not want to be parted from her son, no matter how difficult life became.

'Well, just what will you do if Eddy insists on going to Liverpool?' Susan asked, stirring her tea. She had rushed from the Charing Cross Road to meet Abby for a snack lunch in their usual cafe off Berwick Street.

'I don't know,' said Abby. 'The trouble is, he's so dead keen on the idea of being a partner in a firm. He thinks it's a gift from the gods.'

'So it is,' said Susan, sensible to the last. 'And frankly

207

he'd be a fool to take the shares. Starting up a business in today's financial climate is very hard. I know, because Daddy's always going on about it.' She sighed. 'But that leaves you in one hell of a situation.'

Abby's chin took on that defiant thrust which Susan had seen so often before. 'Well, I won't go – so that's final.'

'You're forcing him to choose between his career and you?' asked Susan.

'Maybe I am, I don't know,' said Abby. 'Please God I never have to find out. I don't want to hurt him. The Carrs have done so much for me. They've been my family since I was nine years old. How can I fight that?'

'You can't,' said Susan. 'And we women have to follow our men whatever we think. It's always been that way, and you won't change the world.'

'Oh, let's change the subject,' said Abby. She drank her tea, then talked about her job at the salon, and the people with whom she worked. Susan spoke about her course, and gave all the latest news from St Martin's. Soon Abby was back in the old life, a carefree student talking and laughing with her friend.

'Oh yes, and I went to a play at RADA the other night and your cousin was in it – Stella Glenister. I saw her name in the programme, and, since Pippa had a friend in the play, we went backstage afterwards and I met her.'

Abby raised her eyebrows in surprise. 'Stella! What ... I mean ... was she any good?'

'She only had a small part. The play was *Measure for Measure*, and frankly I didn't understand a single word of it. She was all right, I suppose.' Susan then looked serious, as though trying to decide whether to say more about the meeting or not.

'What? What is it?' asked Abby, recognizing her expression. 'Did you get a chance to speak to her? What did she say ... anything about Richard?'

Susan looked up from her cup, then bit her lip uncertainly. But now that she had spoken of Stella, it would be impossible to keep anything back from Abby.

'Go on, go on!' Abby's heart was in her mouth. 'What did she say about him?'

'He's in Malaya. Apparently he gave up Oxford and is doing his National Service.'

'Malaya,' Abby repeated quietly. 'Fighting? In the jungle, fighting communists? He wanted this rather than stay in England?'

Susan nodded and said nothing, while Abby digested the news. Her expression showed an inner struggle – pity versus anger. 'Why?' she said at last. 'What on earth made him do such a thing? What a fool he's been. He's wanted to be a barrister since he was fourteen. And now because of me he's thrown it all away.' She tried to fight back the tears she could feel misting her eyes. *Poor Richard! Poor, devastated man.*

'Did ... did Stella say anything more? I mean, it must have come as a blow to his parents.'

Susan nodded and said gently, 'Oh, Abby, I'm a fool. Why don't I learn to keep my stupid mouth shut? I didn't mean to tell you, but ...'

'I'm glad you did,' said Abby. 'And if you ever hear anything else I expect you to tell me. How else am I going to know what's going on?' She lapsed into a long silence, once more thinking of William. *He must be shattered. First, his daughter, who believes she's his niece, leaves without a word, and marries into the Carr family. Then his son walks out on all his dreams and ambitions, to take up arms.* 'Is my ... my uncle all right? Is he well? Did Stella say?'

'Oh, yes, he's quite well, I believe.' Susan glanced at her watch and stood up. 'It's late. I must fly.' Looking down at her friend, who seemed not to have heard her, she said: 'Oh, I do wish you'd confide in me. I know your aunt is behind all the things that have happened, I just know it. What *did* she say to you that day in Harrods?'

209

Abby raised her green eyes as though coming out of a sleep. 'She told me something I could never repeat to a living soul, not even to my best friend. Sorry, Susan. But please try to understand.'

Susan shook her head. 'No, I'll never understand in a million years, but I respect your need for privacy. Anyhow, shall we meet again next Thursday? Same time?'

Their next meeting arranged, the two girls went their separate ways. Abby hardly knew where her feet were taking her, as she thought of Richard in Malaya. He was in danger, and it was all her fault. Shocked, ashamed and humiliated, she had made the wrong decision in trying to protect him, and save her own pride. Richard, hurt and angry, and not knowing why she had left him, was now in deadly peril, when he should be safe at Oxford.

Please God, keep him safe from harm, she found herself praying silently, as she entered Maddox Street.

CHAPTER TEN

'Your Uncle William has died.' The words were just beginning to sink in as the Canterbury train sped on through the fields and woods of Kent. *My father has died*, thought Abby, still trying to come to terms with the fact. It had been only yesterday, during a particularly hectic morning, that Justine had called Abby to the telephone.

'I've some bad news for you, Abby,' Susan's voice had sounded grave on the other end of the line. 'Stella rang me, knowing that I could contact you. I'm afraid that your Uncle William has died. It happened last Friday. Someone found him slumped over the desk in his office. He had a massive heart attack. They say he must have died instantly. Oh, Abby, I am so terribly sorry.'

Stunned, Abby had finally managed to ask, 'Did Stella say when the funeral would be?'

'Wednesday, two o'clock at Ashton Green.' Then Susan had added, 'But your aunt doesn't expect you to be there. Stella just thought you ought to be told, that's all.'

At this, Abby had felt a sudden upsurge of anger. How dare Milicent assume that she would stay away from her own father's funeral? He had been good to her, and she had hurt him most dreadfully. Surely she could at least stand by his grave and bid him farewell.

Now, as she looked out at the orchards and oasthouses set amid hop gardens, she was glad that Richard was so far away. Had he been in England, she would not be making this journey. Poor Richard, she thought. It was unlikely that he even knew of his father's death. How could they get word to him in the jungle? It might be months before he found out. That was sad.

It was a chill November day and brown leaves blew about the churchyard as Abby walked through the lychgate towards the west door of the church. The bus had been late, and as she heard the strains of 'Abide with Me' mingle with the wind soughing through the trees, she paused. The service had already started behind the closed oak doors. Since she was neither expected nor welcome, she decided to wait in the porch until the moment of burial.

Tense, filled with remorse, she sat quietly, a sad figure in a smart black suit. Her red hair had been swept into a neat chignon and was topped by a small half-moon hat made in velvet to match the collar of the suit. She had made this outfit, of her own design, during her long and tedious house-bound days, and found it ironic that its first airing should be at her father's funeral. She might have broken William's heart, she thought bitterly, but at least she was dressed properly for his burial.

The congregation was praying, their murmuring voices muffled by the thickness of the ancient oak door. Abby had never felt quite so outcast as she did now, nor so lonely. Yet loneliness had been her lot since the Carrs had moved to Canvey in August, leaving her at Victoria Place. Each morning she had wheeled Ross to the nursery, worked a long and hard day, then collected him in the evenings. Since Justine gave no quarter to young mothers, he was usually the last baby left, and she was forever thanking whichever nursemaid stayed on until her late arrival. As for Ross, he missed his old routine and Evelyn's confident hands. He cried each morning when Abby left him, yet disliked being taken from the warmth of the nursery back to a cold and damp-smelling house. Maybe Evelyn had been right to talk of having him at Canvey. All Abby knew, however, was that without Ross she had no one.

Now, as she waited for the service to end, she looked down at her gloved hands, thinking that for today, at least, Ross would be happy. Evelyn had rushed to London on receiving Abby's telegram, enabling her to attend the funeral. Victoria Place and Canterbury were a world apart, with only Ross linking that world with this.

Her gaze fixed on the fourteenth-century cottages beyond. She was back in Ashton Green, a place she had thought never to see again. But what a sad homecoming! It hardly seemed possible that William would not be at Ferndene Lodge when she returned to her old home. There was so much she had to say to him, but he wouldn't be there. Instead she would be face to face with her sister and stepmother, yet call them cousin and aunt. *Madness! To hell with them both*. She leaned back against the stone wall, her heart filled with anguish, not just for William's passing, but for the passing of her innocence and happiness.

As the church doors opened, Abby moved out of sight, and watched the procession, intending to merge with the mourners as they progressed to the grave.

The Vicar appeared, then the pall bearers with the wreath-covered coffin. It stabbed at Abby's heart to think of that dear, gentle man who now lay within it. If only she could have seen him before this, to explain, to ask his forgiveness! When Milicent appeared, all in formal widow's weeds, with Stella holding her arm, Abby pulled back, feeling this was not the time for them to meet. There were many mourners, most of them employees of Glenisters, but also people from the village. Mrs Wellings was crying into her handkerchief, so too was Mrs Blackstock, who took Abby by the arm and whispered chokingly:

'I'm so glad you came, dear. Your uncle would be, too. He's missed you dreadfully, and we're all going to miss him.'

So saying she took a firmer grip on Abby's arm and urged her towards the graveside, where she deemed her place should be. Abby tried to stay back, but Mrs Blackstock would have none of it.

Keeping her gaze on the coffin, Abby fought back her tears, but it was useless; once started they would not stop.

213

She glanced up at the mourners on the far side of the grave and froze. Beside his mother stood Richard. He was wearing a black coat, leaning heavily on a cane, and was staring straight at her.

Her eyes met his across the open grave, and in them she saw hatred and accusation. Vaguely she could hear the Vicar's ecclesiastical tones – 'dust to dust, ashes to ashes, in the sure and certain hope' – but her heart was pounding and she felt dizzy. It was a dream, a nightmare. Richard was in Malaya, not standing there in black with those terrible accusing eyes.

When the coffin had been lowered into the ground, Milicent stepped forward. Face hidden behind a black veil, she threw a handful of earth onto the grave, then stepped back seeking the support of her children. Only Stella gave it to her. Richard had not taken his eyes off Abby.

At last it was over. People started walking away, but Abby could not move. Mrs Blackstock beside her whispered, 'Are you all right, dear? Come on. Come back to the house.'

Abby nodded, murmuring, 'Yes. I will, in a minute.'

Understanding the girl's desire to be alone, Mrs Blackstock walked away sadly.

Turning from the grave, Abby headed straight for the rear gate which led into Back Lane.

'Abby!' cried Richard. 'For God's sake, stop!'

Abby hesitated, then hurried forward once more, as if fearful of the man behind her. At his second shout, she paused again and this time turned. Richard was limping towards her as quickly as his injured leg would allow. Then he was beside her, reaching for her hand. At his touch, life returned to Abby and she tried to pull away.

'Oh no,' said Richard, through clenched teeth. 'You don't run out on me again.'

'Let me go. Oh please, Richard, let me go!' Her voice was a sob as she tried to pull from his grasp, but his hold was too strong and her will too weak. 'I . . . I didn't expect you to be here.' She kept her head turned from him. 'I wouldn't have come if I had known.'

Richard dropped her hand abruptly, and when Abby turned she saw hurt and anger in his face. 'Do I repulse you that much, then?' Like a defeated man he sighed and, leaning more heavily on his stick, said: 'Once you spoke of loving me always. We planned our future together. It was unthinkable for us to live without each other.'

'Oh, Richard,' sobbed Abby, tears streaming down her face. 'That was a lifetime ago.'

A young woman approached them from the mourners waiting at the other gate.

'Richard, we're all waiting ...' Stella's voice trailed off in surprise as she saw Abby. 'I didn't realize you were here,' she said coldly.

Abby bristled and thought of her father's body not yet covered with earth. 'No. I wasn't expected and I'm just leaving.'

'No, you're not,' said Richard. 'We're all going back to the house together.'

'I don't believe it!' Stella was looking at him aghast. 'After what *she's* done to us all? I think she's got a cheek coming here today. She broke Daddy's heart and now that he's dead she comes crawling back ...'

'Shut up!' hissed Richard, his eyes blazing. Turning to Abby, he said, 'You came here today for Father, and for his sake and memory I think we should bury the hatchet, and help Mother to deal with our guests.' He put a firm hand on her arm. 'The car's waiting.' His resolute manner left the women no alternative but to do his bidding.

Milicent was already seated in the car when Abby climbed in. Her head lifted slightly but it was hard to read the expression beneath that veil. During the journey home Abby stared at her stepmother. *She's afraid I'll tell them. I wonder if she's cried at all? Well he's gone now, Milicent Glenister, and neither you nor I can hurt him any more.*

The car eased slowly along the lanes and entered the High

Street, where people had drawn their curtains as a mark of respect. An elderly gentleman raised his hat in homage to William Glenister's memory as they passed. No one inside the car spoke. After what seemed an eternity, the Rolls finally pulled up outside Ferndene Lodge.

Inside the house, long-serving members of William's staff mingled uneasily with Milicent's friends. Samantha Fellowes was there standing close to Richard, as he did his best to play the host. He was the head of the family now, and, to those watching, it seemed that Samantha would take her place by his side. Was this what she was supposed to see? thought Abby bitterly. Had Richard brought her back here to hurt her like this?

'He was very ill, you know,' said Stella, standing beside her now.

Abby studied her half-sister. Gone was the puppy fat and rounded face. The dark hair was swept back to reveal high cheekbones, large eyes and full lips. And there was, indeed, a hint of Jean Simmons in Stella's features now. 'What happened to him?' asked Abby.

'He led an attack on a communist stronghold. Two bullets hit vital internal organs and one shattered his thigh.' Stella stared at Abby accusingly. 'We nearly lost him. It was weeks before they let him sail home to an army hospital here. He was awarded the Military Cross for outstanding courage and valour. Daddy was very proud of him ...' Her voice cracked with emotion. 'He's gone through all that and he's still not twenty-two. He's killed and seen men killed. He'll never be the same again, and it's all your fault. How could you have done it to him?'

Abby was trembling, and tears blurred her vision. 'I would have given the world for him,' she gasped.

'Of course, Mother and Samantha have been marvellous,' Stella went on, ignoring Abby's remark. 'They've nursed him back to health. He only got rid of the crutches a week ago. I really don't think he would have made it this far without Samantha. Do you know that girl could have had the pick of the English aristocracy, but she's turned her back on all of them, even that Jeremy what's-his-name, because she loves Richard.'

Stella really knew how to turn the knife, thought Abby, hurting every bit as much as was intended. But the quiet haranguing was not yet over.

'Poor Richard,' she went on. 'As far back as I can remember he's always wanted to be a barrister. And he was doing so well until you did the dirty on him. Then he just seemed to fall apart. Even worse was the way Daddy took it. He was so desolate, so confused about everything. He kept asking where you were and why you didn't come home. In the end, I had to tell him that you had married and would never be coming home again. It shook him badly. He and Mummy had a terrible row and ... frankly I'm surprised the big attack didn't happen then. He cared a lot for you, Abby, and you repaid him in such a cruel way. I agree with Mummy – it was a dark day when you were brought to this house.'

Abby listened to all this with increasing despair. It was intolerable, and the truth would have to be told. 'You don't understand, Stella. I discovered something which left me no option but to ...'

'Oh, we know what you found out,' cut in Stella, waving a dismissive hand. 'There was still no excuse for you to behave as you did.'

'You *know*!' Abby repeated, perplexed. 'But she said you weren't to know. Richard too? Richard knows?'

'Yes, of course.'

'And yet you still ask why I ran away from him?' Abby asked in growing amazement.

'*I* don't,' snapped Stella. 'Mummy told Richard you'd take it badly. He didn't believe her, of course. Never does. But, in the event, she proved to be right. He's a romantic fool. Believes in true love and all that.'

Abby could hardly breathe, let alone reply. Her gaze focused on Milicent standing beside the piano talking to

Willard Moore, the family solicitor. Briefly the women looked at each other, then Milicent quickly turned away.

It was unbelievable that Stella could say such things. 'I must get some air,' gasped Abby, hurrying out of the room into the garden. There she stood, inhaling the cold damp air until her head cleared.

'Mrs Carr? You are staying a little longer, I hope?'

Turning, Abby saw that Willard Moore had followed her outside. 'No, Mr Moore, I'm about to leave.'

'Oh dear. Mr Glenister was most specific that everyone should be together for the reading of his Will, and Mrs Glenister has kindly agreed that, in spite of the sad circumstances, this would be the only time his wishes could be carried out.' Reaching into the inner pocket of his dark suit, he brought out a white envelope. 'Mr Glenister charged me to deliver this letter to you upon his death. I thought you might like to glance at it now. There is also a small bequest, so please stay a little longer. I can offer you a lift to the station, if you have a train to catch.'

When the solicitor returned to the house, Abby tore open the letter.

My darling Abby,

I have, for so long, wanted to tell you the truth – but you must understand my silence was to ensure your welfare.

You are not my niece, but my daughter. I believe you already know this, and am grieved that you should have been so terribly hurt by it. When I told Milicent, she promised not to tell you. Now I think she broke that promise, and that you felt the need to stay away from me thereafter.

I do not know what you were told, but the truth is that I loved your mother, and wanted her to come with me to Folkestone when I inherited the shops. However, she refused to leave London and her ailing father, who died soon after you were born. I was hurt and angry, and our parting was a hostile one, I'm afraid. Only later did I learn that she had married my cousin, when he wrote chiding me for failing the woman I had put in the family way. He thought that I had refused to marry your mother, when, in fact, I had known nothing of her pregnancy. Your mother was a lovely woman of fierce pride and honesty, who did not deceive my cousin into thinking her unborn child was his. Her death was a shock to me. When I found out that you were alive, it seemed that I was being given a chance to put right the wrong I had done.

I know this has hurt you deeply, but I want you to understand that I grew to love you as much, if not more, than I loved Stella and Richard.

God willing you never have to read this letter. I hope to get the chance to tell you all this in person, when the bitterness you feel towards me has softened a little.

Please forgive me for everything, and always remember how deeply I cared for you. Your loving father,

William

It struck Abby to the heart to learn her father had blamed himself for her behaviour. Had he been so blind to her love for Richard? Had he really believed Milicent's revelation had driven her from home? Poor, disillusioned man.

She was putting the letter away when a deep voice said, 'Don't go.' Turning, Abby saw Richard standing in the doorway, one hand on his stick, the other resting on the lintel. He looked tall and much older. The rage in his eyes was replaced by tenderness as he came towards her, and touched her face gently. 'Don't go,' he murmured softly. 'I've tried hating you and I've tried to put you from my mind, but it's impossible. Even in the jungle ...' he smiled weakly. 'Seeing you here it's as though none of it happened. I love you as much as I ever did.' His voice seemed wrenched from him by a passion he could not control. 'Why in God's name did you turn from me?'

Fighting her desire to rush into his arms, Abby shook her head in despair. 'Don't. Please don't. You *know* why we can no longer be together; you know and yet you say such things.'

'But after all that happened between us ...'

'Exactly,' cut in Abby. 'That's what makes it so terrible.'

'We could, at least, have talked about it first,' he said.

'Talk!' Abby looked at him in astonishment. 'Talk! There are some things in this world that no decent person can talk about.' Hurrying away to the rear of the garden, she found herself trembling. One white rose withered on the climbers against the old brick wall; apples rotted on the ground and the air was filled with the rich autumnal smell of wood smoke and fruit. By the gate she paused, listening to the sound of the river beyond, and saw Richard standing where she had left him. He looked so dejected and alone that she longed to put her arms about him, to comfort him and say that everything was all right. But everything was not all right.

Richard stared at her for some time, then turned and, leaning heavily on his stick, walked slowly back into the house. It was then that Abby saw the tall woman in deep black watching from inside the Lodge. Milicent looked apprehensive, and could no longer hide her feelings behind a black veil. *She wants me to go away, right now. Well, damn you, Milicent Glenister! I shall stay for the reading of the Will, as my father wished.*

When Abby returned to the house most of the guests had left. Willard Moore met her in the hallway and ushered her towards the dining room where Stella was already seated at the table. The two girls sat without speaking. Only the loud ticking of the grandfather clock broke the stony silence between them. At length, they were joined by the others. Richard took his place opposite Abby, much to her discomfort, while Willard Moore moved to the head of the table, where William used to sit. The solicitor paused to look at Milicent.

'Your husband changed his Will a few months ago.' He cleared his throat, then began. '"To Mrs Blackstock, for her unfailing kindness and hard work over the years, I leave the sum of one hundred pounds."' The solicitor looked up. 'I see the lady isn't present.'

Milicent nodded. 'She's washing the dishes. I'll tell her later.'

'I did ask for her to be present.'

'And I asked her to get on with her work!' snapped Milicent. 'Please do go on, Mr Moore; it's been a very long and tiring day.'

'"To my daughter Stella, and to Abigail, I leave the sum of eight hundred pounds each."'

Abby gasped in astonishment, ignoring Stella's look of horror. Eight hundred pounds! It was a fortune.

'"The rest of my estate, including my business and home, Ferndene Lodge, I leave to my son, Richard Philip."' Mr Moore glanced up and registered the shock on Milicent's face. Her expression matched that of her daughter. '"There is a proviso here, however, that the said family home, Ferndene Lodge, shall be lived in by my wife, Milicent Ann, until her death or possible re-marriage. Only then may Richard live in it, or dispose of it as he wishes. This I have done to ensure that the estate remains in the family."' The solicitor took off his glasses and stared at the stunned faces without further comment. Clearly William had not trusted his wife, and there had been rumours of an affair when this new Will had been made.

Milicent finally found her voice. 'This is outrageous! I am his widow and have a prior claim to the family home. By all means, let Richard have the business, but the house is mine.'

'Of course it's yours,' said Richard. 'I'm hardly likely to turn you out into the snow, now am

221

I? You can't sell it, that's all. And you can't re-marry.'

Milicent looked at her son long and hard. 'Would you really hold me to that?'

The look she received in return was just as penetrating, but Richard said nothing. Willard Moore could see another difficult situation arising, and quickly added: 'As for money, Mrs Glenister, your husband did have life insurance, so you should have enough to live on.'

'Well, I think the whole thing is a disgrace,' said Stella, suddenly. 'Why should Richard inherit?' She looked around the table. When no one answered, she tightened her lips angrily and said: 'I'm contesting this will, Mr Moore.'

'It specifically states that . . .'

'I don't care what it states,' snapped Stella. 'I'm contesting it, so that's that.'

'Think of the business,' said Richard. 'It can't run in a state of limbo. Who's to manage it? You're at RADA and have no interest in the store.'

Stella gave him a withering look. 'I've no objection to you managing it, but I see no reason why you should own it as well. Don't daughters count?'

Abby listened in growing confusion. How could Stella make such a fuss? It was extraordinary. It seemed perfectly logical to her that Richard should inherit. So why were they talking in this fashion?

The solicitor cleared his throat once more and tapped his glasses on the mahogany table, saying: 'Mr Glenister's instructions were crystal clear. If you mean to contest the Will, then I must warn you that such litigation can take years.'

Stella was in a fighting mood. 'I don't care. I just want justice.'

Mr Moore returned the will to his briefcase and stood up. 'This is hardly the time for such a discussion. I suggest you come to my office, Miss Glenister, and we'll talk about it there.'

Glancing at her mother, aware of her grief, Stella fell silent for a while. 'Very well,' she said quietly. 'Later, then. I'm sorry, Mummy, but I feel very strongly about it.'

Richard got up from the table, murmuring, 'I damn well need a drink.' He went to the sideboard and poured a whisky, before remembering his manners. 'How about you, Mr Moore?'

The solicitor shook his head. 'Thank you, but no. I'm driving Mrs Carr to the station in a minute.'

Richard stared at Abby. 'No. Not just yet, please.' His eyes were pleading. 'We've had no chance to talk properly.'

Abby longed to feel his arms about her once more. But only a sibling kiss was permissible now. 'I do have a train to catch.'

At this Richard turned and limped away. As Abby saw him go, looking so crushed and defeated, her heart melted. She turned to Willard Moore. 'Would you mind waiting one moment longer?' she asked.

In the garden, Richard was standing, with his back to her, beside the wooden garden seat. He did not turn at her approach.

'I still don't understand,' he said quietly, 'why you had to marry so quickly, without even a word to me. After all we meant to each other, why did you run to another man the minute you found out?'

Abby said nothing as she struggled with the uncertainty in her mind. Finally, she knew the truth had to be told, shameful and humiliating though it was. 'We have a son.'

Richard turned slowly, his expression one of growing amazement. 'What did you say?' he whispered.

'Our baby needed a father, and Eddy was there for me.' The look on Richard's face was incomprehensible. Was he shamed, shocked or angry?

'You were carrying *our* child,' he murmured, at last, 'yet

you said nothing to me. Now you justify your marriage to a man I cannot believe you love, by saying that *my* son needed a father?'

'I don't understand you!' cried Abby.

'Nor I, you. You are over-reacting to something I could not help. I told you in my letter ...'

'Letter!' Abby broke in. 'What letter?'

Richard sank down onto the bench, the pain in his leg becoming too much to bear. 'The bloody letter I wish to God I'd never written!'

Abby touched his hand gently. 'I never received it. When was this?'

'The summer following Cornwall.'

Abby gazed at him in bewilderment. 'You knew, even then? But your mother told me she would say nothing to you.'

Richard looked confused. 'How strange. When Mother broke the news to me at Oxford, she tried to persuade me not to tell you. Yet then she told you herself. It makes no sense.'

'No,' murmured Abby, remembering all that Milicent had said that Saturday morning in Harrods. 'It makes no sense at all. Still, that doesn't lessen its shattering impact on both of us.'

Richard was looking at her with hurt eyes. 'Was it *so* shattering?'

'There you go again, making it sound like nothing!' Abby could not bring herself to use the terrible word 'incest'. It was too horrendous. Had Richard no shame, no sense of decency? Was this the man she loved to distraction? She wanted to be far away from this place and this shame. 'Goodbye, Richard. We can never see each other again. Never.'

He caught her by the arm and pulled her down again. 'Why not? I love you, Abby. Why should I let you go?'

'You must,' she cried, tears flowing down her face. 'You know you must, so why make it more difficult?'

224

'I know no such thing,' said Richard, gripping her arm until she winced with pain. 'I want you and I want my son. I won't have him raised by some semi-literate cockney. I won't!'

'You have no choice.' Abby gave a violent tug and rushed away.

As the black Humber drove past the Cathedral, Abby turned to look at the great edifice for the last time, remembering the days when she had wandered the Precincts in search of Richard. That was all so long ago, she thought now.

On the train back to London, she could not forget the bewildered look on Richard's face, and the cry of her name that came from deep within him as she rushed away. Her heart was breaking and it hurt; it physically hurt so much that she thought she might not live through this.

The two other women in the carriage with her pretended not to notice the distraught young woman in black. They kept their heads turned away firmly, one feigning sleep and the other reading an evening newspaper long after there was nothing left for her to read.

Bulldozers tore down the old houses in Victoria Place early in December. The council's decision to bring the demolition forward had come as a shock, and Abby had been forced to find somewhere quickly. It was a small, two-edroom flat in a depressing Victorian house on an equally depressing street, off the Old Kent Road. The sitting room overlooked an old disused graveyard. The trees were spiky skeletons in a foggy cold world, while the church itself had closed down ten years earlier because of severe bomb damage.

It seemed impossible to Abby that Christmas was only two weeks away. Her life had become one endless round of work and mothering. More often than not, it would be after nine o'clock at night before she could collect Ross since, in readiness for Coronation Year, Justine was taking on more work than she could handle and expected her staff to stay late.

Of Abby's inheritance there was still no sign. She was at a loss to understand why it was being withheld from her, and telephoned Willard Moore, only to learn that Stella had carried out her threat to contest the Will. Nothing of William's estate could be touched until legal matters were settled.

'But how long will that be, Mr Moore?'

The solicitor had replied that such disputes had been known to drag on for years. 'But I'm sure it won't come to that, Mrs Carr.'

Abby had been on the verge of giving in to Evelyn's wishes and taking Ross to live in Canvey, but then found a sympathetic nursery-maid who agreed to look after the baby each evening in her own home for the sum of five shillings per week. It made a big hole in her earnings, but she had no choice. Wheeling Ross home through the cold night air, along dark and mean streets where gangs of loud-mouthed youths hung around the pubs, was a task Abby dreaded and hated. It would end, she kept telling herself. This awful time could not go on.

Worn out by the time she climbed into bed, she found herself unable to sleep properly. During the day, her busy life quelled painful memories, but, at night, she thought of Richard's tormented face, and heard again his cry as she'd walked away from him for the last time. Anguish gnawed at her and, at times, she found the pain unbearable. What else could she have done? Did he hate her now, when she was condemned to love him all the days of her life?

After tossing and turning all night, Abby welcomed the work which drove away her tormented thoughts. Not only did she work hard, she was learning fast also. Justine's designs might be 'variations on a theme', but she still had to sketch them out, then make a toile and the pattern, all of which Abby absorbed with the greatest of ease. Progressing from cuffs and buttons, she was now making up whole garments, with seams and boning finished to perfection.

Justine was happy with her little seamstress. 'How lucky we are that you learn so quickly,' she said again and again, causing Abby to think wryly that money would be more welcome than flattering words. As it was, she had cut down on fuel by being out nearly all day, and food was, more often than not, a snatched sandwich at lunchtime and baked beans on toast at night. Only on rare occasions did she find the time to meet Susan in their usual cafe, but when she did, such meetings did more than anything in the world to lift Abby's spirits.

With Eddy's demobilization coming so soon in the New Year, he was unable to return home from Germany for Christmas leave. Abby took Ross to Canvey Island, where Evelyn, who had never known a Christmas without her son, did her best to make something out of the occasion.

'It's awful, this first time without 'im,' she confided to Abby when they were walking along the sea wall on Boxing Day. The sun was shining, but a cold east wind cut through their coats and blew the scarves from their heads. 'Still, we lose one and gain another. Now we 'ave Ross. His first Christmas.' She smiled and gazed across the busy shipping lanes of the Thames Estuary to the Isle of Grain beyond. 'It's kids what make Christmas, after all.'

'Do you miss London?' asked Abby, glad that Ross was inside sleeping so that she and her mother-in-law could have this time on their own.

Evelyn nodded. 'Like the very devil. I didn't realize just 'ow much I would miss it. But Dad's a lot better, thank goodness, and that's what it's all about. We did the right thing, even though I think we all miss the old place more than we thought we would. Well, it's very different, especially in the winter months. Funny, I'd always thought I'd like living by the sea. Now that I do, I'm not so sure about it.'

Abby's gaze followed the line of mud and shingle which served as a beach, but her thoughts were on the letter she had received three days earlier in Eddy's Christmas card. He had made it clear that he was having second thoughts about the partnership, and had been in touch with George Potterton again. They'd agreed that another visit to Liverpool would be the best thing before making a final decision. Although this had come as no surprise to Abby, she felt sick at heart just the same, knowing quite well the decision Eddy would finally make.

Liverpool! It was unthinkable. And so unnecessary, when she had eight hundred pounds coming to her. Eddy should sell the shares, get a decent job with his new qualifications, and buy a small house. She could then continue with her training, and maybe use her legacy to set up her own business one day.

As Abby walked beside Evelyn, she thought about her options. She could put her foot down and tell Eddy to choose between her and the partnership, thus causing him to resent her for the rest of his life; or she could accept this new life in a strange place with a man she cared for, but could not love; or she could leave him, depriving Ross of a decent home, and a stepfather who loved him. She was on the horns of a terrible dilemma, yet found herself chatting on about the weather and Harry's health.

'Well, I'm sure of one thing,' she said in answer to Evelyn's remark, 'had you still been in London, I don't think he would have survived that last peasouper. It killed so many.'

Evelyn nodded. 'She's changed our lives, 'as Mrs O'Connor.'

And how, thought Abby wryly. If only William's legacy could be dealt with as quickly as that of Mrs O'Connor's son then Eddy would not be in such a hurry to venture north. 'Is she homesick, too?' was all she said.

'Difficult to say,' said Evelyn. 'If she was, we'd be the last to know about it. You know what she's like. Mind you, I think the old girl's found 'er niche already. Trots off to the pub every day, and knows more people now than I do.' She paused and turned to Abby. 'I've been thinking. She'll be eighty at the end of January and it'd be nice if we 'ad a bit of a do for her, at the pub. A kind of surprise party. What do you think? Will you and Eddy come? It'll be the first time we'll 'ave seen Eddy for months.'

Abby smiled. 'Of course we'll come. Can't let Mrs O celebrate her eightieth without us.' They had arrived back at the bungalow and Abby caught sight of the wooden name plate which was as old as the house.

'*Four Winds*. It's well named, I'll say that much!'

In the weeks that followed Christmas, it became obvious to all at Maddox Street that Justine was unwell, but typically she refused to see a doctor, claiming it was over-work. 'As soon as the Coronation is over, things will settle down again.'

But as the days passed, Justine became more ashen-faced, and spent more time away from the salon, leaving her small staff to cope with the excessive orders she had so happily accepted.

Abby began to worry. Supposing this was serious? So serious that the salon had to close and they all found themselves without a job? It would be worse for her, still in training. Would anyone else take her on? In the East End, the big chain producers would snap her up, but to what purpose? Churning out frocks for second-rate stores? Tough as things were, Abby liked working with a couturier; she loved the world of fashion and she loved London, and felt that things were really beginning to happen here. If she did not fight her corner, she would end up in Liverpool chained to the kitchen sink.

Eddy arrived home, free of his uniform, and itching to return, at last, to good old 'civvy street'. Happy to be back, he nevertheless missed the companionship of army life. Dismayed to find his wife too busy to spend any time with him, or her baby, he kept urging her to give up work now that he was home. But Abby said there was no way she could leave the salon while Justine was unwell. 'There's so much to do, you've no idea.'

'Well, don't expect me to wheel a pram each evening,' he had replied angrily. Yet he had done just this, collecting Ross as the light faded, and looking after the child until she returned. When Abby did arrive, he invariably found her over-tired, edgy, and pleading fatigue whenever he wanted to make love to her.

'It can't go on,' he said angrily one evening, when she came in long after nine o'clock. 'Dammit, I won't have my wife coming 'ome at this hour, too tired for me, too tired for the baby, too tired to eat properly and too tired ...' he stopped. 'Well, you know. It's ridiculous, Abby. You're working yourself to death — and for what? To make a nice fat profit for some ruddy foreigner.'

'She's sick.' Abby sank into the fireside chair, kicked off her shoes and felt the warmth of the electric fire on her toes. 'She can hardly help being ill.'

Eddy sat opposite and glanced around the miserable little room. 'What a dump this is! Listen, I'm off to Liverpool next weekend to see George. I know how you feel, luv, but at least give me this chance. Next week I'll make my decision, once and for all.'

Abby stared at him coldly. 'You've already made it, so stop all this pretence, Eddy.' Alarmed that the moment of truth was so suddenly upon them, she searched for some way of holding off the inevitable. Then her face lifted, as she remembered. 'Did you say next weekend?' When Eddy nodded, she smiled. 'It's Mrs O'Connor's eightieth and they are having a party for her at the pub that Saturday evening. I said we'd be there.'

Eddy had been expecting rage and fury, and had steeled himself for this moment with some well-rehearsed dialogue. This was the last reaction he'd expected, and it left him nonplussed.

'What? Bloody 'eck, I don't know a thing about it. George is expecting me now, so I can't put it off.'

'You *must*,' said Abby, leaning forward anxiously. 'It's her eightieth, and it's been arranged for weeks. I'm sorry, I forgot to tell you, but I've been so busy lately.' Eddy had been apart from his family for so long that perhaps he had grown away from them. Perhaps Germany was so big and so far that England seemed very small, and Liverpool no distance from London. Her hope lay in reversing such emotions within him.

Eddy stood up and ran anxious hands through his dark hair. 'No, I can't put George off again. The man will think me a fool.'

Abby was filled with consternation as she realized, by this time next week, her fate would be sealed. She had to have more time to think, even if it only amounted to another seven days. Eddy had to be made to reconsider.

'I can't believe this of you, Eddy Carr. Mrs O'Connor's been extraordinarily generous to you and, because of that very generosity, she's to be denied your presence at her eightieth birthday party. It's a very important day for her − and, let's face it, she hasn't had much fun in her life. You're like her own grandson, replacing the family she's lost.'

Eddy looked at Abby and his heart melted, as it did whenever she stared at him with those soft, helpless eyes. 'Oh, hell,' he murmured. 'You make me feel like a criminal.'

Abby could sense that he was wavering. 'It was all decided last Christmas, and I promised your mother that we'd be there. She'd be terribly hurt now if we let her down.' This was stretching the truth, in view of Evelyn's concern over Ross travelling in cold weather, but Abby was past caring.

'But what's George gonna think if I keep messing 'im about like this?' Eddy gave a long sigh. 'Oh, all right. Have it your way. I'll use the box on the corner and see if I can get through to 'im.'

He returned thirty minutes later, having re-arranged the

meeting. 'And nothing's gonna stop me going to Liverpool then, do you understand?'

Abby nodded in mild relief. She had a few precious days in which to make Eddy realize how miserable he'd be away from London. Fresh out of Germany, he'd hardly had time to re-adjust. He would – somehow she would make sure of that, and she only had seven days to do it in.

'It's beautiful, luv,' said Mrs O'Connor as she looked at the cream blouse which Abby had made for her birthday. Nothing else would be acceptable but the high Edwardian collar and tucks down the front. She had also made a long skirt of grey wool, cut to the pattern the old lady had always worn, with a triangular shawl to match. 'They're all beautiful. Oh, Abby, you've worked so 'ard!' Mrs O'Connor kissed the smooth young cheek lovingly. 'What a blessing to 'ave you and Eddy caring so much. You'll never know 'ow much I appreciate that.'

Evelyn looked down at Mrs O'Connor who was sitting by the fire surrounded by flowers, cards and boxes of chocolates. 'You can wear them tonight. Thought we'd all go down to the pub for a celebration drink.' She glanced knowingly at Eddy and Abby, glad that everyone had kept the secret.

The wrinkled face grinned, and the nose twitched. 'Lovely idea. I've got to show my new clothes off some'ow!'

Abby remembered the night in the Chislehurst Caves when Mrs O'Connor had swept into their lives, causing a stir and bringing out a bottle of milk stout. That had been over eleven years ago. Try as she might, Abby had never been able to imagine her as young. To her mind, Mrs O'Connor had always been an old lady. One moment she had not existed and the next – she did.

'I never thought I'd live to be eighty,' said the old woman, looking at her birthday cards. 'Daft thing is, I only feel about thirty.'

Eddy grinned. 'That's fine. Only another twenty before you receive your telegram from the Queen!'

The 'knees-up' in the room above the bar was a success from start to finish. Twenty-eight people sang and danced, while a local friend played the out-of-tune piano. Evelyn and her cousin had spent most of the day preparing food, and taking pride of place on the cold buffet was the birthday cake itself. Eddy proposed a toast as Mrs O'Connor cut her cake, then led her on to the floor for a slow waltz, much to the delight of all who watched. Watching her husband, Abby was proud, and she knew that persuading him here had turned out to be the right and proper thing to do.

As Eddy led Mrs O'Connor back to her seat, the bald-headed man at the piano shouted: 'Come on, Mrs O. We've sung all the old London songs I can think of. It's your choice now. What'll it be?'

Mrs O'Connor thought for a moment, then said, 'Do you know "The Mountains of Mourne"?'

The pianist looked surprised. 'That's Irish.'

'My Dan used to like it a lot. D'ya know it, luv?'

'Irish the lady wants, and Irish she'll get,' laughed the man, turning back to the piano. His fingers flew over the keyboard and the cockney voice boomed out, *'O Mary, this London's a wonderful sight!'*

Abby surveyed the scene, marvelling that one moment she was helping to fit society women into expensive gowns, and the next singing with cockneys in an Essex pub. Quietly and without fuss, she slipped on her coat, put a scarf around her head and waved to Evelyn. She was anxious not to keep the schoolgirl babysitter up too late.

She left the pub and walked out into a bitterly cold night. It was clear, with bright moonlight, but the wind was strengthening. It moaned across sea and marsh, cutting through to her bones, but her spirits were high as she remembered Eddy dancing with the old lady. Surely now that he realized just how important his family were to him,

233

her husband would sell the Liverpool shares? Strains of 'The Mountains of Mourne' followed Abby as she took the road away from the pub, then the low moan of wind took over from the singing. Sometimes it rose to a screaming pitch before dropping again. Lowering her head against the gusts, Abby moved quickly, hoping the others would get home before the weather worsened.

The schoolgirl who had been looking after Ross switched off the wireless as Abby entered the house, and asked if she had enjoyed herself. 'Yes, thank you,' said Abby, rushing towards the fire and rubbing her ice-cold hands before the glowing coals. 'How was Ross? Did he sleep?'

'Like a log,' came the reply. 'Did Mrs O'Connor enjoy herself?'

'She had a marvellous time.' Abby opened her purse, and gave the girl two shillings and sixpence. 'Was there anything good on the wireless?'

The young face shadowed. 'It's awful. A cross-channel ferry went down in the Irish Sea today and most of the passengers were drowned.'

'God, how awful.' Abby shuddered at the thought of the tragedy. 'Poor souls. In these freezing temperatures, too! How on earth did it happen?'

'It was a gale, apparently,' said the babysitter, making her way to the front door.

Abby watched as the girl rode off on her bike, and called after her: 'Be careful!'

Later, as she sat by the fire listening to the BBC late night news, she heard more of the tragedy in the Irish Sea. A warning was given of the possibility of exceptionally high tides in the Rivers Thames and Medway and that it would be 'very cold'. As the BBC closed down for the night, Abby heard the others arriving home and was glad they had not heard the news. Nothing must spoil this evening for Mrs O'Connor.

Sleep was impossible that night for Abby. The wind had become a gale screaming across the coast. Once or twice she drifted into a slumber made turbulent by half-dreams and sounds that cut into them. Awakened by a crash she raised her head slightly from the pillow. Beyond the closed curtains she could see the bright moonlight, but the island was full of strange clangings as corrugated roofs on sheds lifted and slammed down again; gates swung on their hinges, banging against their supports. She thought she heard shouts and a distant whistle, then told herself it was only the wind.

There was a muffled boom, and something heavy thudded against the outside wall. Abby felt the house shake, got up in alarm and found herself standing up to her ankles in water. Screaming for Eddy to wake up, she searched for the light switch. Water was all around her, cold swirling water that threatened her balance. At last she found the switch, and pressed it down. Nothing happened. Eddy's voice called to her in the darkness.

'Abby ...? Hell's bells – the sea's coming in!' As he shouted to the others, she looked out of the window in disbelief. A torrent of water flowed past the bungalow, carrying a caravan with it. Frozen to the spot, she stared as it swept past, followed by a dead cow. The ice-cold water had reached her knees and was rising fast.

Panic-stricken, Abby staggered across the room to pick up Ross.

'Where's Harry? Where's Mrs O'Connor?' Evelyn's voice screamed from another room. 'Abby ... Eddy ... oh, God ... oh, my God ... what's 'appened to the lights?'

'I'm 'ere!' cried Harry. 'It's bloody dark – can't see a thing.'

Mrs O'Connor's frightened voice called out from her bedroom. 'I'm by the door ... there's something in my way.'

The water was rising rapidly, shifting the furniture. 'We've got to get higher before the front door gives way,' Eddy cried. He grabbed Abby and Ross and, guided by the moonlight, led them to the dining table, and lifted them onto it.

'It's moving!' screamed Abby. 'It's giving way ...'

This time Eddy carried them to the sideboard. Sweeping everything off it, he lifted Abby and the baby onto it, then turned back to find the others. 'Up on the sideboard, Mum,' he said, but Evelyn pulled away from him in her anxiety to find the other two.

Suddenly the front door burst open and the sea poured in. Screaming, Evelyn heaved herself onto the sideboard as flotsam filled the sitting room.

Trapped between the bedroom and the sitting room, Mrs O'Connor's old fingers gripped the top of the door in an effort to stay upright. The water had now reached her waist, and she gasped with the cold.

'Where are you, Mrs O'Connor?' Eddy cried.

'I'm all right, son. You look after the others,' came the weak reply. 'I can't move but there's a chair.' After a pause, 'I think I can climb onto the arm of it, so don't worry about me.'

Eddy was frantic by now. 'Don't move, I'll get you.' The water was rising quickly, and he was trying to think as fast. If only they could get out onto the roof − but unlike many of the Canvey homes, this one had no outside staircase. He hauled himself onto the sideboard, and hurled a dining chair at the ceiling until he managed to break through. He helped Abby and Ross onto the rafters, then turned to his mother, who was kneeling on the sideboard, too scared to move.

'No, I'm not going up there. It won't take my weight.'

'It will,' shouted Eddy. 'Come on. There's no time for this nonsense.'

'It won't,' cried Evelyn. 'I'll only bring down Abby and the baby.' The sea reached the top of the sideboard and they felt it shift beneath them. 'Oh, God! Oh, God, it's moving.'

'Get up!'

'I can't.'

Eddy grabbed his terrified mother, helped her to her feet, then placed her hands on the rafters. Still she refused to climb, even though Abby reached out to her.

'Don't let go of me,' cried Evelyn.

Eddy tightened his hold. 'Dad, where are you?'

'I'm all right,' came the weak answer. 'Stay with the women.' Trapped between the settee and the wall, Harry had managed to free his legs at last and was balanced on the window sill with his hands on the curtain rail for support.

From the tenuous security of the rafters, Abby clung to whimpering Ross, unable to believe the horror below. Trees, caravans, cars swept past, and still the gale screamed and the waters rose. As the top of the sideboard disappeared beneath the freezing water, she gripped Evelyn's hand tightly, knowing it was only a matter of time before they all drowned.

The moonlight caught Eddy's face and she could see in his expression all the agony of wanting to save his family, yet not knowing how. Looking up at her, he murmured, 'I love you, Abby.'

The water had reached his waist and Evelyn's chest, when Mrs O'Connor's still form floated below them. 'Don't worry, I'll get 'er. Look after Mum,' Eddy cried, jumping into the water.

'No, Eddy, no!' Abby screamed in horror as he tried to swim after Mrs O'Connor, and, like her, was swept out of the door. The last Abby saw of him was his hands clutching the air. Still screaming, she clung to Evelyn and Ross in utter desolation.

In the grey dawn light, all that remained of Canvey Island were a few rooftops looking like small rafts in a grey sea. Caravans, uprooted trees, human beings and cattle floated in the water. The wind had died, and the North Sea flood tide had eased. To the rescue-workers it seemed a silent dead land. Occasionally, they would find survivors shouting from a rooftop, people who'd been there all night, some clinging to children, others too shocked to speak of those who had slipped into the flood during the long and terrible night.

At seven o'clock, they found those that remained of the Carr family.

Shocked and cold, Abby sat in the small boat, a grey blanket over her wet nightgown, unable to fathom where the island ended, and the sea began. Ross lay still in her arms. He had stopped crying hours since and seemed to be sleeping, his chubby face now grey-blue, his eyes closed, his lips slightly parted. *Sleeping*, Abby told herself dimly. *Just sleeping*.

Harry was barely conscious, his breath coming in short gasps. He had managed to cling on to his precarious position, even though the water had risen to his shoulders. Beside him Evelyn stared ahead without seeing, her mind in darkness and her body suffering from exposure.

At the edge of the flood, the St John's Ambulance Brigade put Harry and Evelyn onto stretchers, then carried them through thick mud, where roads had once been, to a primary school turned into a relief centre and crowded with refugees. As Abby stumbled after her in-laws she felt someone reach out to take Ross from her arms. At once she pulled away, resisting with what little strength she had left.

'Please, dear. Let me take the child.' The woman had a soft voice and a motherly manner.

'He's sleeping, sleeping — that's all,' Abby managed to murmur at last.

The woman did not give up until she prised the frozen babe from its mother's arms, and rushed him to an open stove inside the kitchen. There she laid Ross on her lap, took off his wet things, and massaged his ice-cold body with gentle firmness. The people gathered there watched in silence, glancing at each other from time to time, then shaking their heads in sadness. Someone produced a soft blanket and the baby was wrapped in it, while the hands continued to will life back into his small body.

Abby saw their looks and slowly began to realize what was happening. The warmth of the fire melted the appalling numbness of her body and mind, as she stared down at the tiny, still body of her son. Why was he such a strange colour? A thought took form and grew stronger. Her son was dead. Eddy had been swept away and was probably dead too.

Suddenly, the baby gave a slight shudder and drew in a sharp breath. The woman continued her work until he moved again. There were gasps of joy and disbelief as Ross gave a whimper.

In a daze, Abby found herself sitting in the moving ambulance with other victims of the flood. Someone had helped her into dry clothing but she had no memory of it. All she could see was her son lying in the arms of the ambulance man. Ross had been dead, now he was restored to her once more. Suddenly Abby began to tremble, and shock gave way to convulsive sobbing. The ambulance man leaned forward to comfort her.

'This little chap's going to be just fine. We're taking you to Southend Hospital.'

Once at the hospital, Abby refused to rest, her mind only on her family. When she learned that Ross was over his ordeal, she stayed by his cot for some time just to make sure.

'He's a strong child,' a nurse told her. 'A miracle child, we think. You've nothing more to worry about now. Try to rest.'

'No,' said Abby, rising. 'I must go back. My husband's lost ... dead ... I don't know. But I must find out.'

The nurse checked the casualty list and Eddy was not on it. No one of his age group had been brought in, she told Abby. 'Of course, there's Rochford Hospital. Many people have been taken there.'

'Before I go, could you tell me about Mr and Mrs Carr?'

'Mrs Carr is suffering from shock and severe exposure and her condition is listed as "poorly". But hopefully, she'll be fine in a day or two. Mr Carr, however, is critically ill. His heart and lungs were already weak. We're doing everything we can, but I think you must prepare yourself for the worst.'

Abby nodded. 'I must go back to Canvey. I'll return later, when I've news about my husband.' She looked at the nurse with tearful eyes. 'He might be alive. He could be alive, couldn't he?'

The nurse tried to persuade Abby to remain in the hospital, but to no avail.

'I'll go mad not knowing,' cried Abby. 'I must go back. He could be looking for me, and I must be there.'

Abby managed to beg a lift back to Benfleet in one of the ambulances. All during the journey she kept seeing Eddy's face staring up at her in the moonlight. Then he was in the water, his arms reaching upwards. She put her head in her hands to drive out the memory, but it would not fade.

Cold to the bone Abby left the ambulance, and stepped into eight inches of black mud which had once been a busy main road. All about her were tired, dishevelled people, many of them soaked to the skin and carrying pathetic bundles of the few things they had been able to salvage from their homes. Everyone looked dazed, and most were searching for someone who was missing. There were vehicles everywhere, moving slowly through the mud: ambulances, lorries, buses and private cars involved in the evacuation of eleven and a half thousand people from the island to the mainland.

Abby stood for a moment, not sure which way to turn, then instinctively tried heading for the island. The road bridge was still cut off and everyone was being directed away. She looked across to where Canvey used to be, and saw only the sea. All the houses and bungalows had disappeared. How many people had disappeared with them was not yet known. Horror filled Abby as she thought

Eddy and Mrs O'Connor could be out there somewhere. Into her mind came strains of 'The Mountains of Mourne' and she trembled at the memory. Was it only last night they had been enjoying themselves at the old woman's birthday party?

'You look lost, luv,' said a cheerful voice. 'Can I do anything to 'elp?'

Abby turned to the large woman with two small children trailing beside her. 'I'm looking for my family. They were swept away ... there must be somewhere I can find out what happened to them?'

The woman told Abby to try Benfleet School, pointing to the long column of refugees. 'Follow that lot, I should, luv. Don't worry. I'm sure they're fit and well and looking for you.'

Abby trudged on wearily among the refugees, then found that, without her realizing it, the column had parted after the level crossing, and she'd arrived at the station instead of the school. A train had pulled in and people were trying to board it. Some were still in shock, many were soaking wet, but others were active and cheerful, counting themselves lucky to be alive. All wanted to get away from this terrible place. Abby remembered those nights when everyone had been trying to get on the Chislehurst train. *Eddy, oh Eddy, where are you?* Forcing her way out of the station at last, she eventually arrived at the school. Inside the main hall, Abby paused in astonishment. Where had all these people come from? They were being given first aid, food and warm clothing by the Women's Voluntary Service, the Salvation Army and the British Legion.

Abby asked the first man she saw about Eddy and Mrs O'Connor. Middle-aged and concerned, he brought her a cup of strong tea and some sandwiches, saying: 'I'm sure your husband will turn up. He's young, strong and must be fit if he's just demobbed. Can he swim well?'

'He can swim,' murmured Abby, the hot liquid thawing her body. 'But I wouldn't call him a strong swimmer.'

'Well, you give me all the details and where you intend to go, and let's hope we match you both up. He won't be the only one to have gone into the water and survived. Rochford Hospital is your best bet, if he isn't at Southend.' He did not add that few bodies had been recovered, since first consideration must be given to the living. How could he tell this poor young woman a thing like that?

For hours Abby wandered around, checking list after list, making enquiries and asking ambulance men if they had seen anyone fitting Eddy's description. She waited in an agony of suspense, only to learn that Eddy had not been taken to Rochford either.

By mid-afternoon the evacuation of Canvey was well under way. With the sea defences so badly breached, there were fears that the next high tide would bring even more destruction, so that even those on higher ground became fearful. Horror stories of more than three hundred dead made the rounds.

Abby heard the rumours with mounting panic and refused to leave. 'Any moment now they may have word of him. I must stay! He'll be looking for me.' Frantically she searched the lists, as they were pinned up, until hope began to fade. As darkness fell, cold fear of the place descended with it, and she returned to Southend Hospital. There, Abby found her son and Evelyn comfortable, but Harry's condition had worsened. She stayed beside Evelyn, holding her hand and trying to find words of comfort and hope, but, by dawn, Harry's fight for life had ended.

Mary O'Connor's body was found in a tree, hanging like a rag doll over the branches. Late on the Wednesday, the body of a young man was washed up on marshes four miles from Canvey. Army dental records confirmed it to be that of Edward George Carr.

Eddy was buried with his father and Mrs O'Connor at the cemetery in Benfleet. George Potterton travelled from Liverpool for the funeral, shocked by the death of the young man he had hoped would be his partner. Abby was touched, but seeing him only increased her pain as guilt mingled with her grief. Eddy had so wanted to go to Liverpool, but she, for reasons of her own, had persuaded him to go to Canvey instead. 'Only a week,' she had said, 'just one more week, and something might happen.' Well, now it had — and Abby would never forgive herself. She might not be to blame for the surge of the North Sea merging with the exceptionally high tides in the Channel, but she'd killed Eddy all the same with her selfishness. *Dear kind Eddy,* Abby thought, as she threw a handful of earth into his grave. *How sad that a man of your goodness should have fallen in love with me! I'm sorry, my dear. Please God, forgive me.*

Evelyn was inconsolable. Her despair and grief were terrible to see. 'They didn't want to come to Canvey in the first place,' she cried, after the service had ended. 'I made them come; I wanted the best for 'im, you see. I only wanted the best . . .'

Abby led her weeping mother-in-law from the graves, making a silent vow that she would care for her until death separated them too. Then, like Ruth and Naomi, they made their way out of the churchyard, Abby determined never to leave Evelyn's side.

The following day, in the church at Ashton Green, Richard married Samantha.

243

CHAPTER ELEVEN

Determined never again to let the course of her life be set by others, Abby made plans as she sewed and pinned. She had to make something of herself, for only with financial success could she become independent. And independent she intended to be.

George Potterton had been kindness itself, offering to buy Eddy's shares at a price higher than their worth. But, since Eddy had made no will, the wheels of the legal system ground on slowly, and until matters were completed Abby could touch nothing of her husband's money. Nor could she touch the legacy from her father. From Willard Moore she learned that Richard was as determined to keep the store as Stella was to take it from him, and that, legally, things were deadlocked. 'God, I could kill the silly girl,' she had cried. 'Why *is* she being so stubborn? Can nothing be done to release my money?'

Nothing. All Abby had was what she earned and the possibility of a widow's pension. Meanwhile, when she had paid her rent and bills, there was nothing left to put away for the moment when she hoped to be free of Justine. Having expectations was no substitute for money in the bank, and although her employer had shown some heart after the tragedy, allowing Abby time to organize the funeral and settle her mother-in-law into the flat, she now piled on the pressure as never before.

Added to the grief had come insult, when Evelyn's insurance company failed to pay compensation for her home, deeming the disaster an 'Act of God'. Like many victims of the East Coast flooding, she had to rely on the Lord Mayor's Fund, which had received contributions from all over the world. Even here her need was not thought to be great, since she had a home with her daughter-in-law, and so the hand-out was small. It was to be weeks before she and Abby received grants from the Fund of three pounds and ten shillings per week for being widowed by the disaster.

Many homes on Canvey were beyond repair, but others, like Four Winds, still stood. Mrs O'Connor's gift was slowly being cleared of thick mud and debris and would be left to dry out before repairs could be made. But it would be months, if not years, before it would be habitable once more. Evelyn and Abby never wanted to see the place again, for fear of the harrowing memories. One day, thought Abby, when the sea defences were rebuilt and people began to forget, then maybe someone would wish to buy the little bungalow, but for now, it had to be forgotten.

Memories, however, could not be so easily dismissed, and Evelyn wandered about the flat in a state of shock. Only when Abby had to return to work did she awaken to her responsibilities. One of these was looking after Ross, and raising him was like raising Eddy all over again. The child gave her something to live for. Demanding, always into mischief, he took up every minute of the day, and soon Evelyn found herself saying: 'The dead are dead. I must care for the living now.' Even so, she was like a shadow moving through the shops, anxious to avoid all conversation in case people said 'how sorry they were'. Whatever she did, wherever she went, she would never forgive herself for making the family move from Bermondsey to the coast. She, who had survived the Blitz with all the good-natured cheerfulness of the Londoner, now had nightmares where the sea burst in on her while she slept in her bed, and carried away everything and everyone she loved.

Sometimes Abby wondered at the wisdom of letting Evelyn have complete charge of Ross, but soon saw how this responsibility had saved the woman's sanity. She then wondered whether letting her believe Ross was her own

245

grandson was a cruel deception, and decided the truth would be even worse. In Ross, Evelyn thought she had something left of her own son. She could never be told otherwise. This, in turn, meant that Ross would have to grow up thinking of Eddy as his father, when his true father was in fact alive and well. When the weight of it all felt too heavy for Abby to bear, she remembered Ross was alive, and nothing else mattered. She would make a world for him in which he would want for nothing.

Shortly after the disaster, Justine's illness worsened, and she was taken into hospital for exploratory surgery. Whatever ailed her, no one thought it right or proper to mention. Meanwhile, at the salon, the cutter was beginning to panic. 'How are we to cope?' she kept saying in a high-pitched voice. 'What are we to do about all these appointments? We'll have to cancel them.'

'We can't let our clients down at this stage,' said Abby. 'Half the couturiers in London are working flat out, with the Coronation in three months' time. Why not let me do more? I've met most of the clients personally, and I know what most of them want.' She searched through the order book and saw that two clients were due for appointments. Both Mrs Bruce Bellingham and Lady Crowley had awkward figures and needed a touch of tender loving care, which Justine had never really given to them. Abby had watched in despair as they had chosen outfits never meant to be worn on such frames. This was Abby's chance, and she took it.

Before Lady Crowley arrived, she sketched three flattering designs. Not for her the boned and caged restrictions of the Dior look. Abby intended her customers to feel comfortable in clothes where the cut was all important. She discussed it with the cutter, seeing the interest on the woman's face.

'These are good, Abby. I think Lady Crowley will go for it, and I'm one hundred per cent behind you.'

Lady Crowley did go for it and so too did Mrs Bruce

Bellingham. Both ladies were delighted to see original designs made especially for them. The girl had talent, they decided, and were quick to tell their friends.

Lady Crowley came back for another session before Ascot. 'I've nothing at all for Ladies' Day and from the way you handled that suit and ballgown, I hope you'll design something for me to wear in the Royal Enclosure.'

Abby sketched out a gently-swathed shin-length dress, then showed Lady Crowley swatches of chiffon, saying: 'The soft grey with an underlining of lilac would suit your colouring to perfection. With a standaway collar, and picture hat to match, you'd look very smart.'

When the gown was finished, Lady Crowley studied herself in the full-length mirror, twisting this way and that, happy with the natural swing of the skirt. 'In a light wind it will look most fetching. Puts me in mind of sweet peas. You've a good colour sense, my dear.' As Abby bent to adjust the hem of the dress, she asked: 'How is Justine?'

'Very ill,' said Abby sadly, knowing, in her heart, Justine had only a few months to live.

Cancer! The unmentionable word had been mentioned in hushed whispers by the Maddox Street staff. If the rumour was true, then it was not only the end for Justine, but for the salon as well.

Lady Crowley shook her head sadly. 'Poor woman, she couldn't have picked a worse time to get ill. Still, every cloud has a silver lining, and you're it this time.'

That evening, when Abby entered Justine's flower-filled room at the London Clinic, she found her sitting up in bed, flicking through the latest copy of *Vogue* magazine. Her peroxided hair showed half an inch of dark root, and fell in lank tendrils about her pale face. Shorn of make-up, Justine looked quite different, and Abby could see now that once she'd been very attractive.

'Are you feeling any better?' asked Abby.

Justine glanced up at Abby coldly. 'How can I be better with all this worry? Can it really be true that you have decided to step into my shoes?'

'What?' Abby frowned and shook her head. 'I only made a couple of things . . .'

'Which you designed yourself, I gather.'

'Yes.'

'And which are proving to be quite popular.' She pointed a long accusing finger at Abby. 'Do not presume too much. I'm not in my coffin yet, young lady.'

Abby's eyebrows shot up in surprise. 'I don't presume anything. I only wanted to help. Good heavens, we're all working night and day to keep your business going. I have a gift for design, as well you know, because you've already seen them and used them. I thought you'd be pleased. After all, the designs are successful and they're going out under your name, not mine.'

'Yes, yes, yes.' Justine winced with pain and leaned back against the pillows.

Alarmed, Abby took her hand. 'Can I get you anything? Shall I ring for the nurse?'

'No,' came the hushed whisper. 'I'll be all right in a moment.' When the spasm passed, she looked up at Abby. 'I shall return in a few weeks to see your so-called designs for myself. If I am not satisfied with them, it will go badly for you, my girl.'

'I'm sorry if I've upset you. I didn't mean to.'

Justine's manner softened. She could ill afford to lose staff now, and Abby was the best worker she had. If anything, she should be giving her a raise, and the title of Assistant Designer. But she would do nothing of the kind. 'Well, thank you for coming, Abby. I'll be back soon, and we'll decide then whether you should design for me or not. Please do nothing more until then!'

When Abby left the London Clinic, she thought of the cheque she had received a month ago from Eddy's legacy. George Potterton now had complete control of the company and Abby had a little money to start her own business. But by the time she had paid for rent, overheads and materials, it would not last too long. Still, Abby knew this was the time to start up on her own. Poor Justine was dying, and her clients were looking for a new designer. She must find a small premises in the right neighbourhood: somewhere with room for a receiving salon, a workshop, fitting room and flat.

It was not going to be easy. Abby had never realized how expensive the 'right areas' of London could be. Night after night she searched the 'To Let' columns in the evening papers, yet nothing suited her needs or her purse.

Meanwhile, at Maddox Street, the telephones never stopped ringing, most of the callers wishing to make an appointment with Justine's new designer. When Abby took the calls she pencilled in appointments for herself, but if Mrs Grey got there first, she told the clients that they could take no more orders for now.

Knowing Justine had given the word, Abby stepped up her efforts to search for a place of her own. People like Lady Crowley lived and breathed within an area of six square miles, unless they were on their country estates. Somewhere within that perimeter Abby had to set up her own business, and it would be costly. She would need at least one assistant, and that meant more capital. It was high time Stella stopped tying up their father's Will. Abby entered Justine's small office, and telephoned Willard Moore.

'I realize it's all taking a long time,' he said, 'but I did warn Miss Glenister, if you remember. Look, it might be worth your while having a word with your aunt. She could surely let you have your money from her own personal account. Of course, she would lose some interest, but I'm sure you could make it up once your bequest is paid.'

Ask Aunt Milicent for a loan? After giving the matter a great deal of thought, Abby decided to bury her pride. Desperate needs called for desperate measures. Her hand froze over the receiver. Supposing Richard answered. Dear

God, what would she do then? It was a risk she would have to take. If he answered, her finger was poised to cut off the call.

'You want me to lend you eight hundred pounds?' Milicent's voice had risen two octaves in amazement. 'You upset my husband, nearly destroy my son, and now you have the gall to ask me to lend you money?'

'It's my money I'm asking for,' said Abby. 'I would have it now, had the Will not been contested. Aunt Milicent, I need it desperately.'

'My dear girl, I thought it outrageous that you should have been mentioned in the Will at all. You've caused nothing but trouble. Not one farthing will you get out of me. You've made your bed with that awful costermonger family, so now you can jolly well lie on it.'

'That family was torn apart in the floods last February,' said Abby with growing anger. 'As for saying I destroyed your son, then I might remind you that I had no choice but to leave after you dropped your little bombshell in Harrods. My husband is dead and I have a son and a mother-in-law to look after. Please, Aunt Milicent, it's only a loan, and you'll have it all back with interest as soon as the Will is settled. You have my word.'

There was a slight pause, then Milicent's sharp voice hummed across the wire. 'I'm sorry. I didn't know about your husband. But in any case, I don't see what that has to do with us. I'm sorry, I can't help you.'

How could Milicent have said such things? She was aware of her son's love for Abby and had been for years. Yet she was still prepared to blame her stepdaughter for things she had no control over. Why were they all so against her, when the whole family knew that William was her father?

At the beginning of April, Abby finally found the premises she had been seeking. The Victorian house in Old Church Street, West Kensington, had once been a dental surgery with a large waiting room, two good-sized surgeries and upstairs, two bedrooms, one sitting room, a kitchen and bathroom. The whole place was in desperate need of decoration, and Abby did frantic sums, only to find they did not work out.

The banks proved uncooperative. No banker would give a woman an unsecured loan, any more than they would give her a mortgage. When bankers learned that this particular woman wanted them to invest in the mysterious world of fashion, they thought it frivolous to the point of absurdity, and politely showed her the door. 'Times are hard, Mrs Carr. Money is tight at the moment. Government restrictions are biting hard, I'm afraid. Sorry.'

Had she been a man, Abby knew, they would not have dismissed her without checking her order books and production plans and budget paperwork. No, she was a woman, and, worse than that, she was a woman in a hazy fashion world the bank managers knew nothing about. The premises in Church Street would have to remain a distant dream.

Exhausted as she was, Abby could only sleep fitfully at night. Every time she closed her eyes she saw Eddy being swept to his death on the black waters of the flood. In that memory was another; that of a flickering candle on a ledge of chalk, once thought to have been a Druid altar. If only that little boy with socks falling about his ankles had not grown up to love her, then he would be alive today. Now she would never be free of his ghost.

Justine returned to work looking a mere shadow of her former self. Thinner, constantly tired and in pain, she spent three afternoons a week at the hospital, unaware that her staff had guessed the nature of her illness. Her first task was to check all Abby's work. She studied her sketches and toiles and even rang her clients to ask if they were satisfied. Slightly surprised at the adulation Abby was getting, Justine decided to let her continue doing work which was now quite beyond her own abilities.

'Very well, my dear,' said Justine. 'I've decided to let

you go on – as long as you clear everything with me. Do not forget, this is my salon, and everything you design goes out under my name. You are still under training, so do not expect any change in your pay packet.'

Mrs Grey gave her employer a cold look. Abby was keeping this business afloat: giving it a new lease of life, in fact. Never had they received so many requests for appointments as they did now. 'Come, come,' she murmured to Justine, when they were alone, 'Abby deserves a raise. How can you say she's still in training when she's really your designer?'

'No one asked her to be my designer,' said Justine tartly. 'Until she appeared on the scene, my clients were perfectly happy with the existing fashions. Why should I be out of pocket?'

Mrs Grey could hardly believe her ears. 'She might leave you!'

Justine smiled thinly. 'And where would she go? She has no money and therefore no hope of starting up alone. Other houses might take her, but only on my reference.'

Mrs Grey walked away, unable to continue such a conversation. To make money on the talent of another person without giving that person credit or an increase in salary was completely unethical. Yet Justine was very sick and would not be able to continue much longer.

Early in May, Abby received a letter from Willard Moore enclosing a cheque for eight hundred pounds. Stella, it seemed, had grown tired of the fight and had given up contesting the Will.

Abby read the letter again, then squealed with delight, causing Evelyn to come running.

'Whatever is it, luv?'

'I've got it. I've got it at last,' cried Abby, waving the cheque. 'My legacy! Oh, do you realize what this means?' she said, clasping the bemused Evelyn to her. 'I can start up on my own. I wonder if that place in Old Church Street has gone? The rent was steep, but I'd have enough to keep me going for a year, I think. I'll have to be careful how I cost my clothes. Undercharging would be disastrous and overcharging will frighten everyone off.' Pausing in her excitement, she frowned as a thought struck her. 'Will it worry you if we move?'

Evelyn was still staring at her in open-mouthed amazement. 'Move? Move where? I dunno what you're going on about, luv.'

'To Kensington, where I can start my own business.'

'Kensington!' The voice rose shrill, as Evelyn sat down quickly in the fireside chair. 'Kensington? That's an expensive place, my girl, and not for the likes of us. As for this nonsense about starting your own business, I've never 'eard anything so daft in all my life. You've got a job you like, even if the pay's rotten, and this place ain't too bad now that I've got used to it.'

'No, you don't understand,' said Abby. 'Any day now Justine is going to close her salon. She's very ill. I must be ready when that happens since, God willing, I might get her clients. If I do, they won't travel this side of the river.'

'Oh, won't they indeed,' snapped Evelyn.

'No, they won't. And I certainly don't intend to live in a dump like this for the rest of my life either. And where I go, you go. I want you and Ross to have a nice place to live and ... well ... I just want things to be better, that's all.'

Evelyn shook her head, murmuring, 'Well, I only 'ope you know what you're doing.'

That morning Abby learned that the premises in Old Church Street had not yet been let. Without more ado, she arranged to meet the estate agent to sign a contract. She managed it all in an extended lunch break which had not pleased Justine, who'd been compelled to wait for Abby's return before making an announcement to the staff.

'My doctors tell me I must retire.' Her voice was strained,

her face thin and haggard, her eyes dull and tired. 'I have decided to take their advice.'

It was distressing to listen to that weakened voice, knowing that Justine was going away to die. In spite of the hospital treatments and her indomitable will to live, the fight was almost over.

'I'm sorry to have to do this to you all,' Justine went on, 'but I am giving up the lease on this place at the end of the month. By then, I expect us to have fulfilled all our commitments, even if it means we work late. I do not expect anyone to be let down. Thank you for all your hard work.'

She turned to Abby and took the girl to one side. 'And what about you? Where will you go now?'

Abby explained about her small inheritance and the place she had found in Kensington. 'Don't worry, I'll stay until we've satisfied all our clients. I wouldn't walk out on you now.'

'I hope you realize what you're taking on,' said Justine. 'What about staff?'

'Just myself at the present,' said Abby.

'And you think you can run a fashion salon alone? You'll end up being just another dressmaker and that won't pay the rent for long. Believe me, the overheads are enormous, and then, the long waits for clients to settle their accounts. The richer they are the worse they are. I warn you, people like Lady Crowley only settle up once a year. Can you carry on for that length of time?'

'I shall have to insist on earlier payments, that's all.'

'Then they'll desert you, my dear.' Justine sighed. 'You will certainly need an assistant machinist and a cutter.'

'I can't afford either,' said Abby. 'It would be marvellous to take Sylvia and Mrs Grey with me. We all know each other and work well together, but I couldn't pay them one quarter of the money they get now.'

'Very well,' said Justine. 'However, I can give you a start by letting my clients know that you are setting up alone.'

Abby was amazed at this act of kindness. 'Would you? Would you really? Oh, it would help enormously.'

Justine was as good as her word. She sent letters to each client mentioning Abby's new career, as she informed them of the demise of her own.

London was in the grip of Coronation fever, and was being sumptuously decorated. Heraldic beasts topped the arches in the Mall, and all along the roadside hung gaily coloured banners, each supporting a coronet. The processional route was garnished with similar decorations, and Westminster echoed to the sound of stands being built in the vicinity of Parliament Square. Abby thought the whole city had gone mad, and never wanted to hear the word Coronation mentioned again.

When she, Evelyn and Ross moved into the house in Old Church Street, Susan and her boyfriend, Bernard, arrived close on their heels armed to the teeth with paint, bought at 'cost price' from someone in the trade, and cheerfully set to work on the downstairs rooms, these being the first priority.

Abby had specified a soft sage for the main salon, with white cornices and bosses. From Liberty she purchased brocade to make drapes which matched the period of the house, and Susan managed to find a dilapidated chaise-longue in the Portobello Road, which she re-upholstered to match the gold of the curtains. Four balloon-back chairs from the same antique shop received the same treatment. With a full-length mirror gracing the wall, and a bowl of flowers on the round walnut table between the tall windows, the dingy, dark waiting room had become an elegant salon.

'I'd say that looks pretty good,' said Abby, surveying the room. 'Thank you, Susan and Bernard – I can't imagine what I would have done without you.'

Upstairs, Evelyn set to with a pot of white paint to brighten up the small sitting room and bedrooms. As she painted, her misgivings about the move were alleviated and she suddenly felt confidence in Abby's ability to make a go of things. *Kensington, Harry! Look at your old girl now, and don't laugh.*

'What are you going to call yourself?' asked Susan, as they finished painting the fitting room. 'I mean, in a world of Balmain, Schiaparelli, Balenciaga and Givenchy, you can hardly be Abigail Carr.'

'But that's my name,' said Abby, with an amused smile.

'But it's so boring. Unless you call yourself just "Abigail".'

Abby paused momentarily, then wrinkled her nose and dismissed the idea. 'Sounds like a hairdresser. Anyway, all my cards are printed, and I'm already known to a few people by my own name.' She crossed her fingers and prayed that, soon, many would know it.

'But it's so *English*.'

'Norman Hartnell seems to be doing quite well with his name.'

Two days later, Susan turned up with a house-warming gift. Abby unwrapped the heavy object and found herself holding a shining brass plate with the name *Abigail Carr* inscribed upon it. It was a moment she would always cherish. 'Thank you, Susan. Thank you for being such a good friend.'

Abby's first client, Mrs Bruce Bellingham, arrived at the new salon and gazed around appraisingly. 'My dear, you've made it all so *elegant*!'

Before the week was out, Abby had seen five clients, and taken enough orders to keep her busy for weeks. She desperately needed help, but until she could afford it, she would just have to burn the midnight oil herself. And this she did, working into the early hours, barely finding time to eat or even notice her son and mother-in-law. Evelyn knew the strain she was under, and endeavoured to see that the household ran smoothly around her.

Coronation Day was cold and grey, but nobody minded

as they sat warm and cosy around the new television Abby was slowly purchasing for Evelyn's benefit. Feeling guilty at leaving her mother-in-law alone so much, with all her memories, Abby felt it the least she could do.

Susan came with Bernard, and, after the Hallowing, produced a bottle of wine to celebrate the occasion. As the golden coach and marching columns made their slow way back to the Palace, the skies opened and rain poured down on the thousands waiting along the processional route.

Abby loved it all, and wondered what Hartnell must be thinking, with all eyes turned on the shimmering, jewel-encrusted gown he had created for the Queen. This surely was the zenith of any couturier's career. She wondered how near she would ever get to designing for any member of the Royal Family and decided her chances were nil.

By August, orders were coming thick and fast, and Abby needed more staff desperately. Susan helped her out during the holidays, glad of the experience she was gaining.

'Either make them pay their bills, or make the other clients wait their turn,' she said, as she eased yards of pale blue chiffon beneath the needle of the sewing machine.

Abby smiled wryly. 'I'm not established enough to play prima donna, Susan. Clients of this class settle their accounts every six months, or annually. If I invoice them now, they'll simply turn away. But I'm not in a position to say to Liberty, "Put it on my account, please." And that isn't cost-effective, either. I should be getting my material wholesale.'

'I know, but the banks will just turn you down again.'

'I'm not so sure,' said Abby, working on the hem of a gown that would one day grace a ballroom. 'This time I have a business that's growing. All I want is something to tide me over.'

'They'll send you away with a flea in your ear,' murmured Susan. 'No collateral is like having the plague.'

It was Mrs Bruce Bellingham who finally came to her rescue, when it slowly dawned on her that the salon had no staff. 'My dear, how on earth do you manage?' Abby had rushed to answer her telephone, breaking off their fitting, and now returned full of apologies for the interruption. 'Have you no help at all?'

'For that,' Abby confided, 'I need capital — and the banks won't help me. I tried them last week, six in all.'

'Merchant banks?'

Abby shook her head. 'They only deal with huge firms, don't they?'

'Mostly.' Mrs Bruce Bellingham looked at herself in the mirror, pleased with the grosgrain suit in navy and white for her grand-daughter's wedding. 'My nephew is with Churston and Fox in the City. I could give him a call.'

Three days later, Abby presented herself at the City bank of Churston and Fox, founded in 1784 to create commerce in Britain and the Empire. She was immediately confronted by a hostile-looking receptionist.

'Oh, if you've come about the junior clerk vacancy then you really must make an appointment. Meanwhile, I'll check your details and CV.'

Dismayed, Abby realized that for all her careful dressing in a neat, navy suit and small hat over a French plait she still looked too young to be a businesswoman.

'I'm Mrs Carr,' she said firmly. 'I have an appointment with Mr Bryce at eleven thirty.'

Miss Mansell frowned and pulled her diary towards her. 'I have a *Mr* Carr for eleven thirty.'

'A mistake,' said Abby, determined not to be put off. 'I am Mrs Carr and Mr Bryce is expecting me.'

Miss Mansell went on full alert. Like a dragon protecting her lair, she seemed all set to breathe fire. 'Well, I'm not sure he's free to see you, after all. There seems to have been a blunder.'

'But not of my making,' said Abby pointedly. 'I've come a long way and I do have a business to run. Would you please tell Mr Bryce that I'm here?'

Miss Mansell flushed with anger. How dare this young

slip of a thing speak to her in that manner? 'I think it might help if you told me why you wish to see Mr Bryce.'

'I think not,' said Abby, wanting to hurl something at the woman. 'Mrs Bruce Bellingham has explained something of the matter to him, I believe.' This was sheer speculation on her part but Miss Mansell's attitude changed at once.

Abby's heart was pounding as she entered the oak-panelled office. She had just won a battle, but the war was by no means over. Before her stood a huge desk, and behind it a man sat, bent over some papers. As she entered, he smiled and rose to his feet. About forty-six years old, his features were strong, almost handsome, Abby thought, noticing his dark chocolate eyes, and the brown hair greying at his temples.

'Good morning, Mrs Carr,' he said, extending his hand to her. 'Please take a seat.'

Abby took his hand; it felt strong and firm. She sat down. This man who wore Savile Row suits and Jermyn Street ties was hardly likely to be impressed with her. Determined at the outset to seem in command of herself, she said firmly: 'There seems to have been some confusion in your outer office. As you can see, I am *Mrs* Edward Carr. My husband is dead.'

Wrong-footed from the start, Jonathan Bryce fiddled with his tie and murmured, 'I'm very sorry about that. An unfortunate mistake under the circumstances. Now then, what can I do for you?'

Abby launched into her well-rehearsed speech, backing it up with order books. 'I'm not asking for the moon,' she said, at last. 'Just a loan so I can employ much needed staff.'

Jonathan Bryce sat back in his chair, and tapped his Parker fountain pen on the desk top thoughtfully. 'My problem is putting your case to the Board. We only deal with large companies of long standing. The High Street banks are surely better for this kind of request.'

Abby's heart sank. Slowly, she stood up, disappointment

written on her face. 'I've already tried them.' She held out her gloved hand politely, dignity now restored. 'Anyway, thank you for seeing me, Mr Bryce.'

Jonathan leapt to his feet. 'No, please Mrs Carr. Do sit down,' he said, inexpressibly drawn to this lovely young widow who according to his aunt, worked all hours trying to re-build her life. Furthermore, she reminded him of his late wife, who'd been killed driving an ambulance in the London Blitz. The pain of that loss had never left him, and Jonathan recalled how glad he'd been of the support he had received. So why was he being bloody-minded now?

'These look very healthy,' he murmured, looking down at the order books once more. 'Tell me what your overheads are, and we'll fix a figure to cover those for, say, two years at an interest rate of two and a half percent.'

Abby stared at him in astonishment. At last, someone was offering a helping hand! 'Thank you, Mr Bryce. Two and a half percent will be fine.' She smiled at him, eyes shining with relief, and enthusiasm for the future. 'Now I can really go ahead. I have the clients, I believe I have the talent; all I needed was the backing. I'm very grateful to you.'

Evelyn, however, was not so pleased. 'Borrowing all that money!' she exclaimed. 'I've never owed no one a penny in all my life. Just 'ow do you expect to pay it all back, that's what I want to know? In your line of work I should 'ave thought you'd be the first to say, "cut your coat according to the cloth", not the other way around.'

'It's all right,' Abby explained. 'I didn't go to a money-lender. I went to a respectable bank. It's perfectly normal to borrow in the world of business.'

'What do you know about such things?' cried Evelyn. 'You're a dressmaker, not a businessman.'

It was useless to argue, so Abby quietly let the matter drop. Within two weeks, she'd contacted Mrs Grey, who was happy to work for the two years left to her before retirement age. She also found a girl straight from college, who had the skill and knowledge of dressmaking but no practical experience. Yvonne was twenty-two years old, and eager to learn. Tall and slim, with long dark hair, she could also model when required. Her team set, Abby looked to the future with confidence.

'You'll crack up one of these days,' said Evelyn one night. 'It's nearly ten thirty and you're still in this workshop. I thought hiring extra help would see an end to this.'

Abby was putting the finishing touches to a wedding gown. It was her first big assignment, the society wedding she had dreamed about, and she did not intend to let anything go wrong. From start to finish she'd worked on the dress herself, and now draped the yards of cream duchess satin over the model so that she could check the line of the neck once more. 'I must get this finished,' she said. Her head ached and the last thing she needed was a scolding from her anxious mother-in-law. 'Just another ten minutes. The bride's coming in first thing tomorrow morning and I promised it would be ready then, all save the hem.'

Evelyn made a tutting sound of disapproval. 'Another ten minutes, eh? That's what you said at eight. And what about your son? I swear the poor little mite thinks I'm 'is Mum. God only knows who 'e thinks you are.'

This chiding had become a daily affair and always upset Abby. God had given Ross back to her, and she loved the golden-haired child as dearly as she loved his true father. Eddy lay cold in his grave, yet she still had this sinful love for her brother. Her guilt was already so great, it helped little to have Evelyn add to it.

'You're right. I'm so tired and my shoulders ache,' Abby said, joining Evelyn in the sitting room. 'It's just that this is the first important dress I've been commissioned to design. Lucinda Shergold is marrying Viscount Burnham. Most of London society will be there, so don't you see how important it is for me?'

'I do, of course I do,' said Evelyn, pouring out the tea

261

she had made. 'But you'll be cracking up if you go on like this – and where will we be then?'

Abby sipped her tea thankfully and sat back, feeling the tension ease from her shoulders. 'It's not only who she is that matters, it's her age group. If I'm a success, I hope to capture the younger market. I've so many ideas for the youthful figure ... girls just seem to wear what their mothers wear. I'd like to give them something else. I've given it a lot of thought.'

'Do you ever think about your son while you're at it?' said Evelyn sternly.

'All the time.' Abby leaned forward, and met her mother-in-law's gaze. 'Don't you understand? It's for you and Ross I want this success. Security is everything. It means a place of our own, a position in the world that people respect. Isn't that what everyone wants at the end of the day? I think I can make it happen.'

'In short,' snapped Evelyn, 'you want more than you were born to.'

'Don't we all?' asked Abby. For a while there was a long silence, a silence that often fell between them since that dreadful night, as they remembered their dead. Abby's eyes moved to the small photograph on the mantel which Evelyn had only just found the courage to bring out. Abby had taken it just after the Carrs had moved to Canvey. It had been a warm Sunday in July, with the smell of cut grass, since Eddy had just mown the back lawn. Evelyn had been in the kitchen preparing roast lamb, while Mrs O'Connor shelled peas in the garden. Harry had pottered about, weeding a little here and there. Small sailing dinghies dotted the sea, children splashed in the water, sheep and cattle grazed on the marshes and all had been well with the world. Just before lunch, she'd called everyone into the garden and taken the photograph.

Eddy was holding Ross, who wanted his lunch and looked unhappy. Evelyn and Harry had their arms about each other and were laughing. Laughing also was Mrs O'Connor, who had asked Abby not to take the picture since she was still in her apron. It hurt to look at the photograph and she turned her eyes away. Instinct told Abby when it was right to speak.

'Has Ross been good today?' When Evelyn replied that he had, Abby went on. 'You're right, Mother. I will try to be with him more from now on.'

On a cold March day, guests filled the church of St Margaret's, Westminster, and waited for the bride. Abby stood inside the porch, as she had promised Lucinda, and felt her heart pounding as the Rolls Royce came into view. Once the bride came inside the porchway, Abby set to, and settled the veil over her tiara, then straightened the train of the dress, finishing as the organist struck the first chords of 'Praise My Soul the King of Heaven'. Slowly, the bride and her father walked down the aisle, and Abby took her place in a rear pew.

As Lucinda and her husband left the church, an army of newspaper photographers appeared anxious to get pictures of the most exclusive wedding of the year. Abby smiled as she stood watching. The sun had broken through the grey clouds, causing the dress to shimmer in the bright early spring light. The medieval cut of the gown suited the tall, slender bride to perfection. The family tiara glistened in the sunlight, and the long veil lifted slightly in the breeze, as Lucinda submitted herself to the endless photo session.

The reception was held at the Ritz. Pleased that everything had gone so well, Abby was more than ready to relax with a glass of champagne. She stood, an elegant figure in a cornflower-blue jersey suit, small hat atop the swept-up hair, and a hired three-strand set of pearls at her neck. Warmed and heartened by the favourable reaction to the gown, she found herself in conversation with the bride's mother and her friends. Mrs Shergold had attended most of Lucinda's fittings, behaving like a commander about to launch an offensive. Now that victory was hers, she was relaxed, happy and anxious to tell everyone about Abby.

'Well, well. So Cinders has returned to the Ball, I see.' The male voice was faintly familiar and turning, Abby found herself staring at the arrogant features of Jeremy St John-Tennant. For one stunned moment, the years fell away, and she was back at Wickham Place, feeling his wet lips over hers. Now she could cheerfully have hit him all over again.

'You really must introduce me to your fairy godmother,' he was saying, savouring the moment. Jeremy studied Abby's shocked face, and saw that she was as beautiful as ever: more mature, more elegant, and sophisticated also. Her make-up was flawless and her grooming immaculate. What a pity she was from the wrong class, he thought. No background there. Still, if he played his cards right he should get her into his bed before the night was out. Someone from the wrong side of the park should prove an interesting change.

'Ah, Viscount Kelthorpe, I don't believe you've met Mrs Carr,' said Mrs Shergold, then turned back to her other guests.

'Mrs?' Jeremy's eyes widened. 'Not godmother then, but godfather. *Carr*, did she say?'

'Viscount, did she say?' Abby smiled thinly. 'Did someone die?'

'Grandfather.'

'I'm so sorry.'

'Why should you be? You never knew him.'

'No,' said Abby in biting tones. 'But his death has elevated you and, for that, I'm extremely sorry.'

Jeremy's eyes narrowed in anger. 'Still a shopgirl's sense of humour, I see.'

Abby smiled. 'Still the schoolboy with a schoooboy's petulance, I see.'

'What are you doing here?' asked Jeremy.

'I was invited by the bride, if you must know. What are you doing here?'

'Bride's cousin.' Angry that Abby was turning away from him, when most girls hovered like moths to a flame, Jeremy caught her arm. 'Speaking of cousins,' he said through clenched teeth, 'yours seems to be doing very well for himself these days. Typical of the Glenisters to jump up the social ladder by any means available. But then Sammy always was a pig-headed little fool.'

Abby frowned. 'What are you talking about?'

Jeremy gave a mirthless laugh, angry at the memory of his own hurt and humiliation. 'Oh, don't give me that innocent look. God, you're all the same. Avaricious and full of guile, yet always managing to look so damned noble.' Seeing the bewildered look on Abby's face, he realized that she truly was baffled by his words.

'My dear girl, I'm speaking of Richard's rise to the landed gentry, by way of marriage to the delectable Samantha. Don't tell me you didn't know.'

A flashbulb almost blinded Abby, as she tried to take in the words. Like a rabbit held in the glare of headlights, she was unable to move. Too stunned to speak, all she could do was listen to Jeremy's stream of invective and watch his sensuous lips curl into an ugly sneer. 'Can't go wrong, can he! The son of a shopkeeper marrying into an old family like that. Tainting it with his blood. Samantha will be the loser, of course. She could have had the world. She could have been my wife, with a title. Now she's just plain Mrs Glenister, with a mill-stone around her neck. Well, she'll come to her senses one day, and it'll be too late.'

Abby felt her legs weakening, and gripped a small side table to steady herself. Jeremy's angry voice seemed to be fading away.

'I say, you look the very devil. You're not going to peg out on me, are you? Too much champers, perhaps?'

The spasm passed, and Abby made a supreme effort to sound normal. 'It's the heat of the room, that's all.' Glancing around nervously, she saw that the bride and groom were about to cut the cake. A hush fell over the assembly as the speeches commenced.

Visions of Richard on the cliff-top at Tintagel filled Abby's mind, and she wondered if Jeremy were playing some cruel joke on her. 'He ... he really is married?' One look at that face told her this was no joke. 'When?' she asked in a soft whisper.

Surprised, Jeremy looked down at her. 'You really didn't know? Good God.'

'When?' asked Abby with growing persistence.

'Oh, last February some time.'

February! Abby thought of all she'd been going through when Richard had done this thing. It seemed the cruellest blow of all. Samantha, of all people! She recalled the years he had spent trying to avoid the unwelcome attentions of Ashton's lovely heiress, yet now he had married her!

'It was a bad day when he lost interest in you, my dear,' Jeremy was saying. 'Why the devil didn't you keep a firmer grip on the fellow? Although I doubt you could have done much. Glenister's on the make and knows which side his bread is buttered.'

'Don't say such things. You don't know what you're talking about. You never did, as I recall.'

Jeremy smiled sardonically. 'Ah, how she rushes to his defence! My word, I almost believe you still love the blighter. Maybe Carr isn't such a lucky chap, after all.'

'Be quiet,' hissed Abby, wishing she could run from the Ritz as she had run from Wickham Place. But she was now a woman of some standing, at a society wedding. 'You know nothing about my feelings for Richard, or his for me.'

'His, no. Yours are written all over your face.' Jeremy was beginning to enjoy himself. 'Have no fear, Mrs Carr, when our social-climbing friend thinks he's finally made it, I'll bring him down.'

'*You'll* bring him down?' Abby looked at him with contempt. 'And who are *you* to bring down a man who was awarded the Military Cross for outstanding courage? And while we're on the subject of courage, in which branch of Her Majesty's Forces did you serve for your National Service?' Jeremy compressed his lips and said nothing.

'Medical dispensation? Of course.' Abby sipped her champagne, and realized the speeches were coming to an end. There was applause and laughter, as the bride and groom said their farewells, then she prepared to leave also, glad to get away from the man who'd spoiled the day as once he had spoiled a party. But Jeremy followed her to the hotel lobby.

'Why rush off? Let me take you to dinner.'

'Sorry. Have to get home,' said Abby quickly. 'But if you could conjure up a taxi, I'd be grateful.'

They walked out of the hotel and stood among the other guests. It was rush hour and all the taxis were full.

'I'm parked at St James',' Jeremy was saying, grabbing her by the arm once more. 'If you won't let me take you out to dine, then at least let me drive you home.'

And let you know my address? You must be joking, thought Abby, refusing politely. 'Oh look, there's one for hire.'

Jeremy lifted his arm without enthusiasm. 'This is stupid. Dinner would round off the day rather well.'

'But my little son is waiting for me to put him to bed,' said Abby.

'Lucky beggar,' leered Jeremy, closing the taxi door.

Leaning back in the taxi Abby looked out at Green Park, hardly noticing the bare winter trees. All she could see was the ugly look on Jeremy's face, when he had spoken of Richard's marriage. It had frightened her. This man who always had whatever he wanted, had wanted Samantha also. Instead, his old rival had walked away with the prize, and Jeremy would never forgive Richard for that.

Richard married! It was so hard to believe, but believe it she must. Desolate and heavy of heart, Abby told herself this was how it must be, the only way it *could* be. Even so, it hurt to think he'd been tumbling around in bed with that ice goddess, while she still loved him to distraction.

As the taxi approached Old Church Street, Abby's lips tightened. At least Milicent had what she always wanted. Richard was now her passport into the world of society she'd always felt to be her due.

When pictures of the wedding appeared in *The Tatler*, it was Evelyn who saw them first. 'I often wondered why you took this magazine. Well, blow me, there's a photo of you talking to some nob!'

Abby had been trying to get Ross to eat his porridge, but the little boy kept spitting it out, much to his mother's annoyance. Taking the magazine, Abby found herself staring at a picture of her own face. The eyes seemed to be gazing into the distance, but there was no sign of the shock she had been feeling at the time. Jeremy was looking down at her, his smile belying the acrimony of the conversation they'd been having. It was just like any other normal *Tatler* picture.

The caption read: 'Viscount Kelthorpe talks to Abigail Carr, the London couturier who designed the bride's gown.'

'In *The Tatler*, eh!' said Evelyn, bursting with pride at her daughter-in-law's achievement. 'The dress is lovely. She looks a dream. This ... what's-his-name, this ...'

'Viscount Kelthorpe? What about him?'

'Well, it's just the way 'e's looking at you. Sort of ... well, not like someone you only met at the wedding.'

'Oh, I've met him before. Years ago, long before he was a Viscount.'

At that moment, Ross pushed his bowl of porridge off the table and screamed loudly when Abby smacked him on the hand. 'You're a naughty little boy,' she cried. 'Don't you ever do anything like that again!'

Evelyn came to the rescue. 'All tots do that from time to time. There's no need to shout at 'im, luv.'

She picked up the sobbing child and hugged him tenderly.

'You're spoiling him,' snapped Abby, nerves like taut wire. 'How am I ever to teach him right from wrong if you always take his side?'

'I know, luv. But you've got to 'ave a little more patience when they're this age. All you're doing now is making Ross afraid of you.'

Abby knew her mother-in-law was right. Had she not been on edge at the sight of the photograph, she would not have reacted so strongly. She walked across to her son, still in Evelyn's arms, dried his tears with her handkerchief, and kissed him gently on the forehead.

'Mummy bad,' sobbed Ross. 'Mummy bad!'

'No, Mummy's not bad,' said Abby gently. 'Mummy loves Ross very much, but Ross must not throw food onto the floor. Now love me, there's a good boy. Come on, give Mummy a huge kiss.'

At first, Ross refused, hiding his face against Evelyn's chest and sucking his thumb for comfort. Then he turned, smiled disarmingly and reached out for his mother who took him in her arms and hugged him tightly. 'Mummy loves Ross very much.' Abby kissed his hand and put him back in the high chair. 'There now. Will you eat this new bowl of porridge that Granny's just brought for you? For Mummy, will you eat it?'

Knowing he was the centre of attention, Ross decided to be magnanimous and started to eat properly.

'I must fly, Mother,' Abby said, glancing at her watch. 'Yvonne will be in already and Mrs Grey, too.'

The success of the wedding gown was phenomenal, and Abby was soon swamped with prospective clients. She telephoned Jonathan Bryce at the bank, her heart racing, as she asked him for help and advice. She needed more staff, bigger premises to work in and more capital.

Jonathan had already seen *The Tatler*, which his aunt had waved under his nose on the day of its publication, and half-expected Abby's call. 'And you feel the need to seize the moment. I understand. Look here, we ought to talk. So why not over lunch? Supposing I pick you up at twelve thirty. I'll be in Kensington, anyway: might as well kill two birds with one stone.'

Abby put down the telephone with a sense of dread. He had sounded cheerful enough, but 'kill two birds' had been an odd choice of words. Supposing he were going to say the Board had not been happy about the loan without collateral or guarantors to back it, and were not going to carry the risk of extending it!

She dressed carefully for the occasion, aware that she must look well-groomed and yet slightly vulnerable. She sensed Jonathan's attraction to her, but knew he was a hard-headed banker. She must smile beguilingly, with soft eyes, whilst speaking of cold, hard facts. Businesswomen in a man's world had to learn the art of duplicity, or be swept under the carpet.

Choosing a soft green suit, perfect for her colouring, Abby swept her hair into a chignon, and swathed it within a ring of beige mink, left over from an expensive suit she'd made for Lady Granville. Allowing soft curls to frame her face, she used make-up sparingly.

Jonathan arrived nearly fifteen minutes late, complaining about the traffic. Abby knew she'd dressed correctly, when he stopped his tirade and just stared at her. They lunched at the RAC Club in Pall Mall, where the head waiter addressed Jonathan by name.

When they'd ordered, he leaned back in his chair and talked on about this and that, as though trying to avoid the reason for their meeting. *He's wondering how to let me down gently*, thought Abby with a sinking heart. *He's going to pull the rug out from beneath me, and hopes I won't break my neck in the fall.*

Smiling, she spoke of the wedding and of the success of the gown. 'It was hailed as the wedding of the year, and many people might have expected Lucinda to go to

Norman Hartnell or Hardy Amies. But she came to me. I'm now inundated with orders but, unhappily, I'm forced to book people for months ahead.'

'That's good, surely. It makes you exclusive.'

'Weddings don't wait. If a young society bride can't get what she wants from me when she needs it, then she'll go elsewhere.' Abby looked at her glass, noticing how the light from the window turned the pale sherry to spun gold. 'I need to extend my premises and take on more staff. I've learned I can rent some floor space in Hammersmith.'

Jonathan stared at her for some time, and then asked, 'What exactly are your future plans, Mrs Carr?'

Abby paused before speaking. 'At the moment, I'm trying to keep up with the orders coming in, and for that I must hire more staff. Later, if things keep going well, I'd like to move out of my cramped premises into a bigger place where I could have a full complement of trained staff. It would please my clients and improve my standing in the world of couture. But – and here's the big but – the building would have to be in the heart of London's fashion area, preferably Mayfair. Then, when I get there, I intend to design my first collection, and show it in my new premises. So the salon must be big enough for fashion shows, and if I could have a sweeping staircase as well, that would be marvellous. Dior's first collection practically took place on a stairway. It was called The New Look. You know the rest.' Abby stopped speaking and saw, from Jonathan's slightly astonished expression, that she had frightened the man silly. 'Well, you did ask! That's my ambition, to be a top couturier. Whether it ever happens depends on how I manage now. The orders are there and my popularity is growing.'

Jonathan was impressed by her candour. It was only seven months since Abby had first come to him, and in that time, her business had gone from strength to strength. He could see no reason why the Board should turn her down, even if they did disapprove of loaning money to a woman. 'As you say, first things first. Tell me about these premises in Hammersmith.'

Seeing the relief on Abby's face made Jonathan realize how deep her fears had been. A strange woman, he thought. In fact, he sensed three women there. The first was a pretty and vulnerable girl who knew little about the world, yet whose eyes shone with enthusiasm. But a glance into those dark green eyes revealed a second woman, who had suffered deeply and was afraid; these eyes seemed older somehow. Then, there was the third woman: a determined force, willing to work herself into the grave in order to achieve her ambition.

What on earth could have happened to this lovely creature to have produced such an extraordinary mixture? he wondered, wishing he could protect her from a world she'd already found too harsh. But Abby needed his support and counsel, with no strings attached.

In the drawing room of her London home in Beauchamp Place, Samantha Glenister was glancing through *The Tatler*, when she paused, eyes widening in disbelief. Sensing her shock, the child in her womb kicked out in protest.

'The *London couturier*?' She stared at the photograph of Abby and Jeremy for two minutes, before hurling the magazine across the room in rage. It was unbelievable. She'd heard of the new designer, this Abigail Carr — who had not? But never for one moment had she connected her with that girl from Bermondsey, the slum child Richard had once loved, and still did, she suspected. How on earth had Abby risen to such heights? And what was her connection with Jeremy?

Slowly Samantha's eyes drifted to the silver-framed wedding photograph on the mahogany side table. How happy she'd been on that day. Richard had seemed happy too; therefore it was natural she should think his love for Abby had died. Just why had the girl disappeared from their lives in such mysterious circumstances? No one spoke of it. It must have been serious, or Richard would not have gone away. Those physical wounds he'd received in Malaya mended quickly, but what of the others he had received in England? They had not healed. After his father's funeral, Richard had been like a zombie, caring nothing for the world or anyone in it. She had taken firm control of him, gradually tightening her hold and leading him to the altar. Had she not tricked him with talk of pregnancy, would he have married her? Samantha remembered again that night when he had been drinking heavily. She had wanted him so much, and he had taken her violently. Then, all passion spent, he had fallen asleep, while she made plans to trap him into marriage. Poor Richard. She had known he would do the decent thing, because that was his nature. She only had herself to blame for her failed marriage. Richard was kind and considerate enough, but there was no passion in the man. No passion for her. Though he performed his marital duty, it was usually when slightly drunk. How she had ever managed to conceive at all was a miracle.

'And all because of that Bermondsey trollop!' Samantha shouted the words aloud. *Talking to yourself, Sam? They say it's the way to madness. But you're already mad, surely, to marry a man who has always loved his cousin!*

In her sixth month, bending to pick up the magazine was awkward and uncomfortable, but it had to be done before Richard returned. He was hardly likely to look at it anyway, since he had no interest in her society friends. Nevertheless, it was best to play safe. Samantha shuddered to think what might happen should Richard ever find Abby again. Their marriage would be over – and that, in turn, might jeopardize his position in London where, through her father's connections, Richard was working with a leading publishing house. Then there was his deep interest in politics. An active member of the Conservative Party, he worked long hours and went to as many meetings as possible. Deciding Abby's return to her husband's life would be a disaster, Samantha took the magazine out to the dustbin.

The Hammersmith premises consisted of the length of the second floor above two shops and had plenty of space for machines, tables and a drawing area. It was hardly a class establishment, overlooking the busy Metropolitan Line, where trains rattled past every seven minutes. But it was cheap, light, and roomy, and Abby had been able to pay one year's rent in advance. With four more women on her team, all experienced and well trained in 'making up' garments, Abby could work at Church Street with Yvonne and Mrs Grey, sketching, measuring, fitting and finishing, whilst still keeping a careful eye on the work going on in the 'factory' at Hammersmith.

Two more years, Abby told herself. Two more years to establish herself, then she would turn her attention to Mayfair and her first collection.

CHAPTER TWELVE

Seven-year-old Ross ran down the steps of the Georgian school building, satchel on his back, socks around his ankles and grey jacket flying, as he joined his waiting mother.

Abby bent to kiss her laughing son, then shepherded him to the waiting taxi. She did not notice the green MG which had pulled up some yards away. As the cab moved off, so too did the MG, its hood up against the cold March wind. It followed the taxi to Kensington Gardens, where Ross climbed out, carrying a wooden yacht which Jonathan had bought him for his birthday. He stood with some impatience while his mother paid the driver, then took her hand until they were in the gardens. Then he sprinted ahead to the round pond and was soon happily lost among other youngsters sailing their boats.

Satchel under one arm, leather handbag hanging from the other, Abby followed her son to the pond and stood watching among the mothers and uniformed nannies for some moments, before sitting down to relax for the first time that day.

From the moment she had promised Evelyn to give more time to Ross, Abby had kept her resolve, no matter how busy her schedule. Each day she collected him from school, then brought him to these gardens, which had delighted London's children for generations. Later, she would take him home, where they'd spend more time together before she returned to her work for the rest of the evening. Winning her son's trust had not been easy, but the years of determined care and unbreakable routine had changed Ross from a rebellious infant to a normal, happy child.

Abby was well aware that none of this would have come about but for Evelyn's unflinching support. It was she who bonded all three of them together and without her, Abby knew, she would have been lost.

As it was, her business had continued to grow during these years, only suffering a setback when Chanel returned to the fashion scene in 1954. It had been a bad moment, but Abby persevered with her own lines until she was finally able to move into her new premises in Brook Street, Mayfair, three years later. There she'd shown her first collection, and the success had been overwhelming. Orders had poured in; her designs were in every important fashion journal in Britain, Europe and the United States, always worn by her top model, the tall and willowy Claudia, whose haughty, chiselled features and dark swept-up hair had become synonymous with the House of Carr.

With such success had come more staff, including a new fitter, Madame Duval, who had trained with a top fashion house in Paris, and brought years of invaluable experience to Brook Street. Old friends were not forgotten, either. Susan joined the firm as one of two under-designers, and a welcome friend. Although extremely talented, she was forever saying to Abby: 'I would never have had your confidence.'

As Abby sat in the gardens now, watching her son sailing his boat, she smiled at the memory of Susan's words. It was lack of confidence and sheer fright for the future which had pushed her so hard. Everyone she had ever loved had been taken from her, leaving a chip of ice lodged somewhere in her heart, so that she was afraid to love again. That ice only melted for Ross and Evelyn. No, it was not confidence which had made her a success, but a determination to make herself feel wanted and secure.

Jonathan had been as reliable in business as he had been in friendship, helping Abby to find the finances which made the move to Brook Street possible. Having given up the Church Street house, she had moved into a small West

Kensington flat, but was now interested in a two-storey Georgian house at Hampstead, close by the Heath itself. Today, she'd learned that the contracts were ready to be signed.

The sky darkened, threatening a heavy downpour. The green MG meanwhile had been parked on a side street. Its driver was now standing in the gardens, well back from the pond, where he could see Abby and Ross, yet not be seen himself.

It was the third time this week Richard had followed them to these gardens. Each time he'd stood in the shadows, fighting down his overwhelming desire to clasp Abby in his arms, then sweep his little son high in the air, and hear him laugh for joy. But that could not be, so he kept out of sight. A week ago he had known nothing of Abby's life, although she was always in his thoughts. It had, therefore, come as a shock to find her lovely face staring out at him from a magazine cover in a dentist's waiting room. He read the article but it had given away nothing of her personal life, save that her salon was in Brook Street.

Driving straight from the dental surgery to Brook Street, intending only to go past, Richard had sat in his car for nearly two hours just waiting for a glimpse of Abby. People went in and came out, but of the woman he still loved there was no sign. He had been on the point of leaving, when a taxi had pulled up outside the salon and suddenly there she was. A neat figure in a loose cream woollen coat, her long titian hair curling around her shoulders, she climbed into the cab without even noticing him. He had followed her to the school, then these gardens, trying to summon up enough courage to face her. Then he would remember her last words to him, when she had spoken of being 'appalled' and said that 'they must never meet again, never.' Because he loved her still, and her life seemed to be going so well, he knew he would be wrong to intrude upon it. And so here he was: a love-stricken bystander, a watcher afraid to be discovered.

Ross was running towards his mother now. Richard stepped back quickly, and watched as Abby took their little son by the hand and walked back towards the busy main road. She was so close he could smell her perfume. Only a few feet separated them, but for Richard it might as well have been a thousand miles. Every nerve in his body cried, *Go to her!* but his feet were rooted to the spot.

You poor bastard, he cursed himself angrily. *You poor, bloody bastard. You pitiful wretch of a man. Small wonder she chose that illiterate cockney instead!*

Slowly Richard walked back to the MG, feeling his life was dust. Between Abby and Samantha, he had lost his manhood, his ambitions and his pride. He'd even lost his birthright, since William's bequest had proved to be a source of embarrassment to the Fellowes', who still looked down on 'trade'. It was out of the question for Samantha's husband to run a Canterbury store, and so Milicent ran it for him. Now he lived in London, wore the right suits, went to the right clubs, and gave the air of being more than he was without even trying. In truth, he was a junior member of a publishing firm, desperately trying to come to terms with a world he knew little about. As for all his clubs and well-made suits, Richard Glenister knew he was just marking time until, on the death of Samantha's father, he would take over the running of the estate with its many hop gardens and orchards. Meanwhile, he saw himself for what he truly was: a redundant appendage to a lovely society queen and heiress. Yet he was expected to keep her in comfort at Beauchamp Place, from which she ran up huge bills all over London.

Such a lifestyle could not go on. His own income not being large, he found himself dipping into Glenisters' company profits and knew his father would not have approved. All round he was a failure. Only a career in politics could redeem his shattered life, Richard thought, wondering if his father-in-law could fix that, too.

*

278

The workroom resounded to the hum of sewing machines as Abby walked through to the office where Roland, her under-designer and manager, was on the telephone.

'No, it isn't all right,' Roland was saying. 'Look, Mrs Carr is here right now. Perhaps you could try explaining to *her* why the second batch of satin is a different shade of pink to the first?'

Abby took the telephone. 'Yes, I do understand it's difficult to get the match, but where does that leave me? How can I run my business if yours doesn't come up with the goods? I have clients who rely on me. If I can't rely on you, then I'll have to find another textile manufacturer who won't keep letting me down like this.'

Roland listened, knowing that no matter how many times he said the same thing, it was only Abby who held sway with the manufacturers. Thirty years of age, with a thin, aesthetic face and dark curly hair, Roland Hudson had trained with another fashion house but found the challenge of helping to manage the House of Carr a unique experience, which got better all the time. He knew the coming collection of winter lines would be as successful as the others, and was extremely happy to be working with Abby, though he knew little about her.

Abby liked Roland; his warmth and humour did much to dispel a tense atmosphere, especially before the shows. Suspecting that he was homosexual she was disturbed, at first. Soon, however, she found his slightly effeminate ways more amusing than anything else. He was a good, reliable friend and an efficient worker. Looking at him now, in his pink silk shirt and dark grey cravat, velvet jacket over corduroy trousers, she thought he could only be described as 'dapper'.

'Everything's set for Germany,' he said. 'The papers have arrived with all the info.'

He was referring to a charity fashion show to be held near Düsseldorf in April, a week after the collection was unveiled in London, in order to raise money to help the

International Relief Foundation. This was mainly a British and Franco-German affair which had started after the war to help the many displaced persons in refugee camps. That Abby had been invited to show her collection to the glitterati of Europe was an honour, and she knew that Madame Duval had been instrumental in the arrangements.

Madame Duval had an old friend in Paris who was not only a fashion editor for one of France's top magazines, but also deeply involved in the IRF. 'She adores your clothes,' the French woman had said. 'My dear, she knows everyone who is anyone in Paris. We trained together in couture before the war, then ... well ... after that she did other things that led her to this charity work. I speak of you often, so it's not surprising that you were in her mind when they decided to put on a fashion show.'

Roland now fumbled through the papers on his untidy desk until he found the one he sought. 'Madame Duval's friend, Odile Longet, is the one setting the whole thing up,' he said. 'In a mansion outside Düsseldorf at a place called Wittenhausen. It belongs to some baron who is the Chairman of the IRF. He's laying on a champagne supper afterwards. Good God, programmes are selling at thirty pounds a piece!'

'Thirty pounds!' exclaimed Abby in surprise.

'All in a good cause.' Roland waved a vague hand through the air. 'Dior put on a fashion show at the Krupps' place, in Essen. It was for charity also, and proved a huge success.'

'Dior!' Abby swallowed hard. 'Good heavens, what have they let me in for? Oh, Roland, suppose it's a dismal failure and no one bothers to come!'

They turned their attention to the journey. Roland, who knew Germany well from his National Service days, said he would be happy to drive the large van with the collection, while the models and Abby could travel by air.

Abby looked at him in astonishment. 'You – drive that van all the way to Germany?'

'Why not?' said Roland. 'I served there for eighteen God-awful months. I know West Germany like the back of my hand.'

'Don't tell me you didn't like army life,' Abby teased.

'My dear, I've never been so miz in all my life.' Roland shook his head. 'The people I had to mix with! Well, the less said about that the better. And the *language*! It was all the fault of that stupid PSO. I told him I was artistic, I asked him for something suited to my talents, so what did he do? Sent me to the Royal Engineers, where they trained me to drive lorries. So, I'm your man to take the collection. Leave it with me, luvvy, and all will be well.'

'I'm going with you,' said Abby. 'If you think I'm letting my collection out of sight then you're wrong.'

'You can't. You're the famous young fashion designer. You can't turn up at this place in a van!'

'Rubbish,' said Abby. 'Now make arrangements for everyone else to fly and book us on the ferry.'

Roland sat back in his chair. 'I wonder if I know this mansion? Most of them were taken apart by the Germans for fuel, staircases and floors just ripped out. Those that remained intact only did so because the Allies got to them first and used them as headquarters. *Wittenhausen*. Hmmm ... it rings a bell in my tiny mind.'

Abby left Roland with his post-war memories, wishing the German venture could have waited until after she'd moved to her new house in Hampstead. It had been last September when Jonathan had shown her the house. The interior needed re-decorating, since it had been empty for over a year. The long rear garden resembled a Monet painting, with overgrown grasses and flowers reclaiming the lawn and pathways. She had set about capturing it in watercolour on her next visit. Now, as she talked to the fitter and cutter, she wished she could just walk out into it and relax. Jonathan constantly begged her to ease up. He worried about her and Abby knew his interest went deeper than mere friendship. She pretended otherwise, since she cared for him as a dear friend but nothing more. They had a warm and trusting relationship where the rules were kept and boundaries never crossed.

In the first week of April she and Roland set off for Germany, much to Evelyn's dismay. 'I won't sleep a wink until I know you're back safe.'

The route Roland chose took them south to Tilbury before turning eastwards onto the Harwich road. 'I was only nineteen, I suppose,' he was saying, still recollecting his army days. 'In Berlin people were living under sheets of corrugated iron. Had to feel sorry for the poor devils.'

Suddenly the sign for Canvey Island stood ahead of them. Abby's stomach turned over and all the years fell away, as she craned her neck to see where the island lay in the distance. Then they were past; Canvey and Benfleet were out of sight.

Roland was still chatting on about the crushing of a nation, the clearing of the ruins and finding himself in the middle of an historic relief effort. 'The Russians cut off the western sector of Berlin, which meant we lost all our power supplies. So I found myself working among engineers to provide generators, as well as help with the air-lift. What a time that was!'

Abby drew her mind back to his voice, marvelling that such a dapper man as Roland should have been involved in such an event. The very idea of him driving huge army lorries had seemed incongruous to her, until he sat behind the wheel of this large van as though born to it. Canvey kept flashing back into her mind, and to obliterate it she asked Roland more questions about his army days.

They took a night ferry to the Hook of Holland and Abby lay in her cabin feeling the gentle swell of the sea: the same North Sea which had lost its way one cold winter's night and devastated so many lives. Evelyn's cousin had been kindness itself after the disaster, tending the graves regularly and arranging for the bungalow to be re-decorated with a view to selling it. But six years was not long enough for people to forget that horror. Sixty would not be enough to sweep it from Abby's mind — should she live that long. She recalled the trauma of returning to Benfleet to visit the graves, one year after the tragedy. Since then, it had become an annual pilgrimage. But not once had she and Evelyn crossed the road bridge to the island itself.

They arrived in Holland at seven thirty on a bright sunny morning. Abby gazed across the fields, comparing the flat countryside to the soft hills of Kent. Everything was so fresh and clean-looking, she thought. Pretty, doll-like houses, with tulip-filled window boxes, dotted the landscape. It was a pleasant drive, and soon they crossed into Germany.

As they approached Düsseldorf, the countryside became more undulating, until gentle rolling hills had taken over from the huge skies of the flatlands. Abby peered at the map. Wittenhausen was between Düsseldorf and Dortmund. They approached the village late in the afternoon, and the directions became more precise. 'Go on past the Posthaus, then turn left. The mansion is two kilometres further on. According to this, there are wrought iron gates and two stone pillars with eagles on them.'

'Good God!' murmured Roland. 'Of course. HQ Wittenhausen. It all comes back to me now. I used to drive supplies here. It was the only decent building in the area — well, if you like Teutonic neo-classicism, that is.'

'This baron — does he still live here?'

Roland looked thoughtful. 'If I remember correctly, the owners used to be industrialists, on a par with Krupps. Some of them were tried at Nuremberg because they used slave labour in their factories.'

Abby looked at him in amazement. 'What? Are you saying I'm to show my lovely collection in a place with such hideous connections?'

'Wasn't a prison, my dear, just a house where rich people once lived. Anyway, it was an HQ for years and years.'

'And this baron? Is he the industrialist come home?'

'I thought the baron was the Chairman of the Foundation,' said Roland. 'It's a strange inconsistency if he's also the man who helped build Hitler's war machine.'

In growing alarm, Abby looked at her letter. 'The name's von Schreiber. Dear God, I hope it isn't the same man. If it is, I simply won't meet him.'

'You won't meet him,' said Roland. 'After the war these industrialists were stripped of everything they ever owned.'

Abby frowned. 'I hope you're right.'

Roland saw the turning and headed off the main road. 'I can't imagine what the organizers are going to think when their star designer turns up in this van.'

'Who cares?' said Abby tersely. 'I'm here to work, not to be gawped at.' In her mind, she went over the arrangements for the afternoon. They were to meet the organizers, go over the building and make sure everything was right for their needs; leave the collection there, under guard, then go to their hotel where, hopefully, the rest of the team would be waiting for them.

At length, they came to the tall iron gates which now stood wide open. Roland eased the large van through, then stopped as a uniformed guard came forward to check their identity. When he was satisfied, he waved them through.

The afternoon was mellowing now to a soft golden light which gilded the pale buds on the chestnut trees lining the drive and turned daffodil heads to brilliant yellow. Fields stretched away beyond the trees, and horses whinnied in the distance. As the van rounded a bend, the house came into view.

Abby stared in growing astonishment, then caught Roland's arm tightly, saying: 'Stop. Stop, please!'

Alarmed, Roland slammed on his brakes. 'What's wrong?' Seeing the strange expression on her face, he frowned. 'What is it?'

'I know this place,' murmured Abby. 'It doesn't make

any sense, but I feel as though I've been here before.'

'It's what they call *déja-vu*. You swear you've seen something, or said something before. Only you haven't. You're tired, that's all. The brain's playing tricks.'

He was right, of course. She had never been out of England. Maybe she *was* just tired – tired of being in this van for so long on such a warm day.

'I think I'll walk a bit,' she said, opening the door of the van and climbing down. 'You drive on, Roland; I'll just stretch my legs.'

Roland watched as Abby walked slowly along the drive, staring up at the house as though transfixed. How odd she was at times, but how beautiful she looked just now, in a simple jersey wool dress with the golden sun on her loose slightly dishevelled hair. It made her seem so young. He started the van and eased forward again, coming alongside Abby who was still wandering, as though she had stepped out of this world and into another.

Abby *was* in another world – a world of the past, with strains of the Schubert *Impromptu* filling her head. She was in the drawing room at Ferndene, with Milicent at the piano, sketching the engraving on the golden cigarette case. Every window, every chimney, every doorway of the house which stood before her had come under her sketching pencil. Time and time again she had copied from the engraving, a perfectionist even in those days, until she finally captured the mansion in pen and wash. Incredible though it seemed, this was the very same house. Abby stood still for some time, her eyes slowly scanning the grey stone edifice, until she suddenly had the feeling she was being watched from behind the tall windows. Troubled, she returned to the van, unable and unwilling to answer Roland's concerned questions.

Roland drove the van forward and was met by several more guards who directed him to the rear of the property where there were other cars and lorries, and men in overalls unloading gilt and red velvet chairs. An army of workmen were erecting a marquee in the grounds, while others struggled with cables to fix lighting around the house and in the trees. Sounds of hammering and shouting filled their ears, as Abby and Roland climbed from the van.

Abby saw a tall, elegant dark-haired woman in a Givenchy dress of light oatmeal tweed approaching.

'Good afternoon. I am Madame Longet of the Foundation, and I know that you are Mrs Carr.' She was in her early forties, clearly at home in this extraordinary place. 'Please do come in,' she was saying. 'I am so sorry that Baron von Schreiber cannot be here just now. He hopes to see you tomorrow morning.'

Glad to hear this, Abby followed Madame Longet through the cavernous building along echoing corridors, until she finally found herself standing in the ballroom where workmen were building a cat-walk and scaffolding for the back drapes. Madame Longet pointed out the minstrels' gallery where the Salon Orchestra would play.

'What do you say, eh?' asked Madame Longet, clearly pleased with herself. 'It has to be the best setting for any fashion show, unless you choose the Louvre or Buckingham Palace. Do you not think it *fantastique*?'

'Absolutely *fantastique*. Madame Longet, I hadn't visualized anything quite so large, so Wagnerian,' Abby said, taking in the great stone fireplace, the chandeliers and the massive oil paintings of eighteenth-century figures on the walls. 'How old is the house?'

Madame Longet shrugged. 'Not so old, early nineteenth century. But there was an older house; it was burned down. The baron's family have always lived here.' Stiffening, Abby shot a dark glance at Roland. The industrialist and the baron *were* one and the same, after all. They wandered into the spacious library, where tea was served by a smiling full-figured woman in a plain green dress, who was known as Frau Kruger.

'The housekeeper and a few gardeners are all the staff here now,' Madame Longet explained. 'The baron hardly uses the house any more, preferring to live in his apartment in Dortmund and his villa on the Rhine. This place has only just been returned to his family.'

Abby sipped her lemon tea, thoughtfully. 'Is his title an old one, or something slipped to him by a grateful goverment?'

'Like the Third Reich?' Madame Longet smiled. 'Oh no, my dear. Hitler wiped out most of the old aristocracy after the attempt on his life. The baron was lucky to escape, and only did so because he was needed to keep the wheels of industry turning until the end. The grandfather of the present baron married into the Kleiner family, who owned steel factories. With the death of the Kleiners' only son the daughter inherited, and Kleiner became the House of Schreiber. It was this family who helped to build Germany's strength from the turn of the century. I hope this doesn't bother you too much.'

There was a long and awkward pause. It seemed wrong to speak ill of their host, thought Abby, but truth was truth. She changed the subject. 'My fitter, Madame Duval, has spoken of your great friendship.'

'We spent our youth together, training in haute couture. Then came the war and everything changed. I went to work in another field altogether. Afterwards I found myself back in Paris, on the edge of the fashion scene once more. I worked as an assistant editor, then as an editor, and then became involved in this Foundation. The cause is a good one. I've been in those camps. It was there that I met the present baron, who is one of the founders of the charity.' She looked at Abby enquiringly. 'I do hope the arrangements are to your satisfaction.'

Abby told her the arrangements were perfect and after tea, they walked around the mansion once more, looking at rooms for storing and changing while a growing sense of panic seized Abby. There was so much to do and so little time. She wanted everything to go well, but suppose everything went wrong? Suppose no one liked her collection? What was well received in London did not always go down so well on the Continent.

At last she and Roland climbed into the waiting Rolls Royce, weary to the bone.

'I can't get over the fact that I've sketched that house time and time again,' said Abby, watching the fields and woods give way to the outskirts of Düsseldorf. 'I suppose it's quite a famous house.' That had to be it, she told herself. Milicent had returned from her time in Dresden with a souvenir of one of Germany's famous buildings.

'I'm glad the baron didn't show up,' she murmured quietly, so the chauffeur could not hear. 'I certainly don't relish having a polite conversation with someone who helped to destroy Europe. So now he's involved with charity — trying to buy back self-respect. Typical!' Abby smiled bitterly. He couldn't fool her, this wicked old Nazi who had served Hitler so well. He should be in prison.

Early the following morning, as Abby and her team set off for Wittenhausen in three Rolls Royces, she wondered why von Schreiber should be doing so well when, according to Roland, he had been stripped of everything he owned.

Unable to fathom how she could be so obsessed with the man and his house when they had an important fashion show to put on, Roland became irritated by her distracting questions. 'How would I know?' he said at last. 'Germany has to be rebuilt, and for that you need industrialists. They're a NATO country now. We need them.'

Abby looked out of the window and thought of her stepfather dying on a Dunkirk beach. Then they were turning in through the imposing gateway once more, and she felt butterflies in her stomach. She knew she would have them until the show was over.

At the entrance, Madame Longet was waiting for them, standing beside a tall and distinguished-looking man. Abby walked towards them, then found herself being introduced to von Schreiber. She blinked in mild astonishment as he took her hand, clicked his heels smartly together and

288

bowed slightly. This was not the old and sinister man she had expected to meet. No more than fifty, if that, he was handsome with a strong, kind face, his blond hair now greying, his eyes blue and tender as they held hers.

'Ah, Mrs Abigail Carr,' he said in faultless English. 'The lovely and mysterious young woman who seemed so fascinated by my home. I can't tell you how much I appreciate your coming.'

So she had not been mistaken after all. Someone *had* been watching yesterday afternoon. Why on earth had he not made his presence known? Unsure how to react to this man who had been England's enemy, Abby answered him coolly.

'Yes, I was rather interested.'

The baron smiled and looked at her in a quizzical manner. 'I've always deemed it something of a monstrosity, myself.' He turned then to meet the rest of the team, his manner so courteous that everyone found themselves liking the man. Everyone except Abby. How could she allow herself to be deceived by such charm, knowing the baron's background? Slave labour and the black leather coats of the Gestapo flashed through her mind. No, she was not so easily deceived.

She stood back while he talked to Claudia, and told herself that while she could not be as rude as she would have liked, she could be cool and distant. Hopefully the man would go away and leave them to get on with their work. Suddenly he turned to her, and she sensed he was a little disturbed by her manner.

'What do you *really* think of the house?' he asked quietly.

Abby paused, wondering whether to say anything, then curiosity got the better of her. 'I feel I know it so well. As a child I sketched it from an engraving. I'm sure this is the house, although I could be mistaken. I daresay there are others like it in Germany.'

'Similar, but not quite like this one. Just where did you see this engraving?'

'On a cigarette case, of all things,' said Abby.

Madame Longet hovered, clearly anxious to get rehearsals under way. But as they turned to their tasks, Abby registered the look of surprise which crossed the baron's face at her reply.

By mid-afternoon Claudia and the two other models were rehearsing on the cat-walk. The small Salon Orchestra went through its repertoire, as more flowers and then the caterers arrived. The chaos built until Abby feared they would never be ready on time. Claudia was complaining about everything. The back drapes did not hang properly, and had to be rearranged. At last there was a hiatus as the guests began to arrive. Abby changed into a chiffon gown of cornflower blue, and set her hair in the chignon which suited her so well, then concentrated on the ordeal ahead.

The rich and famous arrived in a fleet of expensive cars. They came from France, Germany, Holland, America, Italy and Switzerland. Press photographers were everywhere, and flashbulbs lit the air as film stars and millionaires ascended the imposing steps of the mansion.

Abby watched in amazement, and whispered to Roland: 'It's more like a film première than anything!'

'Cannes, rather than Wittenhausen,' he agreed. 'Never mind, my dear. It's good for you, and good for the cause. They'll love the collection.'

'Oh, please God you're right.' Abby turned away from the window feeling sick with nerves, wishing the night was over.

At last, everyone was seated, Madame Longet made a welcoming speech and then the show was on. It wasn't until the finale that Abby, at last, breathed a long sigh of relief. Like an empress, Claudia came down the cat-walk wearing the *pièce-de-résistance*: a long evening gown in oyster-pink double duchess satin, cut low at the back and swept into a train. The spectators thundered their approval and Abby knew she'd been a success. The Europeans and Americans loved her designs as much as the British. Her clothes draped the body naturally, and brought a new concept to fashion design.

After Claudia had glided, like a haughty swan, back behind the drapes, Abby went on stage to acknowledge the applause. Someone came forward with a huge bouquet of roses, and she received them standing in the spotlight to a resounding ovation. At that moment, her eyes fell on the baron in the front row, applauding with the others. What was it about him that brought back the sense of *déja-vu*?

Behind the scenes Roland hugged Abby, enthusing over the success of the evening and her clever designs. Madame Longet arrived, and kissed Abby on both cheeks, thanking her for such a wonderful show. 'That collection is *fantastique*! All Paris will be at your feet. There are not too many British designers who can claim that honour,' she smiled. 'The baron has asked me to bring you to the marquee, where everyone is waiting to meet you. I'm sure you're ready for a glass of champagne.'

Abby was more than ready, yet she put off the moment until Madame Longet began to suspect her reasons. 'You are ill at ease with the baron. Why?' When Abby did not answer, Odile Longet went on. 'It is because of the war?'

Abby looked into those warm brown eyes and felt she could trust this woman. 'Yes,' she whispered. 'He was, after all, a Nazi industrialist.'

Odile tensed. 'He was not,' she said firmly. 'It was Karl's father who was the great industrialist of the thirties and forties. Karl was a doctor, forced into the army to serve in field hospitals. His brothers were killed in the war, then the father died from a stroke in 1944 and Karl succeeded to the title, becoming the head of Schreiber Industries. He was forced, by the High Command, to run the company. It was important to Hitler that a von Schreiber be at the helm.' She paused, and her eyes softened. 'When the Allies moved in, they arrested most of the industrialists, but Karl was found innocent of any crime against humanity and released. Since then, he has brought work to thousands, and cared deeply about the plight of Europe's refugees. Believe me, my dear, this man was no Nazi.'

Abby smiled thinly, and murmured, 'Find me a German who was!'

'You are too harsh, too cynical. The man is not responsible for his father.'

'Are you saying he didn't use prisoners to work in his factories?'

'He had no control over that. Himmler gave orders that the SS were to be in sole charge of the labour force.' Odile looked at Abby with pleading eyes. 'Karl has suffered greatly; we all have. But he works hard now to benefit others. Please, do not make him suffer this embarrassment tonight.'

Abby looked at the woman and realized that Odile was in love with the baron. Was he in love with her?

'Very well, I'm ready. Shall we go in?'

Inside the marquee, waiters moved among the many guests with champagne and caviar. A stuffed boar dominated the large buffet table. Chefs stood ready to carve from joints of beef, lamb or pork. There were salmon steaks, frogs' legs, chicken and a variety of salads and fruit. Baron von Schreiber had spared no expense to make his guests welcome, grateful for their support on this and other occasions. Jewels gleamed on richly-dressed women, and the babble of different languages drowned the music from the Salon Orchestra. Soon Abby found herself completely surrounded by women enthusing over her collection. The baron came to her rescue, at last, leading her to a quiet corner.

'Tell me about this engraving,' he said.

Her mind filled with the collection, Abby tried to gather

her thoughts. 'Well, it was on a cigarette case which belongs to my aunt.'

'A golden case?'

'Yes.' Abby became more alert.

'How did your aunt come by such an article?' The baron seemed tense, though his manner was still one of courteous charm, for all the inquisitorial turn the conversation was taking.

'She's always had it, as far as I know. I went to live with her as a child.' Abby sipped her champagne and added, 'I know she lived in Germany for a time, so she must have acquired it then. Your house is obviously very famous.'

'Yes, I suppose it is,' he said quietly. There was a pause. 'Did she live in Dresden?'

Abby looked at him in growing wonder. 'Why, yes. Yes, she did. How on earth could you know that?'

'Her name is Milicent, and she was a teacher of English and the piano?'

Abby nodded in bewilderment. 'Yes. How incredible that you should have met Aunt Milicent! They say it's a small world, but this is ridiculous. Did you know her well?'

A strange smile crossed his face. 'Oh yes, I knew her very well. Her name was Waterton, is that not correct?'

Abby looked thoughtful. 'It's Glenister now, but I'm sure that Waterton was her maiden name.'

The smile faded and a sadness shadowed the eyes. 'So she married.' He added quickly, 'Do forgive me, Mrs Carr, but the whole thing is so beyond belief that I cannot take it in. You see, your Aunt Milicent was once my wife.'

Abby could not take her eyes off his face.

'We divorced many years ago,' he explained, 'but I was the one who gave her the cigarette case, and had the house engraved upon it. I'm afraid our marriage did not last very long.'

It was unbelievable, thought Abby. Aunt Milicent married to a German, and to a man from such a family as this one? All through the years she had kept this secret.

What must her feelings have been during the war? 'She never spoke of it,' she said at last.

'Well, she had her reasons. The war. My family's history.' The baron sighed. 'Oh yes, she had her reasons.' He had never told his own children that once he had been married to an Englishwoman. During the war years they would never have understood. But the war had been over a long time, and it hurt him to think she still had said nothing. 'Is she well?'

'Very,' said Abby, suddenly realizing where she had seen this man before. It had bothered her all day, but now she remembered. 'You once had an Alsatian, didn't you?'

'I still do,' said the baron.

Abby smiled, as memories of the dusty attic came back into her mind. 'I once saw a photograph of you. This house was in the background. I've been puzzling over the fact that I'd seen you before, and that explains it.'

The baron's eyes looked distant and there was a hint of pleasure in his voice. 'She kept that photograph, did she? She left in such a temper, I had expected she might have torn up such a memento.'

'Did she take the picture herself?'

The eyes locked back into the present. 'No. No, Milicent never came to this house. And she's married?'

'Widowed, I'm afraid. She has two children now – grown up, of course.'

'What of my son?'

Abby frowned. 'No. She only has two children.'

The baron looked anxious. 'One of them is a boy, yes? He would be about twenty-seven or twenty-eight. She said she was going to call him Richard. He is well, yes?'

Abby stared at him blankly, then nodded.

The baron sighed with relief. 'Thank God.' His eyes narrowed as he went on. 'She has never said then that Richard is my son?'

The world stopped suddenly, and Abby turned to stone. The baron receded into the distance, still speaking, but her world was silent, without air. Feeling herself suffocating, Abby turned and forced her way through the astonished guests out into the coolness of night, her feet stumbling and tripping across lawns until she came to the lake, shimmering silver in the moonlight. There she paused and leaned against the trunk of an elm in an effort to catch her breath. The words hammered inside her brain. '*Richard is my son! Richard is my son!*'

It can't be, it can't be, Abby told herself, still stunned. Was it possible the baron had said those words? Or had it been the noise, the heat and the champagne befuddling her mind? She was away from all that now, in blessed silence, with the sweet smell of grass. A myriad of coloured lights lit up the terrace, then blurred into each other as tears stung her eyes. The baron was wrong. Richard was William's son, surely. And yet − and yet those eyes and that mouth told her otherwise. Suddenly the years came rushing back, long anguished years which had set her life on a different course because she had believed that Richard was her brother. Then she felt a firm, strong hand on her shoulder, and heard the baron's anxious voice.

'I did not mean to shock you like that. Please, my dear, do forgive me. I should have thought before speaking.'

Turning slowly, Abby looked up into his strong face, clear in the moonlight, and knew that he truly was Richard's father. The resemblance was unmistakable now. Tears poured down her cheeks, as she thought of all those terrible wasted years of misery and anguish brought about by Milicent's desire to keep the truth from her children. A shudder coursed through her, then she felt the warmth of the baron's dinner jacket around her shoulders.

'It's too cold for you to be out. And I am a blundering fool.' If he understood her shock, he could not understand her obvious grief. She seemed devastated, heartbroken almost. Was his name so odious, then? The baron supposed it was. No one who had not been here during the war years could be expected to understand. Yet even so, Abby's behaviour did seem a little excessive.

Groups of people were wandering in the grounds, and some had gathered not far from them. Leading Abby to the terrace, the baron ordered brandy. 'I think you could do with this, and I know I could.'

Absently Abby took the glass, and clutched it tightly as she tried to control her weeping. 'There's no mistake? You're quite sure about Richard?'

Karl looked surprised. 'No mistake, I assure you. When Milicent left me she was three months pregnant. The child was born in a town called Folkestone. She wrote at the time, and said she intended to call him Richard, after her own father. I think that was meant to hurt me.' He paused, and lit a cigarette. 'What does hurt me, however, is that she clearly hasn't told my son. Oh, I could understand it during the war, but to keep it up for ever is a crime against the boy. He must be told. Will you tell him?'

Abby nodded slowly, the desolate emptiness and waste so overwhelming she could not speak. There was an ache in her heart which would not ease. Anger, grief and a sense of futility fought within her against her indescribable relief. Relief that she and Richard had not committed incest, that they shared not one single drop of blood. She wanted to scream at the moon, '*It's too late . . . it's too late!*' but, instead, she put the glass to her lips, and swallowed the cognac as though it were water. Liquid fire burned her throat, and took her breath away. She coughed then and felt the strange warmth bring her back to reality.

Karl smiled. 'You've never had brandy before, I can see that!' He watched her with affectionate concern, sensing now that there had been strong feelings between her and his son, yet still unable to understand why she was reacting in this way. 'Well, I don't normally recommend cognac for one so young as yourself, but for now it might help.'

Abby's thoughts were racing, retracing the past, remembering words spoken. Warily she took another sip of brandy. This time the fire was not so fierce, and she felt her shattered nerves calming. It made her defiant. 'You think Milicent kept her secret because you're German.' She smiled wryly. 'Oh, no. She had another reason for choosing silence.'

'Oh?' Karl was curious, and waited for further explanation of this extraordinary remark, but none seemed to be forthcoming. 'I lost touch with her soon after receiving that letter. All communication was made through lawyers,' he said. 'Ever since, I've wondered about him. Can you imagine what that's like? All those years?'

He looked at her face, pale in the moonlight. 'Tell me about my son. What is he like? What does he do? Is he married . . . dear God, there's so much! Please tell me.'

'What is he like?' Abby thought, as she gazed out over the lake. 'You would be proud of him. He's a good man,' her voice broke with emotion. 'A wonderful man, really. He went to Oxford to read Law, but left after one year and fought in Malaya, where he was wounded and received the Military Cross for bravery.' She turned to the baron and smiled. 'I said you would be proud of him. And . . . and he's married to a young woman whose parents are wealthy landowners.'

'Any children?'

'That I don't know,' whispered Abby. 'I haven't seen him for some time.'

'Why not?' the baron wanted to know.

Abby shrugged and gave a nervous laugh. 'Oh, just one of those things. He's busy — I'm busy.'

'But don't you meet at home — at Christmas, for instance?'

Abby shook her head. 'I left home a long time ago.' She finished her brandy. 'I really should get back and see if everything's all right. The outfits have to be packed in the right order, and the accessories checked. There won't be much time tomorrow.'

Karl placed a hand on her arm to prevent her moving

away. 'Surely you have a team to do that for you. Are you getting cold?'

Abby shook her head, but found herself shivering nevertheless. 'No. I'm fine, really.'

'Why did you leave home?'

'Because I chose to.' Abby's words were spoken with a tension not lost on the baron.

'May I call you Abigail?' When she nodded, he went on. 'I know nothing of your life or background. I do not mean to pry, but I should like to know more about you.'

Abby stared ahead, stone-faced. 'My parents were killed in the war. I went to live with my aunt and uncle in Canterbury. Richard and Stella were my second cousins. Only when I was eighteen did I learn that William was not my uncle, but my father.' She turned to him, her head held high. 'Now do you understand?'

There was a long silence, then the baron spoke. 'Yes, I believe I do. The shock must have been great, especially since you obviously have strong feelings for my son. And Milicent still said nothing?'

'Nothing,' Abby repeated, then said, 'I loved your son, and he loved me. When we thought we were half-brother and sister, we parted. There was no way I could live at home any more. Since then I married, and he's married too. My husband drowned, and now I have my business to run. That's the end of the story. I'm sorry I became so emotional. It was the shock, that's all. Forgive me for embarrassing you like that.' She moved away and this time was not to be detained. 'Now I really must go.' She handed his jacket back to him.

The baron looked down at the lovely, sad and tear-stained face, slowly realizing that this girl might well have become his daughter-in-law. 'Yes, I ought to return to my guests. Shall I see you tomorrow when you come for your things? Have luncheon with me.'

Abby shook her head. 'We have to get back to Holland for the ferry.'

'Coffee, then?'

'Coffee would be lovely. I look forward to it, Baron.'

He took her hand. 'Call me Karl. We were very nearly related, after all.'

As he clicked his heels and bowed slightly, Abby realized that this man was Ross's grandfather. He would never know it, of course. 'Very well, Karl. Till tomorrow then, and thank you for such a wonderful champagne supper.'

All that night Abby tossed and turned in her hotel bed, unable to sleep for the anger and anguish which now engulfed her. When she had stood on the terrace with Karl, the world had seemed a slightly unreal place, almost as though they had been characters in a play. Maybe it had been the champagne, following such a triumph, but whatever it was had dulled everything after the first, initial shock. Now, however, truth stood cold and clear: hard, painful truth. Milicent had deliberately deceived her, and Richard also. She had ruthlessly destroyed their lives in order to get what she wanted. All those years, those terrible years of guilt, loss and pain, had been for nothing.

Her mind fled back to that fateful morning in Harrods' restaurant. Milicent could have told her then, but instead had let her believe that Richard was her brother. How could anyone be that cruel?

'Dear God, woman, you'll have a great deal to answer for one of these days,' Abby said aloud. What kind of mother would break her son's heart, rather than let him live in happiness with the woman he loved? Milicent thought her secret safe, did she? How could she have ever dreamed that one day Abby would meet Richard's real father, the man whose existence no one was meant to know about?

Richard would be told, of course. It would be her first act on returning to England. Why should he go on thinking of their love with shame? Richard would be told, even if he did now love Samantha. He must understand what his mother truly was. Milicent was not going to get away with this!

Thinking of all the happy years she and Richard might

have shared, had they not been raised on a lie, Abby's thoughts turned to Ross. Guilt stabbed at her. Was he not being raised on the same lie? Was she not doing to him what Milicent had done to Richard, and William to her? *But it's different*, she told herself. *My reasons are for his own good and for Evelyn's*. Should Evelyn ever find out the truth, it would tear her apart. Nevertheless, conscience pricked at Abby. Even though she meant well, Ross could suffer one day because of her silence.

Her thoughts returned to Karl. He seemed kind and gentle, yet there was this question-mark hanging over him because of his family and their part in Hitler's war machine. What sort of man was he really?

At dawn, the thoughts began to fade, and Abby finally drifted into a fitful sleep.

The following morning when they arrived back at the mansion Abby was looking tired, but Roland was in fine fettle, unaware of anything other than the overwhelming success of the evening. He had come away with many orders, and deemed the whole venture well worth their time and trouble.

The models, along with Madame Duval and the *vendeuse*, had already headed for the airport. While Odile Longet offered to find staff to help Roland load the van, Abby was escorted into a drawing room by the smiling Frau Kruger, who spoke no English but nodded a great deal as she indicated that Abby should sit by the tall windows with the warm sunlight streaming through. Abby looked around at the elegant furnishings, the pale green damask wallcovering, the strange green-and-white-tiled stove in the corner, which rose up cone-like to the ceiling, and the paintings on the wall. One was a Turner sunset, another by Sisley. Karl knew his art and obviously had the means to pay for it.

Her gaze travelled to the many silver-framed photographs on a long mahogany side table. She peered at each one, wondering who they were, suspecting that the pale, drawn woman seated on the sofa and the tall grey-haired man standing behind her were Karl's parents. *Richard's grandparents*, she thought suddenly, *and Ross's great grandparents!* It was all so unreal. Before them, stretched out on the carpet, was a huge Alsatian, paws crossed neatly before it, ears pricked up at the camera. By the woman's dress, Abby judged the photograph to have been taken some time during the early forties.

She moved on to other photographs, realizing that despite all the important people who must have come to this house, only family photographs were on display. Pictures of those made famous by their infamy had been consigned to the flames, or hidden away in some dark, forgotten place.

Then she saw it. Karl was much younger, and the pretty, dark-haired woman obviously his wife. It was a formal photograph, with the wife seated while Karl stood behind her. On either side stood two little girls: twins, Abby thought. They were about six years of age, with clear, shining beauty, long fair curly hair and eyes that gleamed with genuine amusement. Perhaps the photographer had said something at that moment to make them smile.

She held the photograph for some time, wishing she could take it back to England to show to Milicent. How happy this young family looked! Karl's second attempt at marriage was clearly more successful than his first. The girls, of course, would be grown women by now. His wife would be in her late forties. Why had they not come to the show last night, she wondered?

The door opened and in walked Karl and Odile. Both stood smiling at Abby, as Frau Kruger brought in a trolley with a silver coffee service, porcelain cups and saucers and a large cream gateau. Glad she was not to be left alone with Karl, Abby relaxed.

'A stunning success, my dear,' Karl said. 'Marvellous. But I must admit I'll be glad to return to a world I know more about.'

'Where are you going?' asked Abby.

'Berlin tomorrow, for one week, then back to Dortmund. New York next week for three days, then Paris, then Berlin again.' Karl picked up his coffee.

Abby wondered when he ever got around to being with his wife and daughters, but felt it rude to ask. 'Who will look after this house then, if you're not here?'

'A caretaker staff.' He looked around casually. 'God knows what I'll do with it. Your army had it for years. When they handed it back, it was quite a blow. Maybe I'll throw it open to the public, if anyone wants to clatter around such a mausoleum.'

They chatted casually about this and that, then Odile asked if they would forgive her, but she had much to do and should be getting on with it. Karl stood as she left, then sat down and tried to persuade Abby to eat more of the cake. 'Frau Kruger will be very cross if you don't. She takes it as a personal insult if her cooking is ignored!'

Abby forced herself to eat another small slice, aware that this might be the last piece of food to enter her mouth for the rest of the day, since Roland loathed stopping en route for anything.

'Are you really going all the way back to London in that van?' asked Karl in disbelief.

'Of course. But you already know that, since you saw me arrive in it.'

'Did I?' Karl smiled mysteriously. 'You looked very strange, wandering towards the house like that as though you were sleepwalking. I wondered who on earth you were.'

Abby smiled. 'Why didn't you come and greet us?'

Karl shrugged. 'I don't know. I had no idea what to say to anyone from the fashion world. It seemed best to let Odile handle it.'

Odile! Abby noted his use of her first name. Was he a married man, having an affair and just being cautious about it? He was extremely good-looking and women were drawn to such men. Looking at Karl now, Abby could see how Richard would be in some twenty years' time. That was what she had seen, when she had stood on the cat-walk acknowledging the applause, although she hadn't known it.

She drew the conversation back to the house. 'So you won't be living in it, then?'

'What on earth do I want with a place this size? Always did hate it, even as a child.' He frowned. 'Although that might have something to do with an unhappy childhood and a father who never spared the rod.'

'What about your mother?'

Karl's face clouded. 'I adored her. But you must understand, I was the youngest, the least important member of an important family. My eldest brother was the heir to the House of Schreiber, not I. I was only too glad to leave and start my medical training. I was in Dresden, when I met Milicent. She was teaching a family in the old town. We met at a party and I fell in love with her. It all ended badly, as you know. My father would not accept her into the family.'

'Because she was English?'

'Because she was of the wrong class.'

Abby smiled to herself. Milicent must have been furious! No wonder she'd become so obsessed with class. She listened as Karl went on talking about his strict and domineering father. A German of the old school who cared only about the honour of his word and the honour of his country, he was unimpressed with Hitler, whom he regarded as a common little upstart. He was furious when, upon becoming the new Chancellor, Hitler tore up the Treaty of Versailles. Ordered to produce more steel for the manufacture of weapons, it had been made very plain that if he refused he could always be replaced by someone who had less scruples. That would have meant control of the Company going outside the family. Everything his father had built would be handed on a plate to someone else.

His story finished, Karl stood up, saying: 'Come, let's

take a walk in this warm sunshine. You'll be cooped up long enough in that awful van.'

They wandered back towards the lake, glistening now in the morning sunlight. A swan glided past, eyeing them curiously, then dipping its bill into the water. Soon it was joined by its mate, and they swam on towards the far bank.

Abby looked up at Karl. 'I hope to see Richard again, and I'll tell him of our meeting.' *You can be sure of it!* she thought. 'He will want to know all about you. Marriage, children, your life in general. Of course, if you'd rather he didn't know, then so be it.'

He led her to a bench and they sat looking out across the water at a small, classical temple on the other side. Rhododendron bushes grew at its base, their dark leaves moving slightly in the soft breeze.

'I'm no longer married,' said Karl quietly. 'My wife and little girls were killed when Dresden was bombed. Twin daughters – lovely, happy twin daughters whom I loved very much.'

Abby heard him recalling the bombing in appalled silence. She could hardly believe the little girls and that pretty woman were dead. That was the night Milicent had struck Stella, as the newsreader reported the attack. No wonder she had been so agitated, turning on William and Stella so bitterly. It was not only the children she had taught that concerned her – it was Karl.

'I'm so terribly sorry,' she whispered.

'I blame myself,' Karl was saying. 'That's the terrible thing I have to live with. You see, my father had died, and I was ordered to take over the firm. But the raids on the Ruhr were so bad that I insisted my wife and children remain in Dresden. There they would be safe, I said. Thousands of refugees were pouring into the city, and there seemed no reason for it to become a target.' He paused and stared ahead with burning eyes. 'How dreadfully wrong I was.'

They lived in different worlds, but Karl was like Evelyn:

304

both blaming themselves for the death of their loved ones. Suddenly, Abby felt sorry for him. With all his power and wealth, he was a sad and lonely man. The loss of a child was the worst thing that could happen to anyone.

It was time to leave, and Abby stood with Karl outside the main entrance. 'You'll never know how glad I am that our paths crossed. Had I known about you years ago, my life would have been very different.' She handed him a card. 'That's my new salon in Mayfair. When you're next in London, look me up. With any luck, I might just manage to bring you and Richard together again.'

Karl smiled. 'You won't find that easy. You cannot know what it's like, being thought a war criminal when you are completely innocent. Richard may think the worst also.'

'He'll never think that, never.'

'Ah, but he will,' said Karl. 'Why do you think his mother never told him of me? My very name is odious to the world now.'

Abby shook her head. 'Your name isn't the reason. I told you that last night. Anyway, time heals wounds.'

Karl laughed gently. 'Wise words from one so young. What on earth do you know about time, my dear? You've so much of it left.' He took her hand in his and held it firmly. 'But, yes, I would dearly love to see my son before time runs out on me. He is, after all, my heir.'

'I'll do all I can,' said Abby, meaning every word of her promise. She turned away, then paused as a thought struck her. 'Karl, who is your favourite composer?'

'Schubert,' said Karl. 'Why do you ask?'

Abby nodded. 'I thought it might be.'

Driving away from the great house, Abby smiled to herself. Schubert! That explained a great deal. Remembering the far-away look on Milicent's face as she had played the piano, Abby realized that her stepmother was still in love with Karl. Small wonder

305

she could not love William. As the van rounded the
bend, and made its way through the iron gates, she
wondered whether Richard ever would see his father or
his ancestral home.

CHAPTER THIRTEEN

The Brook Street salon was a solid building of Portland stone. Double-fronted, the impressive mahogany doors were set within a classical Georgian porch that belied the spacious interior. Anyone entering was surprised by the large entrance hall, dominated by an elegant winding stairway.

The drawing room had been converted into an office which Abby used, while opposite stood the fitting room, large and comfortably furnished with armchairs and tall mirrors. To the right of the stairs was the reception desk, behind which were shelves of materials and accessories. A young girl sat there writing in the appointments book. She looked up as Abby entered the building.

'Good morning, Mrs Carr.'

'Good morning, Avril,' said Abby, unbuttoning the cream woollen coat she had designed herself. In the hallway were pictures of the famous clothed in her outfits, duchesses mingling with film stars, all shining with the glamour that the best haute couture could give.

Avril followed Abby into the office and showed her the appointments book. 'I've pencilled in Lady Graham for four o'clock, and said I would ring back to confirm.'

Abby said that was fine, and went upstairs to what had once been a ballroom, and was now the main showroom for the House of Carr. The huge floor-to-ceiling mirrors had been fixtures when she'd moved in, and now soft sage greens and ivory satin gilded chairs had returned the room to its former glory. It made a perfect setting for her collections.

Above the ballroom on the second floor and running the

length of the building were her workroom, Roland's office and changing rooms for the models. Everyone now was under one roof, and life was much easier. Decorating and refurbishing had been expensive, but exciting. Jonathan had arranged the huge loan, and, thanks to Roland's efficiency, the move had gone to plan, in spite of Abby's fears. There had been sad moments, also. Saying goodbye to Church Street had filled her with nostalgia for those first days. She was leaving a home, not a flat over the workshop.

The move to Hampstead, however, had been more traumatic. Ross had cried and lamented this second disturbance to his life. Abby had spent hours comforting the little boy, pointing out that since he was not changing schools he would still see his friends, and that here he'd have not only a garden to play in, but the whole of Hampstead Heath as well.

'But my friends won't be able to find me any more!' he had wailed.

'Of course they will. We'll invite them over as often as you like,' she had said. 'And you are going to have the best bedroom you ever had, with plenty of space for your toys and books. Uncle Jonathan has bought you a desk and chair. There's even a playroom downstairs where you can lay out your railway set. Your friends will love coming out to you at Hampstead.'

Finally, Ross had been won over. But Evelyn had not been so easy to placate. Grim-faced, she had studied the tall Georgian house in its terrace, eyed the well-proportioned rooms suspiciously, and paled at the cost of it all. 'You'll never get this place warm. Look at the 'eight of those ceilings. I mean, it's lovely and all that, Abby, but it's old! Why couldn't you 'ave got one of those small modern 'ouses? Much easier to cope with and cheaper to run.' She mellowed a little at the sight of the large kitchen downstairs, overlooking the long walled garden. She approved of the new kitchen units, then stared at the modern electric stove

308

as though it had dropped from another planet. 'What's all these knobs for, then? And this clock?'

Abby explained the technique of pre-setting the timer. 'The dinner can start to cook while you're still out. When you come home, hey presto!'

Evelyn had stared at her daughter-in-law as though she had taken leave of her senses. 'Me? Go out and leave an oven on! Never in a million years, luv. I wish you'd got gas. I've always 'ad gas . . . this one frightens me a bit.'

'As for the running of the house,' Abby had gone on to say, 'you're going to have help. I've arranged for a domestic to come in every morning for three hours.'

'You're joking!' had come the horrified reply. 'And what am I supposed to do — sit on me bum all day and turn rusty? Listen, I'm not falling to pieces just yet, and I don't want no busybody prattling around our 'ome, poking 'er nose into things what don't concern her.'

'You can't possibly cope, and I don't expect you to,' Abby persisted. 'You'll have your work cut out looking after Ross, and shopping and cooking. Mrs Proctor will take all the heavy chores off your hands. At least give it a try. For my sake. Please?'

After a long silence, Evelyn had agreed. 'Very well. But if I don't like 'er, and if she don't clean the place properly, then she goes. Is that a bargain?'

'It's a bargain,' Abby had sighed.

Now, in the salon as she awaited the first client of the day, her thoughts drifted to Richard and Karl. On her return from Germany, she'd wanted to tell Richard the truth about his father at once, but caution prevented her from writing to Ferndene Lodge. Instead, she telephoned Mrs Wellings, who still ran Children's Wear in Glenisters, and asked for Richard's address and telephone number, thinking she might somehow get hold of him without Samantha knowing about it.

'I don't have it, I'm afraid, Mrs Carr. Your aunt's in her office, though — shall I put you through to her?'

309

'Please, don't do that. I really don't want my aunt to know I've telephoned. It's ... well, it's a surprise, you see. Do you know when he's likely to be in the store?'

'Mr Glenister and his family are in the South of France just now, that much I do know.'

Abby's heart hardened at the cosy domestic picture. 'Does he get to the store very often? I mean ... when will he return?'

'He returns at the end of next week, but he doesn't come to Canterbury much these days. His mother runs the store now. The only time I know he'll be here for certain is when the auditors do the books.'

'When will that be?'

'September. The first week in September.'

September! All these years, and now another four months before she could see him face to face.

'Very well, I'll come to Canterbury during that week. I'll contact you again nearer the time, to confirm the day. But please, Mrs Wellings, don't let anyone know about this conversation. I realize that I sound ridiculously over-dramatic, but there are reasons.'

'I understand perfectly,' said Mrs Wellings. She was no fool. Milicent Glenister had not mentioned Abby's name since the girl had mysteriously departed all those years ago. No mention at all of the niece who had risen to fame in such a meteoric way! All they ever heard about was Stella, the actress. It was shameful. 'Don't you worry, Mrs Carr. This is just between us.'

'Thank you. Oh, and please do call me Abby, the way you used to. Are you keeping well?'

'Very well, thank you. Getting near retirement age now, though. I would just like to say how proud we all are of your success.'

'That's very kind of you.'

'I just wish your uncle could have lived to see it.'

'So do I,' whispered Abby, her heart full suddenly. 'Oh, so do I.'

She had wondered how she would get through the months of waiting. In the event, she'd been so busy that getting through them had proved no problem at all. Now, however, the moment she'd longed for and dreaded had suddenly come. It was the end of August.

Her client arrived and selected an outfit. Joanna Craig was a theatrical star of advancing years, fading looks and growing talent. Still in great demand, she filled every theatre she played in, and was always in the news. Three years ago she had discovered that Abby's clothes were not only the most comfortable she had ever worn, but also the most flattering. Since then, she had been a walking advertisement for the House of Carr. The two women had become good friends, in spite of the difference in their ages.

'Darling, I simply *must* fly,' said Joanna in the strong throaty voice that had made her so famous. 'Now you have the tickets. The play's the best thing I've done in years. I'm wild about it. You will be, too. Come to my dressing room after the show.'

Abby looked at the tickets, and knew Jonathan would be her date as he'd often been these past years. He was the perfect escort and a close friend who never let her down. If only she could love him as, she felt certain now, he loved her! If only she could love any man other than Richard who still dominated her thoughts and emotions. It was madness, she told herself. She was young and attractive, yet she lived like a nun, holding on to a dream which had been shattered years ago. Perhaps September would kill these feelings for Richard, once and for all.

Back in her office, Abby rang Glenisters. When she heard Mrs Wellings' voice her heart quickened, and her hands became clammy. 'It's me — Abby. I wondered if you'd had any more word of the auditors.'

'Of course,' came the reply. 'They're coming next Friday. I should have telephoned you, but you know how it is, everything gets on top of you and ...'

'It's all right, really. Friday, you say? And Mr Glenister will be there?'

'Oh yes. Are you coming to see us then?' The voice was hopeful. 'You're the only couturier whose face is as famous as her chief model's.'

Abby laughed. 'I'd love to. But ... well ... that might be a little difficult, given that my aunt isn't to know.'

'I understand,' said Mrs Wellings, disappointed, but knowing Abby's desire to stay out of Milicent's way. 'Mr Glenister should be finished with the auditors by mid-afternoon.'

'Would you mind giving him a message?' Abby's voice was tremulous, and her heart was beating wildly now. 'Would you ask him to meet me when he's free?' Would he, though? Or would he just ignore such a request?

'Of course. Where and at what time?'

Abby thought quickly, eliminating the centre of Canterbury, since to be seen in the High Street would be asking for trouble. 'Tell him I'll be in St Dunstan's Church at three o'clock. It's extremely important. But remember, not a word to another soul!'

'Don't worry,' came the reassuring voice.

When Abby replaced the receiver, she felt drained. If just ringing Glenisters to arrange a meeting with Richard had this effect on her, what would she be like when she faced him again? *Settle down, you little fool. He's a married man, and probably happy. He's most likely forgotten that he ever loved you at all!*

Unlocking the top right-hand drawer of her desk, she took out a framed picture, a sketch wrapped in tissue. Removing the paper she gazed down on Richard's noble young profile looking out to sea from the ruins of Tintagel Castle. All these years she'd kept the sketch, carefully hidden from the Carr family, from Jonathan and even Susan. It was hers and hers alone.

Jeremy poured more wine in Samantha's glass and studied

312

her, liking what he saw. She'd matured into a cool, lovely young woman, rather like Grace Kelly, he thought, with her hair swept back into a French plait under the Breton-style hat. He thought how perfect she would have been as his Viscountess, and, in twenty or thirty years' time, as his Countess. But, she would be neither now, he thought smugly, and she was living to regret it. Why else did he find it so easy to take her out when Richard was away? She was bored already with the shopkeeper's son. *You've made your bed my sweet, now you must lie on it! Would to God it were mine.*

At this precise moment, however, bed was the last thing on Jeremy's mind. He gazed thoughtfully around the Dorchester Grill Room, with its ornate ceilings and tapestried walls. Lighting a cigarette, he decided to come to the point. Spending time and money on Samantha was a means to an end: the end being the financial ruin of Richard Glenister. 'How is he these days?' he asked suddenly. 'Richard, I mean. Still penny pinching?'

Samantha sighed and stirred her coffee. 'Oh, he's as impossible as ever. I love him, Jeremy, truly I do, but he has such a close hand! I daren't tell him I've bought anything new, because I know it will lead to a row. So now I don't tell him at all.'

Jeremy smiled and eyed her Chanel suit. 'Well, my dear, you don't come cheap. Did it ever occur to you he simply doesn't have the money you're used to spending? Still hell-bent on entering the House, is he?'

Samantha nodded. 'Oh, yes. And Daddy's been marvellous, working all-out for Richard. Things are looking up in the political field, but more than that I cannot and will not say. After all, you are connected with the press.'

'Connected! My dear lady, my cousin practically owns Fleet Street, and I'm being groomed to sit in his chair one day.'

'Which I find odd,' said Samantha. 'After all, when your father dies you'll have the estate to run.'

'Whatever's left of it after death duties. It might just finish us.'

'You'll sell a few Van Dycks, and let in the public,' Samantha smiled. 'Sorry, I forgot. The public already trails through your state rooms.'

Jeremy inhaled deeply. 'You wait. It'll happen to you one day – this State theft. But I don't intend to sit around growing old, waiting to inherit. Anyway, getting back to your dear husband, you know you can always talk to me. Whatever you say will always be held in the strictest confidence.'

Samantha touched his hand affectionately. 'I know. It's just that Richard doesn't tell me what's going on half the time.'

Concern crossed Jeremy's face. 'I hope you understand that if he does become an MP, you're going to be a lot poorer, unless he has money behind him.'

'Only the store in Canterbury.'

'Better than nothing, but less than you're used to.' Jeremy gave her a searching look. 'Still, he must have a lot of excellent investments. Sorry, shouldn't talk about money. Bad form. It's just that I do worry about you, my sweet.'

Samantha looked a shade embarrassed. Money and background were vital in her circle but only background was discussed openly. Finances had never entered her head, until Richard forced her to confront their situation. She had an allowance of her own, and had no intention of turning it into a joint income. 'All I know is that his shares took a dive when an African gold mine he'd invested in was nationalized without warning.' She sipped her coffee. 'He wanted to be a barrister, and that's what he should have been. The stockmarket is a complete mystery to him, I'm afraid.'

This was music to Jeremy's ears. He leaned forward in a conspiratorial manner. 'I really would like to help, not him, of course, but you. I do care, you know that. If

Richard wants to double his money within a year, I know how he can do it. It's safe – you have my word on it.'

Samantha's eyes widened. 'What is it?'

'Langdon Construction.' Jeremy looked at her with hard eyes cloaked in sincerity. 'They're winning all the major contracts, seemingly poised for the big government one which will change the look of London and the provinces beyond all belief.'

'Go on.'

'My dear, there are plans afoot to tear out city centres and build huge new complexes. High-rise flats, like the Roehampton development, and then more motorways. The M1 is just the beginning. And Langdon is set to gain the largest slice of the cake. Richard should buy shares now, like I have. He could use the store as collateral, and go in for eighty thousand at thirty shillings each. They'll be worth three pounds within a year.'

'Where would he get that kind of money?' Samantha was shaking her head slowly. 'Eighty thousand at thirty shillings each – that's . . .'

'My dear, the store is worth that, surely.' He sighed. 'Or whatever he can safely afford. There's no risk, it's a certainty.'

'How can you be sure of all this?'

'I've seen some of the plans and spoken to businessmen and architects. The councils know they have no option but to reconstruct. Like it or not, it's going to happen.' He smiled sardonically. 'You know what they say – every cloud has a silver lining. Even a concrete jungle! But remember, this is a secret.'

Samantha frowned. 'Of course, not a word. But how on earth am I going to persuade Richard?'

'Well, don't bring up my name, or he'll ignore the whole business. Tell him you heard it from Nigel Bingham. He has all the right connections in business, and Richard knows him well enough to trust his judgement. He's bound to go straight to

315

the horse's mouth, so brief Nigel. You can handle it, my dear.'

Samantha smiled at him. 'You are a dear, Jeremy. Sometimes I wish . . .' she stopped suddenly. 'I just wish that Richard knew what a good friend you really are. He still hasn't forgotten New Year all those years ago. Childish, really, holding grudges to that extent.' She drummed her fingers on the table, thoughtfully. 'Even so, he's very cautious at the moment, having had his fingers badly burned in the African venture. I might not be able to persuade him to buy Langdon shares.'

Jeremy drew on his cigarette, exhaling slowly. 'See to it that you do, my dear.'

Returning to his office, Jeremy called in his senior secretary. 'Any word from our source about Langdon?'

'Nothing, sir,' came the reply. Miss Searle had worked for the newspaper group since the thirties, and had been perfectly happy until this arrogant young man joined the business. His casual disregard for her made her wish that she could take early retirement, instead of facing his rudeness for another three years.

'Well, didn't you chase it up as I asked?'

'Yes, sir, but until he reports to his contact, there's no way I can reach him.'

Jeremy looked across his expanse of desk at the grey-haired woman in her navy suit. 'Blast! If he does telephone, put him through to me at once. No one else is to know about him.'

As Miss Searle left, Jeremy studied the Langdon Construction file. The company had been putting in the lowest tenders for some time now, and winning contracts over their major competitors. Maybe they were the best — maybe not. When discontented murmurings had reached his ears, he started a secret investigation, sending a skilled engineer into Langdon to work under cover.

Placing his feet on his desk, Jeremy frowned with

impatience. His initial elation at getting Samantha to bite the bait was already beginning to fade. Suppose Langdon proved to be cleaner than Snow White? Not only would he have no story, he would have handed Richard a gift, instead of a hot potato.

That same night, Abby sat in the theatre with Jonathan, watching as Joanna Craig wooed her audience. She was a powerful actress who held the stage completely, so it came as a shock to Abby when the actress playing the younger daughter came on from the wings. The voice and stance were so familiar. Peering through her opera glasses, Abby blinked in astonishment. 'Stella,' she murmured. 'It's Stella!' Glancing through her programme for the familiar name, she found an actress by the name of Gemma Landis in the part. Again she put the opera glasses to her eyes. It *was* Stella. The stupid girl had changed her name. 'Gemma Landis, indeed,' she whispered to Jonathan, who was bored, waiting for the interval when he could have his gin and tonic. 'Fancy my . . . my cousin, in a West End production. I'd assumed she was swanning around in provincial Rep.'

'It wouldn't do her any harm,' murmured Jonathan, singularly unimpressed. 'Pretty girl, though. Puts me in mind of Jean Simmons.'

After the performance they joined the invited guests hovering in and around Joanna Craig's dressing room. Dressed in a blue silk wrap, but still wearing her stage make-up, Joanna stood amidst her admirers, receiving the adulation she craved, laughing loudly and calling everyone 'darling'.

'Now, darlings, I want you all to meet my dear friend Abigail Carr, who dresses me like a woman, yet makes me feel like a queen.'

Abby blushed as all eyes turned to her, and heard Joanna's next comment with some surprise.

'I'm hoping I can persuade her to design the wardrobe

for my next production. Providing we get the backing, of course.' She kissed Abby lightly on the cheek. 'My dear, did you enjoy the play?'

'Very much,' said Abby. 'My cousin was playing the part of Zena.'

'Stella?' The stage make-up cracked a little in surprise. 'Good heavens, is *she* your cousin? Well, where is she? Do call her in, Charles, there's a darling. Let's see her face when she sees Abby.'

'You won't have to look far.' The deep, laconic voice made Abby turn. A tall man was leaning nonchalantly against the door, looking at her with dark eyes. 'She's always around somewhere.'

'Greg!' cried Joanna. 'Oh, do stop lolling around making the place look untidy, and come and meet Abigail and Jonathan. This is Greg Hadleigh, our esteemed writer.'

Towering above all others, Greg slowly approached Abby. He was wearing a dinner jacket with a bow tie as black as his eyes. Or were they brown? Abby found it hard to tell. His dark hair was a shade longer than normal and his face, although sensitive, seemed to be hewn out of granite. Extending her hand, she was nonplussed when he held it firmly, looking deeply into her eyes. 'I'm glad you came.'

'Glad to be here,' said Abby, her voice too high.

'What did you think of the play?' The eyes twinkled with amusement, as though he could sense her discomfort.

'Oh ... I enjoyed it very much.' This time, when she tugged, he relinquished his hold on her hand. 'This is Jonathan,' she said quickly. As the two men exchanged pleasantries, Abby moved away to the group surrounding Joanna. What on earth could she say about his play? That she had found it thought-provoking and deeply moving? That was true, but to say it to a man who was clearly flirting with her seemed to be asking for trouble. When she turned her head surreptitiously, Greg had gone.

Stella duly presented herself at the 'inner sanctum', wondering why she'd been called. Shed of her make-up, wearing a chunky sweater over drainpipe velvet trousers, she looked remarkably young, and had copied Audrey Hepburn's gamine look by cropping her hair short.

'Abby, darling! What are *you* doing here?' Stella advanced, all smiles, planting a kiss on her sister's cheek. 'How absolutely marvellous to see you again. How are you?'

Abby smiled and said how well she was, and how wonderful she thought Stella was looking. As she spoke, she felt a genuine rush of affection. 'I simply couldn't believe it when you appeared on stage. You were very good,' she added tactfully. 'Wasn't she, Jonathan, wasn't she good in the part?'

'First rate,' murmured Jonathan, wondering how much longer they were to stand around when he was growing hungrier by the minute.

Stella had turned to Joanna, and was laughing with mirthless eyes. 'You know, it's absolutely incredible. We grew up together, but with Abby's career and mine, we simply haven't seen each other for ages. Yet we were always so close, and there hasn't been a day I haven't thought of her.'

Abby could hardly believe what she was hearing. Stella had made no attempt to contact her since William's funeral. Was it ungracious to assume that Stella thought having a relative who was one of Britain's top couturiers, and also a friend of the West End's most famous actress, could be a useful contact? Yes, Abby decided, it was an ungracious thought, but true just the same.

At last, Jonathan and Abby said goodbye. Stella walked with them towards the stage door, then all three stared out in dismay. 'Good Lord, it's pouring,' said Jonathan. 'Wait here, Abby, I'll bring the car round.'

Stella leaned against the wall, and lit a cigarette. 'That was all a bit of a shock. When I heard that Joanna wanted to speak to me, I was worried. What did you *really* think of me in the part?'

Abby smiled. 'I thought you were good, as I've already told you. And look at you, playing the West End. I'd no idea. What else have you been in?'

'Oh, I've been pretty lucky, I suppose.' The voice was crisp now. 'I've played at the Savoy and the Cambridge. Small parts, of course, but it's a start. I'm also auditioning for a part in a television play next week.' There was a long and awkward pause. 'I'm sorry I was so rotten to you at the funeral. It was a beast of a day and I ... well, I'm sorry.'

Realizing how much it had cost Stella to say that, Abby said, 'It's all right. It's all in the past and forgotten.'

'Good. And you've gone on to be a great success. Joanna makes quite a point of telling people about you. Oh, Abby, I'd love to see your salon. Brook Street, isn't it? Of course I could never afford your prices, but I'd love to see the world of top couture at first hand.'

Abby nodded. 'Of course.' She turned and looked out into the dark wet London night, frowning. 'Poor Jonathan. Never gave a thought to bringing his umbrella this evening, yet he's never without it in the daytime.'

'Well, you certainly can't get that dress wet.' Stella eyed the dark green taffeta gown, and sighed with envy. 'I'd kill for something like that.'

If ever there was a hint, this was it. 'I'm up to my eyes at the moment, but I will make you something without charging my usual rate. Let's call it a secret, though.'

Stella's eyes lit up. 'Would you? That would be fantastic. Do you remember that fabulous gown you made for me to wear at the New Year's party? I ought to have known then that my cousin would make it to the top. By the way, who is Jonathan, and what is he to you?'

'Just a very good friend,' said Abby. 'Without him, I wouldn't have made it to the top.'

Stella nodded. 'It seems we women are all in the same boat.'

'No, I don't think you quite understand,' said Abby quickly. 'He really *is* a very good friend, and my banker. That's all.' Clearly Stella's career depended on a very different kind of relationship. 'Stella, there's one thing that puzzles me. Why do you still call me "cousin"?'

'Because you are.' Stella stubbed out her cigarette with a careless heel. 'Everything's changed at home, you know. Ferndene's a very quiet place, now that Richard's married.' She put a hand to her mouth suddenly. 'Of course, you didn't know he married Samantha.'

'Oh, yes,' said Abby quickly. 'I knew years ago. How are they?' Keeping her voice under control was hard. The question had been in her mind from the first moment she had set eyes on Stella.

'They're fine,' came the reply. 'Of course, I haven't been in touch with Richard since that nonsense about the Will. But I do see Sam from time to time and she's very happy. Over the moon, I should say. They have the most adorable little girl. Fiona, they call her. She's the apple of Richard's eye, and he spoils her dreadfully.'

Each word sent a knife through Abby's heart, but she smiled and tried not to think of Richard doting on his little daughter when he had a son who needed him, also. The happy husband and father would hardly be likely to thank his former love for re-entering his life to tell him about Karl.

'Earlier, I asked you why you still called me "cousin". I must say I find that strange, after all these years.'

Stella's eyes widened. 'What an odd thing to say!'

'Not odd at all, given that we're half-sisters. So why not come to terms with that fact?'

The shocked disbelief on Stella's face came as a surprise. 'Sisters! What are you talking about? We're no such thing.'

Now it was Abby's turn to be surprised. 'Of course we

321

are. William was my father. Good heavens, we spoke openly at the funeral. You said then you knew all about it!'

Stella simply stared at her, shaking her head. 'How can you say such lies, such filthy, rotten lies?'

'At the funeral, you said your mother had told you everything.' Abby was covered in confusion.

'I said no such thing!' cried Stella. 'You are my cousin. Your father was killed in the war. Stop trying to steal an identity you don't have!'

At that moment the lights of Jonathan's car came into view. 'We need to talk,' said Abby firmly. 'Can you come round to my salon tomorrow morning? It's important that we get to the bottom of this appalling muddle.'

'Muddle? Lies, yes, but muddle, no.'

'Come to Brook Street, please Stella,' Abby said, and then ran to the waiting car. As Jonathan drove away, she listened to the click of the windscreen wipers, feeling utterly confused by her sister's behaviour. It made no sense at all.

After a late supper, Jonathan drove Abby back to Hampstead, where Evelyn was waiting up. She had never ceased being the worried mother, and could not sleep until her daughter-in-law was safely home. Abby's recent trip to Germany had been an agony for her. Suppose the van crashed or the ferry sank! she had thought, lying awake all night. Now, as the door to the drawing room opened, she put down the book she was reading and sighed with relief.

'You look as though you've 'ad a good time!'

'We had a lovely time,' said Abby, kissing her. 'Was Ross good? Didn't fret, I hope, because I wasn't here to put him to bed?'

'Good as gold, and sleeping like a log. He's got a bit of a cold, I think.' She smiled up at Jonathan. 'Would you like some tea, or coffee perhaps?' When he declined, she went to her bed, thankful Abby had such a friend. He was like a father, yet did not take Eddy's place in her affections. On the other hand, she knew a woman of Abby's youth and looks shouldn't remain a widow all her life. One day a man would come along and take away the only two people she had left in her life. It was a fear Evelyn had lived with for some time now. After all, the man who wanted Abby could hardly be expected to want her ageing mother-in-law, as well. She must learn to come to terms with it and not spoil Abby's chance of happiness. Nevertheless, she dreaded the day.

Stella was shown into Abby's office at nine fifteen the following morning. Flinging herself into a chair, she crossed her legs and folded her arms in a defensive manner. She was wearing a blue mohair sweater, several sizes too large, over the black drainpipe trousers. The short hair exaggerated her fine bone structure and sensuous, sulky mouth. Her eyes were covered in pale blue shadow, the brows brushed into a fine arch. They arched even higher, as she began to speak.

'Well, Abby, you've kept me awake most of the night trying to make head or tail of your nonsense! Would you mind starting from the beginning, please?'

Abby sat down at her desk. She, too, had spent a sleepless night.

'Believe what you will, your mother told me that William was my father. He told me himself, in a letter which I'm perfectly willing to show you. I believe he told Milicent before I went to St Martin's School of Art. It was far more of a shock to me, for obvious reasons, than it can ever be for you now, so if you've come here full of dramatic gestures, then they'll be entirely wasted on me.'

'If it's true, then why hasn't Mummy told me herself?'

'At the funeral you said she had.'

'We must have been speaking at cross purposes.' Stella unfolded her arms, and leaned back as though the fight had gone out of her. 'Dear God, I truly cannot believe it. I thought he was the perfect, loving and respectable father that every child would want to have. It seems I was wrong.'

'Why? He was everything you thought he was. Why change your mind now?'

Stella's lip tightened. 'Why? I learn that my father was sleeping around with working-class women, producing little bastards all over London, and you ask *why*?'

Abby shot to her feet in anger. 'Why, you sanctimonious little brat! Your father's life before he met your mother was his personal business, not yours. Once he met your mother, he was always faithful to her. She did not repay the compliment, so save your anger for her.'

Stunned, Stella stared at her sister and thought how unfair it was that this girl from the slums should end up with all this. And to think, after all the trouble she had caused, she could still wound! The very idea that they were sisters was too strange to contemplate, although she knew Abby was not lying. Abby had never lied in her life.

Abby had fallen silent, and Stella felt bound to say something. 'If you're referring to Mummy and Brian Rivers, well, it's old hat. She still sees him, but she won't marry him because that wretched brother of mine might just hold to the terms of Daddy's Will and throw her out of Ferndene. Brian's paying maintenance for his children and has to live in a grotty cottage out at Sturry. Mummy couldn't bear to live like that.'

Abby was standing before the fireplace, staring into the gilt mirror above the mantel. The woman who looked back at her was too pale by far.

'At the funeral, what was it you thought I was referring to, if not our father?'

Stella had swivelled around in her chair, and was looking at Abby curiously. 'I assumed you were referring to Richard's father. His true father, that is.'

Abby turned swiftly. 'What? Richard knows about his father?'

'Well, of course he knows. Everyone knows.'

'Not quite everyone,' said Abby tersely. 'No one thought to tell me.'

'But Richard did tell you!' Stella's eyes followed her sister's slow progress back to the desk, wondering if she was all right. 'He wrote to you, and you just disappeared. He told me all about it, when he returned from Malaya. As Mummy pointed out, the Germans killed your entire family. She knew it would upset you, and told him not to say anything. But you know Richard. He couldn't go on deceiving you, and he wrote. He expected you to understand.'

The past flashed before Abby and she saw Richard's stricken face in an autumn garden. What had she told him? He had told her he loved her and she had said she was '*appalled*'. 'Dear God,' she whispered, collapsing into the chair, staring ahead with distant eyes. 'What have I done?'

Stella leaned forward. 'You didn't know this?'

'I received no letter,' murmured Abby. She felt light-headed and her voice seemed to be echoing at the far end of a tunnel. 'No letter.' Richard had spoken of a letter, and she'd seen nothing significant in the remark. But it had been *everything*.

'Why did you leave him like that?' Stella was saying.

Abby blinked and returned to the room. 'Haven't you grasped that yet? At the funeral I had the impression that you both knew I was William's daughter, too. Can't you understand?'

Slowly light began to dawn in Stella's eyes. 'You thought ... you thought ... Oh, my Lord, that's terrible. And you had a baby, didn't you? Richard's baby!'

'Why, oh why, didn't Richard tell me face to face, instead of relying on a letter? And why didn't your mother tell you both about me? Why didn't she tell me about Karl? What is the matter with the woman?'

Stella shook her head and said, 'Poor Mummy. Fancy having to live with such secrets! What with the German fellow, then Daddy — it must have been awful for her to learn that you were Daddy's child.'

Smiling thinly, Abby said, 'Spare no tears for your mother, Stella. She has a neat line in deception herself.'

'Mummy? How could you say such a thing, after all she's done for you?'

Abby looked at her coldly. 'She's clever, cunning and completely devoid of feeling. That woman is so wrapped up in her son that she would sooner destroy his happiness than have him marry the wrong woman. The woman he loved.' She stood up, and massaged her brow, frowning. 'Don't worry, Stella. You'll adjust to the situation in good time. I know — I'm something of an expert at adjusting. Look, I've the most awful headache. I . . . I really don't think I can go on just now.'

Realizing how things were, Stella moved quietly to the door. 'Yes, of course. I'm sorry if I . . . well, I'm sorry. If you didn't learn about it from Richard, then just how did you find out about his German father? I noticed you called him Karl just now.' She paused. 'Well, some other time, then.'

Abby returned to her desk, her mind wholly absorbed with Richard. One by one the veils had been lifted from her eyes, and she could see clearly at last. Milicent had played her hand very carefully — and won.

In two days' time she would see Richard, and this time they would not be at cross purposes. This time, however, Richard would not care one way or the other. She had hurt him badly, and that could never be put right.

CHAPTER FOURTEEN

Richard sat opposite his bank manager while the man read through the last company report of Langdon Construction. Ever since Samantha had told him about the company, he'd been curious, but cautious, checking with Nigel Bingham who assured him that Langdon was as sound as a bell and any investment would certainly show a good profit. He could see no reason why anything should go wrong.

The manager took off his spectacles, and frowned. 'Well, yes – it looks impressive enough. How much were you hoping to borrow for these shares?'

Richard swallowed hard. 'I thought about forty to fifty thousand pounds.'

Mr Coniston looked at him in surprise. 'That does seem a great deal to invest in one company: even one with such a good balance sheet as this.'

'I realize that, but I have assets worth far more.'

'Not much more,' said Mr Coniston firmly. 'Profits in Glenisters are well down. Since your father died, they've been dropping steadily. Then there was that gold mine ... you borrowed then against the house, Ferndene.'

'But that was only a small loan, and I managed to pay you back,' said Richard, not adding that he had borrowed from another source to do this, a source which demanded more interest, once again using the house as collateral. 'Look, I know that was a mistake, although who could foresee the nationalization of the gold mines? This is totally different. It's a British company, a public company which, I'm told, is likely to get a huge contract to build more high-rise office blocks and flats. I really don't see any risk. Anyway, I certainly don't intend to hang on to the shares for more than a year.'

'You do realize you'll be borrowing against the store,' said Mr Coniston. 'And don't forget the interest on the loan. Who can say how stable that will remain?'

The disapproving tone began to irritate Richard. Was he still a child in the eyes of this man, to be spoken to in this manner? 'Look, I do understand how you feel. Believe me, I wouldn't even consider this, if I thought there was any risk.'

'The stock market is one great big risk. A gamble, as you've already learned to your cost. I served your father for years and I think – at least I hope – that I served and advised him well. I would like to do the same for you now, Mr Glenister.' He sighed and stood up. 'But business is business and you do have the collateral, so the bank is covered. If I can't discourage you from this venture, let me offer you my best wishes. And Mr Glenister, you must give more thought to the firm, and see why profits are falling. When you've done that, let's have another chat.'

'I will. As a matter of fact I'm going to Canterbury tomorrow, so I'll look into matters as thoroughly as I can.' Richard paused. 'Well, how much can I borrow?'

'Forty thousand at the very most, given the state of the firm,' said Mr Coniston. 'Sorry, but there it is.'

'Forty thousand it is,' said Richard, shaking the man's hand firmly. 'I'll keep a careful eye on the stock market. Depend upon it. Nothing is going to happen to my father's firm.'

St Dunstan's Church stood on a busy corner of the main road not far from Canterbury's huge, fortress-like city gate. As soon as Abby entered the ancient building, the sound of modern Canterbury faded and the silence was broken only by her footsteps echoing along the nave.

Glancing at her watch she saw that it was only twenty past two. Nearly three quarters of an hour to go. It might as well be a year, she thought. Would he turn up? All during the long drive she'd gone over each and every word she would say to Richard. Resolved to be cool and unemotional, she would tell him how they had been so cruelly misled, remembering always that his feelings for her were no longer what they had once been. Then, they would part as friends, she hoped, and she would have recovered her dignity and perhaps some of her sanity at last.

Pausing at the last resting place of William Roper, she stood there in an unholy mixture of fear and longing. She glanced at her watch again. With every passing minute, she was becoming more and more nervous, like a condemned prisoner waiting for the sound of his executioner's footsteps outside the cell. Perhaps she should walk about the town and then return, she told herself, but someone would be bound to see her, and mention the fact to Milicent. She was not ready for Milicent yet.

Beside the tomb, Abby read how Sir Thomas More's loving daughter, Margaret Roper, had brought his head to this church, after his execution at the hands of King Henry VIII, to be laid in the vault of her husband's family.

Then footsteps sounded in the nave: a man's tread. *It's too early*, she thought wildly. *Much too early*. Rooted to the spot, she slowly turned.

Richard walked towards her slowly, his grey suit jacket slung carelessly over one shoulder, his face grim and anxious. He said nothing as he faced Abby, but thought her like a frightened gazelle as she stood there trembling. He wanted to fold her in his arms there and then, yet stood back. Her dark green eyes were large with alarm. Her auburn hair fell in soft curls, the way he had always loved to see it, in each curl a host of memories he would do well to forget. Whatever she had done to him, however much she had made him suffer, he knew now that he loved her more than ever.

Abby opened her mouth to speak, but no sound came

out. Everything she had planned to say fled from her mind. Slowly, tears filled her eyes, and began to fall.

It was too much for Richard, who clasped her to him tightly, feeling her shaking body collapsing against his. With her head on his shoulder she wept. 'I didn't mean to hurt you. Truly I didn't. It breaks my heart to think ... I only found out recently and ...' She choked on a sob. 'I'm still trying to piece together the jigsaw your mother has made out of our lives.'

'What on earth are you talking about?' he asked tenderly. Stroking her soft hair, he kissed her head, murmuring, 'I haven't understood one word so far.' Reaching into his pocket for a handkerchief, he gently wiped away her tears. 'Don't cry, please, darling, don't cry.' Then, tilting her face to his, he kissed her. 'Why are you in such a state?' Sudden alarm crossed his face. 'Our son? What's happened to him? Is he all right? Tell me!'

Abby nodded. 'Ross is fine.'

'Thank God,' said Richard with a deep sigh of relief. 'He's a bonny little chap.'

Her fine eyebrows were arched in surprise. 'How do you know?'

'Because I've watched you both in Kensington Gardens.'

Astonished, she stared at him. 'You were there? So close, yet you couldn't find it in your heart to speak to me?'

Richard's jaw hardened. 'Would you have wanted me to? You sent me packing, remember? In any case, you have your own life now. You're happily married, successful in business. Any more children?'

Still deeply hurt, Abby shook her head. 'Ross is my only child. *Our* child.'

'Oh?'

Abby looked away. 'Eddy died some years ago. Ever since then, it's been just Ross, Eddy's mother and myself.'

A long silence followed her remark, and Richard looked

330

quite lost. 'I thought ... I'm sorry, I'd no idea. What happened?'

At that moment, an elderly woman entered the church. 'We can't talk here. Come on,' Richard said, taking her arm.

Together they walked out into the warm September sunshine, to a Canterbury still crowded with visitors. At the West Gate they turned into the Abbey Gardens, away from the noise and bustle: a small haven in a busy city. Strolling slowly past the rose beds set alongside the shallow River Stour, they paused by the ruined wall of the Abbey to look back at the bridge and the great gate beyond.

Trying to find the right words to tell Richard about William was difficult and Abby wished now that she had written to him instead. So far, nothing had gone the way she had planned. Just seeing him had made her realize that she loved him as much as ever. No, this way was much harder, especially as he was looking at her so intensely. Turning away from those eyes, she leaned over the wall and gazed down at the flowing river. 'I went to the theatre a few nights back.' Her voice was falsely bright. 'Guess what? Stella was in the cast! Oh, it was only a small part, but at least she's made it to the West End.'

'Stella! We haven't spoken since the Will was read. She flatly refuses to have anything to do with me.'

'It's as well we did meet,' Abby went on quickly, 'because only then did I realize that you and I had been duped.' Then she told him everything; from the meeting in Harrods with Milicent, to the meeting with Karl, then finally the meeting with Stella. When she had finished, she slowly turned her gaze from the river to Richard. What she saw in his face alarmed her. 'And so — here we are. I thought you ignorant of Karl's existence, and wanted to come here to tell you the truth. What a fool I would have seemed. What fools your mother made of us both.' She sat down on the seat beside the ruined wall, not wishing to look at that stricken face again. Richard still said nothing. Nervously she added: 'I realize it's all in the past now. But I couldn't go on living with the thought that you might hate me.'

'*Hate* you?' murmured Richard. 'Oh, my love, if you only knew.' He put his arms about Abby, but his eyes were drifting back to Christchurch Fields on a hot June day. Milicent had come to Oxford to give him his birth certificate. She had been worried, vulnerable, begging him to forgive her for not telling him the truth earlier. She had then told him about his German father, a young doctor from Dresden.

'You can see why I found it so difficult to speak out,' Milicent had said. 'You took the name of Glenister, not only because you were just three when I married again, but also because of the war. I was afraid you would be hurt if anyone ever found out the truth. The longer it went on, the more difficult it became, since I knew you would look at me the way you're looking at me now.'

When he had recovered his wits, his first thought had been of Abby and he then made it clear to his mother that he wanted to marry her. 'Do you think it will alter her feelings for me in any way?' he had asked innocently.

How young, foolish and trusting he'd been just eight years ago. Even now he could see that flash of anger in his mother's eyes, followed quickly by the loving smile once more, as she urged him to say nothing to Abby. 'If you wish to keep her, then hold your tongue. The Germans killed her entire family, remember that. Wait until you're both older and more sure of each other. Tell her now and she will leave you. Believe me, Richard, I know what I'm talking about. Trust me.'

Feeling ill, Richard clasped Abby's hand tightly. 'She said nothing to me about William being your father. You just vanished from my life without saying why. What else was I to think?'

Abby looked at his ashen face. 'Did you have so little faith in me, then? Did you think my love such a frail thing that I would leave you because of your father's nationality?' Tears burned her eyes again, and she looked away. 'Couldn't you see that nothing in this world could have destroyed that love? Nothing!'

There was a long silence, then Richard said, 'I thought that then. I believed nothing could tear us apart.'

Abby sighed, and whispered bitterly: 'Except your mother. We certainly underestimated her.'

Richard shook his head. 'No. She didn't mean to deceive, I'm sure of that. Oh, Mother's difficult, I grant you, but she would never do anything that cruel.'

'Wouldn't she, though? Think of it, Richard. She told me that William was my father, which is true. She also made it clear that you and Stella were not to know because of the embarrassment, leaving me with the appalling realization that we ... that ...' Even now she could not say the word. 'I was expecting your child ...'

Richard pulled her against him, whispering, 'Don't, don't.'

Abby composed herself, then continued her indictment of Milicent. 'She then went to work on you, revealing that your true father was German, and that you mustn't tell me because I would leave you. Do you still believe she didn't mean it?' She sighed and shook her head slowly. 'You know, she's just like Tristan's wife, urging you to believe in a black sail.'

Richard smiled. 'Nonsense!'

'Is it?' Abby moved away from him with eyes blazing. Suddenly everything seemed crystal-clear to her. 'She wanted you to believe in a black sail – and you did, Richard. Instead of destroying us with a lie, she did it with the truth, then sat back and let us do the rest. You should have searched for me sooner, my love.' She fell back against him again, and stared at the Abbey ruins. 'She had the luck of the devil. Your letter might have reached me, and I might not have stepped into the path of a taxi. Susan might still have lived in the flat and ...

Oh, Richard, your mother took a huge gamble and broke the bank. What a pity you didn't gamble also — on me, instead of her!'

Richard had become very tense; Abby could feel his heart pounding against his chest. When he spoke, his voice was thick with emotion. 'Then why, in God's name, didn't William speak out years ago?'

Abby thought how his once boyish face had matured beyond its twenty-nine summers.

'All those years,' Richard murmured, his voice like a simmering volcano. 'All those *wasted* years. Christ, when I think of it!'

Abby clasped his hand tightly. 'Don't think of it. Otherwise you'll be destroyed by it. Believe me, I know. It's in the past now, and the course of our lives has been set. You're happily married, and Stella tells me you have a little girl.'

'Happily married!' Richard gave a hollow laugh. He trembled as he struggled to control his feelings. 'These tormented years could have been such happy ones. We're back together now and I refuse to let anything part us this time from what was meant to be.'

Abby shook her head. 'It was never meant to be. I sensed that all those years ago, in Cornwall. Something told me even then that we were only going to have that brief moment. They call it Fate: written by God when we're born. Do you believe that?'

Richard's voice was like ice. 'I believe our fate was written by my mother, and I'll never forgive her as long as I live.'

For all that she hated Milicent, his words made her blood run cold. 'I didn't come here today to turn you into a bitter man. I came because you had to know the truth. What your mother did was unforgivable, but some mothers can be monsters when they think their children are threatened. She thought you were: by Abby Nichols from Bermondsey, with her cockney accent and rough ways. No matter how much I changed, I was still that same little girl to her — the girl from the wrong background who caused her so much embarrassment. Leave her to me, Richard. She's your mother, when all's said and done. And your wife is your wife. I have no intention of breaking up your marriage.'

'My marriage is a sterile farce.'

'Hardly sterile,' retorted Abby drily, 'when you have a daughter.'

'Not born of love, as our son was.' Richard looked down at her. 'Tell me all about him. He's like me in looks, I know that much, but what of his temperament? Is he happy, clever, mischievous?'

Abby smiled. 'He's all of those things, when he's a mind to be. Ross can be quite a handful at times, but he's very bright and impatient.'

'He needs a father.'

'He has a loving mother and grandmother,' came the swift reply.

'He needs *me*.'

Abby glanced up at him. 'What's that supposed to mean?'

'That I should have access to him. That he should know he has a father who cares. That I want to divorce Samantha and live with you both.'

His words had her heart soaring, then it plummeted once more. *Words!* The Richard she knew and loved would not walk out on his wife and child. He might, however, fight for his son. 'Ross has grown up believing Eddy to be his father: his hero father who died trying to save the life of an old woman. Evelyn believes this too, and after all she has suffered I'm not about to tell her, or Ross, the truth. She has raised our son almost as though she were raising Eddy again. I've sworn never to leave her, I swore that over Eddy's grave.'

'You had no right to make such an oath. Eddy is dead — I live. Don't I have rights, too?'

'No, my darling.' Abby felt true pain as she answered. 'No, in this matter you have no legal right, at all. The name on Ross's birth certificate is Carr.'

Richard jumped to his feet, and leaned against the stone wall. 'Christ, does nothing change for us? My father, your father and now Ross's father. Being raised on a lie seems to run in the family. We're like a bloody Greek tragedy, Abby, can't you see that? Look what the lies have done to us. Don't let it happen to our son!'

Tears welled up in Abby's eyes and flowed down her cheeks. 'Don't think I haven't gone over this problem in my own mind again and again. But while Evelyn lives, there's nothing to be done. Nothing, Richard.'

'I meant what I said about leaving Samantha.'

Abby shook her head, feeling her heart might break. 'No, you didn't. Your wife is the innocent party in this. You won't take it out on her. You're not the type, Richard.'

After a long and painful silence, Richard sat down again and took her hand. 'All I know is that I love you as much today as I did in Cornwall, and that our son is the fruit of that love. What harm can there be in letting me see him just once? Why do you want to cast me aside as though I'm nothing? Please, darling – just one day with him. One day to kick a ball around a field, or take him to the Zoo. You couldn't be so cruel as to deny me that. He won't know that I'm his father, that much I promise. You can say I'm anyone – uncle, cousin, friend, I don't care – only let me see him.'

He seemed so lost and despairing that Abby knew she would not be able to resist for long. By now, they should have parted to live the rest of their lives without guilt or hurt. But it was not to be like that, at all. She was faced with a Richard who loved her as much as she loved him. Her feelings were a strange mix of joy for his love tempered by the hopelessness of their situation. 'I ... I don't know. Your one day will go to two, then three and ...'

'It won't. I give you my word,' murmured Richard.

'I'll have to think about it,' said Abby. 'Do you realize your father feels the same way about you?'

For a moment, Richard looked confused, then he frowned. '*Him?* Why? And why should I want to meet him? You see. There's your proof. If you leave me out of Ross's life, he'll have no interest in me whatsoever.' He studied her carefully. 'How did you come to meet my father anyway?'

Abby told him about the fashion show, and his father's position as the head of the large charity. 'If it hadn't been for the house etched on your mother's cigarette case, I would never have discovered who he was. Imagine that, Richard.'

'With great difficulty,' murmured Richard. 'I mean ... well, it's almost unbelievable. The coincidence rate must be ...'

'Oh I don't know,' she broke in. 'Our mutual careers made the impossible possible.' She sighed and looked at her hands. 'Or maybe Fate had grown bored with us, and decided to give the pot another good stir. Anyway, Karl does want to meet you, Richard. You're the only child he has.'

'He'll have to go on waiting.'

'That's a cruel thing to say. You don't know the first thing about him.'

'I don't want to know anything about him.'

'Why are you so bitter towards a man you've never met? He's your father, for goodness' sake.'

'William was my father, in every other sense of the word.'

She stared at him and then said quietly, 'He's a good man, Richard. He was never a Nazi.'

'Did he tell you that?'

'Of course not, the subject never came up. But I learned a lot about him, and I know you'd like him, Richard.'

'Look, let's drop the subject, shall we?'

Suddenly, she realized that his attitude towards Karl had nothing to do with the war, but everything to do with their parting. He was blaming Karl. 'Richard — what happened to us was your mother's doing, not your father's.'

'And what of us?' Richard wanted to know. 'What of our future together?'

Their future together? Abby knew Richard would never walk out on a wife and child, any more than Samantha would give him a divorce so he could marry her oldest rival. 'Well,' she murmured, sinking back into his arms once more, 'we don't have much longer. Let's not waste these precious moments left to us with angry words or hopeless plans. You've been in my thoughts night and day. I've wondered about your life and how you spend your time. We've a lot of catching up to do.'

An autumn chill began to settle over Canterbury as shadows lengthened and they sat talking of their lives, present and past; of Eddy's death and Ross's miraculous recovery, of the years of struggle which followed, and of her success today. They spoke of his fears for the store in Canterbury which, in Milicent's hands, was failing; of his hopes for a political career; his decent and helpful in-laws; his prodigal wife and financial worries and, last of all, his wilful but greatly loved little girl. As they talked, the sun began to set, sending shafts of amber and purple across the western sky. The purple faded to grey, and small bats came out of hiding to flit and dart through the twilight air, swooping low over the water, then skimming past the man and woman who saw only each other.

Finally the time came to part, and Abby was resolved to be firm. She had come to say goodbye to Richard, not break up his marriage. They were adults, after all — decent adults with a strict code of behaviour. How did the song go, she asked herself? '*There are some nice people, with nice manners* ...' Perhaps they were too nice for their own good, but she knew of no other way to live. Yet, as Richard walked her back to the car, then leaned in and

338

kissed her once more, it was 1950 all over again. They were young students with their future before them and if she looked up she would probably see Susan leaning out of the window teasing them mischievously.

When he let her go, she was trembling and had to fumble with the keys to get them into the ignition, while biting back the tears that suddenly blurred her vision. As the engine started, she moved into first gear and felt as though she were being wrenched from Richard as a snail is wrenched from its shell. Driving away, she saw him in the rear mirror, a tall figure standing in the light of the street lamp. Then she was out on the London Road and he was lost from her sight at last.

Mrs Wellings had stayed late to check stocks and go over details with Milicent after the auditors had left. She was just putting dust covers over the counters, when she saw Richard stride through the department to his office. His face was like thunder, she thought, wondering if the storm was about to break. Milicent, she knew, was back in the office. She was angry with her son for leaving her with the auditors to face the issue of falling profits without his support.

Richard walked past the Accounts Department, then burst into the office, causing his mother to look up in surprise. 'And where have you been?' she demanded in a cold voice.

Richard closed the door carefully behind him and stared at her. 'Mother, I think it's time we had a talk.'

On the Friday following the meeting with Richard Abby was in the workroom, when she was called to the telephone.

'Wouldn't give his name, I'm afraid,' Roland said, indicating the telephone in his office. Shutting the door behind her, Abby could still see the workroom staff through the glass partition as she picked up the receiver.

'Hello. Abigail Carr speaking.'

There was a moment's silence before a low voice

339

answered, 'It's no use, darling, I can't bear it. I simply cannot accept that we've said goodbye.'

Gripping the receiver until her knuckles turned white, Abby slowly sat down. Ever since she had driven away from Canterbury, she'd been haunted by the image of Richard standing beneath the lamp light. Fingering her pearl earring anxiously, she whispered, 'Please, Richard, don't do this to me. How can I be strong if you don't stay out of my life?'

'Do you love me?'

'That's an idiotic question, and you know it.' Glancing through the partition, Abby saw Madame Duval looking at her curiously, and became aware that she was in a goldfish bowl. She straightened up, deliberately brightening her expression.

'Please, darling, one more day,' Richard was saying. 'Just one more day, when we can be together with our son. An ordinary family outing — is it too much to ask?'

Abby turned her back on Madame Duval. 'I told you, I won't let you upset Ross.'

'And I gave you my word that I wouldn't.'

As they argued, Abby began to feel that she was being unreasonable. Longing to see Richard again, her defences weakened. 'Very well,' she succumbed, at last. 'I'll bring Ross to the Zoo at Regent's Park on Saturday at ten o'clock, to meet his Uncle Richard. But, darling, this is the end. It has to be, so please don't make things more difficult than they are already. Will you promise?'

'I promise. Ten o'clock on Saturday at the main entrance.'

Ross was first out of the taxi as it pulled up at the Zoo entrance. Abby paid the driver, then saw Richard walking towards them, his face a mixture of relief and joy.

'Thank God,' he murmured breathlessly. 'I was afraid you'd change your mind.' Would she laugh if he told her that he'd arrived forty-five minutes earlier, his heart sinking as the minutes passed, until he'd convinced himself that she had decided not to come? But here they both were. He looked down at his son. 'And you are Ross!'

Ross stared up at the tall, fair-haired man and shook hands, as he had been taught. 'How do you do, sir,' he intoned solemnly.

'Call me Uncle Richard,' said Richard, longing to hug the boy to him.

'How do you do, Uncle Richard.' Ross beamed up at his mother, pulling her forwards. 'Can we go in now? Can we see the tigers first?' He ran off towards the ticket office, while Abby and Richard gazed at each other in relieved amusement. It was a look which said, '*We have this day.*'

It was a cool day, with bright sunshine and an east wind. Abby watched Ross drag Richard from cage to cage, talking at the top of his voice. He had clearly taken an immediate liking to this uncle who'd surfaced from nowhere, and was completely relaxed in his presence. He stood in awe before the lions, and wanted to stroke the tigers, yet refused to ride on the back of an elephant.

'Strange, for a boy,' said Richard later, when Ross was out of earshot. 'I would have jumped at the chance.'

'He's only seven and the elephant is big. He has a right to be afraid at that age.'

'Hmm. He's never had a man in his life, that's the trouble.'

Abby watched as Ross licked at a large ice cream cornet, and made faces at the chimpanzees. 'Look at him now,' she murmured, with an amused smile. 'If a hairy arm came out and took that cornet, we'd never hear the end of it.'

Richard laughed, then the smile faded. 'It's odd to think he has a sister, and doesn't even know it.'

'He'd knock the living daylights out of her if he did,' said Abby, determined to keep things light. 'Your son can be quite a ruffian, even if he has been brought up by women. He can hold his own academically and physically.'

341

'Which school are you going to send him to when he's older?'

Abby sighed. 'I've put his name down for Stowe, but the idea of sending him away is too unbearable to contemplate. So it might be a day school in London. I haven't really decided.'

Richard looked at her in horror. 'A day school in London would be disastrous! Coming home each night to mother and grandmother is no upbringing for a boy. He should go to the King's School, his father's old school.'

'That's impossible and you know it,' said Abby.

'Why?'

She gazed at him with wide eyes. 'How can you even ask? Our son wandering around Canterbury as a Carr? Going to his father's old school without being aware of it? Going into Glenisters and not realizing that his father owns the store? How could you suggest such a thing?' She sighed, as the truth hit her. 'You think you'd see more of him. Well, that would look odd, wouldn't it? And how long would it be before your mother, or Samantha found out? No, Canterbury's out. It was Jonathan who mentioned Stowe.'

'Jonathan?'

Abby then told Richard about the man who had helped her so much. 'Truly, I don't know where I would have been without him. He's my closest friend, apart from Susan.'

'Friend?'

'Yes,' said Abby firmly, 'friend. After Eddy died, life reached rock-bottom for me. Stella was sitting on my inheritance, and there were legal problems concerning Eddy's shares. I worked all hours with a couturier who taught me a great deal. When the chance came to break free and go it alone, no banker would even listen to me — except Jonathan who, bless his heart and, thank God, his head, could see more clearly than those other old fools. Life isn't easy for women in a man's world.'

And where was I? thought Richard angrily. Where had

he been when the woman he loved was struggling and suffering? Grimly he remembered the recent confrontation with his mother. Milicent had turned pale, but denied doing anything to harm either of them.

He'd persisted with his questions until she turned on him angrily. 'So I saved you from a bad marriage! Is that so terrible? What mother wouldn't do everything in her power to save her children from harm?'

At this final admission, Richard had marched out of the office, slamming the door on his mother for ever. He felt no guilt, only anger and hatred when he remembered the wasted and embittered years.

He squeezed Abby's hand. 'This is madness, you know that, don't you? Madness. You are my very life, and I won't let you go.' Before she could respond, he saw Ross running back to them, and stood up. 'Now that your son has teased every animal in the place, how about taking him for a row on the lake?'

'Could we?' cried Ross. 'Could we, Mummy?'

The trees around the lake were changing hue and Regent's Park had never looked lovelier to Abby, as she sat in the boat trailing one hand in the water and watched Richard and their son. They had each taken an oar, and were now rowing the boat in half circles, much to Ross's amusement. The east wind had dropped, and the day had turned warm and golden. For one brief moment they were a family like any other, out in the park on a Saturday afternoon.

Later, Abby and Richard walked hand in hand past the rose beds, as their son ran ahead pretending to be an aeroplane. 'What a wonderful day it's been,' Abby said. 'This is how it was always meant to be from the moment we first met as children.'

'And this is how it *will* be,' said Richard firmly. He stopped walking and looked down at her with smouldering eyes. 'I can't live without you, Abby. Today has convinced me of it. Oh, I realize Sam will be hell on earth about divorce, but in the end I will be free to marry you.'

343

He was saying all the right things, and all the wrong things, so that Abby's spirits soared then fell in seconds. 'No, it's impossible.'

'Why?'

'Where would we live while we wait for our freedom?'

'Well, that's a minor point, darling. We can rent our own place, or I can move in with you.'

'You know I want that more than anything in the world. But aren't you forgetting Evelyn?'

Richard frowned. 'Evelyn? What about her?'

'I told you in Canterbury that I would never leave her.'

'Who's asking you to leave anyone, you little goose? Evelyn can live with us, can't she?'

Abby turned away and tried to imagine a married man, her cousin and the father of her child, living in the house at Hampstead, living a lie. How long would it be before Richard wanted Ross to know the truth? How long would he understand her reasons for keeping that truth from Evelyn? Furthermore, her mother-in-law would be shocked at her living openly with a married man. Samantha would cause trouble, and was not above arriving at the house for a show-down. Evelyn was not well enough to be subjected to that.

Abby shook her head. 'You can't live with us, and I won't leave Evelyn.'

'I've just told you ...'

'It won't work.'

'Why not? At least give it a chance.'

Abby looked up at him, her eyes swimming in tears. 'I can't take that chance. Ross is a happy little boy, content to think his father died heroically. Evelyn is only now coming to terms with Eddy's death through Ross. How then could you sit in our house day in and day out with this terrible secret? We would be living a lie, and it would destroy us in the end. I love you more than life itself, but if I have to choose between

344

having you and not hurting her, I must choose in her favour.'

Richard looked crushed. 'I'm prepared to leave my wife and child for you, but you're not prepared to leave your mother-in-law? It's ridiculous, darling. She can hardly expect you to live the rest of your life as a nun.'

'Of course she doesn't. But −' Abby hesitated and looked up at him. 'I'm responsible for Eddy's death. I killed him.' She told him how Eddy would not have been on Canvey Island that night, but for her selfishness.

Richard smiled, as understanding came into his eyes. 'And Evelyn is the cross you must bear as a penance. Is that it? How would *she* feel if she knew you felt that way about her?'

'That's not the whole reason. She's like a mother to me, a real mother, and I love her as a mother.'

They walked on slowly, then Richard said: 'I killed a girl once. A Chinese terrorist, but a young girl, just the same. I only tell you this now, so you won't feel alone in your guilt.'

Abby put her arms about him, saying softly, 'I'm glad you understand.'

Richard nodded. 'God help me, I do. But moving in with you is the only way to bring Sam to the divorce courts. Without a complete break, our marriage will just drift on and on.'

Abby shook her head. 'You can't live with us. And quite frankly, I don't believe you could ever leave your wife and child. I don't ask it of you.'

Richard fell silent. Until this moment, he had not realized Abby possessed such strength of character. Somehow, he'd seen her as a victim. But how could a 'victim' have achieved all that she had? Abby Nichols from Bermondsey was as tough a Londoner as they made them, and it had been another Londoner who had seen her through. Small wonder then that the strange cockney woman he had never met was pushing him aside now.

Ross came running back to them. 'Are we going somewhere else now? Are we, Uncle Richard?'

'How about tea, with ice cream, and sticky cakes?' Richard bent to his son, and tousled his blond head lovingly.

'Do you think we should?' asked Abby cautiously.

'Why not? I can have tea with my cousin and her son, surely,' said Richard drily. 'Don't tell me there's a law against that too.'

'Well, as long as it's somewhere quiet.'

Richard took them to the Cumberland Hotel where Ross squared up to a plate of cream cakes, sandwiches and ice cream. Abby looked aghast. 'If he isn't sick after that lot, then I'm the Duchess of Windsor.' She took a bite of cucumber sandwich, and felt the sun setting on her happiness. Soon, she and Richard would say goodbye. Oh, they would smile and pretend to be normal and light of heart, for Ross's sake, but the heartache would be there, just the same.

'Did you like the Zoo?' Richard asked Ross.

Munching on a cream cake, Ross nodded, his cheeks bulging.

'Would you like to go again?' Richard kept his eyes averted from Abby.

'Yes!' cried Ross with his mouth full.

Abby stiffened. 'What are you doing?' she whispered. 'We agreed. You *promised*.'

'What harm is there, for God's sake,' he answered quietly. Smiling at Ross, he said loudly, 'Then why not meet again, next Saturday? Same place, same time, and back here again for tea.'

'Can we?' Ross was looking at his mother. 'Please, Mummy, *please*! And can I bring Bannem? He's my best friend, Uncle. He comes to the house sometimes because it's by the Heath and he lives in Ealing and you can't play football there. So can I bring him? Please?'

'Bring anyone you like,' said Richard. 'That's if your mother doesn't mind.'

It was too cruel, thought Abby, urging her head to dominate her heart. She must put her foot down now, and make an end of it. Yet in the end, her heart prevailed. This was not to be their last day, after all. Someone had pulled back the blinds and let sunshine into her soul.

'Only one more time, because Uncle Richard is a very busy man and has to go away.'

Ross turned to Richard and wanted to know where he was going. A bond had been established between them already, a bond which neither wanted to break.

Later, Abby asked Ross to sit in the hotel lobby, since she had to speak to Uncle Richard alone.

'You're making things even worse and going back on your promise,' she whispered to Richard.

'I know, I know,' he murmured. 'But, darling, is it too much to ask that we see each other from time to time? What harm is there in that? Don't send me away again, Abby; I couldn't bear it now.'

Abby looked at him with pleading eyes, now shining with tears. 'I'm trying to be strong, and I can't be strong alone. You ask what harm is there? Oh, Richard, can't you see that we'd end up meeting in second-rate hotels, always afraid that someone might see us. In the end, you'd return to Samantha and we'd both feel shabby somehow. I don't want our love to end that way, in recriminations and hurt. I don't want to feel guilt and shame. I've had years of that.'

'What we feel for each other could never become shabby or shameful,' Richard replied angrily. He glanced towards Ross. 'Poor little chap. He's tired. We can't discuss our life now. Let's meet tomorrow.'

Abby shook her head. 'Tomorrow's Sunday. It's impossible. I have a family to think about.'

'Monday, then,' urged Richard. 'I'll collect you at six o'clock.' He gazed down at her troubled eyes. 'You *do* love

347

me?' When she nodded, he went on. 'And you see that we must be together?' She shook her head and then, unable to stop herself, the negative gesture became a positive nod. Richard let out a sigh of relief. 'There is a future for us, darling. It's all going to be all right, you'll see.'

'Monday, then,' she whispered. 'Just for an hour or two.'

Richard drove Abby and Ross back to the house in Hampstead. Stopping the car, he turned to Ross and said, 'Until next Saturday, then. Ten o'clock sharp at the Zoo entrance, and *don't* let your mother be late.'

Abby stood watching as the MG sped away and suddenly felt all the worry lift from her heart. It *was* going to be all right. Richard had said it would be, and she was desperate to believe him. Somehow, someday, Richard would get his divorce and then they could be man and wife. The question of what to tell Ross and Evelyn would have to wait. It was different now. Richard would be by her side. All through Sunday and Monday Abby thought about nothing else but the moment when she and Richard could be together again.

Richard drove her out to the green woods and fields of Surrey, where they dined in a seventeenth-century coaching inn.

Gazing across the table at her lovely face, made iridescent by the light from the log fire, he took her hand and spoke of their future together. He was already searching for a flat and had seen one he deemed perfect. 'A place of our own.'

'A hiding place,' murmured Abby, 'where we will meet for a few hours after lying to those we care about. I don't know, darling. It's not our way.'

'Until I can marry you, it's the only way,' said Richard. 'Oh, darling, I know how you hate all this hole-in-the-corner business, but the important thing is that we should be together. We must keep our love secret for now. If

Samantha should ever cite you as co-respondent, it could harm your career and you've worked far too hard ...'

Abby squeezed his hand gently. 'And what about *your* career, the one you hoped for in politics? Are you prepared for that sacrifice?'

'Yes,' said Richard firmly. 'There are no ifs or buts, as far as I'm concerned. Life without you isn't worth a damn to me. I've tried it, so I know.'

Abby looked at him with melancholy eyes. 'You talk of our future as though you truly believe that we have one together.'

'We do,' said Richard.

'Samantha will make life hell. Will you keep to your resolve or will your courage fail you?'

Richard smiled. 'I've got the Military Cross. I can do anything!'

Abby laughed, knowing there was no other way for them now. She felt light and happy at the thought of lying in Richard's arms and re-living that afternoon in Cornwall: not once but time and time again, until they were too old for such passion, content just to be with each other until death parted them.

The following morning Abby arrived late at Brook Street, the business of the day bringing her back to reality. Richard had wanted to see her again that night, and the night after, but Abby sensed the danger in this. 'Wait until we've found our own safe haven.'

She was doing the right thing, she told herself now. Caution was everything if they were not to throw away their future happiness. Even so, the hours of this week would stretch into eternity for her, until Saturday arrived once more.

Only a week, she told herself. But, as she gathered some muslin in her hand, she felt a chill course through her veins. In one week, her life had once been changed completely.

By Wednesday Abby's fears and worries had vanished.

Richard was right. Things would work out in time. If his marriage was as bad as he maintained, then surely Samantha would be glad to end it. Light of step, she walked into the foyer where Avril was arranging white roses.

'Good morning, Avril!'

'Isn't this weather lovely?'

'Marvellous,' beamed Abby, smelling the roses. Leaving her things in the office, she almost ran upstairs to the workroom, where she then spent most of the morning going over the designs for the forthcoming spring and summer collection, to be shown in October. Surrounded by pleated shantung, chiffons and crepes, she looked again at her designs and felt sure she had a collection which surpassed all the others. 'Well, we've had the A-line, the H-line, the Trapeze-line and every other line you can think of. These designs go one step further.'

Susan nodded as she eyed the black strapless gown the model was wearing. Softly sheathed, it hugged the body in floating chiffon and, in her opinion, was a 'knock-out'. 'You're sure about the length though, bearing in mind Yves St-Laurent has sent hems soaring?'

'Let Paris shock if it wants to. Just below the knee is quite flattering.'

'Below the knee it is,' said Susan.

Roland was looking at Abby curiously. 'What's happened to you? You look like the cat that licked the cream.'

Abby blushed a little and murmured, 'I'm just pleased at the work coming out of this place. You're all marvellous.'

It was almost noon when Avril called for her on the intercom. 'I'm sorry to trouble you, Mrs Carr, but Mrs Glenister is here to see you.'

Abby's heart missed a beat. *Milicent, here?* Had she come to lock horns in Brook Street, of all places? She could tell Milicent that she was too busy and hope the woman would go away quietly, or meet her and risk an hysterical scene. Glancing at her watch, she remembered that the Marchioness of Twyneham would be arriving at two thirty. Milicent had to be a hundred miles away from here by then. The only thing for it, was to face her now.

'Very well, Avril,' she said, hoping her voice sounded calm and collected. 'Show her into my office. I'll be down directly.'

Heart still pounding, she turned to Roland, and smiled casually as she inspected the mint-green linen he was holding out for her approval. 'Yes. That's fine. And the trimming?' Only when she had seen the piping did she nod in full agreement, and remove the smock she always wore in the workroom. Pausing at the door to her office, Abby took a deep breath and walked in.

A woman stood with her back to the door, hands on the mantelpiece, head bent to the hearth in a gesture of despair. Slowly the head turned at Abby's approach.

'Samantha!' Unable to disguise the surprise in her voice, Abby stood there trying to recover her wits. 'I thought ... never mind. Sit down, please.' This was worse, this was infinitely worse than she had ever imagined. Richard's wife knew!

Samantha made no effort to move or speak and just stared at Abby in a cool, calculating manner. Groomed to perfection in her favourite Chanel, this time in navy jersey, she remained at the fireplace.

The silence was as unbearable as the stare, thought Abby. 'Please, do sit down.' Gesturing to an armchair she sat down herself and waited.

At last, Samantha sat down and crossed her long, shapely legs. She seemed poised, but Abby noticed now that her hands were trembling slightly, and that the brown eyes were moist as though she had a bad cold. 'I've come here today, not to reproach you, but to beg you,' she said softly. 'This doesn't come easily to me; but Abby, please, please let Richard go. Let him come back to me.'

Nonplussed, Abby stared at her. This was the last

351

approach she had expected Samantha to take. 'I ... I wasn't aware that Richard had left you.'

'Oh, don't play games with me. I know what's happening. I know you went to Canterbury to see him, to say wicked things. Your aunt told me everything. She was in a terrible state. You set her own son against her.'

Abby looked at Samantha coolly, understanding everything. 'I see. Just what did Milicent tell you?'

'That you and Richard were lovers years ago and are lovers again.'

'She seems to know a great deal for a woman stuck in Canterbury all the time.'

'And that he intends to leave me for you.'

'What does Richard have to say to all this?'

Samantha shook her head. 'I haven't mentioned it to him. But that's just it. He never speaks to me, and since you came back into his life he's been more distant than ever. You actually sought him out, I understand. Why are you doing this? Why? We were so happy until now.'

'And yet he never speaks to you?' Abby probed, though she felt wrong-footed. Bitter words and recriminations would have found swift answers, but all this pleading, from the proud daughter of the manor, left her powerless.

'I meant he's always so preoccupied with work. But I love him, and he loves me.'

Abby heard her, but did not believe her. Samantha was lying to save a marriage which had died long ago. 'He loves me,' she whispered at last. 'We've always loved each other.'

Uncrossing her legs, Samantha leaned forward, her face pinched into bitterness. 'You left him of your own free will to marry someone else!'

'Is that what you've been told?' Well, thought Abby, that was one blessing. The idea of people like Samantha knowing the truth was too horrendous to contemplate. 'If you really loved him, you would let him go. You wouldn't want him chained to you for the rest of his life.' She paused and waited for the sparks to fly. 'Yours is a loveless marriage.'

'A loveless marriage?' Samantha's voice had risen to hysterical proportions. 'Is that what he told you? Oh Abby, if you only knew how happy we were and how much he loved his little girl. But since you came back into his life, our happiness has slipped away and ... and I don't know what to do.' Suddenly, she broke into sobs. 'Please, leave him alone, and let us find that happiness again!'

Liar, thought Abby, then recalled a distant memory of a proud young girl riding a chestnut pony across Stapledown. She had been in awe of the haughty rider. Was this the same ice goddess, weeping so uncontrollably before her, begging Abby Nichols not to ruin her life? Or was it just a very good act? When Samantha tried to stop the flow of tears, without success, Abby decided that she was not acting.

'Please, Samantha, don't – '

'Have you given a thought to Richard?' Samantha sniffed and dabbed at her nose with a lace handkerchief. 'He'll be ruined at the first whiff of scandal. Because of you he gave up Law. Now, because of you he'll give up his dream of entering Parliament. I can't bear to see him hurt all over again ... I can't ... I can't.' She buried her face in her hands and sobbed wildly. 'And ... and if you take him from me, I won't live without him.'

'Stop it. Stop it!' cried Abby, in growing dismay. She stood up and moved across the room towards the window. The day had darkened with her mood and now rain swept across Brook Street. What kind of a woman was she? Here was a young wife pleading with her not to steal her husband. Could she ignore such a plea? Richard had said he hadn't known a moment's happiness with her, but did Samantha realize that? Whatever his feelings towards his wife, Richard would never say a harsh word, choosing to keep his distance instead. Such a man might make a false impression on a woman who looked at the world through blind eyes. There were many such Englishmen. It was, in fact, the English way. And what of Samantha? That she cared for Richard was not in doubt. That she cared enough to let him go, was.

'I don't have the power to take Richard from you unless he really wants to leave anyway,' she said.

'But you do, you do. You have the power to destroy both our lives and separate Fiona from the father she loves. God help you if you succeed. I shall never forgive you and neither will your clients, many of whom are my friends. It's no good your trying to pretend you are innocent.' The tears had stopped, and the voice had taken on an edge which was more like the old Samantha. 'You were both seen at Regent's Park Zoo last weekend. You had your little boy with you. Richard's son, no doubt.' Seeing Abby start, she smiled thinly. 'Oh, did you think I didn't know about the child? I've known for some time.'

Abby's shoulders fell. 'Stella?'

'Stella. You were also together on Monday night.' The thin edge in her voice turned to outright anger. 'I know, because I was trying to get through to Richard by telephone. He came in at one o'clock in the morning, smelling of your perfume. You're wearing it now.'

'You have a vivid imagination, Samantha,' murmured Abby, facing the window. Her heart was pounding, and she felt ill. How could she lie? Yet she must. The Zoo could be deemed innocent enough. But Monday night was something else, and, for Richard's sake, she would lie through her teeth. 'I really am very busy. You're wasting my time with this fantasy.'

'Fantasy! If you go on, I shall put an end to my life. I cannot live without Richard. Believe me, I don't say this lightly.'

Abby smiled and turned to face her adversary with cold eyes. 'On the contrary, I think you said that very lightly, far too lightly to convince me.' It was the age-old ploy, of course, and one which had kept many a man chained to a loveless marriage. Samantha was full of such ploys.

Richard had told her how this wilful and selfish daughter of the manor had trapped him into marriage. Now she wanted to trap him by a moral dilemma. *Over my dead body!* thought Abby angrily. 'If you and Richard are no longer happy in your marriage, then it's a matter for you two. Coming here was just a waste of time.'

'That's debatable,' said Samantha, with a slight air of triumph. 'You see, before I came here, I went to your home at Hampstead.'

'My *home*? How dare you?' For all her steady gaze, Abby felt unnerved. 'Would you mind explaining why?'

'I went, hoping we could have this conversation there, but the woman who answered the door said you had already left.' Samantha smiled and lit a cigarette before going on. 'I naturally assumed she was your charlady, until she said she was your mother-in-law. The little boy was there also. Does your mother-in-law know that Richard is the boy's father?'

Abby did not reply, but the look in her eyes said everything.

'I see she does not,' said Samantha, inhaling deeply. 'Well, well. I wonder what she would make of it all if she did know. It's up to you, Abby. Leave Richard alone and you have nothing to worry about. I really couldn't care less about the boy or that cockney woman, but I do care for my husband, whatever you may think.'

Stunned by her words, Abby stared at her. 'Why, you bitch. You god-awful bitch of a woman!' This was unendurable. 'How dare you make such threats. I'd like to know what Richard would make of your blackmail. Do you really think that would tie him to you?'

Samantha smiled, knowing she had won. 'Tell him if you like. He will, of course, be extremely angry, just as your mother-in-law will be very shocked. Because the moment Richard learns of our talk will be the moment she discovers the true father of her grandson.' The smile faded and the eyes glinted like ice. 'It's no idle threat. If you see my husband again, I will carry it out.'

Turning back to the window, Abby saw the rain was easing slightly. But she hardly noticed. How on earth had Samantha latched on to the one thing she'd always dreaded? She had won; it was over. *Over.*

'That you're prepared to go to such lengths must mean that you care something for Richard,' she murmured. What pain this appalling decision was causing! 'I just wish you cared enough.' She sighed and felt her throat constricting. 'I always knew you were a hard woman, but I had no idea how hard until this moment. You needn't worry – I shan't see Richard again.' The finality of her words seemed to echo around the room.

'Is that a promise?' The voice sounded immensely relieved.

'Yes.' The lump in Abby's throat was becoming harder and more painful with each passing second. 'Tell him. You must tell him.'

'I couldn't do that, and you know it. Richard would be furious.'

'Then let him be furious,' cried Abby. 'It's no more than you deserve.' She was shaking now and the cry gave release to her pent-up emotions. She wanted to scream and tear the place apart. She wanted to kill Samantha with her own bare hands. 'Go. Please go – now, this minute. You've got what you came for. But remember this. If my mother-in-law ever does find out the truth, then I shall take Richard from you without a moment's hesitation.'

Still facing the window, Abby heard the door open and then close again. She did not turn her head or move. Samantha had gone, and with her had gone all hope of happiness. She had just promised the woman that she would never see Richard again. *Never?* Could she truly keep that promise? She must. Otherwise Evelyn would suffer along with Ross. It occurred to her then, that Samantha was

356

very like Milicent. Selfish and possessive, they would both stoop to any ploy to keep the men they loved chained to their will.

Devastated, Abby collapsed into the armchair and wept. Only a short while ago she and Richard had been planning their future. Now they had no future. When would she learn?

A gentle knock on the door brought Abby back to reality.

Susan took one look at Abby's stricken face, then rushed to her in alarm. 'What is it? What's happened?'

'It's nothing,' Abby whispered, in a broken voice. 'Just some bad news, that's all.'

'Ross is all right?' When Abby nodded, Susan stared at her troubled friend, wishing she could help. But once again, it seemed that Abby meant to shut her out. 'Who was that woman who just left?' she asked suspiciously.

Abby stood up, studied her face in the mirror, and decided she looked as though she had influenza. 'That was Richard's wife.' These words were greeted by a stunned silence. 'What was your impression of her?'

'Elegant and cold. I can see she's upset you. Is Richard all right?'

'Oh yes,' said Abby briskly, her voice making it obvious that the matter was closed. 'How are things upstairs?'

Sensing the mood, Susan stuck to business. 'One or two problems. I just wanted to check the design for the ballgown once more. You were re-thinking the shoulders, remember? But it doesn't matter, we'll leave it until you're feeling better.'

'Oh, I just need a minute or two to gather my thoughts,' said Abby. She glanced at her watch, blinking to restore focus to her blurred eyes. 'It must be lunchtime.'

'And you should stop working and eat,' said Susan, like a scolding aunt. 'I'll send Avril out to get some of the open Danish sandwiches you like so much.'

Abby shook her head. 'Thank you, but no, Susan. I

couldn't eat a thing just now.' She smiled at her anxious friend. 'Go along now, and don't worry. I just need time to think. I'll be in my studio when the Marchioness arrives. Will you ask Avril to call me then?'

At that moment, the door opened and Avril walked in. Susan smiled, saying, 'Someone's ears were burning, I see.'

'I'm sorry to bother you, Mrs Carr, but there was a strange telephone call earlier, when you were with Mrs Glenister. He wouldn't give his name, but said: "Saturday, same place, same time." That was all.'

When she was alone once more, Abby steeled herself to write to Richard saying she could not break up his marriage, and would not be able to meet him the following Saturday. Mentioning nothing about Samantha and her threats, she begged him to accept her decision, told him she would always love him, then gave the letter to Avril to post at once.

When it was done, she sat down at her desk, feeling very cold.

Through the rest of the week, Susan and Roland became more and more worried about Abby. She was a mere shadow of the woman they all knew and loved.

'Diabetes,' said Roland to Susan one morning. 'I've seen it before. She's pale and drawn, and I'm sure she's lost weight.'

Susan shook her head. 'No. I think it's her heart.' The words were spoken quietly, in Roland's office so that no one else could hear.

He looked at her in alarm. 'Her heart? Dear God, not at her age surely?'

'It's a weakness of the heart and she's had it years. Ever since I first met her. I had hoped she was over it, but I was wrong. It isn't physical. Well ... I'm not sure if heartache isn't physically painful when all's said and done.'

Roland let out a sigh of relief. 'God, you gave me a

fright. Well, dear, if it's love, she'll get over it. There are plenty more fish in the sea and she's a good looker.'

Smiling at such naivety, Susan returned to her work, wishing that Abby could meet someone else, someone who could knock Richard out of her head once and for all. The mystery of those years had never been revealed. In Susan's opinion, Abby had been wrong to keep her secret, for by so doing she had made a heavy load even more unbearable.

In the house in Beauchamp Place, Samantha looked at the neat, hand-written envelope which had arrived in the afternoon post.

It posed something of an enigma, since hand-written mail was usually for her, or for both of them, and the correspondent easily recognized by the writing. This, however, was different, and she was suspicious.

She peered at the postmark until she could make out the letters stamped W1. Then, swiftly eliminating her own friends in that area, her suspicion increased. Brook Street fell between W1 and W2 and Abby's salon was closer to Bond Street than Grosvenor Square.

'That makes it W1,' she murmured to herself. 'Abby!'

Did that woman have the gall to break her promise so soon? If Abby had written to Richard, then what might she have told him? Samantha's thoughts raced. She had banked on Abby not saying a word. Yet here was a letter from the vicinity of Brook Street.

Slowly she walked into the drawing room, and stood gazing down at the vase of dried flowers in the hearth. If Abby had told Richard, then it would be necessary to act without further delay. 'There's only one way to find out,' she said decisively, and headed for the kitchen.

There, she boiled a kettle and steamed open the envelope, trying to unstick the flap without damaging it. She failed, and knew the tell-tale tear would give everything away. Snatching the letter from the envelope, she read it through three times, then felt like kicking herself. Abby had done exactly as she'd promised, and had not mentioned their meeting. The letter said it was over, yet she couldn't let Richard have it.

Rushing into the drawing room, Samantha sat down at the bureau, and tried to copy Abby's neat handwriting onto a new envelope. For an hour she sat there, as her failed attempts piled up around her. It was useless! The writing did not match up, no matter how hard she tried. Worse, there were elements of her own hand which could not be disguised. A confrontation with Richard over Abby was the last thing she wanted.

Finally, Samantha tore up the letter and burned it in the grate, placing logs over the charred remains.

'But you promised!' Ross was looking up at his mother with accusing eyes. 'You always say people should keep their promises. Uncle Richard wants to take me to the Zoo – he said so.'

Abby looked at her son's disappointed face as they sat at the evening meal. 'But he can't help it if he's had to go away sooner than he thought,' she sighed. 'You know he wouldn't do this deliberately. He was looking forward to it so much.'

'Where's he gone then?'

'I'm ... I'm not sure. Away.'

Ross gazed at her warily. 'That's what they told Fisher when his mother died. They said she'd gone away, and when he asked where, they said the angels had taken her. What they meant all the time was that she was dead. Is Uncle Richard dead?'

'No, darling, of course not.'

'Because if he is, I wouldn't want you to talk tommyrot about angels.'

'I wouldn't dream of it,' said Abby. She glanced across to where Evelyn was sitting. 'Whatever happened to innocence?'

Evelyn finished her fish pie. 'Don't ask me. They seem to

know more than I do these days. Ross, if you've finished, then outside with you. Pick up all those things you left on the terrace and bring them in.'

When the child had gone she looked across at her daughter-in-law, sensing there was something wrong. Abby had been behaving strangely all week. 'It's a pity your cousin's gone away. I expect you was looking forward to seeing 'im again. I know Ross was.'

'Yes,' murmured Abby, trying not to choke on her food. 'Still, there it is.' Evelyn was digging and she knew it. It was wrong to keep her in the dark like this, but what else could she do? 'Now then, I'll do the dishes but then I've work to catch up on.'

'Then clear off to your room and work on it,' said Evelyn, gathering up the dishes. 'It won't take me long to get rid of this lot.'

'Leave it for Mrs ...'

'Not on your life.' Evelyn gave her a dark look. 'What, 'ave 'er come into a messy 'ouse?'

'That's what *she's* meant to do – clean it.'

'I know, but I 'ave my pride.' Evelyn paused and looked at Abby. 'Poor little chap's very disappointed. It's a good thing that friend of 'is couldn't make it, otherwise you'd 'ave two un'appy kids on your 'ands.'

Abby nodded. 'I'll go and talk to him.' She walked down the stairs and out into the garden. The terraced area was littered with books, a football, several wind-up cars and an empty beaker which had contained milk. The new term had started, and Ross was sitting amidst his own toys, his crestfallen face staring at the chaos around him. Bending to pick up one of the toy cars, Abby smiled at him, saying: 'Did you have a friend in today after school?'

Ross nodded. 'Bannem came, but he's a bit of a pain these days.'

'But you've always been such good friends, and you had a good holiday with his family in Devon.' Abby tried to sound light-hearted.

361

'I liked last Saturday better,' murmured Ross, still sulking.

Of course he had, thought Abby. He had been with his father and they were so alike. Now she was denying him the company and love of his father, in order not to hurt his grandmother. How much it hurt her, Ross would never know.

'Isn't he ever coming back?' His question was more of a plea and it tormented Abby.

'Yes,' she replied, 'one day, he'll come back. Look, I know he promised, darling. Like you and like me, Uncle Richard deems a promise to be a promise. But it isn't always possible for promises to be kept. Someone connected with your uncle's work has sent him away, and he has no choice but to go.' Too choked to say any more, she busied herself picking up Ross's things. Soon he joined her, sensing that she was as disappointed as he was.

On Saturday, Richard stood outside the main entrance of the Zoo eagerly waiting to see Abby and his son again. He had lived for this moment, counting the days, the hours and finally the minutes. As each taxi drew up he watched expectantly. Time passed, and still he waited. At two o'clock, he finally turned away, a lone and desolate man in a bustling London. He walked for miles without seeing or hearing anything, without even knowing where his feet were taking him. All he knew was that Abby had lost heart and faith in all that he'd proposed.

All day, Abby tried to concentrate on her work, but it was hard. Now most of the staff had gone, and she was sitting alone in her studio when the telephone rang.

'Abby?' Richard's voice was thick and constrained.

'Yes,' she whispered, feeling her heart would break. It was the call she'd been expecting for the past two days. The call that had not come.

'Why, Abby, why?'

'I explained ... Oh Richard, you must try to understand. Your wife ... your child ...'

'We've been through all that. I don't understand what's changed.'

'Don't you?' Abby tried to go on, but her heart was too full. At last, she said, 'Perhaps you underestimated Samantha. She knows about us, Richard. She was here in my office only the other day. We were seen at the Zoo and she's put two and two together about Monday night.'

There was a long pause as Richard tried to take all this in. 'But how? Why?'

'I told you. The Zoo and, of course, your dear mother.' Abby's voice had a bitter edge to it now. 'She's said nothing to you?'

'Samantha? No, not a bloody word. How dare she go to you and start trouble?'

'Well, she did. It would be quite wrong now for us to enter into something which could only end badly, maybe even tragically.'

'Tragically? What on earth are you talking about?'

Abby sighed. It was no use. She would have to tell him. 'Samantha threatened suicide, should you leave her.'

'And you *believed* her? Oh, don't fall for that old chestnut, darling. I've seen Sam when she doesn't get her own way. If you had too, you'd ignore all her threats as everyone else does.'

'She made another threat which I can't ignore,' said Abby. 'She intends to tell Evelyn that you're Ross's father. She was there. At my house.'

It was some time before Richard spoke again. 'Even so, I think it's just a bluff.'

'Dare we risk it?' asked Abby. 'I can't, not after all that Evelyn's been through. I won't let her be hurt. And you must say nothing to Sam. If you do, she's promised to tell Evelyn right away. Darling, we must be strong. If you want to help me through this, then get on with your life and let me get on with mine.'

'You can't know what you're asking,' said Richard, his voice breaking up.

'Oh, believe me, I do, and I find the situation as unbearable as you. I once said if I had to choose between having you and hurting Evelyn, then I must choose in Evelyn's favour.' Tears blurred her eyes and she was trembling. 'I love you more than life itself, and I know how much you love me. We have that at least.'

Abby replaced the receiver, and stared into emptiness. It really was over now. Ice-cold shudders went through her; and her heart tightened as though held in a vice. Then she leaned forward, holding her head in her hands as sobs racked her body.

CHAPTER FIFTEEN

Few of the invited spectators, seated on gilt chairs in the salon, could have guessed at the fraught nerves behind the scenes, as haughty models sauntered along the cat-walk to the soothing strains of Mantovani.

All the tension of the past weeks had built to this moment and Abby watched, her stomach tied in knots. Only now, as she heard the clapping, did she begin to relax. Her spring and summer collection was a success, after all. She'd known from the start that it was good: well-balanced, but with a touch of the new and daring. So why all this self-inflicted torture?

Among the spectators sat Evelyn, tears of pride in her eyes, as Abby appeared briefly to acknowledge the applause. Until now, she'd always stayed away, saying she would be a 'fish out of water', uncomfortable among all those 'posh people'. This time, however, Abby had refused to take no for an answer. Added to which, Mrs Proctor, the domestic, had raised an eyebrow at Evelyn, saying, 'Good Lord, if she were my daughter I know where I'd be. She must think you don't care!' That had been enough to spur Evelyn into action. She'd arrived with Jonathan earlier that afternoon, tried to keep out of everyone's way and wished secretly that she had stayed at home. Now she could not wish to be anywhere else.

When the fashion editors and sketch artists had left, Evelyn made her way through the general throng towards Abby and threw her arms about her, murmuring, 'I just wish Eddy could 'ave been 'ere to see it. It was smashing, luv, really smashing.'

Abby hugged her mother-in-law. 'I told you it would be fun. Not the frozen event you expected. You liked the clothes?'

'Can a duck swim?' laughed Evelyn. 'It was all lovely. Just − lovely.'

'Darling!' The voice came from the distance and Evelyn stood back as a tall, auburn-haired woman wafted across to Abby, both arms outstretched.

'Darling, it was absolutely *breathtaking*. I particularly like the sweet-pea range.' This had been one of the highlights of the show: flowing chiffon in overlapping colours of grey, pink and mauve with large picture hats covered with the same material. 'I simply *must* have one of those outfits for Ascot, and at least two of the linen outfits, to say nothing of the evening gowns.' She sighed and spread her arms in mock despair. 'Whatever shall I do? I have to choose, yet I love them all.'

'Thank you,' said Abby, smiling. 'This is my mother-in-law, Evelyn Carr.'

Suddenly aware of the small woman standing beside her, Joanna turned and gave her a dazzling smile. 'Oh, I'm so sorry. How very rude of me, bursting in like that. How do you do, Mrs Carr.'

'This is Joanna Craig,' said Abby to Evelyn, who was staring up at the famous actress with her mouth slightly open.

'Your daughter-in-law is just about the most talented designer in this country. She's taken Paris down a peg or two.'

Evelyn swallowed, and smiled. 'Yes,' she said at last, 'I am very proud of Abby. Very proud.' Her voice trailed off with uncertainty. What else could she say to this legend of stage and screen? How often had she queued to see her films? Now here she was, face to face with her, discussing Abby. The last thing she wanted was to embarrass Abby with her South London accent. 'Least said, soonest mended', had always been her motto. The other was 'practise what you preach'. So she smiled, and said nothing more.

'But do you know, Mrs Carr,' Joanna went on in a conspiratorial tone, 'she's been working much too hard and I think she's looking rather peaky. So I want you to help me to persuade her to stay with me in the country for a quiet weekend; that's if you don't mind my tearing her away from you!'

Evelyn glanced at Abby. 'I think that's a very good idea. She does work too hard.' Thank God she had managed to say her aitch this time, even if she did have to work at it. 'And I don't mind at all.'

'There you are!' said Joanna. 'Abby, you're coming to Breedon for a houseparty the week after next, and I won't take no for an answer. I'm having a few of my friends, and Robert will be having some of his old fogeys. Please do come, and bring that nice Jonathan Bryce with you. Robert got on with him quite well that night at the theatre. Bankers, you know ... I believe he shoots?'

Abby blinked, trying to switch from high fashion to country matters. 'Shoots?'

'Pheasants!' Joanna smiled. 'Our woods are full of them.' She turned back to Evelyn. 'My husband thinks about banking, shooting and his wife, in that order. I, on the other hand, like creative people, so we've learned to compromise.' She laughed lightly, and looked back at Abby. 'I daresay it's the reason our marriage has lasted so long. We've absolutely nothing in common, and therefore nothing to quarrel about. How can we fail? Please, do say you'll come. I want to show you off to my friends, and I promise not to discuss the wardrobe you're designing for the play. No, this is to be a "switch off" weekend. The country air will do you the world of good. Anyway, I must fly, darling. I'll be in touch. Goodbye, Mrs Carr; it was so nice meeting you.'

Jonathan looked after her, saying: 'Did I hear my name mentioned?'

367

'We're to have a dirty weekend away,' whispered Abby, with an amused smile. Seeing his shocked expression, she added, 'We've been invited to a houseparty at the famous Breedon Park. I think it's a shooting party – wellies, labradors and dead pheasants. You're invited to keep Robert company, I understand. Mother is shocked!'

'No, I'm not,' said Evelyn. 'When you're with Jonathan, I know you're safe.' With that she walked away to talk to Susan.

Jonathan frowned. 'What's that supposed to mean?'

Abby laughed. 'I think it was meant as a compliment,' she murmured. 'I'm not sure about going. It would mean leaving Evelyn and Ross for a weekend and I see so little of them as it is.'

Jonathan gave her a serious look. 'Frankly, I think you should go. Something's been eating away at you for weeks and I wish you could confide in me. That's by the way, and I'll say no more about it. But a change of scene would do you good. It's time you put your sorrows behind you.'

How does he know? wondered Abby. Had Susan said something? How could she, when she knew nothing! No, what Jonathan knew, he knew because she'd been wearing her heart on her sleeve all this time.

Safe, Jonathan thought, leaving Abby to more admirers. Did Abby really want to be 'safe' with him? Did she not wonder why he never tried to make love to her, as he so longed to do? Perhaps not. Perhaps he was just a father-figure, dependable old Jonathan, who was so 'safe'. A weekend away with Abby could come dangerously close to changing that image. He would have to be careful, and go on being 'safe'.

Later that night, Evelyn sat in her dressing gown drinking her usual cup of tea in the drawing room. Abby was curled up in an armchair, still trying to unwind after the strain of the day.

'I've kept you up too late, Mother. It's been quite a day.'

'It's been a beautiful day,' murmured Evelyn, her eyes still hazy with memories, her head a little light. 'All those people, and Joanna Craig! Wait till I tell Mrs Proctor. That'll 'ave 'er green with envy. But your clothes, luv – they was smashing. I can just see Anna Neagle in them. Smashing, really smashing.' The mist cleared from her eyes and she frowned. 'I know I 'aven't made things easy, all that moaning and groaning, but I was afraid for you. Still, I needn't 'ave been. You've made it, girl. And do you know what? You'd 'ave made it even if you 'adn't gone to that posh aunt of yours in Canterbury. You've too much spunk to accept what God dished out to you.' Her face clouded. 'Not that I believe in God any more.' She sipped her tea thoughtfully. 'Victoria Place, and all that went with it, was not for you. I knew that the first time you came back to us. I knew it when you married Eddy, and that worried me. Even now, I sometimes wonder what would 'ave happened if you and Eddy 'ad gone to Liverpool.' Her eyes glistened with tears. 'I don't suppose ... well, it would all be different. Dear God, I'd give anything ...'

'I know, I know.' Abby went to her and put a comforting arm about the quivering shoulders. 'But things are the way they are, and we must live in the present, not the past.' She frowned. 'You're lonely, that's the trouble. I've dragged you away from your old roots to a place where it's difficult to make friends. You can't exactly chat over the garden fence here, can you.'

Evelyn touched Abby's face gently, and made a supreme effort to gain control over her emotions. 'Don't you mind me, luv. Just got a bit weepy, that's all. I'm over it now. Anyway, I'm not lonely,' she lied, feeling she had spoilt Abby's triumph by bringing up the past. 'Mrs Proctor chats to me in the mornings, then Ross is 'ome later and when Mrs Bannem brings him back, she often pops in for a while.' She patted Abby's hand and stood up slowly. 'So now it's me for bed. You want to get on up, too. Now that the collection's been shown, you can ease off.'

'That'll be the day,' smiled Abby. 'Now the orders will come in thick and fast and I'm still up to my eyes designing Joanna's wardrobe for her next play. I'll be up shortly.' She sank back into the armchair and picked up a magazine, flicking through the pages vaguely. She tried to concentrate on an article about house renovation, but soon her eyes started to wander, as did her mind. '*Things*.' Mrs O'Connor's words came echoing back across the years, as Abby took in the understated comfort and elegance of the room. '*I 'ad a flat full of things once. Took a lifetime collecting them and they all vanished in one second.*'

Since the room faced north, Abby had painted the walls in pale peach to give it warmth. It was a large and comfortable room with easy chairs and two sofas and a white marble fireplace. The walls displayed the fine paintings Abby had bought from various galleries over the years. Of late, she'd developed a keen interest in the works of John Piper. Her own efforts, and those of Susan, who had been more prolific in her art output, lined the hallway and stairs, along with sketches produced in their student days.

The dining room was more formal, with Chippendale furniture and Waterford crystal. Silver candelabra decorated the long table — a gift from Susan, and crystal decanters stood on the sideboard. Those who came to the house were always surprised that a modern designer should have such a traditional home when their own homes had the latest in teak or Scandinavian furniture. Mahogany and walnut were the heavy trappings of the past. But Abby felt differently and furnished this old house accordingly. Even so, she would trade it all for the chance to live out her life with Richard — who *was* her life.

At last, Abby rose from the armchair, switched off the lights and went upstairs to her bedroom. From the dressing table, she pulled out an envelope of old photographs taken with the Box Brownie that William had given her for Christmas one year. Seeing Richard as he had been, fair and smiling, all hopes of Oxford before him, gripped her heart. Abby asked herself why she kept doing this; why hang on to the past when it brought so much unhappiness?

Seated at the dressing table she brushed her hair, then caressed a lock, as Richard had, remembering the sensation it had aroused in her. If she lived to be ninety she would never stop loving him. Yet she was only twenty-seven! Her youthful prettiness had mellowed to womanly beauty. One day it would fade, and she would go to her grave with the memory of one afternoon of passionate love-making.

Was that all the love she was to have? Surely one day there would be another man in her life. She smiled wryly. *How, you fool? No one's allowed to get near.* She knew she'd built a fortress around herself; mainly to keep Jeremy at bay. After they'd met at that wedding, he had made quite a nuisance of himself. Abby's loyal staff knew better than to let him anywhere near her, and finally he'd given up. But she still lived with the anxiety of his possible return. Her thoughts returned to Richard once more and, as always, she fell asleep thinking of him.

Three days later, Avril entered her studio with a calling card.

'The gentleman is waiting in the salon, Mrs Carr.'

Abby took the card and read it aloud. 'Baron von Schreiber! What on earth is he doing in London?' Abby nodded. 'Yes, tell him I'm just coming.' Glancing at herself in the studio mirror, she saw that her hair needed pinning up. Long and slightly tousled, it made her look so young, and it was unfashionable these days to have hair so long, when most women had short bouffant hairstyles. Quickly, she twirled it into a chignon, dabbed some powder on her nose, and nervously tried to think of diplomatic words. But how did you tell a father that his son simply did not wish to meet him?

Karl was seated on the sofa, a sombre businessman with weighty problems on his mind. Having arrived in London late the night before, he'd spent the morning at a business meeting, then asked his chauffeur to bring him directly to Brook Street. Now, as Abby entered the room, he stood up and gave a slight formal bow before kissing her outstretched hand. Still holding her hand warmly, he said, 'How good it is to see you again, Abby. I hope my sudden arrival does not inconvenience you?'

Abby smiled and said she was delighted to see him again. 'What brings you to London?' she asked, dreading the reply.

'Impatience,' said Karl. 'Business, too, of course. However, that could have waited.' He paused and frowned. 'Where is my son, Abby?'

Feeling apprehensive, Abby resorted to a lie. 'I ... I don't know. I couldn't find him.'

Karl smiled wryly. 'Oh, come now. If Richard owed you a thousand pounds you would find him soon enough. You only have to ask your aunt.'

Abby clasped her hands before her, twisting them slightly in her nervousness. 'I don't speak to my aunt. We ... we don't get along.'

'I see. But, even so, England is a very small country.'

'London is a very large city.'

There was an awkward silence, then Abby sighed. 'Look, we can't talk here. Come to my office.'

In the office, they sat facing each other while Abby tried to find the difficult words. If only Karl were not so tense, so eager for his son! 'I wasn't truthful just now. I *have* seen Richard. It was our first meeting in years.' She rose from her chair and walked slowly across the room to the window, remembering the conversation with Samantha. How long ago was that? Five weeks – six, perhaps? It seemed like years. 'When we met, we spoke of many things – painful things. By the time I brought you into the conversation, Richard was angry and dismissive.' She sighed, realizing how hurtful this must be to Karl. 'I'm sorry. I misjudged the moment. My timing was terrible.' Keeping her back turned, she went on. 'You see, he's always thought of

William as his father. To find out the truth as a grown man has been hard for him. He's hurt and angry and still hasn't come to terms with things.' She turned swiftly and looked into those wounded eyes. 'Oh, Karl, give him time. I'm sure he will want to meet you one day.'

'Are you saying that *you* had to tell him about me? That he had no idea of my existence?' Karl was looking at her with astonishment.

'He did know. Milicent had told him . . . well, sometime earlier. What she told him exactly, I really couldn't say. He didn't want to discuss it.'

Karl smiled sadly. 'I said it would not be easy. With my family background and the war, perhaps it will be impossible. They say if we do not know our parents, we do not know ourselves. Maybe that is what frightens Richard. He does not know what he will find.'

Abby shook her head. 'I'm convinced his feelings against you are connected to us. You see, in a sense, your being his father was the cause of our parting. It was a terrible mistake, and our lives have been ruined by it. That's why he's so bitter. It isn't you, Karl. It's . . . oh . . . I don't know.' She sighed deeply. 'I'm sorry — so very sorry.' To speak of Milicent as she'd like would put her in a bad light, so she would have to leave him ill-informed.

'I've distressed you,' said Karl, with deep concern. 'Oh, my dear, that was the last thing I intended. Do please forgive me.' He glanced at his gold wrist-watch. 'Look, it's past noon. No German can think on an empty stomach, and they have excellent cuisine at the Dorchester. I always stay there when I'm in London. I would be most honoured if you would allow me to take you to luncheon.'

Abby tried to gather her thoughts together. 'That would be lovely, but . . .'

'No buts! I hate eating alone, so please indulge me. I've come a very long way.'

Looking into his troubled eyes, Abby felt sympathy for him. 'Yes, you have. I would be happy to have luncheon

373

with you.' Struck by a thought, she went to her desk and took out the sketch of Richard. Showing it to Karl, she murmured, 'He's very like you.'

'Very,' said Karl. He stared at the sketch for a long time. 'It's excellent work. Yours, of course.' When she nodded, he handed it back to her, saying, 'Thank you for showing it to me.'

In the Terrace Restaurant, Abby ordered Dover sole, then glanced around the light and airy room with its silk and pastel decor, feeling thoroughly spoiled. Her eyes fell on a familiar figure seated in the far corner. At the same moment, Jeremy looked up from his plate, and saw her. She averted her gaze quickly, praying the three businessmen at his table would make him forget her presence completely.

'How often do you come to London, Karl?'

The baron shrugged. 'I haven't been here for over a year.' Glancing at the wine list he added: 'I hope to start a small subsidiary company in the North. Schreiber was built on steel, but we have long since expanded into other engineering projects.'

Abby looked at him curiously. 'It must be strange to spend all those years in medicine, then end up running a huge industrial company. Don't you miss being a doctor?'

Karl nodded. 'Of course. My ambition was to be a surgeon. Neurosurgery was my intended specialization, but, when I should have been training, I was in a field hospital, patching up soldiers as quickly as possible under heavy gunfire. I did my neurosurgery the hard way. I'm afraid I lost a few patients.'

'I still find it hard to understand why you should have been removed from that, and forced into a world you ...'

'Knew nothing about?' Karl smiled. 'Exactly. At the time, I was told it was all to do with morale. And, for my part, I was not too happy at the idea of losing my

inheritance, which would have happened had I not obeyed.'
He smiled wryly. 'In those days, we all had to obey without
question. I had some romantic idea of salvaging something
for the future. We all knew that Germany was finished, yet
the High Command fought on. Madness! Albert Speer was
forever on my tail. After your RAF bombed the factories,
he was everywhere, making sure production went on. Had
he been less efficient the war might have ended much
sooner.'

Their food arrived, wine was poured and Karl asked her
how the Dover sole was.

'Delicious,' said Abby.

He cut into his fillet steak and went on. 'I thought I
would eventually return to medicine. But it was not to be.
The Allies gave us aid and, as an industrialist, I was asked
to participate in the rebuilding of my country. How could
I say no? And so the course of my life changed completely.
It took years, but Schreiber rose out of the ashes, and now
gives employment to thousands.'

Abby sipped her wine and said, 'Then this is really a
company you built up from scratch. How can you say you
were born to medicine?'

'I've often wondered. Anyhow, be that as it may, my
Board grow anxious for me to name my successor. They
already have someone in mind. A young man of ability
and talent who, by the time I die or retire, will have the
experience to take over. But it has always been a tradition in
my family that the firm goes to the eldest son. I want to keep
it that way, otherwise Schreiber will disappear under some
God-awful corporate name and be managed by a Board
of Directors. It has already happened to most of the old
firms. Only Richard can save it happening to ours.'

Abby listened with growing astonishment. Richard at
the head of an industrial giant? It was inconceivable.
'But you're still young. And a good way from retirement,
surely.'

'Richard has to be trained. I could have a heart attack,

or fall under a lorry — whatever. That's why I must find him quickly. Not only because he's my son, but because I must assess his ability.' He leaned forward and touched her hand gently. 'You see, my dear, I know what it's like to be hurled into a position for which one is not trained.' He sighed, and thoughtfully sipped his claret. 'But, when all's said and done, I just want to see my son. I want him to say for himself whether he wishes to carry on the name of Schreiber. Do you think he will?'

Abby sighed. 'You want Richard to live in Germany and run the company. Then I must warn you that his wife is a social butterfly, and would never be uprooted. And Richard has already made up his mind to go into Parliament, if he can get elected.'

The blue eyes darkened. 'Then after one hundred years of all but dominating German industry, the House of Schreiber will be no more. I built that company up from the ashes, and I want Richard to have it — as well as the title.'

Title! Abby's heart sank. Poor Karl didn't know how much he was asking Richard Glenister to accept! Wittenhausen and the industrial Ruhr were as far away from his experience as the earth to the moon. How could she convince Karl of this?

Reaching into her handbag, she took out one of her cards and wrote Richard's London address on the back of it. 'All I can do is give you this. The rest is up to you. I'd rather not contact him again, to be honest.' She paused, and swallowed hard. 'We've said our goodbyes. It wasn't easy. In fact, it was very painful. You do realize what I'm saying?'

Karl stared at her with shrewd, yet sympathetic eyes. 'I do.'

At that moment, there was some movement from the table in the far corner and Jeremy was on his feet, looking straight at Abby, as he walked towards her table.

'Well, well, if it isn't Mrs Carr. Crawled out of Fortress

Brook Street, have we?' His small eyes opened expectantly as the baron began to rise to his feet in a courteous manner.

'May I present Viscount Kelthorpe,' said Abby to Karl. This was the last thing she had wanted. 'Baron von Schreiber.' She saw the curious light in Jeremy's eyes, and knew he was filing away the name. Only recently had she learned that his second cousin, Lord Hexgrave, owned half of Fleet Street, and had made Jeremy one of his editors.

After a few pleasantries, Jeremy left, saying, 'I'll be in touch, Abby. I never take no for an answer.'

'You obviously do not care for that man,' said Karl, as the waiter brought coffee. 'I did not exactly take to him myself.'

'He once threatened to harm Richard. He's a newspaper man so I suppose he could, if Richard became famous.'

They drank their coffee in silence, until Abby realized it was time for her to leave.

'It has been most pleasant seeing you again,' said Karl.

'I've enjoyed it, too,' murmured Abby. 'I'm sorry I failed you where Richard's concerned.'

'I think now I was wrong to come searching for my son. I have been selfish. He must come to me in his own good time. It may be many years before he does so; then again, it may be that he never does.' He bowed slightly, took her hand and kissed it lightly, making her feel like a queen. 'I am sad that you and he parted. I could not have wished for a more lovely and gracious daughter-in-law.'

Outside the hotel, the baron ordered his chauffeur to drive Abby back to Brook Street. As the Rolls pulled away, Abby looked back and waved through the window. Karl raised his hand, but did not move from the entrance until the Rolls slipped into the traffic towards Hyde Park Gate.

Settling back against the luxurious upholstery, Abby wondered if she would ever see Karl again. She liked the man and felt deeply sorry for him. His surname might be odious and forever linked with the Third Reich, but he was a lonely, kind-hearted being, who had only ever wanted to be a surgeon.

Her thoughts drifted to Milicent. Not once had Karl mentioned her name. What would she think of the step-daughter she so hated, dining with the former husband she still cared about? Abby could hear again the Schubert *Impromptu* echoing through Ferndene. Poor Milicent. Keeping Karl's photograph locked away in the attic, just as her stepdaughter kept Richard's portrait locked away in her office drawer. Loving someone inaccessible to them was the one thing the two women had in common. As Abby gazed out the window, she realized this was her weapon for revenge.

Viscount Kelthorpe walked into his outer office. 'Any news yet?'

Miss Searle looked up. 'Langdon, sir? Yes. The report arrived from our source soon after you left this morning. He urges you not to publish until he gives the all-clear.'

'What, more delay?' Jeremy walked into his office, thinking that in all these wasted weeks, the Langdon shares had soared, leaving Richard better off than he had ever been. Still, all that was about to change. He smiled and turned his attention to the report.

It was as serious as Jeremy had hoped. Langdon's success was based on ruthless cost-cutting. While the competitors' materials had been thoroughly checked, Langdon's long term use of bribes and, consequently, blackmail, had ensured him a large number of contracts. It was clear that his building materials, including concrete for foundations, were of an inferior standard. In certain cases, this might lead to structural problems. Even should such faults be discovered in time, the cost of repairs would be prohibitive. One building was already suspect, and the source was now investigating it.

Sighing with relief, Jeremy walked across to the window and looked down on the cars and lorries in the street below. As soon as word hit the stock market, the Langdon shares would plummet. The scandal following the newspaper's revelations should ensure high sales for weeks. Jeremy loved the newspaper business. Thanks to his relations, he'd been propelled to the top in a few short years, and was now being groomed to step into Lord Hexgrave's shoes when he retired.

His thoughts drifted back to the Terrace Restaurant. *Schreiber*. What on earth had Abby been doing lunching with a man old enough to be her father? Baron von Schreiber. Why did that name ring a bell in his memory? He pressed the intercom. 'Miss Searle – find out all you can about a Baron von Schreiber.'

'Can you give me more information?'

'If I could, I wouldn't be asking, would I? There can't be too many titles knocking around Germany these days. Name's linked with the war. Industry possibly. I was only a child at the time, but you should have memories of that period.' He switched off, murmuring, 'Stupid bloody woman. It's high time she retired.'

It was half past five. Karl had been sitting in his Rolls for twenty minutes, watching the house in Beauchamp Place, the house where his son lived. He was nervous, wondering what he would do should Richard suddenly appear. Rush across and introduce himself? No, that would be unforgivable, bursting in on the man's life in such a blunt manner. That was why he had asked Abby to intercede for him.

Unable to sit there any longer, the baron got out of the car. He strolled up and down the street for ten minutes, then worried that his movements might be regarded as suspicious. Returning to the Rolls, he decided to wait for another thirty minutes. After that, he had business people to meet. Maybe Richard would return home early this evening. Just to catch a glimpse of his son, was all Karl wanted.

Suddenly a green MG turned the corner, and pulled up outside the house. Karl stiffened, and leaning forward, watched as the driver, a grey-suited, fair-haired young man, left the open-topped vehicle, and walked into the house.

Karl leaned back in his seat, feeling a little shaken. He had just seen his son. After all these years, he'd finally seen his son. Even without Abby's excellent sketch, he would have known Richard anywhere. It was like looking at himself some twenty-five years earlier.

The overwhelming temptation to knock on the front door had to be resisted. Richard *must* come to him. If and when that day came, then Richard could easily find him; everyone in the City had heard of Schreiber Industries. Milicent and Abby both knew of the mansion at Wittenhausen. Karl gave one last glance to the house in Beauchamp Place. Yes, he thought, Richard would find him when the time was right. He only had to ask.

Breedon Park was a stone mansion standing in rolling countryside between Cirencester and Cheltenham. Sheep roamed its green fields and pheasants filled the thick woodlands. It was a place of stone terraces and rose gardens with avenues of rhododendrons sloping away to a distant sward which ended in woods.

As Jonathan turned off the main road, Abby could see the lights of the estate in the gathering twilight. A soft evening mist mingled with smoke curling up from the tall chimneys of the house.

'Hope you remembered to bring stout brogues and a plaid skirt,' said Jonathan. 'Oh, and a shabby tweed jacket.'

Abby smiled. 'I have a brand new country jacket, thank you.'

'That won't do at all! It's *de rigueur* to look as though the jacket has been handed on from generation to generation. The shabbier the better.' He grinned, then looked at her teasingly. 'Wonder why I was invited along? You don't suppose ...?'

His meaning was clear enough, and although Abby knew he was joking, the thought began to bother her. 'I don't suppose anything, other than that Joanna and her husband like you.' At least, that had been her assumption until this moment. Now she was no longer sure. 'I'm sure they don't think ... well ...'

'That we're having an affair?' Jonathan laughed. 'Why can't you come right out with the word? I'm sure they don't think any such thing. Who cares anyway? We're here for a relaxing weekend.'

He drove across the forecourt, rounded the rose bed and parked the car. 'Well, here goes. If they do think the unthinkable, we'll just have to put a brave face on it,' he said, and winked.

A fine thing for him to say, thought Abby dismally. No one, of course, would mention their suspicions outright, so there would be no opportunity for her to set the matter to rights. Would they believe her anyway? To many, the kind of platonic relationship she enjoyed with Jonathan simply did not exist between man and woman. Her life was her own, she told herself firmly. What she did had nothing to do with other people, and was no business of theirs.

Some of the other guests had already arrived. Abby and Jonathan joined them in the large drawing room for tea and toasted muffins around a blazing log fire. Two golden labradors stretched out before the hearth, one twitching in sleep, the other staring ahead with half-closed eyes, as Joanna kept up an animated flow of conversation. Her husband, Robert, sat quietly, the warmth of the fire and the boredom of having guests slowly overcoming his efforts to stay awake.

At six o'clock they all went to their rooms to rest, and dress for dinner. Everything Joanna could do to make her guests feel at home had been done. There were flowers, bars of perfumed soap, boxes of tissues, jugs of water, magazines and a few bedside books. The bed was a modern and comfortable surprise in a room of sixteenth-century origins, but the bathroom was antique, frozen somewhere between wars, and had to be shared by the guests.

Before all the hot water went, Abby managed to soak lazily in water softened with perfumed oils. Then she returned to her room, and lay in her silk kimono on the bed, relaxing for the first time that day. So far, she decided, the guest list came heavily down on Robert's side: gentleman farmers, bankers and their wives. True, there was one theatrical producer, Joanna's agent and an actor she'd never seen in any play or film. Everyone was in their mid-forties and fifties, and the talk was all of shooting, hunting and racing. One could hardly have expected the Oliviers, but then, at Joanna's level, one had hoped ...

At that moment, there was a commotion outside. Abby hurried across to the window and saw the two labradors leaping up at a car, determined to prevent an Alsatian from getting out. From the open-top vintage Bentley, a man was shouting at the dogs, trying to extricate a case from the back seat.

'Quiet, Nelson! Be quiet!'

A light beamed on him as the front door opened, but he had his back to the window. Joanna's voice rang out, half-laughing, half-scolding.

'Fancy bringing him! You know what he's like. It'll be chaos. Quiet, Luke! Down, Sam, it's only Nelson.'

Chaos was right. All three dogs were chasing each other round in circles, barking and snapping, leaping and growling, before they answered the call to enter the house. The light went out, the door was closed and peace restored.

Abby dressed carefully, brushed her hair until it shone, then swept it into a chignon. Slipping into a dress of midnight-blue chiffon, softly draped from the waist, she knew the only jewellery to wear with it was her pearl earrings set in small diamonds. Deciding she'd hit the right note, she picked up her evening bag, just as Jonathan knocked on her door.

'What on earth was all that noise?' he asked.

'Some idiot arrived with a dog,' said Abby. 'Don't leave me, Jonathan. I've already been asked if I ride to hounds. I haven't the heart to tell them I've never been on a horse in my life.'

Jonathan looked at her, remembering the shy young girl who had almost cried in his office. She was now looking every inch a woman of the world with colouring that would have Renoir reaching for his palette.

Abby saw him as soon as she entered the large drawing room. Towering head and shoulders above the other guests, he stood with a group by the window, his eyes sweeping the room in a bored fashion. When they fastened on her, they flickered into life, and a smile played on his lips.

'You remember Greg Hadleigh, don't you,' Joanna was saying, as she led Abby and Jonathan across to him. 'I'm sure you met in my dressing room once or am I wrong?'

'You're never wrong, Joanna,' murmured Greg, gazing into Abby's wide green eyes. 'Of course we met.' He dragged his gaze from her face, and nodded to Jonathan.

'Let me get you a drink, Hannah,' Robert was saying, hovering about them. Abby asked for a dry sherry, and heard Joanna correcting her husband as they walked away, then his bumbling reply. 'Oh, well, I knew it was something biblical!'

Smiling, Abby looked up at Greg, saying, 'Are you the one who arrived with the Alsatian?'

Greg nodded. 'You heard our stealthy approach, then?'

'I did,' said Abby. 'Do you take him everywhere with you?'

'More or less. Especially to the country. He loves houseparties. He's a Yank, you see, and has to be trained in English ways.'

Joanna returned, put an arm on Greg's massive shoulder and said: 'This giant of a genius has just finished the best

383

play I've ever read. And do you know, the bastard hasn't created a part for me in it! Honestly, I could murder him. And now he's off to the States, to be corrupted by Hollywood.'

Abby sipped her sherry and tried not to sound as nervous as she felt. 'What are you going to do there?'

'One of my plays is to be filmed, and I'm working on the screenplay. That was the condition of acceptance.'

'How exciting!' Abby was duly impressed. 'What's the play about?'

'A murder trial.' Greg looked bored with the subject, as Jonathan interjected.

'And how long will you be in Hollywood?'

'Six months — possibly more, possibly less. I hope less.' His voice was deep and vibrant. His face put Abby in mind of a rugby player's, but his eyes were deeply sensitive, as was his mouth. He took a silver cigarette case from his pocket, and was offering it to Abby, when Joanna suddenly dragged him away to meet another group of her guests.

'Rather full of himself, don't you think?' Jonathan said. 'Met his type before. Think they're God's gift to women, so be careful.'

Surprised at his tone, Abby smiled. 'I suspect you're hungry. You always start growling then.'

'No, I mean it, Abby. I just don't want to see you hurt.'

This was unbelievable. 'Good heavens, we've hardly said two words, and he's just off to the States! He isn't interested in me, and I'm certainly not interested in him,' she snapped. But she suddenly felt hot, and her face was flushed. From time to time, her eyes drifted to where Greg stood. Why did he make her feel so uncomfortable? Like a star-struck schoolgirl unable to speak in 'the presence'. There could be no other man for her but Richard. And Greg was so different! Whereas Richard had a noble profile, Greg's had been hacked out of a mountain-side. The jaw was strong and square, and the mouth bold and sensuous. Greg Hadleigh, she decided, had to be the most masculine man she had ever seen. Yet he had a sensitivity which enabled him to write some of the best plays in the English theatre. Unlike his contemporaries, he was neither working-class, nor angry. Cynical, thought-provoking, yes, but not angry.

Matters were not eased for Abby when she was placed directly opposite him at dinner. His eyes were constantly on her. She tried to avoid them by conversing with the banker beside her, but once or twice found herself drawn to those dark eyes, like steel to a magnet.

As the dinner progressed through its many courses, she became more tense, finding it difficult to eat with someone watching her so intently. The conversation had now taken a theatrical turn, and Anouilh's *Becket* came under scrutiny. Then the talk turned to financial backing versus freedom, and Greg was forthright in his views that backers should 'back off' when it came to content.

'Hold on there,' said the producer. 'You snipe at what you call an endless stream of mindless comedies, but there are queues at the box office, and that's what counts in the end. Plays that depress, or are too deep for the public to understand, just mean empty theatres. It's as simple as that.'

'Then so are the general public.' Greg sipped his wine and looked across at Abby. 'Do you find my plays too deep and depressing?'

Nonplussed, Abby shrugged. 'I never did understand what the angry young men were so angry about, so your last play was a welcome change to me.'

'Maybe the angry young men just want their wives to notice them occasionally. That's all Jimmy Porter ever wanted.' His voice was strangely cold.

After a strained silence, Jonathan said, 'Personally, I enjoyed *Salad Days*. We should have more productions like that.' He turned to Abby. 'Which theatre did we see that in?'

385

Seeing Greg's dark stare, Abby shook her head, murmuring, 'I can't recall.'

'*Salad Days*,' sighed the banker's wife. 'I thought it was simply wonderful. And so very ... well, so very *English*.'

Joanna cut in quickly. 'But Abby is more of an opera fan, I believe. Which is your favourite, Abby?'

Without a moment's hesitation, Abby replied: '*The Magic Flute*.' Her mind flashed back to an evening at Covent Garden with Richard beside her. If only he were here now to stand between her and this man, whose eyes kept saying 'come to bed'! She met the languid gaze with a cold stare, and was glad when the talk shifted to the loss of the Empire.

At last, Joanna led the ladies into the drawing room, leaving the men to their brandy and cigars. Pouring coffee, she talked freely, as women do when unshackled by the presence of men. Everyone fell about laughing at her outrageous stories and remarks. Decorum was restored when the men joined them again and the rest of the evening passed pleasantly with Joanna at the concert grand, singing Noël Coward songs in a clear melodious voice, while her guests listened with quiet delight or, like her husband, fell asleep.

That night Abby lay in her bed, thinking about Greg Hadleigh. Why did she find him so disturbing? Was she so vulnerable, so susceptible after sending Richard away?

Hearing a scuffling sound outside the door, Abby listened for a moment, then heard a whisper, and the sound of heavy breathing. Nervously, she crept out of bed, opened the door the merest notch and found herself looking into the brown eyes of the Alsatian.

'*Nelson*.' The whisper caused the dog's ears to prick up, and he turned and sloped away. Abby opened the door wider and looked out. Greg was standing on the landing, still in his dinner suit. He grinned broadly, his eyes raking her body, clearly admiring her form through the Grecian-style silk nightgown. Suddenly, feeling naked, she tried to cover herself.

'Sorry I disturbed you,' murmured Greg. 'But ever since his months in quarantine, Nelson is paranoid about being shut in. So I've rescued him from the stables.' He winked, and put a finger to his lips. 'Not a word to Joanna!'

Abby nodded, and returned to her room smiling to herself. What a strange man he was: curt, morose, sure of himself with women, yet soft as butter when it came to his dog.

On a golden autumn morning the 'beat-out' started. Abby watched in a field, as the beaters, walking side by side, made their steady progress towards the burnished woods, clear now against the pale blue sky. At the edge of the woods, pheasants flew up in alarm, and shots rang out. Labradors retrieved the birds in their soft jaws and presented them to the keeper. Fascinated, yet saddened by the scene, Abby watched for some time, then returned to the house with Joanna and the non-shooting guests to enjoy a tour of the grounds. Later they rejoined the others for a picnic lunch.

As they approached the woodland clearing, the smell of woodsmoke mingled with cordite, and the day seemed to have become more hazy, threatening an early mist. 'I do hate all this,' Joanna whispered. 'Why we can't have a quiet, restful weekend, I really don't know.'

Looking at Joanna now, Abby could have sworn the actress really was the 'lady of the manor', with her woollen tweed jacket and hat. Calling her dog Luke to heel, she was saying how utterly useless he was. Grinning, she added, 'I'm as dotty about my dogs as Greg is about that wretched Alsatian. Do you know, he sneaks the dog into his bedroom every time he comes here? He thinks I don't know. Doesn't seem to realize there are dog-hairs left all over the room.'

Abby stroked Luke's head. 'What did Greg mean when he said his dog was a Yank?'

'Nelson's the legacy from his divorce. It was a traumatic affair and we never mention it. His last wife was an American. They lived in New York. Then ... well ... it all ended with him keeping the dog. He's never parted from it now. Even takes it to the theatre with him during rehearsals.'

Two of the household staff were preparing lunch on trestle tables, now covered by white linen cloths. Steak and kidney pie, potatoes, wine and rolls, preceded by spirits for those who felt the need, and sherry for others.

With gun barrels broken, the shooters were heading towards them. Jonathan was in earnest conversation with Robert, while behind, in a shabby jacket, strode Greg, with two of the bankers.

Abby found herself constantly looking at Greg. What was it about him that said he 'belonged'? Was it that easy blend of guns, battered country clothes and confidence which those not born to it found so difficult to achieve? They all had it: the people who were here today. After the war, she recalled how everyone had spoken of great social change. Socialism would make everyone equal. The people who had said such things had forgotten that inbred quality of the English upper classes who, even if forced to live in a hovel, would do so with an air which said they 'belonged'.

'You look pensive.' Greg had walked across to her, wine glass in one hand. 'You've no wine. Take this.' His penetrating eyes looked into her embarrassed ones. 'Aren't you enjoying yourself?'

Abby took the wine, swallowed a mouthful of pie and nodded. 'Yes ... well ... I'm astonished at the eagerness men show to kill anything that moves once the season's in progress. But then you must have heard that so many times.'

Greg nodded. 'You're right. And it's difficult to understand. But these birds are bred and reared here for the express purpose of being killed. Some – many, in fact – do survive.' He looked at her and grinned. 'So you're against blood sports, but you join a shooting party. Why?' Nodding in Jonathan's direction, he added, 'I suppose he dragged you along.' Shaking his head, he frowned. 'He's old enough to be your father, for God's sake!'

Abby stared up at him angrily. 'What has that to do with anything?'

Greg put up his hands in mock defence. 'Hey, steady on, little lady. I just think it's an appalling waste, that's all.' With that, he walked away from her.

During the afternoon, Abby could endure the slaughter no more. Turning away from the guns, she headed into the woodland, breathing a deep sigh of relief, as the noise retreated in the distance. Peace at last. The earth smelt damp and as she kicked at last year's leaves, her mind filled with memories of the copse that led up from the River Stour to Stapledown.

Don't look back, she told herself, following a small track which led downhill to a narrow stream. Wandering along its silent bank, and climbing over fallen branches, she sat on a tree stump for a while and realized how deeply she was missing Ross. What was she doing here so far from her little son? If only she and Jonathan could return home tonight. As it was, they would leave on Sunday afternoon. Who would take Ross to church? She always did, every Sunday morning, and he always moaned, even pretended he was ill. Tomorrow he'd persuade Evelyn that he had a stomach ache, then would make a miraculous recovery in time for his lunch.

Suddenly Abby felt cold, and realized the light was fading. Poor, sad woods she thought. No birds sang here today. Wending her way back she cut up from the stream through a thick carpet of fallen beech leaves into darkening wood. Realizing that she was in unfamiliar territory, Abby retraced her steps, hoping to see some familiar landmark.

Hearing gunfire in the distance, she tried to work out

how far away it could be, then realized with dismay that she was lost. How stupid! 'Oh, this is ridiculous,' she said aloud. 'Put your thinking cap on, girl! The woods aren't that large.'

Her one aim now was to get back to the clearing before anyone noticed she was missing and started a search, but the path remained as elusive as ever. There was a volley of fire, this time to her right. It was immediately followed by another which seemed to come from the left. Echo? Of course not, she told herself, there was nothing for it to bounce off. Not knowing whether to turn left or right, she decided to head straight on, and tried to stem her rising panic. *Don't be a fool. They're not going to return to the house with a guest missing! Jonathan, at least, would realize I wasn't with them*. Which was worse? she wondered. Being alone in this wood all night, or being found by a search-party and having Joanna dine out on the story for weeks?

'What in God's name do you think you're doing?' Greg's voice thundered, the anger in it startling her as much as his sudden appearance. He strode towards her, his face dark and anxious. 'Don't you know it's damned dangerous to go wandering off like this in the middle of a shoot? Bloody embarrassing if the labradors dragged you out instead of the pheasants!'

Her relief at seeing him was immediately swamped by indignation at his tone. 'I'm touched by your concern,' she said coldly. 'Really, there's no need to worry. I'm not lost, and the guns are miles away.'

'Nevertheless,' said Greg, quieter as he approached her, 'accidents have been known to happen. Come on.' He led her through the trees and down the hill, where she now saw the old track. 'Why the hell doesn't he look after you?' he muttered grimly.

'I'm perfectly capable of looking after myself, thank you.'

'Of course you are,' came the sardonic reply. He took

her firmly by the arm and led her on, until they came at last to the clearing. Joanna was standing by the Land Rover with a few of the women, and waved as she saw their approach.

'I'm sorry,' murmured Abby. 'I didn't mean to alarm you, but I was perfectly all right, truly I was. My ears couldn't take any more, that was all.'

Joanna glanced up at Greg, and smiled. 'He was more worried than I was. I haven't lost a guest yet.'

Jonathan approached, his face red with the open air and joy of shooting. 'Hello, Abby. Have you had a good afternoon?'

Abby could not look at Greg, as she replied. 'Lovely. I took a walk in the woods.'

'Good.' Jonathan walked on towards the truck which was filled with dead pheasants. 'Robert certainly keeps well-stocked woods.'

Abby felt annoyed with Jonathan for showing Greg how lacking he was in concern; and with herself for being unreasonable. Was she beginning to believe the myth herself? But if everyone thought she and Jonathan were having an affair, they might as well think he really cared, otherwise the insult was doubled. Perhaps Greg put her in the same category as the businessman's 'little bit of fluff'. She would have to put him right. But how? When?

That evening, after dinner, they settled down to bridge, and Abby found there was one thing she could thank Milicent for after all: the endless hours that she'd spent teaching all three children the game she loved so much herself. Not having played for years, Abby had to admit to her partner, the banker, that she was rusty. At least she was playing and did not have to endure Greg's hard stare.

Breakfast the following morning was a quiet and casual affair. Abby wandered into the sunlit dining room, and helped herself to bacon, scrambled eggs and mushrooms, ignoring the kedgeree, sausages and kidneys. She sat down at the table where the banker and his wife were already eating and looked through tall windows onto lawns, brilliant in the morning sunshine. In the distance, she could hear church bells. As the maid poured coffee into Minton cups, she explained that their hosts were at church and that Matins would be at eleven for those who wished to go. Abby thanked her, and ate her breakfast, making polite conversation and wondering when the other guests would arrive. Her thoughts were on one in particular. She had gone to bed thinking of him, remembering his firm hand on her arm, as he had led her out of the wood. What a fool he must think her! She hoped to be out of the dining room before he arrived. Seeing him last night in a room full of people was one thing, but if he should sit down at this table now, she knew she would be covered in confusion. Someone had entered and was looking under the dish covers. Abby's heart started pounding, as she buttered her toast slowly. Then Jonathan sat down beside her.

'Did you sleep well?' he asked, surprising the other two at the table.

'Yes, thank you,' murmured Abby, with deep relief. 'Our hosts are at church.'

'They always go to the Communion service,' said the banker.

Jonathan tackled his kedgeree with a healthy appetite. 'Haven't been to church for years. Excluding weddings, of course.'

'Well, I'm going later,' said Abby. 'Is the village far?'

Oak and beech trees lined the lane winding downhill from Breedon Park to the small village. Church bells pealed across meadows still heavy with dew, and the gentle warmth of the morning sun fell on Abby's face as she walked along. She felt glad to be away from the house, where most of the guests were reading the Sunday papers. Most – but not Greg. There had been no sign of him all morning.

Wearing the brown velvet suit she'd arrived in, her own creation with a full skirt and fitted jacket, she had put on a beret of the same material. Jonathan had once observed that it made her look like Rembrandt.

In the distance she could see a stone cottage, its side wall completely covered with crimson Virginia creeper. Her instructions had been to turn right at this point into Church Lane. At that moment, a dog appeared by the cottage: a large Alsatian, ears alert and twitching, eyes turned to her, as it came up the hill.

Abby walked on, remembering how one of her school friends in Ashton Green had been savaged by a dog of the same breed. This one, she decided now, looked decidedly offensive. *Keep walking. Don't let it see you're afraid*, she told herself. If it attacked, would the people in the cottage hear her cries for help? Suddenly, the dog broke into a run, and headed straight for her. Abby stopped dead in her tracks, frozen with fear.

'Down, Nelson.' The deep, familiar voice came from somewhere by the cottage and the dog dropped to its belly at once. Abby breathed a sigh of relief as Greg came into sight, swinging the dog lead casually. Abby had never been so glad to see anyone in her life. Nelson, meanwhile, had risen to a sitting position, tail twitching from side to side, as he whined and quivered with contained excitement.

'Hope he didn't frighten you,' said Greg, slipping the leash on Nelson's collar. 'This lane's usually quiet and he needs a good run. He won't hurt you,' he added, without smiling. 'There's no need to look quite so scared.'

The sight of Abby had stunned Greg at first, since she seemed to have walked straight out of the landscape, like some ancient earth goddess. Her titian hair blowing gently in the breeze, she was like autumn personified: richly coloured, beautiful, yet with a hint of sorrow about her. It was in her eyes, those deep green eyes. He longed to know what had put it there.

Abby bent to pat the dog. 'Of course I wasn't scared. Just

393

didn't want muddy paws all over my suit!' She wondered at the strange look in Greg's eyes, and said lightly, to hide her growing shyness, 'You must have breakfasted very early.'

'When it was fresh. Then I took Nelson on a four-mile walk, and now I'm ready for my coffee. You look as though you're heading for church.'

'I am,' she answered, wondering why he rarely smiled.

'Alone?'

'Why not?'

'No reason, I suppose. Still, it does seem a little odd. Mind you, I'm no churchgoer myself, so I've no idea what people get up to these days. Sad though. He allows you to wander into danger, ignores you, then lets you go to church alone. The man's got one foot in the bloody grave.'

Abby looked at him in astonishment, then said coldly, 'I'm going to be late. Goodbye.'

With that she turned on her heel and walked down the hill, aware that he was looking after her. She could feel his eyes boring into the back of her head, and wished her face would stop burning. Had it turned that dreadful tell-tale red? Well, what if it had? At least he couldn't see it. How dare he say such things about Jonathan?

But why on earth had she left him thinking she was having an affair with an older man? On the other hand, 'We're just good friends' was such a hackneyed phrase, it would only have produced a laugh. Let him think what he liked! She would not dignify such unworthy thoughts with an explanation.

There were no more than twelve people in the church and most of them were elderly women. Abby prayed for the peace and repose of Eddy's soul, then William's and then Mrs O'Connor and her father-in-law. She prayed for her dead mother and sister, and finally for Justine, who had died, in Bath, six years since. So many in just twenty-seven years of life! People she had loved and needed; all had been taken from her, including one who still lived. She asked God to keep Richard safe and grant him the wisdom to seek out his true father, then prayed for Evelyn and Ross.

At the house, Abby found everyone on the terrace, having pre-lunch drinks: everyone save the one person her eyes sought. It was some time before she learned that Greg had returned to London early to prepare for his flight to the States. The news brought a rush of disappointment which surprised her, but also a bonus of information.

'I absolutely adore him, of course,' Joanna was saying to the producer. 'But one never knows where one *is* with the man. I'd no idea he was going this morning. He didn't say. Just came out with it, like that. No warning. Strange.'

'Bloody rude, if you ask me,' murmured Robert into his gin and tonic.

Joanna winked at Abby, as though they shared a secret about her grumpy husband who'd continued to call her 'Hannah' throughout the weekend. 'Oh, he's always been like that. Here one minute, gone the next.' She sighed. 'Still, he's the best. I only hope the Americans don't tempt him away from us this time.'

'He didn't marry again, then?' asked Abby, hoping her voice sounded casual, unaware of the glance Jonathan had thrown in her direction.

Joanna shook her head. 'I'm not sure he'll ever marry again. He's had two attempts already and the last ended in terrible acrimony!'

'Hadleigh,' murmured the banker's wife. 'Any relation to . . .'

'The plane people?' Joanna cut in. 'Yes, he's the younger son. He was also a pilot in the war — and decorated, at that. It seems strange that having been involved with planes all his life, he should suddenly turn to writing, but the family's loss was the theatre's gain.'

Long after the subject of Greg Hadleigh had been dropped, Abby continued to think about him. Small wonder he 'belonged', and did not write working-class plays about angry young men. What would he know of working-class life? He had been born to everything, and had the added advantage of being highly talented as well. He ought to be over the moon, yet how tense and unhappy he seemed.

Only when she arrived back home, and was hugging her little son and telling Evelyn all about her weekend, did she put Greg Hadleigh from her thoughts. The houseparty was over, and already consigned to the past.

On Christmas Eve, Abby threw a party in Hampstead for her staff and close friends. Susan came with Bernard, the young man she had known since her St Martin's days, discarded, then found again, when he was more 'mature'. Roland escorted Madame Duval, while Claudia arrived on the arm of a French Count who owned a château in the Loire Valley. It was inevitable that Abby would lose her one day to the aristocracy. It seemed to be journey's end for most top models, who then became valued customers.

A tall Christmas tree stood in the hallway and, above that, peering through the banisters, was Ross. Abby climbed the stairs to him. 'Time you were in bed, young man. The sooner you go to sleep, the sooner Santa will fill your pillow case.'

'Why can't I come to the party?'

'Because you're too young. This is a grown ups' party and very boring for you. We shan't be playing party games.'

'Not even musical chairs?'

Abby shook her head and wrinkled her nose. 'See what I mean? Boring.'

'Sounds it,' said Ross, getting to his feet. 'All right. Goodnight, Mum.'

Walking to Evelyn's room, Abby knocked on the door and sighed. 'Oh, Mother, please come out. Why on earth are you hiding away in there?' There was no reply, and she opened the door to peek inside.

Evelyn was standing before her full-length mirror in her new gown of pale blue silk. Her grey hair had been cut and re-styled by Steiner, and Abby had applied her make-up sparingly and cleverly, so that she glowed and harmonized with the gown, looking younger than she had ever looked.

'Well,' said Abby, approaching. 'What do you think?'

Evelyn touched the gown and said apprehensively, 'I think I'm a long way from Victoria Place. Oh, don't get me wrong, I know you mean well, and the dress is lovely. But I wouldn't feel right, not with all the people you've got out there.'

'But you've already met most of them, so what's the problem? You look lovely; you look younger, slimmer, prettier and ...'

'Classier?' said Evelyn a shade too quickly. 'I might look it, luv. But the minute I walk out there and open my mouth, everyone'll think I'm your char.'

'It's a Christmas party, for goodness' sake, not an Embassy Ball. Most of the people know you, and those who don't jolly soon will. Who are you so afraid of?'

Evelyn was now fiddling with the shoulders of the gown nervously. 'No one. Everyone. Well ... it's ... you don't seem to understand that I don't fit into this world you've made for yourself.'

'Not again, please. We've been through all this before. When you came to Brook Street you thoroughly enjoyed the whole day, remember?'

'I know. But all I did then was sit and look. Didn't 'ave to make polite conversation with people I know nothing about. I'm a Bermondsey woman, luv. I used to like chatting to people in the street and popping in and out of friends' 'ouses. Now all that's gone. I mean really gone, with them pulling down the streets to build these awful flats. Now I'm 'ere, in this lovely 'ouse – and quite 'appy, luv, so don't go thinking otherwise. All I ask is that you don't expect me to step into your world. You was cut out for it, and I wasn't. You can't make a silk purse out of a sow's ear.'

This last sentence Abby chorused with her, since she had heard her mother-in-law say it so often. 'No one is trying to change you. All I ask is that you be *yourself*. That's the secret. Just be yourself and come and meet my guests. It's Christmas Eve and I'm certainly not going to let you spend it in here.'

'What about Ross?' Evelyn was twisting and turning in front of the mirror, still unsure about her new image.

'Gone to bed saying the party sounds very boring,' laughed Abby. 'He's waiting for Santa.'

Evelyn clapped her hand to her mouth. 'Santa! Ooh, I almost forgot. Someone brought this here the other day, and charged me to give it to you on Christmas Eve.' She walked across to her wardrobe and reaching onto the top shelf, pulled out a small package wrapped in golden paper, and tied with crimson ribbon. 'Now I reckon 'e thought I was your char. So that just shows you.'

'He? Who was it?'

Evelyn shrugged. 'Never seen 'im before in my life. Just 'anded me this and left.'

Abby's heart was racing. 'What did he look like?'

'Oh, fair-haired, tallish, nice-looking fellow, I thought. Who is he?'

He had been to her home. And she had not been there. How deeply that hurt. Desperate as Abby was to open the package, she would have to wait until Evelyn was elsewhere.

'Well? Aren't you going to open it?'

She forced a light laugh. 'We mustn't keep our guests waiting. I can open this later.'

'You really think I look all right, then?' asked Evelyn nervously. Taking a deep breath, she said firmly: 'Right. Let's go!'

'It's a Christmas party, Mother, not the long walk to the scaffold!' said Abby, as she felt Evelyn's hand tightening on her arm. They walked down the staircase, past the Christmas tree and into the drawing room where fifty people were laughing and chatting. Jonathan met them on the threshold, kissed Evelyn on the cheek and told her she looked radiant. A steward walked past with a tray of champagne cocktails. Jonathan took two, and offered them to the women.

'Happy Christmas to you both,' he said, touching their glasses with his.

'Happy Christmas,' they replied, walking on with him into the drawing room, where Claudia was holding court. Surrounded by men, and standing close to her French Count, the model was dressed in a strapless, full-skirted gown of salmon-pink taffeta, which fell just below the knee. The Count de Courteil was charming, and spoke to Abby and Evelyn of his chateau in the Loire, and of the wine his family had made for centuries. Evelyn listened and said nothing. She had no idea where the Loire was, or what it was, but tried to look as though she did, content to let others do the talking.

Realizing that her mother would be fine, Abby wandered into the dining room and checked the table with a critical eye. The caterers had come up trumps and chefs stood ready to carve behind a table laden with roast meats, fresh salmon and all manner of salads, to be followed by crème brûlée, mousse, fruit salads and coffee. Candlelight shone on crystal and Abby thought her dining room had never looked so lovely. But her mind was on the small package upstairs. As soon as it was possible to slip away unnoticed, she went to her bedroom, closed the door and held the package lovingly, overwhelmed by sadness. He had been here, to this house; had stood on her doorstep hoping to see her; and she had not been here for him. Holding back the tears, she untied the ribbon and removed the gold paper to reveal a black velvet box. Picking up the card that rested upon it, Abby read Richard's neat handwriting.

*

O thou soul of my soul! I shall clasp thee again
And with God be the rest!

Browning! His favourite poet, she recalled. Raising the lid
of the box, Abby gasped in disbelief. Inside lay a pearl
choker necklace of three strands, with a diamond clasp.
Never had she seen anything so exquisite or given with
so much love. Now the tears fell freely, for this was a
memorial present, and Richard meant her to remember
him every time she wore it. Did he not know that the
little imitation pearl was loved just as much, and that he
was never out of her thoughts, and never would be?

Later, sipping champagne, smiling and chatting, she
thought only of Richard, wondering what he was doing this
Christmas Eve. No doubt he and his wife and daughter were
at Ashton. They would go to the Christmas Day service, and
the manor house would be decked out with holly and ivy, as
it had been on that Christmas ten years ago. Ten years! This
time next week, they would be toasting in the new decade.
What lay ahead? What would the sixties be like?

'Are you all right?' Jonathan sounded concerned as he
took her arm and led her to a quiet corner. 'You seemed
to be in another world.'

Abby sat down beside him on the sofa, and smiled. 'Did
I? Christmas does that to people. But the party's going
well, don't you think?'

'I most definitely do think,' smiled Jonathan, producing
a small package from his pocket. 'Happy Christmas,
Abby.' Smiling, Abby took the package and, from her
evening bag, drew out her present for him.

'Open yours first,' he said.

She did, and found a lady's gold wristwatch, small and
exquisite. It was far too expensive and said a lot more than
she wanted to hear. 'Oh, Jonathan, it's beautiful. But you
shouldn't ... I mean it's ... well, it's simply lovely, but
so expensive!'

'Acceptable, though,' he said in a strange voice. 'And

we've known each other nearly seven years, so I don't think you're being compromised.' Grinning, he tore the paper from his package and opened it. Taking out the silver cigarette case with his initials engraved upon it, he laughed. 'Now who just ticked me off for buying expensive presents? I shall treasure it always.' He leaned forward and kissed her gently on the cheek.

Abby's eyes misted over and she smiled at him with a deep warmth which bordered on love. 'Jonathan, you really are the best friend I've ever had. I wouldn't have come this far without your help.'

'Oh yes you would, young lady.' Jonathan put the cigarette case into his pocket. 'If the hounds of hell were snapping at your heels you'd kick them back and climb out of their reach. When I first set eyes on you, I saw a frightened young girl with enough determination to make her plans work.'

'Frightened? Good heavens, was I that obvious?'

'You were that young.'

'How awful,' giggled Abby. 'But that was your Miss Mansell's fault. She unnerved me.'

'She guarded me with her life,' said Jonathan. 'I miss her now that she's retired.' He raised his glass. 'Well, here's to Miss Mansell and to us.' They touched glasses. 'Happy Christmas, Abby.'

Moved to tears, Abby's lip trembled. 'Happy Christmas, Jonathan.'

CHAPTER SIXTEEN

Richard peered through the windscreen of his MG, but the wipers could do little against the torrential downpour which had brought traffic almost to a standstill. The lights of oncoming cars dazzled him, and his headache was growing stronger with each passing minute. Every bone in his body ached; he burned hot, then felt cold. *'Flu. The perfect ending to a bloody awful day!* he thought. A day he'd spent going over the books and stock at Glenisters, in an effort to pinpoint the reason for the store's decline since his father's death. His mother's attitude had been far from helpful. Still angry with him for turning on her, she had been in no mood for more accusations. Yet who else was at fault, if not she? Obdurate in her ways, unable to keep staff for long, she had lost her hold on the class of people who used to frequent the store. Glenisters was not keeping pace with the times, and their prices were high for the goods they sold. In her own defence, Milicent had said that since the 'right' people were no longer coming to the store, there was little point in buying expensive lines. 'In this day and age, when even the working classes have cars, people travel to London to shop when they want the best.'

'Rubbish,' Richard had said. 'Canterbury has good shops, and people come here from miles around.' And so it had gone on, accusations and recriminations. Rates were up, profits were down. Something had to be done. As Richard approached London, he knew, without a doubt, that he had influenza. *Not now – when I've so much to do.*

In the morning he had to meet his bank manager, who

was bound to ask him awkward questions about Glenisters' falling profits. In the afternoon, after a literary luncheon, he had to get to local Conservative Party headquarters, where talk of a by-election was bringing forth nominees for selection as candidate. To be laid low at such a time was too unfair for words.

He arrived home at eight o'clock where Samantha, on seeing how ill he looked, promptly sent him to bed. He slept fitfully throughout the night, and in the morning, when he fell into a deep sleep, Samantha telephoned his office. 'Honestly, darling, he'll keel over if he goes. Anyway, you don't want all those horrid germs floating about your head, now do you?' Remembering that some of her Chelsea Set friends had promised to telephone later, Samantha took the phone off the hook so that Richard would not be disturbed. The domestic was told not to vacuum, and Fiona was taken out by her nanny.

It was late on the afternoon of the following day when Richard surfaced. Slipping on his dressing gown, he crept downstairs to find Samantha lounging on the sofa, drinking tea and reading a book. She looked up as he entered and smiled. 'Feeling better? I was going to bring you a cup of tea, but you've saved me the trouble.' Her smile could not have been sweeter, he thought, watching her pour from the silver tea pot. Her face was carefully made-up, and she was wearing the cream jersey dress usually reserved for socializing.

'Been out?' he asked.

'I lunched with Henrietta. Thought it best to let you have the house to yourself. How's the head?'

'Still muzzy,' he murmured, feeling as though someone had driven a herd of elephants over him. Had she really been with Henrietta? If only she *would* have an affair, then he'd be released. As it was, he could hardly say, out of the blue, 'I want a divorce'. Still, he would never forgive Samantha for what she had done. Could she not see the look in his eyes that must, surely, mirror his feelings for her?

'Drink this.' Samantha stood over him with the tea. 'Would you like some more aspirin?'

Richard drank the tea thirstily, then sank back in the armchair, feeling weak. 'Another cup if there is one, and yes, I would like more aspirin.'

Samantha poured the second cup and walked out of the room, returning with the aspirin bottle. 'Just as sure as God made little apples, I'll go down with the wretched thing next.'

'Sorry. Must've caught it at the office.'

'Yes. When I rang them, I was told you were three down. You might have warned me! I'd have taken Fiona to mother.' She pursed her lips. 'If there's one thing I hate, it's illness.' Had Richard expected sympathy, he would have been hurt. As it was, he reached for the newspaper, and dragged his tired eyes over the print. When he saw the name 'Langdon,' however, his eyes opened wide.

'The firm Langdon Construction has been ordered to cease all building work pending a ministerial investigation after severe cracks appeared in the walls of a London block of flats. Allegations of dangerous building practices have been made by an expert construction engineer, who spoke of inferior materials being used in the reinforced concrete foundations, which could cause serious faults in high-rise buildings. A full report from the Ministry will be made available at a later date.'

Richard felt the blood drain from his face. Stunned and rigid, his hands gripped the paper tightly as the room span around him. *Oh God, dear God — it can't be happening.*

Samantha glanced at him in alarm. 'Richard, you look terrible! I'll call the doctor. Why are you staring at me like that?'

At last he found his voice. 'This. Didn't you read it?

Don't you ever look at a newspaper these days?' He waved the paper at her angrily.

'I've been busy. Why? What's the matter?'

But Richard was already on the telephone. His broker answered at once, and said he'd been trying to telephone all day. 'It's the Langdon shares.'

'How bad is it?' asked Richard, dreading the answer.

'As bad as it could be. Rumours hit the stock market before today's press reports. I tried to contact you yesterday, but your phone was engaged all day. By the time I tried to sell, nobody wanted to know.'

'What are the shares worth now?'

'Not even the paper they're printed on, old boy.' The tone lightened. 'All you can do is hang on to them in the hope that the ministerial report won't be as bad as forecast. God, you should have seen the floor yesterday! It was like the fall of Icarus. I'm sorry, old boy, but I did try contacting you.'

Feeling that death would be a welcome release, Richard replaced the receiver and turned to Samantha. 'He says the phone's been engaged all day. What's been going on?'

'I took it off the hook,' she replied, absently, then turned back to the newspaper, frowning. 'This is awful. Has it made any difference to our shareholdings?'

Richard smiled to himself, wishing he had a revolver to put to his head. In one stupid gamble he had lost his home, his father's firm, his integrity and his future. He stared at the wall for a full minute, unaware of his wife gazing at him, her face a mixture of confusion and irritation.

'Well, have the shares lost some of their value?' When Richard turned, Samantha saw the truth in his dead eyes, and felt her legs go weak. 'It can't be true. It can't! Jeremy promised, he was so sure. He said ...'

'Jeremy?' Richard's eyes flicked back into life. 'What the hell has Jeremy do with this?'

Realizing she had put her foot in it, Samantha would not demean herself by trying to recover the situation. 'Well, if you must know, it was Jeremy who first mentioned Langdon.' Seeing the strange look on Richard's face, she felt unnerved. 'He meant well, truly he did. He had shares too, he told me so. He's lost just as heavily as you, you know.'

'No, I don't know.' There was a long silence while Richard tried to take this in. 'Jeremy ... but I thought you said the tip came from Bingham. Why didn't you tell me the truth at the time?'

Samantha fingered her pearl necklace nervously. 'Because – well, because he knew you wouldn't buy if he had advised it.'

Richard stared at her, something akin to hatred in his eyes. 'Too damned right I wouldn't.' This woman had ruined his life. First Abby, and now this. 'Doesn't Jeremy edit this paper? Well, doesn't he?' When Samantha nodded, he went on angrily, 'Then surely he had wind of this long before it went to press. If he meant well, then why the hell didn't he try to warn us? One phone call was all it needed.'

'You forget,' said Samantha quietly. 'I took the phone off the hook.' Her voice was as weak as her knees now. She had never seen such a look on Richard's face before, and it frightened her. 'I didn't want to disturb you.'

'You didn't want to disturb me.' Richard repeated the phrase like a sleepwalker, then suddenly wanted to laugh. It bubbled up inside him like an erupting volcano and he knew he was on the verge of hysteria. Sinking into the chair once more he buried his head in his hands and took three deep breaths until the spasm passed. Jeremy had set him up. He had no proof of it, of course, but he knew it just the same. 'Sam, get it into your head that he did not phone us. Get it into your empty little head that he never bought any shares in Langdon, no matter what he told you. The man is my enemy. You knew that.'

Suddenly he realized how cold he was, with the deep gnawing cold of sheer despair.

*

In the drawing room at Ferndene, Milicent was white as she listened to her son. He'd arrived without warning on this Sunday morning, while she had been awaiting Brian Rivers, who was taking her out to lunch. She had expected Richard to apologize for his rudeness of late; instead he was telling her they were ruined.

'I ... I can't believe I'm hearing this,' Milicent murmured in a quivering voice. 'You stand here, in the home where you were so lovingly raised, and tell me you've gambled away everything your father took so many years to build? All because of your stupid greed?' She turned from his shamed face, and stared out of the window at the cold February day. It had begun to snow and already, beneath the chestnut tree, the lawn was covered with fine white powder. 'Stella was right. The estate should have gone to her.' Swinging round, she stared at her son with blazing eyes. 'What on God's earth possessed you? Did you once think of me, or your sister? Did you give any thought at all to your employees, most of whom have been with us for years? What's to become of them now?' Tears blurred her vision. 'First, my husband stabs me in the heart, then my son turns the knife. What made you do it, Richard?' she asked, trembling with shock.

Richard walked across to the fireplace and gazed down at the glowing coals. 'You have only yourself to blame, Mother. You turned Abby away from me, because you wanted me to marry the daughter of the local squire. But you forgot one rather important thing. The landed gentry are used to spending, and women like Samantha think nothing of running up large bills.'

Lighting a cigarette, Milicent drew on it, murmuring, 'You're Samantha's husband – you should have put your foot down. But no, you buy shares you can't afford, using the store as collateral, and now it's gone, you're blaming me. That's disgraceful, Richard. You've changed. My God, have you changed!'

Richard looked down at the hearth. 'Yes, I've changed,

and I've been bloody stupid too, because I trusted when I should have known, by now, not to trust a living soul.' He turned and faced his angry mother. 'It seemed that Langdon couldn't put a foot wrong. Oh, I had it on very good advice — advice given to me by your adorable Samantha, who had been used, just as I was used. How did I know Langdon was a crook? I really thought I was safe, Mother.'

'Yes, I daresay you did. Meanwhile, what's to happen to our staff? How long will it be before the store goes into receivership?'

Richard sank into the fireside armchair, wondering how he was going to break the next piece of news to his mother without her collapsing completely. 'The bank is not unsympathetic, and will give me one month to come up with the money. After that, they have no other course but to take the store into receivership.'

'We might as well give the staff a month's notice tomorrow,' Milicent sighed. 'Now I have no job, no role in life any more.'

'Why don't you marry Brian Rivers?'

'Well, that's a fine thing to say,' she snapped. 'You destroy the family firm, and then have the gall to say, "Why don't you get married"!'

'It may well be the only answer, for you.' Richard's voice was very quiet, and his knuckles had turned white.

Milicent's eyes narrowed. 'What's that supposed to mean?'

'Rivers has a house, I understand. You could live there with him.'

'Live in a damp little cottage out at Sturry? No thank you! This is my home as long as I don't marry. The Will was clear on that point.'

'The fact of the matter is that Ferndene goes under the hammer, too,' Richard said quietly, then quickly went on. 'I've been robbing Peter to pay Paul. Last year, I borrowed money for some shares against this house. They did badly, and, in order to pay back the bank, and save Ferndene, I had to borrow from another source, only this time the interest rate was higher. I can't go on. I'm broke. Ferndene goes too.'

'My home?' Milicent was leaning against the piano for support. Thinking she was going to faint, Richard rushed to her side but she pulled away from him, her mouth twisted with bitterness. 'You're saying that I no longer have a roof over my head?' Her face was ashen. She looked up at him, with accusing eyes. 'I shan't leave. They'll have to drag me out. I came here in the thirties, and turned this modest house into a home. I raised you all here, and suffered the war here. Now . . .' She covered her face with her hands and burst into tears. Richard hovered awkwardly. His burden of guilt was strong, but he felt no love or pity as he looked down at his weeping mother. 'What's to happen to me, Richard? Where am I to live?'

'I've already told you. Marry Brian Rivers.'

Milicent threw him a dark glance. 'And Stella? What of her? This was her home, too. Shall we move in with you and Samantha? You have a heart of stone. Ever since you met Abby again, you've been hostile to me. I think you've done this deliberately!'

'Oh, don't talk such rubbish.'

'It isn't rubbish. That girl has been nothing but trouble to me ever since I first set eyes on her.'

Richard could hardly believe his ears. 'Abby did no harm. You did it all yourself, Mother. Had you left us in peace, we would be married, I would still own the store and Ferndene would be your home.'

Milicent jumped to her feet, and squared up to her son angrily. 'My God, I do believe you're enjoying this. It's revenge, isn't it? You could save Ferndene, if you wished. What's it worth – eight, nine thousand pounds? You could find the money somewhere. Samantha has plenty, for God's sake. Won't she help?' Her mouth curled into a bitter smile.

'No. You'd rather see your mother thrown out onto the street.'

'You must be mad if you believe that.' Richard felt his head throbbing. He was still not over the 'flu and the journey to Canterbury had not helped. 'Don't you think I would give the earth to undo all this? Yes, I've been stupid and greedy, a complete bloody fool, and I lost the game.'

'We've all lost,' groaned Milicent, the fight going out of her. 'I'm surprised you think of it as a game.' Choking on a sob, she ran from the room, slamming the door behind her.

Richard paced the room, weighted down by the depression deep within him. Samantha had been as shocked as his mother, making it plain that she was not in a position to help, since her own money was held in trust until she was thirty. From this she only had a small annual allowance. 'I suppose Daddy arranged things that way so that ... well, so that no one could marry me for my money.'

When he'd said, 'It's a damned shame you couldn't live within your allowance,' she had resorted to tears, reminding him that he had a large store, and a good job, which her father had secured for him. How could he say she had driven him to ruin? It was unmanly and untrue.

Wandering across to the piano, Richard absently picked out a few notes. Into his mind came a picture of Jeremy, standing in the snow with a bloody nose, promising never to forget that day.

What was left? He had lost Abby, his store, his home and all hopes of a political career. No party would back a man who couldn't even keep his own firm from going under. Fine politician he would make! He would never recover from this blow. Never.

'And so if we're to move with the times, then we must change our thinking, and embrace ready-to-wear, as well as couture.' Abby sat behind her desk, surveying the dumbstruck faces of her top staff.

'*Prêt-à-porter?*' Madame Duval was unable to hide her horror. 'You cannot do this. Pierre Cardin was ... what you say ... blackmailed by the Chambre Syndicale for doing such a thing.'

Abby smiled. 'I think the word you mean is "black-balled".'

'Well, whatever it is, Cardin was thrown out. He shocked all Paris.' Her high voice could not contain her indignation, and she visibly trembled. 'And I came to you for haute couture, not this ... this ... *prêt-à-porter* nonsense.'

Abby sympathized with the woman, but she had been quick to sense a change in the fashion world. New young designers were stamping their style on ready-to-wear garments which had caught the eye of the young middle classes. Boutiques were springing up everywhere, bringing to the fashion-conscious a fresh appeal at half the price that couture could offer.

'But you *will* be working in couture. I shall double up on the collections, offering one in traditional couture, and the other for the ready-to-wear line. Of course, my designs will be expensive still, but accessible to those who cannot afford couture prices. I think Cardin was quite right. Fashion should be for everyone. And it will be, I'm sure of that.'

Roland was enthusiastic. 'I think Abby's right. If we try sticking to the old way, we'll find ourselves a moribund little outfit, instead of a thriving fashion house.'

Abby turned to Susan, knowing she had her full support, since they'd been discussing the matter for some time now. 'I know for a fact that we could have outlets in Harrods, Harvey Nichols, even in New York. If things go well, I intend to open my own boutiques. However, our couture side must remain strong.'

'It's a great idea,' said Susan. 'After all, we never make more than twenty of any one design, no matter how

411

popular, and, in that way, we stay exclusive. But this cannot sustain us against the competition we're going to be up against. It's changing.' Susan addressed her remarks to the rest of the group. 'New young designers are invading the fashion world. Take this Mary Quant, for instance. She's already cornered a large part of the ready-to-wear market. We'd be crazy to stand back and let it all happen without us.'

Roland was tapping his pencil on the side table next to his chair. 'But where are the funds to come from? We're still heavily in debt to the bank. I can't see them extending their loan.'

'They don't have to,' said Abby. 'We have backing from a textile company. They've served us well in the past, and we've been good for them. I propose the first ready-to-wear collection be ready for next March, along with a separate showing of our couture line. That gives me a few months to find a factory, and come up with designs.'

'What about the boutique?' asked Susan.

'I know of a place in Old Bond Street. The lease expires at the end of next year, and the present owner isn't going to renew. I want that lease, if possible.' Abby's eyes shone at the thought. Already she could visualize the shop, dramatically different from her usual conservative elegance. 'So keep your fingers crossed.'

'My God.' Roland's eyes opened wide, as he shot up from his chair. 'We shan't have a minute to breathe from this day on. A year is less than no time in this game.'

'That's why I depend on you all so much,' Abby said, knowing they were enthusiastic, save Madame Duval, who would come around in time.

As the meeting broke up, the intercom brought Avril's disembodied voice into the room.

'Mrs Carr, I've had a telephone message from a Miss Glenister. Are you alone?'

'Yes, come in, Avril,' Abby said, wondering what on earth Stella was phoning about now. Avril entered the room, saying in a hushed voice, 'There's something wrong, I'm afraid. Miss Glenister was very upset, and said a terrible thing had happened in the family. She asked if you would wait here for her to ring back. I'm afraid I had no time to get her number. She rang off so quickly. But the call wasn't from London.'

Listening in growing alarm, Abby felt certain that something had happened to Richard. A car accident! Was he injured, or dead? Stella must have been calling from Canterbury. In panic, Abby dialled Milicent's number. There was no reply. Why would there be! If Richard was lying in a hospital somewhere, his mother and sister would be there with him. *Oh God, I should be there, too.* The panic grew steadily and, for the rest of the afternoon, Abby paced her office like a caged lion, willing the telephone to ring.

It was a quarter to six when finally it did. Pouncing on it, Abby heard Stella's voice with a mixture of relief and disbelief. Richard was alive and well, but had lost Glenisters.

'What? I don't understand, Stella. You're not making any sense. Calm down, please. What do you mean, he's lost the store?'

'He's ruined us, Abby!' cried Stella. 'All because he gambled on the stock market and lost. Even the house is going.'

'Ferndene!' Abby gasped. 'Are you sure you've got this right?' Richard would never do anything so blatantly stupid, surely. Not unless he had been pushed to the brink of madness. 'Is Richard all right? I mean, he hasn't done anything ...'

'Hasn't jumped off Beachy Head?' snapped Stella, suddenly shed of hysterical tears. 'No such luck.'

'That's a terrible thing to say.' Abby was trying to sound calm, when all she felt was despair. 'You owe it to him to be supportive.'

'I owe him *nothing*! It's how much he owes everyone else that's causing the problem.'

413

'And how much is that?'

When Stella told her, Abby closed her eyes in horror. 'He borrowed all that to buy shares in one company? *Why*?'

'That's what *we* would like to know. He's become too greedy, I suppose. Sammy likes the good life, and I daresay my brother has a taste for it, too, by now. I could kill him, Abby, honest to God I could. Daddy should have left the estate to me, his only true and legitimate child. But no, the son of his wife was *far* more important. Men!' She paused for breath, then added more calmly, 'Anyway, you're family, and I thought you should know. I wish someone could help him out of this mess. I'd do anything to save Glenisters.'

Abby replaced the receiver, her heart going out to Richard. At the same time, she found it difficult to understand why he'd behaved so recklessly. Richard, of all people! He was the last person to take such a risk. All that money! Far beyond anything she could hope to raise. She was already over-committed with the expansion plans for the months ahead. Yet she had to help him. His life was in ruins, and he must be in the depths of despair. Such a man might feel ending his life was the only way out. Something had to be done. But what? Who was there who could help?

At the Oxford Playhouse, Stella made her way back to her dressing room to prepare for the evening's performance. Having such conversations backstage, while members of the cast and stage hands were constantly walking past, had not been easy. She sat at her mirror, her thoughts on Abby — rich and successful Abby, who still loved this idiot brother of hers; Abby with her expensive salon, her Hampstead home, her lovely clothes and face. Let Abby come to Richard's rescue.

Leaning forward to paint her eyelids, Stella smiled faintly, congratulating herself on her performance just now. Abby would be in quite a state, if she knew her half-sister. Somehow the money would be found. Abby had always had a soft heart and people like that were easy to manipulate.

That same evening, Abby telephoned Willard Moore, explaining how Richard had lost Glenisters, and asking if he could mediate with Richard's bank manager as to the sum owed. Shocked at the news, barely able to contain his anger, the solicitor listened to her request.

'I can't say more just yet, but if the money could be found, it would have to be transferred to Richard's account. Since you and the bank manager have known each other for years, I thought you might work together with me to try to save Glenisters. I just need to know the sum owed to the bank. His other debts he must clear himself.'

Completely mystified, Willard Moore agreed to do what he could, leaving Abby with one more call to make. She took out her personal address book, found the number she sought, then placed a call to Düsseldorf.

Karl was at the airport to meet her the following afternoon and, as they drove to Wittenhausen, Abby struggled to find suitable words. How could one turn up in a foreign country, meet the unwanted father of the man one loved, and then ask him for over forty thousand pounds? Yet here she was, doing just that on a cold, snow-bound February day.

'I absolutely insist on your staying at Wittenhausen the night,' Karl was saying. 'Hotels are depressing, and Frau Kruger loves having people to cook for. She's already preparing one of her very fattening dinners in your honour, so you'd better be hungry or you'll hurt her feelings.' He glanced at Abby with true pleasure. 'Then you must tell me what it is that brings you to Germany so suddenly. Richard is well, you tell me, so it is a great mystery. Nevertheless, your being here is a delightful surprise.'

Delightful surprise! 'Oh, Karl. I can't accept your kind

hospitality unless you know why I'm here. Believe me, you won't be so pleased. In fact, I think you're going to be very angry with me.'

'You mean, Richard still does not want to meet his father?' Karl lit up a cigarette and smiled. 'No, you wouldn't have come all the way to Germany to tell me that. Bad news comes better after a good meal. When we've rested and dined, you may tell me what it is that will make me so angry.' The Rolls turned into the long driveway, white now with snow. When the mansion came into view, shed of its marquees and workmen, Abby thought it looked dead, empty and forlorn, a spectre from the past which nobody wanted any more.

Frau Kruger and her husband were the mainstay of the old mansion now. They lived alone in the servants' quarters, kept fires burning, furniture polished, rooms aired and looked after the baron on the occasional weekends when he brought guests to his ancestral home. Ever since the baron's telephone call the previous evening, the Krugers had shot into action, preparing for Abby's visit.

As Frau Kruger led her up the impressive stairway, Abby glanced again at the oil portraits on the walls, wondering if they were all Karl's ancestors. If so, his lineage was a very long one. Small wonder he was so anxious to find his son and heir! Following the German woman along the landing she looked down to the hallway below, remembering when the house had been filled with people and music. She had been too nervous to enjoy it then, and too shocked to care about it later, but that night had marked a turning point for her. The vow she'd made after her bitter discovery still held good. If Milicent was sorry for her actions, she would weep before Abby was through with her.

Frau Kruger stopped at an open door, and stood back for Abby to enter. The bedroom was dominated by a four-poster bed with a crimson canopy, which matched the velvet curtains. The mahogany dressing table was heavy and ornate. In one corner of the room was a wood-burning stove and a large armchair with a tapestry-covered footstool. In the other stood a wash-stand with a marble top.

'I do hope you'll be comfortable.' Karl was standing on the threshold. 'We call this the Kaiser's room. Wilhelm came here for a shooting weekend around the turn of the century. He slept in that bed, so it's always been highly valued in the family.' He walked through a mahogany door which led into a narrow corridor-like room. 'This is your bathroom.' Indicating the deep bath with its wooden panelling, he smiled. 'The very essence of modernity when my grandfather had it installed! He had been to visit Queen Victoria at her home on the Isle of Wight, and saw Prince Albert's bath. When he came home, he copied it to the letter. It's old, but it still works.'

Abby laughed. 'Karl, it's lovely. But I feel badly, putting you to all this trouble.'

'Nonsense! The room should be used. I hate museums, and if I'm not careful this house will become one.'

Abby looked at him warmly. 'You spoil me, Karl. Yet all I ever bring you is pain.'

The blue eyes that reminded her of Richard shadowed slightly. 'And is it pain you have brought me this time?' Before Abby could speak, he added, quickly, 'No matter. All things can be overcome. You must not be so tragic, Abigail.'

Tragic! Was she tragic? Thoughtfully, Abby unpacked her suitcase, hanging up her short cocktail dress of sea-green crêpe de Chine, laying out her negligee and nightgown. Tragic, indeed! If Karl really saw her that way, then he could prevent more tragedy by putting funds into Richard's account. She sank down onto the bed, and gazed around the opulent room. Oh, Lord! What a thing it was to be treated like this, when she had come a-begging. Why should Karl give Richard that money? What love did he have for a son he had never met; a son who refused to meet him? Karl von Schreiber was, after all, a businessman, a top industrialist. To get where he was, a man would have to be astute, without sentiment.

Suddenly Abby knew that this was a terrible mistake. Karl would see Richard as a weak-minded, wayward son, certainly not trustworthy enough to take over his inheritance. Schreiber Industries would end up under a corporate name, managed by a Board of Directors. This house would become a hotel or a nursing home, and the Schreiber dynasty would end with Karl.

They dined in the small dining room, waited on by Herr Kruger, who watched Abby keenly to see if she was enjoying his wife's cooking. Abby cleared every course without any trouble, since each dish was superb: rich and with a light sprinkling of garlic, to which her English palate was unaccustomed. She enjoyed every mouthful. Only after Kruger served the coffee, were they left alone.

'Brandy?' asked Karl, holding the decanter.

'No, thank you.' This was it – the moment of truth, thought Abby, stirring her coffee carefully. 'I suppose you're waiting to hear why I've come to you like this, out of the blue.'

'Well, I *am* curious,' admitted Karl, pouring brandy into his glass. 'Come now, out with it. It cannot be so bad, surely.' He saw the candlelight dancing in her eyes, eyes that were as green as her dress. Her hair was loose, and burnished in the glow. Already he was a little in love with Abby, and the thought shocked him. She loved his son, and whatever had brought her here now had something to do with Richard, he was sure of it.

Abby began to speak, her manner beguiling, anxious and appealing, as she told Karl all that had happened. 'Oh, I know he's been a fool, but what Richard did was completely out of character. I wish you could know him, Karl. You would understand what I mean. He's just not the type; he must have been desperate. As far as I can judge, he acted on good advice about Langdon Construction. He

418

wasn't the only one to get his fingers burned. It caused quite an upset in the City.'

'Yes, I read about it,' said Karl. 'So now he's up to his neck in debt, and is going to lose his company.'

Abby nodded. 'And when he loses that, he's lost everything. He wanted to become a politician: fat chance he'll have now.'

'His integrity has taken quite a dent,' said Karl. 'Politicians cannot be seen to be weak in judgement.'

'It could happen to anyone.'

'Yes. But people who buy shares in such quantities must have the money behind them to laugh at such a loss if it happens. The boy has been a fool. I am disappointed in him.' He sipped his brandy thoughtfully. 'And you have come here to ask me to cover his debts, is that it?'

How terrible it sounded. What must he think of her now? 'Yes,' murmured Abby. 'I'm sorry. It's unforgivable of me, but I cannot help him myself, and I don't know anyone else who can. Karl, I'm afraid for him. Afraid that he might . . .' Her voice trailed off.

Karl lit a cigarette, then, picking up his brandy, walked over to the fireplace, where he stared down into the flames. Abby watched the crystal brandy glass shimmering in the glow of the fire, then her eyes followed the smoke which Karl exhaled. It curled upwards over the mantel, then evaporated, and she wished she could evaporate also.

At last he turned to her, and said, quietly, 'It took a lot of courage for you to come here and say all that. You must love him very much.'

The green eyes filled with tears. 'Yes,' whispered Abby, 'I love him very much.' Oh, this was far worse than she had imagined. 'He's suffered so much. If only you knew! Oh, I realize that you've suffered even more, but that was war. His suffering was . . . unnecessary. We could have been so happy!'

'Yes,' murmured Karl. 'You thought you were sister and

brother; then, on that evening you came here, realized that was not so. But it was too late.'

Abby sat quietly, wondering what Karl would think if he knew that Richard had a son. 'If only Milicent had told me about you!'

Karl gazed into his brandy. 'Milicent. Ah, yes. And what has she to say to all this, I wonder?'

'I think I can imagine.' Abby sighed, feeling her venture had failed. 'I'm sorry. It was wrong of me to come to you like this. Disgraceful, in fact. But I simply had to try to do something to help him.'

'But Abigail, if Richard will have nothing to do with me, why would he accept money from me? It is a great deal of money. If he should find out, would he not be angry with you, and return the money, anyway?'

Abby nodded. 'Yes. Yes, that's exactly what he would do. He has so much pride, you see.'

'So then — he must never know.'

It was some moments before his words registered. Then Abby's eyes opened wide in astonishment.

'You mean ... you mean you'll do it? You'll help him?'

Karl shrugged. 'He's my son, isn't he? Of course I shall help him — on one condition. That he does not learn who his benefactor is. As you say, he has his pride, and will only return the money.'

'On the other hand,' said Abby, smiling through tears of relief, 'he might come out here to thank you personally. And then ... well, this could be the very thing which brings you together.'

'You forget,' said Karl sternly, 'I have my pride also. I do not want my son coming to me because I was financially useful to him. So, is it agreed that you will keep this secret?'

Abby nodded. 'Yes.' What fools men could be when pride was at stake! They both needed their silly heads knocked together. Nevertheless, she would have to keep this promise, and that was not going to be so easy. 'Richard will probe and probe until he finds out.'

'From you?'

'No. When I make a promise I stick to it. But the bank will have to be told. I can take the cheque in on my return to London, but a covering letter from you should accompany it. They will never disclose the source then.'

As Karl started walking towards his study, Abby had another thought. 'Karl, when you write that letter, could you add one other proviso? It would help Richard enormously if the decision to sack his mother was taken out of his hands. You see, since Milicent has managed the store, it has declined steadily. She has to go, Karl. Either Richard runs it himself, or he appoints a professional manager to do it for him.'

Karl smiled, and nodded. 'Sounds like good business sense to me.' He paused, adding, 'If that is the reason — the true reason?'

Could this man see into her mind? 'Of course. How can he sack his own mother? But the anonymous benefactor can't be accused of anything, and Richard is let off a very sharp hook.' *And I shall have one small part of my revenge.*

When Karl had written the letter, he placed it in an envelope with the cheque and handed it to Abby, smiling.

'There. It is done. But if that son of mine gets into any more financial difficulties, he will have to fend for himself.' Breathing a deep sigh of relief, Abby placed the envelope in her handbag and held back a great desire to kiss Karl.

From the study, Karl led her to the huge drawing room, where Kruger brought fresh coffee. 'The last time you were here, you asked me which composer I favoured above all others,' Karl said, walking over to the concert grand by the windows.

'And you said Schubert,' replied Abby, pouring the coffee.

'And you seemed to expect that reply,' said Karl thoughtfully. 'Why?'

Abby took his coffee to him. 'Oh, it was just that when I was a child, Milicent used to play Schubert a great deal. One particular piece has always stayed in my mind. Somehow, when I saw this house, it came back to me, and now I connect it with you.'

Karl sat down at the piano and began to play. 'Was it this, perhaps?' As she heard the *Impromptu*, Abby was immediately transported into the past. She could almost smell Ferndene again, and feel Richard's presence. Closing her eyes, she saw him, looking up at her from the hallway, as she leaned over the banister. He had quarrelled with his mother, and, from behind closed doors, had come the strains of this melody. When troubled Milicent had always taken refuge in it. Now she knew why.

'Your favourite of all favourites.'

'She used to play it for me in the old days, since her touch was a good deal better than mine. We both loved it, and each other . . .' He stopped playing suddenly, as though the memories were painful. 'Still, that was a long time ago.' When his fingers touched the keys again, the room echoed to a Chopin waltz.

Sleeping in the Kaiser's bed should have been a thought-provoking experience, but Abby was too tired to care. From the moment her head touched the pillow, she slept until awakened by Frau Kruger with a breakfast tray.

The snowfall in the night made the drive to the airport slow and hazardous, and Karl rushed her to the flight desk with only ten minutes to spare. 'Do call me to let me know that you arrive in London safely, and that the cheque is in Richard's bank.'

Abby thanked him again. 'I wish Richard knew what a father he had in you. He will one day, Karl; I'm certain of it.'

Karl took one last look at the striking woman in her fur-lined coat, wondering if they would ever meet again.

422

Each time he saw Abby he was a little more in love with her, and last night had been hard for him, playing the father role when he wanted to be the lover. 'Goodbye, Abigail. When I come to London in June, we will meet again.'

From London Airport, Abby took a taxi direct to Pall Mall and delivered the envelope to the manager of Richard's bank, then went on to Brook Street. From her office, she telephoned Evelyn before anything else, and learned that all was well on the domestic front. Evelyn still could not grasp the reality of the past twenty-four hours.

"'Ave you been then? All the way to Germany and back? But you only left yesterday morning.'

'Well, I didn't walk. I took a plane and then there were cars driving me everywhere.'

'Why did you go?'

'Business,' said Abby, looking at the day's appointments.

'Business! In Germany?'

'Yes – business.'

When Evelyn put down the telephone her face was grim. 'Business, my eye! There's a man in this somewhere,' she murmured to herself. 'Please God, Abby 'asn't fallen for a foreigner.'

For Abby it was a relief to get back to work, and the rest of the day was divided between her studio and the workroom where the autumn collection was slowly being assembled for March.

It was Samantha who found Richard. He simply vanished for three days, making her frantic with worry. She telephoned Ferndene, alarming Milicent, then her parents, who'd not seen him, then friends – so very tactfully – only to draw a blank. Panic had then set in, and Samantha had spent hour upon hour driving around London until she was exhausted. *This is crazy*, she'd told herself. *Like looking for a needle in a haystack. Oh, Richard, where*

423

are you? Her mind raced back to the Sunday morning he'd insisted on driving to Canterbury to face his mother with the disaster. What had he been wearing? What identification did he have on him? She remembered him slipping his wallet into the inner pocket of his greatcoat. He would also have his driving licence. Had there been an accident then she would have been informed. Thoughts of ringing the police were tempered with caution. If Richard wanted to be alone with his thoughts, he would be furious if the police found him, and started asking questions.

Then, she had rung the salon, and learned that Abby was out of the country. 'I see. When will she be back?'

Avril had started at the sharp tone. 'Tomorrow.' Then the receiver clicked, and the line had gone dead.

So that was it! He'd gone rushing back to Abby, and she'd taken him away. Unable to believe Abby would do such a thing after her promise, Samantha rang her parents, saying Richard had left her.

'*Left* you?' Lydia's voice had been disbelieving. Her daughter was throwing another of her tantrums. Nevertheless, Richard's disappearance, at such a time, was cause for grave concern. 'Think, my dear. He's hurt and deeply unhappy. Where is he likely to go for solitude? You alone can know. Is there some place he's been especially happy? Maybe somewhere you and he have spent some time together? Think about it.'

Samantha had thought about it, and come to the slow realization that there had never been a place where she and Richard had been truly happy together. She recalled last September, when Milicent had told her of Abby's visit to Canterbury. Not a week later, a friend mentioned seeing Richard at the Zoo 'with a female friend'. The friend was being diplomatic, trying to alert Samantha in the most tactful way she could. It was this, more than Milicent, which had sent Samantha in tears to Abby's salon that day. The thought of it made her shudder. How she had demeaned herself before that guttersnipe. The Zoo? Had he been happy that day with Abby? It was a long shot, but anything was worth a try.

And so she had found him, sitting on a bench, huddled against the cold, his face unshaven, his complexion ashen, his eyes red-rimmed. Richard had wandered without knowing where he was. He had spent one night at Covent Garden around a bonfire with some tramps, and another in a small, seedy hotel. Early that morning he had ended up at Regent's Park, and entered the Zoo, since it was the only place where he could sit without being stared at.

Samantha's relief was immense, but he seemed to want no part of her warmth, taking himself off to bed with more aspirins and a raging temperature. When he finally awoke, it was to see her standing at the end of the bed, a smile on her face.

'Ring your bank manager, at once! I think your troubles are over.'

When Richard heard about the secret gift of money, he hardly knew what to make of it. 'But I *must* know. I can't accept that amount without ... yes, I realize what the letter says but you can understand that to accept money from a complete stranger could lay me open to ... well ... anything.'

'Allow me to reassure you on that point,' said the bank manager. 'It is from someone who wishes you well − I can say no more than that. It clears the debt completely. You have your store once again. However, touching the store, there is another proviso. Your mother is no longer to run Glenisters. It must be managed by you yourself, or by a professional manager. It's a term of the gift that I must adhere to as strictly as the pledge of secrecy.'

Richard could hardly believe he was hearing all this. Was he dreaming still? Who could it be? The only person capable of making such conditions was Abby. But where on earth would Abby get forty thousand pounds to give away? She was doing well, but all her profits were ploughed back into

425

the company. Where on earth could she have found such a sum?

When Stella telephoned and learned of the gift, she whooped with delight. 'I thought as much. I was on the phone to Abby the day Mother rang me. I know it's her, Richard. She's as rich as Croesus – but look, if it's to be a secret, then let it be one. Otherwise, who knows, she might take the money back again!'

Richard scratched his head, his mind spinning on a carousel of relief, confusion, happiness and guilt. 'I can't let her do this – not Abby. I can't accept it from her.'

'You must, you fool! You should thank your clever little sister for thinking of Abby in the first place. If I hadn't told her, you would be ...'

'Yes, I know what I would be. Anyway, you'd better tell Mother. Right now, I'm too ...' Unable to finish the sentence, he handed the phone to Samantha and walked into the bedroom, not wishing his wife to witness his emotions. There, he sat on the bed, put his head in his hands and felt the tears release the tension in his body. The pent-up emotions of the past week spilled out of him. He had been saved; pulled back from the brink by the woman he loved and he could not even thank her.

The following day had been a long and busy one for Abby, culminating in a painful afternoon, when the Countess Revedon had selected outfits for herself and her daughter to wear in the coming season. The daughter, who was rather large, and always under her mother's stern command, had wanted to wear dark turquoise taffeta.

'Don't be silly, Edwina. You'll look like a hot air balloon. Let Mrs Carr guide you.' Having said that, she then insisted on seeing design after design, taxing Abby's skills to the limit, to find something that would give her daughter the illusion of slimness and height.

Satisfied at last, she swept out of the salon with the

unfortunate Edwina, leaving Abby with a sheaf of designs and notes.

Susan entered the office with a cup of tea, and laughed. 'My God, I'll bet you're glad that's over. The Countess doesn't get any easier with the passing years. That poor girl of hers ought to start dieting.'

Abby had collapsed in the armchair, tired to the bone. 'I know we aim to please, but there are limits. I feel sorry for Lady Edwina, having to run the gauntlet of her coming-out year, when I know she'd rather give it a miss.'

At that moment, the intercom buzzed, and Avril's voice broke into their conversation. 'I've a Mrs Glenister on the line. Shall I put her through?'

Abby sat bolt upright in the chair and felt her heart sink. Samantha? What now? Had Richard refused the money, or had the thing she dreaded most actually happened?

Susan was heading for the door, mouthing, 'I'll leave you in peace,' as Abby went to the phone.

'Samantha? What is it?' she asked, her heart pounding.

'Abby, oh, Abby – something dreadful has happened!' Milicent's voice sobbed on the far end of the line. 'Oh, God, you must help, you must!'

'It's Richard!' cried Abby. 'What's happened to him?'

'Don't talk to me about him,' came the reply. 'He's responsible for all this. He lost the store on the stock market, and now I'm to lose my home!'

'But ...' Abby bit her tongue just in time. 'Yes, Stella told me about the store going into receivership.'

'Oh, that's old news. In any case, someone stepped in and helped him.' There was a pause. 'Was it you?'

'Me? No, I'm afraid it wasn't, although I'm very glad to hear that Glenisters won't be sold after all.'

'Yes, it's a great relief, although the bank is insisting on some very strange conditions.' Another pause. 'Are you sure you know nothing about this?'

427

'Nothing, I assure you,' Abby replied, smiling to herself. 'Why are you so upset?'

'It's Ferndene. That is to be sold over my head. Abby, I'm homeless!'

Milicent's pitiful voice, the cry for help, the weeping, pleading tone, did not move Abby.

'I don't understand,' she said coldly. 'You say someone had helped him keep the store. Why not the house?'

'Because he borrowed from another source against Ferndene, and now the creditors have to be paid. At least, that's what he says. But I think he could hang on longer.'

'Not if he's having to pay large sums of interest, he can't,' said Abby, wondering how many more shocks Richard was going to produce before this month was over. 'In any case, he doesn't live at Ferndene any more.'

'But *I* do!' Milicent's voice rose hysterically. 'Abby, I'm to be turned out of my home. I've nowhere to live unless I can buy back my house. Abby, my dear, couldn't you help me? A loan, that's all I'm asking: a loan which I will pay back, with interest, if you like, in order to keep the house for Richard.'

'For *Richard*?' Abby bristled with anger, as all the years of hurt came flooding back in one second. 'I can't see how it affects him. After all, he's married to the daughter of the manor. When Samantha inherits her father's estate, Richard will be living with her in splendid style. Why would he want Ferndene?'

There was a moment's pause, as Milicent became aware of Abby's intent. When she spoke again, her tone was conciliatory. 'Your father only bequeathed it to Richard on the condition that I remain there until my death, or re-marriage. Well, I'm not dead, and I certainly don't intend to re-marry. But because Ferndene is now in Richard's name, he has to hand it over to his creditors. I've only got a few weeks to find somewhere to live. I don't have enough money to buy a

428

place of my own, and no bank will give a mortgage to a woman.'

'Yes,' said Abby icily, 'I know that only too well.'

'So I'm asking if you could lend me ten thousand pounds. That is the estate agent's estimate of Ferndene's worth.'

'That much? Well, Ashton is an up-and-coming village, close to Canterbury and within commuting distance to London.' Abby let out a long sigh. 'But I really can't help you. That's Richard's job. My father bequeathed you to his protection. I can't save Ferndene.'

Milicent's voice was trembling with anger now. 'I don't believe that! You're rich and highly successful.'

'I'm also heavily committed financially.'

'But, Abby, this is your home.'

'Really? I seem to remember you turned me out of it.'

'Nobody turned you out. You just went, and we all missed you dreadfully.' Milicent's efforts to change tack were lost on Abby, who knew she must be choking on humble pie. 'Please, Abby, I tried to make you happy in this house. Now all I'm asking for is a loan. That's all, just a loan.'

'As I once asked you. Remember?' Abby was trembling now, and her voice contained simmering anger, held under control at some cost. 'Do you remember how you answered? First, you laughed, and then you said, not one penny would you loan me, desperate though I was. And I was asking for my own money!'

'I see. You're holding that against me still, after all these years. How can you be so heartless?' Milicent's voice rose in anger.

'I wouldn't know how, if I hadn't learned it from you,' said Abby quietly. 'I can't help − I simply don't have the cash. All my money goes back into the company. I'm sorry for your troubles, but I can do nothing.' Replacing the telephone, Abby sat rigid, trembling from head to foot. At last, she had her revenge. Not only was Milicent out of her job, she was out of her home also. Her stepmother

429

had made a supreme effort to swallow her strong pride, and actually begged from the young woman she disliked so intensely. Heart still pounding, Abby tried to relax. Now it was Milicent's turn to scrimp and save, and live in some God-awful flat, with no hot water.

Of course, it would never be that bad. William's life insurance would keep Milicent from poverty, but it wouldn't save her from a drastically lower standard of living. Milicent was reaping the harvest she had sown at last. Poor woman! What would she do now? Marry Brian Rivers and live in his run-down cottage? She just might. Her dented pride would send her fleeing from those who called themselves her friends. Even shopping in Canterbury would be fraught with hazards. How else could she explain away the sale of Ferndene, but to say she was marrying again, and moving to her bridegroom's house on the other side of Canterbury? Of course, she would never be able to entertain those friends in her new home, and they would never know where she lived. But Milicent would survive this inconvenience, without ever enduring the pangs of anguish she had forced on others.

The next morning, when a letter arrived at the house in Hampstead, Abby was so astonished at the handwriting, she didn't notice Ross rush off to school. Only as she heard the front door shut, did it occur to her she had not kissed her son goodbye. Vaguely aware of Evelyn clearing the breakfast dishes, she tore open the envelope.

Darling,

What a fantastic thing to do! It's all right, the bank insists on keeping your secret, but I'm not that much of a fool. Who else would have cared? Who else would have made certain that Mother was removed from the hot seat? She's furious, of course, and suspects you're behind it all. But you were quite right, my love. You've saved Glenisters, my reputation and my sanity.

I still hope to get into Parliament given a year or

*so, and I do mean to repay you one day. I cannot
have you the loser, when you've obviously borrowed
yourself to help me.*

You are never out of my thoughts, darling.
What a damn shame it all is!
Richard

*P.S. Please don't write back denying any knowledge
of all this, because I simply won't believe it.*

Abby read the letter with a mixture of joy and dismay. It
was all wrong for Richard to thank her, when he should
be thanking his father. She wanted to write back, telling
him the truth, but she'd promised Karl. At last, she put
the letter in her handbag to lock away in her office desk
with the sketch and Richard's other letter. If he thought
she was his benefactor, then so be it. At least it would
keep him from asking more questions.

CHAPTER SEVENTEEN

In Sotheby's auction rooms, Abby tensed, ready for the bidding, as the John Piper was placed on the stand. Certain the painting would never be hers, she was enjoying this brief respite from work just the same.

It was the end of May and the weather was as warm as England was colourful. She had found the perfect premises for her 'ready-to-wear' factory; her last collection had been very well received, and she had just launched her first perfume. *Autumn* had just the right blend of fragrances for the House of Carr, not too heavy yet with a hint of the exotic supplied by the experts in Grasse. The one great drawback to this phenomenal success was the amount of administration Abby found herself dealing with, instead of designing at her drawing board. It all seemed a far cry from those simple, hard-working days in Kensington.

As the auctioneer started speaking, Abby leaned forward in her chair, and gave a curt nod, her pre-arranged signal, from time to time. Soon, however, the bidding climbed out of her range and she left the fight to two determined collectors. One was a middle-aged man with a grey beard, and the other was somewhere behind her. The grey bearded man raised his programme one last time, the movement barely perceptible. The gavel came down and the Piper was sold. Though disappointed, Abby told herself it was just as well. Susan would have thought the painting a hopeless extravagance, Evelyn would not have liked it, and she never would have heard the end of the matter.

A collection of lithographs followed. Intrigued, Abby waited until the sale was at an end, then glanced across the room to see who had bought them. To her astonishment,

Greg Hadleigh was speaking to the salesroom assistant. His eyes met her startled gaze, and he strode across the room towards her.

'You look as though you've had a bad day,' he murmured, grinning.

She must say something, instead of just standing there frozen to the floor! 'For someone who just purchased those superb lithographs, I'd say *you* are having a very good day.' *Why was her voice so high?*

'It's good to see you again, Abby. What were you after?'

'The Piper.'

Greg nodded sympathetically. 'It went to the goat-headed one. I suspect he's bidding for an American millionaire.'

'I had no idea it would fetch so much.' Her face shadowed. 'Is it really going to America, do you think?'

'Doesn't everything, in time?' he answered curtly. 'They're buying up our inheritance, and we're too crippled with high taxes to fight back.'

Abby looked up at him, thinking how much taller he was than she remembered: attractive, too, in his silk cravat and suede jacket. 'Sometimes things that belong to England finally return to England. When did you get back?'

'A week ago,' he said. 'I have to collect my lithographs. Will you wait?'

Abby waited, wondering why she was doing so, and then he was standing before her once more, a curious expression in his eyes. 'I didn't have you pegged as an art lover,' he said candidly. 'Or were you bidding for him?'

Abby frowned. 'I'm sorry?'

'Were you bidding for your husband?'

As they emerged into Bond Street, Greg noticed how the bright sunshine fell on her hair, lifting the colours, as it had one Sunday morning in a quiet country lane. Then she had been in autumn hues; now she was all in cornflower blue. She was the most desirable woman he had ever seen.

433

'I have no husband,' Abby said quietly. 'What made you think ...?'

Greg looked confused. 'I was under the impression, at Breedon, that Jonathan ... well, I was obviously wrong. It was the wedding ring. A natural mistake, considering.'

Abby glanced at her left hand. She had worn Eddy's ring for so long it felt like part of her finger. 'My husband died many years ago.'

'I'm sorry to hear that. He must have been very young.'

'Yes. He was.' She felt compelled now to set his mind straight. 'And Jonathan ...'

'It's all right. Explanations are not necessary,' he said curtly.

Oh, but they were, thought Abby. Very necessary. Yet, how could she even begin without giving Greg the impression that her interest in him was all he wanted it to be? She would rather die than kow-tow to such conceit.

'Tell me about Hollywood. Did everything go well?'

'Not entirely,' he said, as they walked along slowly. 'It all comes down to compromise in the end. Like most writers, I hate having to write to suit commercial considerations. There were some bad moments, but the film goes into production soon. I might have to return to do more re-writes, especially if the director doesn't like the ending. Right now, though, I'm here for my new play. Rehearsals start next week.'

'Good heavens,' laughed Abby, 'your head must be spinning. You have to be the busiest writer around.'

'Not so busy that I can't take you to tea.'

Abby smiled, but shook her head. 'I'd love tea, but I'm already late.'

'Very well. How about a drink later on this evening?'

Abby paused, then shook her head. Something was warning her not to get involved with this man. 'No. Sorry, I've masses to do. Taking time out like this has put me way behind. You do understand?'

The dark eyes glinted like steel. 'Oh, I understand only too well. Does he keep the leash that tight, then?'

Abby stopped walking, and looked up at Greg in astonishment. 'What exactly is that supposed to mean?'

'The pity is, your sugar daddy's old enough to be your grandfather.'

The cheek of the man! The barefaced impertinence! Abby's cheeks burned. 'How dare you say such a thing? No man keeps me, Mr Hadleigh, either on a leash or in high luxury. Good afternoon.' With that, she turned, and quickly walked away. Greg caught up with Abby at the junction just in time to prevent her pitching forward into the busy traffic.

'Leave me alone! I could have crossed then.'

'Having saved you from being shot to ribbons, I'd as lief not have to scrape you off the wheels of a car,' Greg said, swinging Abby around to face him. 'Come down off that high horse, for God's sake. I didn't mean it.'

Abby's eyes blazed. '*Please* — will you just go away from me!' She crossed the road, turning into Brook Street, and walked at a rapid pace towards her salon. But it was useless. When she reached the building, Greg was right behind her. 'It's not any of your business,' she said, 'but Jonathan is a very close friend, one of the best I've ever had. I don't like your nasty insinuations, and think you should know you're way off beam.'

Greg leaned against the wall nonchalantly, a smile on his sensuous lips. 'Just good friends, eh! A man and a woman that close, and just good friends? It simply isn't possible. Especially when the woman is young and beautiful.'

'Of course it's possible,' said Abby, giving him a defiant look. 'Oh, not for the likes of you, I daresay. But among decent, caring people who rate friendship more highly than ...'

'Sex?' He grinned broadly, eyes dancing with amusement. 'Well, if that's what you think, little lady, then you're sadly in need of an education. Believe me, if you and Jonathan aren't sleeping together, that sure as hell isn't his choice. How on earth can you be so naive?'

His arrogance was too much. Abby hurried up the steps, then glared down at Greg furiously. 'Think whatever you like. But I will say it once more to make sure you understand the truth. Jonathan Bryce is a business colleague, and good friend of seven years' standing. I don't want his reputation damaged by silly gossip. My life is my own, Mr Hadleigh, and this is my company. Many people depend upon me for their livelihoods and a scandal of any kind will harm them quite as much as me. In future, I would be grateful if you'd keep your offensive comments to yourself. If not, I shall have no alternative but to sue you for slander.'

Greg looked at her for a moment, then said, in a mocking voice: 'My word, but you're magnificent when you're angry!'

'Quoting your own trite dialogue?' Abby gave him a cold, withering stare, then went into the salon while he gazed after her, with an amused and intrigued expression.

In the blessed quiet of her own office, Abby tried to calm herself but still trembled with anger. *How dare he*, she thought. *How dare he!* No man had ever spoken to her with such mockery and rudeness. No man, save Jeremy — but he didn't count. She sank into the armchair, suddenly fatigued.

Whatever made her think that Greg Hadleigh was fascinating? The man was a womanizer of the worst possible kind. It was obvious he held women in contempt. What a far cry he was from her beloved Richard!

When Abby had calmed down sufficiently, she went upstairs to the workroom, where Susan was working on a design.

'Any luck?' she asked.

'Luck?' Abby blinked for a moment, and then remembered. 'Oh, the Piper. No. Far too expensive.'

Susan smiled. 'Still, at least it made a pleasant break for you. You needed it.'

Like a hole in the head, thought Abby grimly. She examined the sketch, pushing all thoughts of Greg Hadleigh from her mind.

An hour later, a huge bouquet of flowers arrived. Called down to the office by Avril, Abby stood looking at the flowers in utter surprise, and frowned as she read the card, finding the strong scrawl difficult to decipher.

I was unforgivably rude and beg your forgiveness. If you have any charity in your heart, you will let me take you to dinner and tell you all this in person. Greg

Abby read the card twice, then tapped it irritably on the desk, torn between anger and sympathy. The flowers were lovely, and it must have been hard for a man like Greg to apologize. On the other hand, if he thought a bunch of flowers could make her forget the insult, he'd miscalculated. Walking into the hallway, she had a quiet word with Avril.

'If a Mr Hadleigh telephones, thank him for the flowers and tell him I accept his apology, but not his invitation.'

'Very well, Mrs Carr. I gather then, that you're out if he telephones?'

'You gather correctly. Thank you, Avril.' Abby returned to work, thinking her secretary-cum-receptionist an absolute treasure. Always unruffled, always diplomatic, Avril's convent education made her the perfect front for any business.

Greg Hadleigh did telephone; on that day, the next and the next, until Avril began to run out of excuses. Still the receptionist was unprepared for the determined figure who burst through the doorway one afternoon.

'I'm Hadleigh, and I wish to see Mrs Carr. Now don't tell me she's out, because I saw her come in some time ago.'

Avril remained calm and looked him in the eye. 'Mrs Carr is with a client. She has two other appointments, and will not be free this afternoon.' Her eyes swept over his tall, masculine body. She knew who he was, of course. That face had been in many magazines, and she'd seen him interviewed on television. In her opinion, he was a dish. Why on earth was her employer so anxious to avoid him? she wondered, her heart beating a little too quickly, as she sat under his intense gaze. 'I'm sorry, but all I can do is tell Mrs Carr you called in.'

'Tell her now,' said Greg, smiling gently. 'Please. I won't keep her more than one minute, that I promise you.'

'That I promise *you*,' said a voice from the stairs.

Greg looked up to see Abby in a turquoise cotton dress, her hair loose and slightly dishevelled, design sketches under her arm. The sight of her standing there, stunned him momentarily. Then he grinned, and said quietly, 'Call off your guard, Mrs Carr.'

The shock of seeing him turned to mild anger, as Abby walked down the stairs. The impertinence of the man! Still, now that he was here, she could hardly throw him out like a brawling fishwife. 'You'd better come into my office,' she said coolly.

Greg followed her into the office. 'My God, I think the Crown Jewels would be safer here than in the Tower! She's good, your secretary. Better than a Rottweiler, any day.'

Abby was still on her guard. 'Well? Why *have* you come here?'

Greg leaned against her desk, his eyes meeting hers. 'I've come to see you. I was idiotic and incredibly rude, and I want to make it up to you. When I thought that you and Jonathan were married I was, to say the least, bemused. Then, when I realized you weren't, I was jealous and angry. I thought you were throwing your life away on a man years older, and that you'd be hurt. I didn't want that to happen to you. So I lashed out with my tongue. Since then I could happily have bitten it off. Do you understand?'

'I see,' said Abby, after a long pause. 'Even so, there was no need for you to come here. Your flowers were lovely and said it all.'

'They didn't begin to say what I would have said personally.'

His intimate manner threw Abby into confusion. She retreated to familiar ground. 'Yes, well, you've said it now. Thank you for coming. I really must get back to work.'

'Stop being so haughty, Abby. You haven't the face or personality for it. It's time we stopped this silly feud, which I started and you seem determined to carry on.'

He was too close to her, his masculine presence almost overwhelming. Her legs weakening slightly, Abby sat down behind her desk to put a wall between them. 'I have no feud with you. I simply dislike your arrogance and contempt where women are concerned.'

'Contempt?' Greg seemed genuinely puzzled by this. He leaned forward to look into green eyes which avoided his. 'Oh, Abby, if you only knew,' he murmured softly. 'What is it? What's eating at you? I saw it at Breedon. You were unhappy then, and you're unhappy now. Is it a man? If so, he hasn't brought you much happiness. Maybe it's time you cleared the decks and started all over again.'

Abby's lips twisted into a bitter little smile. 'With you, I suppose. Look, I'm not interested in any involvement just now. I have a busy fashion house to run, and a son and mother-in-law to look after.'

'Listen to yourself,' said Greg. 'It's positively frightening for a young and beautiful woman to talk that way. If you were forty-five, fine. But you're not even out of your twenties, for God's sake. There must be more in your life than work and duty.'

'Such as love?' Abby's eyes were cold. 'I've had about as much love as I can take. It's brought me nothing but heartache, and I've decided never to get involved again. Don't talk to me about love.'

'All right then. What about fun? Enjoying life. Loosening up a little. Surely a simple dinner with a friend won't commit you.' His eyes were soft now, and his smile tender. Suddenly Abby found herself warming to him.

439

Friend! Warning bells sounded in her head once more. Greg Hadleigh was not the 'friend' type. Yet what could she say? He had a power which she found irresistible.

Sensing that she was beginning to waver, Greg seized the moment. 'A friendly dinner. Where's the harm?'

'Very well,' she murmured, at last.

'Tonight?'

'No. That's impossible.' She had promised to help Ross with his reading that evening. Such moments with her son were precious.

'Tomorrow, then.' Greg stood up, striving to control his strong desire to embrace her there and then. 'I'm at the theatre all day, but I should be able to get here for seven. I'll look forward to it.' With that he walked out of the office, leaving Abby wondering if she had made a dreadful mistake.

All during the following day, she was certain that she had. *Stand him up*, she told herself. She could always leave a message with Avril. But that seemed churlish and unsophisticated. Oh, well — let him take her to dinner. Refusing only made him more persistent. Let him find out how boringly uncompromising she could be. What was exciting about a widow with a child and mother-in-law? He'd be unlikely to ask her again.

After a busy day, Abby went up to the top floor to dress for dinner. Here she showered, made her face up in the models' mirror, then slipped into the chiffon dress she had worn for last year's Ascot. Softly draped at the shoulders, it fitted snugly at the waist, then fell in gentle folds of changing hues to below the knee. Sweeping her hair up into a chignon she added pearl earrings, then dabbed *Autumn* behind her ears and on her wrists.

Finally, she returned to her office to wait. The longer she waited, the more she wished she'd refused Greg's invitation. She was nervous. Sitting down at her desk, she took out the sketch of Richard, and suddenly felt as if she were betraying him. What on earth was she doing? In agreeing to meet Greg, she was pretending to herself that she was free. The plain truth was that she would never be free for anyone but Richard. There was still time to stop this silly nonsense, she thought.

As she entered the salon, she saw him. He was lounging on the sofa, reading a bound copy of his play, and making notes. He looked a little untidy and thoroughly out of place.

At her approach, Greg looked up and grinned. 'Your guard told me to wait, so I made myself comfortable. I'm early.' He stood up and walked towards her. 'Abby, you look lovely! But I've never felt so out of place in my life. It's unnerving, to say the least.'

His mocking eyes and voice caught her off guard, and she found it difficult to reply.

'Nevertheless, Dior, Hartnell and Amies all flourished in such an environment. It isn't the preserve of women.'

Her heart sank as she took in his sartorial efforts. Greg was still wearing his beloved suede jacket, although the shirt was white, and he wore a sober silk tie to go with it. As though reading her thoughts, he said: 'Sorry, didn't have time to go home and change.'

Feeling slightly put down at his over-casual approach, Abby tried to go one better. 'To be perfectly honest it's been such a hectic day here, that I forgot all about this evening until a little while ago. It's a good thing I keep a couple of dresses on the premises.' Hoping he felt deflated, she took his arm as he led her down the stairs.

'Since it's such a lovely evening,' he was saying, 'I thought we'd drive out of town.'

Greg was right. It *was* a lovely evening, warm and golden as they drove out to Goring and pulled in at a riverside hotel. Greg reached into the back seat and retrieved the dark suit jacket he had placed there earlier that day. Seeing the surprised look on Abby's face, he smiled. 'Come now – I'm not that irresponsible.'

She was even more surprised to discover that he had

already booked a window table, and that the waiters called him by name, smiling in welcome.

'You're clearly no stranger here,' said Abby, settling into her seat and gazing at the tranquil scene before her. Swans glided on the Thames, a small boat made its way upstream and a slight breeze stirred the green willows. 'It's beautiful – simply beautiful,' she murmured.

Leaning back in his chair, Greg studied Abby, remembering the first time he had met her in Joanna's dressing room. She had struck a chord within him immediately. Seeing her again at Breedon had only strengthened that feeling. In Los Angeles, his mind constantly drifted from work to the vision of Abby standing lost in an English wood. He had thought her married, and tried to put her out of his mind. Now, at last, she was seated opposite him, and his body burned for her.

Picking up the menu, he suggested dishes she might like, yet food was the last thing on his mind. Here was a woman of a different mould from his other conquests: a woman with class and independence; a woman with a fiery temper and some hidden tragic secret. Her dead husband? Was he the reason for that look in her eyes? Whatever it was, he would have to tread carefully with this one. He wanted her, and meant to have her, but she would never have him. No woman would have his heart again.

Embarrassed at the way he was looking at her, Abby said, 'Do you come from this part of the world?'

'I was raised in Hertfordshire,' he said, sipping his Scotch. 'My brother still lives in the family home, which is why Nelson had such a good time when I was away. I'm fetching him home this weekend. I miss the old boy very much.'

Abby was beginning to change her mind about this man. He was more human than she had given him credit for and she warmed to his presence.

'And what does your brother do?' she asked.

There was a moment's hesitation before Greg answered,

almost as though he felt her remark to be an encroachment upon his privacy.

'My brother builds planes.'

Allowing her eyes to open, with dawning realization, Abby said: 'Hadleigh! Of course. You're the Hadleigh ...'

'Aircraft Corporation? I'm not, but my brother is. I opted out of the family business long ago to become a writer, incurring much wrath and general disgust. Now I'm famous, everyone at home's very pleased with me.' He grimaced and drank more whisky. 'Let's hope I'm still in favour when I write myself out, and want to return to aircraft design.'

'Of course you won't write yourself out,' said Abby, sensing a brooding intensity below the seemingly light words. Here was a man with a terrible sense of insecurity, she thought.

Leaning forward, he smiled. 'Now that you know something of the man, tell me about the woman.'

Abby smiled and picked up the menu. 'She's very hungry, I can tell you that.'

They settled for Chateaubriand, with pâté to start with, then Greg asked suddenly, 'How long have you known Jonathan, did you say?'

Abby smiled with amusement. Was he still determined to believe his fantasies? 'Seven years. I like being with him.'

'But not in his bed.' The words struck like a whiplash.

Abby stiffened. 'Now you're being insulting again.'

'Sorry.'

'No you're not,' said Abby lightly. 'And frankly, I don't care. Believe what you will — my life is none of your business.'

The look in his dark eyes disturbed her, as he murmured, 'It will be.'

Pretending not to have heard, Abby asked about Hollywood. As they talked, she began to relax a little and, by the time the coffee came, she knew that Greg was thirty-eight, had flown Lancaster bombers during the war, was working on a new play for television, and wrote a column for a Sunday newspaper.

Abby spoke of her work, and the wardrobe she'd designed for Joanna's new play, currently running in Shaftesbury Avenue. Then they spoke of Joanna herself, Greg making her laugh at old theatrical stories about the actress.

When they left the restaurant, it was dark outside but the air was still and warm and filled with sensuous fragrances. As they stood by the river looking at the lights of the ancient building reflected in the water, Abby felt a stirring for this man standing so close to her. It was the air, she told herself: this heady perfect summer's night.

They drove back to Hampstead in bright moonlight. Greg parked outside the Georgian house, then looked at the still woman beside him. The moonlight had turned her skin to alabaster, and her eyes were shining. Gently, he took the radiant face between his hands and kissed her tenderly on the mouth.

Feeling Greg's lips pressing hard and hot against her own sent Abby's senses reeling. His arms slipped around her and she melted into the warmth of his embrace. He searched her eyes before kissing the lids softly and letting his lips brush her cheeks. Then, reluctantly, he released her, leaving Abby astonished at her reaction and trying to recover her composure.

Greg escorted her to the front door, watched as her trembling fingers tried to fit the key into the lock, then took it from her, and opened the door.

Abby said nervously, 'It's a little too late to invite you in for coffee. Thank you for a lovely evening, Greg.'

He nodded. 'It *was* a lovely evening.'

That night Abby slept hardly at all. Her senses had been re-awakened, and her body craved love. Richard's love? Greg's love? She was confused, and blamed the wine.

The following morning as she drove to Brook Street, she felt alarmed at the effect Greg Hadleigh was having on her. He made her react in a manner she found positively shocking. It totally negated her determination to be in control of her own life. With a man like Greg, she was not in control, she was all at sea. Was it simply physical, or was she beginning to fall in love? Was it possible that she could feel this way about anyone other than Richard? On the other hand, love had brought her nothing but heartache, and she was resolved to love no more.

Ignoring Avril's surprised look, Abby instructed her to tell Mr Hadleigh, if he telephoned, that she was out or otherwise engaged.

But Greg did not telephone, either that day or the next. At first, Abby was relieved, but when three days passed without a word from him, she started to worry. Why? Why had he pursued her as he had, held her as he had, only to ignore her now? Slowly, confusion turned to anger. He had been laughing at her, after all. Thinking her a cold fish, he'd hauled her down from her ivory tower, and must be feeling very pleased with himself. What on earth had made her think she had seen something else in those dark eyes of his?

On the third day, Avril buzzed her office. 'There's someone here to see you.'

Abby stiffened and her heart quickened. 'Oh? Who is it?'

'Miss Glenister,' came the answer.

Stella! Abby's shoulders fell with a mixture of relief and disappointment. Not a word had she heard since that frantic telephone call, but here Stella was, no doubt wanting another couture creation on the cheap. After the last outfit, Abby decided there could be no more favours.

'Very well. Show her in please.'

The office door opened, and Stella stood dramatically on the threshold, a fixed smile on her face. Her hair, now longer, was combed back to reveal a widow's peak. She pressed her cheek lightly to her sister's face, murmuring: 'Lovely to see you again, darling. Oh, I do hope I haven't interrupted anything very important.'

'As a matter of fact,' said Abby glancing at her watch, 'it's a very busy day.'

Stella sighed. 'I've just come from some dreary church hall in Acton, where I'm rehearsing for a television play. It's a murder mystery, and I get strangled halfway through the first episode, so it isn't much of a part. Still, what's television? Never watch it myself. The stage is where I belong. In fact, I might have drawn a lucky straw there.'

It was amazing, thought Abby, how Stella came and went in her life without mentioning the long periods of silence in between. 'What do you mean?'

Stella threw herself into the armchair and stretched like a cat. 'Well, this actress was in a car crash, and there's a panic on to find a substitute. I'm up for the part. The play's already in rehearsal. It's only a small role; still a lucky break, don't you think?'

'Not for the poor actress in the car crash. Was she badly hurt?'

Stella flicked a finger through her hair then shrugged. 'Haven't a clue. I don't know her. Anyway, her bad luck is my gain. It's the way of the world, Abby. You have to look out for number one in this life, as well you know.'

She stood up, walking across to Abby who was now at her desk. 'That's why I'm here, really.' Her eyes shone with excitement. 'You see ... well, there'll be the usual opening-night party, and I simply have to look my best. You'll never know how important it is. But ...' she flung her arms out in despair, 'I haven't a thing to wear. And you made such a marvellous outfit for me the last time, so I wondered ...' She waited, adopting the child-like expression she always used when trying to persuade.

'You wondered if I would play fairy godmother again,' said Abby. 'Look, Stella, it isn't that I won't, but that I can't. My staff are fully committed at the moment; the

446

order books are full. You would have to wait a good three months, at least.'

'Three months!' Stella's jaw dropped open. 'But I need it in four weeks!'

Abby laughed. 'Oh Stella, you really have no idea. It can't be done.' Then, she remembered a dress she'd made for a client who fled the country, without collecting or paying for it. Abby had altered the dress to fit herself, and worn it only once. 'There is a possibility. But first tell me how things are at home.'

'Home!' Stella's eyes clouded. 'We have no home any more. Ferndene was sold over Mummy's head. I know she rang you asking for help.'

'Which I was not in a position to give,' said Abby quickly. Stella gave her a strange look, and went on. 'Well, it was terrible. Poor Mummy. They practically had to drag her out of the house in the end. She really believed that someone would come forward, and save Ferndene for her. It was terrible, simply terrible.'

'Yes,' murmured Abby wryly, 'I daresay it was. And Richard? Is everything all right with him now?'

Stella's eyes gleamed with triumph. 'Ah, so it *was* you. I thought as much. You gave yourself away then, Abby. It's as clear as day that you knew he was off the hook.'

Abby thought quickly. 'Your mother mentioned it, if you really must know.'

Stella smiled in disbelief. 'What I don't understand, darling, is why having saved Richard, you then let Ferndene go without a fight.'

'Look,' said Abby firmly, 'you really must believe me. I had no money to help Richard, and I didn't save the store. Furthermore, you must make Richard believe it, too.'

'I haven't spoken to my idiot brother for ages, and don't intend to, either. Oh, don't worry. Your secret's safe with me. We're not supposed to know, so we don't know.'

Stella paused, and looked at her stepsister curiously. 'He disappeared, you know. As soon as he heard he was ruined, he went to see Mummy. Then he vanished for three days. Sam nearly went spare. Do you know where she found him? London Zoo, of all places! Honest to God, Abby, I really believe my brother is cracking up. Sam thinks that he contemplated suicide. We know that he drove to Dover, after leaving Ashton Green. My theory is that he stood on Shakespeare's cliff, and couldn't find the courage to jump.'

'Don't,' cried Abby in horror. 'Don't say such terrible things.' Heart pounding with alarm, she stood up and walked to the window. If anything ever happened to Richard, she was sure it would kill her, too. 'He's all right, though? Tell me he's all right now?'

Stella sighed. 'Of course he is. Why on earth does our conversation always come back to him? Thanks to Richard, we no longer have a home.'

Abby moved back to her desk, her mind on Ferndene. In her zeal to hurt Milicent, she'd allowed Richard's home, and William's pride and joy, to be taken from the family. The idea of returning to Ashton Green, but not to that lovely old house, filled her with depression. 'And where's your mother living now?' she asked.

'She married Brian Rivers, to my absolute horror.'

So Abby's surmising had been correct after all! 'Is she happy now?'

'Not very.'

A smile of triumph lit Abby's face at the thought of Milicent trapped in a small cottage with the man she had deceived William for. 'Then why did she marry him? I'd no idea things were that serious between them.'

'They weren't,' said Stella. 'But what else could Mummy do? He's so boring. Has no interests at all, save for bridge, which is how they met in the first place. I could never understand what Mummy saw in him. Still, I suppose she was lonely after Daddy died, and a woman alone never gets invited anywhere. So there you have it.'

Just as I want it, thought Abby, as Stella went on, saying

448

that all Milicent's fine furniture, including her beloved piano, had gone into store, until they could move into a bigger house.

'Not that such a time will ever come,' Stella added. 'Brian isn't the go-ahead type. More of a rut person really. Can't see what Mummy likes about him. And did you know he was a Roman Catholic?'

'Goodness, that means no divorce, whatever happens.' Abby looked thoughtful, and frowned. 'But I thought Brian was already divorced.'

'Separated. Mummy just told us he was divorced to stop us thinking of her as a home-breaker. But that's just what she was; he left his wife and children for her. Now the wife's dead, the children grown up, and Brian, having previously given his wife the family home, now finds himself without two pennies to rub together. At least he has the cottage.'

'Yes,' murmured Abby, with some satisfaction. But she was not finished with Milicent yet. Karl was coming to London next week and she had invited him to the opening of the Summer Exhibition at the Royal Academy. With a spare ticket in her possession, the opportunity was too good to miss. Smiling, she said, 'It's a shame your mother doesn't get out as she used to. I think she'd jump at the chance to visit the Summer Exhibition and I have a spare ticket for the opening. It's for two.' She took one of the tickets from the desk drawer. 'Give this to her, but for goodness' sake don't say where you got it. Tell her it was yours. If she thinks I have anything to do with it, she'll probably refuse to go.'

'She *was* pretty bitter about you when we last met. I wish she knew how kind-hearted you are!'

'Now, about your opening-night party,' said Abby. 'There is a dress which might look all right. It's a sea-green, with a cut-away panel in the full skirt to reveal green lace. If you like it, you can borrow it this once.'

Stella followed Abby up to the workroom, where she

tried on the gown. It fitted perfectly. 'Problem solved,' smiled Abby.

'You're a saint,' said Stella. 'And I'll never forget what you've done for me ... I'll never forget it.' She twirled in front of the mirror, her mind on the great event to come. So much depended on it. This gown made her look stunning. How could she fail?

Karl von Schreiber stood in front of a painting, stroking his chin thoughtfully. 'Portrait of a Man', by Augustus John, was one of the finest things he had seen in the exhibition.

'So much that is modern, I find difficult to like. But this is one of the most striking pictures I've seen in years.'

Abby nodded in agreement, then gazed about the room. The galleries of the Royal Academy of Art were so filled with people that she began to despair of coming across Milicent. As her eyes searched the crowds, she prayed her stepmother had used the ticket. If so, then today would be her final act of vengeance. Milicent could go from her life and mind for ever. At last the curtain would fall on the tragedy that had taken years to unfold, and marred every character performing in it.

They walked on, consulting their catalogues. Abby studied each painting with deep interest, but Karl preferred the representational oils and water-colours. He liked Sir Winston Churchill's 'Villa at Cap Martin', admired Annigoni's 'Eliza', showing Julie Andrews waif-like in *My Fair Lady*, but frowned at Lowry's exhibit, unable to understand what Abby liked or saw in the picture.

'It's child-like,' he said.

'It's evocative,' she replied. 'Can't you smell the smoke belching from those chimneys?' When Karl shook his head, she laughed. 'Well, you'll be in the North yourself tomorrow. Perhaps you'll remember this painting then.'

Karl frowned at the unwelcome reminder. His new engineering plant was already in trouble. Shop stewards kept calling for wild-cat strikes. Tomorrow morning he would meet them all: directors, managers and shop stewards.

'If there is no meeting of minds, then I may have to pull out of Britain. That's the last thing I want to do.'

It was the last thing Abby wanted also. For Karl was family, even though he did not know about his grandson.

Earlier, when they'd lunched at the Dorchester, his first words had been about Richard. Had she seen him? Had she heard if he was well? Abby had answered as well as she could, adding that it was high time Karl told his son about the money. At this, he had tensed, and quickly changed the subject.

At that moment, Abby glimpsed the unwelcome figure of Viscount Kelthorpe, and stiffened as he turned towards her. Briefly their eyes met. Jeremy nodded and glanced at Karl, his nose almost twitching with curiosity, then turned back to the elegant woman at his side.

Abby led Karl into the next gallery, praying Jeremy would keep his distance. They walked on until they came to a sculpture of Sir Winston Churchill, a small-scale version of the statue at Woodford. Karl admired the work as much as he admired Churchill, and would not be drawn away. Abby's eyes scanned the gallery for some sign of her stepmother. Only when she finally despaired of her ploy, did she catch sight of a familiar woman in blue, walking through the doorway. It was Milicent. *Thank you God. Oh thank you!* She must keep Karl in this gallery a little longer.

'I'd like another look at that large abstract, Karl. Do you mind?'

'Of course not.' Innocently following her, Karl frowned at the huge oil, his face a study of puzzled disapproval.

'What do you think of it?' Abby asked, knowing what he would say.

'The painter is an artist of sorts,' he said. 'A con artist.'

Stepping back from the painting, Abby saw Milicent moving towards them. She had put on weight and seemed quite middle-aged. The grey-suited man beside her was a good head shorter, and looked very bored as he stared around with vacant eyes.

Abby took a deep breath, and went into action. 'Good heavens! I just don't believe it.'

Karl turned. 'What is it?' He followed Abby's gaze and could see nothing to produce such a strange expression on her face. 'What is it? Tell me.'

'The woman in the blue suit. When she turns, you'll get the surprise of your life.'

Abby left her confused guest, and walked over to Milicent. 'Hello. I really don't know what to call you these days. I suppose it should be Mother, but that doesn't seem right, does it? Milicent sounds a little impertinent, and you're not my aunt.'

Turning at Abby's voice, Milicent's surprise was quickly replaced by hostility. 'You! I've nothing to say to you. Please go away.'

Abby smiled. 'Nevertheless, I think you might have something to say to the gentleman I'm with. I do believe he's recognized you, which is amazing after so many years.'

Brow puckering with puzzled irritation, Milicent sighed. 'Look, I would like you to . . .' Her voice trailed off as she saw the distinguished figure approaching her. The grey eyes opened in disbelief, and a hand went up to clutch at her throat. Motionless, she stood staring, as Karl drew close, and smiled down at her in amazement.

'Can it be true?' Karl murmured. 'Am I seeing things?' His astonished expression relaxed into a broad grin. 'Milicent, what a coincidence.'

Suddenly, Milicent came out of shock, murmuring weakly, 'Karl? *Karl?* What on earth are you doing here?' Painfully conscious of her years and faded looks, she patted her hair beneath the matronly hat, and made a supreme effort to recover her composure. Thirty years had changed her beyond belief, while he was more handsome than ever.

Now Karl became aware of the small grey man, whom everyone had forgotten, and looked at him expectantly.

'This ...' murmured Milicent faintly, wondering why God hated her so much, 'this is my husband, Brian Rivers.' As Brian shook hands with Karl, she added: 'This is Karl von Schreiber, my first husband.'

It was clear from Brian's expression that Milicent had made no mention of her first marriage and, although he tried to conceal it, Abby knew that he was angry.

Karl looked bewildered. '*You* are Milicent's husband? But I thought ...'

'They were married six weeks ago,' said Abby quickly. 'Congratulations to you both, by the way.' She beamed at Milicent. 'Stella told me. I'm so happy about it.'

Milicent smiled thinly, then looked Karl straight in the eye.

'And you? Did you bring your wife to London?'

'I am a widower,' said Karl softly.

Milicent had turned quite pale. A widower! And she a newly-wed. Oh, it was too cruel for words. 'It's been so long. Thirty years at least.'

Sensing that it was time to leave them alone, Abby turned to Brian, drawing his attention to a painting on the far wall. 'It's by Roger de Grey. I do like his work, don't you? This is a particularly good example.' So saying, she led him away gently, unwilling as he was to go. When they stood before the painting, she whispered: 'Look, I hope you don't mind. It just seems right to let them catch up a little after thirty years. There are things they might want to talk about.'

Brian stared at her coldly. 'It seems a strange thing. She's married to *me* now. And, if you want to know, I wish she hadn't come here today.' He felt like a third sock, unwanted and totally useless. His wife had been married to a German, and this was the first he had heard of it. What other secrets had the woman kept from him? he wondered.

From time to time Abby glanced back to see Milicent staring up at Karl with melting eyes. She had not been wrong. Milicent *was* still in love with her first husband. Abby wondered how, with love as strong as that, she could have left him. Then she recalled that Milicent had been a young woman a long way from home, and not accepted by her husband's family. Added to that were the sharp emotions of pregnancy.

Instead of sticking it out, Milicent had fled. By the time she had realized her mistake, pride, and a stubborn refusal to admit her error, had forced a wedge between the young couple. So, here she was, face to face with the man she'd been dreaming of all these years, and it was too late. Six short weeks stood between the longings of thirty years, and the possibility of those longings being fulfilled. It was almost possible to feel sorry for the woman, thought Abby. But she'd lured her stepmother here to show her what could never be. In the moment of finding Karl again, Milicent had lost him by marrying Brian Rivers.

After seven minutes had elapsed, Brian could tolerate it no longer. Duty done, he returned to the couple, who were so deeply engrossed in each other they barely noticed his approach. When Karl did, he immediately drew Brian into conversation. Then it was Milicent's turn to be drawn away by Abby, who whispered: 'I hope I did the right thing. Thought you and Karl might have things to talk about.'

Milicent still looked a little dazed. 'I don't understand, Abby. How long have you known Karl?'

'Surely Richard told you about the fashion show at the von Schreiber mansion at Wittenhausen?'

'The house at Wittenhausen!' murmured Milicent, remembering how she had never been allowed to set foot in the family estate. 'Yes, Richard did say something about a fashion show but ... he didn't elaborate.' Her eyes lost their dazed look, and became suspicious. 'And this is the first time you've seen Karl since then?'

'Oh no. I've seen him on and off during the past year.'

The grey eyes opened wide. 'And you said nothing to me?'

'Should I have done?'

'Of course,' hissed Milicent. She could have hit the stupid girl there and then. 'Did he never ask about me, or wonder where I lived? Did he never want to know whether I was married or widowed?'

'Why, yes. But I managed to evade his questions, knowing that you wouldn't want him to get in touch after all these years.'

So earnest were these words that Milicent could only stare at her in dumbfounded shock. 'What? Why wouldn't I want him to contact me?'

'Because in all the years I've known you, not once did you mention the man's existence, even when it meant everything to Richard and to me. I was forced to the conclusion that you must hate him. Many divorced people do hate each other, after all.' She smiled. 'Just before Christmas he became so insistent, it took some duplicity on my part to keep him out of your hair. Then, when Stella told me about you and Brian, I just knew I must keep him from you. But now that you're married it doesn't matter.'

In the tense silence that followed, Abby thought Milicent was going to strike her. Her face, contorted with barely-controlled rage, had turned quite pink. 'You should have told me,' she whispered, at last. 'You should have told me!'

'Why?' Abby's eyes had lost their innocence now, and Milicent detected a harsh note in the voice. 'Does he mean so much to you, after all?'

Milicent stared at her stepdaughter coldly. 'You did a dreadful thing in not telling me.'

'And you did a dreadful thing in not telling me.' Abby's voice was bitter, for all it was low. 'He does mean a great deal to you. And Richard meant a great deal to me. If you suffer one third of the anguish you put me through, you might understand what suffering means.'

Milicent's eyes opened wide as truth slowly dawned. 'This meeting was no coincidence, after all!'

'I gave the ticket to Stella, urging her to pass it on to you,' said Abby. 'I'm *so* glad you came. I'm sure Karl is, too. Did you know his elder brother died in the war? When his father died, he inherited Wittenhausen and the title. It becomes him: Baron von Schreiber. And the house is lovely. But then you never saw it, did you?'

As Milicent looked at Abby, she remembered the scruffy little cockney girl screaming, 'I 'ate you, I 'ate you!' That little girl was a cultured woman now, much celebrated in the fashion world, yet the message was still the same. She saw it in those green eyes, and realized how deeply felt hatred could be.

Karl was approaching them, his arms held out like a shepherd gathering his flock. 'Why don't we all go across to the Ritz and have tea?'

Weary and jealous, Brian shook his head. 'Thanks, but we've got a train to catch. We want to get to Charing Cross before the rush hour, otherwise we'll be standing all the way to Canterbury.'

Surprised at the lamentable dullness of the man, Karl shrugged. 'Then wait until the rush has abated. We shall have tea, then drinks perhaps.' He was looking at Milicent now, and wondering why her face was so ashen.

Brian was obdurate, however, and, holding Milicent's arm, started saying goodbye. She pulled away from his grip, then looked up at Karl with moist eyes, knowing she would never see him again.

'I would dearly love to stay a little longer,' she began. 'But it's better that we go.' Her lips trembled slightly, as she whispered: 'Goodbye, Karl.'

Karl raised her hand to his lips, and kissed it gently. 'Goodbye, Milicent. Maybe we shall meet again one day.'

She gave him one last lingering look, then rushed into the crowd, followed by her astonished husband.

Watching them go, Abby thought, *I hope your heart breaks, as you made mine break*. Then she sighed, doubting Milicent had a heart to break, in the first place. All she would feel was anger and resentment which would, no doubt, be hurled at her present husband.

As Karl stared across the room with an unfathomable expression, Abby thought of the tender look in his eyes and the tears in Milicent's as they had said goodbye, and wondered whether, in hurting Milicent, she had hurt Karl also. Suddenly, victory did not taste quite so sweet: 'Well,' she said, at last, 'that must have been a strange experience for you, after all this time.'

'Yes,' murmured Karl, eyes still focused on the distance. 'Yes, it was.' With an effort, he brought his attention back to the present and smiled at Abby. 'I hardly recognized her, at first. But then we've both changed a great deal after thirty years.'

'I don't suppose you got around to telling Milicent about the money?' she asked.

'No. We did discuss Richard though, and she has promised to try to persuade him to meet me. But it seems they have a poor relationship these days.' He sighed.

'Then let me tell him, Karl. If Richard knows the truth, he'll want to meet you. I'm sure of it. After all, what harm can it possibly do now? He's spent the money paying his debts, so there's no going back. What do you think?'

'I think,' said Karl, smiling down at her, 'that it is high time we had tea.'

Not to be put off, Abby continued the conversation, as they sat over tea in the Ritz. 'Richard thinks I'm the one who paid off his debt, and I cannot go on letting him believe that. It's time he learned the truth. I'm asking you now to release me from my pledge, Karl.'

Karl bit into a cucumber sandwich, and looked at her thoughtfully. 'If it makes you so unhappy, then do what you must. But I want my son to come to me because I'm

457

his father, not because I was useful. That was my reason for not telling Milicent.'

'I do understand, truly I do,' said Abby, sipping her lemon tea. 'But how will we ever know if your fears are justified, unless we put them to the test? Release me from my pledge and I'll write, telling him everything. After that, it's up to Richard. But even if he came to you, initially because his good breeding demanded it, the fact of his coming at all is a start. Something for you both to build on, don't you think?'

After a long silence, Karl said, 'Very well, Abby. I've been very selfish placing you in such an embarrassing position. You may tell him if you wish, but don't expect him to dance with joy at the news. Go ahead with my blessing.'

That same evening, Abby penned a letter to Richard telling him everything. She gave Karl's address, his full title and several telephone numbers where he could be reached.

You once said you had no intention of ever meeting him, but I beg you now to reconsider, and put from your mind any preconceived notions you may have. See him first, then make up your mind.

I said we must never communicate again, and this letter breaks that rule. But, my darling, I would like to hear that you will look upon Karl kindly and meet him. It would mean as much to me, as to him.

Your gift at Christmas was overwhelming, but you must never do anything like that again, never.

Stella told me that Ferndene is up for sale and that your mother has re-married. By coincidence, I was with Karl at the Royal Academy, when your mother and Brian walked in. It was quite a reunion. I believe she still loves Karl, but now she has Brian.

Ross thrives and I've put his name down for Stowe, because I think you are right. As he grows older, the

*environment of being raised by a grandmother and a
working mother can hardly be the best thing for a boy.
So now I only have a few more years of him, before
he's lost among hundreds of boys, tutors, tuck boxes
and trunks, coming home only at exeats and holidays.
They say it makes a man of a boy, but I dread the day.
Ross, however, is looking forward to it immensely.*

  *Meanwhile, my darling, I hope to hear that you and
Karl have met at long last. Please do not disappoint
me. Write back soon.*

I will love you always,
Abby

She read the letter through, hoping it struck the right note,
then stepped out into the cool evening to walk the short
distance to the pillar box. It was dusk. Lights appeared in
windows; people strolled past her on their way to pubs or
restaurants. She could smell the Heath, rich and earthy,
and suddenly wished she too could have someone to share
this lovely evening with.

At the postbox Abby paused, wondering if she was
doing the right thing after all. Deciding that she was,
she posted the letter, then stood with her hand on the
Victorian pillar, suddenly drained of energy. It had been
a day of triumph, surely, the *coup de grâce*, so why did
she feel like weeping?

'If the contents are that bad, then you shouldn't have
written it.'

The deep voice came from behind her. Turning swiftly,
Abby found herself staring up into Greg's concerned face.
Surprise robbed her of speech. 'What on earth ...?'
Unnerved, she shivered slightly.

Greg slipped out of his suede jacket, and placed it gently
around her shoulders. 'What is it? You look as though
you're trying to hold up the world and crumbling beneath
the weight.'

Abby wanted to lean against him for comfort and

459

support, but remembering how he'd slighted her, she stiffened instead. 'No, I'm fine, thank you. There's nothing wrong.' Frowning, she went on. 'I asked you . . .'

'You were going to ask, what the hell am I doing here,' said Greg. 'Well, I brought the dog for a run on the Heath, then found myself close to where you live. I was contemplating ringing your doorbell to ask you out for a drink.'

'Were you indeed!' she said coldly. It was only then that she realized how tired and unkempt Greg looked, rather like a man suffering from a terrible hangover. His shirt was crumpled, his tie loose and crooked, and he needed a shave. Glancing at his parked car, she saw the Alsatian sitting upright in the passenger seat. Ears alert and twitching, Nelson stared back at her.

Abby looked at Greg, wondering if he intended explaining his neglect of her after their one evening together. It seemed not. She moved away, determined that, whatever her feelings, she would not give this man the satisfaction of seeing them. She would be cool and offhand, preserving her dignity. 'I'm afraid a drink is out of the question. I only stepped out to post this letter. My family are expecting me back.'

'Then we go back to the house, and tell them,' said Greg.

'No.' Abby was walking quite briskly now. 'I've had a long and difficult day.' She handed Greg his coat, but he merely replaced it around her shoulders.

'Then I'll walk you back. It's getting dark. You shouldn't be wandering so close to the Heath by yourself.'

'It doesn't bother me,' she said, wishing him gone.

'No, but it certainly bothers me,' he said, taking her firmly by the arm. 'If you won't drink with me tonight, then how about tomorrow?'

His timing was way off, thought Abby wryly, her head still filled with thoughts of Richard. She was in no mood for dalliance, especially with a man who'd insulted her with his silence. 'I take it you live in this part of London, then?'

'No, I live by the river at Chiswick.'

'And yet you bring your dog to Hampstead Heath for an evening run? Do you do that often?'

Greg nodded. 'I've a lot of friends living in this area.'

Abby was no longer angry, but curious, wary of this man who could blow hot one minute, cold the next, and then turn up on her doorstep as though nothing had happened. 'What an extraordinary person you are, waiting outside my home like this. Most men would use the telephone.' She looked at his tired eyes. 'Have you been ill?'

Greg smiled. 'Only in my head. But the crisis has passed. Of course, there could always be a dangerous relapse if you insist on playing Turandot, the ice princess.' How could she possibly be expected to understand, he thought, when he hardly understood himself? After his marriage failed in bitter recriminations and a tragic loss, he'd decided never to allow a woman to gain the upper hand on his emotions. *He* was in charge, and *he* would call the shots. This had worked well enough until Abby stepped into his life. After a week of mental and emotional upheaval, he could not put her from his mind. It was his own fault. He should never have chased after her in the first place. Breedon Park had been a warning; he did not heed it and now the battle was lost.

That afternoon, he'd telephoned the salon to be told that Abby was out. Certain he was being given the brush off once more, he'd come here. Then he'd hesitated, and taken the dog for a run instead, telling himself he was behaving like Freddie Eynsford-Hill in *My Fair Lady*, hovering about on 'the street where she lived'. The thought disgusted him. Then Abby appeared, just as he was returning to his car. She was *here*, and it was a miracle. How on earth could he tell her this?

There was a movement at the window as Evelyn drew the curtains on the gathering darkness. She paused as she saw them both standing by the steps, and Abby could sense her curiosity.

'Goodbye, Greg,' she said abruptly. 'I must go back in.' She almost ran up the stairs to the front door which opened at her approach. Briefly she looked back to see Greg smiling up at her.

Evelyn closed the door, watching as Abby rushed to the window in the drawing room. 'Who was that, luv?'

Abby was staring down into the fading light. Greg had started walking back to his car. 'Oh, just someone I ran into,' she answered quietly, wondering why she hadn't gone for a drink with him. He had been so charming this evening. Yet he'd offered no explanation for his silence.

'Lives in these parts, does 'e?' asked Evelyn, a shade too casually, her fingers clicking away at the needles holding the sweater she was knitting for Ross.

'Chiswick, I think. He's a playwright, and a good one too. He's quite famous.'

'Good-looking,' came the response. The hands stopped driving the needles and fell into repose. 'Are you ... well ... will you be seeing 'im again?'

Blinking at the notion, Abby wanted to reassure her mother-in-law. 'Oh, goodness – I hardly know the man!'

'It isn't the feller you went out with the other night, then?'

'Yes. As a matter of fact he is.' There was a strange silence.

'Abby, I want you to know I don't expect you to go through the rest of your life without another man. No woman should 'ave to do that when she's widowed as young as you was.'

'Please, this really isn't necessary,' murmured Abby.

'Oh but it is,' came the firm reply. 'One day Mr Right is gonna come along – and when 'e does, I expect you to marry 'im. Eddy loved you as deeply as I do and, like me, 'e'd want you to be 'appy. If that means re-marrying, then it's fine by me. It'd probably be good for Ross too. So you're not to mind about me, luv. I'm not 'elpless. I can look after myself.'

Only then did Abby realize how much the thought had occupied Evelyn's mind. They were brave, self-sacrificing words, and even though the speaker meant every word of them, Abby knew there would never be any question of her mother-in-law living alone. She forced a nervous laugh. 'All this, because I chatted to a man just now! Mother, really.'

It was then she noticed Greg's jacket still around her shoulders.

The following day was very hot and Abby sighed with relief when she left her salon. It was seven o'clock and London's cafe society was out in full force. Espresso machines hissed in coffee bars, where youngsters gathered for the evening; the pubs had opened, and people sat outside chatting and laughing. In Hyde Park the Serpentine was crowded with small boats. Longing for the peace and quiet of her garden, Abby walked quickly towards her car. The day had been busier than usual, and she'd telephoned Evelyn warning her she'd be late home.

Abby was just about to climb into the car when a hand grabbed her arm, causing her to jump, and turn in surprise. She found herself staring up into the flaccid features of Viscount Kelthorpe.

'Did you enjoy the paintings?' asked Jeremy, a cold expression in his eyes.

Abby could hardly believe it. 'Did I *what*? Where on earth did you spring from? And I'd be grateful if you would take your hand off my arm.'

Jeremy released his grip and frowned. 'I called in, but was told you were all tied up.' He smiled suggestively. 'My mind ran riot, I don't mind telling you. So I waited in my car until you were untied.' The smile vanished. 'I've been waiting for thirty bloody minutes.'

Abby frowned. 'That keen, eh? Why this sudden interest?'

'You see, my dear, I'm a curious sort of chap. In my profession one has to be. So I keep asking myself why a nice young Englishwoman, such as yourself, should be seen in the company of an ageing German industrialist such as von Schreiber.' The thick lips curled into a sardonic smile. 'Or has the day come when the glow of Baron can melt the ice chill of Nazi?'

Shocked at his words, Abby could have struck him. Of course, Jeremy had done his homework and, of course, he'd got it all wrong. That was the nature of the beast. 'Jeremy, the older you get, the more boring you become. For one thing, the baron never was a Nazi. As to your other point, our meeting was connected with the charity he heads. Or have you something against charities now?'

Jeremy gave a mirthless laugh. 'I see you *have* been mesmerized by the title. But that's hardly surprising, given your background. And speaking of the Glenisters, just how did he get away with it?'

'You're talking in riddles, which is even more boring,' snapped Abby, but the alarm on her face told Jeremy that he had touched a raw nerve.

'I'm speaking of Richard, and, yes, I daresay that is boring. One minute the man is ruined, the next he's walking tall. Who saved him? His ex-love, perhaps?'

Puzzled, and worried by his knowledge, Abby was finding it hard to think straight. 'What on earth makes you believe that Richard was ever ruined?' she said, trying to sound casual.

Leaning close, Jeremy whispered: 'Because I was the one who ruined him. It was so easy! A word or two in a certain pretty ear was passed on to him, and the greedy fool fell for it.'

Dear God! Abby's mouth went dry as she looked into Jeremy's malicious eyes. '*You?*' It was the only word she could utter as her hatred culminated in a resounding slap across his cheek, that sent him reeling. Trembling with anger, she found her voice. 'You despicable bastard!'

Grabbing her arm, Jeremy glowered at her. 'Still the little slum girl at heart!'

'Would you mind taking your hands off the lady?'

Greg removed Jeremy's vice-like grip from Abby's wrist. 'What in God's name do you think you're doing? Lord Kelthorpe, isn't it? Quite an exhibition for Mayfair. Could even make a good story for your paper. I suggest you leave. At once.'

For one awful moment Abby thought the two men would come to blows. She looked around nervously, noticing that a few people had stopped to watch the ugly scene. 'Stop it, Jeremy. Leave now, and take your grimy thoughts with you.'

Much to her relief, Jeremy stepped back and, without another word, went to his car.

Seeing that Abby was trembling, Greg placed a comforting arm around her. 'What on earth was all that about?'

Never so glad to see anyone in her life, Abby shook her head. 'Thank you, Greg. It was all getting very unpleasant.'

'So I could see. I thought he needed rescuing.'

Tyres screeched, as Jeremy sped off in the direction of Grosvenor Square. Abby winced. 'How's that for a temper? The man is raving.' Trying to gather her thoughts, she stared up at Greg. 'And where did you come from?'

'Me?' Greg shrugged and grinned. 'I merely came for my jacket which you so kindly made off with last night. I can't work without it.' His eyes roamed from her face to her neat, high breasts, tight against the fitted bodice of her blue voile dress. 'Getting a shade fresh, was he?'

'Yes,' answered Abby, her mind still on Jeremy's veiled threat. *He had been responsible for hurting Richard and would try again*. The appalling thought that he might make the connection between Karl and Richard was pushed away as being an impossibility. Nevertheless, she was glad she had written that letter to Richard. Forewarned was forearmed. Suddenly aware that Greg was staring down at her anxiously, she said: 'I'm very grateful to you for stepping in just now. But I hope I haven't brought trouble you don't deserve.'

'Trouble?' Greg shook his head. 'Don't worry about it.'

'But I do worry. You've no idea how nasty he can be. I know from bitter experience how long that man can bear a grudge.'

'Then God rot him, as Handel would say.' Seeing how tense and afraid she felt, Greg took the keys from her hand and locked the car. 'Come on. You're in no state to drive anywhere just yet.' Taking her arm, he led her to his Bentley. 'How the hell did you ever get mixed up with him?' Climbing into the passenger seat without giving a thought to what she was doing, Abby replied, 'We first drew blood ten years ago. He got fresh, and I slapped his face.'

'So it's becoming a habit, then,' laughed Greg, as he eased the car out into the traffic.

Settling back in her seat, Abby watched his strong hands on the steering wheel and a feeling of peace descended on her. Yesterday she had found Greg's powerful presence out of sync with her sad mood. Today she welcomed his strength and his comfort. There was no tension in him now, and, for the first time, she was at ease in his company.

As they cleared the West End, she felt the wind lifting her hair. 'Where are we going?'

'To take Nelson for a walk,' came the reply. 'The poor animal's been chained up in the garden for most of the afternoon.'

'Your dog?' Abby looked at him sharply. 'But you live at Chiswick, you said.'

'Strand on the Green, to be precise. You'll like it there

by the river. This is just the evening for it. I'll take you to Nelson's favourite pub.'

The house by the Thames was early nineteenth century. Built of brick, it stood on the embankment wall, protected from high tides. Facing onto the river, its tall windows shone orange gold in the setting sun, almost giving the impression that the house was on fire. The river was low and inland seagulls waded through mud at the water's edge.

Greg opened the side gate which led to his garden and Nelson bounded out, his muscular body quivering with excitement as his barking shattered the quiet. Laughing, Greg dodged the rough tongue which tried to plant kisses on him, then brought him to Abby.

Still nervous of the animal, Abby made no sudden movement, and let him come to her. The brown eyes looked at her with keen intelligence, as if he remembered her, then his soft, cold nose nuzzled into her hand. Gently she stroked Nelson's head until he chased off after seagulls. They flew up screaming in alarm, and in no time, the dog's gleaming coat was covered in mud.

Laughing, Abby said, 'Do you have to bath him every night? Look at him.' The antics of Nelson banished Jeremy from her thoughts. 'My son's for ever asking me to let him have a dog.'

'Why don't you, then?' Greg stood with his casual shirt unbuttoned at the neck, one hand thrust in his trouser pocket, the other swinging the dog's lead. 'All children should have pets. Particularly dogs.'

'I never did. That's why I hesitate, I suppose. There were no animals in the house where I grew up.'

'And where was that?'

Abby told him, then let her eyes roam across the river. 'What an evening,' she murmured. 'And what a lovely place to live.'

Greg nodded. 'I don't think I could live away from the river now.'

'Aren't you worried about floods though?' As soon as

467

she'd spoken, she heard her own voice echoing back across the years. '*Suppose there's flooding?*' and the estate agent's casual reply, '*Oh, there's little danger of that.*' Shuddering as the horrors of that night came rushing back, she slowly became aware of a firm arm around her shoulders and Greg's concerned voice close to her ear.

'What is it? Are you all right?'

Abby nodded, forcing a flicker of a smile. 'It was nothing. Someone walked over my grave, that was all.'

'I think,' said Greg, 'that we should go back to the house. I'll cook some dinner. I'm a dab hand with omelettes.'

Abby smiled and shook her head. 'No. Really, I'd much rather walk along by the river. Anyway, we can't disappoint Nelson.' Feeling uneasy beneath the scrutiny of Greg's dark eyes, she suddenly found herself blurting out, 'My husband drowned in floods. I ... I saw him being swept away and ...' She stopped abruptly, embarrassed that she should have allowed this man to see so much of her life so quickly.

His compassion fighting a ridiculous surge of jealousy, Greg touched her hair with his fingers, and drew it back from the nape of her slender neck which he longed to kiss. 'I'm sorry. I had no idea he died like that. Come on. I think we could both do with a good drink.'

Nelson appeared with a sodden tree branch for his master, and barked. Absently, Greg hurled the branch along the path, watching as the dog chased after it.

'How old is he?' asked Abby, still feeling the touch of Greg's hand on her hair.

'Nearly eight now.' They walked on.

'At Breedon you said something about his being a Yank.'

'He is. I acquired him in New York soon after I arrived there.'

'And how long were you in New York?'

'Three years.' Greg stopped walking and gazed across the river, as though staring back through time. He seemed

468

so troubled, Abby said nothing more. 'The three years of my marriage,' he said, at last. 'When all that ended, Nelson came home with me.'

'Now it's my turn to be sorry,' said Abby. 'I didn't mean to pry.'

'You didn't. We're divorced, and that's that.'

'Children?'

Greg shook his head and for some time was silent. 'They say that good steel is tempered by searing heat. When I returned to London, I was able to write better and with more conviction. I was in my own environment and had no failing marriage to contend with.' He turned and smiled at her. 'So that's me! Successful writer, morose old bachelor, living in a house by a river with a dog for company. End of story.'

Oh no, it isn't, thought Abby. *There's something more, something about you which says 'Danger'.*

When they came to the City Barge, an ancient pub which had become fashionable with Londoners, Greg steered Abby through the people spilling out onto the river path. Their laughter and conversation disturbed the still summer air.

'Too crowded,' he growled, walking on until they came to a quieter pub farther along. 'This is my local. What'll it be?'

Abby asked for a glass of white wine, then sat down on a bench outside, watching the sky fade from red to purple. Gnats hovered on the air; voices floated across to her: and always the smell of the river that reminded her so much of Victoria Place. But in Bermondsey the river smells had mingled with industry and oil from the ships. Here it was simply mud at low tide with inland seagulls screaming at each other. Same river, different location, different world.

As she sat there, her thoughts returned to Jeremy. The man was obsessed with revenge. And who was the owner of 'a certain pretty ear'? Could he have meant Samantha?

Had Jeremy used Samantha to ruin Richard? He could only do that if she had complete confidence in him. And to have such confidence would mean seeing a great deal of the man who had once wanted to marry her.

Abby tensed at the thought. Could it really be true that the woman who'd fought so hard for Richard was now deceiving him? The man she claimed she could not live without? 'My God, you're a hard bitch, Samantha.'

'What was that?'

Abby blushed to the roots of her hair and smiled. 'Oh, nothing.' She watched as Greg set down the glasses, then joined her on the bench. 'I ... I must have been thinking aloud.'

Greg said nothing, sensing that her mood had changed. She seemed more brittle, more on the defensive, as they spoke of different things. He whistled to Nelson. The muddy dog settled next to Abby while she stroked his head gently.

Greg found himself talking about the play, and the difficult director, who wanted changes made in the text. 'The atmosphere's getting more tense every day. I always wanted a shake-down tour of the provinces before going to the West End, but the backers ruled it out.'

'What's it about?'

'A trial that took place after the Monmouth Rebellion. It rocked the land and made the notorious Judge Jeffreys a more hated and feared figure than ever. The prisoner was a woman in her seventies, a woman of high class and breeding with an estate in the New Forest.'

'What happened to her?'

Greg drank his Scotch and soda. 'She was executed.' He lapsed into uneasy thought. There was another problem which he could not discuss with Abby, and this was the director's insistence on bringing in Stella to take over a part. The actress playing the part of the old woman's chamber maid had been involved in an accident: hence Stella's sudden arrival. She had been a thorn in his side far too long, and he'd hoped she had gone to some provincial repertory company. Now she was back, making things very awkward. Greg was almost glad that Hollywood had summoned him.

'I'm flying to Los Angeles tomorrow. They phoned last night. Last-minute changes to the script. They're determined to change the ending, which ruins the whole thing.'

Abby heard him with a mixture of disappointment and relief. This was no time for Greg to be crowding in on her. Yet she would miss him. It was good to have a man in her life, she realized now.

'How long will you be gone?' she asked.

'A week, maybe two. I can't stay longer with my play in the hands of that idiot.'

The sky had deepened to a purple-grey now; street lights blinked on all over London. It was time to go. Greg tried to persuade Abby to have dinner with him, but she insisted on returning home.

As he held the car door open, Greg looked into her eyes and thought, *Christ, but I love you!*

Abby met his gaze, read the thought behind it, and averted her eyes quickly. As they drove back to Brook Street, she felt the beginnings of alarm. Physically she responded to this man, but that wasn't love. She loved Richard. He still dominated her mind, body and soul. She could never feel that for another man.

When the car came to a stop, fearful that Greg might want to kiss her, she put her hand on the door handle to step out.

Seeing this, Greg restrained her. 'You really do want me to scrape you from car wheels, I see.' He smiled gently, aware of her fear. 'Please, allow me to play the gentleman occasionally.' With that, he walked around to her side of the car and helped her out. 'When I'm back from the States, I'll be in touch.'

*

Still in her white satin negligee, Samantha picked up five letters the postman had just delivered, and glanced at them one by one. The handwriting on an envelope addressed to Richard was devastatingly familiar. As she heard him approach, she quickly pushed the letter into her pocket.

'Did I hear the post?' Richard was fiddling with his tie. 'Anything interesting?'

'Bills mostly. Two for you and two letters for me.' Samantha walked over to the breakfast table to pour coffee. 'Why? Were you expecting anything special?'

Detecting a harsh note in her voice, Richard looked at his wife curiously, then shook his head. He drank his coffee then rushed from the house.

Samantha watched him go, then took the letter from her pocket. *Abby again!* At any time their communication would be intolerable, but now, when Richard was so close to achieving his life's ambition, she could allow no hint of scandal to destroy his chances. It had taken years of hard work for Richard to be invited to Conservative Central Office for an interview. Thanks to her father and his influential friends, that was where Richard was heading in three days' time. He was a popular man in the Party, and a very hard worker. God willing, he would soon be an MP. He was very young to be a Member of Parliament, but his years of unstinting work had given him much experience. In ten years he could be a member of the government — in twenty, who could say? Number Ten, perhaps? Was all this to be put in jeopardy by that jumped-up creature from Bermondsey?

Tearing open the envelope, Samantha wondered why Abby was taking such a risk. Did she believe that threat had receded with time? She took out the letter and read the words meant only for Richard.

At first, her thoughts homed in on the gift which Abby chided him for sending. How dare he? Pale and shocked, Samantha sank down onto a chair and read on, trying to take in everything.

She'd known that Richard's true father was German, and that they'd never met. He had told her that his name was von Schreiber, and that his father was a doctor. Yet here was Abby telling Richard that his father was a wealthy industrialist and a baron to boot. A baron, for heaven's sake! That would be one in the eye for those friends who thought she had married beneath her class. The first rush of pleasure left her as Samantha realized she could tell no one, not even Richard. Worse, she had placed herself in the unenviable position of letting Richard go on believing Abby had saved him, when she now knew it was not so.

Samantha paced the room like a caged lion. What would she not give for the chance to tell him the truth: to watch his face fall with disappointment and see Abby for what she truly was. Sighing with despair, she poured herself another cup of coffee, wishing she hadn't opened the damned letter.

For a time, she wondered if she could get away with the old chestnut of 'Sorry, darling, I opened it by mistake'. No, not when the letter came from Abby. Richard would never believe it. There would be an horrendous scene which would push him into Abby's ever-beckoning arms, throwing his wife and his career to the wind.

Angrily, Samantha destroyed the letter.

CHAPTER EIGHTEEN

Abby sat in the gathering twilight, listening to a lone blackbird singing from the rooftop. She loved this beautiful walled garden, which had been a wilderness when first she'd seen it. Now, thanks to her efforts, and Evelyn's, it was a riot of colour, with flowering shrubs, borders, and roses. Clematis climbed along the walls, and in early summer, deep pink candle blossom shone among the new green leaves of the chestnut tree. It was a tranquil garden and a place where Abby always found sanctuary after the rigours of a hectic day.

This evening, however, she could find no tranquillity in spite of the surroundings. Two weeks had passed since she'd written to Richard — two whole weeks, during which she had waited for some response. Telephone calls and letters there were in plenty, but from Richard there had been only silence.

Wondering if her letter had gone astray, Abby had written again. Still there had been no word from him, and she was desolate. He was angry, she told herself. Angry and hurt that she could have deceived him. Her explanation had not been enough. The pain of his silence twisted her heart. How could he ignore her when she'd reached out to him? Perhaps he just needed time to come to terms with the truth, she told herself.

Then Abby saw the morning paper — and there he was, staring out at her from the front page, dressed in sober grey, his eyes kind and smiling as he posed briefly for the cameras. Richard Glenister had been selected as the new Tory candidate for Chiltingham in Kent, where the retirement of the sitting MP now meant a by-election.

This was why he had turned his back on her and Karl. They were embarrassments to him now. He had received the letters and, no doubt, they had given him pause for thought, but, in the end, he had put his ambition first.

Abby sighed. Apart from the pain Richard had caused, it was so unlike him to accept nomination, knowing the truth about Karl. If it ever came to light that he was the son of Baron von Schreiber, it could be an embarrassment for both him and the Party. Yet he had gone ahead, as though placing himself on top of a time bomb, saying, '*What the hell.*'

She looked up at the blackbird still singing on the rooftop. Richard no longer loved her. It was hard to take in. At least she had done the right thing by him in the end.

Abby went into the house and switched on the lamps in the drawing room. As soon as she had settled down with her sketch pad, the telephone rang. As she picked up the receiver, her heart was pounding. Maybe, maybe this time it *would* be Richard.

'Abigail Carr speaking.'

'Hi, Abigail Carr,' came the cheerful, deep voice. 'I'm back.'

Abby's heart took a crash-dive, then she realized it was Greg. 'Oh ... it's you. You're back, then.'

There was a slight, bemused pause. 'That's what I said. Hey, are you all right? You sound strange.'

Abby tried to get back on an even keel and mask her deep disappointment. 'I'm fine. Why?'

'As I said, you sound pretty strange, honey.'

'And you sound more American every time I hear you,' she replied, with a light laugh. 'How are things?'

'I didn't think I'd make it back in time, but here I am, a hair's breadth away from First Night. I don't usually attend them. I'm like old W. S. Gilbert, wandering around London until the final curtain. But I've a hankering to go to this one and I'd like you to come with me.'

'When is it?'

'Tomorrow.'

'That's very short notice, even for you, Greg.'

'I know, honey, but I only got in this evening, and half of me is still in California. So will you go with me?'

Abby thought of Richard's long and terrible silence, then lifted her head in a determined manner.

'Yes. I would like to. I've heard so much about this play, I've got to see it for myself.'

'Good,' said Greg, sounding deeply relieved. 'There'll be the usual bun-fight afterwards where we celebrate or hold a wake, depending on reviews.'

Abby replaced the receiver thoughtfully. Greg had a reputation where women were concerned and she was in no hurry to be just another in his long line of conquests. And there was something else about him, some deep and hidden thing which warned her to stay clear of this man.

But what harm could there be in going to the theatre? After all, it was up to her how Greg behaved. At least someone wanted her, she mused bitterly. Damn you, Richard! *Damn you!*

As the curtain came down on the final scene, the audience rose to its feet in thunderous applause. Glancing at Greg, seated beside her, Abby was glad for him. He had been so quiet and tense before the performance, drinking a shade too much whisky to calm his nerves, but now, as cries of 'Author!' rose from the auditorium, he grinned, and turned to her saying, 'This is where I have to leave you, honey. Won't be long.'

As Greg walked onto the stage, the applause rose to a crescendo, and foot-stamping joined the clapping.

Abby watched in amazement and sheer delight. The play deserved this applause. It was a piece of superb craftsmanship and she felt proud to be with Greg on this night. Even Stella had given a good performance. Later, she would see her backstage, glad to surprise her, since they had not been in touch for so long.

Greg gave one last wave to the audience, followed by a short bow, then left the stage. Returning to the box, he murmured, 'Thank Christ that's over. They seemed to like it, anyway. Now we have to read what the critics say.'

Abby laughed. 'With applause like this, does it matter what they say? It was fantastic, Greg, and I'm glad you asked me here this evening.'

At that moment a spotlight came on the box, blinding Abby, at first, while Greg immediately stood and took another bow.

Lined up on stage with the cast Stella stared up at the box, and the smile on her face froze. When the curtain came down, she rushed backstage, feeling her world crashing around her. *Abby!* Abby with Greg? It was unbelievable. In a daze, she sat in the dressing room removing her wig and stage make-up. Now she understood why Greg had ignored her for so long. Was there no one else in London, other than that wretched half-sister of hers? And to think she had gone crawling to her for a gown to wear on this special evening! How Abby must have been laughing to herself as she gave the impression of the kind and dependable sister. Bitch! *Bitch!*

Slipping into the lovely dress Abby had loaned her, Stella now wondered whether she should go to the party. To go would be humiliating, yet not to go would give Abby the biggest laugh ever. *Damn her, I will go and I'll have a ball*, Stella thought angrily. *And what's more I'll shine like a diamond and show Greg what a terrible mistake he's making.*

The party was held at Claridges. A small dance orchestra played, champagne and caviar were in abundance, and everyone was animated after the success of the evening.

When Greg arrived, with Abby on his arm, people turned and applauded. He made a short, warm speech, thanking the cast and their director. Then the director made his speech, congratulating Greg and the cast, and

477

the formalities ended.

Joanna arrived, and bestowed a dramatic kiss on Greg's cheek, saying, 'Darling — you did it again! I haven't seen it, I've only just come from the theatre myself, but everyone's talking and saying very nice things. Congratulations.'

From the far side of the room, Stella stared at Abby, thinking how serene she looked in her white silk crêpe gown. Her hair had been dressed high, with soft curls at the crown, the front combed straight across her brow. Greg's eyes never left her face, and Stella felt close to murder. Earlier, when Abby had looked for her, she'd managed to keep out of sight, but now the Queen of Fashion was gliding across the room towards her.

'Stella,' said Abby, smiling happily, 'I'm so sorry I missed you backstage. What an evening! Isn't this fantastic? I'm so glad for you all. It'll run and run, I just know it.' Her eyes ran a professional scan over the dress and she nodded approvingly. 'Perfect. It's perfect on you. I knew it would be.'

Aware of a strange hostility in her sister's eyes, Abby frowned. 'What is it, Stella? Is there something wrong?'

'What on earth could be wrong? After all, *I* don't have to live with the guilt of treachery.'

Nonplussed by the remark, Abby could only stare, then the reason for Stella's words became clear. 'Oh, you mean that business at the Royal Academy! I thought she would be pleased to see Karl again. If she took it badly, it was hardly my fault.'

Stella's eyes turned dark. 'Are you being deliberately obtuse? It's always the same old cry: "What, me? Oh, it wasn't *my* fault."' With that, she walked away.

'Problems?'

Abby turned to see Greg, who looked a shade anxious. Fingering a pearl drop earring absently, she shook her head. 'Strange. I thought she would be pleased to see me but ...'

'What did she say?' he asked, in a strange voice.

Abby looked up at him and smiled. 'Oh, it was nothing. A family matter, and I'm not yet forgiven.'

Assuring her that first nights always took people in different ways, Greg led Abby on to the dance floor, and, pulling her close to him, guided her through a slow foxtrot. Every so often she would catch Stella glaring at her with pouting lips and hard eyes. As though aware of this, Greg's arm tightened about her, his intoxicating closeness overwhelming her senses and driving all thoughts of Richard from her mind.

Suddenly, Abby felt loved and cherished. She told herself it was just the heat of the moment; still it felt good. Greg's sensuality had always set her off-balance, but she was not off-balance tonight. In fact, her head was surprisingly clear, even if her emotions were a little mixed up.

By the early hours, many of the guests, including Stella, had melted away, but the war-hardened stayed on until the morning papers arrived. A moment's anxiety plunged the party into deep silence, as the director read out the reviews.

'A work of profound significance,' said one.

'Greg Hadleigh shows us ourselves through the past. He is a gifted writer and never disappoints,' claimed another.

Abby felt herself carried along on the wave of euphoria, and was surprised to see the sky lightening slowly in the east.

'Time we were off,' said Greg. 'The Hanging Judge left half an hour ago, looking much the worse for wear. Hope he'll be all right for tonight's performance.' He touched the wisp of hair that had fallen over her brow, remembering the autumn sunlight kissing it. 'You must be tired,' he whispered.

Abby looked into his black eyes, her lips relaxing into a soft smile. She *was* a little tired, she realized now, but it didn't matter. Greg was weaving a spell about her which she didn't wish to break.

They drove through the deserted London streets, where

only dust-carts and milk-vans moved. Snug in her seat, black velvet cape pulled about her, Abby closed her eyes, and rested her head against his shoulder. To Greg, she looked like a tousled angel, lovely and a little crushed. Suddenly, he changed course, heading west to Chiswick, instead of north to Hampstead.

The house was comfortable, cluttered and badly in need of a woman's touch. Books and papers lay everywhere, but Abby hardly noticed, as Greg pulled her into his arms, kissing her with a passion and force that took her by surprise. She tried to move, but he strengthened his hold so that it was impossible to push away from him. Not that she had any such intention. At this moment, Abby desired him as much as he desired her, and her entire body went limp, as he gently eased his tongue into her mouth. His lips slid down her neck and he buried his face in her perfumed flesh, his desire for her deepening as she yielded to him. Slowly his hands slid down her back, and the white dress slipped to her feet. 'Dear God, how I love you,' he murmured, picking her up and carrying her to his bedroom.

She could hear the seagulls crying overhead, as she lay naked in the bed, and saw his strong, suntanned body leaning over her. Placing her arms around him, she stroked his back, feeling his muscles beneath her fingers; her body was on fire and, as his hands caressed her breasts, all the sensuality she had thought never to feel again coursed through her being. His lips sought her nipples, and they hardened under his tongue; his hands slid down to stroke the smooth silk skin of her belly, then moved on, and she quivered under his touch. He wanted her then, but held back, arousing her to exquisite rapture, before finally taking her. She moved and moaned against him, her body reaching the heights of ecstasy as their lovemaking exploded in its climax. Then she clasped him to her, and was content.

*

480

When Abby awoke, she was lying snug against Greg's naked body, her head nestled in the crook of his arm. He looked so peaceful in sleep, she thought, quite unlike the dominant man who had brought her to the peak of ecstasy with a passion almost bordering on violence.

Slowly she eased away from him, and, pulling the quilt around her nakedness, walked across to the window. The sun had risen now, its bright summer rays making the Thames dance and sparkle before her. An early morning train rumbled across the bridge, and gulls still cried overhead.

Abby glanced back at the large bed, remembering the searing passion of a short while ago. She had never experienced anything like it, not even with Richard. How many women had Greg lain with over the years? How was it he knew so much about them? she wondered, brushing back her hair. Had he made love to others in the same way he'd made love to her? Somehow he'd made her feel very special, like the only one. Could a man make love in that manner unless he really cared? She hardly knew him, yet she had been compliant, allowing him to dominate her completely. The memory of it now should shock, but it didn't.

Greg stirred and opened his eyes, surprised and perturbed to find Abby gone from his side. Then he saw her by the window, the light of the sun forming a halo around her head as she gazed at the river.

Pulling on his silk robe, he walked over to her, and kissed her neck, then her mouth.

'You cried out in your sleep.'

'I did?' Abby almost moaned as his touch sent small shocks through her body. She looked up into his dark, tender eyes and tried to remember. Had she dreamt of the flood again? How many times had she woken trembling in the darkness, trying to still her pounding heart? Now she recalled a moment, when she had awoken to find Greg holding her tightly, trying to calm her down. He was

481

so protective and loving that she'd clung to him like a frightened child. Then he had kissed her and taken her once more, only this time with loving gentleness. Yes, she thought now, that had been the best moment of all.

From that moment on, Greg was determined to sweep Abby off her feet, leaving her breathless, unable to guess at his next move, and unable to think straight.

In London they dined mostly at Rules and the Café Royal, where his friends soon became hers. They made passionate love in his house by the river, but were suitably restrained at her house in Hampstead, where Greg became genuinely fond of Ross and Evelyn.

Ross took to Greg straight away and adored Nelson, running with him on the Heath, and grooming him until his coat shone. Evelyn, too, began to like Greg, but it took a little longer, since she did not give of herself so readily and needed to get the measure of this man who was about to take Abby and Ross away from her.

For the first time in years, Abby felt truly happy. The past was consigned to the past, and her life was starting anew. Was she in love? She hardly knew in the whirl of parties and love-making. By day, she worked so hard there was little time to think. All Abby knew for certain was that Greg now dominated her completely. Gone was the strained intensity which had earlier put her on her guard against him. His play was a huge box-office success, the film had opened to critical acclaim, and he was already at work on another stage play. Somehow, in all this excitement, his thought processes were firing on all cylinders. Greg Hadleigh was a happy man, a man deeply in love.

Then, quite suddenly, everything changed.

Greg became quiet and moody. Abby feared he was tiring of her. When he told her that he needed a little more space, solitude and time to think about his play, she knew it was the end.

They were driving back to Hampstead, after dining with friends, and, in the long pause that followed, all she could take in were his hands on the wheel, those strong hands which had caressed her so tenderly.

Trying to hold back the tears, she answered in a shaky whisper: 'Yes, well, I too have been neglecting my work. And we are both professional people, after all.'

Glancing at her quickly, Greg frowned. 'I'm like this, Abby. I have to get away from people, even you. It's part of my nature. Part of being a writer, I suppose. But it's how I am.'

Abby heard him in silence, her throat aching, her eyes brimming with tears. What a fool she had been to allow herself to be carried along like that! Greg was telling her he no longer loved her. It was over. Ross would be broken-hearted once more and she would say to herself, *never again*. Why couldn't she learn? Why was she so good at running a large fashion house, yet incapable of managing her own love life?

When they arrived at the house, she turned to him, eyes glistening. 'So then, I shan't be seeing you again. Is that it?'

Greg stared ahead, his jaw tensing. He swallowed hard and murmured thickly, 'Abby, I can't share you with anyone. I can't go through all that again.'

Surprise flickered across her face. 'What? That's a strange thing to say.' It was Jonathan, of course. She had been forced to cancel an evening with Greg to meet Jonathan in the course of business. Now she realized he was jealous and it made her angry. Why couldn't he trust her? 'I thought we'd gone beyond all that,' she said, opening the car door. 'But if we're going to have all this nonsense every so often, it's best we say goodbye now. I won't be treated like this.' With that, she got out and slammed the car door.

Greg said nothing, and drove off, leaving her standing there in disbelief. He was angry with her, and all over nothing.

Evelyn was still up, and asked why Greg hadn't come

in. Abby forced a cheerful smile, although her heart was heavy, and said he had masses of work to do. 'He's burning the midnight oil. We ... we shan't be seeing so much of each other for a while.' She glanced at her mother-in-law. 'And you should be in bed. That's where I'm going. So goodnight, darling.'

Evelyn watched as Abby climbed the stairs. 'Are you gonner marry 'im?'

Abby paused, then turned her head slowly. 'It seems not.'

Frowning, Evelyn started up after her. 'You 'aven't fallen out already, 'ave you?' She seemed genuinely distressed. 'Because I'd like you to know right now that I think 'e's a lovely man. Just right for you. I'd love you both to marry, I would. Ross would like it too. Just wanted you to know that.'

Keeping her head averted, so her tears could not be seen, Abby murmured, 'Thank you. But it's not likely that we shall be getting married.' With that, she went to her room and sank onto her bed with a feeling of deep dismay. What could have happened? What had she said or done to bring about such a devastating change in Greg? Now that she thought about it, she realized it could have little to do with Jonathan. No, Greg was tired of her, and on the look-out for fresh conquests. She'd been a fool; she had ignored the warnings, and fallen under his spell.

A week later, in the house at Chiswick, Greg stared out of his study window. The sky was dark and threatened to storm. The Thames was choppy and grey before him. A rowing eight sculled past, and he could just hear the coxwain's shouts.

Having written two lines all day, smoked three packets of cigarettes and finished a bottle of malt whisky, his mind now returned to Stella's words, as she'd sat in this room, accusing him of playing God with people's lives. At first, her sudden arrival had embarrassed him. He was happy, working well and deeply in love. This was the last thing he needed. Having listened to her words of anger, he asked her to leave.

'Look, Stella, I've no time for all this. You knew that our relationship was nothing serious, just a . . .'

'One night stand that went on for three months?' Stella's lips had tightened, and she glanced out of the window on a dismal rain-swept scene. 'God, what a place to live! So dreary in this weather. You should have taken my advice and got this room redecorated. It wants lighter paint on the walls.'

'Stella, I've a great deal of work to get through, so please . . .'

'Is Abby just a rather long one night stand, as well?' The smile that played on her lips was mirthless. 'I suppose that turned you on a bit, tossing me aside for my own cousin. I'll bet you haven't told her about me. If I know Abby, she's not the type to want my cast-offs. She had too much of that when we were young.'

Angry now, and dispensing with all pretence of good manners, Greg walked to the door, opened it and stood waiting for her to leave. What a mistake he had made in Stella. Most of his women were mature enough to understand when an affair was over. But not this one. She was a spoilt child. 'I have no intention of discussing Abby with you or anyone.'

'Then say nothing and just listen,' said Stella. 'She'll never love you and you'll never have her, because she's still desperately in love with my brother. She has been since childhood. When he married someone else, she never forgave him. She's been pestering him ever since, trying to break up his marriage. It was only a few months ago that Richard sent her packing for the last time. He and his wife are very happy, you see. They have a darling little girl.' Seeing the expression on his face, she knew she had made an impact. 'You're just rebound, my dear, whatever else you might think.'

485

'Get out, Stella.' Greg's voice had a dangerous edge to it.

She walked slowly towards the door, pausing to smile. 'Oh. One more thing I should have mentioned. The little boy — Ross, I believed he's called. No doubt Abby's told you he's the son of her late husband. Well, it simply isn't true. Ross is Richard's son. Abby was already pregnant, when she and Richard had a blazing row. He married her greatest rival, and she managed to hook poor, gullible Eddy. Recently, she and Richard took Ross to London Zoo, would you believe? They could have been a little more discreet. But then Abby had her reasons not to be. She wanted to break up his marriage, you see, and was thwarted when Richard's wife found out. Then you came along.' She smiled bitterly. 'I thought you should know, that's all.'

'And now I do know,' he had answered, fighting back a strong urge to strike her. 'Goodbye, Stella.'

Before she left, Stella had turned to make a last stinging comment. 'Forget her, Greg. You're useful to her, that's all. Just as Eddy was once useful.' The rage he had felt must have shown in his eyes because her triumphant expression was replaced with doubt, bordering on fear. 'Goodbye, Greg. I came in good faith to warn you, although goodness knows you damn well don't deserve it.'

From that moment, Greg had been unable to push her words from his mind. He told himself the whole thing was ludicrous. Stella was a woman scorned and, as everyone knew, hell hath no fury like one. She would do anything to hurt him now. Well, he would ignore her. Abby loved him as much as he loved her. Their love-making proved that. He would forget that Stella had come to him with such nonsense.

It hadn't been so easy. Every time he'd looked at the woman he loved, he had found himself wondering if he really knew her at all. That she had loved before was nothing new, but, until now, he'd assumed his rival to be drowned

486

Eddy. Now it seemed she mourned not the dead, but the living. Jealousy had fed on doubt, and taken such a hold that he had let the whole thing spin out of control. If she still loved Richard, then he would have nothing more to do with her.

There could be no peace or happiness with a woman if her heart was elsewhere. He had been down that road before, and the living hell of his last marriage would not be easily forgotten. He had sworn never to go through it again. *Rebound!* He had been played for a fool. But no amount of booze could drive away his aching despair.

Abby could make no sense of it. How could a man love the way Greg had loved, and then suddenly not love? Unhappy, confused and deeply hurt, she was glad of her work, and wondered how she would have got through life without it. Thankfully, she was busier than ever with the coming spring/summer collection to be shown in October.

At home, Evelyn kept up a cheerful front, although she yearned to comfort her daughter-in-law. Since Abby said nothing about Greg, however, it seemed more diplomatic to respect her silence.

Every time the telephone rang, Abby nearly jumped out of her skin, but the call was never from Greg. She could, of course, drive out to Chiswick. She had a door key, after all. Maybe he was expecting her to do just that. A test, perhaps? To see if she would run to him as all his other women had done? Well, he could sit there until the crack of doom. Her pride was every bit as great as his.

At night, she lay in her bed asking herself if she had really loved him. She needed his strength, his warmth, his masculinity and, most of all, his passionate love-making. Did that add up to love? Probably not, she decided. She had known the real thing. Richard would have her true love until the day he died, no matter how much he hurt her. Did that mean, though, that she was wrong ever to seek happiness with someone else?

*

487

'Mirrors. I want more mirrors,' Abby snapped, as she looked at the designs Roland had submitted for the Bond Street boutique. 'Here, and here. And hidden lighting, soft and muted. And I'm not sure about this colour scheme.'

Roland sighed. 'Fine. More mirrors, lots of hidden lighting in the display alcoves and rethink the colour scheme.' Gathering up the plans he marched out of her office as Susan came down the staircase with various materials draped over her arm.

'Dear God, what's got into the lady?' he murmured, shaking his head. 'And don't tell me it's love, because I simply don't want to know.'

'You too, eh?' Susan frowned. 'Well ... it'll all blow over.'

'She's chopping and changing her mind like crazy,' said Roland. 'I've never seen her so edgy.'

'She'll get over it.' Susan's conciliatory tone seemed to calm Roland's jagged nerves. As she walked on she wondered if Greg was at the source of this particular crisis. Abby, however, had said nothing about him. Of course, Susan reminded herself, it might not be Greg, but Richard who was responsible for this latest emotional upheaval. Only that morning the newspapers had announced that he had won the Chiltingham seat by a comfortable margin. There had been a picture of him with his elegant wife and pretty little daughter outside their London home. All that had been missing was the family dog.

It was almost nine o'clock that evening when the doorbell rang. Abby had been reading the newspaper article about Richard's success and would have felt happy for him had it not been for the picture of Samantha smiling so sweetly beside him. They looked like the perfect happy family. How could he go wrong? She stood up and sighed. 'Who on earth can that be?'

Evelyn put down her knitting, and glanced at the carriage clock on the mantel. 'At this time of night, too! Maybe you shouldn't answer, luv. Mrs Proctor thinks we should 'ave chains on our front door like what they do in America.'

But Abby was already in the hall. Leaving the newspaper on the long mahogany table, she opened the door.

'Greg!' Her voice echoed the surprise she felt.

Standing there in the gathering dusk, his face dark and shadowed, Greg murmured huskily, 'I had to come.' He moved forward into the light, and Abby started at how tired and strained he looked. His face was ashen, and his eyes red-rimmed.

'You look terrible,' she said. 'You've been ill. Why didn't you tell me?'

'We can't talk here,' said Greg, seeing Evelyn hovering in the background. 'Let's walk.'

Abby's heart tightened. *I'm not sure there's anything to talk about. Your silence said it all.* The look in his eyes made her change her mind.

'Very well,' she said, at last. 'You've come to say goodbye, haven't you?'

'No.' Greg stood perfectly still, looking down at her with intense black eyes. 'I'm sorry,' he whispered thickly. 'God, I'm so sorry. Can you forgive me?'

'That rather depends ...' Greg stepped forward, and caught her rigid body in his arms, burying his face in her sweet-smelling hair. His mouth found hers, and they kissed with a passion so intense that Abby was lost. She had meant to be firm, cool-headed, sending him on his way with a few haughty words, but now she was lost.

When he lifted his head and gazed into her tear-filled eyes, he knew then that regardless of her past or present loves he could not live without her.

'You still haven't told me why,' Abby was saying.

Greg stroked her face gently. 'I had this terrible fear I was going to lose you to someone else.'

'What made you think that?'

'Am I going to lose you?'

She shook her head, but remained silent. What did he know? Why was he asking such a question?

489

Greg held her face firmly in his hands, his heart heavy with a wordless answer which told him Stella had not been lying. 'If you mean that, then marry me,' he whispered. 'If there's no other man in your life, Abby Carr, then prove it by becoming my wife.'

Abby was taken aback. She knew she wanted Greg in her life, but marriage was so final. Her eyes drifted to the newspaper on the table, and she saw again Richard's smiling face with his radiant wife beside him. *So much for undying love*, she thought bitterly.

Greg knew her thoughts. He, too, had read the newspaper and knew that Richard Glenister was Stella's brother. It had galvanized him into action. He would seize the moment when she was at her most vulnerable. 'Well, darling?'

Abby's eyes looked into his and she murmured, 'Yes, Greg. Yes, I'll marry you.'

Afraid that Abby might change her mind, Greg swept her off to Caxton Hall before she could organize the wedding she truly wanted.

'I'm a divorced man,' he'd said impatiently. 'I can't have a church wedding, and what's the point of a big show at some dreary Registry Office. All that matters is that we're man and wife, and it doesn't mean a tinker's damn where or how that happens.'

Now, as she faced the Registrar for the second time in her life, Abby wondered if she had not been too hasty. What did she know of this man she was swearing to stay with for the rest of her life? He was an enigma to her, and she had allowed him to sweep her off her feet on a wave of anger against Richard. Yet when Greg had left her, she had felt bereft. Was she wrong to take this chance after all: a chance to be happy; a chance for a normal married life and a father for Ross; a chance to put the past from her and start afresh?

Jonathan gave Abby away, smiling to hide his feelings of loss and distrust where Greg was concerned. Susan stood as maid of honour, hoping that this time Abby had found true happiness, while behind her Evelyn was thinking back across the years to the last time she'd watched her daughter-in-law take her marriage vows. But Abby deserved to be happy, and looking at her now in her peach shantung silk jacket and matching skirt, her upswept hair swathed in a silk band to match, Evelyn was determined to endure this day without tears.

At that moment, Abby glanced at her with eyes that said: '*I know, I know. But nothing has changed between us.*' Evelyn smiled back bravely, but her bottom lip quivered as she gripped Ross by the hand a shade too tightly. The little boy bore it as long as he could, but when the grip tightened even more, he yanked his hand away, frowning up at his grandmother and wondering why she was crying.

Outside Caxton Hall, press photographers jostled for the best places, as Abby and Greg appeared on the steps, surrounded by friends from the worlds of fashion and theatre and family from the famous Hadleigh Aircraft Corporation. It was too good a story to miss. London's traffic was brought to a halt before the couple climbed into their Rolls Royce to be driven to the reception at the Dorchester.

The following day their photograph appeared in every national newspaper: the famous playwright and the famous couturier, two highly successful and attractive people who could not fail.

Richard almost choked on his breakfast when he saw it, while Samantha smiled with deep satisfaction. She was safe at last and so was Richard. Knowing that sustained her through the dark days which followed, days during which Richard became deeply depressed, hardly speaking to anyone. *He'll get over it*, she told herself. *All I have to do is say nothing and let time take its course.* Nevertheless, seeing him this way, at a time when he had achieved his greatest ambition, was a shock. It confirmed Samantha's belief that had she not destroyed those letters, he and Abby would be together now.

Richard worked through this dark time, spending most of his days at his Chiltingham surgery in Kent, and his evenings at the House of Commons, where late-night sittings suited him very well. Samantha played the politician's wife for a while, accompanying him whenever duty demanded, unaware that her superior manner did less to help her husband than she imagined. Eventually, fitting in such duties with her own busy social life became difficult and slowly she disappeared from his side altogether.

After a brief but happy honeymoon in Capri, Abby and Greg returned to London and their work. The question of which house to sell was shelved since Abby loved her Hampstead home and Greg needed solitude and plenty of room for his endless supply of books. In the end, they decided to keep both houses. By day, Greg worked at the river, then, at night, he and Nelson would drive to Hampstead in time for a civilized meal with his new family, and bed with his wife.

The following year the first ready-to-wear line was shown, and judged to be a huge success. With outlets in Harrods, Harvey Nichols and on Fifth Avenue in New York, the line sold well. Abby inspected all the work personally, ensuring that everything under her label was the best that could be bought outside of haute couture itself. Her prices were such that her customers expected the best, and she resolved that they should have it.

At the same time, she was determined that the couture side of her business should not suffer, and watched over it like a mother with an ailing infant. Couture was painstaking hard work, building up a collection a slow process, each garment fitted and re-fitted so that none of the traditional way of working was lost. With customers coming from France, Germany, Italy and the United States, she was determined to keep her flag flying high.

Being a hard taskmaster and a fair employer left her little time for a private life, much to Greg's growing annoyance. 'I pack up writing at six, drive home like the wind, only to find myself sitting with your mother-in-law or reading to Ross. Are we married, or what? Is it worth my coming here at all?'

Abby tried to calm him, saying: 'It will settle down. It's just getting this ready-to-wear line started.'

By the time the second ready-to-wear collection was launched, Abby had opened her first boutique in Old Bond Street. Celebrities from stage, screen, society and fashion rubbed shoulders and raised their champagne glasses to the new venture. Her world was coming together. Greg could moan, but they were happy, and Ross had a father at last.

Then Abby received a telephone call from Mrs Proctor saying that Evelyn had collapsed in a shop and had been taken to hospital. By the time Abby arrived, her mother-in-law was sitting up in bed, looking a little cross.

'I just got dizzy, that's all. Can't think why anyone called an ambulance.'

'What's all this about chest pains?' asked Abby anxiously.

'Indigestion, luv. I've been getting it a lot lately. But that's all it is.' She sniffed and glanced about her private room with disapproval. 'This must be costing. Don't go into rooms like this on the National 'Ealth, I know.'

Later the doctor took Abby to one side and said, 'We've made a few tests. It's her heart. She's had a mild coronary attack.'

Abby listened as he tried to explain the problems that had built up over the years for Evelyn. 'I know these medical words mean little, but try to think of it as a tired heart.'

'Tired heart,' Abby repeated the words, as though in a dream. 'Yes. She has suffered a great deal. First the war, then the loss of her family. That same night she stood for hours in freezing water.' She looked up at the doctor. 'In the flooding on the East Coast back in '53.'

The young doctor nodded sympathetically. 'It must have been a dreadful experience for her, and helps to explain the condition she's in.'

Abby looked at him in alarm. 'Her condition? How bad is she, doctor?'

'With care she could go on for a few more years. These things are unpredictable. There's no saying when she might have another attack. We'll keep her in for another week, at least. But when she returns to you, stairs are out. Only very light exercise, a careful diet and regular medication. The essential thing is that she must rest.'

Getting Evelyn to accept that she must rest was like getting a domestic cat to take a swim. 'Listen, Abby. If you want to get old and be put in your box before time, then just sit around all day doing nothing. I want to live a decent life, not the life of an invalid.'

Abby, with the help of the doctor, finally persuaded her that she could do just that as long as she was sensible.

'When you take a walk, you go with Mrs Proctor, that's all,' said Abby. 'Ross is old enough to shift for himself.'

'Poor little mite. He's no such thing,' came the reply.

But Evelyn knew, deep inside, that she was a very sick woman, and that fighting to maintain her old way of life was only causing worry. And so when Abby managed to persuade Mrs Proctor to live in as a full-time housekeeper and 'Evelyn minder' the situation was accepted calmly.

'Well, as long as it's 'er, I don't mind,' said Evelyn. 'At least I know where I am with the woman, and I do trust 'er.'

'She's a veritable treasure, and you know it,' laughed Abby, with deep relief.

Strangely, Evelyn made no fuss when the large downstairs study became her bedroom, and eyed the new arrangement with philosophical acceptance. 'Well, those stairs do puff me a bit. Seems funny though, sleeping downstairs.'

Greg then pointed out the alarm he had fixed beside her bed. 'Ring this, and bells will sound in every room in the house.'

'Just like a ruddy fire station,' scoffed Evelyn. 'When I go, I'll go quietly, if you please.'

'You're not going anywhere,' said Abby firmly, trying to sound cheerful, for all that her heart was full. She then drew Evelyn's attention to the get-well cards and flowers that had arrived. 'Ross wanted you to have this.'

Evelyn looked at the model galleon on the window sill, and gasped with astonishment. It was his most treasured possession, something he had worked on for days, and painted meticulously. She walked across and picked up the card standing beside it. A tightness crept into the back of her throat as she read the neat, childish writing.

I love you, Gran. Welcome home. Ross.

How lucky she was, Evelyn thought, to have such a family. This was her home. This was where she belonged.

On arrival at the plain Victorian cottage in Sturry, Stella was shocked at her mother's appearance. Milicent looked much older and was clearly taking little interest in her appearance. Not that Brian would notice, she thought wryly, watching him through the window as he worked in the garden.

'Look, Mummy, you've got to snap out of this depression,' she said impatiently. 'Ever since that visit to London you've wandered around like a zombie. It was ages ago: eighteen months at least.'

Milicent turned dull eyes on her daughter, as she poured tea from the service she'd used since the thirties. 'Frankly, dear, I really don't care about things any more. Neither life nor death. It was twenty months ago, incidentally.'

Stella sighed with exasperation. 'Oh, Mummy, you're acting like an old woman long before your time.'

'You forget, I'm married to an old man. Not in years, but

in character. It's hard to flourish with such a partner.' The grey eyes misted over as they stared into emptiness. 'When I think what might have been . . .' Her voice trailed off.

'Oh, I could kill Abby for what she's done to us!' cried Stella angrily.

Milicent sipped her tea and raised an eyebrow. 'Us? I don't recall her doing anything to you, my dear. Except use you. But then you shouldn't have been so gullible, allowing yourself to become an adoring fan of the Queen of Fashion.'

Stella's eyes narrowed. 'Abby took the only man I ever loved, the man who was about to ask me to marry him.'

Unimpressed by her daughter's histrionics, Milicent smiled. 'Did she, now. More fool you for letting her.' Then, as though just understanding the full weight of Stella's words, she went on. 'I'm sorry. That must have been hard for you, my dear. I know what it's like to lose someone you've cared about for so long. God, I didn't know anyone could hate that much. You should have seen the look in her eyes, Stella. It was in her power to reunite me with Karl. He wanted to meet me again, and I could see by looking into his eyes that he cared for me. But that bitch chose to part us for ever, and I'll never forgive her as long as I live.' She turned to look at her daughter. 'Such a man! Oh, my dear, he was such a man. I do wish you could have met him. He's hardly changed. While I . . .' She sighed. 'I must have looked like an old lady. Yet he was interested, I could see that. Now I'm stuck with this man . . . Oh, don't get me wrong, Brian is good and kind, but . . . Oh, why was I fool enough to marry him?'

Stella's mind was on her own heartache. She had stopped weeping over Greg, but the bitterness remained. He had spurned her, humiliated her, and ignored her warnings. If the day ever came when she could spoil their happiness, she wouldn't hesitate to do whatever might be necessary.

'Did I tell you that he is the baron now?' Milicent asked.

'Yes, Mummy,' snapped Stella, 'several times, in fact.'

'You see, I've been thinking about that.' Milicent lit a cigarette, and gazed out at her husband who was now pruning a rose bush. 'Richard is Karl's heir. Even if there are other children, Richard is the eldest and of legitimate issue. When Karl dies, Richard will be the next Baron von Schreiber. He should inherit Karl's industrial empire and the mansion at Wittenhausen. To that end, I want Richard to get in touch with his father. But that stupid son of mine won't talk to me.'

'I met Sam recently. She came to the theatre the other day.' Stella had left the cast of Greg's play long since, and was now in a comedy at the Savoy Theatre. 'I don't think she enjoys being the wife of an MP as much as she thought she would.' Stella looked at her mother with cold eyes, still jealous of Richard's place in her affections. 'Did you know Richard was going to leave her for Abby? Oh yes, Abby went that far. Sammy soon stopped it. They're happy together again, but he's no angel and it's time you stopped grieving over him.' She looked at her mother, and whispered, 'Why couldn't you love me the way you loved Richard? Was it because I was William's daughter and not Karl's?'

Milicent remained silent, and turned her face away to the fire. It was answer enough. Stella watched her for a moment, then stood up. 'I must go. I have to get back to the theatre.' She pulled on her coat and gloves. 'You should have loved me more, Mummy. If you had, then you wouldn't be here now, without your position at Glenisters, without your beloved piano and all that meant home. You should have let me go on contesting that Will.' She paused, and eyed her mother warily. 'You talk about Richard's inheritance – have you forgotten that Richard has a son?'

Milicent turned quickly. 'No. Of course I haven't forgotten. How could I? My grandchild being raised by that ... that ... If I could take him from Abby I would, don't think otherwise.'

'I wonder if Karl knows about the child?'

Milicent shrugged. 'I've no idea. He could only learn it from Abby, and I doubt she would want to tell such a proud man that his grandson is illegitimate because of her wanton ways.'

'*Exactly*,' murmured Stella, her eyes widening as the thought began to take hold. 'What would he do if he ever found out, I wonder?'

'I don't know what you have in mind, but this is surely between Richard and his father. It has nothing to do with you, so leave well alone.'

Stella gave her mother a sharp look. 'You always did know how to make me feel a spare part, Mummy.' Her mother made no answer, and she had not expected one. 'Wittenhausen. That was the name of the estate and village, wasn't it? Where did you say it was?'

'Look, I've just told you not to meddle. I want no more trouble from Richard.'

'Mummy, I've no intention of meddling in anything. I asked a simple question.'

Milicent gave her daughter a long and hard look; she knew her too well. 'Why do you want to know?'

'Because, if I ever go to Germany, I'd like to have a look at my brother's inheritance. Hanover, isn't it?'

'No,' sighed Milicent. 'And you've been looking at the house all your life. It's engraved on my cigarette case.'

Stella's eyes opened wide in astonishment, then she threw her head back and laughed. 'I don't believe it. Why on earth didn't you ever tell us?' At her mother's expression she deemed it wiser not to press her further, and returned quickly to her other question. 'Right, so it isn't Hanover. Where, then?'

Milicent sighed, wearying of the whole topic. 'Somewhere north of Düsseldorf and west of Dortmund, I believe. I was never there, so I could be wrong.'

A twisted smile played about Stella's lips. She had failed to stop Greg marrying Abby, but that did not mean she'd given up. Anything that put a strain on the marriage was surely worth a try.

In late May, the Paris boutique opened on the Avenue Montaigne, sandwiched between the famous couture houses of the Faubourg Saint-Honoré and the Seine. For Abby it was the culmination of a dream, only shadowed by Greg's refusal to accompany her. 'Darling, one boutique opening is enough to last me a lifetime. I simply could not endure another.'

She'd been deeply hurt by his remarks, and thought of the many times she had given up precious time to support him in his world. She pointed this out, only to receive a short reply.

'But, darling, that's different. You're my wife.'

Standing now among the specially invited guests, Abby gazed around in satisfaction. *Paris!* At last. Was she mad, bringing British fashion to a city renowned for couture, and highly critical of any other country's styles? Perhaps. But right now, she'd brought a buzz of excitement to the Paris scene, much of which she owed to Odile Longet, whose famous fashion magazine had hailed the British designer. During the many visits Abby had made to Paris over the past months, one thing became clear. Odile and Karl lived happily together either here or in Düsseldorf. Now, as Karl arrived with Odile on his arm, it was obvious how much they loved each other, something which Abby was pleased and strangely relieved to see.

Abby moved forward to greet them. 'Karl, I'm so glad you're here! Odile, why didn't you tell me he was coming?'

Odile shrugged. 'When I knew he was coming to Paris, I told him to come a day earlier, or else.'

'When the lady commands, I obey. Now just hand me the champagne. I'm a fish out of water at these affairs.' Karl's blue eyes swept over Abby, in her black off-the-shoulder gown, wondering why she was standing there alone. 'Where is your new husband? I have not met him yet.'

Abby's eyes clouded momentarily. 'He couldn't make it, I'm afraid. But when you come to England we'll all get together.'

As Odile was distracted by one of her friends, Karl took Abby's arm, and murmured, 'I must speak with you alone. This is not the time. Tomorrow morning?'

His serious expression made Abby anxious. 'Is there something wrong?'

Karl shook his head. 'Tomorrow. I'll tell you then.'

Abby sighed. 'No, the morning's out. I'll be busy with fashion editors and photographic sessions. I could probably get away around four o'clock.'

'Very well. I'll be here then.' With that he moved on into the crowd, and Abby was immediately surrounded by women eager to talk to her. Among them was Claudia, who'd married her Count, and wanted Abby to visit them at their Loire château.

'September is the best time,' Claudia insisted. 'Oh, I know you've got the collection in October, but you simply have to see the vineyards then, and you'll love the château.'

Abby said she would love to visit them, but knew in her heart that it was hardly likely to come about. Wistfully she wondered at the life she had, and the life people thought she had. In the eyes of the world, top couturiers lived like princes, not suburban housewives. She was forever being asked to join the fashionable set on some luxury yacht, or a villa on the French Riviera. It would be fun, she thought, for a little while. A palace here, a private island there, and all the trappings of life for the rich and famous. Yet to enjoy that, one would have to be free of loved ones waiting for you, needing you as much as you needed them. Still, Claudia's château sounded lovely. She would try to persuade Greg, providing Evelyn's health continued to remain steady.

As good as his word, Karl arrived at four the following afternoon to find Abby ready to meet him. The last fashion editor had left, and the photographers were packing up their things. In the shop itself customers looked at the outfits with a critical eye at first, but soon their expressions changed to surprised approval as they found Abigail Carr's clothes elegant and easy to wear. She had brought chic to the French, as one might take coals to Newcastle, and she had won the day.

'Congratulations,' murmured Karl as they walked out into the warm May sunshine. 'Paris has taken you to her heart.' He offered her his arm as they headed along the busy avenue toward the river.

'Would you say so?' asked Abby, recalling how Odile had suddenly remembered an urgent appointment before Karl's arrival. *She knows something*.

'Karl, do please tell me what's wrong. I can't bear it one more minute. And where are we going?'

'On the river,' he replied curtly.

'The river? Why?'

'Because when you hear what I have to say, you might be tempted to walk away. Anyway, it's years since I saw Paris by boat. And you?'

Frowning, Abby stared up at him. 'Never. Oh, Karl, you really are beginning to frighten me. For God's sake tell me what's wrong!'

'All I'm prepared to say, for now, is that I've had a letter.'

Abby stopped in her tracks, her face brightening. 'From Richard? At last! Why didn't you . . .'

'It isn't from Richard. Come on.'

They crossed the busy Place de l'Alma and headed for the Bateaux Mouches just in time to board one of the pleasure boats pulling away from the quay. The sun was mellowing to a soft gold as they passed the Grand Palais. Paris looked beautiful, but Abby was watching Karl, waiting for him to speak.

He sat beside her, his eyes a curious mixture of hurt and anger. 'How is your son?' he asked suddenly.

It was the last thing she'd expected him to say. 'Fine. Always into mischief. He's just the right age.'

'Any photographs?'

He's stalling, Abby thought. Whatever he had to tell her was so bad he was making polite conversation to put off the terrible moment. Opening her bag, she pulled out a small leather folder. Inside were two framed pictures of Ross. 'The one on the left was taken when he was seven and the other more recently.' Handing the photographs to Karl, Abby tensed, aware that she might be making a dangerous move. He had seen Richard's sketch. Surely he would see the likeness between father and son now?

'He has such a lively face,' said Karl. Without smiling, he handed the folder back to her. 'Why didn't you tell me, Abby?'

They were passing under the eighteenth-century Pont de la Concorde now, and Abby could hear the sound of traffic across the busy square. She had been a fool. What had made her think she could deceive Karl?

'This letter you spoke of,' she said at last, 'has that something to do with your sudden interest in my son?'

Karl nodded. 'I could show you photographs of myself at the same age and you would find it hard to tell the difference between us.'

'Tell me about the letter.' Abby looked away from him, feeling as though something in her had died. 'Was it from Richard's wife?'

'No. It was from his sister.'

Shocked, Abby turned to him. 'Stella? Are you sure?' When he nodded, she frowned. Samantha had been her main threat, not Stella. 'What did she say?'

'That your son, Ross, is Richard's son, also.'

'But why? Why would she do such a thing?'

502

Karl looked angry. 'And if she had not, would I have gone to my grave in ignorance, Abby? Would I?'

Abby turned away from his penetrating blue eyes. 'I've always wanted you to know, but it was impossible. For one thing you would have disapproved – and for another, Ross doesn't know that Richard is his father.'

'I see.' The tone was one of sadness now. 'But that's wrong. I simply don't understand. Why in God's name did Richard leave you carrying his child?'

'I left him,' said Abby in a flat voice. 'And you know why. I was married and widowed before I found out the truth.'

'But, Abby, you must have known how much a grandchild would mean to me. Especially since my own son has not been in touch and never will be.' Karl placed a hand under her chin and turned her face to his. 'My grandson, Abby.'

'I don't mean to hurt you, Karl, but he's only a little boy. He's already living under a threat which would not only hurt him but his grandmother as well.' She then explained and, by the time she had finished, the boat was passing the Ile de la Cité beneath towering Notre-Dame. From somewhere a guide explained in different languages the history of the Cathedral, the voice echoing across the river as Abby went on. 'It would kill Evelyn if she ever found out. Oh, I know what you're thinking; it's wicked of me to deceive her like this, but it's the only thing I can do.'

'But Ross has to know sooner or later,' said Karl gently.

'When he's older and able to accept ...'

Karl shook his head. 'Supposing someone tells him before you get around to it?'

'Stella?' Abby shook her head. 'But why would she?'

'Because her letter to me was not well meant, although she tried to cloak it with good intentions. She has some reason for trying to hurt you, my dear. Be wary of her.'

It seemed hard to absorb, and Abby searched her mind

for some way in which she had hurt Stella. 'Stella's young and silly, selfish too at times, but not wicked and scheming. I can think of no reason why she'd interfere in my personal life. She doesn't even care about Richard. So why on earth she decided to . . .' She broke off, and shrugged. 'It simply doesn't make any sense.' She thought again of that opening night, when Stella had accused her of treachery. Was this attempt to cause mischief a way of avenging her mother? Even as she thought it, Abby dismissed the idea. If Milicent had wanted a shoulder to cry on, she would have found Stella's too hard for comfort.

The cruiser had now begun its return journey, and Karl's eyes drifted across to the Left Bank of the Seine. 'Truly, Abby, I fear the consequences of Ross finding out the truth from someone wanting to cause trouble. Of course, I also must admit to my own selfish reasons for wanting him to know he has a grandfather. Abby, there's so much I can do for that boy.' The sad eyes lit up suddenly. 'I can show him the world and give him an education few of his contemporaries would enjoy.'

As Abby watched, the light which had leapt into his eyes diminished, and she knew that reality had crushed his dreams even as he spoke of them. All his hopes were on her and she could offer him nothing.

'You have had a sad life, my dear,' Karl was saying now. 'I want to ease it for you, not make things more difficult.' He leaned against the railings and looked down at her. 'The saddest thing of all is that by the time you tell Ross about me, both he and I will be too old for any of this to happen.'

The look on his face then reminded her of the look on Richard's face when she left him in the garden at Ferndene. 'Oh, please don't be hurt, please. I couldn't bear that. I can't involve Ross. You have no idea what sacrifices Richard and I have made to that end. Would you have all that go for nothing now?'

Karl shook his head. 'Of course not. But do you know

how hard it is to have a son who does not wish to meet you and a grandson who does not even know you exist?' Turning from her, he looked over the rail at the river rushing past. 'If Richard won't be my heir, then it must be Ross. I may never have the pleasure of knowing him; but please, Abby, do not deny him his birthright. Give him a good sound education and prepare him well. Make sure he studies German and French and speaks both languages as well as he speaks English. For one day, God willing, he will head Schreiber Industries. Maybe that is how it should be. Richard's too close to the war years. Ross's generation will grow up in a different world. Hopefully, the bitterness will have gone, along with the people who caused it. I think Europe will change a great deal before I'm put in my coffin, and I want my grandson to be a part of that change.' He glanced at his watch with an air of agitation. 'I have to be at the airport. How much longer are we going to be stuck on this damned river?'

She had never seen Karl like this before. He was angry, hurt, and trying to hold on to the familiar patterns of his life, the rush to the airport, the first-class flight: anything to take away the pain of longing for his family.

Odile was back at the boutique, anxious that Karl should not miss his Berlin flight. She handed him his plane tickets, passport, briefcase and overnight case, saying with a gentle laugh, 'Our all-efficient German industrialist tends to go to pieces in Paris! I tell him he will forget his head one day. But he tells me he lost it many years ago. It is a quarter to six, Karl. Now go, or the rush hour traffic will keep you here all night.'

Karl kissed Odile gently on the lips, and Abby noticed his anger had gone, as he bade her a more formal farewell. Once inside the car, he beckoned to her.

'I am sorry I lost my temper. That was unforgivable. I know the decision must be yours. I want my grandson to be happy. Will you ever forgive me for spoiling your triumph here in Paris?'

505

Abby nodded and smiled. 'Will *you* ever forgive *me*, Karl? I'll find a way to bring Ross to you. I promise you – I *will* find a way.'

Karl smiled, his eyes still showing anxiety. 'Find it before Stella does. That is all I ask.'

When the car was out of sight, Odile turned to Abby, determined to cheer her up. Karl had not said why he needed to speak with her so urgently, but she loved and trusted him enough to keep out of the way.

Beside Odile, Abby always felt a little gauche: young and English. Wearing a white jersey dress with a coloured scarf tied casually about her neck, she looked *soignée* as only French women can look, without working at it. She also had sex appeal, although her face was more handsome than pretty, and this, too, made Abby feel she had just stepped out of a convent. Add to all this her way of life, and Odile represented to Abby all that was free, emancipated and sophisticated in an older woman. How she envied her!

'Come,' said Odile firmly. 'We will go back to my place for a drink.'

Odile's apartment was on the Boulevard Saint-Germain. Abby's eyes swept over the French marble fireplace graced by a porcelain clock, the fine paintings and prints decorating the walls, and chairs covered in nineteenth-century brocade. She walked to the windows and looked down on the wide tree-lined boulevard below.

Odile entered the room with a tray of canapes and two large glasses of Dubonnet. 'And where is your husband?'

'Busy writing. The fashion scene bores him, I'm afraid.'

Odile shook her head. 'Only an Englishman could be so unimaginative as to let his wife loose in Paris. It would serve him right if you came with me tonight to a dinner party and met a most romantic nobleman.'

Abby smiled. 'Will there be one, then?'

'Ah, but yes. An aristocrat to be sure. It would serve your husband right, eh?'

Thinking her accent would have sent Greg into raptures, Abby decided it was just as well that he was safe in Chiswick scribbling away with Nelson beside him. She accepted the glass Odile held out to her, then sat down on the sofa. 'Would you mind if I asked you a very personal question, Odile?'

'Of course not.' The brown eyes were alert. 'Although I think I can guess what it is.'

'Oh?'

'Since Karl and I are so close, and have been for many years, why aren't we married? Is that it?'

Disarmed, Abby could only reply: 'Something like that, yes.'

'That is easily answered,' said Odile. 'I am already married. But I am a Catholic and, although the marriage ended about seventeen years ago, there can be no divorce.' She shrugged, and smiled. 'It does not matter. If I were free tomorrow I should still think twice about becoming Karl's wife. I am set in my ways, and love Paris. Karl, on the other hand, has his life and work in Germany. So there we are, two people living as we must. And it works. I want it all ways, you see. My Paris, my lovely apartment, my freedom and Karl. What is so wrong with that?'

Abby looked thoughtful, frantically discarding her very English, Protestant upbringing. 'Nothing,' she said at last, realizing she meant it. 'In fact, there seems to be a good deal right with it.'

A long silence followed, while Odile wondered at Abby's remark. Karl had told her something of his son's love for this woman, and the sad manner of their parting. Now she had a new man in her life, a man who had not bothered to accompany her on a night which meant so much. 'Are you happy with this marriage, Abby?'

'Oh, yes,' said Abby, a shade too quickly. That Greg seemed content to let her run around a foreign city alone didn't mean he had ceased to care, but that he trusted her implicitly. In any case, why should he worry about her?

Then it crossed her mind that, had she not been married to Greg, he would have been with her here, come hell or high water. Marriage had made him complacent. *Damn him!* How dare he treat her so casually? 'Oh, yes,' she said again, 'we're very happy.'

She glanced at her watch, then stood up to leave. 'Thank you for all you've done, Odile. Without you I never would have cracked Paris. Now I've just time to get back to the hotel and pack. My flight leaves at nine.'

'Cancel it,' said Odile, lighting up a Gauloise. 'Come with me to this dinner. You would find it interesting. The house is in the Bois de Boulogne, close to the Windsors.' She smiled and twitched her nose mischievously. 'Go on. Ring your husband and tell him you're going to dine with a French Count.' She laughed. 'Of course you do not have to tell him that the Count is nearly sixty and probably homosexual.'

'Don't tempt me,' laughed Abby, thinking it would serve Greg right. Thanking Odile again, she took a taxi back to the Georges Cinq. There were more pressing matters than causing Greg a moment of discomfort. Her problem was Stella. What on earth was her game? Why had she written such a letter to Karl? Abby sighed with despair. How would it be possible to go on protecting Evelyn and Ross, with the odds increasing against them in this way?

She was tired as she arrived at the door to her luxury suite and looked forward to a relaxing bath before checking out. Opening the door, she gasped in surprise.

'Where in God's name have you been?' Greg was standing beside the window, holding a glass of Scotch, his eyes dark with anger and disappointment.

Abby stared at him in dumbfounded surprise. 'When ... when did you arrive?'

'Early this afternoon, thanks to the bloody plane being an hour late. When I finally found the dress shop – sorry, boutique – no one there could tell me where you were.' The eyes searched hers suspiciously. 'Perhaps you can enlighten me.'

Disliking his tone, Abby stiffened with anger. 'For someone who shows no interest in my business, and couldn't even accompany me to my opening night, you're remarkably curious all of a sudden.'

'Well, what the hell do you expect? I drop everything to be with you on your final day here, thinking we can have some time to ourselves, and now it's all too late.'

Abby felt a wave of sympathy for him. 'Oh, you are a fool sometimes! Had I known you were coming I would have been there. But you didn't even bother to telephone. Am I supposed to be a mind reader or something?'

'I wanted to surprise you,' said Greg sullenly.

'Well, you certainly managed to do that,' came the terse reply. 'And now I have to pack.' She was angry at his childish behaviour which had backfired so badly. She was also alarmed and unwilling to mention the fact that she had spent the afternoon with Karl. That would be difficult to explain away. Yet supposing someone at the boutique had mentioned the baron's arrival? There had been no secrecy attached to it. She turned to Greg with a cold stare. 'Had you been with me last night, then this silly nonsense could have been avoided. What happened to make you change your mind, anyway?'

How could he tell her? Until last night, he had thought of her Paris visit as business. She and Roland had talked about the venture until Greg had been bored to distraction. But last night, as he lay alone in their large bed, missing Abby dreadfully, Stella's words had crept back into his mind. He had no reason to suspect his wife of being unfaithful: no reason at all. But there was always a nagging doubt about a woman who had loved another for so many years. On the other hand, would Richard Glenister jeopardize his political career over a woman he had spurned in the past? Hardly. But still, Abby was in Paris alone, meeting many glamorous people. Who could say what might happen? What kind of an idiot would allow anything to happen? And so he had arrived at the boutique, hot and bothered, late and angry, only to find that his wife had left ten minutes before. 'Alone?' he had asked. 'No, Monsieur, with a friend,' had come the reply. Greg had returned to the hotel to wait for her, his suspicion and anger deepening by the minute.

'You can forget the evening flight,' he said quietly. 'I cancelled it. We're booked on a mid-morning plane.'

Abby looked at him in astonishment. 'You did *what*? Greg, you had no right. I have clients at the salon tomorrow.'

'Not until the afternoon, you don't,' he said. 'I'm not that irresponsible. I checked with Avril first.'

Abby grew more indignant at his high-handed manner. 'You've no right to interfere in my business. When we married, you knew I had a career. I don't try to stop you writing, so why can't you understand that my time is just as important?'

'Isn't your husband important too?' he growled, swallowing the contents of the glass quickly.

'Isn't your wife?' Abby sighed in exhaustion. She looked around the suite with its floral tributes from well-wishers. There had been nothing from Greg. 'If she were, then you would treat her with as much consideration as you expect her to show to you.'

Greg's eyes glinted dangerously as he moved towards his wife. 'You still haven't told me where you were this afternoon.'

Abby faced him coolly. 'I took a trip on the Seine, if you really must know.' She knew what was coming next, and what her answer must be.

'Alone?'

Shaking her head, she smiled up at him, aware of his scowling features and dark jealousy. 'No. As a matter of fact, I was with a man. An old friend.' She almost enjoyed saying it, then saw the expression on his face, and became alarmed. 'Really, Greg! You refuse to come to Paris with me, then put me through the third degree because I was here alone. Well, I won't have it. Not once have you asked me about the opening last night. Instead you leave Evelyn alone, when you had promised to stay with her, and come swanning out here, demanding to know why I wasn't standing around waiting for you.'

Greg reached out and took her arm roughly. 'Who was he?'

Wincing, Abby looked up at him with shock. 'You're hurting me! Let go.'

Suddenly aware of his action, Greg released his grip on her arm, noticing with shame the tell-tale finger marks. 'Stop playing this silly game, Abby, and tell me the truth.'

Swinging away from him, Abby moaned, 'Dear God, this is terrible. What on earth has got into you? The man I met was the German baron who once put on a charity fashion show. He's Odile's very close friend, if you get my meaning. He sent us the crystal decanters and wine glasses for a wedding present.'

Greg was taken aback. 'Him? I don't understand ... why on earth ...?'

'Because he could see I had some time to kill, and very kindly took me sightseeing. I've done little of it in the past. All my visits to Paris have been for work. And, in case you're wondering, he's well into his fifties and madly in love with Odile.'

At this, Greg looked and felt deeply relieved. He knew nothing about this strange German aristocrat, but he had met Odile very briefly in London and thought her fascinating. If she and the German were a couple, then he had been worrying over nothing. At least Glenister was out of the picture.

'I'm sorry, darling. I've been pig-headed and selfish. I missed you like hell and ... well, I suppose I let disappointment get the better of me.' He looked into

511

her anxious eyes, realizing that he had not yet won her back. 'Evelyn's fine, Ross is fine and Mrs Proctor has this number, should she need us. Evelyn practically kicked me out of the house. Stop worrying and tell me all about last night. Did everything go well?'

Before she could speak, he pulled her to him and his mouth covered hers, leaving her breathless.

All anger had melted now. The evening sun filtered through the net curtains, filling the suite with amber light. From outside came the distant noise of traffic, but for them, there was only this moment.

CHAPTER NINETEEN

When Abby learned that she was pregnant, her first reaction
was one of horror. She had neither the time nor inclination
for more children and long ago had pushed such thoughts
to one side because of her work. But when, on a cold March
night, she gave birth to a daughter of doll-like prettiness,
she forgot her qualms, and the pain of the last eighteen
hours, and cradled the child lovingly in her arms.

'A daughter,' she murmured, touching the tiny fingers,
which immediately folded over hers. It was wonderful,
and still too strange fully to comprehend. A daughter,
who would be close to her; a daughter, who would want
for nothing and, God willing, would inherit her mother's
talent. And who might, one day, take over the House
of Carr!

Greg was over the moon, completely besotted with his
child. Bending over the crib, he gazed down at the bright
blue eyes, the pink cheeks and rosebud mouth. 'She's
exquisite. As beautiful as her mother.'

Smiling at him from her bed, Abby said, 'And will, no
doubt, be spoilt by her father.' She bit her lip thoughtfully.
'We never did decide on a name.'

Greg shrugged. 'Thought you favoured Helen. I must
say I prefer Tamsin.'

'Tamsin!' said Evelyn, when she heard. 'She'll be called
Tammy, I 'ope you both realize.' Cradling the baby to her,
she recalled the last time such a scene had been played out,
and her heart was too full for words. But she was happy
for Abby, and felt herself to be a grandmother again, even
though there was no blood tie this time. A baby in the
house was a shot in the arm for everyone, she thought.

When the Norland-trained nanny arrived to take over, however, Evelyn suddenly felt bereft. She knew she was no longer young enough or well enough to look after a baby. Even so, it hurt to see her authority being snatched away from her, as the baby was taken to her nursery.

Ross had become very quiet, feeling that his position in the family had become less important to his mother and stepfather. He had been shocked at the arrival of the infant, even though there had been months to get used to the idea. *A baby!* And a girl, at that! It was horrendous.

Abby and Greg did their best to make Ross feel that he was loved, and would not be pushed out by the newcomer. Taking his duty as a stepfather more seriously than ever, Greg took Ross to soccer and rugby matches in autumn and winter, then to Lords and Wimbledon in the summer, so that the bond between them grew stronger, much to Abby's relief.

The Profumo scandal came and went, the Beatles were becoming more popular, skirts were rising, Jonathan was arranging a financial deal for a third boutique in Rome, and Abby was busier than she had ever been in her life. Then, in the chill of November, President Kennedy was assassinated, and the world seemed to stop.

Greg's world had already stopped, although he tried to keep it from his wife. His latest play had caused him more problems than he had ever known during his writing career. Halfway through, he became blocked, and panic set in. Was it over? Had he lost his talent and his voice? Or was it just a temporary failure? Writing was all he knew — all he really cared about. To lose his ability to write would be like losing his very life.

Abby's first hint of his private agony came when she noticed that Greg was drinking too much. It worried her, yet, when she spoke to him about it, he turned on her in such fury that she quickly dropped the subject. She became frightened to see this change in someone she thought she knew so well. Moody and morose, he brought a dark

514

shadow to the house which his drinking did little to lift. Unable to help or endure Greg's private agony, Abby buried herself in her work. This was all too easy with the amount of designing she had to get through, but deep down she knew Greg needed her, and that she should be there for him. It was Evelyn who told her as much in her usual blunt manner.

'You work all hours God sends, Abby. I just don't know why. In the past it was different, but now you've all those people working for you. It ain't right. You've an 'usband to think about now, yet you treat 'im like dirt. Greg loves you very much, and 'e's a good man. If you go on like this, then something terrible is gonner 'appen, you mark my words.' She had then turned from Abby, and walked back into her own room, murmuring: 'It's 'appening already.'

Abby had stood in the hallway, realizing how cruel she'd been to Greg. She was his wife, and he was in trouble. She was the mother of two children, who rarely saw her. She spent more of her life in Brook Street than in her home. *Delegate*, she told herself firmly. *Reorganize your life to include those you love, before you find yourself alone with no one left to love.*

After much rescheduling Abby managed to spend more time with her family. Although Greg was still quiet and morose, he took comfort in her presence. She could sketch and design just as easily at home, find time to play with her baby, discuss school with Ross, talk to Evelyn and curl up in Greg's arms. She learned not to worry about his long silences, as they walked across the Heath together, or dined in a quiet restaurant. Slowly, she broke through the barrier he'd built around himself, and calmed his fears. As the drinking lessened, she gave herself to his passion, and he would hold her tenderly, as they talked late into the night. But no matter how much they talked, they each kept a secret locked away inside themselves. Then, as if by a miracle, Greg started writing once more and the Hadleigh family was happy again.

At the Cambridge Theatre on the first night of his new play, the audience gave him the usual applause, but Greg felt it more a polite gesture, than enthusiasm. After he had taken his customary bow during the curtain calls, he knew that he had failed.

Abby turned to him, sensing his disappointment. 'Well, they liked it! Listen to them.'

'They hated it,' he hissed through clenched teeth. 'I thought I had given them something different, something more profound, but they didn't want it. That, my dear, is the kind of sympathetic applause one gets when the audience isn't rude enough to throw things.'

'You're just being pessimistic,' said Abby, as they made their way backstage. 'It was a good play, and the critics will agree with me. You wait and see. Now then, where's the telephone? I want to call and see if Evelyn's all right.'

'Don't bother,' snapped Greg. 'I think we might just as well drive there right away.'

'Nonsense,' Abby said. 'There's the party. Everyone's expecting you, and if they see you despondent like this, it's likely to rub off on the cast. So come along. Put on a good face, because there's no need to wear that one.' She genuinely believed in the play. It *was* good. It just wasn't the kind of thing Greg's followers had come to expect. He had changed his voice, his style and pace, so that the play might have been written by someone else.

Evelyn was playing cards in her room with Mrs Proctor and the nanny when the telephone rang in the hallway. The housekeeper put down her cards, then walked out of the bedroom to pick up the receiver.

'Hello, Mrs Hadleigh. Yes ... fine ... absolutely. We're playing gin rummy. Your mother-in-law is fine, so you can go to your party.'

Evelyn sighed and shouted, 'Gawd give me strength! Tell 'er to stop worrying about me, or she'll be in the ground before I will.'

Mrs Proctor interpreted. 'Mrs Carr says she's feeling very

well and she's going to bed when we've finished this hand. The baby's sleeping like an angel. How was Mr Hadleigh's play?' There was a short pause. 'Good. We were all sure it would be a success.' Mrs Proctor returned to the card table. 'Mrs Hadleigh won't stay too long at the party. She's just going to put in a brief appearance and expects to be home soon after midnight.' Turning her strict gaze on Evelyn, she added, 'She expects you to be in bed and fast asleep by then.'

'It's like being a kid all over again,' muttered Evelyn, frowning as she reorganized her cards. 'Don't seem so long ago when I was saying such things to 'er. Funny isn't it, the way everything turns on its head as you get older. Anyway, she won't find me asleep when she comes in. She never 'as done yet. I'm not tired these days, somehow.'

'You were reading very late last night,' said Mrs Proctor, in a disapproving manner. 'I saw the light under your door. It was nearly one o'clock in the morning.'

Evelyn shrugged. 'You know me. I never like leaving off in the middle of a chapter. I'll be awake when she comes 'ome tonight, you see if I'm not.'

The party was a slightly subdued affair, with everyone saying good things about the play, yet each thinking that although they understood it, the audience had not. 'I think,' said Joanna quietly to Abby, 'it's ahead of its time. One day it will be a classic, but just now, people aren't ready for it.' Having no role in the play had put her on the same wavelength as the audience, and she could see their struggle to understand Greg's complex mind. She also felt it would fail, and feared for Greg, knowing his vulnerability. 'Be patient with him, my dear,' she whispered in her throaty voice. 'If things go badly, he'll need lots of loving care and deep understanding.'

Sensing Greg's tension, Abby was torn between staying with him until the early hours and going home to Evelyn, whose condition had deteriorated over the past few months. 'Need you stay for the reviews?'

she asked anxiously. 'You'll read them at breakfast, anyway.'

Greg smiled grimly. 'Of course I must stay. The condemned prisoner has to hear the sentence pronounced. But I don't want you here when that happens. Go home. I'll be along as soon as I can.'

But still she stood beside him for another forty minutes, her charm and sparkle helping to lighten the mood of the party. It was nearly a quarter to one as Abby climbed the steps to her front door. Through the window, she could see Evelyn's bedside light sending a glow into the dark night, and, on entering the hall, she heard music. She crept into the room softly and saw Evelyn sleeping in the armchair with her radio on. Abby walked across to the chair, and gently shook her mother-in-law by the arm. 'Come on, my love. Into bed with you.' There was no response, and she tried again. 'Wake up, Mother. You can't sleep in the chair ...' Abby's voice trailed off as Evelyn's eyelids did not even flutter. She touched Evelyn's face, and as her fingers felt the cold flesh, alarm swept through her. Frantically, she felt the wrinkled hands. Cold. Cold as ice.

Panic-stricken, Abby telephoned for an ambulance, but even as she did so, she knew it was too late. Evelyn had died quietly in her chair whilst awaiting her return. She should have been here for her. She should have been here with her dying mother-in-law, instead of partying and drinking champagne.

Abby began to tremble. Was it possible that this woman who had meant so much to her had gone without the chance to say goodbye? Her mother-in-law was cold – so cold. Hardly knowing what she was doing, Abby pulled a blanket off the bed and wrapped it around Evelyn, as if trying to warm the life back into her. Then her eyes came to rest on the photograph Evelyn always kept beside her bed: the picture she had taken of Eddy with his mother, father and Mrs O'Connor in the garden of the house at Canvey.

'All gone,' she murmured, in a stricken voice. Then looking back at the woman who had been her loving support since childhood, Abby sank to her knees and wept like an orphaned child.

On a cold and bleak February afternoon, Evelyn Carr was laid to rest with her son and husband at the cemetery in Benfleet. The funeral was a small affair, and particularly harrowing for Abby as she watched the coffin being lowered into the earth.

Understanding her terrible grief, Susan whispered, 'Don't be sad, darling. She's reunited with them all at last.'

But she left me, thought Abby, desolate. *Her long heartache is over, but when will mine ever end?* She looked down at the graves and said, 'They're all gone now. An entire family taken before its time.'

Greg stood with a warm and protective arm about his wife, helpless to assuage her grief. He too was strangely affected by Evelyn's death, and the knowledge that Abby blamed herself for being with him and not with her mother-in-law left him feeling that he had failed both women. Useless to tell Abby that, according to the doctor, Evelyn's death had been so sudden that even had she stayed home, she wouldn't have been any the wiser.

Ross touched him on the arm and gestured towards Eddy's grave. 'That's where my father is buried. He was a hero, did you know that? He died trying to save an old lady from drowning.'

Greg gave the boy a strange look, then placed a hand on the blond head, saying: 'Yes. I did know that. He was a very brave man and so must you be now, for your mother. She's going to need you to help her through this.'

Ross frowned, wondering how he could help, then glanced at his mother, her face ravaged by grief. He had never seen her cry before and it frightened him a little. He was glad that Greg was here to keep a steady hand on everything, now that his beloved Granny was gone. 'I'll stay home from school, if you like,' he whispered solemnly. 'I don't mind.'

Greg smiled, and told him that would not be necessary. 'It was a nice thought, just the same.'

Abby's grief went deeper than she had ever thought possible. The loss of Evelyn left a void in her life that Greg was unable to fill. For the sake of her family, she kept her emotions to herself, especially since Greg was wrestling with serious problems of his own. After only two weeks, his play had been forced to close. It had shaken him badly. 'I thought I'd given them something really worthwhile,' he kept murmuring, unable to accept the fact that people expected certain things of a Hadleigh play. Even his most devoted fans had made their feelings plain by staying away in droves. His way of dealing with this crushing blow was to turn to the whisky bottle and no amount of reasoning from Abby could change this dark side of his nature.

She was desperately concerned, but her own work was at its peak with collections looming, a visit to Paris to check on the boutique, and making plans for the Rome venture. She had no time to play nursemaid, and was grateful when Greg took himself off to the house in Chiswick, ostensibly to write, but in reality to nurse his wounds. There he remained, holed up with Nelson, refusing to answer the telephone or the door, until Abby, in frustration and growing anger, simply gave up trying. Whatever state he was in, she told herself, she would rather not know. But she did want to know, and all through the showing of her collection she thought of little else.

Two days after the collection had been shown, Greg arrived in her office looking fit, clean-shaven and without a trace of alcohol on his breath. He strode across the room towards her, and, taking her left hand into his, produced a small jade bracelet he had bought in the Burlington Arcade only that morning. Placing the bracelet on her wrist, he looked down at her bewildered expression, and murmured quietly, 'I know, darling. The Crown Jewels themselves couldn't make up for the way I've treated you. Can you ever forgive me?' Placing his other hand around her shoulder, he pulled her to him, murmuring in her ear, 'I love you. Always remember that.'

'But I've been out of my mind with worry,' whispered Abby, responding to his closeness, as she always did. 'How could you do such a thing?'

'Some madness, I daresay.' His lips brushed her cheek. 'But I woke up two days ago feeling like death, and told myself it had to stop. Believe me, darling, it's the last time I go on a bender. From now on, I'll face whatever life hurls at me sober.'

She turned her head and gazed up at him. 'Truly? Have you really given up drinking?'

'Truly,' he said, pulling her closer. His lips bent to hers, then moved up to brush her temple. 'It won't happen again, I promise you that. I've missed you, Ross and little Tamsin more than I can say.'

'What made you do it?' she asked, fearful that to some degree she was responsible for his unhappiness.

'Pride, I think. I kept comparing your success with my failure. As a man, it's difficult, darling. Try to understand.'

Abby understood only too well. Eddy and Greg had one thing in common, and that was the idea that women must play second fiddle to their careers. While Greg had been on cloud nine, he'd hardly noticed her success, but when his cloud evaporated, he was as prejudiced as any man.

He moved away and thrust his hands into his pockets. 'I've been walking a lot lately, thinking about things.' He smiled. 'I've an idea for a new play.'

And if that doesn't work out, what then? she thought anxiously. *Will we go through this hell again?* Abby let the thought go, knowing she would never be able to change him, and glanced at the bracelet with shining eyes. 'Oh,

Greg, this is beautiful. You didn't have to buy this to say you're sorry. Just your being here is enough for me. I do know what you've been going through. I do understand, even though you may think I don't.' She looked up at him. 'Now, tell me your idea for this new play.'

He grinned and shook his head. 'Ah, no. It's a mere seedling waiting to germinate. When it does, then I'll discuss it with you.'

There was a knock on the door, and Avril poked her head around. 'Excuse me, Mrs Carr. I have the plane tickets for you. I thought you might like to have them now.'

'Thank you, Avril.' Abby took the tickets from her receptionist, unlocked the top drawer of her desk and placed them inside, wishing she did not have to go to Paris the following day.

'Mrs *Carr*?' Greg repeated, his tone making Abby look up with anxiety. 'Bloody hell! You'd think she'd have the courtesy to call you Mrs Hadleigh in front of me.'

She groaned inwardly. 'A slip of the tongue, that's all. We agreed it was impossible for me to change my name. I'm Abigail Carr of the House of Carr. Hadleigh would only serve to confuse. Once I enter these premises, I'm Mrs Carr. There's no insult intended – you know that.'

The intercom buzzed and Avril's voice pierced the air. 'Lady Lloyd-Farrar is here, Mrs Carr.'

Abby glanced at her watch and sighed. 'Sorry, darling, but I simply must go. This one is an autocrat from the Victorian age, so I dare not keep her waiting.'

Greg looked disappointed but resigned. 'Very well. I'll collect you for lunch at one.'

Abby frowned. 'Greg, I've so much to do. There's no way I can take time out for lunch.'

His face darkened. 'Dear God, do I have to make an appointment too? Surely one hour for your husband wouldn't make such a hole in your exciting day?'

'I really have to go.' She paused, and looked up into his dark, hurt eyes. This was no time to turn away from him – not when he needed her to help him through this trial. Who could know what strength of willpower he had summoned up to bury the weakness which threatened to maim him? In that moment, her heart melted.

'Very well,' she said, smiling. 'As soon as I've finished with Lady Lloyd-Farrar, then we'll have lunch together.' She picked up the length of blue silk she had been examining along with the sketch. 'What do you think of this, used in conjunction with a deep sea-green for this gown I've sketched?'

Greg nodded with approval. 'It would look marvellous on you.'

Abby shrugged. 'Unfortunately it's for a debutante.' She headed for the door, then looked back at him tenderly. 'Darling, I'm so glad! See you at one.'

'I'll be here,' he murmured, smiling.

Her sense of relief growing by the minute, Abby laughed light-heartedly. 'That's a date, Greg Hadleigh. Don't stand me up now.' Then her expression became serious again. 'Everything's going to be all right. This was just a hiccup, that's all. Everyone has them from time to time.'

Not you, thought Greg, as he watched the door close. As he was leaving he noticed Abby's keys were still in the desk drawer. He was about to return them, when it dawned on him that he had no idea what time her flight would be the following day. Without hesitation, he opened the drawer, and checked the airline tickets. Then, as he replaced them, he noticed a package wrapped in white tissue below a small notebook. Curiosity overcoming him, he unwrapped it carefully. Inside was the framed sketch of Richard. Something fell softly to the ground, and looking down, Greg saw several small photographs at his feet and two folded letters. The fair-haired young man in all the photos resembled the profile in the sketch. He knew that face. Had he not seen it splashed all over the newspapers a few years ago? It was Richard Glenister.

For a moment, Greg stood frozen to the spot. So she

kept him locked away in the shrine! With sinking heart, he opened the letter and read the note which had accompanied Richard's gift of a necklace three years earlier. He stared at it bleakly for a long time, unable to accept the truth. Even now, it was Richard she loved, just as he had been warned. Angry and dismayed, he wondered how any woman could be so devious as to love one man in this way, yet marry and bed another. Had she been pretending to herself that it was Richard, and not he, who made love to her during those long and passionate nights?

Shocked and sickened, Greg replaced the picture, letters and photographs, locked the drawer and returned the key to Abby's handbag. Why he did all this, he was not quite sure. All he knew was that he desperately needed a drink.

After a difficult session with her client, Abby quickly retouched her make-up and returned to her office expecting to find Greg. Glancing at her watch, she saw that she was eight minutes late. Walking across to her desk, she spoke into the intercom.

'Avril, has Mr Hadleigh telephoned?'

'No, Mrs Carr.'

'I see. He must have been held up in the traffic; in which case I shall probably be later getting back this afternoon. What time is Mrs Treece coming?'

'Two forty-five.'

Abby frowned. 'Well, I'll certainly be back in time for her, so don't worry. You can go to lunch now, Avril, and take your full hour.'

'Thank you, Mrs Carr.'

Abby sat waiting, unable to work. What on earth could have happened to Greg? After all that had been said that morning, he wouldn't leave her waiting like this unless something, some force beyond his control, had prevented him from returning. By two o'clock, she'd telephoned her home and the house at Chiswick. Mrs Proctor had not seen him, nor had she received any message from him. The

524

telephone in the Chiswick house rang and rang. Thoroughly alarmed, Abby toyed with the idea of ringing the hospitals. But what could she say? That her husband was one hour late for a luncheon engagement? As she returned to the business of the day, she was certain that Greg would contact her and explain everything.

When four thirty came, Abby could stand it no longer. Unable to concentrate on anything other than Greg, she left for Hampstead, telling herself that he would be there, cuddling his adored little Tamsin and talking to Ross. Then she remembered that Ross was spending the evening with the Bannems.

The first thing she saw as she approached the house was the vintage Bentley parked outside. Surprise gave way to relief, and relief to anger. Greg *was* all right. He was here, safe and sound, just as she had prayed he would be. Why, then, had he stood her up?

Greg was standing beside the fireplace, whisky tumbler in his right hand. The glass was half full. Her heart sinking with apprehension, Abby stared at him, nonplussed. 'What on earth ...? You *promised*. Only this morning you promised to stop all this drinking.'

'This morning is in the past.' His manner and tone sent a shudder through her. He drained the glass in three gulps, then walked across to the drinks table and refilled it.

'Don't,' said Abby weakly. 'Please, Greg, don't! What's happened? Why didn't you come for me at lunchtime? I waited and waited. You might at least have telephoned. I've been worrying.'

'How good of you,' murmured Greg, shooting her a dark look, and taking another large swallow from the glass.

'*Please*, Greg, stop this,' she pleaded. 'I don't understand. Only this morning you were so eager to start again, so keen on your idea for a new play.'

'Damn the bloody play.' He walked, a little unsteadily, over to the fireplace, and stood with his back to her.

After a long silence, Abby was forced to the conclusion

that, within two short hours, Greg had decided his idea would not work and, in despair, returned to the bottle. He must have spent lunchtime in a pub. Putting herself between him and the drinks table, she said, 'Look, I know how you feel, but ...'

'The devil you know how I feel!' he growled.

'Yes, I do know,' she said quietly. 'I create for a living, too, and it's hard, very hard sometimes. I'm expected to produce something new for each collection. If I don't, then I'm boring; if I do, and it's too different, then I'm being frivolous. With four collections a year it doesn't get easier. I can't afford to fail and I can't afford to feel sorry for myself either. There are times when my mind is a blank and everyone's waiting for it to produce something that will bowl them over. It's a problem we have in common, Greg.'

'Rot,' he snapped, heading towards the drinks table once more. 'You've a team to support you, while I'm on my own.' When she tried to bar his way, he pushed her to one side roughly, and poured more Scotch into his glass.

'Then it's just as well you *are* on your own,' whispered Abby, with growing anger. 'Dear God, if you had a company to run, with hundreds depending on you for a job, you wouldn't be so quick to run to the bottle when things get tough.'

With that, she walked out of the room, and went to her bedroom, shocked that the man she had married could suddenly turn into this hostile stranger. She should have listened to those warning bells in her head; she should have realized what they were trying to tell her. Shattered at his rough handling of her, when he had always been so gentle, Abby sat down at her dressing table, and felt her heart pounding. Was she afraid of her own husband? Suddenly, she knew that she was. Had this been the dark and dangerous thing she'd sensed in Greg, when first they met? How could she live with it? Drunkenness was something she had never encountered before. Friends

526

might become merry at parties, and she had seen plenty in their cups, but drinking on this scale was completely alien to her experience.

The bedroom door burst open. Startled, Abby turned to see Greg standing there, rage emanating from him. Yet, for all he had drunk, he seemed in control of his movements and speech. Only the fire in his eyes revealed the ugly transformation.

'Would you have walked away from Richard, the way you just walked away from me?' he asked in a threatening tone.

Abby's heart took a violent leap. *How on earth had he learned about Richard?* 'I ... I don't understand.' Her voice was shaky and fearful.

'You understand only too well. Aren't you ever going to grow out of it, for God's sake? Isn't one man enough for you?'

Wide-eyed she stared at him, confused and unable to understand how or what he'd found out. 'Richard is my cousin,' she said, trying to sound firm and in control.

He laughed. 'Your very *loving* cousin, so I believe.' Closing the door he went on. 'I've known about it since before our marriage.'

Abby stared at him dumbfounded. 'And just what do you think you know?'

'That you love him still, but were quite prepared to marry someone else.'

'Who told you such a thing?'

'Why, your other loving cousin, of course.' He leant against the door in a manner which suggested he meant to keep her a prisoner in this room.

'*Stella?*' Abby's confusion was giving way to growing alarm at the expression on Greg's face. This was not the man she had married. He had become someone else.

'She shared my bed long before you did.'

It took some time for Abby to absorb this news, but as she did, a lot of things fell into place. Most of all, it explained

Stella's hostile manner since that fateful first night. Clearly she had been in love with Greg, and had seen her half-sister as a usurper. So she had attempted to destroy Greg's love and their marriage by spiteful revelation.

'I see,' said Abby numbly, feeling somehow cheapened. 'You should have told me.'

'Did *you* tell *me*? Did you tell me that you loved another man, the man who is father to Ross? Did you tell me that you were prepared to destroy his marriage? Oh, Abby, I knew all of this before we even married. I had hoped that it was over, that I could replace him in your heart.'

'You have a strange way of trying,' said Abby. 'I haven't seen Richard for years. Can you say the same about Stella?'

Greg gave her a strange look. 'I don't keep Stella's picture and letters locked away in a secret shrine. It's a good sketch, by the way, and one I would have expected to see decorating a wall had he meant nothing to you. I read the letter with Browning's doggerel on it. *Browning*, for God's sake! Can't he even tell you he loves you in his own bloody words?'

Abby's eyes blazed with anger. That anyone should intrude on something so precious and twist it into something dirty, was bad enough, but that it should be Greg who had done this, was too much. 'You've gone too far,' she hissed. 'How *dare* you read my private letters? How *dare* you?' Her voice rose. 'You had no right!' She leapt to her feet, lips trembling with rage, fists clenching and unclenching. 'What do you know of my past? And when did I ever encroach on yours? I demand an apology. And when you've given it to me, finish what's left of the whisky, and get out of this house.'

Her words were like a red rag to an angry bull. Greg moved towards her quickly. 'Don't try sending *me* away, little lady. I'm your husband, not bloody Richard, and I'll make you forget him, if it's the last thing I ever do.'

As Abby backed away behind the bed he followed her,

his eyes black with anger, his mouth twisted in bitterness. Before she could get into the dressing room, he had caught her, pulled her close, and was pressing his lips so hard on her mouth that she gasped for air, and tried to pull away from his alcoholic breath. Her struggling only angered him further, and his hard body pressed over hers, forcing her back onto the bed. Then he was tearing at her dress, his hands tightening painfully on her breasts, his lips moving down to her exposed nipples, heedless of her cries to stop.

'You won't shut me out, you won't,' he murmured, as his hands moved down to her groin. 'I love you.'

Love? Recoiling with horror, she cried out again, 'Stop it! Have you gone mad?'

Her words seemed to stun him. Lifting his head, Greg saw her terrified face and, with a shudder, moved away from her. Without a word, he stood up, stumbled towards the door and out of the room.

Too shocked to move, Abby lay there, feeling ill. Then, somehow finding her feet, she went to the door and locked it before falling back on the bed, where she lay shaking and sobbing with fear and disgust.

She heard the front door slam, and prayed Greg had gone. Some time later, Mrs Proctor knocked on her door.

'Is everything all right, Mrs Hadleigh?'

Abby sat up quickly. 'Yes, thank you.' The argument must have been heard all over the house. 'I'll be down in a minute. Mr Hadleigh has gone out, I take it?'

'He has, Mrs Hadleigh.'

'Then will you bolt the front and back doors, please?'

'How will Mr Hadleigh let himself in?'

'He won't be letting himself in, not unless I give orders to that effect. Right now, he's not to re-enter this house.'

Abby went to the bathroom, where she splashed cold water on her face, before getting under a shower. *He'll never come back, never, not while I have any say.* She put on her nightgown, checked that her face and lips weren't too bruised, even if one side of her cheek seemed a little swollen, then went downstairs to make sure Mrs Proctor had locked the doors. The bolt was in place. It would take six men to break down that solid Georgian door.

'Dinner is ready, Mrs Hadleigh,' said the housekeeper gently. 'I think you should try to eat a little.'

For her sake, Abby tried to eat some of the roast beef that had been so carefully cooked earlier that evening, but she could hardly swallow. Ashen-faced, she moved about the house like a shadow, wishing, with all her heart, that Evelyn were still there with her. How could Greg have behaved in that manner? But it had been the drink talking. No wonder his last marriage had ended in such acrimony. Her thought fled to Richard, and what might have been. *Dear, gentle Richard!* Tears of longing filled her eyes. But Richard wasn't here, and there was always the danger that Greg might return. Supposing he tried to snatch Tamsin away from her? This was no time to be going to Paris.

The following morning the bruised lips had more or less returned to normal, but Abby was still pale and shaken. Worried about the baby, she gave strict instructions to both the nanny and Mrs Proctor that Greg was not to enter the house while she was in Paris.

'Don't worry, Mrs Hadleigh. We'll take care of everything, so put your mind at rest.'

Abby smiled at Mrs Proctor's reassuring words. No one had mentioned the ugly scene of the night before and she was glad of their diplomacy and support.

Although Abby hated being away at such a time, Paris lifted her spirits. The boutique was doing exceptionally well. Parisians, it seemed, liked her styles almost as well as they liked Chanel's.

Odile had arranged for her fashion magazine to do a profile on Abby, then whisked her off to the Bois de Boulogne where a Count had arranged a small dinner party in her honour. To Abby's surprise, Maria Callas was among the guests. Great though this honour was, Abby's thoughts kept returning to Hampstead, wondering what Greg might do. Each time she telephoned, she was assured that all was well. Mr Hadleigh had not returned. The relief Abby felt was tempered with growing concern.

By the time she was airborne once more, she was blaming herself for Greg's fatal step backwards. Only that morning he'd come to his senses, and was looking forward to the future. What a fool she had been to keep Richard's picture and letters locked away like that! The picture should have been hanging on a wall, and the letters long destroyed.

To think he had known all this time and yet said nothing! She could have killed Stella for destroying the happiness they might have known. She began to pity Greg. He had known the truth, yet married her anyway. There was a great deal of love in that. And she, too, had loved him. Oh, not in the way she loved Richard, but with as much love as she had left to give. Until the failure of his play, their marriage had been successful. Was it all to go down the drain then, all that love and passion and hope for the future? Abby remembered the look on his face. That night he had hated her, and had tried to rape her in his drunken rage. How could she ever forget that?

By the time the plane landed, she had determined on her only course of action. Divorce!

Her solicitor gently pointed out that 'desertion' would be better grounds than 'cruelty', which was hard to prove. Drunken husbands beat their wives all the time, and probably raped them, too. The wife had no recourse to law in matters of this kind, unless there were witnesses to prove that her life was in danger. Rape in marriage did not exist. It would be seen by the court as a man's right, and a domestic matter between a man and his wife.

'If he is agreeable, then adultery on his part would be the easiest way. It can all be arranged. These things usually are, you know.'

Abby looked at the bespectacled, bald-headed man, who

531

had represented her affairs for years, and could hardly believe she was hearing this.

'Brighton, you mean,' she snapped. 'The maid walks in and discovers two people in bed together and that is grounds for divorce, whereas a man can practically beat his wife to death, and rape her at will, and that is not?' Sensing she had made him uncomfortable, she added: 'Of course, that did not actually happen, but he *was* violent — which is how he gets when he drinks.'

'He has got to want this divorce as well, otherwise it's going to be a long, expensive and ugly affair, Mrs Hadleigh. Separation is unmessy and more discreet, but it takes years and, in that time, the parties must not meet, or you have to go back to square one.'

Abby sighed. 'Then adultery it must be. I'm sure I can find the grounds.' But, as she left the office, she knew she could never hire a sleazy detective to spy on Greg. Later, when tempers had subsided a little, maybe then he would agree to the divorce. What did it matter how long it took? She would never marry again. Not after this.

Susan was horrified when she learned the marriage was over, although she had guessed things were not going well for Abby. For some time now she had looked like a woman about to break. Discreet probing had caused the shell to soften, and release the human being locked inside. Susan had listened with true sadness and had not sought to advise, only to be there for Abby at such a time.

'Better no marriage at all than a bad one,' Abby said. 'That's one problem you and Bernard will never have, I'm certain of it.'

Susan's marriage had been a huge success. Bernard was regarded as highly talented in the world of stage and television set design. Their small flat in Chelsea was usually filled with friends who'd 'just drop by' in the evenings or at weekends so it had become almost an art centre. Abby had always envied this aspect of Susan's life, although she sometimes wondered what she did for privacy. Now she asked herself how Susan could possibly be expected to understand the darker side of married life when she and Bernard lived only in the light.

'Look, darling,' said Susan, 'you're not to spend time alone at Hampstead. Come to us for a while. We've got a spare bedroom and ...'

'It's very tempting, but I have children. Ross is already asking questions.'

Susan sighed. 'He would have been better at boarding school as things are. Bring him, too. Your nanny can look after the baby. You should be with people at such a time, not with your own gloomy thoughts. If Greg should return, then ...'

'Then I ought to be there,' Abby cut in.

'I was going to say, you'd best not be there,' said Susan. 'I thought the idea was that he was to keep away.'

Abby was thoughtful, then looked up at her friend. 'It's very tempting, Susan, and you're very kind. But I really wouldn't be very good company right now.'

Nodding with understanding, Susan murmured, 'Just as you like. But don't feel you're alone with this one. We can help.' She walked to the door. 'Must get back upstairs. This is no way to get Lady Tiptree's ballgown finished. We're having a party on Saturday evening – nothing fancy, just a 'bring a bottle' bash. I wish you would come. You can stay in the spare room. It'll do you good.'

Abby nodded and grinned at her friend. 'I might just take you up on that. A bottle party, eh! Rather like old times, except no one could afford a bottle in those days. I'll bring something rather special.'

'You just bring yourself,' said Susan. Before she shut the door, she looked back to see Abby still sitting before her desk staring into emptiness.

Abby did not get to go to the party, since at six o'clock on Saturday the police contacted her with news of Greg. He had been found lying face downwards on the river path late one night, with Nelson standing guard over his body, barking at anyone who tried to approach.

Shocked and frightened, Abby drove to the Hammersmith Hospital where she found a curt doctor. 'Alcoholic poisoning is one problem, concussion the other. He took a heavy fall and cracked his head badly.'

'How bad is he?' she asked anxiously. This all seemed like a dream; hopefully she would wake up before she heard any more bad news.

'Conscious now,' said the doctor. 'He's been here for two days. No identification on him, you see.'

'Then I'd like to see him straight away,' said Abby. 'Which ward is he in?'

The doctor looked a little embarrassed. 'I'm afraid that Mr Hadleigh is not well enough to see anyone.'

Abby's eyes widened. 'You said he was conscious. How ill is he?'

'He's going to be all right as far as the concussion goes. It's a matter of drying out. We've done all we can for him, but now he needs specialist help. I can recommend an excellent clinic which he should be transferred to as soon as you give your consent.'

Abby blinked, and looked at him in puzzlement. 'You think he's an alcoholic, don't you? Well, he isn't. He's only started drinking like this because he's been under a lot of strain lately.'

The doctor nodded sympathetically. 'Even so, he's in a bad way now, and needs professional help. I'd leave it to the experts to say whether he's an alcoholic or not. He certainly needs to dry out and spend some time in counselling. He's also going through something else — self-disgust. I've had strict instructions that he wants no visitors, especially his wife. Oh, please, Mrs Hadleigh, don't worry about that. It's all quite natural and understandable. Give him time. Meanwhile, I'll give you the address of the clinic and tomorrow we'll have him transferred there. I would wait for another week before visiting, and check first with the doctors there before you do. They're experts in the field, so I think you should take their advice.'

In a daze, Abby returned to her car. *Clinic? Alcoholism? Greg in the hands of white-coated men who would tell her when she could see her own husband? What had happened to her world?*

A week later, she drove to a village in Hertfordshire where the clinic, situated in a large Victorian house, was set back among woodland in two acres of grounds. The trees lining the long driveway were still bare of leaf; daffodils swayed in the cold April wind, and the sun was trying to break through scurrying clouds.

Eight days had passed since Greg had arrived: eight days in which Abby had tried to reassess her future without him, fearing that her rejection could cause a set-back. Dreading the coming encounter, she parked the car outside the large entrance porch and removed a suitcase, packed with day clothes, toiletries, reams of blank paper and pencils. Suitcase in one hand and portable typewriter in the other, she walked into the building and down the tiled corridors, fighting a strong desire to flee.

One of the attendants led her to the old conservatory where Greg stood alone, in hospital pyjamas under a striped candlewick dressing gown, staring out at the woods beyond. Turning at her approach, he looked at her in amazement.

'Why did you come?' he said in a gruff voice. 'I told them, no visitors.'

Abby put down the suitcase and typewriter, and stood unsmiling in the doorway, her blue, mink-trimmed coat buttoned to the neck, hair loose and windswept. Dark shadows beneath her eyes accused him, filling him with remorse so that he looked away quickly, but not before she had registered shock at his appearance. The only colour in his face was the hideous weal on his forehead, where the stitches could still be seen. He was thinner too, she noticed, feeling a wave of pity flow through her. *Stella,*

535

you bitch! she thought grimly. *Like mother, like daughter.
You have a great deal to answer for, and one day you'll
answer to me.*

At that moment, the sun broke through the clouds once
more, filling the conservatory with warmth and life. Abby
removed her suede gloves, still shocked at the sight of Greg
and a little afraid of him. 'I brought your clothes and your
typewriter,' she said quietly. 'I thought ... well, I thought
you might want to get on with that play you were about
to start.'

Greg turned slowly, keeping his eyes averted from her.
'That was a million years ago. As for clothes, I doubt if
I'll be allowed to wear them. They keep me dressed this
way so that I can't leave. Can you believe that?' Then
he looked at Abby, aware of her frail beauty and how
much he had hurt her. What on earth would she think
if she knew that within these walls alcoholics raved and
drug addicts screamed? One look at some of his fellow
patients had been enough to put him off drink for the
rest of his life. What would Abby know of such things?
'But I suppose it's all for my own good.'

'Yes,' Abby whispered, wondering how to break the
long and awkward silence which followed. 'Are you feeling
better?' she asked at last.

'Oh yes,' he answered, a shade too briskly. 'Heaps better.
I'll be out of here shortly.' For a moment their eyes met,
but this time it was Abby who looked away, fear mingling
with love and understanding.

'Your wound looks pretty horrible. Does it hurt
much?'

Greg forced a light laugh. 'You can blame Nelson for
that! Oh yes, I'd had a few, but I wasn't so drunk I
couldn't stay on my feet. He ran straight across my path,
I lost my already precarious balance and fell. I remember
thinking, "Thank God it's low tide," before blacking out.
Where is he, by the way?'

'With me, of course.' Abby stayed on the far side of the

room, the large coffee table between them, and sat down in a rather shabby armchair. 'They said you could have died. Nelson's barking alerted someone, and then he refused to let anyone get near until the police came. I'm told you'll be here a little longer. Anyway, your clothes are in the case ...' Her voice trailed off. She had not prepared herself for the shock of seeing him so much thinner, his face drawn and haggard, with only the eyes to remind her of the old Greg. 'This has happened to you before, hasn't it?'

For a long time Greg leaned on the window ledge, looking at the light on her soft, curling hair. 'Not quite like this,' he said at last. 'I went on a bender in New York after ... after the marriage failed. But that wasn't the reason. We had a small son. He was not quite one year old, when she walked out on me. It was winter and snowing badly. She was driving to her parents in Connecticut when a lorry skidded into her car. The baby was killed outright.' His voice thickened and it seemed he was on the verge of weeping.

'Oh, Greg. Why didn't you ever tell me? I'm so sorry.'

'This is the first time I've been able to speak of it,' he whispered. 'Anyway, after that I hit the bottle. Things got bad, but not as bad as this. I recovered. For months I didn't touch the stuff, then I found that I could drink socially once more without any craving. Until a few weeks ago.' Their eyes met: hers anxious and confused, his reflecting the love he still had for her. 'Dear God,' he murmured, 'how in the world did I get to that appalling night? I can't ask you to forgive me, darling, because I'll never forgive myself. But I want you to know that I love you, and the last thing I ever meant to do was hurt you in any way.'

Until this moment Abby had been quite certain that divorce was her only way out. But now, seeing him so desperate, so filled with guilt and remorse and nursing such painful memories, she knew she couldn't go through with it. He needed her. How could she turn her back on him now? Was it love she still felt for him, she wondered, or pity? Whatever it was had something to do with three happy years — years that could not be tossed aside quite so easily, after all. Then there was Ross to think about, Ross who now saw Greg as his father.

From across the room, Greg watched the small hands twisting in Abby's lap and sensed that she was still afraid of him. If only he could remember what had happened that night! These past days had drifted by in a semi-conscious haze, so that it was difficult to tell reality from dreams. Had he dreamt about the attack on his wife which had caused her to scream? If not, then God help him. After that, his brain had turned to scrambled egg, and only the memory of Nelson sending him flying on the river path shone through that mess. Perhaps he should be in prison. As it was, he would live in a prison of his own making, as he had done since his little son was killed.

Greg moved towards Abby, saw the shadow of fear in her eyes and stopped. Would she ever lose that look?

'I love you more than anything in the world,' he said. 'You can't know how much it hurts to see you afraid of me.'

Suddenly, Abby felt a heart-melting pity and her fear vanished. She walked slowly across the room towards him, reached out, and let him take her hands into his. 'Not any more,' she whispered. Seeing the love in his eyes, she went on. 'Oh, Greg, we should never have kept such secrets from each other. Had you told me about Stella, then I would have explained about Richard. As it was, I was afraid to speak of him for fear of losing you.'

Greg's hands tightened on hers. 'And I thought that if you knew about my old relationship with Stella, I would lose you. I simply hoped to replace Richard in your heart. When Tamsin was born, I truly believed it had happened. We were happy then, very happy — or so I thought.'

'I thought so, too,' murmured Abby. 'But how could I have known of the suspicion lurking in your mind? I don't know what Stella told you, but I can guess. As for Richard, well, I sent him from my life a long time ago. Now, he's happily married, just as I was until ...' She sighed, and turned her face away from Greg's intense gaze. 'As for the picture you found, it's been in that drawer for years. I couldn't let Evelyn see it because, as you can see for yourself, Ross bears a strong resemblance to his father. Evelyn never knew the truth and neither does Ross. I know that some day he will have to be told, but I shall choose the time and place for that.' Abby knew he was thinking of the letters, also locked away, but made no mention of them. Reaching up, she stroked his face gently. 'Try to understand there are things which even now I cannot share with you, things that go deep into my very being. I don't ask you to tell me of your feelings before you met me. That would be quite wrong, and in the end we would only end up hurting each other unnecessarily. When we met, we started anew, and put our past behind us.'

'Did we?' murmured Greg, in a strange tone. 'How far behind us would it be if Richard were suddenly free to marry again?'

She let her hand fall quickly. 'That's a silly thing to say! You just told me you still loved me. Are you now trying to say you want a divorce?'

He grabbed her hands once more and, holding them tightly, looked into her eyes. 'Do *you*?'

A sense of dismay crept over Abby. She thought she had reached through to him, but now realized she had merely been chipping away at ice which could not be broken so easily. *Give it time to melt*, she told herself.

'At first I thought that I did. Now, seeing you again ... I know that I don't. But you haven't answered my question.'

His tense hold on her hands relaxed. Why were they dancing around each other like this when all he really wanted to do was clasp her to him and never let her go? His only desire had been to love and protect her; instead, he had hurt her. Even if she were prepared to forgive him, would she ever completely trust him again?

He pulled her against him. 'The last thing on God's earth I want is to spend my life without you, my love. Will you forgive me, and have me back? Can we make another start?'

She nodded, looked up at him and smiled tremulously. Gently he kissed her on the mouth, a kiss of sweet tenderness that told her more than passion could ever say. Placing her arms about him, she leant her head against his chest and felt his heart beating. 'Battlefields have a way of becoming havens of peace. Well, our battle is done. I think, when you leave this place, we should go away to somewhere warm for a short holiday, and give ourselves a break. Meanwhile, Tamsin and Ross will be glad to see you back. Tamsin's been fretful. A late tooth, I think.'

'Poor little mite,' murmured Greg. 'I'm longing to see her again, and Ross, too.' He frowned. 'What explanation did you give him for my sudden disappearance?'

'At first, I said that you were away doing research. Eventually I had to tell him you'd been involved in a slight accident. He was very worried and wanted to visit you, but I told him that the hospital didn't allow children to visit.'

'You're sure he has no inkling of . . .'

'No,' cut in Abby quickly. She moved away and pulled on her gloves once more. 'Leaving already?' Greg sounded disappointed.

Abby indicated the male nurse hovering outside the door. 'I don't think I have much choice. Anyway, I've brought you the tools of your trade. So *write*, Greg, and put everything else from your mind.'

He walked with her to the front entrance. 'Will you come again tomorrow?'

Opening the door of the car, Abby nodded. 'Every day, until they throw you out.' Climbing into the driving seat, she felt a sudden swell of emotion which set her eyes stinging with tears. Greg tapped on the car window. She wound it down and they kissed.

'Drive carefully,' said Greg with a worried expression. 'Looks like some heavy weather coming up. Ring me when you get home, so that I know you're safe.'

Promising that she would, Abby started the engine and eased slowly along the drive. Glancing in her rear mirror, she saw him standing there looking after her, a forlorn figure in a striped dressing gown. *Poor, poor Greg.* What he must be going through was a despair infinitely worse than her own. It had always been there, this dark abyss which kept trying to claim him. It was up to her now to see that it did not.

She had married him for his strength and found herself to be the stronger; she had married him for his warmth, passion and intellect, only to find how easily this could turn into something terrifying. Lastly, she had married him so that Ross could have a father, and found herself lying to her son to keep him from the truth. Now she knew that she loved Greg because he needed her. For better or for worse she had vowed to keep him unto her. Well, she had seen the worst. Things could only get better with each passing day. They would start again, and this time she would not allow Richard to come between them.

CHAPTER TWENTY

Samantha yawned sleepily and held out her glass for more champagne. Jeremy filled it at once.

She lay on the sofa in his Eaton Square drawing room, her satin negligee falling open to reveal a bare leg. Since Richard had become an MP she saw little of him. If he was not at his constituency surgery, he was at all-night sittings in the House of Commons. Jeremy, on the other hand, always made time available for her needs, and with him she could be a very different person to the one Richard knew. She liked the rough way Jeremy made love to her: sexual behaviour which would shock Richard – and would have shocked her, too, had she cared for Jeremy. As it was, he was uncomplicated fun, and her lack of feeling for him stripped her of all inhibitions, allowing her to play the part of whore. She felt no guilt at deceiving Richard, telling herself that any husband who ignored his wife to the extent he did deserved to be cuckolded.

She looked up at Jeremy, as he refilled his own glass, and stood gazing down at the traffic cruising past his London home. It was late May and the evening was exceptionally warm. He opened the window, and sighed. 'It's nights like this when I think we should get air conditioning installed.'

Samantha stretched like a cat. 'You know, Jeremy, darling, with all your wealth and two fantastic homes, I can't understand why you haven't made a good marriage by now. Instead you waste your life on silly old me.' She had said this so many times in her little-girl voice, she knew the answer by heart.

'You were the only one I wanted, my love,' he said

casually, not even bothering to look at her. *The stupid bitch!* Did she really believe she was the only woman he ever brought here? He had failed to ruin Richard, but he could still use and humiliate Glenister's wife whenever he chose. Besides, his relationship with Samantha was his way of keeping tabs on Richard. She talked too much for an MP's wife. He suspected that Richard knew it and kept important things to himself. Even so, he lived in hope.

Samantha sat up and frowned at him. 'Seriously, Jeremy, why haven't you married? A man like you should have the pick of the bunch.'

He gave a curt laugh. 'The pick of the English roses? Good God, what a prospect. I shall probably marry some flamboyant American whose father owns a huge stud farm in Kentucky. You think I'm wealthy? God's teeth, when one has an historic house to look after, money doesn't go anywhere. No, it's a rich American or nothing. Meanwhile, you'll do very nicely.' Jeremy turned from the window to look at her languorous body, thinking her as desirable as a perfectly carved statue: something to admire, not to love. Abby had been a different prospect. But he had made a fool of himself over her and even now, that hurt. Nothing Samantha did could touch him in any way.

He forced a smile. 'I'm waiting for you to divorce that idiot you married! How can you stay with him, when I can offer you wealth and a title? Wouldn't you like to be a Viscountess, my dear?'

Samantha moved voluptuously, and purred. 'Wealth I shall have one day. Oh, not like yours, of course, but Daddy's already made the estate over to me to avoid death duties later. As for a title, well ... as it happens, Richard's father already has one.'

Jeremy looked so bemused, it sent her into gales of laughter. 'It's true! Oh, darling, your face is a hoot. Richard's father is a baron, no less. William Glenister was Richard's stepfather. Now do you understand?'

Jeremy frowned. 'No. Why does he call himself

Glenister? It's unusual to take the name of the stepfather, surely?'

'Apparently not, and it's all quite legal. Richard prefers it to remain that way.'

Sensing a good story, Jeremy sat down beside Samantha. 'Why?'

'Because his father happens to be German. During the war it wouldn't have been so nice for him, running around with a name like von Schreiber.'

Jeremy looked thoughtful, then stared into her eyes with an intensity that should have sent a warning note. 'What name did you say?'

'Schreiber. Baron Karl von Schreiber, and he's loaded. Has a huge business empire and a lineage to equal yours.' She swallowed the rest of her champagne and held it up for more. 'I'm empty again.'

'Schreiber,' murmured Jeremy to himself, his mind flicking through dates and names until it suddenly focused. 'Good God. So *that's* who he was. Glenister's father. Well, well, that goes some way towards explaining why Abby was with him.' Seeing the look of confusion on Samantha's face, he smiled. 'I met him once. He was lunching with Richard's cousin.' He took the bottle of champagne from the ice bucket and returned thoughtfully to Samantha's side. 'Now, what do you suppose he was doing lunching with her?'

Samantha looked at him sharply. 'I have no idea. I've never met the man, and neither has Richard. What's more, he doesn't wish to. Can we drop this very boring subject now, please?'

Jeremy ran a hand up her leg, feeling a thrill of excitement which had nothing to do with his hand on her flesh. At last he had a weapon he could fire at Richard with complete accuracy.

'Wealthy, you say? Then Richard's a fool not to get closer to his Dad. What kind of business is he in?'

'Industry of some sort,' shrugged Samantha, wishing

544

she had never raised the subject. Jeremy was too full of questions. 'Look, can we drop the subject, please?'

Jeremy shrugged. 'Very well. But I did see him with Abby – twice, in fact. Strange, don't you think?'

'Abby!' Samantha sat up, her eyes flashing with anger. 'Why do you keep bringing her name up? What's so interesting about her, for goodness' sake?'

'Because one can't simply ignore her.' Jeremy paused, then said, 'And who but she could have found the money to stop Richard from going bust after the Langdon fiasco?'

'Don't mention that. It was all your fault for not warning me in time. Richard's convinced you did it deliberately. Anyway, Abby had nothing to do with the money, as it happens. It makes my blood boil to think that Richard, and just about everyone else, believes that she did.'

Feigning surprise, Jeremy shook his head. 'It was Abby, all right. No one else could have done it, given that no one else knew.'

'It *wasn't* Abby,' cried Samantha. 'Why don't you listen to me? It was the baron. She got him to give Richard the money, that was all.'

As soon as she had spoken, Samantha realized she'd said far more than prudence allowed, and stared at Jeremy in alarm. 'Now look ... what I just said ... all that has to be a secret. I'm not supposed to know. And you mustn't tell a soul. Please, Jeremy, promise me you'll keep this to yourself.'

Smiling, Jeremy let his fingers stray a little further up her leg. 'Of course. Everything you say to me is strictly off the record. You know that, my sweet. You can always trust me.'

A week later, Richard Glenister took his place on the platform of the Town Hall which was housing the public meeting to determine once and for all whether or not his constituency would have a bypass. The question of where this road should be had been a thorn in his flesh for far too long. One or two local newspapers had sent reluctant reporters along, and only one national saw fit to report the outcome. The national belonged to the group owned by Lord Hexgrave.

One by one the panel put their case to the public who, for the most part, sat in horrified silence as the death sentence on their land was passed. Questions were then invited from the audience, and Richard was about to answer one, when a man stood up to shout in a loud voice:

'I have a question, sir, which concerns the country as a whole. Is it not a disgrace that the son of a Nazi war criminal should be the Member of Parliament for this constituency? Furthermore, is it not a disgrace that the Member in question should receive large sums of money from this man?' Seeing the stunned look on Richard's face the man went on. 'Is it fair to all our boys who lost their lives in the war? I call upon our Member of Parliament to resign.' With that, the man walked out, leaving the audience shocked and silent.

Suddenly a flash bulb dazzled Richard, followed by another, and another. The hall filled with the babble of four hundred voices raised in disbelief. Still trying to make sense of the man's words, Richard waited until the chairman called the meeting to order once more, then stood up and said, 'I'm very sorry for that outburst. It was quite meaningless to me, I'm glad to say. Now then, I'm here to answer questions, so let's get on with it, shall we?'

Concentrating as hard as he could on the question of the bypass, Richard was still in shock from the words that had been shouted through the hall. As the evening wore on he began to feel a cold fist squeezing his heart, sending shivers of foreboding through him.

'I suppose it's going to be very hot in Rome at this time of year,' said Abby, smiling at Greg across the breakfast table.

'Steaming,' he answered, as he poured himself another cup of coffee. 'Couldn't you have opened your boutique in the autumn instead of June?'

'Autumn is Collection time. Although things seem so chaotic there it might have been wiser to put it back a week or two. Roland's gone on ahead, and the stock arrived in good time, but I'm uneasy about this one. No Odile looking after things! I wish you would change your mind and come with me, it would do you good. Give you a break from all the writing you've been doing lately.'

Greg shook his head. 'Someone should stay with the children. Since I'm glued to the typewriter, it might as well be me. Also I'm going great guns at the moment. Can't be torn away from the thought process.'

She would miss him, even for a few days, but Abby was glad he would be here for the children. Since their return from Bermuda, Greg had been his old self, writing well, walking with Nelson on the Heath, spoiling little Tamsin and being a good father to Ross. She felt she could leave the country without due concern.

Outside a car horn blared and Ross came racing down the stairs.

'It's the Bannems and I can't find my violin anywhere!'

'It's where you left it,' said Abby with amusement. 'In the study.' She lifted her face to his as he came to kiss her goodbye, then gave him a warm hug. Next year he would be at Stowe, and she would miss him dreadfully.

'I'll miss you, darling. Be good for Greg and Mrs Proctor.'

'You have a good time in Rome,' said Ross. 'Will you bring me back a present?'

'Of course,' said Abby, laughing. 'Now off with you, or the Bannems will be driving to Kensington minus one very important passenger.'

Abby went with her son to the front door, and waved

547

goodbye. Then, feeling weepy, she returned to the breakfast table, wishing she did not have to go anywhere. All she wanted was to be here with her husband and children.

Turning her attention to the morning paper, she scanned the front page when suddenly the sub-headline caught her eye.

TORY MP ACCUSED

Mr Richard Glenister, the Tory MP for Chiltingham, has been accused of being the son of a Nazi war criminal. The accusation came yesterday evening during a meeting of the Chiltingham Council and the public to discuss the new bypass route. Mr Glenister had been answering questions, when a man stood up and made the accusation.

Questioned later, the man, who refused to give his name, claimed that Mr Glenister's father is Baron Karl von Schreiber, the German industrialist and the only remaining member of the notorious family who built up German industry from the late nineteenth century, culminating in the huge war machine of Hitler's Third Reich. The accuser further suggested that a large amount of money was paid to Mr Glenister by his father to clear debts after heavy losses on the stock market.

Abby felt the blood draining from her face. She could hardly breathe. It was impossible that anyone could say such things! Impossible also that anyone should connect Richard with Karl.

Greg wandered back into the dining room, suede jacket slung over his shoulder. 'Isn't it time you were on your way, little lady?' He frowned as he saw the strange expression on her face. 'What is it, darling? You're as white as a sheet.'

Abby's eyes were fixed ahead. 'It's nothing. Nothing.'

'Yes, it damn well is,' said Greg, in growing alarm. His

eyes slid to the newspaper she was clutching so tightly, and gently he took it from her. When he had finished reading, he looked at her coldly.

'We don't seem to be able to get away from him, do we? Is it true what they're saying?'

'No,' Abby sighed. 'How can you even think it? They're wicked lies. Karl isn't a war criminal or a Nazi. Good God, do you think I'd have anything to do with him if that were true?'

Greg glanced back at the paper. 'But his family were the famous industrialists with all those factories on the Ruhr?'

Abby looked at him, aware of his thoughts. 'Yes, but ...'

'Have you any idea what went on in those factories?' asked Greg harshly. 'Have you never read about the slave labour, the Poles and Slavs who were literally worked to death as part of Himmler's policy?'

'You don't understand ...'

'No, Abby, it's you who doesn't understand. And you wouldn't be so quick to anger over this if von Schreiber weren't Richard's father.'

'That's a dreadful thing to say,' cried Abby. 'And what do you know about it, anyway?'

'What do I know about it?' The anger in Greg's voice was barely under control. 'When you and your lover-boy cousin were mere children, I was risking my life bombing von Schreiber's bloody factories. Do you know what that cost in human lives? God, when I think about the men who didn't return from those missions ...' His voice trailed off in despair. 'You're wasting your sympathy on the wrong side, Abby. If Karl feels he's been hard done by, then let him sue. That goes for Glenister, also. They're old enough to look after themselves. It has nothing to do with you. Meanwhile, I have work to do, and so have you.'

He strode to the front door and, turning, saw Abby standing behind him, her face pale. 'Dear God, what's

549

the matter with us, arguing like this? It's hard on your cousin − I do understand that. But he should never have placed himself in such a vulnerable position. It's unfair, darling, I know, but the sins of the fathers will always be visited on the children. It's what *we* feel that counts in the end.'

'And just what am I supposed to feel?' asked Abby coldly.

'Nothing. It has nothing to do with you.'

Abby shook her head. 'God, you're slow at times! If Ross is Richard's son, then he's also the grandchild of Karl von Schreiber. Or didn't that thought occur to you?'

For some time, Greg looked at her in silence and then, seeing her despair, he moved forward and clasped her face between his hands. Tears brimmed in those lovely green eyes, and, as they began to fall, he kissed them tenderly. 'Don't cry. Ross has Carr for a surname. He'll never be told anything different.'

'Oh, yes, he will. Too many people know, including Stella. She has already threatened to tell him; so has Samantha, and one day Milicent might ...'

'That's only supposition.'

Abby looked away. 'I promised myself I would tell him, and, when Evelyn died, I truly meant to. But each time I tried to broach the subject, I couldn't do it. I just couldn't snatch away my little boy's happiness. But the longer I put it off, the more danger there is of his being hurt by it.'

'At the moment, I would say that your instinct for not saying anything is the right one.'

'Meanwhile, I must let Karl know what is being said about him. I must give him the chance to clear his name, and Richard's too.'

Greg's eyes darkened. 'Stay out of it, for God's sake. You have your own life to lead. Think only about Rome and the boutique. By the time you return, all this will have died down.' He held her close, and kissed her passionately. 'Have a safe journey, my love, and ring me as soon as you reach your hotel. I'll be waiting for your call. And now I have to be at the theatre in thirty minutes.'

Abby stood on the steps watching as his car sped away. How could Greg be expected to understand that the man she had always loved was part of her very existence, a thing apart from her marriage? That man was now in deep trouble, and she had to do something.

Picking up the newspaper, she re-read the article, still unable to believe that anyone could say such things. Then she realized: this was one of Lord Hexgrave's newspapers. *Jeremy!* Of course. Her thoughts travelled back across the years to a smart wedding reception, and those full moist lips saying, '*I'll bring him down one day.*' Well, he had chosen the wrong man. When she acquainted Karl with the facts, he would slap a lawsuit on Lord Hexgrave before he could say 'hot metal'.

Walking back into the drawing room, she placed a call to Düsseldorf, only to be told that the baron was away. She then placed a call to Paris.

Odile was surprised to hear from Abby at such an early hour, and soon gleaned that something was wrong. Karl, she said, would be in Paris that evening, but would be rushing off to Geneva at the crack of dawn.

'I have to talk to him urgently, but I can't talk about it over the phone,' said Abby. 'Look, I'm on my way to Rome today, but I'll make a detour to Paris for a few hours.'

'Tonight then, my dear.' There was a click as Odile replaced the telephone. Abby then put a call through to Brook Street and asked Avril to change her plane booking. 'But Avril, I'd be grateful if no one knew of this change. Only Roland. No one else – no one at all.'

In Beauchamp Place, Samantha was feeling physically ill. She had read the newspaper and realized how Jeremy had used her. The thought of his naked sweating body over hers now made her shudder with shame. She felt like a

Shepherd Market whore, and had been treated in much the same way. Trembling with anger, humiliation and guilt, she watched as Richard read the article, and saw his face turn ashen.

'It's lies — all bloody, rotten lies,' he said at last. 'How dare they? I don't know my father, but I'm sure he wasn't any of these things. Damn it, he wasn't even an industrialist, just a doctor! Mother told me. And what's all this about money?' He threw down the paper, and glared at his wife. 'If I catch the devil who burst into that meeting, I'll sue him for every penny he owns. Why did he *do* it? It's senseless.'

'I shouldn't make too much fuss, Richard,' said Samantha, nervously pouring coffee into his cup. 'Best to let these things die a natural death.'

'*My* death, you mean — my political death. Members of Parliament don't have Nazi war criminals as fathers. Someone is out to damage the Government, and with this coming so close on the heels of the Profumo affair, they might well manage it. It's up to me to scotch the lies before it's too late.' At that moment, the telephone rang. Richard answered it, then returned to the dining room. 'That was the Chief Whip's office. I'm called to the Presence already.' He looked utterly despondent. 'Now it all begins. This is your friend's doing! He swore long ago to destroy me and he failed last time, but now ... who can say?'

'Be careful,' said Samantha. 'The onus is on you now to prove the newspaper wrong. Take that money, for instance. How do you know where it came from?'

Richard was pulling on his jacket. 'Oh, I know, and I can prove it. Have no fear on that score.'

Samantha stared at him, with narrowing eyes. 'You think it came from Abby, don't you? But supposing you're wrong? Why don't you check with your bank manager?'

Glancing at his watch, Richard shook his head. 'The bank isn't open yet. Meanwhile, I can't keep the Chief Whip waiting. As for you, don't say anything to anyone.'

'Oh what it is to be the wife of an MP. Shall I hide in a broom cupboard?' Samantha walked with him to the front door then froze at the sight of press reporters and photographers outside her home. 'You can't go out there! You can't, Richard. I'll call the police and have them removed.'

Richard pushed her gently to one side. 'Don't be such an idiot.' He forced his way through the reporters, who fired off questions in rapid succession.

'Is there any truth in the allegations against you, sir?'

Richard smiled. 'I thought the allegations were made against my father.'

'And what have you to say about those, sir?'

'Nothing. I have never met, nor had any dealings with, my father – my true father, that is. I was raised in Canterbury by my English mother and English stepfather. That is all I can tell you, gentlemen.'

'But was your true father a Nazi industrialist, sir?'

Richard climbed into the car, shaking his head. 'As far as I know, he was, and still is, a doctor.'

'But what about this money, sir? It's been alleged that you accepted vast sums from Baron von Schreiber.'

Richard started the ignition. 'That allegation is quite false,' he replied, then closed the door and drove as quickly as he could to Westminster. Once there, he made his way along the corridors of power to his office and telephoned his bank, insisting on the information denied to him four years earlier. The old manager had since died, and he was told his successor would have to check back through the files.

'That's all right, I'll hang on,' said Richard, heart pounding with anxiety and the rush to get to the House in time for his appointment with the Chief Whip. Impatiently he waited, tapping his fingers on the receiver until the manager's voice crackled in his ears.

'Mr Glenister, this will take some time, but it might help you to know that my secretary remembers the occasion quite well. The cheque was brought in personally by a Mrs Carr.

553

I understand that the lady in question is quite famous, and that my secretary has never quite forgotten the occasion. Does that help you for now?'

Breathing a huge sigh of relief, Richard said, 'Thank you. Thank you very much indeed.'

'We will, of course, continue our check, and confirm it to you in writing. Since you needed the information so urgently, I thought I'd pass on my secretary's comments.'

'It ties in with my own information exactly. Thank you.'

The stern eyes of the Chief Whip stared at Richard from the far side of a large desk as he tried to explain his side of things.

'So as you can see, from all I know of my father, these allegations are quite untrue.'

The Chief Whip sighed and, taking off his spectacles, turned them between his fingers thoughtfully. 'I see. Most unfortunate — surprising too, to find such things written in a quality newspaper. Lord Hexgrave is usually factual as well as discreet. According to you, this time he has been neither. What do you intend to do about it?'

'I shall, of course, sue,' said Richard, without having really thought the matter through.

'Sue!' The grey eyebrows shot up. 'Oh, no, you must never do that. Even if you win the case, you still end up the loser. Apart from the cost, it's the old thing of mud sticking. Anyway, the Government has had enough mud slung at it with the Profumo affair. Now this comes along out of the blue. Did you not make it plain, during your interview at Central Office, that your father was German?'

Swallowing hard, Richard answered. 'Scant attention was given to the fact, since I had never seen him. I was raised by my English stepfather, and that is why I bear his name. I only learned of my true father whilst at Oxford and I was told then that he was a doctor — nothing more.'

The eyes narrowed. 'Can you prove then that your father is not Baron von Schreiber, the industrialist?'

Richard hesitated, trying to recall what Abby had told him beside the River Stour that afternoon. 'His name is von Schreiber and I believe he runs a large charity now. As to a title ...' He shrugged.

'But did your mother never speak of him? She is still alive, I take it?'

Looking the Chief Whip coolly in the eye, Richard said, 'Suffice it to say that we have not spoken in years. A family matter.'

'Dear me. How very sad.' The voice held a hint of disapproval. He put on his spectacles and clasped his hands before him. 'Given that your father's name is von Schreiber, it might be a matter of false identification. If that proves to be the case, then certainly you should demand an apology. I'm surprised at Hexgrave for printing something that could be so damaging to us. He's always supported the Tories.'

'I would still like to sue,' Richard said.

'Don't even consider it! Taking on the big guns would be cripplingly expensive. And what of this other allegation: that you lost heavily on the stock market, and received money from your German father to get you out of a jam?'

'I did lose money when Langdon went down, but a good friend helped me out. I spoke to my bank only this morning, and they have confirmed who my benefactor was. It was *not* my father. Do you still say I shouldn't sue?'

'I still say it.' The Chief Whip looked grave. 'Hmmm ... the inference, of course, is that you received Nazi money. You will have to issue a denial to the House, and to the Press. Really, Glenister, this stock market fiasco was another thing you should have made plain at Central Office.'

'Why? It was over long before I decided to stand for election. No one outside my family knew of it.'

'People always find out, Glenister. Ordinary people might shrug it off, but MPs are not ordinary people. They must be trusted and held in the highest esteem by their constituents. It remains to be seen if, in the next twenty-four hours, you can regain that trust. To do that, you will have to disprove all allegations.'

'I will. Have no fear on that score.'

'But should you draw a blank . . . ?'

'Then I would have to do the honourable thing and resign.'

Richard left the office, still trying to come to terms with everything. Could it be that his father — his detested father who had come between him and Abby — was now set to ruin his future hopes in Parliament also? Of course, the papers were wrong, but he had yet to prove it. Twenty-four hours was not long to fight for his career, his good name and his dignity.

Entering his shared office, he found he was no longer alone. At the opposite desk sat the other backbencher, chatting loudly on the telephone. Richard sighed impatiently. Of all the days when he truly needed privacy, he was clearly not going to get it.

'Ah,' said his colleague, placing a hand over the mouthpiece. 'A call came for you. Could you ring your bank urgently?'

Suddenly Richard felt chilled. There was something wrong — he just knew it. Within seconds he was speaking to an embarrassed bank manager who was explaining that, although the cheque had been paid in by a Mrs Carr, it was actually signed by K von Schreiber, and had come from a Düsseldorf bank.

Replacing the receiver Richard realized that his hands were clammy, and his heart was racing. It was unbelievable. For some moments he sat at his desk, his thoughts on Abby. Why had she let him go on thinking that she had been the benefactor? And why had his father been so generous to a son he had never even met? Then another uncomfortable thought struck him. If Jeremy had found out this much, what else did he know that might come as an unwelcome revelation?

'I have to go,' he said, standing up and pushing paperwork into his bulging briefcase. 'I'll be in Canterbury, should anyone come looking for me.'

His colleague looked understanding. 'Fine. This is bloody for you, and all I can say is that I'm very sorry. Don't believe a word of it myself.'

Richard smiled thinly. 'Neither did I, until just this minute. That's why I have to go to Canterbury.'

Later that afternoon, as Abby sat in the airport waiting to board her Paris flight, she bought the early edition of the *London Evening News*, and read Richard's denial of Karl, with growing disbelief.

When questioned, Mr Glenister said he had never known his father, nor had he ever had any dealings with him. Asked about the money his father had, allegedly, given to him, Mr Glenister replied that the allegation was false. He further stated that his father was not an industrialist, but a doctor.

She read the paragraph three times, unable to believe that Richard could say such things. The picture above the statement showed a confused young man, and she felt deeply sorry for him. But that did not excuse such careless lies. Had he changed so much that he could turn his back on those who cared for him in order to enhance his career? By the time Abby was airborne, she had decided that no man could change that much. Richard had never been devious, nor had he ever lied to her.

When she reached Orly, a fine drizzle had clouded Paris. Her taxi pulled up outside an elegant building sandwiched between a smart restaurant and an art gallery. As she paid the fare, a door opened, and Odile was walking towards her

557

with a black umbrella. Even in the rain the Frenchwoman looked chic in a cream and black linen suit, her dark hair swept back into a smooth chignon, her high heels clicking across the paving stones, as she greeted Abby warmly.

'I feel so terrible not driving to the airport to meet you,' she was saying, as she led Abby through a courtyard where geraniums bloomed in terracotta pots, and a small fountain played. They climbed a spiral staircase, as Odile went on. 'Only I had three appointments this afternoon, and Karl was so late arriving, there simply was no time.'

Abby stood with her hand on the wrought iron balustrade and looked up at her friend. 'Karl is here, you say?'

'Yes,' said Odile with a slight frown, 'but I can tell you that he is a very worried man just now. He is convinced that something simply dreadful has happened to his son. Has it?'

'Richard is well,' said Abby, following Odile into the apartment. The window in the drawing room was open and the noise of traffic rose from the tree-lined boulevard below. Seated at the walnut desk in the far corner, Karl looked up from the letter he had been writing, rose to his feet and greeted her warmly, though he was unable to conceal the anxiety in his eyes.

'How lovely to see you again, Abby. Did you have a good journey?'

'Bumpy over France, but the sun was shining when I left London.' She sank into a sofa.

Odile smiled brightly. 'First, we will have a civilized glass of champagne, and then we shall dine at our favourite restaurant.'

Abby looked at Karl. 'You will not feel like drinking champagne when I tell you why I'm here. Please, do not be alarmed. Richard is safe and well.'

Reaching into her briefcase, she removed the morning newspaper, having discarded the *Evening News* as an unnecessary addition, and handed it to him.

'I hate bringing such a thing to you, but you had to

know.' Abby looked away, so that her eyes rested on the fine paintings instead of Karl's horrified face. Finally, when she found the courage to look back at him, she saw anger in his eyes, but he spoke calmly and sadly.

'The sins of the fathers shall be visited on their sons. It is so unfair though – so damned unfair. Richard has done nothing!'

'You'll sue, of course,' said Abby. 'They mustn't be allowed to get away with such dreadful libel.'

Rising to his feet, Karl threw the paper down onto the desk. 'Of course it's libel, but does that mean I should go into their three-ringed circus to perform like a dancing bear? That is what they want. Think of the newspapers they can sell then! The profits will far outweigh any damages payable to me or to Richard. No, I will not give them that satisfaction.'

Abby stared at him. 'But ... but people will think it true if you don't take action. You *must* sue, Karl. Think of your reputation. Think of Richard.'

'I *am* thinking of Richard.' The pain in Karl's eyes was distressing to see, and for a brief moment it seemed to Abby that he would fight. Then, turning back to the window, he said, 'Nazi – war criminal – Abby, I have always had to live with such accusations from others who were ignorant of the facts. No, I was never a member of the Nazi Party, although my father and brother were made to join under duress. And no, I was never classified by the Allies as a war criminal, as the newspaper could have found out quite easily. But the name I bear is enough. Everyone knows that my family helped to build up the machinery which made the Third Reich possible. Everyone knows also that Poles and Slavs were used as a slave labour force in our factories on Himmler's orders. So how can I sue your newspaper, Abby?'

He was silent for a while, then looked at Abby sternly. 'I loathe everything the Nazis stood for and did, but I've always loved my country, and would do nothing to harm

559

or betray Germany. To go to England now and try to clear my name would put me and the German people back on trial simply for the benefit of entertaining people at their breakfast tables, and selling more newspapers. I'm sorry for Richard, but there is nothing I can do. God, how he must hate me now!'

'Hate you?' Abby stood up slowly and faced the man who should have been her father-in-law. 'How can you say such things? He knows these allegations aren't true. He knows you're innocent.'

'Innocent!' Karl drew a cigarette from the silver box, lit it and exhaled slowly, keeping his eyes averted from Abby all the time. 'I killed seven Polish prisoners. I pointed them out to the SS Commander, and he had them executed. I am *not* innocent.'

Abby's blood turned to ice. What had he just said? She could only stare at him in horror. At last, he sank down once more onto the sofa.

Karl went on speaking, as though, having said the worst, he could speak more easily. 'They came each day from the camps, half-starved and sick, to be worked to death, as a race of sub-humans, on Himmler's orders. The Third Reich would grow and conquer the world on the backs of such sub-humans – that was the plan. I never saw conditions inside the camps, but what I saw inside the factories shocked me to the core. The SS had complete control over these prisoners, while my job was to keep up production. I was told to think of my wife and twin daughters safe in Dresden. They would remain safe while I did my job and let the SS do theirs. And so I, too, had to learn how to look the other way. So there we are, Abby. I cannot help my son. And I was a fool to think we could ever get to know each other.'

Odile walked across to where Karl stood and placed a comforting arm about his shoulders, while Abby sat on in silence, unable to make the move she now felt was expected of her. In the event, it was Karl who did instead.

560

'This has been a distressing time for all of us.' He stubbed out his cigarette into the ashtray and murmured, 'I have a meeting this evening, which I forgot to warn you about, Odile. And so, ladies, please excuse me.' Ignoring the surprised look on Odile's face, he turned to Abby. 'I am letting you down, when you came all this way seeking my help. Try to understand, my dear, that I can do nothing.'

With that he was gone, leaving her staring blankly into space, as she tried to come to terms with a Karl who was very different from the one she thought she knew. Had he really ordered the execution of helpless prisoners?

Following Karl out of the apartment, Odile returned after a few moments. 'That man takes the guilt of the world on his shoulders.' She walked back to the drinks table and refilled their glasses. 'Forget what he said. It is not what it seems.'

'Those prisoners who died. Did . . . did you know about that?' Abby asked. 'Did Karl ever speak of it before?'

There was a long and awkward pause. 'No,' whispered Odile. 'But it is not what it seems. Karl would never defend himself, because for one thing he is too proud, and for another, he believes there can be no defence for such as he. I was with the Resistance during the war, Abby. Many of my colleagues were caught and tortured to death. Do you think I could ever love a man who could condone such things? Do you think I could ever love a Nazi?' She smiled. 'Did you know that when his father refused to join the Nazi Party, the Gestapo took the eldest son, Dieter, and threw him into Ravensbruck until the baron changed his mind? Dieter was only released when he, too, joined. Karl they did not care about − he was the youngest and nothing to them at the time. Just a young army surgeon, of little consequence. Dieter was the heir; I am told he was killed in an air-raid in 1944. And so I say to you now, all is not what it seems. Believe me.'

Still confused, unable to get the thought of the seven

prisoners out of her head, Abby rose to her feet saying:
'I'm so sorry, Odile. I've brought you nothing but misery
this evening. I think it's best if I go now . . .' She stumbled
over her words. 'I don't want to be here when Karl returns,
and he won't want to see me here. Thank you, Odile, for
your hospitality, and please forgive me.'

As the taxi sped away along the Boulevard Saint-
Germain, Abby was still unable to shake off Karl's
words. What did she know of the man, after all? Greg
had been right.

The following day, as Abby flew to Rome, other British
newspapers took up the story of the Tory MP and his
Nazi war criminal father. They demanded the truth. 'The
British public', they said, 'has a right to know.' In Fleet
Street, meanwhile, Lord Hexgrave was sitting in his office,
staring across the desk at Jeremy.

'I hope you're sure of your facts, my boy, because I
have to tell you that I don't like the smell of this one bit.
You should have cleared the story with me first.'

Jeremy shook his head and smiled. 'When you offered
me the editorship, you said I was to use my own judgement.
I did. The result is that distribution has almost doubled.
That's more than it did during the Profumo affair. Isn't
that what it's all about?'

'Not exactly.'

A corpulent man, in his sixties, Lord Hexgrave owned
three of the country's top newspapers, and had been
grooming Jeremy to step into his shoes. Now he wondered
if he'd misjudged the young man, after all. 'You know that
it's never been my policy to instigate scandal of any kind.
That I leave to less scrupulous tabloids. Of course, if it
becomes a national issue, then I have no alternative but
to take up the story. But initiate it — never.'

'Sir, we did not initiate it. We took up an accusation
made by another source, and merely reported it.'

'By reporting accusations from someone who has since
vanished off the face of the earth, we have, in effect,

initiated the scandal. Can't you grasp that fact? This is a top quality newspaper, yet we have accused this baron — who, incidentally, has an engineering plant in this country and provides work for hundreds — we have accused him of outrageous things and in so doing have pilloried a Tory Member of Parliament. What proof have you for all this?'

Jeremy began to look a little uncomfortable. He uncrossed his legs and leant forward, clasping his hands before him tightly. 'Trust me, sir. I know all about von Schreiber. I've been looking into his background for some time.'

Lord Hexgrave frowned. 'And found him to be a Nazi war criminal? Well, I hope to God you can provide absolute proof before he decides to sue. As it is, you've queered my pitch all round. If you're right, and Glenister is forced to resign, it will look bad for the Government, and probably cause them to lose the election. If you're wrong, then we're going to look the biggest bloody fools since Chamberlain cried "peace in our time".'

'The man was a Nazi industrialist, like Krupp,' said Jeremy. 'Trust my judgement. I really do know what I'm doing.'

Richard drove into Beauchamp Place, and pulled up outside his house, steeling himself for the encounter to come. Forcing his way through the phalanx of waiting reporters, he stood on the doorstep and faced the press, his expression solemn.

'Gentlemen, I have just returned from the House where, in the best interests of the Party, I have resigned my seat in the Commons. Thank you. That is all I have to say.'

The front door was already open. Thankfully he walked into the hall, as his housekeeper, Mrs Howe, closed it quickly on the pursuing press. Leaning against the door he murmured grimly: 'Let that be an end to it.' Devastated, unable to come to terms with events which had moved so quickly, he knew only that his world had come to an end. He had lost Abby years ago, then his son, and now his political career. Damn it, they had even taken away his dignity! What else did they want from him?

'Where is everyone?' he asked.

'Mrs Glenister is upstairs,' Mrs Howe replied, looking a trifle embarrassed. 'Can I get you something, sir?'

'No thank you,' said Richard. He had telephoned Samantha from the House immediately after resigning, and was in no mood now for her histrionics.

Entering the drawing room, he poured himself a large Scotch, then sank into an armchair thinking of the events of the past two days. His mother had not been surprised to see him turn up at the cottage, and all former hostility was forgotten in her shock and anger at the press. Brian had sat impassive, as Milicent explained to Richard all that she knew of his father's family background.

'Until I met him that day at the Royal Academy, I had not seen him for years – thirty years, at least. I know time changes people, but one look told me he was the old Karl. He had little to do with his father. But, because he is now the baron, the press have jumped to the false conclusion that he is tarred with the same brush as his father. I'm sorry, my dear. It is grossly unfair on you. What I'd really like to know is how the press ever got hold of this information, linking it to you. Christ Almighty, who would tell them such things, and why?'

All during the drive back to London Richard had pondered the mystery of how the press had managed to dig up such information. He was certain now that the man at the meeting had been a plant: just the sort of tactic that Jeremy would use.

But how was it that Jeremy knew the identity of the secret benefactor? If the bank had refused to tell their own client, they were hardly likely to blab it to the press. There was only one person who could have known – the one person who had placed the cheque from Karl into the bank. *Abby*! But Abby loathed Jeremy as much as he did. It was all so senseless.

A loud thump from above drew Richard back to the present. Draining his glass, he walked up the stairs, to find his wife hauling suitcases from the landing cupboard.

'What's all this?' he asked.

Samantha lifted her stubborn chin and turned defiant eyes on him. 'What does it look like? Fiona and Nanny caught the train an hour ago. Piers is collecting me in a few minutes and he's driving me home. Oh, don't look at me like that! Life has become impossible in this goldfish bowl.'

Following her into the bedroom, Richard thrust his hands in his trouser pockets, and murmured quietly, 'Perhaps it would be best to get away for a bit — just until things have quietened down. Have you packed my things yet?'

Pausing, with a pink satin nightgown in one hand, Samantha looked at him nervously. 'You don't understand, Richard. I'm going to Wickham Place without you. Well, what the hell do you expect? My life is in ruins. So I think it best that we ... well ... that we part. I'm not Valerie Profumo, standing by her husband like a saint! I'm *me*. It isn't my fault that your mother married into a notorious family with Nazi connections. So, quite frankly, I see no reason why I should play the good little wife.'

Richard stared at her coldly. 'Good wife! When did you ever play that particular role? I'm not the bloody fool you take me for, my dear, and I'm damned sure you've been seeing someone else. You can't take this appalling scandal, and you're using it to end what I can only describe as an even more appalling marriage. I'm all for that. All I ask is that you stop treating me with contempt and do something honest for a change.'

Samantha turned her face away, feeling her cheeks burning. Quickly she moved to the window at the sound of a car pulling up outside. 'Good, Piers has arrived. It's good to think I have at least one friend left, even if he is my own cousin.' Slipping a mink coat over her shoulders, she turned and stared at her husband. 'You're wrong about the affair — I've always been faithful to you. But I really cannot take any more of this hiding from the press and being afraid to answer my own telephone.' She paused at the door, wishing he would say something instead of staring at her. 'I'll ring you from Mummy's. You must see that I have to go. It's for Fiona's sake, as well as mine. The poor little thing has gone through a terrible time.'

'Wouldn't she learn more by riding out this storm?'

'Richard, that's a terrible thing to say! She's a child, a child who, quite suddenly, has no friends. She should have been attending a birthday party this afternoon, but the mother telephoned to suggest that it might all be rather awkward.' Samantha's mouth twisted at the memory. 'You think you know people and then, suddenly, you realize you don't know them at all. I wonder how many friends we have left at this moment, Richard?'

From the street below a car horn blared. Richard picked up the suitcases. 'Well, as you said, there's always Piers. And if you want him to remain your friend you'd better get out there fast, before the press frighten him off.' As he carried the suitcases down the stairs, he murmured, 'What a field day they'll have when my wife drives off with another man.'

Samantha swept out of the door, then climbed into the waiting Jaguar. She sat quite still, her face impassive, as the car moved away from the excited reporters. From the drawing room, Richard heard Mrs Howe close the front door, and wished he could close it as easily on his life.

It was nearly seven thirty that evening, when he heard the sound of a taxi outside his house. Richard's first thought was that Samantha had returned, then he told himself how unlikely that was. Peering out through the gauze of net curtains, he saw a woman stepping out of the taxi. She was tall, with sleek, dark hair, and wore a red and black suit. She paid the taxi driver, gazed about her in mild surprise at the motley collection of reporters and photographers, then walked to the door and rang the bell.

'Who the devil ...?' Richard frowned as he heard Mrs Howe clattering along the hall.

'Excuse me, sir, but there's a lady to see you. A foreign lady. It's important, she says.'

'Tell her to go away, Mrs Howe. She's bound to be another reporter.'

Mrs Howe shook her head. 'I don't think so, somehow. She gave me this card to give to you.'

Richard read the card, which had the name of the baron's foundation on it, and frowned. 'Madame Odile Longet?'

'She asked me to tell you that she knows your father personally and has come to offer her help.'

'How on earth can anyone do that?' murmured Richard wryly. He sighed and nodded to the housekeeper. 'Very well, you'd better show her in.'

Odile entered the room quietly and introduced herself to Richard. 'I flew in from Paris earlier today. I am your father's friend and have been for many years.'

Richard thought that, whatever else his father might be, he was a man of extraordinary good taste.

'Please, Madame Longet, do sit down.'

Odile settled herself in an armchair and crossed her long, shapely legs. 'I have come to tell you about your father, because I know you have never met each other. Your English newspapers have treated him quite disgracefully and I want to help put matters right.'

Richard stared at her for some time, then asked: 'Can you clear his name?'

Odile gave him a dazzling smile. 'I can only tell your press about the man they don't know, the one who has done so much for humanity since the war. Your father is a good and kind man.'

For one moment, it seemed that the sun had come out inside the dark drawing room, and Richard smiled. 'Would you care for a drink?'

'I think I should like one of your gin and tonics,' said Odile.

Richard poured her drink, then filled his own glass with a liberal helping of Scotch. 'Well, if my father's innocent and there's anything you can do to help clear his name, then I'm very happy to see you.'

'To Karl,' said Odile, as they touched glasses. 'We would have known nothing of all this, had Abby not turned up in Paris with a copy of the newspaper. She wanted your father to sue, but he will not, because it will bring only further embarrassment to you. But I have been in London seeking people who have worked with the Foundation and who have known the baron for years. They are prepared to come forward with statements to the press and television.'

'Are they now?' Richard leaned back in his chair and began to relax for the first time in days. 'Do go on, Madame Longet – I'd like to know more.'

The new boutique in Rome stood close to the Spanish Steps in the Piazza di Spagna, Rome's most elegant shopping area. When Abby arrived at noon, the sun was brilliant but the heat in the piazza was nothing to the heat building up within the showroom.

'They promised faithfully that everything would be ready on time!' Roland's voice held more than a hint of panic as he greeted Abby, and his appearance was proof enough that he had slept little. 'The painters can't get on until the electricians have finished, and Gina, poor darling, can't begin on the displays until everything's finished. Look at it, Abby, just look at the place! We can't open, of course. We simply won't be ready in time. I'm ready to sue this interior decorator for every penny he's got. You can see how it is.'

Abby could see exactly how it was. Roland on the edge of panic was a Roland who laid aside all diplomacy, and turned to blustering instead. He had clearly upset the volatile Italians, including Gina, who had been chosen to manage the boutique because of her experience and calm efficiency.

'We can't and won't cancel,' said Abby firmly. 'We have forty-two hours to lick everything into shape, and we *will* do it.' She ought to have felt panic-stricken, but was strangely calm, her thoughts and fears still centred on Richard and the appalling trial he was going through. It was this measure of calmness, coupled with her looks, that settled everyone down. For the 'bella Signora Carr' electricians and decorators drew on reserves they were not prepared to find for the dictatorial Englishman and, by a hair's breadth, with just fifteen minutes to spare, the boutique was ready for the grand opening.

Shattered as she was, Abby moved among her guests talking and laughing, aware that this last *prêt-à-porter* collection was one of her best yet. Well-received and publicized, it had sold well in London, New York and Paris. Now it remained to be seen whether Italian women too would fall for the English look.

Awakened early the following morning by the telephone, Abby struggled to open her eyes. When the operator told her, in halting English, that the call was from London, they shot open. *Greg!* She had completely forgotten to contact him as promised. These past forty-eight hours had driven everything from her mind.

'Is that you, Greg?' she murmured, sitting up in the bed.

'I've been trying to reach you. I've been worried sick.'

Abby's heart turned a somersault at the sharp tone of his voice and her thoughts fled to her children. 'Is it Tamsin? Ross? What's wrong, Greg?'

'We're all fine, but I've been going out of my mind trying to get through to you. The hotel said you didn't book in on Tuesday evening. They said you had cancelled your booking and were arriving the following morning.' There was a long pause, followed by a sharp 'Abby? Are you still there?'

Trying to collect her thoughts, Abby ran a hand through her tousled hair, and forced a light laugh. 'Oh, how silly! But this is Italy, and you know what the Italians are like. I can't tell you what chaos it's been ever since I arrived. I'm sorry I didn't manage to get through to you, but with all the problems I've encountered ... The place was a shambles. It's been terrible.' Desperate to avoid more awkward questions, she prattled on about the boutique. 'I'm so exhausted! My plane doesn't leave until four-thirty. I've masses to do, but I refuse to leave Rome until I've seen the Sistine Chapel.'

When Greg spoke again, there was a note of disbelief in his voice, and she wondered at the wisdom of keeping her brief visit to Paris from him.

'Well, I'm glad you're safe. It's strange they should tell me you hadn't booked in.'

After a short pause Abby answered. 'Yes. I'm sorry, but it really has been a madhouse.'

Greg was silent, as though expecting her to add more. When she did not, he said sharply, 'Well, I know how busy you are. I'll meet you at the airport. Enjoy Rome.'

Abby replaced the receiver with a sense of deepening anxiety. He knew. Exactly what he knew, or thought he knew, was anyone's guess, but he knew she had not been in Rome that first night. That edge in his voice disturbed her. To tell him the truth now would send him into a rage of jealousy, yet not to tell him was even more dangerous. Who could say what he was thinking now?

It was a welcome relief to see Roland all sprightly and chirpy at breakfast. 'I didn't think we'd do it, but we did, thank God. I'll show you something of Rome. Lightning tour, Madame.'

Rome was overwhelming in noise, colour and sheer

life. Abby had never been anywhere with such danger, excitement and vitality: danger from the traffic, excitement from the sheer fact of being there, and vitality from the people who treated their city like a never-ending party. She was left with an impression of terracotta, ancient ruins, grandeur, and slums where washing hung across narrow streets. In the Sistine Chapel they stood in the echoing nave staring up at Michelangelo's ceiling until they both felt dizzy. And back at the Spanish Steps they paused, while Abby glanced with envy at the couples sitting there without a care in the world and time to enjoy life.

Later, with one eye on their watches, they sipped cool drinks at a pavement café, listening to the trickling water of the fountain in the middle of the piazza. Beyond the fountain Abby could see a newsstand.

'Do you suppose they've any English papers?'

Roland followed her gaze. 'They'll be yesterday's, or probably even some from the day before. Do you want one?'

'Please.'

Roland looked at the traffic moving around the fountain and sighed. 'Your wish is my command.'

Filled with anxiety, Abby watched as he crossed the piazza and examined the papers on the stand. At last he bought one.

'Well,' gasped Roland, breathless on his return. 'My dear, scandal upon scandal! Do you remember that German baron from the fashion show at Wittenhausen? Well, he's hit the headlines in a big way. Read this.'

Abby took the tabloid from him, and saw Richard's unsmiling face peering back at her. The caption above it read: 'Member of Parliament resigns over Nazi link'.

Oh no, she groaned inwardly, casting her eyes down the long column of misinformation wrapped up in 'the people's right to know' jargon. Only one fact had they actually managed to get right. Richard Glenister had, indeed, received money from the baron.

But, on the whole, supposition and speculation had taken the place of hard facts, and, with Karl refusing to do anything, the papers had the game to themselves with no risks attached.

CHAPTER TWENTY-ONE

As he had promised, Greg met them at the airport, and dropped Roland off at his Ebury Mews flat before driving on to Hampstead. He was quiet, as he listened to Abby's endless tales of problems and triumphs, all too aware of the desperate strain in her voice that told him how tense she was. It was proof that she had been lying to him.

'Well,' he said grimly, 'you've talked and talked, which is unlike you, yet I'm still waiting for you to tell me where the hell you were that first night. And *don't* tell me you were in Rome. I had the hotel staff check and re-check, only to be assured that the Signora Carr would not be arriving until the following morning. So where were you, Abby?'

'Dear God, you don't let up, do you? Where do you think I was?'

At this angry outburst, Greg pulled the car into the kerb, and switched off the engine. Turning, he gave her a look of desperation. 'I dare not think. Try telling me the truth, in your own words.'

Abby bit her lip, then sighed. 'Very well. If you must know, I decided that Karl should be warned about the allegations being made against him by the press. Someone had to. Since he was in Paris for a conference, I called in on my way to Rome.'

Greg's brief sense of relief at this unexpected explanation was quickly dampened by the realization that only her love for Richard could have sent her on such a mission.

'It was that important to you?' His hands were still tight on the steering wheel as he stared ahead into the dimly-lit street. 'And who went with you?'

Abby turned to him angrily. 'I went alone. And I stayed at the Georges Cinq alone. If you don't believe me, then I daresay you could go there and check out the register yourself.'

Greg started the car and eased out into the road once more. 'And all because your precious Richard was in trouble! My God, it amazes me how quickly you move for him.'

Shifting a little in her seat, Abby looked down at her hands. 'Now you're being unfair. Richard is my cousin! An attack on him is an attack on the family.'

Greg gave a mirthless laugh. '*Family!* My God, if Stella's anything to go by, that's one family you could do without.'

His mood remained grim and sullen that whole night. Abby could sense his tense body close to her in bed and, using her genuine exhaustion as an excuse, turned away from him and pretended to sleep.

She awoke at dawn, and looked out of the window on the grey morning light just breaking. Greg was still sleeping, so she crept out of the bedroom and looked in on Ross, who was slewed across his bed with all the covers on the floor, and then Tamsin. The toddler lay with her thumb planted firmly in the rosebud mouth, eyelids flickering above long lashes, and Abby felt, then, how much she was missing of her child's progress.

She left early for Brook Street, not wishing to speak to Greg. When she returned at six o'clock that evening, he was still at Chiswick.

'He said he would be back quite late tonight, Mrs Carr.' Mrs Proctor placed a tea tray beside her chair, but Abby's attention was held by the television news.

The male announcer spoke of new evidence in the von Schreiber affair which would clear the baron of all accusations made against him. The picture then changed to a grey-suited Frenchman, who told his interviewer of the work Karl had done for the International Relief

Foundation. He also explained how Karl had been a doctor, only coming into the family business towards the end of the war, and of his innocence in the matter of the prisoners. This last was backed by the appearance of a man who spoke, in very halting English, of his own experiences as a Polish prisoner at the age of twenty-three. Looking older than his years, he was visibly moved as he recalled those terrible times. He had been young and strong — he had also been lucky. Living now among the Polish community in London, he had seen the newspaper reports of von Schreiber, and felt that he should speak out.

'When you see only evil and terror and know only fear and pain, you feel there is no humanity left in the world. Then, one day, a man, a German of high rank, tries to help, and you realize that decency and humanity, still exist, after all. It was von Schreiber who made me see that. Word had gone around that the old baron had died. One day, in the steelworks, we saw the Standartenführer enter with von Schreiber, the son. The group I was working with were older, and most of them were too ill to work. I knew, as they did, that when they could no longer work, they would be finished. I remember the look on von Schreiber's face when he saw us. He seemed shocked, as though he had never seen such things before. I heard him arguing with the Standartenführer. He was angry that men so weak and ill were being treated in this way and said it was inhuman. The Standartenführer was angry, also, and called the guards to bring out my seven companions. Then the guards led me away with the other workers. I was afraid. This SS Colonel was the most evil man. We were led outside the works into a yard. In two groups the men were taken to a wall, and then shot. When von Schreiber realized what was about to happen, he turned on the Standartenführer, but the guards held him back, and he was forced to watch the executions.

'I thought my last moment had come and felt angry that this newcomer should have brought about my death

575

by his interference. Did he know nothing? I waited for the moment when the guards would drag me to the wall. But after seven men were shot, they led us back to the factory, and told us to get on with our work. von Schreiber's lesson was over. After that, we saw very little of him. We were the property of the SS. They had the power of life or death over us. That was the lesson the baron learned that day.

'Now, when I see von Schreiber being accused of crimes committed by the SS, I must come forward and tell what I know. I have no love for the German people. They killed my entire family. But this man is innocent.'

The interviewer then turned to the camera, saying: 'Why then did an accusation from a stranger at a public meeting suddenly become a witch-hunt, leading to the resignation of a Member of Parliament and a slap in the face to a man who has done so much to help the refugees of post-war Europe; to help restore the German economy and bring work to thousands? These are disturbing questions which cannot be ignored in a country which prides itself on fair play.'

Abby switched off the television, wondering why Karl had said nothing of all this. Instead, he had led her to believe the worst of him. And how readily she had done just that! He could have killed the lies, and yet had chosen to keep his council and his dignity. 'Witch-hunt' was right, she thought bitterly, and she had almost become one of the screaming rabble crying 'Burn! Burn! Burn!'

She recalled Odile's words, *'It is not as it seems'*, then rose from her chair, a sense of deep relief and exhaustion sweeping over her. It was finished. Karl had been exonerated by one of the very prisoners held in the factories. There could be no better advocate.

Ashen-faced, Jeremy switched off the television in his office and, with legs like lead weights, walked back to his chair. Before he reached it, the telephone rang and Lord Hexgrave's voice barked in his ear.

'Well? Did you see it? *Did you*?'

'Er . . . yes, sir.' Jeremy swallowed hard and said weakly, 'How do we know that the Pole isn't lying?'

'As he's a survivor of the Holocaust, I should think it highly unlikely.' The tone was like cold steel. 'Come over to my office at once!'

The line went dead. Jeremy felt a dryness in his mouth, and his hands became clammy. How could things have gone so horribly wrong? He had Richard in the palm of his hand, and now the bastard had slipped away again.

Lord Hexgrave looked up from his desk as he entered, and the anger in those grey eyes sent a shudder through Jeremy.

'Von Schreiber won't sue,' he said. 'He wouldn't dare.'

'Why not?' Lord Hexgrave's voice had a dangerous edge to it. 'He seems to be holding all the cards now. Where's the proof you promised me that he was a war criminal? Well? Where is it?' At Jeremy's long silence, he sighed deeply and shook his head. 'I see.'

'Well, you can't blame me if the staff are so bloody inefficient they can't get the story right! I rely on the researcher and . . .'

'My staff have always been exceptionally good at unearthing facts when they've been asked to do so. Did you ask?'

'Yes, and they found payments made by a German bank into Glenister's account.'

'That seems to be the only thing you did manage to get right,' came the scathing reply. 'Presumably, because it was the only thing you asked them to research. The names of all war criminals are on record. I should have thought that even a cursory check would have told you not to go with this one. A few hours' further research would have revealed this massive charity organization which von Schreiber founded. But you were looking for a quick sensation – and to hell with the facts. You've embarrassed the Government to such an extent that we could possibly wind up with Labour winning the next election. And we've been made to look fools. If we're not facing a libel suit, we'll be bloody lucky fools.'

Jeremy gave him a baleful look. 'It won't come to that, sir. His position is too precarious, coming from that notorious family.'

'*His* position is precarious!' Lord Hexgrave gave his cousin's son a withering look and lit a cigar, as he contemplated his next move.

'Our only honourable path would be to print an apology. But that would leave us without a leg to stand on should von Schreiber or Glenister decide to sue. No, von Schreiber is powerful enough to damage us badly, not just financially, but in reputation. I don't think we've heard the end of this, not by a long way.' He glanced at his watch. 'Haven't you got a paper to get out?'

In Düsseldorf, Karl's staff were beleaguered by news reporters from England, desperate to interview the baron. Frustrated at being cold-shouldered, the photographers were left only with pictures of the industrialist getting in and out of his car, or with long shots of the mansion at Wittenhausen. At last, Karl relented, and gave a statement to the press, confirming that he'd never met his son. He would very much like to do so, but Richard had been raised in England by a stepfather he loved very much. It was difficult suddenly to burst into another person's life. But, yes, he had tried to help his son out of a financial difficulty, charging the banks in question to say nothing about the source of the gift, and therefore his son had thought it came from a close friend in England.

This interview was shown on the BBC's nine o'clock news, and filled Abby with deep relief. Karl had been totally exonerated, and Richard had told no lies. Both were innocent, and the press had egg all over their faces.

When Richard was interviewed, he was as courteous as his father had been, only displaying anger at Viscount Kelthorpe for destroying, not just good names, but the reputation of what had always been a quality newspaper. 'Now that he's dragged it into the gutter a public apology is the very least we can all expect from him.'

'Will you reconsider your decision to resign from Parliament now?'

Richard shook his head. 'No. I've resigned, and that's that. Thank you, gentlemen.'

Abby watched with sadness. She could have strangled Jeremy. This had been a personal vendetta and he had used one of Britain's top newspapers to pursue it. It remained to be seen whether or not he would have the grace to apologize.

Throughout the rest of the evening she waited for Greg to return home. When he did not, she telephoned him at the house in Chiswick.

'Sulking or working?'

There was a long pause, then Greg answered. 'Working. I've seen the news. You must be feeling very relieved right now. Your Paris trip did some good after all.' The hint of sarcasm in the voice changed with his next sentence. 'Go to bed, darling. I'll be home in the early hours. I'll try not to awaken you.'

Wondering if he was alone, Abby put down the receiver. If he returned to her drunk, then their marriage was well and truly over. In the event, she was asleep when he came in, and she left early the next morning.

Most of the newspapers carried the story of the television interviews, the Polish prisoner taking most of the spotlight. Only those papers owned by Lord Hexgrave completely ignored the event. Furious at this, and seeing no apology forthcoming, Abby drove to her office wondering what Richard would do about it. But as the morning wore on, it dawned on her that he, like Karl, would do nothing. In the end, she placed a call to Lord Hexgrave.

'Hello. Am I speaking to Lord Hexgrave's personal assistant?' On learning that she was not, and that her contact was the junior secretary, she went into action.

'I'm Abigail Carr, the couturier. He's meeting me for lunch, but I'm not sure where.'

Realizing she was speaking to a famous celebrity, the girl was helpful.

'Lunch ... oh, I see. He'll be at the Ritz at one o'clock.'

'The Ritz. What a good thing I phoned! I was convinced it was the Savoy. Thank you very much.'

Curiosity growing by the minute, Jonathan sat in the lobby of the Ritz Hotel, wondering why Abby had telephoned him out of the blue, asking him to meet her for lunch. He contemplated her marriage, and it dawned on him, with a pang of guilt, that if it had failed he would not be too devastated at the news. Abby's love for Hadleigh had affected him more deeply than he had expected, and he still held reservations about the man who was not to be trusted with his precious Abby. Since the marriage, the days of being her confidant and friend were over, and he missed them dreadfully.

It was impossible for people not to glance twice at the young woman who entered the hotel. She looked stunning in a classic suit of blue linen with a standaway collar which suited her to perfection. A double row of pearls decorated her neck and her hair fell to her jawline, turning under slightly, beneath the pill-box hat. Her eyes shone as they settled on Jonathan who was walking towards her. 'Quite like old times,' he said, kissing her lightly on the cheek. Although she looked as lovely as always, he noticed a pallor in her complexion and sensed a strain in her manner. There was something wrong, and that's why they were meeting. It couldn't be business, he told himself, because that was doing very well; therefore it had to be the marriage.

'It's wonderful being with you again,' said Abby, with genuine affection. As they were shown to their table, Abby's gaze swept across the dining room until she saw

Lord Hexgrave, seated by the window with two other gentlemen. She had met him twice: once at Ascot, when his wife was determined he should meet her couturier, and again at a charity ball.

Jonathan ordered dry sherries and looked at her curiously. 'Come on, out with it. What's wrong?'

Abby glanced at the menu, and shrugged casually. 'Nothing.' Looking up at him, she knew she would have to do better. 'Oh, it'll blow over. Greg's just being unreasonable, that's all. We went through a bad patch a few months ago, but it sorted itself out in the end. I daresay it will again.'

Sensing the lack of confidence in her voice, Jonathan felt anxious for her. 'Do you want it to? He's a dark horse, your husband.' He took a sharp breath. 'You know you can always look to me when you need a good friend.'

For one overwhelming moment Abby felt the desire to tell Jonathan everything. 'Oh, I've missed you so much,' she said at last. 'But I didn't come here to be sorry for myself.'

'I should hope not,' said Jonathan, smiling. 'I hope you came to have lunch with a dear and rather ancient friend. In which case we should concentrate on the menu, then talk afterwards. What do you fancy?'

Abby found it hard to concentrate on food. She felt unwell and put it down to the Rome visit. 'Salad ... something very light, I think.'

Throughout lunch they talked of everything, from Ross and the baby to the business, old times and Evelyn. Not once did either of them mention Greg. From time to time, Abby's eyes drifted to the table by the window. Lord Hexgrave had reached the coffee and brandy stage now. Soon she would make her move. Searching inside her handbag, she drew out one of her business cards and, to Jonathan's surprise, wrote something on the back, then beckoned a waiter to take the card across to Lord Hexgrave's table.

'What are you doing?' asked Jonathan.

'It's just a note,' answered Abby.

'But ... do you know who that is?'

'Oh, yes.' Abby watched as Lord Hexgrave picked up the card, read it, then nodded to her without smiling, and said something to the waiter, who then returned to Abby.

'Lord Hexgrave would be happy to see you for a few minutes after his guests leave, if you don't mind waiting, madam.'

Abby nodded, smiled across at the newspaper magnate, then looked back at Jonathan innocently. 'You don't mind, do you? Seeing him there gives me the perfect opportunity to ask him something, that's all. His wife is a client of mine.'

'I see,' said Jonathan in a disapproving tone. 'It's not like you, Abby, to move in on someone enjoying a quiet lunch. A breach of etiquette, my dear. Do you think you're being wise?'

'No,' murmured Abby, 'but when will I ever get the opportunity again? It's easier to meet the Prime Minister.'

'Well, have a care, that's all I ask,' whispered Jonathan anxiously. At last, the great man stood up and gave a curt nod to Abby. She felt her heart turn a somersault and wished she had never been so reckless as to start this silly nonsense. What on earth did she think she was doing? She would only anger him further. It was too late now, however. 'Well, here goes,' she sighed. 'I won't be more than five minutes. Will you excuse me, Jonathan?'

Lord Hexgrave stood to greet her, then gestured to one of the vacant chairs, saying, 'Mrs Carr, good to see you again. Please sit down. It's some time since we met, but I do remember you. Nothing wrong, I hope? My wife's account is not outstanding; no more than is usual, that is!'

'Good heavens, no!' said Abby, forcing a light laugh. Her smile faded. 'No, I'm afraid I have something far more serious to discuss with you.'

'More serious than unpaid accounts?' Lord Hexgrave leaned back in his chair and looked at the woman opposite with shrewd eyes. Had she not been such a looker, and his wife's couturier, he would not have received her.

'It's very difficult for me to say what I have to say,' murmured Abby. 'But it ... well ... the fact is that I have known Lord Kelthorpe for many years now, going back to 1950, in fact, when he and my cousin came to blows. It was a stupid, boyish fight and Jeremy came off rather badly. I had forgotten the incident until I met Jeremy some years later. He reminded me of the fight and told me then that he would destroy my cousin one day. Oh, not just because of the bloody nose he received, but because my cousin also married the girl of Jeremy's dreams.' She paused and added quietly, 'My cousin, I should now point out, is Richard Glenister.'

She saw a slight flicker in those impassive eyes. 'Public humiliation is total destruction, wouldn't you agree? Unfortunately for him, Richard's character was good and true, so Jeremy could find no way to bring him down. That was why he used the father — wrongly, as things turned out. I thought you ought to understand that your newspaper has been used by Jeremy to pursue his own personal vendetta against my cousin.'

Lord Hexgrave listened to all this in total silence, his only sign of emotion being the tightening of his fingers on the brandy balloon. When at last he spoke, his voice was calm. 'I see. Well now, Mrs Carr, was there anything else?'

'One thing,' said Abby, growing angry. 'Why have you printed no apology?'

'Apology?' Lord Hexgrave frowned. 'Never explain, never apologize. I live and die by that maxim.'

'Even when it means refusing to put right an appalling wrong? Are you afraid the baron will sue? Because he won't, I can assure you of that. He should, of course. But he's a fair and honourable man. Until recently, I had assumed that you were.'

The flaccid cheeks flushed with anger. 'My reputation was made before you were even thought of, my dear! If one of my editors has been remiss, then I must take the blame. I am sorry that your cousin and his father have been put through so much. Truly I am.'

'Then say so publicly, and regain your reputation,' said Abby. She stood up and extended her hand to him. 'Anyway, thank you for seeing me. And please do give my kind regards to Lady Hexgrave. Goodbye.'

She moved back to the table where Jonathan was waiting for her, and felt the pain in her head increasing. She was hot, and growing hotter, as she heard Jonathan's voice in the distance. 'Are you all right? You're as white as death.'

'Take me home, Jonathan, please,' whispered Abby. Swiftly, Jonathan led her out of the hotel and into a taxi.

'Hampstead Village.'

'No,' murmured Abby, 'Brook Street. I've so much to do.'

Jonathan looked at her in growing alarm. 'You need a doctor.'

At that moment, she collapsed onto his shoulder in a dead faint.

Jeremy felt a spring in his step as he walked into Lord Hexgrave's office. Nothing more had been said about the von Schreiber affair and it seemed consigned to the past already. 'You wished to see me, sir? I do have an editorial meeting in fifteen minutes' time.'

Lord Hexgrave was standing by the fireplace, one hand holding a cigar, the other clasping the mantelpiece. His thinning grey hair made him look almost bald in the dim shadowy light of the late afternoon. Churchillian, thought Jeremy vaguely, hoping he would not be kept too long.

'What do you think of this office?'

Surprised at the question, Jeremy gazed around at the art deco of the thirties without enthusiasm. 'Not a period I like. Why? Are you thinking of changing it to something more up to date?'

'No. What changes I have in mind have nothing to do with the room. It's just that I remember when this building was erected. Better days — better times. We held our heads up high then, and ruled nearly a third of the world.'

Jeremy sighed inwardly, feeling he was in for yet another bout of nostalgia for the 'good old days'.

'When this room was built, things were very different.' The old man sighed. 'Now the whole country seems to be going to the dogs.' He turned and faced Jeremy. 'But I won't let that happen to my newspapers. While I live and breathe I will uphold my standards, even if I have to fight like a lion to do it.'

Jeremy began to feel uncomfortable, aware that the crusty old newspaper king was getting dangerously close to the subject he had hoped was forgotten. 'Yes, sir, of course.'

'I had an interesting lunch today.' The piercing eyes stared at Jeremy. 'Oh, yes. I met a most charming lady, a beautiful lady, and a rather angry lady. She knows you very well.'

'I know a great many beautiful ladies,' said Jeremy, with a nervous laugh.

'Oh, but this one had quite a lot to say about Richard Glenister.'

Jeremy looked startled. '*Samantha?* You met Glenister's wife?' Samantha had been furious and had attacked him in what he had found to be a rather amusing telephone call. Now, of course, she was out for revenge. Yet what could she have said that would reflect so badly on him? He grinned sheepishly. '*Lady!* I doubt you would call her that if you knew her. She's very free with her favours — if you understand me, sir.'

'And if you were a gentleman, you wouldn't speak of a lady in that fashion,' snapped Lord Hexgrave. 'Now do you see what I mean by standards slipping? If people of our class don't uphold them, what hope is there for the rest of the country?'

'Mrs Glenister does not deserve to have your ear,' said Jeremy quickly. 'She would only lie.'

Lord Hexgrave moved slowly to his desk and looked thoughtful. 'I understand that you and she were once ...'

'That was a long time ago.'

'Still, these things hurt, and sometimes the pain lasts.'

Stung into defending his pride, Jeremy said quickly: 'Fidelity doesn't!' Unable to resist a grin, he went on. 'MPs leave their wives alone far too much.'

'Like that, is it? Strange choice she made, turning her back on wealth and a title, in order to marry a would-be politician. What is Glenister's background?'

'He's the son of a jumped-up tradesman, who thought he could climb the social ladder by marrying into an old family.'

'You mean she gave up all for love.' Lord Hexgrave smiled. 'Sounds like a fairy story. So you're back together again, in a fashion. And you'd still like to have her as your wife?'

'Good Lord, no! If she's happy to have extra-marital affairs, then who am I to send her away?' Jeremy's lips tightened in an ugly fashion. 'She's made her bed: let her lie on it, with or without Glenister.'

The venom in the voice was not lost on Lord Hexgrave, who stared at his protégé with eyes of cold steel. 'It was she then, who told you about her husband's German father?' The question was so casually tossed into the air that Jeremy answered without even thinking.

'Samantha never was the most discreet of wives.'

'And now her husband is a destroyed and humiliated man. That was the aim of the exercise, was it not?'

Realizing he'd been caught off guard, Jeremy stiffened.

'Sir? I don't quite understand your meaning.'

'Oh, you understand, all right. By the way, who was the fellow who appeared out of thin air to accuse Glenister, then vanished again? How much did you pay him? I'd rather like to know before that, too, is made public.'

The thunderous voice and the sheer overpowering presence of the man made Jeremy feel small. 'Two hundred pounds,' he murmured. 'Well, how else could we get the story going?'

'Your love life and petty jealousies are your own affair, but how *dare* you use my newspapers as a battlefield!'

'That is wholly unfair, sir,' said Jeremy, rising to his feet rather shakily. 'As a journalist it's my job to seek out information and report it. Am I to blame if some people are more indiscreet than they should be?'

'For a man who causes so much trouble, I find it quite remarkable that you're such a helpless creature. I'll have to let you go, Jeremy. You will leave Fleet Street. Don't bother trying to return – because I shall see to it that you never edit another newspaper in London. Go home to your estate. I'm sure your father needs your help. Maybe that's where your talents lie.'

Jeremy looked at him in stunned disbelief. 'But ... but my editorial meeting!' He glanced at his watch. 'I'm late and ...'

'I'll take it for you. Meanwhile, I have newspapers to run and a public apology to make in tomorrow's editions. Goodbye, Jeremy.'

Stunned, Jeremy walked slowly to the door. There he turned, and faced Lord Hexgrave, saying bitterly, 'You prefer to take the word of that slut against mine? I'm telling you that Samantha Glenister is ...'

'Samantha Glenister? I've never met her in my life. The charming lady I met at luncheon was Mrs Abigail Carr.'

CHAPTER TWENTY-TWO

For days, Abby lay in St Thomas's Hospital, fighting the pneumonia which had attacked her so suddenly.

Greg paced the corridors of the hospital, frustrated that he could not be close to his wife until the danger was over. At last, after the crisis had passed, he was allowed into her room and gazed with guilt and alarm at her pale face on the white pillow.

Bending to the still, sleeping figure, he kissed her gently on the forehead, then lovingly lifted a tendril of hair between his fingers, his eyes moist with tears. He had come very close to losing her altogether during the past three days, but now, thank God, she was coming through like the fighter she was — no thanks to him. It was his fault, surely, that she had gone through such stress at a time when she was already overworked. And what had he done to ease her load? Walked out on her like a jealous schoolboy.

As he sat there, Abby's eyes began to flicker. They opened momentarily and looked at him, then closed again as her lips moved. He bent closer to catch her words, but the whisper had been so faint, that he could not be sure he had heard her rightly. She had uttered one word. '*Richard*.'

Dismayed, he sat back quickly, then told himself that he could have been mistaken. At that moment a nurse appeared and took Abby's pulse.

'How is she?' asked Greg anxiously.

The nurse smiled reassuringly. 'She'll be fine if she gets lots of rest.' The soft Dublin accent was calming as she went on. 'There's nothing more you can do, Mr Hadleigh.

Come back tomorrow when she's that much better. By then, she'll realize that you're here.'

Greg stood up, his face grim. 'Maybe I'm not the one she expects to be here.' Abby had seen what she wanted to see, he told himself as he left the room, unable to bear the thought of the disappointment in her eyes when they focused, not on Richard Glenister, but on Greg Hadleigh.

When he returned the following day, he found Abby propped up against her pillows, smiling brightly. Her face was pale still, and there were shadows under her eyes, but she was obviously much better.

She put out her hand to him as he moved quickly towards the bed. 'What a woman has to do to keep her husband's interest!'

Putting his arms about her gently, Greg kissed her tenderly. 'Dear God, you gave me a fright. I love you. Don't ever do that to me again.'

Once back at her Hampstead home, Abby's recovery was swift. Greg hardly left her side, as visitors came and went. Susan and Roland reassured her that all was well at the salon, while Jonathan still had not got over the fright she had given him in the taxi. Flowers bedecked the house, as they had the hospital room. As Abby recalled those awful days, when she'd thought she was drowning, she marvelled that anyone could get pneumonia in the summer. 'It's ridiculous! One moment I was in fine fettle and the next . . .' She clicked her fingers.

'Overwork and stress,' said Greg. 'You were at your lowest ebb when the virus struck.'

In the days that followed he helped her to regain her strength by walking with her on the Heath, and taking her for drives in the warm summer air. But no matter how he tried, he would never forget how she had called for Richard, not for him.

Susan came every evening with reports from the salon, but the one thing which helped Abby the most towards

589

recovery was the newspaper which Susan had kept for her to read.

Lord Hexgrave had printed his apology to Richard and, furthermore, had compensated him with a large sum of money. Abby could hardly believe it. Subsequent newspapers reported that Viscount Kelthorpe had been forced to resign his job as Editor as a direct consequence of the affair.

'Susan,' Abby said, 'there *is* a God, after all.'

Having decided that his loveless marriage finally was over, Richard found himself thrust into mourning at the sudden death of his father-in-law. Sir Gerald had succumbed to a massive stroke which, some whispered, had been brought on by the dreadful events of recent weeks, and the unwelcome publicity to which his family had been subjected.

Distraught with grief, Samantha had telephoned, pleading for his return to Ashton. 'I'm sorry ... so very sorry for everything. Mummy's in a terrible state. Poor Daddy! One moment he was fine and the next ...' Her voice faltered. After a pause she said quietly, 'Fiona keeps asking for her Daddy – and I need you too, Richard. So please, forgive me for being such a beast to you, and come home.'

Saddened at the thought of that kind, hard-working man being struck down because of him, Richard had returned to the fold, where he'd taken charge of things. He tried to comfort his wife and mother-in-law, telling himself that when things settled down, he would break free for good. Now was not the time. He could not be that cruel.

Having sought legal advice on whether or not to sue Lord Hexgrave, Richard had been advised to 'sleep on it'. And he had, only to awaken one morning to see the public apology spread across the front page. It was the least Hexgrave could do, he thought, but the icing on the cake was Kelthorpe's dismissal. Since then there had been a call from his constituency to have Richard reinstated as their MP. But it was too late for that. He had resigned, and no one from Central Office had asked him to reconsider in any case.

Now he was walking through the grounds of Wickham Place with his mother-in-law. The evening sun cast long shadows across the verdant lawns, as they strolled towards the rose gardens nestling below Stapledown. The air was sweet with newly-cut grass and perfumed roses.

'We lean on you far too much,' said Lydia, clipping some blooms and placing them in her basket. 'But I want you to know that at no time have we ever regretted your being our son-in-law. We both grew to love you very much. Do you understand that, Richard?'

'Of course I do,' said Richard, for one brief moment forgetting his worries and giving himself up to the fragrant beauty that surrounded him. On such an evening as this, Wickham Place was a sanctuary away from the world.

Lydia cut another bush rose, smelt its fragrance and placed it in her basket with the others. 'This was Gerald's favourite time of year.' She looked at him, her dark hair now almost grey, her face still young for all her fifty-nine years. 'I have this awful fear that you feel somehow responsible for Gerald's death. But you know the doctor said he died of a massive brain haemorrhage, which had been building up for years, ever since he fell from his horse. He was concussed by the fall and then seemed fine. He was told to return for another check later, but never bothered. You know what he was like. He said everyone was just making a silly fuss over nothing.' She pulled a dead head off a bush. 'He was wise enough, however, to make the estate over to Samantha some time ago to avoid crippling death duties, but she really has no idea of the work that goes on here. Gerald and his estate manager used to manage six hop gardens and eight orchards – eight hundred acres in all. I was wondering . . .' She paused and looked up at him anxiously. 'I was hoping that you might take on Gerald's mantle, and run the estate. I'm afraid that Samantha ...' She paused and shrugged. 'Well, it's your daughter I'm really thinking about. Fiona will inherit this place one day — God willing, we can keep it going till then. For her sake, Richard, will you help us?'

For a moment Richard felt as if he were drowning. This was surely the moment to tell her he wanted a divorce. But how could he? Lydia Fellowes was one of the kindest women he had ever met.

'There are many things for me to think about,' he murmured, unable to look her in the eye. 'Changes to be made.'

'Of course,' said Lydia swiftly. 'How thoughtless of me, when you've so much on your mind! In any case, I dare say you'll be asked to reconsider your resignation now. That would be the right and proper thing for the Party to do, surely?'

Richard shook his head. 'No, I resigned on a matter of honour. There can be no going back.'

Lydia looked at him compassionately, knowing how his pride had been shattered. No one could have worked harder for his constituents than Richard. 'Well, it's something to think about — the estate, I mean. There's no hurry.'

No going back, thought Richard, as they strolled slowly towards the house. All through this horror story he had wondered about Abby, half expecting her to turn up at Beauchamp Place; but that had been stupid and fanciful. Why would she jeopardize her marriage and success to be seen with him?

No going back. He'd wanted to meet his father but to do so now, when the danger was past, would make him seem like a 'fair-weather son' only. Having refused to meet Karl earlier, he now had no option but to go through his life without ever meeting him.

No going back. With so many doors closing behind him, what on earth did the future hold?

As they approached the house, Richard could see

Samantha at one of the tall windows. What was it about her expression that reminded him of Milicent, staring out from the windows of Ferndene on the day of William's funeral? Guilt, perhaps? Anxiety? Was she afraid he might find out about her affair? He smiled wryly to himself, having long suspected such a thing and welcoming it as grounds for a divorce. Which one of her socialite friends could it be, he wondered? He'd dismissed the idea of Kelthorpe immediately, since, after the Langdon business, even Sam would have had more sense than to get involved with that viper again. *Women!* Why were they so devious? Even Abby had let him go on thinking she had supplied that money. *Why?* Whom could he trust? He simply did not understand the world any more.

'You were treated disgracefully,' Lydia was saying. 'I thought Samantha was quite wrong to come here, leaving you to face it all alone. I know you insisted, and that was kind of you, Richard, but a wife should stand by her husband. I told her so in no uncertain terms.'

Smiling to himself at these words, Richard went into the house, remembering the day his wife had walked out on him. Could he really blame her? The long shadow of Krupp and emaciated prisoners working in the factories of the Ruhr would hang over the world for a very long time. Enveloped in the same shadow was that of his own father.

In the drawing room Samantha was arranging flowers, her gaze averted from his cold stare. Understand her, he might – but he would never forgive her.

And so Richard drifted on through the warm summer days, his actions automatic, his mind inattentive, his anger still smouldering.

It was Greg who brought up the thorny problem of telling Ross the truth. Two things had convinced him of the need: firstly, Abby's close brush with death, and secondly his own close brush with a hostile Stella who turned up out of the blue at a rehearsal of his play. Greg had treated her with polite courtesy which, he felt, she really did not deserve. She'd enquired after Abby, then, smiling thinly, asked how Ross had taken the news about his grandfather's appalling history, and his father's fall from grace.

Unprepared for such questions, Greg simply ignored them, pretending to be engrossed in the rehearsal.

This had angered Stella all the more. 'Don't tell me the boy still doesn't know the truth?' When this too had met with no response, she had continued. 'He must be the only one who doesn't! All children should be told the truth about their parentage — Abby would be the first to tell you why. But I doubt she ever will. It would be too embarrassing.' She rose to her feet. 'I can see I'm about as welcome as rain at a Buckingham Palace garden party, so I'll take myself off. But Ross is my nephew, and I shall make certain he is told the truth.'

The threat had occupied his mind throughout Abby's illness, compelling him to become Ross's shadow in case Stella was waiting to pounce. He collected the boy from school each afternoon, making certain he was safe in the house and doing his homework before the evening meal. Then they would take Nelson for a walk on the Heath and, on their return, Ross would be allowed to watch a little television before going to bed. So far, so good. But how long could he keep this up? Now, as he and Abby sat in the garden one dusky evening, he broached the subject, without mentioning Stella's visit.

Abby sighed at the question, which tormented her night and day. 'But he's so young still! Karl wanted me to tell him ages ago, but I've never found the courage. Every time I try to mention the subject, I look into those trusting eyes and I just can't bring myself to do it.'

Greg was frowning. 'The German knows, then?'

'Karl knows, yes,' said Abby, slightly miffed at his tone. 'Stella wrote and told him some time ago. I think the idea was to cause general mayhem in the family.'

More secrets, thought Greg, recalling once more with a sinking heart how Abby had called for Richard in her illness. He had never felt so bereft in his life. Leaning forward in his garden chair he gently took her hand. She was still so pale, her delicate beauty now more fragile than ever, reminding him of a Pre-Raphaelite painting. He hated to cause her more stress, but this could not wait. Until now he had no idea Stella had already tried to hurt Ross. Her failure would only drive her to further action.

'Has Ross received any mail lately?'

Abby shrugged. 'Only a couple of party invitations, nothing special. Why?'

Forced to tell her of Stella's sudden visit and threat, Greg added: 'Don't worry, darling. He's a sensible little chap. I don't pretend it will be easy, but in the end he'll come to terms with it. You'll see.'

Abby's mind raced back across the years to the motionless baby, lying on a woman's lap before a kitchen stove, the little body blue-grey and as cold as the grave itself. She had nearly lost Ross then. Could she go through that hell a second time? 'But he's only twelve. Far too young to hear such news.'

'When is the best time to hear it?' murmured Greg. 'The longer you leave it, the more difficult it gets. All I know is that it should be now, before he finds out from someone else.'

How many times had she heard that? Abby sighed, unable to keep back the tears which sprang to her eyes so easily since her illness. 'I've tried protecting him for so long. First it was for Evelyn's sake, now ... Well, now I think it's for mine. I'm so terribly afraid.'

Greg stood up, thrust a hand in the pocket of his suede jacket and pulled out an envelope, saying, 'You tell Ross, and I'll cheer you up afterwards with these.'

Looking at him in surprise, Abby took the envelope from his hand and removed the Glyndebourne tickets from it. '*The Magic Flute*,' she murmured, seeing again the small stage of Covent Garden Opera House as it looked from the gods. She could almost smell the damp rising from Richard's rain-sodden overcoat as they huddled together and could feel the sheer joy and rapture at being so close to him.

'Well?'

Greg's voice burst into her memories. 'Marvellous! My favourite opera. How did you know? I don't remember ever mentioning it.'

'You did,' he replied. 'At Breedon Park. Now then, who shall we take as our guests? Whoever they are, they'd better like eating a picnic on a damp summer evening, praying it doesn't rain on them.'

'July.' Abby was thoughtful, then glanced up at Greg apprehensively. 'Karl will be here that week. He's already written to me, suggesting we have lunch. Odile's coming over with him. Would you object if we took them along as our guests? Karl's a great music lover.' Somehow, it seemed only fitting that if she could not have Richard by her side during *The Magic Flute*, then she should have his father instead.

Greg was looking perplexed. 'Are you sure that's wise, after all the unwelcome publicity?'

'It's *because* of all the unwelcome publicity that I think we owe it to the man to extend the hand of friendship.'

'Do we?' Greg gave a curt laugh and turned away. 'When all's said and done, the fact remains that his family built the factories that produced weapons designed to be used against this country. Don't you think our little foursome might prove a touch embarrassing?'

'Embarrassing or not,' said Abby, feeling her anger rising once more, 'Karl is Ross's grandfather. When I tell my son about Richard I have no option but to tell him about Karl. What Ross makes of it is up to him. Since you're involved, you might as well make the best of the situation, and meet Karl now. Who knows, you might even like him.'

And pigs might fly, thought Greg. But, as he faced Abby, his stern countenance relaxed in a smile. 'Very well, if it pleases you, my darling. Do I take it that you intend Ross to meet him also?'

Abby shook her head. 'No. First things first. Ross has to come to terms with the fact of Richard, before anything else.'

Greg's smile faded. He knew the terrible risk he was taking for the sake of his stepson. Abby and Richard would be in touch once more. Supposing this rekindled her love – the love which, clearly, had not been extinguished? It was a chance he would have to take. If she could meet Richard and return to him unchanged, then the thing he dreaded most would be buried for ever. If not, then their marriage was not worth holding on to.

'The Bannems have asked me to go to Cornwall with them for two weeks,' said Ross excitedly, on the last day of term. 'Can I go, please?'

'Of course,' said Abby, knowing how much he enjoyed going away with his best friend. And yet, once she had told him what he had to know, he would surely need to be close to her. She watched him now, thinking how like a colt he seemed: all limbs and a too-slender body. But his eyes were bright, his fair hair shining like golden corn, just as Richard's had at that age. They were in his bedroom, where Ross was deciding what changes should be made to incorporate the loudspeakers he needed for the electric guitar Greg had promised him.

'I'm going to start a group, with Bannem, so that when I leave school I can be like Paul McCartney, and write songs. We'll be famous, just like the Beatles! Bannem's good, he can play very well. Of course, his parents bought him his guitar last year, when you wouldn't let me have one.'

Later that evening, as Greg lifted Tamsin high into the air so that the little girl squealed with delight and demanded more, Ross said, 'I think we should call ourselves the Scorpions.'

Greg smiled across the drawing room to where his stepson sat on the sofa, hands behind his head, large eyes thoughtful as he mused on his future. Putting Tamsin down again, he said, 'Why don't you let me show you the real theatre, Ross? I'll take you on a tour backstage, and you can meet the people who make things work.'

The eyes widened. 'Famous people, too?'

Greg nodded solemnly. 'Of course, although they might not seem famous to you since they won't be rock and roll stars. But they'll certainly be famous to people who like plays.'

Ross glanced down at Tamsin, who was now sitting at his feet fingering his shoes. 'I'd like to go. When?'

'Whenever you like, young man. I'll enjoy taking you.' With that, Greg swept Tamsin up into his arms and made soft growling sounds as he buried his face into the wriggling little body. Tamsin shrieked with delight as Abby entered, followed by Nanny Williams.

Smiling, Abby let out a long sigh. 'There now, you've got her all excited again! She'll never settle down.'

'Of course she will,' said Greg, handing the child over to the nanny's outstretched arms. 'Won't you, my lovely? Be a good girl and go to sleep now.'

Fat chance, thought Abby, as her daughter was taken away complaining loudly. It was the same story every night. But what else could she expect from a man who had gone through the agony of losing a child? It was a wonderful thing that she had been able to give him another and she could see, even at this early stage, that the relationship between father and daughter would be a very close one. Unlike the relationship between mother and son, when Ross found out the truth! Icy fingers closed about her heart at the thought.

That night, after Ross had gone to bed, Greg looked at his wife sketching at the easel in her study and thought how tense she seemed. Behind those lovely eyes lay such turmoil. Was he mistaken to insist that Ross be told the truth? Could it be that her female instincts were more accurate than mere male logic?

He walked to where she sat and placed gentle hands upon her shoulders, massaging them as he spoke. 'Ease up, darling! You'll make yourself ill again with all this worrying.' She touched his hand but continued to stare ahead at the design she was working on. He tried to introduce a lighter note.

'The Beatles have a lot to answer for. Fancy, all this expensive education – and what is Ross's ambition? To play a guitar.'

Her eyes flickered. 'I'm afraid he'll turn from me, Greg.' As she spoke, she remembered Mrs O'Connor growing into old age without setting eyes on the son she had loved so much. Could that happen to her?

'He'll do no such thing,' murmured Greg, kissing the nape of her neck. 'It's all a matter of choosing the right moment, that's all.'

In the event, it was Ross who chose the moment, by bringing up the visit he had made to London Zoo four years earlier.

It was early evening and Abby had arrived home at five o'clock, still not quite strong enough to put in the hours she was used to working. Tamsin was going from flower to flower, bending to sniff some and trying to pull the heads off others, until Abby intervened to save what was left of her precious garden.

Now she sank onto the lawn beside her sprawling son and encouraged Tamsin to play with her toys. 'So you remember that day, do you?'

'Vaguely,' said Ross quietly. He looked up from the book he had been reading and took a bite of his apple. 'Did Uncle Richard die?'

Staring at her son warily, Abby said, 'What a strange question! What made you think of Uncle Richard so suddenly?'

'A lady,' said Ross, looking up at his mother and

frowning a little. 'She came to the house just before you came home. Mrs Proctor was in the kitchen, and Nanny had taken Tamsin for a walk, so I answered the door. This lady asked if I was Ross. I said yes. Then she asked me if you were in. She seemed pleased when I told her you were out, which was odd. Then she said she had come to talk to me about the man I called Uncle Richard. Just then, Mrs Proctor came out, and told me to go into the garden. The lady went away without speaking to me again.' He looked at his mother thoughtfully. 'I think Mrs Proctor sent her away. Didn't she tell you?'

Abby shook her head slowly. 'What did the lady say her name was?'

Ross shrugged. 'I didn't hear.'

'What did she look like?'

'Pretty. She had dark hair.'

Abby's heart sank. 'Yes. I believe I know who it was. She's . . . well, she's a relation of ours, only you've never met her because we grew apart over the years.'

Sitting up straight, Ross stared into his mother's alarmed eyes. 'A *relation*? But she must be someone you don't like. And why did Mrs Proctor send me into the garden so that I couldn't talk to her?'

Dear God, she really means to do it, thought Abby wildly. *Is Stella still that much in love with Greg?*

'I really don't know, darling,' murmured Abby at last, knowing the time had come. Seeing Nanny Williams enter the garden, she asked her to take Tamsin. 'I'll come up to her in a while.' When her daughter had been taken into the house, Abby gave her full attention to Ross, trying to find the words she had rehearsed to say to him. Now, suddenly, she could not recall a single one.

'But what did she mean, she was going to tell me something about Uncle Richard? He never came back. He didn't like me very much, did he? Otherwise he would have kept his promise.'

Abby looked into her son's hurt eyes, and hugged him

600

to her. 'Oh, darling, you're so very wrong! He liked you a great deal.'

Ross was silent for a moment, wondering at the passion in his mother's voice. 'He *is* dead then, isn't he?'

'No.' After a long silence, Abby finally managed to find the words to explain to Ross that the man who lay in Benfleet Cemetery was not his father, but his stepfather. When she had finished, she paused and looked into those blue eyes, seeing again the hurt she had once seen in his father's.

'He was *here* all the time? He was here and didn't come for me?' The boy's lips began to tremble.

'He wanted to very much, but I asked him to stay away, because it seemed the right thing to do at the time. There were ... certain complications.'

Ross tried to take this in, then shook his head slowly. 'But Wilkinson's parents are divorced and he sees his father a lot.'

'Divorce is rather different. I did what I did to keep you safe, to protect you from things which would only have confused you. But now you're older and deserve the truth. You'll be a young man soon, and I think you can accept it. Your father truly wants to see you again.'

'Well, I don't want to see him,' cried Ross, leaping to his feet, his eyes filling with tears. 'All this time I did have a father, and he didn't come near me except that one day.'

'I've explained why,' said Abby in alarm. 'Please try to understand. I told him to stay away because it was the right thing to do at the time.'

'No, it wasn't. And if he really cared, he wouldn't have listened to you,' said Ross, then fled into the house, leaving Abby shaken.

For a moment she sat there, listening to the blackbird on the rooftop, trilling his territorial song. She had failed. Slowly she rose from the chair and walked into the house, wishing Greg were there. His presence would have calmed

601

Ross and his way with words would make the boy see things in a different light.

Ross was in his bedroom when she found him, seated by his desk staring at a model galleon he was working on. His cheeks were streaked with tears as she walked over to him and placed her hands on his shoulders. At once he twisted away from her touch, and said sharply: 'Granny didn't know, did she? She thought I was her real grandson.'

'Of course she knew,' Abby lied. 'It made no difference. To Granny, you *were* her grandson, and her pride and joy. When God took her son, he gave you back to us. That was a miracle, darling. You are special – very special – and you are loved not only by me, and Greg, but by your true father, as well. It's hurt him all these years to know you were growing up without him. But, darling, there are things which I can't tell you just yet. When you're older, you'll understand. At the moment, I'm asking you to accept all that I say because it is true.'

She waited for his reply, but he said nothing, and went on staring at the galleon. She left him there. What he needed now was time, and she would give him that time. Her words had caused a deep wound which had to heal.

It was a full week before Ross began to return to the human race and Abby was more than grateful to Greg, who had laid aside his work to be with the boy. He took him to the theatre to watch a rehearsal, then went boating with him on the Thames, and drove him out to the Hadleigh Aircraft factory to see the planemakers at work. Ross slowly came to accept the truth and, on the eve of his Cornish holiday, found his mother in his bedroom packing a suitcase.

'If it's all right, then I would like to meet my father,' he said quietly. 'I talked to Greg about it and he thinks I should.'

Abby turned to look at him, her face breaking into a radiant smile. 'Oh, darling, I'm so glad! I'll fix up a meeting between you when you've returned from your holiday.' Her face shadowed. 'I shall miss you dreadfully these next two weeks.'

Ross looked embarrassed. 'Why? You think I'm a baby and treat me like one.'

'Be very careful where you bathe. The currents are treacherous, so stay in shallow water. Do *not* swim out of your depth.' She smiled. 'Apart from all that, have a marvellous time and get yourself a good tan. I wish we could have taken you away ourselves, but with Greg's play, and some of my staff away, we just ...'

'I know,' said Ross cheerfully. 'Anyway, I like going to the Bannems' cottage and I like sailing their dinghy. You'd probably stop me, saying I was going to drown or something.'

Abby looked surprised, then laughed. 'Oh, I see! You can't wait to get away from us, you little monster.'

The following morning as she and Greg stood waving from the doorstep, Abby felt an aching loss at her son's going, and knew she would worry until his safe return. Greg placed a comforting arm about her.

'Don't fret, darling. He'll be fine. It's good that he's going now; it'll give him a chance to settle down and think things out for himself.'

Abby's eyes were tear-filled as she nodded. 'I know, I know, but even so ...' She stopped speaking as her throat seemed to close up, and made herself think ahead. With two seamstresses and Susan on holiday, it would take a lot of work to avoid falling behind with the couture collection. She was looking forward to meeting Karl and Odile for lunch at the Dorchester Grill, and tomorrow evening she and Greg were taking them to Glyndebourne.

The respite would be brief, however. When Ross returned, she would have to draw on all her reserves of strength to make contact with Richard, yet still keep him at a distance. Would she be able to do this, she wondered with growing anxiety.

*

Abby glanced across the gardens at Glyndebourne, the verdant lawns dotted with opera lovers who sat around picnic hampers, champagne corks popping, the sound of gentle chatter wafting on the balmy air.

Karl sipped his champagne, lit a cigarette and gazed about him in a satisfied manner. 'Strange to have an opera start at four, then take two hours' interval to eat a picnic dinner, and return afterwards to hear the rest of the opera! Strange, but beautiful. And so very, very English.'

Smiling, Abby agreed with him. Their Fortnum and Mason's hamper had provided them with luxuries, and they'd dined off her garden table with a lace tablecloth and silver knives and forks, and drunk champagne out of her best glasses. She had even taken the trouble to arrange a floral centrepiece, which sent Odile into gales of delighted laughter. The first half of *The Magic Flute* had been perfect and Odile pointed out to Abby and the others that too much champagne might have them falling asleep through one of the finest performances of the opera she had ever heard.

Having been ill at ease at the thought of Karl and Greg meeting, Abby need not have worried. Greg had been tact itself, surprised to learn that Karl had seen two of his plays and was able to speak of them with true interest. Now, as they sat on garden chairs eating like kings, Greg thought how strange it was that he'd once hated this man and the idea of Abby's friendship with him. How stupid and prejudiced he had been! There was something about Karl which spoke the truth. It was in his eyes, his soft voice, his manner and his quiet sense of humour. Greg knew humbug when he saw it — in the theatre, he'd seen a great deal of it. Karl was no actor. He was what people saw: a quiet, decent man.

Greg could hardly take his eyes off Abby. For the first time since her illness, she was looking radiant in a gown of amber silk. From the shoulders floated two long panels, which the soft breeze lifted as she moved. Her hair had been swept back off her face into soft curls, accentuating her bone structure, just as the colour of the gown exaggerated her green eyes, titian tresses and porcelain complexion.

Abby caught his eye and smiled, suggesting that when the picnic paraphernalia was put back in the Rolls she'd hired for the occasion, they should all take a stroll around the grounds before the opera continued.

Karl and Greg walked back towards the car park where the chauffeur took all the equipment from them, while Abby and Odile started across the lawns to the lake. As they strolled and chatted, Abby nodded to those clients who came each summer to Glyndebourne simply because it was part of the season, along with Ascot, Henley and Wimbledon.

Suddenly she stopped dead in her tracks, her eyes drawn to a tall woman with blonde hair who was standing with a group not far away. Abby went rigid. She knew that shape all too well. The last time she had seen it, the figure had been dressed by Chanel. Now Samantha's form was covered in a black, slinky crêpe gown with a low-cut back.

Heart pounding, Abby's eyes searched frantically for Richard. Then she saw him. He was standing with his back to her, talking to another man in the group. Their chatter seemed to fade suddenly and in the following hiatus Richard turned slowly and looked straight across the lawns until his eyes met hers. She knew then that she had willed him to look in her direction, and that he had felt her will.

Odile was looking at Abby in alarm. 'Are you all right?' she asked. 'What is wrong?'

'Richard. It's Richard! I should have realized ... *The Magic Flute*.' Following the green eyes, Odile saw the fair-haired man in the dinner jacket heading away from the group towards them. Abby had forgotten she had anyone with her as she stepped forward to meet him. Odile stopped and saw Karl and Greg in the distance looking for them. When she looked back at Abby, she was heading toward the trees which overhung the lake, where Richard waited for her. Odile moved away and walked slowly back to the men in an effort to forestall them.

Abby walked along the lake, golden now in the evening light, then stood before Richard. For a moment they just stared at each other, unable to believe this moment was happening. Then, slowly, they reached out and clasped each other's hands, both feeling the old desire returning.

Almost laughing with joy, Richard blurted out: 'God, I must be dreaming! Oh, darling, I never thought I would see you again.' His eyes drifted over her. 'You look fantastic — bloody fantastic. It's a miracle. *You're* a miracle.' Suddenly the light went out of his eyes as reality took hold. 'But married. Is he here?'

Abby nodded, and when he asked if she was happy, she gripped his hands more tightly and asked only, 'Are you?'

Richard looked grim. 'You know the answer to that one. How's Ross?'

'Fine. I've told him about you.' Aware suddenly that they were still holding hands, Abby glanced around nervously, then pulled away from Richard. 'He wants to meet you.'

'Good God,' murmured Richard, hardly able to take this in. 'How did he react when you told him?'

'It was hard for him, at first. But he's come to terms with everything, and wants to meet his real father.'

'You're sure about that?' Richard asked. 'He isn't saying it just because he thinks it's what you want to hear?'

'Quite sure,' laughed Abby. 'It's going to be all right, truly it is.'

A deep sigh of relief escaped from Richard. 'God, that's marvellous! Bloody marvellous! When? How soon can we do this?'

'Well, your son's in Cornwall at the moment. He loves Cornwall, too. So you'll just have to wait another two weeks. I was wondering how on earth I could contact you. During this awful business — about you and Karl —

I tried telephoning, but the line was busy all the time. And you didn't answer my letters. Oh, darling, I was so sorry about everything.'

Richard was looking at her strangely. 'What letters? When did you ever write? And why did you go on letting me think you were the one who paid off my terrible debt?'

Utterly bewildered, Abby started walking along the lake. 'But that's just it! I didn't let you, not after Karl said it was all right to tell you. I wrote to you twice, but you never got in touch with me.'

'When?'

Abby blinked. 'About four years ago. I told you everything, about the money and Karl. Who he was, and how much he wanted to see you ...' Her voice broke off at the expression on his face. 'Don't tell me you didn't receive them!'

'I received no letters, Abby,' said Richard, feeling a familiar coldness creep over him.

'One letter might go astray, but not two!'

'No. Not two,' repeated Richard. 'Tell me, could my wife know your handwriting?'

'I ... I really don't know.' But suddenly Abby did know. What other explanation could there be? 'Oh, Richard! You can't think Samantha would ...'

'Sam would do anything,' came the bitter reply. 'Anything.'

Abby's heart sank with dismay. 'It seems that letters are dangerous things for us, Richard. Very dangerous.' Seeing how angry he had become, she tried to distract his thoughts. 'There's something else you don't know. Your father is my guest here this evening. Oh Richard, he'll despair if he ever knows he was so close to you without your meeting. Please, darling, agree to see him.'

Richard looked at her in surprise, then let his eyes roam across the groups of people scattered about the grounds. 'Where?'

Glancing around, Abby saw Greg, Karl and Odile

standing staring a short distance away. Greg had a face like thunder. She had no way of knowing if Karl understood who this mysterious intruder was, but he looked uncomfortable, sensing his host's growing anger. 'Please, Richard. Meet him now.'

Richard looked across at Karl, who was now looking at him. 'Very well. But I think it's too late for us — much too late.'

'Wait just there.' Joy lit Abby's face. 'I'll send him to you.'

'We don't have much time.' Richard smiled. 'And suddenly I feel very nervous.'

Hating to leave him, Abby returned to her husband and guests. She looked at Karl. 'I think you know who that is.'

Karl nodded. 'Slowly, it began to dawn on me. Will he see me?' When Abby nodded, he crossed the lawn and made his way to the lake. Richard stepped forward and, after a moment's awkward hesitation, the two men shook hands. Offering Karl a cigarette, Richard lit it for him, then father and son walked side by side until Abby could see them no longer.

Only then did she notice the look on Greg's face. 'I'd no idea he would be here! I had to tell him about Karl, and Ross.'

'Of course,' said Greg, glancing at his watch. 'What an evening it's turning out to be. Grand reunions all round.' The cynical tone was not lost on the women.

'It is something Karl has dreamed about for so long,' said Odile.

'Good,' said Greg curtly, darting a black look in Abby's direction. He saw her cheeks flush, like a woman caught out with her lover, and felt, suddenly, that his world could turn to ashes. It could have happened at any time, given that he himself had urged Ross to meet his father, but not on this golden, happy evening surely. Not now, when their marriage seemed to be getting back on an even keel.

Only when the second half of the performance was about

to commence, did Abby see Richard and Karl come back into sight. They walked slowly, talking like two people completely at ease with each other. Then Karl put a fatherly hand on Richard's shoulder, and the two parted.

Seeing how moved Karl was on his return to them, Abby deemed it tactful to say nothing. They walked back into the Opera House beside the old mansion, and as the strains of Mozart rang out in the auditorium, Abby felt as though a weight had been lifted from her shoulders. *It was done.* Richard had met his father at last, and the meeting had been a good one. God willing, it would go as well when he met Ross.

The only thing that would never be resolved was her love for Richard. It was as overpowering as it ever had been. Suddenly it seemed that Greg was a stranger, a powerfully-built stranger, with a rugby player's face and a Savile Row dinner jacket, sitting beside her now and gazing sternly at the stage.

As Mozart's score flooded the night, Richard could not keep his mind on the opera. Too much had happened for his thoughts to settle. Meeting his father had been a strange, incredible experience, which he had kept from Samantha. He felt her presence beside him, his thoughts returning to the disappearance of two letters containing secret and intimate details meant for his eyes only. Information of great importance had been kept from him, and he had been publicly humiliated as a result. Suddenly everything was falling into place at last. The letters. His wife's affair. Jeremy's exceptional knowledge, leading to the *coup de grâce* from which he would never fully recover. It was his own wife who had ruined him and kept him from being with his father, just as she'd kept him from being with Abby. His mind fled back to the Langdon business. Even as far back as that she had been cuckolding him, and with the man who was his sworn enemy. It was not to be borne. Rage flared and grew stronger, until he could bear it no more. Jumping to his feet, he stumbled past the people sitting in his row, then marched along the aisle to the exit.

Seeing him go so abruptly, Samantha murmured an excuse to her friends and hurried after him.

Turning at the mild disturbance, Abby saw her passing, and wondered what was going on. As Samantha flung a black stole around her shoulders, light sparkled off her diamond bracelet and then she was gone.

In the car park Richard was fumbling with the keys to his car when Samantha caught up with him.

'I've never been so embarrassed in my life! First you walk out on your guests during the interval, leaving me stranded and looking ridiculous, and now this. We shall be blackballed by the Glyndebourne Committee after this charade.' Her eyes narrowed as Richard turned the key in the lock. 'It's Abby, of course. I saw you talking to her. Whenever she turns up, trouble follows.'

Richard turned to her, eyes blazing. 'Those letters, Sam. Tell me about the letters you destroyed.'

Samantha stared at him, then pulled her stole more closely about her. 'I ... I don't know what you mean.'

'Oh, come on! It might be four years ago, but I'm sure you remember. Don't go on treating me like the idiot you've always thought me.' Richard opened the passenger door. 'Get in. We're going home.'

Nervousness gave way to incredulity. 'We *can't*! What about Piers and Fenella? They're our guests.'

'Are you going to get in, or do you want me to leave without you?'

Frightened by his accusations, Samantha hesitated. 'I think I'd better stay with our guests. I shall have to order a taxi –'

Before she could finish the sentence, Richard grabbed her by the arm and pulled her into the passenger seat. She barely had time to shut the door before he drove out of the car park at such speed that he almost lost control on the turn.

'For God's sake be careful,' cried Samantha. 'What on earth has got into you? And just how do you suppose Piers and Fenella are going to get home?'

Richard stared ahead grimly as his foot pressed down on the accelerator. 'Not one word to warn me my own father had given me that money! You knew everything about Karl, yet not one bloody word could you spare for me. My God, you could find plenty for Kelthorpe. When I think of it — how you've used me all these years — I could kill you.' The car raced along the Lewes road, gathering speed so that Samantha's hands clutched the seat in growing fear. 'You prevented me from being with my father, you threatened Abby through her son, and you cuckolded me with the very man who had sworn to destroy me. Is there anything else you have in mind, Samantha?'

'You're driving too fast,' she cried, close to tears. 'Slow down, please, Richard. Slow down!'

But Richard's anger had boiled over into violence, and a desire for self-destruction. In this moment of madness, his foot pressed even harder on the accelerator. 'Bitch! You bloody rotten bitch.'

With tyres screeching around the sharp Sussex bends, the car sped on into the night.

Leaning back against the upholstery of the Rolls, Karl smiled as he thought about his meeting with Richard. Until this day, he had never believed in fate; yet fate had brought him face to face with his son, at last. They had only had fifteen minutes together, but the ice was broken. They could go on from there. 'What an evening it has been,' he said. 'I don't want it to end.' He smiled. 'Will you both join us at the Dorchester for a light supper? After all, we did eat rather early and I am famished.'

Still dreaming of her own encounter with Richard, Abby was happy to accept. 'It certainly would round off a lovely evening. Thank you, Karl.' She glanced across at Greg; for all his light chatter, she sensed his anger and dreaded the inevitable scene when they reached home. But home seemed a long way off just now. She closed her eyes. *Let him rant and rave all he likes. But I was with Richard this evening, and he can't take that away from me.*

At that moment, the car came to a halt. Winding down the window, Abby saw a policeman and lights ahead. 'Oh dear, it looks like there's been an accident.'

'Damn.' Greg looked through the rear window. 'We can't back up. Half the Glyndebourne crowd are on our heels.' He poked his head out of the window and spoke to the policeman. 'What is it, officer?'

'An accident, sir,' came the reply. 'Could be some time, I'm afraid.'

Greg sighed. 'That's all we need! Can't go back and can't go forward. We could be here for hours. Wonder how bad it is?'

'I'll see,' said Abby, opening the door.

'Stay here,' said Greg, offering cigarettes all round. 'You might see something you'd rather not see.'

'I might see how long we're going to be stuck here.' Abby climbed out of the car, glad to leave his black mood and feel the cool night air on her face. Slowly she moved down the line of cars, and asked one driver how long he had been there.

'Nearly fifteen minutes,' he replied. 'The fire brigade were called to cut the poor devils out.'

Abby could see the horror before her now, and felt her stomach churn over. A car lay on its side, steam escaping from the crushed engine. Clearly it had lost control on a sharp bend and crashed into an elm tree before overturning. As ambulance men eased someone out of the wreckage, she looked away quickly, remembering Greg's words of warning. How right he had been! She was about to return to the Rolls, when curiosity forced her to glance back. The body of a woman had been placed on a stretcher, and was being covered by a blanket. Before Abby became aware of the blonde hair and black dress, she glimpsed something

612

shimmering on the arm. *Diamonds*, she thought. *Only diamonds shine like that*. Ice-cold fear swept over her.

The stretcher was carried into an ambulance, which immediately sped off, only to be replaced by another, as the firemen continued their work.

Rooted to the spot, Abby watched in growing horror, as they brought the still figure of a man from the wreckage. Unaware that Greg was now standing beside her, urging her to return to the car, Abby's eyes were on the victim, his hair darkened by blood, his black dinner jacket torn. Somehow, life returned to her legs, as she moved forward. At first, her lips could only mouth his name silently, then she let out a piercing cry.

'Richard! Oh, my God. Richard!'

Before Greg or the police could stop her, Abby was running towards the stretcher, crying: 'Please God, no, please, no . . .'

'Stand back, miss,' said one of the ambulance men, as he made a quick examination. 'Still alive. Just.' They rushed the stretcher to the waiting ambulance.

'Wait,' shouted Abby. 'I'm coming with you.'

'No, you're not,' said Greg, trying to pull her away.

'Let me go,' she screamed. 'It's Richard. Let me go!' Striking out at her husband, Abby ran after the ambulance men.

'He's my cousin. Please – his father's in one of those cars, but he mustn't see this.'

'All right, miss,' said one of the ambulance men. 'But no hysterics. We'll need you for details.' He turned to Greg who was standing in shocked disbelief at the ambulance door. 'It'll be Brighton Hospital, sir.'

Greg stood back, watching as the doors closed on Abby and Richard. At last he walked back to the convoy of cars, pausing to compose himself for the dreaded moment when he must face Karl.

Inside the ambulance, Abby sat staring at Richard's still face, thinking how strangely peaceful he looked. 'Will he live?' she asked, staring at the ambulance man with pleading eyes.

The man turned, and smiled reassuringly. 'They'll do all they can. But it was a bad smash. You say he's your cousin?'

Abby nodded, her hysteria giving way to exhausted despair. It seemed unbelievable that a few hours earlier Richard had been with her in a sylvan setting, and there had met his father for the first time. How cruel life was – how unrelentingly cruel. Her thoughts returned to the woman on the stretcher, the diamond bracelet so incongruous among the carnage. 'His wife. Is she ...?' One look at the man's face told her the answer.

Samantha was dead! Abby's mind simply refused to register the fact. Samantha dead and Richard close to death – could this really be happening? 'We've just come from Glyndebourne,' she heard herself saying in a small, faraway voice, '*The Magic Flute*. A lovely opera and so beautifully sung ...' Her voice faded away and her eyes took on a glazed look.

The ambulance man looked at her sympathetically. 'A sad end to an evening out. He's got a fair chance, though. Don't despair.'

The ambulance raced on towards Brighton, the clanging bell reminding Abby of the time she'd sat with Ross after he had returned from the brink of death. Please God that Richard could return also!

She closed her eyes and prayed.

CHAPTER TWENTY-THREE

Abby sat in the busy Casualty Department of the hospital answering questions in a dull, vague voice. A nurse brought her a cup of tea and words of comfort, but nothing could ease the numbing fear which now enveloped her.

When Greg arrived with Karl and Odile, he found his wife staring at the wall and shook her gently. 'Abby. How is he?'

Slowly, Abby turned her head and looked up at him, her face pale and tear-stained. 'They're operating now,' she murmured in a small, tense voice. 'That's all I know.'

Greg glanced at Karl's anxious face, wondering what kind of hell he was going through. Only an hour ago, he had found his son; now it seemed he was about to lose him. Calling a nurse to his side, Greg explained who Karl was, and she promised to tell the father any news immediately. Returning to Abby, he took her by the arm.

'Look, this could be a long business. There's nothing you can do here, so let me drive you home. Karl will ring us when there's news.'

The look she gave him struck into his heart like a knife. 'Of course I can't leave. He's dying. Don't you understand anything?'

He understood everything. At this moment, Greg Hadleigh no longer existed for Abby. It was time to leave. Then he hesitated. Abby was in a state of shock and hardly knew what she was doing or saying. He must wait and hear the doctor pronounce Richard's fate. If it was death, then his wife would need all the love and understanding he could give her. If it was life, then he knew their marriage was over. Glenister was now a widower; all things were possible. Heavy of heart, Greg leaned back against the wall, wishing he could down a bottle of Scotch there and then.

After two hours, the surgeon appeared and talked quietly to Karl, before moving on to the next case.

Karl returned to Abby and Odile, who stared at him with frightened eyes. 'They've managed to stop the internal bleeding, and there's no sign of brain damage. He had internal injuries and three broken ribs, sustained, they believe, when he was thrown against the steering column. It seems that the passenger side received the worst damage. His wife must have died instantly.'

'But he's out of danger?' Abby asked.

Karl nodded and breathed a sigh of deep relief. 'They think so, yes. Thank God! But he's still very ill.'

Greg gave Abby a long, measured look. 'I think we should go home, get some rest and contact the hospital again later. Agreed?'

Abby only partially heard him. Richard was going to live! Her mind held no other thought. Richard was going to live. She felt Greg's fingers tighten on her arm, trying to pull her from her seat.

'Abby, come on home.'

She gave him a strange look, and shook her head. 'No, I can't leave him. I must be here when he comes around. I must.'

'That's Karl's affair, surely,' said Greg, in growing anger. 'Come home with me where you belong.'

Sensing trouble, Karl approached them. 'Please, Abby, go home with your husband. You look very tired. Odile will go with you. Perhaps you wouldn't mind dropping her off at the Dorchester, Greg.'

Abby shook her head, wondering why they refused to understand. 'No, I'm staying.' She looked at Greg. 'You go — you and Odile.'

Greg looked into Abby's eyes. 'You do realize what you're saying?' he asked. 'If you stay now, then it's all over between us.' He waited for her reply, but she stared at him as though he were an alien from another planet. His shoulders fell, as he sighed with despair. 'There's no point in my hanging around any more – no point at all.' With these words, he left her, said goodbye to Karl and Odile and walked out.

Abby watched him go, but nothing could move her from this place now. What did he know? What did any of them really know of her feelings for Richard?

Lady Fellowes arrived, distraught and in a state of shock. Abby did her best to comfort the poor woman, but how did you comfort someone who had just lost their only child? Fifteen minutes later, Milicent walked in with Brian, demanding to see her son. Abby tried to calm her, but Milicent turned on her stepdaughter with startled eyes.

'And what, may I ask, are *you* doing here? I learn that my son has been involved in an accident, no one will tell me anything, and I find *you* here! I might have known.' As Brian tried to soothe the frightened woman, she pushed him off, glaring at Abby. 'What happened? For God's sake, someone tell me!'

Glancing into the small room where Karl and Odile had been asked to wait, Abby saw Richard's father sitting with his head in his hands. Odile had her arms about his shoulders. She turned to Milicent. 'Please keep your voice down. He's going to be all right, but he's still very ill.'

Milicent's eyes had filled with tears. 'My son,' she murmured, breaking into a sob. 'My dear, darling son.'

When Abby told her about Samantha, Milicent sank slowly onto one of the waiting room chairs, her mouth half open, her eyes glazed in shocked disbelief.

'Lady Fellowes was here a little while ago,' murmured Abby. 'Poor, poor woman.' And what of Greg? What was it he'd said when he left? Abby tried to remember. He had been angry, but she was in no mood to worry about that now. When she returned home, they would talk things over and he would understand.

People shuffled past and nurses rushed to help incoming patients, some with serious injuries. 'We can't sit here,' said Abby. 'They've been very kind and are letting us use a quiet room.' It struck her then that Karl should be forewarned of Milicent's presence. 'Wait here — I'll be back.'

When Odile heard what Abby had to say she stood up at once. 'It is better that I wait outside.'

Returning to Milicent, Abby explained to the bewildered woman that Karl had been with them at Glyndebourne and was now waiting here for news of his son. Then, taking her stepmother by the arm, she led Milicent gently to the room where Karl was standing ready to greet her.

For one moment, Milicent stood there, then she rushed forward, flung her arms about Karl and wept upon his shoulder, leaving Brian hovering helplessly on the threshold.

As Abby watched them a strange numbness crept over her. Tiredness, shock and tension were now taking their toll. Turning, she left Karl and Milicent and almost staggered back to the main waiting room to sit beside Odile, whose tact and measured words proved so comforting.

It was four in the morning when the duty doctor told Karl that Richard had come round from the anaesthetic and was able to see his parents for a short while.

Karl looked past the doctor to see Abby standing behind him. She was like a taut wire and her eyes were wide and pleading. 'Please, doctor,' said Karl, 'let Mrs Hadleigh go in first. It means so much to them both.'

Milicent, who had been sitting next to Karl, looked up at him as though he'd taken leave of his senses. '*What?* You can't mean ...'

'Yes, I do mean it,' said Karl gently. 'It's more to her than you'll ever know.'

The doctor looked perplexed. 'In cases such as this, only next of kin ...'

'Please,' urged Karl. 'Make an exception. I'm sure her visit will be brief.'

The doctor escorted Abby to the recovery room, lecturing her on the dangers of exciting the patient. 'He must keep calm. He can't talk, but he might try. Don't let him. Do *not* mention his wife – that must wait. It won't do him any good to hear it now. You can have just two minutes. Then the parents must go in.'

Abby thanked him, then walked to the bed, where Richard lay, a profusion of blood and saline dripping into his body. His face beneath the head bandage was whiter than the pillow and his right eye was half-shut from the bruising over the brow.

She put a hand to her mouth to stifle her gasp, and tried to still the emotions welling up inside her. 'Darling,' she whispered. 'Richard, darling. It's me, Abby.'

A flicker of a smile softened his white face, and the lips moved as he said her name in recognition. She put her ear to his mouth and heard his faint whisper. '*Stay here.*'

'I've been here all the time,' she murmured. 'Oh, my darling, you must get well. You *must*.'

She pressed his arm gently, longing to hold him. 'I'll stay, darling, just as long as they let me. But you mustn't try to speak.'

For another full minute, she stood looking down at him as he lapsed once more into sleep. Then the doctor entered and nodded to her curtly. As she left, Karl and Milicent entered, leaving her to wonder at Richard's reaction when he opened his eyes and saw the two of them standing there.

It seemed an age to Abby before they returned. It was Karl who spoke first, his voice filled with emotion and relief.

'He recognized us ... but he's unable to speak.' He turned to Abby. 'I feel better now, knowing he's going to get well. All the signs are good. Thank God.'

'Thank God,' said Brian in a constrained voice. He hardly knew Richard and had no liking for a son who refused to see his own mother. Nor did he like the way his wife was behaving around this German aristocrat.

Aware that she had flung on the first dowdy thing before racing off to the hospital in panic, Milicent stood beside Karl wondering what on earth she looked like. What could this man think of the pretty young girl he had taken to wife all those years ago, suddenly turning into a middle-aged woman?

After their meeting at the Royal Academy, Milicent knew what a fool she had been to leave him and vowed that if their paths ever crossed again she would not let him go. Somehow, she would arrange to spend the rest of her life with the man she had dreamt about for over thirty years. This time Abby could do nothing, and Brian could go to hell. Was it not fate, then, that their son's tragic accident should fling them together once more? Karl's presence during these dark, terrible hours had been the one blessing of this night. When he had placed comforting arms about her she knew, without a doubt, that she still loved him. And now, after all they had endured, she was certain that her feelings were mirrored by his. If he asked her to return with him to Germany, she would not hesitate for a single moment. She stared across the room at Abby's pale, tired face and thought bitterly, *That little bitch won't have her revenge after all. What part has she played in all this? My son lies critically ill and my daughter-in-law is dead.* Yet there she is.

Suddenly Odile appeared on the threshold, still glamorous with the black taffeta cloak over her black and white evening gown. Her face looked strained, as she smiled at Milicent, then asked Karl for news of Richard.

Karl walked across to her. 'Tonight we have witnessed a miracle.' He turned and said to Milicent: 'May I introduce Madame Longet, a very, *very* close friend of mine?'

The implication was understood immediately, and it seemed to Abby that Milicent's face crumpled. How old she looked — old and defeated, a world away from Odile's vitality and chic.

'Madame Longet,' murmured Milicent, nodding. The shock of the woman's appearance had not receded as she felt Karl's hand take hers.

'Well, Milicent,' he said, 'it was a sad way for us to meet again. Tomorrow I return to Germany, but I shall see Richard before I go. I have a villa on the Rhine that is an ideal place for him to convalesce.'

A strange pang of jealousy swept over Milicent then. Not just jealousy of Odile, but also Richard. 'Oh, well, I'm not too sure about that. His wife is dead, don't forget. Richard will have a great duty to his mother-in-law and . . .'

'Yes, of course. But he has to mend first, in mind and body. For that he needs to be away from stress. I can send a private plane for him. He will be handled like porcelain — you need have no fear.'

Wishing that someone would handle her like porcelain for a change, Milicent wanted to hit out. 'You do know, I suppose, that Richard has a son, by Abby? They have never met. Isn't that so, Abby?' Her voice was a shade close to hysteria, as she added, 'What a family we are! What on earth must your . . . your friend make of us, I wonder?'

Recognizing now the Milicent of old, and remembering why their marriage had failed, Karl smiled patiently. 'Oh yes, I know all about Ross, and am looking forward to meeting him. Abby has promised this will come about soon.'

'Yes . . . well . . . that's good, then,' said Milicent, feeling as though she had tried to light a very damp firework. 'Just as long as you know.' She glanced around, unsure what to do or say, until her eyes fell on Brian. 'I think we'd better stay in Brighton for the day so that we can visit Richard.' She gave Karl one last, lingering look, said goodbye, then took Brian's arm and walked out into the cool morning air.

*

621

It was almost ten thirty as the Rolls Royce pulled in to the drive of Abby's Hampstead home. The chauffeur looked through his rear mirror and saw the lovely, dishevelled woman still fast asleep in the back.

'Wake up, madam,' the driver said. 'You're home.'

Abby stirred, raised her head and peered at the man through half-closed eyelids. Realizing, with a shock, that she had slept through most of the journey, she thanked him, then slowly walked to her front door. It opened at once, and Mrs Proctor was helping her into the house.

'You poor dear, you poor dear! I heard all about the accident. Dreadful, simply dreadful. How is your cousin now, Mrs Hadleigh?'

'Out of danger, thank you,' Abby replied. As Nelson came running into the hall to greet her, she patted the dog's head and gazed about her nervously. Soon she would have to face Greg, who had left her looking so angry. If only she could remember what she had said and done last night. Everything was confused, like a terrible, mixed-up dream.

'Where is Mr Hadleigh?'

'Upstairs,' came the quiet answer.

'Then I'll go up as well,' said Abby. She had to face Greg some time. Would he cause a scene, or would he be kind?

Anxiety shadowed Mrs Proctor's face, but she assumed a light-hearted tone. 'Oh, by the way, Ross telephoned from Cornwall last night. He wants you to know he's having a marvellous time, hasn't drowned and the weather is hot and sunny. He's spent the last two nights camping in the cottage garden and has been bitten by midges and mosquitoes. Mrs Bannem has covered him with calamine lotion, apparently!'

Abby's thoughts reached out to her son. How she longed to hold him at that moment! He had come close to losing his true father almost at the moment of accepting him. 'Good,' she murmured, 'I'm glad he's happy. Cornwall's so lovely at this time of year ...' Her voice trailed off. 'I'll go up.'

'What about breakfast first?' cut in Mrs Proctor quickly. 'You look all in. Why not relax in the drawing room? I'll bring you a tray.'

Sensing the housekeeper's discomfort, Abby's heart lurched a little. 'I couldn't eat a thing just now, but coffee would be wonderful. Would you mind bringing some up in a little while?'

Thwarted in her purpose, Mrs Proctor walked slowly towards the kitchen.

As Abby started up the staircase, Greg appeared on the landing. He had showered, shaved and changed into his corduroy trousers and old suede jacket. Over one shoulder was slung a raincoat, and he carried a leather holdall.

'What's this?' asked Abby, frowning. 'Are you off to Chiswick? Greg, how can you possibly work after ...?'

'Is he still with us?' His sharp tone cut into her sentence, as he descended the stairs in a determined manner.

Nodding, Abby whispered, 'They say he's out of danger, but when I saw him it seemed hard to believe. He's very ill, Greg – so very ill.'

'But conscious when you saw him?' The dark eyes glinted, although the tone had softened a little.

'Yes. He recognized me, so that's a good sign.'

The lips curled scornfully. 'What a touching moment that must have been!'

Abby's face crumpled. 'Don't. Please don't, not now. I couldn't bear it.'

As she turned from him, he grabbed her arm and said angrily, 'Do you think I can bear it? Do you think I shall ever be able to forget last night?' He walked past her into the drawing room.

Slowly, Abby followed him, unable to grasp what was happening. She slumped onto the sofa, and sat hunched forward, cold, exhausted and shattered.

For some time there was a terrible silence between them as

Greg stood gazing into the empty hearth, feeling his world had come to an end. When he spoke, his voice was barely audible. 'I thought we had come through it. I wanted so much to believe that Richard was in your past, that I had driven him from your heart, but last night showed me how terribly wrong I was. From the moment you set eyes on him, I ceased to exist for you. Even before the accident, that much was evident.'

Abby looked up at him, her mind still on last night's horror. 'But ... Richard was dying.'

Realizing he was not getting through to her, Greg turned slowly. 'When you were told that he was going to live, you should have returned to *me* – your husband. You had no business remaining there.'

Abby shook her head vigorously. 'No! I couldn't have left him. If I had ...' She swallowed hard, recalling that distant night in her childhood when she had failed to keep her vigil. Common sense told her it could have made no difference to the fate of her mother and sister, but some deep, primeval instinct caused her to feel otherwise. 'If I had, then he would have died. I know it.'

'Rubbish.'

Abby sighed. How could Greg possibly understand, when she hardly understood herself? If only she could think straight. As it was, all she wanted was to clasp Tamsin in her arms, and then sleep and sleep.

Greg remained where he was and spoke on in quiet, measured tones. 'I've often wondered what you would do if Richard were suddenly free to marry again. After a decent period of mourning, he will be free to marry you, and I have no intention of standing between you. My luggage is already in the car. There seems little sense in prolonging the agony.'

Abby stared up at him uncomprehendingly. Richard free to marry her? The thought had not entered her head; she had difficulty in registering the fact. 'What are you saying?'

'That I'm going to give you your freedom.'

Slowly, Abby rose to her feet. 'You're *leaving* me? You said you loved me.'

'It's because I love you that I'm leaving you.' Greg walked towards her, then placed firm but gentle hands on her shoulders. 'It isn't me you want, but Richard. It's always been Richard, and always will be.' His eyes burned as he gazed at her shattered, disbelieving face. 'I once told you that I could never share you with anyone, Abby. Well, he's played the spectre at our feast for quite long enough. Believe me, it takes a great deal of love to let someone go.' He let his hands fall to his sides and moved towards the doorway. 'I've kissed Tamsin goodbye.' His voice broke and, for a moment, he could not go on. 'That was the hardest thing of all. I can't bear to lose her too, Abby. I shall want to see her regularly, so don't try to deny me those rights.' He paused. 'Don't worry, I'm not going to bury my sorrows in drink. That's one thing that *is* very much in the past, believe me.'

He walked into the hallway and whistled for Nelson, who came running to his master.

In astonishment, Abby watched as Greg opened the front door. She blinked, as though suddenly coming to her senses. 'You can't mean it. Oh, Greg . . .' She shook her head and sighed, suddenly angry. 'This is idiotic. Where are you going? Will you be at Chiswick?'

Greg shook his head. 'No. I won't be anywhere that you can find me. This has to be a clean break. Any further contact between us must be through our solicitors. I'll furnish you with good reasons to divorce me, so long as I still have the right to see my daughter.' His face softened and the eyes were sad. 'I wish to God I could have said goodbye to Ross! I feel so sorry for the boy. As it is, I must leave it to you to explain. Ask him not to think too badly of me, and tell him I love him as though he were my own son. And that's true.'

The voice disappeared somewhere into the back of Greg's

throat as he walked through the door and down the steps, followed by Nelson. 'Goodbye, honey.'

Still in a state of disbelief, Abby stood watching as he and the dog climbed into the Bentley and drove out of her life.

Slowly, Abby shut the front door and walked back into the house. Climbing the stairs, she told herself Greg was just angry and would return when he had calmed down. As she entered the bedroom, her eyes went to the door of his dressing room. Had he *really* gone? His words had sounded so firm and so final. She opened the door and walked in. A full length, oak-framed mirror faced her, and she hardly recognized the grey-faced dishevelled creature reflected in it.

One cursory glance inside the huge walnut wardrobe was enough. Her heart sank. Greg *had* gone – and she was alone, truly alone. If only Evelyn were still here!

She needed to think, but her mind refused to oblige. Instead, scenes of the night before flashed by: Richard's face in the evening sunlight; Karl and Richard walking together; the shimmer of diamonds as Samantha rushed from the opera; the diamonds again, only this time gleaming on a limp arm hanging from a stretcher; and Richard being lifted into the ambulance. Somewhere in her memory was the sound of a scream. Her scream?

She fell back onto her bed and lay looking up at the high Georgian ceiling as her mind began to clear. *Letters*. She had spoken to Richard of the letters. Even now she could see the anger in his face. Then he had walked out, in the middle of his favourite opera. Clearly, he and Samantha had fought over those stupid letters and, in anger, Richard had driven recklessly. A shudder coursed through her body. It was all her fault! What a fool she had been even to mention the letters.

'You had everything, Samantha,' she murmured. 'Except the wit to appreciate it. Yet even in death you score over me, since I will have it on my conscience for the rest of my days.'

How strange all this was, when the evening had started out so well. Now Greg was gone and she had no idea where. She needed sleep, but how could she sleep? The only way to get through the day ahead was to go to Brook Street and work. There the normal routine would drive away the pain and confusion she was feeling. Standing in her long satin underslip, her hair now falling loose to her shoulders, she removed the golden necklace she had worn to Glyndebourne, and placed it in her jewel case. There, among the diamonds and sapphires that Greg had given her, she pulled out the little imitation pearl hanging from its chain.

Richard still loved her, while Greg had walked out on her for good. But what else could she have expected from a husband she had hurt so badly? Not long ago, she had sworn never to hurt him again, yet last night she had been unable to help herself. What on earth was happening to her?

Her eyes returned to the locket, the symbol of innocent love untarnished by hurt and betrayal. Suddenly, all the pent-up emotion of the past hours caused Abby to fall back onto the bed, clutching the pearl locket in her fist, weeping uncontrollably.

When Mrs Proctor arrived with the tray of coffee, she found Abby curled up and sleeping like a child. *Poor girl*, she thought pityingly. *Fancy coming home to this after such an ordeal*! She had come to like Mr Hadleigh very much, but never would she understand him. What a strange man he was — and so unpredictable! But then he was a writer, and people with artistic temperaments were different somehow.

In the days that followed, Abby tried to find Greg, only to learn from his brother that he had left the country, having dropped Nelson off at the old family home first.

'But where did he go?'

'I can't reveal that to you, I'm afraid,' said Tom. 'Sorry,

Abby, but I gave him my word. Look, if it's anything to do with ... well ... legal matters, I can give you the name of his solicitor.'

Abby's hand tightened on the receiver. How cold and hollow it all sounded! And even if she could speak to Greg, what would she have to say to him? That she didn't love Richard? 'No. Don't bother, Tom,' she said, at last. 'It doesn't matter.'

At the hospital in Brighton, Richard had been moved to a private room but, on reaching it, Abby found her way barred by a ward sister, who informed her that Mr Glenister could only receive visits from immediate members of his family.

'I am family,' Abby assured the sister. 'He will want to see me. I'm Mrs Hadleigh. But if you tell him Abby ...'

The look she received was kind but firm. 'I'm sorry, Mrs Hadleigh. Your name is not on our list.'

Abby frowned. 'Carr. It used to be Carr.'

The white-capped head shook slowly from side to side. 'No, Carr isn't on the list either.'

Abby became alarmed. They were hiding something from her. 'He *is* getting better, isn't he?'

'Of course. Don't worry on that account. Mr Glenister is recovering, but I have strict orders from the family that no one else is to be allowed in.'

Abby smiled and nodded. 'Well, that makes sense. But Richard and I grew up together — I'm his cousin. He will want to see me, if you just go in and ask him.'

The ward sister was showing signs of impatience. 'I'm sorry, Mrs Hadleigh, but the answer has to be no.'

Dismay sweeping over her, Abby glanced at the door dividing her from Richard. Two steps was all it would take: two short steps and a twist of the handle before this dragon lady could do anything about it.

'Please, Mrs Hadleigh. He's sleeping after a bad night,' said the sister, reading Abby's mind and resolving to prevent a nasty scene, even if it meant resorting to a lie.

Mrs Rivers had been so firm in her intent to sue the hospital should anyone get near enough to her son to cause him more stress. This Hadleigh woman was one of the people specifically mentioned: Mrs Abigail Carr-Hadleigh.

Abby nodded and sighed. That closed door between her and Richard seemed symbolic of their love. She held out grapes, flowers and two paperback books. 'Then would you please give these to him? Tell him Abby was here and that I hope he will be completely well soon.'

'Of course,' said the sister, nodding. 'I'm sorry about everything, but I have my orders and ...'

'I understand.' Abby smiled and turned away quickly, so that her tears could not be seen. She drove straight back to London, thinking how ironic it was that the mother Richard had come to hate, and a sister who'd ignored him for years, could now be considered close family and least likely to cause stress.

If the weeks that followed were bad for Abby, they were devastating for Ross. No matter how carefully she explained, or how much love she showered upon him, the boy just wanted to keep to his own room. He missed Greg and Nelson more than he had ever thought possible. Added to which, his real father was badly injured and lying in hospital.

'You're the man of the house now,' Susan told him one day as she watched him putting the finishing touches to his model Lancaster Bomber. He'd started this for Greg, to surprise him, then put it away when he learned Greg had left him. Then he'd received a letter, with no address upon it, in which Greg explained how much he missed his stepson, and hoped he would understand that grown-ups quarrelled as much as children and, very often, they had to part company because of it.

Now Ross looked up into Susan's familiar face, thinking that aunts were not the sort of people with whom a chap could discuss his most intimate feelings. He had two fathers, but would be returning to school in two weeks' time without setting eyes on either one of them. His mother had told him he was very lucky, with all these people wanting and loving him, but in truth, no one wanted him except her. When he grew up, he would be free to live where he pleased and do what he pleased. There would be no fathers making promises they had no intention of keeping. He would live by himself in another country and not expect anything from anyone. That was the only way to avoid being hurt. But how could he say all this to Aunt Susan?

'You're pretty good at this,' murmured Susan, running an appraising eye over the model. 'You're good at sketching too. Have you thought about art school?'

Ross shook his head. 'I like mechanical drawing, and I'm seriously thinking about architecture, but your kind of art ... I don't think so. Mum wants me to learn French and German and boring stuff like that, but I don't have to take German if I don't wish, so I won't. I tried it. It's hard. Harder than French − and I hate French.'

'Still, if you want to get on in the world, languages are important.'

Ross looked up at Susan and frowned. 'Paul McCartney didn't have to learn all that rubbish and he's done pretty well.'

Susan looked about her. Ross's room had been transformed into a sound studio by the look of things. 'How's the guitar-playing going?'

Ross sighed, and looked at her balefully. 'Not too good. I was going to have lessons. Greg said ... well, anyway, it didn't happen. I've tried to teach myself but it isn't very easy.'

Susan looked thoughtful, and got to work at once. When she had found a good tutor willing to give him daily lessons, she returned and told him: 'It's a present from me.'

From that moment on, Ross stopped lounging about the house, got up early to be ready for his tutor, then spent the day practising, until he steadily improved.

*

On the last Sunday in August, as Abby drove into the High Street at Ashton Green, a million memories came flooding back to her.

The village looked exactly as it always had, pretty with its ancient houses, sun-dappled by the trees, and quiet to the point of listlessness. Somewhere a cock crowed — the only sound to break the silence. She stopped the car and glanced at Ross, who had nodded off beside her, knowing he was unaware of her reason for bringing him to this part of Kent.

They had spent the morning in Folkestone, where Ross had swum in the Channel, got slightly sunburnt and enjoyed the picnic lunch they had eaten on the sands. It was one of those rare treats for Abby: a quiet day out with her son.

'I think we'll go home via Canterbury,' she had said, handing Ross a chicken drumstick.

'Why?'

'Because I want to show you where I used to live.'

The tour of Canterbury had been a quick one, slowed down only by Ross insisting on a boat ride along the Stour. This, and seeing Glenisters department store again, looking smarter than ever, had sent the years rolling back. They walked to the Cathedral and into the Precincts where she had spent so much of her youth waiting for a glimpse of Richard. Now she was back in Ashton, and not far ahead lay Ferndene Lodge itself.

Three days earlier she had learned that Richard had been discharged. She'd telephoned Beauchamp Place, only to be told Mr Glenister was at his residence in Kent. That had placed Abby in a quandary. Given that she felt responsible for the accident, how then could she have the gall to ring that bereaved household, and possibly find herself talking to Lady Fellowes?

In the event she had not telephoned, but her desire to see Richard grew with every passing minute and so, saying nothing to Ross about his father, she had taken him for a day out by the sea.

631

As she started the car once more, Ross stirred and opened his eyes. 'Come on, sleepy head,' she laughed, glad of human company once more. 'I brought you here to show you the village I was raised in. Well? What do you think?'

Ross stifled a yawn and looked out of the car window without interest. 'It's very small, and very quiet. Didn't you get bored?'

'Ahead is the house where I used to live.' Why was she here, taking a trip down Memory Lane? Was it to exorcize ghosts? She had vowed never to return, yet here she was showing the place off to her son.

As she drove on she noticed a few small changes. There were 'No Parking' signs outside the shops which had previously been unnecessary, since few people had owned cars. Turning the corner, she wondered what the new people had done with Ferndene; and then she saw it. The 'For Sale' notice by the gate was the first thing that caught her eye on rounding the bend. Two cars were parked outside the Lodge. Pulling alongside the vehicles, she stared at the house and frowned. The garden was badly overgrown, no curtains hung at the windows and the paintwork was chipped. All in all, the old house had an unloved and unlived-in appearance.

The front door opened and a middle-aged couple walked out into the shadows cast by the chestnut tree. They were joined then by the estate agent, who locked the front door, and walked them to their car.

'Wait here, Ross,' said Abby. She walked over to the estate agent, who was watching as his clients drove away. 'Are you showing people around? If so, I'm very interested in the house.'

'Of course,' said the agent. 'Only too delighted to let you see the property.'

Abby's eyes raked the windows disapprovingly. 'It looks so uncared for! When did the owners leave?'

Holding his clipboard to his chest, the agent smiled.

'Well, to tell you the truth it's been owned by a couple who live abroad. They bought it some four years back, intending to retire here. Since then, the man died, and his widow has decided to sell this place and live with her sister instead. It's very sad to see property of this quality left unlived in for four years,' he said, leading her along the overgrown pathway, and unlocking the front door. 'It's a good solid house of great character. They just don't make them like this any more.'

Abby glanced inside the hall and felt a stirring in her heart. Empty! Poor old Ferndene, so sad and empty all these years. 'Is it all right if I just wander about on my own?'

'Of course. I'll wait by the car.'

Abby looked back at Ross, who was frowning at her, thoroughly bored. 'I won't be long. Would you like to see the house too?'

He wrinkled his nose and shook his head. 'I'll wait here.'

So Abby stood alone, recalling her first sight of the house with the lady from the WVS beside her. Taking a deep breath, she stepped over the threshold, and entered the house she had sworn never to enter again.

Walking into the drawing room, she was astonished at its size, now that all furniture had been removed. The windows needed a good clean, and there were marks on the walls where pictures had once hung. But, despite its neglected appearance, for Abby it echoed with voices from the past.

Abby gazed across to the bay where the grand piano had stood, and again she could hear the Schubert *Impromptu* which Milicent had played so often. She could almost smell her stepmother's perfume, mingling with smoke from William's pipe and the aroma of hot coals burning in the grate. It seemed she was a girl once more, sketching away quietly and dreaming of Richard.

So much of my life is locked away in this room, she thought sadly.

Moving into the kitchen, she wondered how long it would be before newcomers could exorcize the ghosts of the Glenisters and saw, to her surprise, that the old kitchen table had been left behind. Somehow everything seemed much the same, along with the gas stove, the old enamelled sink with the wooden plate-rack high above the huge pine dresser, and the Aga stove.

'*Is it true that you've been living in a cave?*'

'*We have bombs here too, you know. We were evacuated but . . .*'

Upstairs she wandered from room to room until she came to her own. *Apples!* It was once used for storing apples, her stepmother had told her. It took weeks before the smell of apples left it, putting her off the fruit for life.

Through the window she looked out at the long garden with the late afternoon sun tipping the tall poplars. A fair-haired boy was moving through the grass, and for a brief moment, Abby thought she was looking at Richard. Ross could have been his father, but for his jeans and summer shirt. He looked up and waved. She waved back, smiling, but her heart was heavy.

Then, in her mind's eye, she saw someone else. A woman in a blue dress and '40s hairstyle, standing beside a small bonfire. Abby remembered how much the doll had meant to her, and thought bitterly: *Even then, Milicent. Even then!*

The agent was waiting for her as she walked with Ross back towards the car. 'Have you seen everything you wish to see?' he asked.

'Thank you,' said Abby, 'I'm quite finished now.'

Leaving Ferndene she drove to the church, with two pink roses which she had cut from a climber that grew wild. Then she stopped once more, oblivious to Ross's groans of despair. She walked across the cemetery to William's grave, hurt to see how sadly neglected it had become. Weeds overran the kerbstone and, judging by its dry condition, no flowers had stood in the vase for a long time. Placing one of the roses on the grave, she stood there for some minutes before moving slowly towards the Fellowes' family plot.

Two new graves lay within the white rails, and one still had flowers from the funeral fading upon it. Sick at heart, Abby stared down at the withered wreaths, unable to think of that fair goddess lying beneath the earth. Not Samantha, surely! Not that haughty, striking woman in her Chanel outfits. But here she lay, just the same, because of a few thoughtless words. *I shall never forgive myself – never.*

Kneeling, she placed the other rose on Samantha's grave, then walked quickly back to the car.

'When are we going home?' Ross asked, stifling another yawn.

'We're on our way,' came the patient reply. 'Just one last stop.'

Now she drove along the country lane she had once run along at midnight, when it had been covered in snow. Turning the car through the gates of Wickham Place, she eased along the drive, hoping against hope that Richard would see her, and come out of the house.

Someone did come, but he was a stranger to her. Grey-haired and tall, he stood in shirt-sleeves and frowned. 'Can I help you?'

Abby climbed out of the car, feeling exposed and slightly embarrassed. 'I've come to see Mr Glenister. I'm his cousin. Is he at home?' She spoke quietly, not wishing Ross to hear.

'Ah, you've come to pay your respects. Sad business, very sad. I'm the estate manager, by the way. There's no one in, I'm afraid. Lady Fellowes has taken her granddaughter out for the day.'

Abby's heart sank with disappointment. 'I've come from London. Mr Glenister went with them, did he?'

'No. I've no idea where he is,' came the reply. 'He might have gone walking somewhere. Sometimes he's gone for hours. I've only seen him twice in the three days he's been home. I suppose it's the way grief takes some people. Did he know you were coming?'

Abby shook her head. 'I meant to surprise him.'

The man smiled. 'Well, I'll let the housekeeper know you've been, Mrs ...?'

'Hadleigh. Abigail Hadleigh.'

She thanked him and slowly walked towards the car. A thought then occurred to her: a thought that grew until it became a certainty. She was sure she knew where to find Richard.

It seemed strange to be walking once more across the narrow bridge that spanned the Stour. She stood for a moment, listening to the rustle of green willows along the banks, then looked down at the river. This beautiful place was filled with such poignant memories.

With Ross trailing in her wake, she walked on through the shaded spinney and up the hill, until they came upon Stapledown, bathed now in a golden haze.

'How much farther?' complained Ross. 'I'm so hot!'

'We've arrived,' answered Abby. 'From the brow of the hill you can see Canterbury.'

Ross sighed. 'I've already *seen* Canterbury.'

Ignoring him, Abby walked on, until the huge Cathedral appeared in the distance, towering over the city under a pale blue sky, solid, unchanging, enduring. A skylark sang above her, and she remembered how once the only noise had been that of Spitfires droning overhead.

On she walked until she stood on the brow of the hill.

She saw him at once. He was seated on a wooden bench, gazing out over the city. Her heart melted at the sight of him, and she turned to Ross.

'It's been five years since you last saw him. You know who it is, don't you?'

The boy followed her gaze. He stood for a while staring at the man, not recognizing him, yet knowing him nonetheless. Who else could it be? Why had she done this? Why had his mother brought him here without warning him? He was unprepared and shy. He wanted to go home.

Sensing his nervousness, Abby smiled down at him. 'I want to speak to your father alone, first. Then will you meet him? It's time.'

'Does he know I'm here?' whispered Ross. When his mother shook her head, he added, 'Then perhaps I'd better go back to the car.'

'You'll do no such thing,' said Abby. 'Be kind, Ross. Your father has suffered a great deal.'

Reluctant, yet curious, Ross nodded and sank to the ground, aware that his stomach felt the way it had when he'd waited outside the headmaster's office after a fight with another boy. But this was his father, and he had always longed for a real father. Why then was he so afraid?

He watched as his mother walked on towards the wooden seat, the full skirt of her light blue cotton dress lifting slightly in the breeze. His mother, he thought, was a very pretty woman. So why had Greg gone away? And why had his real father married someone else?

Abby's step was quiet, yet Richard knew she was there. He tensed, felt her hand on his shoulder, and reached up to clasp it firmly. For a full minute they stayed like that, silent and too moved to speak.

'Oh, my darling,' Abby murmured. 'I'm so sorry, so very sorry.' She felt his hand tighten on hers and, moving around the seat, looked down at his face. Dark circles framed his eyes, and he was much thinner. 'When you weren't at the house, I somehow knew you would be here.' At that moment she noticed the brass plaque nailed to the back of the seat. Engraved upon it were the words: 'In Loving Memory of William Glenister'.

'What a lovely thought,' she said.

Gently, Richard pulled her down beside him, still trying to find his voice. When he did, it sounded weak and hoarse. 'He was the one who first brought me here, before the war started. Later, after Malaya, he came here with me when I was convalescing. He once said this place cried out for a seat so people could relax and admire the view. But as far as I'm concerned, this has always been *our* place, Abby.'

She reached for his hand and pressed it gently, her eyes gazing into his, her heart filled with love and compassion for him.

'I used to come here alone, to be close to you. Now it's the only place I can get away from *her*. She's everywhere in that house. Wherever I go, her presence is strong: haunting me, accusing me.'

His face was so troubled that Abby felt alarmed. 'No, my dear, she's doing no such thing. It was an accident, so you mustn't go on torturing yourself in this manner.'

'You don't understand,' he said quietly. 'I killed Samantha.'

She shook her head, hating to see him this way. 'An accident, darling – a terrible accident.'

He returned her gaze. 'I killed her! I wanted her dead, and so I killed her. *Now* do you understand?'

Abby blinked, then dismissed such words. 'You don't mean that, you know you don't.'

They lapsed into silence once more and then she summoned up the courage to ask: 'Was it because of the letters?' When he made no answer, she closed her eyes and said bitterly, 'I should have known better and held my tongue, but I really believed you had read them.'

Richard's hand closed over hers and held it tightly. He saw the golden sunlight playing on her loose hair which blew softly in the breeze. 'How could you have known otherwise? But there was more, much more – and learning the truth about the letters was like . . .' He paused and searched for the right words. 'It was like being handed a key which opened a door onto daylight, and I, who had been in darkness, could suddenly see all she had done.' He clenched her hand even more tightly. 'I hated her then. God, how I hated her! Some terrible madness came over me. I wanted to kill her, or at least frighten the life out of her. She cried out for me to slow down, but it just seemed to goad me on. Then came the sharp bend. I saw the tree in the headlights, heard her scream and . . . that's all I remember.'

Releasing Abby's hand, he stood up, and gazed out at the city stretched before them in the evening sun. 'I killed her, Abby.' His voice was thick with remorse. 'And now I'm not sure I can live with myself any more.'

Hearing him speak like that, Abby felt her heart was breaking. Samantha dead, it seemed, was even stronger than Samantha living. She had won! She had parted them for good! Their guilt at her death was her final victory.

Leaning back against the seat, Abby found it difficult to speak. 'Do you remember, in Cornwall, how we used to count the waves? The seventh, you insisted, was the largest and the most dangerous.' She took a deep breath, and expelled it slowly. 'Well, I feel it has just washed over us. We've been dashed against the rocks, left stranded and badly hurt.'

Richard turned at that, saw the tears streaming down her cheeks and walked over to her quickly. He sat down, took her face into his hands and kissed her tears lovingly. 'For me, yes, but you . . . well, you have a good marriage and . . .'

'No,' Abby cut in. 'That's all over now.'

A look of disbelief crossed Richard's face. 'But he was at Glyndebourne with you. What happened?'

Abby searched into her handbag for a lace handkerchief and wiped her eyes. 'I really don't want to talk about that night. Suffice it to say that Greg has gone from my life.' As she said these words she realized suddenly how deeply his going had affected her. So much had gone with him. How empty her life was going to be!

Taking her hands once more, Richard sat back, suddenly exhausted. 'It's bloody ironic, isn't it? I had already decided on divorce before that fateful evening. When the chips were really down, she walked out on me. I knew then it was over,

639

and so did she. I didn't want her and she found me a social liability. I was going to be free at last. Free, Abby! Then her father died suddenly and ...' He shrugged.

'And you had to give her your full support, of course.'

'What else could I do?'

Abby smiled, her eyes misted with sadness. 'You, being you, my love, could do nothing else. You were her strength, and she was your weakness. And now, because of your kindness to her, she's managed to part us for ever.'

Richard's grip on her hand tightened but he knew she was right. Seeing his distress, Abby stroked his hair, then let her hand drift down to his cheek. 'What will you do now?'

Richard forced his mind back to the world about him. 'Oh ... Karl wants me to spend some time with him in Germany. But it'll be harvest-time soon, and I must look after things here.' He smiled wryly. 'Strange to hear that! I wanted to be a barrister, then a politician, yet here I am at the end of the day prattling on about the harvest. I must hold this estate together for my daughter. Then I shall give more time to the store. Who knows, I might make William's dream come true one day and expand.'

'And Karl?'

Richard smiled. 'I like him very much, and curse those wasted years now. Do you know he came to see me four times while I was in hospital? Flew in from Germany in his private plane especially to see me, then flew straight back again. Wasn't that something? I've promised I'll go to him when I feel the time is right. Just now I can't leave Fiona — she's confused and desolate without her mother. Lydia, of course, is distraught with grief. The least I can do now, having deprived one of a mother and the other of a daughter, is to stay here for them.' His voice became bitter. 'It's a funny thing, but I kept telling the police, and the doctors, that I killed my wife. They made comforting sounds, said "There, there", and put it down to natural shock and remorse. I ought to be hanged for murder, but instead they'll probably charge me with reckless driving.'

'Richard, you're one of the most gentle men I've ever known.' She glanced around, remembering Ross. 'But I didn't come here for yet another sad farewell – I came to bring you your son.'

Richard stared up at her in surprise. '*Ross?* Here?'

'Here.' Abby gestured with her head. 'Do you see that scruffy little individual halfway down the hill? He's shy, Richard, and nervous, I think. He's had a rough time lately.'

Slowly Richard stood and looked down the hill. Ross was kneeling back on his heels, plucking the grass, and staring up at him. As Abby rose from the seat he caught her by the hand. 'Don't go! Stay – please stay.'

Abby shook her head. 'You two must get to know each other again, but without me. It has to be that way now. I'll wait for him below, on the bridge.'

'Don't rush away, please, darling. Not yet.'

He looked so distraught that she wanted to hug him close to her, but checked her emotions. 'Don't try to hold on to something you must let go. You have Ross. You have Karl. Love your son, as I love him, and let him feel free to wander between us as he wishes.'

Reluctantly, he let her go, his heart filled with aching love and his eyes stinging with tears.

Abby stood there, seeing his face blurred through her own tears, then managed a whispered 'Goodbye.' For a brief moment, she stopped by her son, said a few words, then watched as he went up towards Richard.

As Abby took the path towards the spinney, she knew she had truly turned her back on 'what might have been' for good. Maybe she and Richard would see each other again – but lovers they could never be. It was not only Samantha who had come between them, but time and life itself. Nothing could bring back those young lovers with all their dreams before them. They were two different people now, with their own separate responsibilities and commitments. Having taken different paths in life, they had ended a long way apart.

She stopped walking and stood on the hillside. Something had changed; something deep inside her had changed. She had become aware of it even as she and Richard had sat together, but now the feeling was growing stronger. It was almost as though the huge wave had not engulfed her, after all, but had simply picked her up and tossed her back into reality.

It was over. Released, at last, from the spell which had bound her all these years, Abby knew quite suddenly that her future lay with Greg and no one else. Until that moment she had never believed it. She had been a woman possessed, with Richard always there, blinding her to the truth.

She gazed down on the trees before her, wondering what kind of madness had allowed her to let Greg go from her life. In her despair, confusion, grief and anxiety, she had thought of no one save Richard, even as the man she really loved and needed had walked out of the door.

A new beginning, she thought, *after the clamour and turmoil*. Wherever Greg was upon this planet, she would find him and tell him how wrong she had been. Would he come back to her after all the hurt she had caused him? Maybe not. But surely he would come home for Tamsin and the stepson he had grown to love? Resolution began to fill her, as it always had when she was at her lowest. She *would* get him back, come hell or high water, and they would make a new start together. This time there would be no secrets between them, and this time their relationship would endure.

Turning, she looked back up the hill to see Ross approaching his father. Their outlines stood dark against the evening sky. As Richard placed his hands on his son's shoulders, she knew she would never stop loving him. But it was a love she could live with now. In some strange way, it seemed that Richard *was* more like her brother.

With spirits lifting, she walked down the path towards

the river. A light gust of wind blew from the east, carrying upon it the distant sound of Canterbury's bells ringing out across the city, fields and woods, calling people to Evensong.

Child of the Phoenix
Barbara Erskine

The long-awaited new novel by the bestselling author of
Lady of Hay and *Kingdom of Shadows*.

Born in the flames of a burning castle in 1218, Princess
Eleyne is brought up by her fiercely Welsh nurse to support
the Celtic cause against the English aggressor. She is taught
to worship the old gods and to look into the future and
sometimes the past. But her second sight is marred by her
inability to identify time and place in her visions so she is
powerless to avert forthcoming tragedy.

Extraordinary events will follow Eleyne all her days as,
despite passionate resistance, her life is shaped by the
powerful men in her world. Time and again, like the phoenix
that is her symbol, she must rise from the ashes of her past life
to begin anew. But her mystical gifts, her clear intelligence
and unquenchable spirit will involve her in the destinies of
England, Scotland and Wales.

ISBN 0 00 647264 8

The Egyptian Years
Elizabeth Harris

The mysterious disappearance of Genevieve Mountsorrel in the Egyptian desert in 1892 was a longstanding family puzzle. Newly married, the young and vivacious Genevieve had sailed for Egypt, happy at the prospect of a new life. No one could explain the tragic turn of events. Only her parasol had been found, hastily discarded in the hot and dusty sand.

A century later, Willa, a distant relative, discovers Genevieve's diary. Drawn immediately into an astonishing story, she learns of Genevieve's secret life and the child she was forced to abandon, the truth about her sinister husband, Leonard, and the extraordinary drama of what really happened to Genevieve Mountsorrel . . .

Acclaim for *The Herb Gatherers*:

'Enormously enjoyable. Elizabeth Harris writes with sensitivity and skill.'
Barbara Erskine

ISBN 0 00 647191 9

Shadows on the Sun
Kathryn Haig

Helen . . .

To Michael, her husband, lonely and reserved, she is both angel and whore . . .

To Adrienne, fleeing the destruction of her homeland by the Kaiser's army, she is an unnatural mother . . .

To Hector, shell-shocked and tormented, she is the woman who has ensnared his brother and brought two families to the brink of tragedy.

After a war that has savaged a generation both physically and spiritually, the affluent classes find themselves cast dangerously adrift from their Edwardian certainties. For Michael and Helen – for all of them – nothing will ever be the same again.

From the last golden summer of a dying era, through the senseless carnage of the Western Front, to the savage gaiety of the jazz age, *Shadows on the Sun* is the story of a terrible obsession.

'An overwhelmingly compelling read. I was captivated.'

Barbara Erskine

ISBN 0 00 647137 4

Tomorrow's Memories
Connie Monk

The Gowers of Denby are a picturebook perfect family. There is Tim, Jane, twins Richard and Liz just sixteen, and Hartley, almost one of the family. Even the onset of World War II can't touch them here in the safe haven of their Devonshire farm, or so Jane believes. In her thankfulness, she finds space and love to spare for two London evacuees and for Meg, a disturbingly beautiful young woman who arrives with a babe in arms.

But Jane is soon to find that no one is beyond the reach of tragedy, that no city, no village, no individual is untouched by war, that sometimes each new day can be a hurdle . . .

Tomorrow's Memories is the touching story of one family's war, of its relationships with one another, and above all, of Jane, as she holds on to memories of yesterday and looks towards tomorrow . . .

ISBN 0 00 647095 5

King's Close
Christine Marion Fraser

Evie Grainger has left behind her beloved Scottish country-side to live with her husband David and her parents in the Close. In the desperately hard conditions, she must fight to bring up her children and keep her family together as the poverty of twenties Glasgow threatens to destroy already fragile family relationships.

Evie's heart is big enough for everyone, it seems. All her friends and relations run to her when tragedy and heartbreak enter their lives. Yet Evie is beginning to feel trapped and is constantly haunted by memories of her childhood in the country. But most of all she can never forget Gillan . . .

'Lively characters and vivid settings . . . will easily captivate both new and old Fraser fans'   *Western Mail*

ISBN 0 00 647002 5

☐	NOVEMBER OF THE HEART LaVyrle Spencer	0-00-647608-2	£3.99
☐	THE NIGHT WALKER Diane Guest	0-00-637781-5	£4.99
☐	WILLIAM'S WIFE Jean Plaidy	0-00-647299-0	£4.99
☐	THE LIVERPOOL BASQUE Helen Forrester	0-00-647334-2	£4.99
☐	THE SEVENTH WAVE Emma Sinclair	0-00-647294-X	£4.99

All these books are available from your local bookseller or can be ordered direct from the publishers.

To order direct just tick the titles you want and fill in the form below:

Name: _____

Address: _____

_____

Postcode: _____

Send to: HarperCollins Mail Order, Dept 8, HarperCollins *Publishers*, Westerhill Road, Bishopbriggs, Glasgow G64 2QT.

Please enclose a cheque or postal order or your authority to debit your Visa/Access account –

Credit card no: _____

Expiry date: _____

Signature: _____

– to the value of the cover price plus:

UK & BFPO: Add £1.00 for the first and 25p for each additional book ordered.

Overseas orders including Eire, please add £2.95 service charge.

Books will be sent by surface mail but quotes for airmail despatches will be given on request.

24 HOUR TELEPHONE ORDERING SERVICE FOR ACCESS/VISA CARDHOLDERS –

TEL: GLASGOW 041-772 2281 or LONDON 081-307 4052